THE

Rouwen made his atta........
to pull Kwuway to hi............ .... the
glass dagger. The wizard jerked hard and ripped
his tunic sleeve to win free. His lips moved but
no sounds came out. Rouwen renewed his attack,
jumping atop the worktable and kicking hard. His
foot smashed into Kwuway's chest and sent the
wizard reeling across the room. Kwuway crashed
to the littered floor, but his lips kept moving.

And Brion Rouwen began to smoulder. His arm
had blistered when the grimoire heated. Now his
entire body threatened to burst into intense flame.
His clothing popped out in tiny sparks, and the skin
beneath turned black as Kwuway continued to weave
his spell.

'You cannot die, but you can suffer,' Kwuway called
triumphantly, getting to his feet when Rouwen
stopped to swat at the tiny fires appearing all over
his body. 'And suffer you will, for all eternity!'

THE ACCURSED

I: The Lord of Death and Life
II: Legion of the Air
III: The Flame Specter

Robert E. Vardeman

NEW ENGLISH LIBRARY
Hodder and Stoughton

This edition first published in Great Britain in 1994 by
Hodder & Stoughton
A division of Hodder Headline PLC

A New English Library Paperback

ISBN 0 450 58840 8

Typeset by Hewer Text Composition Services, Edinburgh
Printed and bound in Great Britain by Cox and Wyman Ltd.

Hodder and Stoughton Ltd
A Division of Hodder Headline PLC
47 Bedford Square
London WC1B 3DP

Book One

THE LORD OF DEATH AND LIFE

For Vicky Bevan, My #1 British fan

1

The Hour of Treachery

Brion Rouwen, Captain of the Intrepid Guard and Deputy Defender of the Realm, walked slowly along the castle's lofty battlements. He frowned until his handsome face contorted into a furrowed parody of itself, as he worried about discharging his duties effectively. Castle Gan had successfully withstood sieges, major battles and minor skirmishes, for more than four hundred years. Rouwen took his office seriously, even if others under his command seemed to think only minimal effort was required from them.

It might be that his ambitions knew no bounds. He was a commoner, but it was assumed widely he would be elevated to Third Baron of Gan at the Spring Festivals in a week's time. It might be ambition to title that drove him, or it might be Rouwen's total allegiance to his king. Those under him debated this endlessly, but only Rouwen knew for certain which it was and he saw no reason to enlighten the soldiers prone to barracks gossip. Keeping them guessing also kept them alert.

Brion Rouwen stopped at the highest point along the battlements hewn from shining white stone and stared at the simple wood plank extending two paces into thin air. *Almost* two paces, he mused. He had sent more than one of his subordinates along this plank a full two paces to their deaths for crimes as varied as treason and insubordination. If his platoon of spies working in the castle's lowest levels were right in their accusations, more would step to their death before the Spring Festivals, affirming to King Priowe his captain's devotion and unstinting vigilance in defense of the realm.

On impulse, Rouwen stepped onto the sturdy oak board. It swayed slightly, as much from his weight as the wind whipping down off the distant, dark Shield Mountains. His gray eyes stared straight ahead as he placed both booted feet on the plank. Rouwen settled his rapier and looked at the tallest peak in the ring of mountains completely encircling Valley Gan.

'Mount Glid,' he muttered, thinking this might be the last sight of anyone he condemned to death. Tonight the peak was crowned with the feeble light from the Lesser Moon. The Greater Moon would not rise for another two hours – signalling the hour of treachery. 'Souls travel to your peak and from there to Paradise.' Glid stood half again the height of neighboring peaks. It was only fitting that those about to die were confronted with their destination and the promise of either eternal prosperity or poverty. If he made a mistake and wrongly sentenced one to die, powers greater than his would rectify it atop Mount Glid.

But was that what the condemned really saw? Cold gusts of wind caused Rouwen to widen his stance slightly. His lank, dark hair became mussed; Rouwen should have worn his guard captain's cap. He blinked and edged forward a half-pace, his boots on the brink of the drop into the jagged spires of granite known as the Fingers of Providence. What thoughts went through a traitor's mind during those twenty long seconds before impalement on the stony needles?

'Repentance?' Brion Rouwen wondered aloud. 'Or are they cursing me and King Priowe and the Empire of Gan?'

Twenty seconds to death alongside the huge stony spire holding Castle Gan. A short enough time that might seem an eternity to the guilty.

Another blast of wind tugged at Rouwen's crimson and gold cloak and sent it snapping behind him like a battle pennant. He kept his balance and looked downward into impenetrable darkness, trying to imagine the kind of man – or woman – who would betray king and kingdom and risk such a death. Rouwen could not see the Fingers below, but small puddles of lava bubbled around them and lit the gloom of the pit with murky orange and yellow flames. His nose wrinkled at the imagined smell of the sulfur rising from those small, intensely hot fumaroles, though he could not possibly catch any scent this high in the castle.

Even the rotting flesh from the traitors' bodies was beyond his ability to detect.

Rouwen took a deep breath of the pure night air, then turned to retreat along the plank. A dark figure blocked his way back to the safety of Castle Gan's battlements. Cloak whipping around his muscular body, Rouwen fought to keep his balance. He reached for the silver wire-wrapped handle of his rapier. To fight here was the height of folly. He could never hope to win.

He had been foolish to indulge his whim to see the last sights of the condemned. Now he might never live to serve King Priowe and Queen Diarra – and never again would he share Princess Sorinne's bed. Rouwen moved so that his heel touched the edge of the plank; beyond this point he dared not retreat. He worked to free his rapier from its sheath. A quick charge might be enough to bowl over his darkness-shrouded foe.

'You live dangerously, Captain,' came a soft voice.

Rouwen did not relax his stance, but he knew there was no need to fight. Although he did not know the man's identity, the spy worked for the betterment of Gan.

'You bring proof of the plot?' he asked.

'I do,' the shadowy figure said, 'but I will not give it to you there. You must accept it here.' A scrap of paper fluttered whitely in the breeze as the informant held up the evidence he had unearthed. Rouwen took a quick, sliding step that brought him to the battlements, then jumped down to the castle's solid white stone. He tried not to look too relieved at the solidity under his boots. Showing betraying emotion weakened his position of authority.

'What have you found?' Rouwen asked, reaching for the sheet of paper. It was snatched from his grip at the last possible instant and held as an enticing morsel.

'Captain, please. I am not the patriot you are. This is not a matter of treason and punishment for me. I need motivation for my betrayals.' The dark figure turned slightly and Rouwen saw the jut of the man's long, sharp nose. This was the most he had ever seen of his informant's face. Any other he would have mistrusted, but his spy's details had always proven accurate.

'The usual,' Rouwen said. 'Full pardon for any crime committed obtaining the evidence.'

'And?' teased his informant. 'What else is there for me to risk life and limb exposing this terrible conspiracy against the Empire of Gan? A thank you and fare-thee-well is polite and virtuous, but I am neither. I need more than thanks to fill both belly and treasure chest.'

'Land?' suggested Rouwen. 'Or something more portable?' He fished for information beyond what the man was likely to give. There was so little land available within Valley Gan that any man would be a fool to turn down such a munificent offer. But Rouwen was not surprised when his spy rejected the chance for growing food and becoming one of the prosperous landed gentry.

'Fifty pieces of silver might be recompense enough,' the shadowy figure said in his soft, mocking voice. He turned and watched as the Lesser Moon rose high above Mount Glid. Witch light danced over the mountain's rim, making it appear to be a silvered dagger ready to gut the sky. The Greater Moon had yet to launch itself across the star-studded dome of the night.

'Forty,' bargained Rouwen. He still sought additional information. Whatever was brewing in the castle's lower levels was enough to frighten this rat into leaving the safety of both castle and valley.

'Fifty is fair. Fifty pieces of gold would be even more to my liking.'

This musing demand rocked Rouwen. Prices for betrayal seldom rose once dickering began. He fingered the hilt of his rapier, wondering if threats might lower the price or loosen the man's tongue. It was obvious this spy's utility was at an end.

'Fifty pieces of silver,' the tall captain said, coming to a quick decision. 'And safe passage through the Demon's Throat.' Rouwen kept his gaze squarely on his spy, but the dark figure turned and looked toward the narrow ravine, the only public exit from the Empire of Gan. Huge armies had smashed like the ocean's waves against a distant shore attempting to flow inward and had been turned back.

By the time those huge armies fought through the Demon's Throat, they were smaller armies. And then they had the mile-high column of rock balancing Castle Gan on its tip to surmount. After fighting up the twisting, turning road with all its clever entrapments, only then did they face the foot-thick steel doors and stalwart stone walls of the castle proper.

For more than four hundred years, no conqueror had added Castle Gan to his tally of victories. None would breach the castle's gates while Brion Rouwen was Captain of the Intrepid Guard.

'Watch the kitchens closely,' came the softly spoken warning. 'All the nobles are slated for poisoning, even your precious Sorinne.'

'Do not speak ill of the princess,' snapped Rouwen. His fingers tightened on the wired grip of his sword.

A mocking laugh met his order. 'I never disparage those who pay my wages. But it is not the princess they seek to destroy. The king and queen are their first targets. Only then do they consider the lesser nobles.' The dark figure flipped the hem of his hooded cloak about one arm. He made a strange gesture in the air as he added, 'Sorinne is more likely to be their prey than Prince Sped.'

Rouwen almost laughed. He held his tongue. This spy knew too much about his assignations with the princess. He need not know Rouwen's contempt for Sorinne's brother, though few in Gan had a high opinion. Sped lived for his bizarre

6

foods and peculiar hobbies. Where Sorinne had inherited the queen's beauty and the king's sharp intelligence, Sped had his father's ill-favored countenance and his mother's petulant, petty conceits. There was even talk of a wizard's spell on the younger son of King Priowe, but Rouwen discounted this. Into the finest of lineages there came genetic blundering.

Even a noble of Priowe's stature and attainment was sometimes cursed by cruel fate to make him the stronger. Sped certainly accomplished this vexation with his immoderate choices in life and love.

'So they will use poison?' asked Rouwen. 'Who is responsible?'

'Ah, there are many petty conspirators. Two cooks are included, perhaps as much through incompetence as intent.'

Rouwen grew impatient. He had no desire to listen to a catalogue of the realm's culinary deficiencies. He wanted names, he wanted methods, and he wanted them now.

'I understand your eagerness to be about the – executions,' the spy said, motioning in the direction of the oaken plank. 'Cook's apprentice Zeegon and master chef Clanna Beg-Nonn await their orders to place ground *thouse* beak in the king and queen's soup.' The spy chuckled. 'It would only improve the taste. Have you sampled the master chef's leek soup? No? Count yourself among the lucky. She poisons out of hand, from poor preparation and implementation.'

'You say they await orders. From whom?' Rouwen did not miss the small turn as his hidden informant glanced toward the Demon's Throat. This threat to the realm came from without, not from within Gan's roster of restless nobles.

'King Nishor has long gazed down the Demon's Throat and wondered what it would be like to sit high atop this rocky column. He finally takes this longing and translates it into action.'

'You have done a service for the empire,' Rouwen said. He let out the deep breath he had been holding. Even in times of peace, there was a silent war raging. Nishor had neither the army nor the magicks needed for a successful assault on Castle Gan. Those impoverished of soldiers, money and wizardry always resorted to subterfuge and assassination. A response worthy of such perfidy would have to be composed.

'Do not begin your campaigns until I have departed this uneasy land,' the spy said. 'And, of course, after you have given me my due.' A mocking bow accompanied this. Rouwen caught his breath again and tensed. His anger mounted. A plot to kill the king could not be tolerated, and this shadowy agent made light of the assassination. Indeed, the spy was no patriot.

'The money is in the usual place,' Rouwen said. He never carried coin with him. The jangling while he patrolled defeated any attempt at silent movement. Awakening sleeping guards wasn't his intent; preventing them from sleeping on duty was better served when he could discipline the malingerers. 'There will be no action against Nishor for a few days, either.'

'Of course not, my dear *Deputy* Defender of the Realm. Without Duke Sosler's cooperation, no troops can be used outside the valley.' The spy cleared his throat, then laughed outright. 'Without the good duke, no troops can be used – ever. Or will you retaliate in kind, with poisons and slender daggers in the back?'

Rouwen seethed. The spy put him in his place. He was only a commoner, in charge of the king's castle guard but not authorized to deploy the army. Only the Empire's Lord Protector commanded troops beyond the castle's walls.

'Go. It is best if you never return to Gan.'

'I am no fool, Captain.' Again the mocking bow. A soft rustle of the expansive dark cloak marked the spy's exit. Rouwen paused a moment and swallowed his anger. There was something more in the spy's words, a hint, a promise, something known but not shared, that gnawed at Rouwen. He pushed it aside. Such gossipmongers always maneuvered for the edge to gain an extra coin or two for their information.

Rouwen looked around and found himself alone on the parapet. The sentry was nowhere to be seen, and the informant had melted back into the shadows with the cockroaches where he belonged. Rouwen walked slowly, hands clasped behind his back, as he considered his best course of action. Two cooks entrusted with preparing food for the king and queen plotted with King Nishor of Mion to seize control of Castle Gan. Knowing little of politics outside the castle, Rouwen wasn't sure if this was a realistic attack. What he did know was that any such endeavor had to fail. That was his duty.

And if he was to prove worthy of elevation to the rank of third baron, he had to bring this to Duke Sosler's attention to prepare for any possible armed invasion by Nishor's army. It did no good assassinating Priowe without an armed invasion following the royal death. Rouwen and the duke had never been anything more than formally polite to each other, because of their different backgrounds. In truth, Rouwen admitted he had done as much to create tension between them because of his insistence on iron control of the castle guard, with no advice sought or accepted from Duke Sosler.

Rouwen stopped on his patrol and stared toward the Demon's Throat. The narrow pass had withstood more attacks than Rouwen could count. He knelt and fumbled out the magic window stored in a box at this sentry point. It took several minutes for the captain to settle the magical device on its tripod and aim it at the Throat.

The smooth silver tube hummed with magical energy as Rouwen bent over and stared into the dark chamber. The hair on his head began to rise and flutter about wildly. The long, dark hair stood on end, turning his head into a spiked ball as Rouwen began to discern a faint outline that turned into dancing red and green lines. A few more seconds passed and the night evaporated, allowing Rouwen to see the defensive positions along the Demon's Throat.

Fires wavered in green and red outlines showing soldiers moving restlessly. The longer he stared through the magic window, the more distinct the images became. Careful examination of the distant positions showed nothing unusual. All was well at the empire's periphery. The only decay came from within Castle Gan.

'Two cooks,' muttered Rouwen. He had two of the castle staff to send to the Fingers of Providence, but first there were other considerations. Rouwen started to put away the magic window, then hesitated. He looked toward Mount Glid. Illumination from the Lesser Moon caused the dancing, gauzy, pale witch light to leap far into the sky from the rock, making it seem that the mountain itself had turned to liquid ivory flame. Rouwen started to turn the magic window toward Glid, then stopped. He had been warned against such foolish surveys. He knew nothing of the magicks locked within the silver tube but more than one wizard told him he would be blinded if he should ever look at Mount Glid and the souls leaping from the rocky surface to Paradise.

Rouwen wasn't certain if they told the truth. Wizards sought to defend their arcane knowledge and weren't above lying or sowing the seeds of fear to do it. Souls might depart from the slopes of Mount Glid, but he wasn't certain the burning witch fires were the physical manifestation and that he would go blind if he tried to view them. He wasn't sure if the witch fires weren't some trick of light from the Lesser Moon, but he didn't turn the magic window in Glid's direction. Rouwen carefully dismantled the silver tube and tripod and stored it in

9

the special compartment. Now was not the time to test his own theories of soul and death and magic.

Rouwen continued his deliberate pacing along the battlements, checking the few soldiers on duty and finding them comfortingly alert. They knew better than to sleep when their captain might check their vigilance at any time, night or day.

'Anything out of the ordinary to report?' Rouwen demanded of the sergeant of the watch. He glanced toward Mount Glid. The Greater Moon rose. The hour of treachery was upon Gan.

'Some activity lower in the castle, Captain,' came the answer. The sergeant was old, battered and had endured more commanders than battles. Still, Rouwen trusted the man's judgment. 'A buzz among the scullery workers.'

Rouwen blinked. He had not found out from his spy when the assassination attempt was to be made. The informant had distracted him with mention of Princess Sorinne. Was this deliberate? The spy knew of Rouwen's affair and so much more.

'Sergeant,' snapped Rouwen, coming to an immediate decision. 'Continue my watch. There is trouble brewing.'

'Do you want the guard roused, Captain?'

'No, let the Intrepids sleep,' Rouwen said. 'This isn't the time to show force. Subtlety is needed.'

'As you wish, Captain,' the sergeant said, his expression sour. The machinations of the nobles – and those longing to be noble – did not interest him.

Rouwen hurried to the tower and took the steps down the tightly turning staircase as quickly as he could. His rapier banged against the steps as he raced to lower levels, found the trap-step and jumped over it, then came to a halt at the base of the stairs. Two sentries should have been stationed here. Rouwen saw no trace of them. He considered following the sergeant's suggestion and calling out the guard. Assassins moved through the castle at will, and he had only learned small parts of the plan.

'What if the poisoning was to be a diversion from the real crime?' he mused. Too many details went unreported and Rouwen felt a growing sense of limited time.

'You spoke, Captain?' came the question from down the corridor. Rouwen spun, hand on his sword hilt. He saw a pair of guardsmen pacing slowly in his direction.

'You left your post,' he accused. 'Why?'

'We heard noises down the hall. It was – nothing,' the guardsman said. He swallowed hard and his eyes darted away for a split second. Rouwen didn't know what the man hid, but it bothered him. He did not want to believe any of his

Intrepids were involved in Nishor's plot to kill the king and queen.

'Near the Princess Sorinne's quarters?' he asked, trying not to sound overly concerned.

'It was nothing,' the guard said with more determination. 'The princess is secure in her quarters.'

'You saw her?'

'Of course not, Captain,' the other guard said with some irritation. 'We spoke with her servants. Her dresser assured us the princess went to her sleeping chambers more than an hour ago.'

Rouwen remembered how the Greater Moon had risen, Mount Glid between it and the Lesser Moon. The hour of treachery. Poisoners in the castle's kitchen. King Nishor deciding he coveted the Kingdom of Gan more than he did peace. And Sorinne was in her chambers, asleep – or so said her servants. Rouwen knew them all and trusted their devotion to their mistress, but he also knew apprentice cook Zeegon and master chef Clanna Beg-Nonn and had personally approved their employment. What inducement had been offered Beg-Nonn? Rouwen couldn't tell. He had thought the woman to be above mere bribery. If anything, the master chef's devotion to her craft had seemed to transcend political manipulation.

Rouwen felt as if he had walked into a pleasant glade dotted with fragrant yellow and red spring flowers and covered with gently swaying grass and found only quicksand beneath his feet.

'Continue your rounds, but be alert. Betrayal stalks everyone in Castle Gan tonight.'

'Yes, Captain Rouwen,' the guards responded in unison. They waited for their commander to rush off in the direction of Princess Sorinne's chambers. Only then did they proceed along their watch, both whispering at the same time about their captain's infatuation.

Rouwen stopped in front of the carved wooden door festooned with bright brass studs. How many times had he entered this door and made love all night with the princess? Rouwen could not remember, even though each time had been sweet and special for him. He reached out, then paused. Did he dare go farther?

Did he dare not to?

Brion Rouwen opened the door slowly and peered inside to the princess's sitting room. A light meal sat on the table. Rouwen turned cold. He rushed inside and looked around, searching for the princess's tasters. Rouwen spun in a circle, his heavy cloak swirling out in a wide crimson circle. From a side room came

11

soft sounds he knew well, a giggle and a sigh and soft moans of passion.

Rouwen strode to the door and opened it. In a smaller room were the princess's tasters, a man and a woman. They were so passionately engaged that they did not notice him. Rouwen closed the door and rushed to a far door, one inset with jewels and bearing the crest of the Princess of Gan. He barged in.

Sorinne lay in her bed, turning and tossing restlessly. She let out a low moan that might have been one of pain. Rouwen ran to her side and dropped to one knee. He touched her forehead. Sorinne's eyes fluttered open, and it took several seconds for her to shrug off the clinging vestiges of sleep befuddling her senses.

'Brion?' she asked. 'What is it?'

'The meal on the table in your sitting room. Did you eat any of it?'

'What? No, yes, no, no, I didn't.' She sat up in bed, rubbing sleep from her eyes. Rouwen's heart almost stopped beating with relief. Sorinne wore only a thin nightgown. Through the translucent folds of pink and green Rouwen saw the slow rise and fall of the breasts he had fallen asleep against so many times. The princess's color was good and now that sleep was fleeing, she looked more alert.

'You feel well?'

'I have not been sleeping well. Dreams of . . .' She bit off any further explanation. 'What is wrong?'

'Nothing, now that I know you are safe.' He kissed her lightly, then hurried to the door.

'Brion, wait.' The steel edge of imperial command halted him. 'Something is not right. Tell me what it is.'

'Go back to sleep. All is under control.' She started to order him to speak. He forestalled her with, 'I'll explain when I return. Stay here – and do not eat or drink anything.'

'Very well.' Sorinne looked mildly piqued but did not pursue the matter. 'Brion?'

He had to see to his job, and she insisted on holding him back. Rouwen looked back at Sorinne. She smiled a little and said, 'Hurry back to me.' She patted the bed beside her.

For a moment, Rouwen almost forgot the danger facing the rulers of Castle Gan. He nodded and then closed the door behind him. He leaned against it for a moment, then strained to hear the sounds of lovemaking still coming from the adjoining room. The tasters acted as a protective wall between the princess and those who might seek her injury. Not only were they to sample all

12

food and drink, they were to remain in this room to intercept any unwanted visitors.

They had failed on one count in their sworn duty. Rouwen wondered if Zeegon and Beg-Nonn had already struck, putting their vile fast-acting powdered *thouse* beak poison in the princess's midnight repast. Rouwen went to the outer door and looked up and down the long, quiet corridor. Just as he started to call out for the guard, the two he had rebuked earlier marched into view at the far end of the corridor. He waved for them to hurry. They broke into a trot and came to a halt in front of him, standing stiffly at attention.

'Yes, Captain?' The one who had avoided his gaze before now stared past him, again avoiding his cold gray eyes. Rouwen recognized the reason. The guard had tried to protect the two, through whatever misguided motive.

'The princess's two tasters are in the side room. Take them into custody and put them in the dungeons. The lowest level.'

'Sir, what have they done?'

'Dereliction of duty.' Rouwen cocked his head to one side and listened to the laughter coming from the adjoining room. 'See to it immediately.'

He received no answer, but both guardsmen hurried to obey. Rouwen wondered what held back his soldier from reporting this failure of the princess's staff earlier. When the guardsmen pulled the tasters from the room, neither fully dressed, Rouwen read the answer on the woman's face.

His guardsman and this woman shared more than a roof over their heads.

'The food,' Rouwen said, stopping them from leaving immediately. 'Have you sampled it for the princess?'

'Yes, of course. We know our duty,' protested the man. Rouwen didn't recognize him, and this worried him. As Captain of the Intrepid Guard, he should have approved all Sorinne's protective staff. Petty details grew into overwhelming duties, but he needed to get a tighter grip on what was happening inside the castle.

'Eat it. All of it,' Rouwen ordered. The man shrugged. One guard released him as he began eating. Rouwen waited for any reaction and saw none. The man finished every last crumb, then washed it down with the entire contents of the wine goblet. A slow smile came to the man's face and he turned to the woman, reaching for her.

Rouwen saw the taster's response, and it astounded him. They paid no attention to him, only to each other as they began kissing.

'Take them to the dungeons as I ordered,' Rouwen said. The food had been safe. That did not alter the pair's delinquency or insubordination in front of their commander. Sorinne had been left at risk.

He followed the guards and their protesting amorous prisoners into the corridor and watched until they descended the far staircase leading to lower levels. Rouwen looked over his shoulder into the sitting room and at the door to Sorinne's sleeping quarters. He wanted to go to her, to comfort her, to tell her of the plot against her and her parents. Rouwen held back. It was better for him to stand guard until another patrol came by.

For all his attention, Brion Rouwen did not see the shadow-cloaked figure duck back into an alcove. A soft chuckle escaped the figure's lips. All proceeded well, better than anticipated.

2

The Queen's Indiscretion

In less than ten minutes another pair of guardsmen marched into the corridor, heels clicking loudly as they tramped along. Brion Rouwen motioned to them. They exchanged curious glances, then hurried to their captain.

'What's wrong?' asked the senior of the pair, a man Rouwen had recruited himself from a failed horse farm on the outskirts of the Valley Gan. 'We're at your command, Captain.'

'Post yourselves here and let no one through. The princess's guards have proven themselves inadequate for the task. I'll have no more failure.' He started off, then paused. He remembered Sorinne's loving smile and the invitation to return to her bed. Rouwen shook off the urge to obey his princess in favour of pursuing the murderous cabal within the castle.

'Is there something more, Captain?'

'Let no one bearing food enter. Do not allow the princess to dine until I've cleared it.' Rouwen forestalled any argument by turning and leaving. He heard the two guards whispering their questions. Such orders were more than unusual coming from him. They were unheard of in the guardsmen's memories. Rouwen preferred for his eccentric orders to spur rumors rather than activating the Intrepids at this moment. If he could quell the assassins without unduly arousing anyone else in the castle, his job would be more perfectly performed.

He began the descent to the dungeons where his guardsmen held the two tasters. He had to issue immediate orders to arrest the cooks, also, but he needed to know how far this cancerous plot had spread. If the princess's tasters were guilty only of lust, he would rest the easier for it. That would not lessen the punishment he intended for them; they had failed their princess by their immoderate coupling.

If they had been employed by Nishor, the plot would have to be revealed instantly to King Priowe. Rouwen continued down the spiralling staircase leading hundreds of steps into the heart of the rocky spire cradling Castle Gan. He glanced down the corridor where his quarters lay. Dozens of Intrepids were asleep in barracks farther away. Alerting them when there was no urgent need rankled, yet Rouwen was beginning to feel uneasy. He was missing some salient fact, some part of the scheme that might trip him up.

A mistake now meant the death of those he both served and loved.

'Brion, a word with you!' A crippled man waved to him from the room next to Rouwen's quarters. He dragged his twisted left leg behind as if it were a heavy log, more a burden than a help to movement. What caught Rouwen's eye was the swirling purple sparks left in the air as the man gestured.

Nespizio made a second gesture, trailing crazily spinning silver scintillants behind his finger this time. Whenever the wizard went to such trouble to capture his attention, Rouwen gladly offered it. Of all those he dealt with, Nespizio had the best sense of importance and never wasted his time.

'I'm on my way to an interrogation. Would you accompany me?'

'The princess's tasters, eh? You finally caught them in a lover's tryst?' Nespizio chuckled a little, then turned solemn once more. 'They are nothing. Do not concern yourself with them, Brion. There is more afoot this night.'

'The hour of treachery,' Rouwen said, remembering how the Greater Moon had been slipping into place above Mount Glid.

'Yes, yes, that, but there is more. I have found out about betrayal within Castle Gan. You must be aware of it and act immediately.' Nespizio looked at him through a filmy left eye. Of his right eye, only a gaping socket remained. Rouwen often wondered why the wizard did not wear an eye patch. His only conclusion had been the stark effect it had on those unaccustomed to viewing such a twisted caricature of a man. Nespizio used his infirmity as a weapon, a diversion, a crutch. It had never worked with Rouwen, and that had forged the bond between them, commoner and wizard, that had endured for more than five years.

'I've learned of it already,' he said softly. 'The king must be told, but I want to remove the threat before informing him.'

'The king? The plot is against *you*, my boy.' Nespizio stabbed a finger out that shot purple-white sparks. Rouwen had no time for such theatrics.

'There is no plot against me,' Rouwen said in irritation. 'Nishor has bought assassins to kill the king. My spies have given names.

This very night those two lovers whom you dismiss so easily might have allowed Princess Sorinne to eat poisoned food.'

'Who is this spy?' demanded Nespizio. 'You never tell me his name, yet he uncovers such fine – hidden – tidbits.'

Rouwen knew what the wizard meant. The spy had never revealed his identity, yet Rouwen had never found the spy's facts wanting. Part of their relationship had included Rouwen's agreement not to put a name to him. Rouwen thought he caught hints of the spy's identity now and again, in fragments of speech pattern, in ways of movement and dress, yet he had never been positive. And it did not matter. The informant had always been right.

'You worry that you don't know the spy's allegiance,' Rouwen said. 'I worried on this when he first came to me, but he has proven himself. Never has he betrayed my confidence.'

'Why? Why would such a highborn sell out his companions for a few coins?' Nespizio cocked his head to one side, fixing the filmy eye squarely on Rouwen. The captain knew this almost blind eye saw more than most men, and Nespizio never stopped thinking. The wizard turned over every detail in his mind, putting them together in new and unexpected ways until truth was his for the taking. But he had never learned who Rouwen's spy was, either, and this rankled.

'What makes you think he is highborn? He might be a guardsman or a gentryman with strong interest in maintaining his prosperity. Food is scarce, even in the good years, outside the Valley Gan.'

'He is highborn,' Nespizio declared. 'I have tried to scry his face and always he is protected by potent magicks. You met with him this night on the battlements, yet I saw only shifting mist where he stood. I cannot even tell the source of the protecting spells, though they might come from within the castle.'

'He is cautious,' Rouwen said, dismissing the wizard's concern. There were a few other wizards within the castle's walls, and they all harbored suspicions about each other. The king's wizard, Kwuway, trusted no one, and few save Priowe trusted him. Thus it ever was among the spellcasters. 'Why did you stop me? My time is precious.'

'The plot is against *you*,' Nespizio repeated. 'Of all those in Castle Gan, you are the most honest and diligent. I do not want to work with a new Captain of the Intrepid Guard.' Nespizio made another gesture that formed an emptiness in the air that Rouwen found irresistible. He stared into – blackness. There was nothing

17

in this bobbing dot and yet there was a captivating, swirling chaos that befuddled him.

Rouwen threw up his cloak and shielded his eyes. 'I should run you through, Nespizio. Never try to bind me with your magicks. Never!'

'It is for your own good, Brion. I do not apologize for having your best interests at heart. Go with care, and remember that those who seem to be your friends are not.'

'Such as you?' Rouwen shot back. He saw the flash of sadness on the old wizard's face and immediately regretted his sharp, inconsiderate words. Rouwen reached out and took Nespizio's shoulder, giving it a reassuring squeeze.

'You have no allies,' Nespizio warned. 'Trust no one, and you will be far safer than you are at this instant.'

'I trust you, old friend,' Rouwen said. 'Now I must begin the interrogation. Even if there is nothing sinister about the tasters, they forsook their duty for a quick tumble.'

'Duty weighs too heavily on you, except with the princess, eh?'

Rouwen snorted at this and went back to the staircase. His spy and Nespizio both knew of his romance with Sorinne. Who else did, in spite of his caution to protect her from salacious gossip? After elevation to baron, there need be no further secrecy. He could petition King Priowe for his daughter's hand and, from all indications, receive his liege's blessing for a marriage. Priowe thought almost as well of Rouwen as did his daughter.

Or perhaps he only deluded himself as to Sorinne's intentions. Rouwen stopped and put his head against the cold stone of the wall. Even Nespizio befouled his thoughts. Sorinne loved him with as much passion as he did her. The seeds of doubt required only the rocky soil of suspicion to grow. He cursed Nespizio, but not what the wizard thought he was doing.

Rouwen was loyal to Priowe and would die in the king's defense. For his daughter, he would starve in Paradise.

He spiralled down to the dungeons, finding the level where his guards had brought the tasters. The man and woman were chained, still half-naked, and shivered in the coldness – or from fear. Rouwen would have to determine which it was.

'Confess now and your souls might be granted some small favor when you ascend from Mount Glid,' he said without preamble. They read no hint of mercy in his words. They were to be executed, if not for attempted assassination, then for dereliction of duty. To Rouwen's mind, one was akin to the other and differed only in degree. A moment's reckless passion might have allowed assassins to slay Princess Sorinne.

'Captain, we did nothing but give in to our desires,' the man pleaded. 'We would have heard anyone entering the princess's chambers and given our lives to protect her!'

'I entered, watched you, then spoke with Sorinne, left and summoned the guards. At no time did you take heed of my presence. If I had meant harm to the princess, she would have died and you would never have known until your vile cravings were sated.'

'You are a man,' sobbed the woman. 'Take pity on us. We know nothing of any plot to kill the princess. We sought only a moment's diversion. Nothing more.'

'Show them the instruments of torture,' Rouwen ordered. The two miscreants paled and began to babble. An assistant torturer whose work Rouwen considered adequate came over and began laying out the implements he would use. Ritual had to be followed.

The question had been put and a request for confession made. The prisoners had not confessed. The torturer would show the instruments, request a confession, then begin using only those devices he had displayed. At periodic times a demand for confession would be made. When it came, Rouwen would accept it and order the two off the plank on the battlements. The Fingers would grip their miserable lust-surfeited bodies before dawn.

'Keep me apprised of the progress,' Rouwen ordered. The guardsmen looked surly but nodded agreement. The one couldn't take his eyes off the woman and her terror at the impending torture. Rouwen worried again that the plot had spread throughout the Intrepid. He had best review the other guards before reporting the assassination conspiracy brewing in the castle's kitchens to King Priowe.

The captain considered awakening his officers and putting them on direct duty protecting the king and queen, but Nespizio had been successful in creating misgivings. There was no one he could trust totally, save for the old wizard and Sorinne.

Rouwen mounted the stairs, found a crossing hall to the queen's wing and stopped when he came to the sentry point at the juncture of two corridors. Three of the Intrepid looked at him, hands on sword and dagger and crossbow. None relaxed when they saw it was their captain. Rouwen had trained them well.

'Any disturbances this night?' he asked.

'None. No one's entered the queen's chambers since she

retired.' The sergeant of the guard's lip curled slightly as he spoke. 'She's just up to her old tricks, that's all.'

Rouwen did not question the man directly. All the Intrepid had stories of the queen's peculiar nocturnal rituals. Weird chants and loud cries of inhuman shrillness were among the reports. Rouwen had never spied on the queen's quarters directly, but he had determined she was always alone when the sounds echoed up and down the corridor. Few considered the lovely Queen Diarra to be of sound mind.

'What of her meals?'

'She's taken no food for the entire lovin' day,' came the report. 'Leastwise, not since her breakfast at first light. Cannot say why, save that she's in one of her fine moods. Been dancin' away, she has. Up and down the halls, listenin' to music only she hears.' The guardsman glanced past Rouwen, alert for anything. Rouwen swelled with pride at such diligence. The sergeant was not being lulled into complacency because he spoke with his superior.

'See that she gets no more food until I authorize it,' Rouwen said. 'When was the last check past her chambers?'

'An hour back. There's no need to annoy her with our marching, Captain.' The sergeant sounded a little defensive about the lack of direct patrol, but Rouwen had permitted it, agreeing the queen's privacy was more important than minute-to-minute protection.

'You are doing well. Put your squad in for a food bonus at the Spring Festivals.'

'Thank you, Captain,' the sergeant said. Even this reward did not slacken his wary attention.

Rouwen started off to report to the king, then paused. He had the eerie sensation of someone watching him, watching and laughing. Back along the corridor he had just traversed were few doors, all securely locked. The staircase at the end of the hall loomed hollow and empty. Rouwen shook off his uneasiness as being caused by Nespizio's ill-considered warning. He found himself jumping at shadows and doubting the loyalty of men he had commanded for five years. Many of them he had been with for the full ten years he had spent with the Intrepid.

'I'll look in on the queen. No servants?' Rouwen knew the answer before he heard it from his sergeant. Queen Diarra did most things for herself, preferring to have no dresser or servant near her. This was met with great relief among the castle's attendants. For them Queen Diarra's strange flights of fancy were too much to be borne. Strange dancing to unheard music was only a part of her peculiar behavior. Ofttimes, like a mad dog, she snarled and snapped at her servants over the most picayune details.

Rouwen walked down the broad corridor, slowing as he approached the queen's chambers. He heard soft music coming from inside, then realized it was the queen singing. Pausing, wanting to be sure she was alone in her chambers, Rouwen found himself leaning toward her door as if he were some sneak thief in the night. He straightened, made his decision, knocked and waited for a reply.

Getting none, he opened the door slightly and called out, 'Queen Diarra? Is all well?'

The music swelled as the queen hummed and put nonsense words to the tune. Rouwen opened the door a little farther and saw the queen dancing naked through her lavishly appointed chambers. She spun and whirled and leaped onto chairs and tables, as graceful as any of the Spring dancers – and far more attractive.

Rouwen saw that Sorinne had come by her beauty honestly. The queen had married at fifteen and had borne the princess when she was scarcely sixteen. The difference in their ages was only eighteen years. For the first time Rouwen realized that he was seven years older than Sorinne and only eight years younger than the queen. This sudden realization made Rouwen strangely uneasy. Taking the queen as lover was as possible as her daughter.

'Excuse me, Your Majesty. I did not mean to intrude –' He started to close the door, but Queen Diarra spun through her elaborate dance, leaped like a young gazelle from the table and whirled past him into the corridor, her naked body flashing like washed ivory in the corridor's dim light.

'Please, come inside,' he urged. Rouwen was acutely aware that his guardsmen at their post were watching the naked queen cavort about like a drunken tavern wanton. He reached for her and somehow she melted into his arms, a perfect fit. Pressing against his body, she caught him off balance and spun him around in a parody of a high cotillion dance popular years ago. Like a frolicking colt, she tossed her head and sent streamers of blonde hair flying. He was all too aware of the lushness of her body and how her beautiful face upturned slightly to meet his, her full red lips parted and her eyes hooded as if passion controlled her totally.

'You are my prince, and you must dance with me,' Diarra said, laughing gaily. In her dark eyes Rouwen saw only burning madness. The queen had slipped into a realm beyond the rule of any man and possibly beyond reach.

21

'Please, Majesty, let me summon the court physician. He can . . .'

'He cannot cut in!' she cried. 'I want this dance with you, just you, my lovely, loving lover.' Diarra swung him around powerfully, causing Rouwen to lose his balance as he stumbled over his cloak and became entangled in his sword's sheath. She laughed in delight at his clumsiness and continued to pull and tug, keeping him off balance and struggling.

He was increasingly aware of her body pressing nakedly into his own as she rubbed herself against him in feline greeting. In size she was so much like his beloved Sorinne. But there the comparisons ended. The madness lurking in the queen's dark eyes drove away any hope of reasoning with her.

'A wizard,' he suggested, getting his feet under him. She clung to him, her breasts flattened against his chest. She hooked a leg around his waist and rubbed herself up and down, then seemed to break down and placed her face into his shoulder. Diarra began crying softly, as if she realized her plight and was unable to change her unseemly behavior.

'I can see if Nespizio can cast a spell to ease your pain,' Rouwen suggested uneasily.

'Pain? I feel no pain. I feel only – excitement. I crave stimulation, and you can give it to me!' Diarra's mood shifted suddenly and she moved closer, her slender leg lifting and circling his waist again. She settled down over the hilt of his rapier and began a sinuous movement that again took Rouwen by surprise. Agitated, not knowing how to cope with the outrageous behavior, he tried to step back.

He found himself pinned against the wall by her full weight. She smothered him with kisses, even as her hips continued working against the rounded hilt of his sword. Her fingers began working over his body, seeking ties and snaps and buttons, pulling and tearing, stripping the uniform from him.

'Your Majesty, stop!' Rouwen twisted to one side, grabbing the queen's slender wrists in a wrestling hold. If Diarra tried to break free, he would throw her to the floor. Rouwen worried that he might harm her as she fought against him.

'You're hurting me,' she protested. 'I order you to release me. I am your queen, and I demand to be obeyed!'

Rouwen relaxed his hold and immediately regretted it. Queen Diarra surged forward, her arms circling his neck. She pulled his face down to hers and kissed him hard on the lips. Her legs twined around his body and prevented him from escaping easily.

'You taste so tasty!' she cooed. She bit his neck and forced him to yelp in pain at the unexpected attack. 'Even your blood is so good!' She began licking at the wound she had inflicted on him.

'Your Majesty, I come with news of an assassination attempt,' Rouwen said desperately. He tried to get her to pause for a moment. He dared not harm her since he was pledged to protect her, yet he could not countenance her promiscuous behavior, even if it sprang from the well of a sick mind.

'Who cares? Let them kill us all!'

Rouwen shifted his weight slightly and Diarra followed the movement. He grabbed her wrists again to hold her at bay. He started to call to his men to summon the court physician and wizard. One man's expertise might not be enough if Queen Diarra's malady was more than physical, more than magical.

To his surprise, she reversed the hold on him, gripped his brawny wrists and sank to one knee. He found himself somersaulting across the room. Rouwen smashed into the queen's bed and fought to keep his balance. He lost the battle when the naked woman swarmed over him, forcing him to the soft feather mattress.

'Do you find me attractive?' she asked. 'I am so lovely that it brings a catch to men's throats. Let me loosen the compliments so you may tell me how desirable you find me!'

Just as Diarra bent forward with Rouwen trapped beneath her on the bed, the door to her chamber slammed hard against the wall.

'Treachery!' shouted the man standing there. 'Is this how you protect your queen?'

Rouwen looked over and saw Duke Sosler, Lord Protector of Gan. What brought the commander of the empire's army to the queen's chamber at this time of night was less on Rouwen's mind than the compromising position he found himself in. But he knew he could explain to Sosler. The man was clever and might find a way to turn this to his own advantage, but Rouwen would not suffer for it.

'Duke, I . . .'

The words became tangled in Rouwen's throat. Behind Duke Sosler stood King Priowe – and behind him were arrayed a dozen or more of the king's personal guard.

3

Despair and Hope

'Majesty!' cried Brion Rouwen, struggling underneath Queen Diarra's pinning weight. The woman refused to stop kissing and caressing him although her husband stood watching her blatant infidelity. Her nakedness only served to infuriate Priowe more. The king's eyes flashed angrily as he raised his meaty fists and shook them impotently in the air. He started to speak but only sputtered in his rage.

For all the king's anger, Duke Sosler showed none. In a cold, level voice, he ordered, 'Take him to the dungeons. Immediately!' He motioned to the king's guard, six of whom pushed past the nobles and rushed to the queen's bedside. Rouwen heaved and threw the woman to one side. His uniform tunic was ripped off, but his crimson-and-gold cloak was still fastened around his neck. He tried to put his clothing into order and found himself being strangled by the cloak's broad wrought-silver catch. The time it took for Rouwen to free himself allowed the king's guard to grab his rapier and jerk it free from its sheath.

His dagger followed quickly, and Rouwen found himself half-naked and unarmed.

'Majesty, there is something wrong,' he pleaded. His mind raced. Nespizio had claimed the conspiracy was against him, but he had doubted this. Even now Rouwen thought there was something more afoot in Castle Gan. He simply couldn't order his thoughts and put the right words into a convincing argument.

'Don't torture him until I get there,' Priowe said, not even looking at his Captain of the Intrepid Guard. The king's attention went to his wife. Diarra's dark eyes were wide and wild. She licked her lips and held her arms out to her husband, lewdly inviting him with both gesture and word.

The king slapped Diarra, sending her across the bed to fall off the far side. She tried to get up, became tangled in the bedclothes and fell heavily. Priowe circled the bed, his rage growing with every step he took.

'Your Majesty, wait,' Rouwen cried. 'It's not her fault. There's more than there appears to this seeming indiscretion.'

'He will never believe the evidence provided by his own eyes,' Duke Sosler said in a low voice that only Rouwen heard. He shoved Rouwen out of the room, then followed with the guards. Sounds of King Priowe repeatedly striking his wife echoed down the corridor until Sosler closed the chamber door.

Rouwen looked to the Intrepid guardsmen posted at the end of the corridor. The sergeant pointedly ignored him, his eyes going past to stare at a blank wall. Rouwen's heart almost exploded in his chest when he realized he was no longer a captain in the castle guard. A moment's misunderstanding, a crazy woman's uncontrolled lust, his own insistence on personally inspecting his queen's quarters had ruined his career – and possibly cost him his life.

King Priowe was a just king, but no one had ever thought him merciful. Life, even in the prosperous Kingdom of Gan, was difficult and often called for the imposition of harsh authority. Another year of drought and even the well-fed within Castle Gan would begin to sleep with growling bellies.

'So our ambitious commoner thinks to have for himself what rightly belongs to the king,' Sosler said as they spiralled down to the dungeons. Rouwen couldn't help remembering his last trip to the lower levels of the castle. It had been to order the torture and confession from Princess Sorinne's tasters. Somehow, each step downward felt quicker and more final for Brion Rouwen this time.

'There is a plot to kill the king,' Rouwen said.

'Indeed? You confess to wishing our king ill? As well as so senselessly humiliating him? I never thought you would endure much torture, but this sudden urge of yours to divulge all your transgressions astounds me. Perhaps it is best that one of such weak moral fiber be removed from command, no matter what the crime.'

'I'm not confessing to anything,' Rouwen shouted, struggling in the guardsmen's grip. 'There is a plot in the kitchen to poison the king and queen. Two cooks. Princess Sorinne's tasters will give corroborating testimony. They . . .'

'Ah,' said Sosler, stopping to stare at Rouwen, as if he had just found a cockroach in his food. The tall, thin duke touched his nose in an unconscious gesture, then adjusted his floppy, gold-chased cap to push thin, sandy hair back under it. 'The traitor thinks to muddy the waters of thought with false allegations. Is it ever this way?' the duke said in disgust.

25

'Clanna Beg-Nonn is to use *thouse* beak poison to . . .'

'Silence him,' Sosler said, pointing to the guard at Rouwen's left. The guardsman crammed a filthy rag into the captain's mouth. Rouwen tried to pull it free, only to be held firmly by three powerful guards. A thin rawhide cord looped around his head and tightened on the gag, keeping it securely lodged against his tongue.

'I take my duties as Lord Protector of the Realm seriously,' Sosler said tendentiously, as they continued to walk through the dungeons. The duke cast a sidelong look at the guards to see if his message had been well received. He sniffed in disgust when he saw that they paid him no heed, concentrating entirely on their captive.

The party of prisoner and captors came to a smaller door leading to the lowest depths of the dungeon. Only a few prisoners ever merited such close imprisonment. Rouwen had thought his situation perilous but not hopeless until this moment. That he would be taken to the few cells below drove home how ignoble his standing had become in just a few minutes with Queen Diarra.

'I am responsible for defending the kingdom from all enemies beyond the walls of Castle Gan. You, as Captain of the Intrepid Guard, were supposed to defend those within the castle against all other enemies. Together we would have concocted defense for the entire realm had you been elevated to noble rank. I tell you all this in the hope that you can explain lucidly why you sought to betray not only your liege but your kingdom.' Sosler took his duties as seriously as Rouwen, but there was no reason for him to assume power within the castle – until now. Rouwen struggled to speak.

Sosler pointed to a set of manacles dangling from an overhead beam. The guards securely fastened Rouwen before pulling the gag from his mouth. Rouwen almost choked as his tongue was freed of the filthy fabric.

'I do not want to assume the onerous responsibilities of patrolling inside the castle,' Sosler said in an offhand manner, 'but you have forced this upon me. Why, Rouwen, why? Explain yourself.'

'Poison,' Rouwen gasped out. His tongue felt as if it had puffed to double its normal size.

'You prattled about *thouse* beak and chef Beg-Nonn. There is nothing to this vile calumny,' Sosler said. He paused for a moment, then added, 'I have conducted a lengthy investigation for King Priowe and those whom you indicted are honest and hardworking, not the sort to plot overthrow and assassination.'

'Not a deadly poison,' Rouwen said, pieces coming together to form a more coherent picture. 'The food is contaminated. Princess Sorinne's was. Her tasters . . .'

'They have regrettably died,' Sosler said. The duke paced slowly, hands clasped behind his back and bony chin lowered to his chest. As he moved, his sword clanked and his dagger hilt whispered softly across voluminous, dangling gray silk sleeves. 'They did not bear up well under the regimen of torture you ordered. Did you have to kill them to hide your own guilt? What did they know that you wished to conceal from your liege?'

'Aphrodisiacs,' Rouwen blurted. 'There wasn't poison put into the food, but aphrodisiacs. That explains their behavior. The tasters were conscientious servants, yet they allowed their baser instincts to run free.'

'You attribute their behaviour to sampling the princess's food?' Sosler almost smiled. The corners of his mouth twitched and lines began to form around his deep-set eyes. The grin faded before it formed fully. 'That is quite good, Rouwen. Innovative. Perhaps you will amuse us further during torture. We are bringing in Baron Chertude to perform the necessary manipulations.'

Rouwen fought to keep himself from quaking in stark fear. Chertude was the realm's master torturer. In the past few years his sophisticated services had not been required often. Rouwen could remember only one instance where the baron's subtle and slowly escalating techniques had been used. A diplomat, trusted with delicate state secrets by the king, had betrayed his position to King Nishor. Chertude had worked on the diplomat for more than a week until the full details were brought forth. The torture had been as masterful as it had been painful.

Rouwen remembered it, and he considered how Chertude might proceed on him. He would confess secrets he did not even know he held before the pain master had finished with his shining knives, heated pins and entrails-boring cutworms.

'Queen Diarra ate a full meal yesterday morning. She must have consumed a large quantity of the aphrodisiac. See how her tasters fared during the day. This will prove my theory!'

'You are suggesting they engaged in activity similar to yours with the queen?' Sosler shook his head at such a feeble attempt to escape true confession and repentance. 'For twenty years I have commanded the armies of Gan. Never have I heard such utter nonsense. Privates have alibied their inattention on duty to powerful wizards ensorcelling them. Officers have tried to make me believe souls from Mount Glid had taken control of their bodies and forced them into obscene and traitorous behaviors. But never have I heard such marvelous invention. I do not know whether to congratulate or condemn you for your ingenuity, Rouwen.'

'Check for yourself. See if it is so. It must be.'

'What is the purpose of such an aphrodisiac poisoning? Our enemies seek to make us screw ourselves to death?' Sosler continued pacing but fell silent as he worked over the possibilities inherent in such an attack.

'Nishor is behind this plot. He has always coveted the wealth and power of Gan. We have secure food crops that do not exist in the Kingdom of Mion. Drought destroys his land and causes unrest among his citizens. He needs our harvests!'

'How have you learned all this?' Sosler stopped and stared at his prisoner. Rouwen saw no sympathy in the duke's pale blue eyes. 'Do you go through the Office of Intelligence? Baroness Freya knows of your data gathering?'

'She knows nothing of it. I have a spy in my pay.'

'Who? Name him,' demanded Sosler. 'Let him come forth to tell us of these terrible plots. But it still does not excuse your behavior with Queen Diarra.'

'I do not know the spy's name. He has always remained an enigma. But his information is reliable.' Rouwen realized how feeble this sounded as a defense. He had never wanted to know his informant's identity because he was afraid of losing the source. The power his spy's details had given him helped keep him in power and allowed him better to serve his king.

'I have always been loyal,' Rouwen went on, knowing nothing would convince the duke. He had never thought of Sosler as being a ruthless power seeker, but now he wondered about the noble's motives. When the duke paused in his high-strung pacing, Rouwen asked, 'How did you happen to be at the queen's quarters at that precise moment, with King Priowe and his personal guards?'

Sosler snorted and shook his head. His thin hair swirled into wild disarray and the duke did not notice. 'You are not the only one with sources of information. It is necessary that I find out what happens beyond the Valley of Gan. Among the tidbits I have received recently from my own sources included mention of your damnable illicit, amorous – activities.'

Rouwen started to reply, then clamped his mouth shut. Nespizio had been right. If Sosler's spy had told of assignations between Diarra and her Captain of the Intrepid Guard, that meant the aphrodisiac had been carefully administered and that he had been maneuvered to go into her chambers at precisely the time Priowe and Sosler came by. This wasn't coincidence or simple bad luck for not making the proper obeisance to the gods. Rouwen swallowed hard as he imagined the strangler's expert noose tightening around his neck.

'Someone seeks to destroy us from within. This is part of it,' Rouwen said, the words tumbling out in an unconvincing rush. 'Find out for yourself – but beware of your informant. And I should have been more cautious of mine.'

'You are guilty of high crimes against the realm, Rouwen. There is no other conclusion I can reach given the evidence furnished by my own eyes.' Sosler cocked his head to one side, listening hard. He stepped to one side and King Priowe entered. Behind the king stood a man hidden by deep shadows.

'That is my verdict, also,' the king said. 'You and Diarra. I trusted you. I loved her!' Priowe's face turned livid with rage. 'Never again will you betray me.'

'I sought only to defend your life and realm, Majesty,' Rouwen said. There was no hope of convincing his liege. The best he could hope for was mercy from Sosler or the mysterious man hidden behind King Priowe.

'Silence!' bellowed Priowe. 'Get Chertude to work on this soulless insect. I want the showing of the instruments by morning and torture to begin within the hour following. And as each bloody piece is plucked from this worthless filth's body, I want it put on display for all in the Kingdom of Gan to see. I want it to make the grand circuit, I want everyone to see what happens to traitors.' Priowe swallowed hard, out of breath, and then added, 'and to adulterers.'

King Priowe spun and stormed from the dungeon. The faint light from the torturer's shallow metal bowls filled with coals gave the furious monarch a supernatural appearance. His cape fluttered like an agitated bat's wings, and the gleam off the jewels in his circlet might have been a feral animal's eyes.

Filling the space vacated by the king was the tall man cloaked in long robes. Face in shadow, all Rouwen saw was a large nose. From this small clue, he knew it was not the diminutive Baron Chertude. The hidden man waited for Sosler, caught the duke's ear and whispered for several minutes. Sosler stiffened and tried to push away. The hooded man grabbed the duke's arm and held him firmly.

To Rouwen's surprise, the duke did not order the guards to strike the man down, nor did he reach for his dagger. He looked angrily at Rouwen, then stalked off after Priowe. The shadow figure paused for a moment and then chuckled.

'Goodbye, my dear Captain,' he said softly. 'It has been so nice knowing you.'

Rouwen found himself unable to speak. He now recognized the mysterious man. Sosler and he shared the same source of information – and Rouwen had ended up in the dungeons, stripped of rank and in disgrace. If a similar fate awaited Duke Sosler, Gan would find itself without its two most loyal and adroit defenders.

'He's been sent by King Nishor!' Rouwen called, more pieces of the crazy puzzle falling into place. 'He seeks our downfall!'

The words echoed through the dungeon's lowest level. Sosler had gone. Priowe had long since returned to the vast castle's upper levels. Only the guards remained.

Not speaking, they came and took Rouwen down from his chains, dragging him to a nearby cell. They slammed the heavy door behind him and left. Only the torturer's bowl gave light for Rouwen to see, but he might have been in the bright spring sunlight and still have his heart and soul in eclipse. His unknown informant had plotted well, too well for Rouwen's liking.

Rouwen made a slow circuit of his new dwelling and found it hardly as long as he was tall and less than his outstretched arms in width. Rouwen reached up and felt heavy stone ceiling inches above his head. He knew what lay under his boots. The stone center of the column supporting Castle Gan reached to the core of the world. Tunneling out was as outrageous an escape as turning into a vapor and slipping between the heavy planks in the door.

Still, Rouwen began working. He forced open a small crevice to the side of the door and discovered he could touch the heavy padlock on the door's exterior. The cold iron hasp failed to yield under his fumbling attempts to pull it free, and only by straining to the utmost and cutting his arm in the attempt, could he touch the cold stone floor outside his cell.

He sank down, wondering if they would feed him. He doubted it. Baron Chertude preferred to weaken his victims before showing the torture instruments. The baron was a master of his craft, but this worried Brion Rouwen less than the danger to his kingdom.

As he gathered his resolve to begin working on the small crevice again, he heard the soft, silken sounds of movement outside. Rouwen bent over and peered out into the dungeon. He wasn't able to see who approached, but he heard a light rapping on his cell door.

'Brion?' came the almost imperceptible whisper. 'It's Sorinne. What have they done?'

'Sorinne!' Rouwen reached through the crevice, fingers seeking her. He touched the princess's dress. She caught his hand and clutched it in her own. Tears came to Rouwen's eyes, and for a moment he found it impossible to speak.

'I cannot stay. They might see me,' came the almost indistinct whisper. 'I'll do what I can to free you.'

'Sorinne, there is a plot,' Rouwen started. He clawed wildly to hold her when the woman pulled away from him. 'Sorinne, wait! I love you!' He extricated his hand from the split in the wood and pushed his face to it. He saw nothing beyond. Sorinne had gone, leaving both the dungeon and his heart desolate.

Sorinne had gone. Somehow, the brief contact had both buoyed his spirits for a few fleeting seconds, and then her absence sent them plunging to new, unexplored depths. Rouwen sat and worried for Sorinne's safety even as he wished she would petition her father immediately to release her lover.

This thought also presented Rouwen with a heart-twisting dilemma. If Sorinne admitted her love for Brion Rouwen, how would King Priowe respond? Did he want to expose her to such rage? And if the princess did not plead for his release, Rouwen would never leave the Gannian dungeons. Pieces of his body would be lopped off and sent on a grand parade around the valley for all to see and revile. That had been Priowe's sentence. Baron Chertude was so expert, a strong victim might linger for a month or more.

The Spring Festivals Rouwen had anticipated so eagerly, along with the elevation to baron, would be celebrated differently this year. His death rather than his triumph would be the whispered gossip on everyone's lips.

'Sorinne, my love,' he muttered. He worried for her but there was also his brother to consider. Adan Rouwen was four years older and a successful farmer, but his prestige and even his livelihood rested on his brother's rank inside Castle Gan. Few were accepted into the kingdom's service and fewer yet attained the rank of captain. For a commoner to be elevated to nobility would be a source of discussion for years. Without Brion's position – with his brother's incredible disgrace – Adan would never be able to supply foodstuffs to Castle Gan or be able to sell easily outside the valley.

Rouwen waited for Sorinne to return – or for Chertude to begin his grisly work. Without the sun to mark the passage of time,

31

without moons or stars or any external measurement, Rouwen was not certain how much time passed. After what might have been hours, Rouwen wondered if they had forgotten him. When his belly growled from hunger, he worried that they would starve him to death.

Drifting in and out of sleep robbed him of ever hoping to estimate how long he had been in the cell. But sleep carried a penalty he was unwilling to pay. As Brion Rouwen would drift off to a troubled sleep, emboldened rats would commence gnawing on his arms and legs. Once he came awake with a start, his hands grabbing the enormous rat beginning a meal on the softness of his throat.

Rouwen crushed it with his hands. Then he ate it. And it was the last meal for a long, long time since the rats became wary of him, circling just beyond his reach and chittering angrily. Only brackish water trickling down the stone walls provided any liquid or sustenance after this.

Time floated without reckoning until Rouwen was shaken from a stupor by loud singing. He had been dreaming of rats devouring him, and somehow the rodents had begun a song appropriate for a tavern.

'Where are you, you little traitor?' came the drunken words. 'You haven't escaped, have you? Join me in a swig of wine. It is unsurpassed. I mixed it with pepper and mulled it with a new leather strap. Where are you, Rouwen? Where, where, where? Come on and show yourself, my mother-loving friend.'

Rouwen recognized the voice after his brain had cleared. Prince Sped had blundered into the dungeons. Or was it a drunken blundering? Rouwen had never understood the young prince or his appetites.

'Here,' Rouwen called, startled at the croaking voice that came from his throat. He coughed and tried to speak. 'Sped, in the cell. I'm over here. Has Sorinne sent you?'

'My dear sister? Of course not. I have come to see the man who is cuckolding my dear father. What a joke. I would have thought Mamma would have chosen better. Or are you a real stallion between the silkens? Is that what she cherishes most in a guardsman?'

Sped laughed again and sloshed wine onto the floor. Through his small crevice, Rouwen saw the wine puddle flow across the stones. He longed to reach out and dip his fingers in the prince's demon brew. Even if the pepper made his thirst worse, it would be worth the price.

'Let me out. There is danger, a plot to kill you all.'

32

'Oh, yes, yes there is,' cackled Sped. 'Our valiant Lord Protector told me all about it. He and Duke Drioway . . .'

'Who's Duke Drioway?' Rouwen croaked out.

'Why, he is Sosler's confidant. From Mion, I think. A renowned world traveller, a noted diplomat from King Nishor's fabulous court and certainly the finest epicure to come into this demon-racked valley in years.'

'Drioway,' Rouwen said, rolling the name over his tongue to be certain he never forgot it. Duke Drioway might be the cause of his problems – and the primary threat facing the Kingdom of Gan.

'Ho, you look like you've acquired a fierce headache, Rouwen. Would you care for a sip of my fine Mionese wine?'

Rouwen recoiled as a flood of wine splashed into his face. He sputtered and then tried to drink. Too much soaked into the tatters of his clothing and not enough reached his mouth. Rouwen tried wringing out his filthy, sweat-stained tunic but the taste was secondary to the moisture provided.

'You've heard what Chertude plans for you, Rouwen. See you around – everywhere!' Sped laughed at his alcohol-fed joke. The drunken prince let out a yelp and crashed to the floor. Rouwen pressed his eye back to the crevice in time to see Sped sitting up. He had slipped in the puddle of spilled wine. He rubbed his bruised buttocks and then shakily got to his feet.

Rouwen's heart almost exploded when he saw a large ring of keys fall from Sped's belt. He tried to keep both prince and keys in sight, fearing the drunken noble would notice he had dropped Rouwen's only hope of escape from the dungeons. Shadows darted about and then Rouwen lost sight of Sped.

And the keys remained in the puddle on the floor.

Rouwen moaned as he thrust his hand through the crevice. Blood flowed down his torso as he jammed himself harder against the wall and opened small cuts along his shoulder and upper arm. He tried to widen the crevice and failed after his first attempts. Hands shaking from lack of food as much as anticipation, Rouwen's fingertips brushed across the cold metal ring.

He failed to bring the keys closer. Sagging, Rouwen quickly tried again and again. Blood flowed down his chest from the scrapes garnered by his desperate efforts and soaked his once proud uniform tunic. Just when he thought he would never bring the keys closer, his thumb circled the iron ring. He tensed and pulled back slowly. It was a clumsy effort but he finally brought the keys up to the other side of the crevice.

But what would he do now? The crevice was too small to bring the keys into the cell, and this would avail him little. The padlock was on the outside. He fumbled the keys around until he found one that might fit a padlock the size and bulk of the one on his cell door.

Again time moved in strange spurts, accelerating and stretching into eternities, but Rouwen kept working. He almost cried when he felt the key slip into the keyhole. And then he began a new battle. Because of the awkward angle, turning the key almost broke his wrist. A final effort was required to get the lock free of the iron hasp.

Rouwen tumbled into the dungeon, free after unknown days of imprisonment. He lay face down, licking the wine on the floor that had provided the means for his escape. He had never thought highly of Sped, but now he wanted to kiss the cruel, drunken prince. And then drive a dagger through his black heart.

Running on the thrill of freedom, Rouwen rolled over and pulled the keys from the lock. He considered the situation, closed the door and secured the padlock. Only then did he turn his attention to the other keys on the ring. He recognized one as opening the outer dungeon door. The others he could guess at, but they were less important for his purposes. From where Sped had stolen the keys was a mystery, but they would now serve him better than they ever had the drunken princeling.

'Sorinne,' he said softly. The princess hadn't been able to free him, and he worried as to the reason. Had King Priowe put her under guard in her own quarters? Or had Nishor's plot succeeded in killing her? Sped might not have mentioned it in his intoxicated fog.

'Sorinne,' Rouwen repeated, fixing the princess's lovely image in his mind. His legs refused to work at first, then held him upright as he strengthened. He staggered through the dungeon, then started up the steps to the cells a level above this lowest bank of cells. Rouwen slowed and cautiously looked out when he reached the dungeon's routine level. A guard slept in the far corner of the dungeon.

He walked slowly, then reached the staircase leading upward to the main levels of the castle. Rouwen found a door locked, but used the key and opened it easily. Glancing over his shoulder to be sure he hadn't awakened the jailer, Rouwen slid through the door and fastened it behind him. If anyone chanced to look in on his cell, it would seem he had simply vanished. That might not hold back a systematic hunt throughout the castle, but it could slow the guards.

Who wanted to stumble across a demon capable of walking through solid walls?

Moving like a specter hunting for its grave, Rouwen worked his way higher and higher into the castle. He crossed to a less travelled route, dodging where he knew the guards were thickest. After all, he had designed the security for the royal chambers and knew the few weaknesses.

What Rouwen did not know was the time of day. He stole to a window and looked through a narrow slit in the thick stone wall. He caught sight of the Lesser Moon working its way higher in a cloud-dotted nighttime sky and thought he saw reflections of the Greater Moon on the clouds' silvery underside.

'Time of treachery,' he murmured, worried at his bad luck. Rouwen had escaped during the period when the guards were most active. He considered finding a small closet and resting or possibly stealing food to regain his strength. Such a course would work against him, he decided, because his escape would be discovered eventually.

'Better to find Sorinne and let her help me directly.' The thoughts of food and wine and perfumed sheets and Sorinne's soft embrace spurred him on. Rouwen smiled to himself when he reached the corridor leading to the princess's chambers. The two guardsmen on duty would soon begin a circuit of the entire floor, checking all staircases. He waited less than ten minutes before the two Intrepids left their post near Sorinne's door to begin their rounds.

Counting slowly, Rouwen reached ten to be certain the guards were gone. Only then did he hurry down the corridor to the princess. He hesitated, not wanting to frighten her. Rouwen knocked softly and called, 'Sorinne?'

'Enter,' came the reply.

Brion Rouwen opened the door. Duke Sosler and six guardsmen with drawn swords greeted him.

4

Cursed . . . and Cursed Again

'Where's Sorinne?' Brion Rouwen demanded, fighting to keep his raging emotions under control. His gray eyes darted around the princess's sitting room and saw that it had been stripped bare, as if she had never lived here. The tables and other furniture Rouwen remembered remained, but the personal belongings he was accustomed to seeing had been removed. 'What have you done with her?'

'She is safe. For whatever reason, Duke Drioway thought you would come here. It seems he knows Gannians better than I. Take him back to the dungeons,' Sosler ordered the guards surrounding him. He stepped to one side, allowing the soldiers to rush forward. A split second of indecision passed for Rouwen, and he took advantage of the change in positions within the room.

Sosler blocked one guard for the wink of an eye. The other five had to converge on the narrow doorway and bumped into each other, rather than sending just one man at a time forward to seize Rouwen. A spin and a well-placed kick sent two men toppling into the others, arms and legs and swords flashing throughout the room in the confusion of their tumble. Rouwen didn't stop to admire the effort.

On legs shaky from too little food and too much fear, Rouwen whirled and slammed the door. He lacked anything to bar the heavy wood portal – and such would have availed him little. The two Intrepids who had been on patrol along the corridors were now returned. One sighted him and broke into a run to catch him. Rouwen had a solitary chance of freedom and took it without hesitation. He knew better than to race the guardsman for the other end of the corridor and the spiral staircase's dubious escape. In his enervated condition, Rouwen scarcely would reach the stone stairs before the guard overtook him.

A slit window through the castle's thick wall opened into the night. Rouwen had nothing to lose by foolhardiness. He jumped to the slanting ledge, and thanks to his emaciated condition, squeezed through the narrow stone window and swung outward.

'Stop! By all the demons between here and Paradise, stop!' the guard cried. A sword blade slashed at Rouwen's legs, missed and sent fat blue sparks leaping off the stone. The guard recovered and thrust through the narrow window, unable to do more than flail about. His bulk prevented him from following his former captain.

Rouwen's toes balanced on a ledge he had never known existed even as his fingers scrabbled to find purchase on the uneven outer wall of Castle Gan. He tried not to look down but had to move when the guard's sword tip found an exposed leg. Blood flowing down his leg and into his boot, Rouwen inched away from the window.

'Get Smel,' the guard ordered. 'He's the only Intrepid tiny enough to fit through the window and fetch the prisoner.'

The prisoner.

The word rang in Rouwen's head like a carillon tolling a death knell. He had gone from respected officer to hunted traitor in a few short days. And none of what had happened was his fault. Rouwen pressed his forehead against the cold stone wall and tried to overcome a sudden urge simply to relax and plunge down onto the Fingers of Providence far below.

He remembered his brief excursion onto the wooden plank a few stories above his head. Rouwen tried to see it outlined against the dome of stars. He wasn't able to locate it. A glance over his shoulder showed Mount Glid, but saw little detail along the wraith-haunted slopes. From where he clung to the wall, Rouwen was in almost complete darkness, emotionally and physically.

'Come in, Cap'n,' urged a small guardsman, worming his way through the window. Rouwen recognized the corporal. Smel had always performed well and honorably and was on the list for promotion to sergeant when such a position came available. 'You can't get away and goin' out to kill yourself isn't honorable.'

Where did honor lie? Rouwen wondered. To be tortured to death by Baron Chertude? To die of starvation in Castle Gan's lowest dungeons, taunted by the likes of Prince Sped?

As if Smel could hear his thoughts, the corporal said, 'I've been told Chertude won't work on you.'

'I demand a hearing,' Rouwen said. His fingers were cramping and the fingertips were turning slippery with blood from the stone scrapes. To stand on the ledge for another minute would be suicidal. He shuffled his feet from side to side attempting to get a better foothold, only to find himself at the lip of the modest ledge. There was nowhere he could flee.

Rouwen looked up and saw scaling the wall was impossible, and to go down? It was a long fall to the Fingers, as so many traitors had learned. Brion Rouwen was no traitor and would not willingly die in that manner.

'Who gives his word that Baron Chertude will not put me to the torture?' Rouwen asked. The disgrace of the Fingers might be better than torture at the hand of the pain master, even if he had to endure an eternity of poverty and degradation just outside Paradise's bounty.

'No one less than King Priowe,' said Smel with some fervor. 'On this I give you my sacred word, Cap'n. I heard him say it with his own mouth, I did.'

The wound on Rouwen's leg throbbed painfully, and his fingers slickened with blood and salt-burning sweat. He began edging toward the window. Smel reached out to grab his former captain's leg. Rouwen winced but allowed Smel to hang onto the wounded limb. With a sudden rush, Smel jerked hard, upending Rouwen. He shrieked as he fell back into nothingness – and dangled upside down, the small corporal clutching his leg tightly.

Slowly, others joined Smel to drag Rouwen through the narrow window. He lost more skin as they tugged him into the corridor. He lay face down on the cold stone for a moment, trying to compose himself. Then he looked up, wondering if Smel had lied about Chertude.

'His Majesty awaits your presence in the dungeons,' Duke Sosler said, arms crossed and looking dour.

'I was allowed to escape to give me false hope,' Rouwen accused. 'Sped intentionally dropped the keys.'

'This was part of Chertude's plan to weaken your spirit,' Sosler said, 'but after much deliberation the king has chosen another route for you. Chertude's skills will not be used now.' From the way Sosler spat out the words as if they burned his tongue, Rouwen knew where the duke's sentiments lay – and it was not in the guard captain's favor.

'I want only to explain to King Priowe what happened. He and Queen Diarra are in dire danger from Nishor's plot to . . .'

'If he tries to speak again, cut out his tongue,' Sosler said. 'I will explain such an injury to the king, if he bothers to ask.'

Smel pulled Rouwen to his feet. Rouwen towered over the diminutive guardsman. The others in the corridor were more than a match for Rouwen's size, speed and fighting prowess, especially now that he was weakened from hunger.

'Do not worry, Cap'n,' Smel said softly. 'Chertude *has* been muzzled.'

Rouwen went more easily. Smel needed only to remain silent, if Sosler had planned otherwise. That the corporal took it upon himself to reassure his former commander settled Rouwen's nerves. He allowed the Intrepids to support him as they spiralled their way back down into the dungeons. Rouwen found himself worrying over Sorinne's departure from her quarters. He hoped that her father had realized the danger within Castle Gan and had moved her to safer quarters, but Sosler's acerbic words did not suggest that.

'We go only to the dungeon's upper levels,' Smel said. 'I am sorry, Cap'n. Really I am. You deserved better for all your good work.'

'What is this outrage?' Rouwen cried. He looked around and saw Sosler, King Priowe and Queen Diarra. His heart almost exploded when he realized the queen had been imprisoned as he had been. King Priowe had not even allowed his wife clothing. She was gaunt, pale and chained to the wall.

'You know nothing of outrage,' Priowe snapped. 'My soul burns for revenge.'

'Chertude . . .' he began.

'He has been dismissed,' Sosler said in his soft voice that carried more menace than if he had screamed. 'That was told you in all truth. Have you made the acquaintance of the kingdom's premier wizard?' The duke stepped back and bowed in the short, pudgy man's direction. 'You will rue the day you met Kwuway!'

Rouwen was past emotion. The escape after so much starvation had drained him, but failing to find Sorinne had been even more draining. Any slight relief he had felt at not being given over to Chertude was erased at the sight of his queen dangling naked, bruised and utterly degraded. Rouwen had spent his career defending the rulers of Gan and had fantasized about giving his life for them. The past few years were dreams come to fruition, and his love for Sorinne was hardly more than that for Diarra and Priowe.

But so much had changed, and he could not adapt swiftly enough. King Priowe refused to listen to the truth, to the dangers stalking him through Sosler's alliance with Duke Drioway. And his liege now presented him as an experiment to the most notorious wizard in Gan. The stories of Kwuway's magical shape-changing experiments were incredible, yet Rouwen knew them to be pale in comparison with what the mage truly did. Kwuway, for all his soft appearance, was hard, harsh and utterly ruthless.

His king, the man he revered, was ordering the wizard to unleash his worst spells. Rouwen could not react. All inside him that made him a loyal soldier died.

'No, no,' moaned Diarra. 'You can't. It's all *his* fault. He forced himself upon me. He was stronger. He was not to be denied!' She thrashed about in her manacles, dark eyes wide with fear. She tried to point at Rouwen as the villain but the chains prevented her from putting the finishing flourish to her accusation.

'Silence!' roared King Priowe. 'There are nothing but lies in this dungeon. I will have the truth before you are cast from my sight forever. Kwuway.' The king stepped back, his face screwed into a scowl that would have caused lesser men to back off. Rouwen simply stared, exhausted in both body and spirit. Any protest he made would fall on deaf ears, but he had to try.

'Queen Diarra was given an aphrodisiac that forced her to . . .' he began. The guard beside him struck him with the hilt of his dagger. The sharp rap caused Rouwen's head to snap to one side and ring like a bell. He sagged to his knees. The guards made no effort to lift him.

'There are many ways of obtaining truth,' Kwuway said in an unctuous voice. 'Does Your Majesty have any particular method?'

'Any will do, if your spell is effective enough.'

'It will be,' Kwuway said, bowing slightly. From his vantage on his knees, Rouwen saw the gleam in the wizard's pale, ice chip-colored eyes. The man wanted to torture with his magicks in ways Chertude could never achieve with mere instruments. Kwuway would attack the soul, the essence of his victim, before releasing that deformed, tormented soul to Paradise.

'Take him, do it to him!' shrieked Diarra. She tossed her head to get stringy blonde hair from her eyes. Any beauty she had once possessed was driven from her by stark fear. Rouwen wasn't sure he could fault Diarra for trying to place all blame on his shoulders, but any respect he had was evaporating like fog in the spring sun. Diarra should have shown more courage, even after being threatened with Kwuway's magicks. As queen she owed her subjects that, her Captain of the Intrepid Guard most of all. More than once Rouwen had saved her life.

'She must confess,' Priowe said. His scowl deepened until it became a permanent part of his countenance. Rouwen wondered if the king would ever again show joy – or mercy.

'I have served you well, Your Majesty,' Rouwen said, fighting to keep from passing out. The blow to his head had caused pain to echo throughout his body, increasing in magnitude until he was almost at the point of screaming. Rouwen fought his own body for supremacy. 'I have served you well and deserve a hearing in this.'

King Priowe ignored him. He pointed at his wife and then clenched his hand so tightly that his fingernails cut into his own flesh. Tiny drops of blood dripped unnoticed onto the stone floor.

'As you wish,' Kwuway said. The wizard began a low chant. Rouwen tried to force its beguiling rhythms from his mind but found himself being pulled in and whirled around – and he was not even the object of the spell. Diarra jerked hard against her chains, her joints popping and fear sweat trickling down her body to leave grimy trails. Kwuway chanted louder, made new gestures in the air that left small red vestiges of magical symbols. And those symbols drifted slowly toward the captive queen, floating like smoke, burning like sparks from a newborn volcano.

Diarra howled like an animal when the swirling magical symbols touched her body and burned deeply into her tender flesh. She broke one chain holding her but the others held her back.

'Your husband the king orders you to speak the truth,' Kwuway said in a silky voice. His pale eyes shone like hellfire as his enjoyment grew. Rouwen wondered if the wizard had ever used this spell before. He looked like a small child given a sweet. 'You will answer any question he asks of you.'

King Priowe banged his clenched fists together and stepped forward. 'How long have you shared your bed with Rouwen?'

Diarra moaned and tried to clutch her chest where the magical symbol scorched her flesh. She opened her mouth to speak but nothing came out save pitiful whimpers. Diarra tried to reach out to her husband, but he stepped back and looked as if he would spit on her.

'How long has Brion Rouwen been your lover?' Priowe shouted now, his rage boiling over. 'Answer me. Answer!'

Diarra gasped and mewled, doubled over with pain. Try as she might no words came out. Rouwen wondered what the words would have been. Condemnation for him? Possibly. She had been anxious enough earlier to place all blame on his shoulders to keep from being tortured by Kwuway. But Rouwen saw something

41

more in the woman's pain-racked body. Diarra was slowly coming to realize no answer would satisfy her husband. Priowe's wrath could not be turned, no matter what she said now.

'She is not giving me what I want to hear,' Priowe said sharply. 'Why not, wizard?'

'There are forces opposing my spell,' Kwuway muttered. 'I cannot understand how any other wizard could penetrate this far into the heart of Castle Gan. It might be – no,' the wizard denied swiftly, cutting off his thought. 'I can work differently, another spell, perhaps.'

Kwuway began chanting faster, louder, moving his fingers in the air to generate new and more potent magical symbols. The burning figures shot forth and embedded themselves in Queen Diarra's flesh, causing her to twitch. Her earlier struggles were gone. She only jerked feebly as spell after spell burned through her.

'Speak only the truth, Diarra,' ordered Kwuway.

'How long have you conducted this illicit affair with Rouwen?' shouted Priowe. 'Tell me, tell me, tell me!'

Diarra sagged in her manacles, dangling limply. Only spittle came to her lips, not the confession that King Priowe demanded of her. Priowe turned angrily on his wizard but before he could speak, Duke Sosler tugged softly at his liege's sleeve.

Priowe jerked away, fury etched on his face.

'Please, Your Majesty, a word,' urged Sosler. 'Let Kwuway refine his spell. If there is interference with his magicks from outside the castle, he needs to find the right counterspells.'

Rouwen saw the look of pure hatred the wizard shot Duke Sosler. There was no affection between these men. Sosler led King Priowe to the far side of the dungeon and spoke quickly with him. Rouwen saw a darkness lurking among the shadows, bright eyes moving in the midst of gloom. That must be Duke Drioway, Nishor's damnable envoy, giving clandestine counsel.

Kwuway sent repeated truth spells burning on Diarra's skin, but the queen only gasped and groaned. No verity slipped free of the bonds of exhaustion to satisfy king or wizard. Kwuway grunted and turned from the queen, going to a grimoire placed on a low stool. The wizard knelt and began leafing through the pages of the magical tome, seeking the precise curse or chant or deviating spell to force the truth from Diarra.

Rouwen looked up at Diarra. Her eyes were sunken with pain, but her lips thinned when she looked at him.

'My queen,' he began.

'May you starve in Paradise for all you've brought onto my

head and house,' Diarra snarled. 'They will never believe me, and now *his* hideous spells gnaw at my guts.'

'We must convince him nothing happened,' Rouwen said. 'King Priowe is falling under Sosler's influence too much. And Duke Drioway is . . .'

'I hate you, Rouwen. You are responsible for this. My misfortune is your fault. You brought this horror to me, and now you do not confess.'

'We are not enemies, Diarra. We must not lose sight of that. We need each other more than ever.'

'I hate you,' Diarra repeated venomously. Her body quaked, and she reached with her freed hand to touch the red welts on her belly and chest caused by Kwuway's truth spells.

'Kwuway!' shouted King Priowe. 'Attend me!'

'Yes, Your Majesty,' the wizard said, bowing deeply. From Rouwen's position he saw the look of contempt creeping across the wizard's face. He obeyed Priowe for his own purposes, not through loyalty. For the first time Rouwen realized many in the Kingdom of Gan were not devoted to their rulers – or not as devoted as he had once been.

'Forget her for the moment. I want the spell Sosler discussed with you prepared for use on Rouwen.'

'All is ready,' Kwuway said, bowing more deeply. He turned a moon-shaped face toward Rouwen and smiled wickedly. The wizard covered this movement and touched his forehead in obeisance to his ruler. 'I will perform the spell immediately.'

'Do it, do it,' ordered Priowe. 'No hesitation, no mercy.'

Rouwen prepared himself for the magical symbols to burn on his flesh and the magical urge to tell the truth to boil up in his writhing body forcing away all inhibition to lie. But he need not lie. This was his chance to convince Priowe of the truth, of the danger, of the plots against him and his queen and his guard captain. Nespizio had warned him, and he had ignored the old wizard's advice. Now he had to reverse the terrible mistakes he had made if he wanted to save both his liege and his kingdom.

Kwuway began chanting, but the tempo and sound of mystical words carried no resemblance to the spell he had cast on Diarra. In spite of himself, Rouwen watched in rapt fascination as green and yellow and red symbols writhed in the air like vaporous snakes, tumbling and turning and merging into a darker figure. The figure grew and darkened and yet also burned with an inner light that confused Rouwen.

How could there be darkness like a storm cloud, yet brilliance flashing throughout more potent than any lightning bolt ever witnessed? And it all tumbled and boiled before exploding with stark ferocity in Rouwen's face. The former guard captain tried to escape but reacted too slowly.

'By all the demons,' muttered Corporal Smel, holding his captain. 'They shouldn't do this. Not right, just not right.'

Rouwen stiffened as Kwuway's spell worked its way through his body. He tried to fight the magicks but couldn't resist. With a power transcending that of any human, Rouwen jerked free of his captors and fell face down on the dungeon floor. His fingers clutched wildly at the stone and scraped out thin furrows, leaving his fingers bloody and aching. Even with such localized pain Rouwen recognized a larger problem, and it ground into his guts.

'Get him to his feet,' Kwuway ordered. Smel muttered to himself but obeyed. The other guard was slower to obey. Kwuway flicked a small, bright speck at the guardsman, causing him to yelp in pain. This magical goad brought a burst of speed to comply.

Rouwen startled himself with the strength in his legs. He had been starved and tortured with magicks and he felt better than he had in a week or more. Not understanding, he watched as Kwuway stepped toward him. Rouwen wondered if he might break free and reach out to snap the pudgy wizard's neck. Smel was strong but too much the bantam to resist. The other guard still smarted from the magical tweak Kwuway had given him and paid scant attention to his prisoner.

Kwuway continued a chant while reaching into a pouch at his belt to pull out a silver locket. The locket spun slowly, hypnotically, and Rouwen realized he could not fight the wizard. No matter how he tried to energize his leaden arms to reach out, he could not. All Rouwen could do was watch the locket spin and twist, moving in a circle, an arc that caught his full attention.

Rouwen wondered what Priowe had ordered his wizard to do. He felt no compulsion to speak of the night with Diarra, of how she had attacked him and pulled him to her bed. Indeed, Rouwen found that no words came to his lips when he tried to speak. His throat tensed and constricted, as if unseen fingers throttled him.

More frightening, no one looked at him. All eyes were on Diarra. Sosler and King Priowe and Kwuway and the guards all stared at the pathetic figure of the naked queen dangling in her blood-stained chains. The magical symbols flaring on her fair skin faded slowly and nothing seemed to replace the spell.

'Is it done?' demanded Priowe.

'There is some more to be done, Majesty,' Sosler said. 'Do you wish to remain?'

'No, but see to it personally.'

'As Your Majesty commands,' Sosler said, bowing low. 'May your meeting with Duke Drioway proceed well.'

King Priowe stalked from the dungeon. Rouwen tried to call to him, to say that Drioway had overheard all Sosler had said to him in confidence just minutes earlier. But Rouwen's voice had been stolen from him. All he could do was watch and wonder what spells were being cast.

'Duke?' asked the wizard. 'Are we to complete the second spell?'

'Of course,' Sosler growled. 'Are you a fool? Never stop that spell halfway through.'

'Do not think to instruct me in magical matters, Duke,' Kwuway said. Rouwen caught more than a hint of rivalry between the men. He saw no way to turn it to his own advantage, not with his voice held captive and his arms imprisoned by his own guardsmen.

'Finish the spell,' Sosler said, stroking the hilt of his dagger.

Kwuway turned and began a new chant, a faster one, one more beguiling and captivating than the one before – and still Rouwen did not understand what its purpose might be. He did not, could not, vocalize. How could he be forced to confess if they prevented him from speaking?

With a sudden move, Kwuway caused the silver locket to vanish. The chanting stopped and the wizard rubbed his hands together. He turned and bent, picking up his grimoire. He started to leave the dungeon when Sosler stopped him.

'Is it done? The spell? Both spells?'

'Of course they are,' Kwuway said irritably. 'Do you doubt my abilities?'

Duke Sosler looked skeptical. The pudgy wizard moved with more speed than Rouwen would have believed possible. He reached out and pulled Sosler's dagger from its sheath. The wizard spun, set his feet shoulder-wide on the stone floor and drove the point of the dagger to the hilt in Rouwen's belly. Then he pulled the sharp blade upward, opening the guard captain like a gutted fish.

Agony exploded like fireworks in Brion Rouwen. He clutched at his stomach, trying to keep his intestines from spilling out. Pain overwhelmed him as he died.

5

Eternal Death in Life

Brion Rouwen had died. He knew he had. No one could take a dagger driven so deeply into his belly and live. Yet the pain refused to go away as he struggled to open his eyes. He should be on his way to Paradise, his soul captured by the magicks dancing along Mount Glid and then dispatched skyward for judgment by gods and demons. Rouwen had lived his life honorably and well, serving his liege lord without fail. He would not be sentenced to an eternity of starvation and want, when all Paradise stretched around him.

But the pain!

He groaned and tried to free the dagger from his belly. His eyelids flickered weakly and faint light blinded him. He was surprised to see Diarra still dangling by her chains, but he was even more shocked to see the wizard standing above him.

Kwuway's dun-colored robes brushed across his chest, tickling him. The mixture of pain and teasing torment brought him more fully awake. The wizard stepped back and stared at him, a look of immense pleasure on his pudgy face.

'It is done,' Kwuway said.

'I fail to see how this can be,' Duke Sosler said, coming into Rouwen's limited field of vision. The former captain rolled over and got a better look around him. The guardsmen stood a few paces away. The expression on Smel's face was one of sorrow. Rouwen realized the small guardsman was loyal to him – but was more loyal to the Kingdom of Gan. If King Priowe ordered an officer killed, so be it, no matter how much the corporal admired him.

'I'm not dead,' Rouwen croaked out. The paralysis that had seized his throat slipped away. He wished the pain would magically disappear, also, but he doubted it would happen. Sitting up, he held himself together. Blood flowed, not as much as he would have thought, but never had Brion Rouwen imagined such pain was possible without dying.

'He isn't dead,' Sosler said.

'I used your dagger for the demonstration,' Kwuway said. 'I am expert in casting certain spells. This one is not to be reversed this side of Paradise.'

Sosler laughed harshly and said something Rouwen missed. Kwuway responded, 'Even *he* would have great difficulty reversing this spell. It is complete. Your captain and queen will suffer, this I guarantee.'

The wizard bent over, grabbed the dagger's handle and twisted hard. Rouwen screamed as new waves of pain washed across mind and body. He watched in sick fascination as Kwuway withdrew the dagger from its fleshy sheath in his abdomen and tossed the bloody blade to the duke. Sosler caught it dexterously, stared at the gory tip, then threw the dagger away from him with a backhand toss. It clanked harshly as it slammed into the dungeon's far wall and fell to the stone floor. Rouwen's eyes followed the dagger's flight, and he wistfully wished he could move quickly enough to get the discarded weapon.

It would find a better resting place in Sosler's putrid heart. And for Kwuway such a quick death would be too good. He wanted to wrap his hands around the wizard's thick throat and strangle the life from him, second by second, breath by breath. Rouwen wanted to do this, but he had to hold himself together.

Kwuway pushed past Sosler and left without another word. Rouwen sucked in his breath as new pain hit him like a war hammer. When he spread his bloodied fingers, he expected to see nothing but sliced open entrails. To his surprise there was little blood and some healing had occurred magically.

'He's healing me,' Rouwen got out before new pain made him retch. Smel came to help him, but Sosler angrily waved the corporal away.

'Healing you? That's rich,' Sosler said. 'He's *cursed* you. King Priowe ordered it, and I have approved. He's doubly *cursed* you, you ignorant peasant!'

Rouwen knew little of magicks and wizardly ways. His duty had been the defense of the castle and all its occupants. For whatever reason, he had been told when he assumed the position of Captain of the Intrepid Guard that no magicks could harm the royalty he was to protect from more common, physical assaults. And none had been launched against Priowe, Diarra, Sorinne, or Sped that he knew of.

His fingers were caked with clotting blood, but the gash in his vitals was almost closed. Rouwen sank back to endure the pain that refused to go away as quickly as the wound. Deep inside he felt vital parts alternately grating like grit in a bird's gizzard and sliding wetly across one another.

'I don't understand,' Rouwen said. 'What did Kwuway do to me?'

'To both of you. Note this, traitor.' Sosler walked around behind Diarra and pulled free a strangler's cord. He knotted it and expertly dropped its loop over the queen's neck. She turned to try and fend him off. The duke jerked with a skill that had not been learned on a practice dummy. Rouwen knew little of the Lord Protector's history but now saw that violent death had been an important part of it.

Sosler's muscles bulged as he pulled back on the cord. The large knot ground down on Diarra's neck, compressing cartilage to strangle her. Sosler put his elbows hard into the woman's shoulders, then added his knee to the middle of her back and jerked as hard as he could. Diarra's tongue thrust out and began to turn black.

And still the duke continued to strangle. Diarra's eyes bulged and she died even as Rouwen watched with conflicting emotions. His duty had been to protect Diarra, and yet she had tried to blame him for her misfortune. Perhaps if he had been a little more astute he would have discovered the poisoning plot earlier, but he had come to realize how well planned it had been.

Sosler? Possibly. Duke Drioway? Definitely. The aphrodisiac had been a part of the trap, and both he and Queen Diarra had fallen into it at the precise moment needed to discredit both. Whatever negotiations King Priowe engaged in with Nishor's emissary, he would be distracted – and two of the king's staunchest supporters would be removed permanently, wife and guard captain.

'Suffer, bitch, suffer!' shouted Sosler, pulling the cord so tight Rouwen thought he would decapitate the woman. Only when Smel protested did Sosler release his garrote. The leather cord slipped off Diarra's once-white throat, leaving behind a blue and green bruise on the front of her throat and a wicked red band where the cord had cut savagely into her flesh.

'What will King Priowe say? I heard nothing from him telling you to kill Diarra.' Rouwen winced as pain lanced through him, but the feelings within him were decreasing. Pain was a fact of his life, but it no longer debilitated him. With the curious strength he had felt immediately after Kwuway had begun his spell, Rouwen stood. Smel and the other Intrepid moved quickly to stand beside him, swords drawn.

'Say about what?' Sosler said, regaining his composure. He

poked Diarra with his finger. To Rouwen's surprise, the woman stirred and fought weakly against the chains holding her. A few seconds later, Diarra's hot eyes fluttered open and focused on Sosler. The stark hatred in that look raised the temperature in the cold dungeons until Rouwen wondered if Sosler might perish.

The duke laughed harshly. He coughed and stepped away from the captive woman. He swung his garrote, lashing her across the face. Rouwen saw that the quarrel between the two was longstanding and had little to do with marital infidelity or kingly decrees.

'Do you understand, Rouwen? You cannot die. And neither can she!' Sosler reached over and grabbed Smel's sword. He lunged and drove the steel into Diarra's body, then recovered and handed the blade back to the guardsman. 'She cannot die, and you will suffer forever. Consider every minor pain to be prelude to mutilation and the agony you will be forced to endure magically.'

'You, you are responsible,' Diarra grated from between clenched teeth. She looked not at Sosler but at Rouwen. He had become the target of her hatred, and he was the only one trying to defend her life and honor. More and more he felt betrayed by her. Where was the loyalty to match his devotion?

His former devotion?

'Put them into a cell,' Sosler ordered. The guardsmen hesitated, exchanging confused looks.

'Together, Duke?'

'Of course together. They deserve each other. Let them express their undying affection to their heart's content.' Sosler stood to one side as Smel unlocked Diarra's manacles and helped her to a cell. The other guard nudged Rouwen forward with the tip of his sword.

'Not so gentle. He can't be killed. Here!' Sosler grabbed the sword from the guardsman and lunged at Rouwen. The former captain sidestepped enough that the cut missed its intended target and only opened a gash more bloody than serious. Sosler seemed not to know or care about the extent of the injury. He kicked Rouwen into the cell and slammed the heavy door behind him.

In the darkness Rouwen heard Diarra's stentorian breathing. She fought for air through her damaged windpipe, just as he strove to keep from bleeding to death. He sat against the far wall and held his midriff, feeling the evil magicks of Kwuway's spell work on him. The wound closed but the pain remained. He would never die of sword cut or infection, but he had to endure their debilitating effects.

'Are you better?' Rouwen finally asked of Diarra. All he received was a snarl that was more feral than informative. He tried to go to Diarra's side, but the woman pushed him away.

'I may not be able to kill you with my bare hands,' Diarra said, gasping for breath, 'but I know you feel the pain as I do. I saw it in your face when Kwuway rammed the dagger into your foul guts. I swear by all the demons between here and Paradise that I will give you so much pain you will be driven out of your mind!'

Rouwen backed off, content to sit quietly in his personal misery. Diarra would come around to understanding what had happened. She must, if they were to convince the king of the plot, their plight and how Nishor sought to gain the Kingdom of Gan for his own.

Diarra's breathing became easier hours after Sosler's garroting, and Rouwen drifted into pain-filled sleep. When he awoke it was to the cell door being flung open. Fingers of pale yellow light filtered in, outlining the man in the doorway. Although he was unable to make out the face, Rouwen recognized the silhouette.

'My king!' he cried. 'You've come. We . . .'

A hard fist knocked Rouwen sprawling across the cell, his arm flailing out to fall across Diarra's bare breast. She struggled to force him away, but weakness kept her from succeeding. Rouwen came to a sitting position and waited for what must come. Words no longer convinced his own benevolent liege, but what actions would force Priowe to reverse his slanderous opinions of wife and captain?

'She is not dead!' Priowe roared. 'They do not suffer! What vile double-dealing spell has Kwuway wrought? I'll have his ears for this!'

'Your Majesty, let me explain,' Sosler spoke from behind the king. 'There might have been a misunderstanding. Nothing can kill them. That was the intent of the wizard's first spell.'

'But the other one, what of the other?'

Brion Rouwen sat up in the cell, attentive to the byplay. He had not been aware of a second spell, but he had been distracted by small matters such as a dagger in his belly and the overwhelming abandonment he felt.

'Kwuway assures me it is fully activated. The spell casket is proof of the spell's power.' Sosler moved into view, king and duke sharing the narrow cell door.

'They deserve one another,' Priowe said after staring into the cell for a long minute. 'Release them, even if he hasn't yet killed her.'

Rouwen tried to make sense of all he had overheard, but it

encompassed more matters than he understood. Magicks were something to whisper about in the barracks, not to speak of boldly or with any confidence that some wizard wouldn't overhear and cause extreme calamity to befall the irreverent. He allowed the guards to pull him to his feet and push him from the cell. Rouwen was sorry to see that Smel was not among the small knot of Intrepids standing watch at the entrance to the dungeons. He wanted to thank the small corporal for both kindness and loyalty.

'Out,' ordered Sosler. 'Get them both out of Castle Gan immediately. The king will not tolerate their foul presence even one more second.'

The sharp sword points pricking his flesh kept Rouwen walking at a brisk pace. He remembered the burning pain of steel, well-honed and slippery with blood, go through him and did not want to tempt any of the guards to test Kwuway's spell of immortality.

They traversed well-remembered corridors and eventually came to a postern on the far side of Castle Gan. Rouwen had used this very gate many times to receive delegates from the valley on their way to petition King Priowe. Neither secret nor well-used, it led to the main road winding down the side of the thick spire of rock on which the castle stood.

Rouwen watched as the gate was unbarred and opened. A cold wind whipped through the small opening and chilled him, bringing forth an uncontrollable shiver. Beyond, miles away, he saw the soft green of fields growing the food needed to maintain the castle and all the populace within the valley. He looked longingly at the valley. Nothing kept his loyalty prisoner inside the castle now, nothing save for one thing.

Rouwen turned and looked up at the soaring towers of the purest white stone, the graceful battlements and arches and walkways atop Castle Gan, and wondered where Princess Sorinne was and what she did and what she thought of him.

What lies had Sosler told? Or had they said anything to her? Sorinne's apartments had been stripped and the poor girl had been forcibly moved elsewhere. Was she caught up in Sosler and Duke Drioway's plot to turn Gan over to King Nishor?

'No,' came the command from his side, a sword prodding him in the ribs, 'don't think of it, Cap'n. We got orders to run you through if you try anything other 'n leavin' the castle.'

Rouwen respected the guardsman's orders. As much as he longed to find Sorinne and hold her again in his arms, he said nothing about the princess and made no move back into the castle. A few paces away Sosler and Diarra faced off. The woman was still naked, but her spirit had not been broken by her tortures and the spell cast on her. She spoke in a voice that carried, even against the wind, and conveyed the full measure of her loathing for Sosler.

'Your treason will not go unpunished, Duke,' she promised him, her body set for fighting. 'Priowe will discover your plot and will not be gentle with you.'

'You have brought nothing but disgrace on Gan,' the duke shot back. 'You were little more than a peasant when he married you, and you shall return to your roots. You will suffer, Diarra, suffer as no woman ever has before!'

Sosler moved quickly, a blade flashing silver in the sunlight. The queen gasped as she clutched at her throat, slit from side to side. Horror crossed her face as she realized what Sosler had done. Sinking to her knees, she tried to stanch the flow.

'Throw her out. Throw them both out. They are banished forever from Castle Gan!' Duke Sosler cried. He waved his blood-dripping dagger at the pair, as if this might speed them on their way to eternal poverty and hunger in Paradise.

The guards carried the weakly struggling Diarra and threw her out the gate. Rouwen followed of his own volition, not wanting to resist the men he had worked so diligently to train. He watched as the gate slammed behind him. The last he saw of Castle Gan's interior was Sosler's sneering face. He turned to Diarra and knelt, prising her fingers away from her slit throat.

'Kwuway's spell still works,' he said. 'The cut is almost healed. Can you speak yet?'

'Yes, you fool,' she croaked out. Diarra coughed blood, then rubbed her injured throat and got her breath. 'And it hurts! By the bountiful fields of Paradise, it hurts so!'

'Sosler says we've been banished. I'm not sure what he intends, but if we start for the base of the spire, we can . . .' Rouwen stopped when he saw the look of utter contempt on the woman's beautiful face. She spat more blood, narrowly missing him.

'You don't know, do you? The first spell Kwuway cast on you?' Diarra's expression was one of hatred and contempt for something she considered less than human.

'No, what was the spell?' Rouwen felt whole. Stretching produced minor twinges of pain left over from the stabbings and other torments, but otherwise Rouwen felt fit. He had no idea what the wizard might have taken from him magically.

'The second spell made you immortal,' Diarra told him. 'The first using the silver spell casket was different, affecting only those around you. Any you love will die!'

6

Radiance of Love, Horizons of Death

Sweat poured down Rouwen's body as he plodded along the steeply spiralling road around the spire bearing Castle Gan. Now and again he stopped to look at the huge castle with its graceful, soaring arches and stone supports, the gleaming stained-glass windows, the silvered medallions, each marking the death of a hero of Gan. Brion Rouwen knew his name would never be entered on that roll of gallantry.

He heard Diarra cursing as she made her way ahead of him on the dusty road. He called to her, 'Please, Majesty, take my tunic. The sun will burn you to a crisp.'

The naked woman turned and glared at him with enough hatred to silence him. Repeatedly he had offered her any of the bloodied tatters of the uniform he still wore. He was tan enough to tolerate the sun until they reached the valley and found better clothing, but it wasn't fitting for a queen to walk along naked, dirty and bruised, her feet being cut to gory ribbons by the sharp stones along the roadway that had once led to her throne.

'I'm no longer queen,' Diarra said with utter venom in her voice. 'Given the chance, I'd slice that fool's tongue out and stuff it up his nose.'

It reflected more on his mental turmoil that he didn't know which fool Diarra meant. Priowe had been duped and betrayed, never understanding the depth of duplicity; he should have been more trusting in wife and captain than he had been. But Sosler was selling out the kingdom to the ruler of Mion, a traditional enemy. Duke Drioway had done much to sway the duke. Or did Diarra refer to the wizard who had laid such onerous spells on them?

'Your shoulders and . . .' Rouwen's sentence trailed off. Even though Diarra was correct in her flat statement that she was no longer queen, he found it difficult to speak frankly with her. Long loyalty to the throne prevented him from arguing.

'My breasts? Is that it, Captain?' Diarra said, words laced

with intense sarcasm. 'You know all about them, ever since you drugged me and had your way.'

'What?' Rouwen was shocked at this accusation. 'The plot,' he sputtered. 'Aphrodisiacs were in your food. That made you behave in the manner you did.'

'So *I* seduced *you*? What an incredible lie!' Diarra laughed harshly at the notion. She stalked off around the next curve in the steep road, leaving him behind.

'Wait,' Rouwen called, racing to catch up with her. He grabbed her arm and spun her around. 'Sosler is the root of this evil growing under Castle Gan. I have been nothing but loyal to you and King Priowe. I would have died for you!'

'Now you must live forever,' Diarra said, a sneer on her lips. She shoved him hard. Rouwen stumbled and tried to regain his balance. A heel caught on a large rock, and he fell to the sloping shoulder of the road. He tried to regain his balance and found himself sliding faster. The sappers designing this road had not wanted siege equipment moved to the doors of Castle Gan. The slope worked against Rouwen as he slid faster and faster.

The abrupt edge of the road caught him by surprise. Rouwen screamed as he fell more than fifty feet to the roadbed below. He flailed about and smashed hard into rock. The world turned black as new pain hammered his body.

Rouwen's eyes snapped open. He stared up at Diarra's naked form. She kicked him in the side and pain racked him. Ribs had broken and liquid sloshed within his chest from the long fall. But he had not died. He was only crippled.

'I can't move,' he told Diarra, gasping for breath. 'Please. We are cursed together. We need to help one another regain . . .'

'Regain nothing!' shrieked Diarra, her face wild and animal-like. 'I will bring down Priowe and make him regret the day he did this to me, the mother of his children, his consort, his queen! I will kill him, I will kill him!'

Rouwen had been so caught up in the horror encapsulating him that he had forgotten the queen's idiosyncrasies. His guardsmen had not seen anything strange the night of her aphrodisiac poisoning because of so much earlier eccentric behavior. She often wandered the castle corridors humming to herself, dressed in rags or ball gowns, handing out coins to any who came near. Or she might try stealing their purses, and who would accuse their queen of thievery? Rouwen had heard rumors of even more peculiar behavior in her private chambers.

He had simply thought her recent conduct caused by agitation over Sosler's accusations. Considering the past week, Rouwen realized her actions had been predictable, normal, and even expected considering the upheaval throughout Castle Gan.

Diarra kicked him again and stepped over him. She smiled without any humor and, singing a bawdy drinking song, left him in the road, under the burning sun to fry. Rouwen closed his eyes and listened to her off-key song slowly fade until it passed beyond the limits of his hearing.

Sun heated him and sweat drained him of needed moisture. In any normal situation, he would fear dehydration and death. Now he longed for departure to Paradise. Pain mounted within him and never vanished. His tongue puffed up from lack of water, and he felt his face beginning to peel from overexposure. Only when the sun danced behind the tall spire of rock holding Castle Gan did Rouwen get any relief. He lay on his back, feeling his internal organs healing themselves, painfully, but with a speed that he wished he could have experienced under less trying circumstances.

As the Lesser Moon rose, so did Rouwen. He struggled to sit up, his back against the rocky cliff on the inner side of the road. He worried that no commerce had passed along the road all day long. Castle Gan needed a steady flow of food to maintain its larder. Artesian springs fed fountains throughout the castle, but Priowe had never allowed the food reserves to dip too low. At any given time, the castle was internally sufficient for almost a year. Sosler, as Lord Protector of the Realm, had declared no siege for that length of time could ever succeed.

Rouwen closed his eyes and tried to force back the hot waves of pain tearing at his mind by concentrating on tactical matters. Any army fighting its way through the Demon's Throat would be reduced by half – more. An invader then had to fight up the spiralling road to the thick steel doors of Castle Gan, and from there the Captain of the Intrepid Guard would defend the citizens within the walls.

He would never be that defender. He had failed because the attack came not through military might but subversion. Never had Brion Rouwen thought that any within Gan would turn traitor and betray the richest, most powerful kingdom on the continent.

'Rot, not power,' he groaned. His world had putrefied from within rather than being cut apart from outside. By the time the Greater Moon slipped into the sky above Mount Glid, Rouwen had passed out from pain. And when the morning sun rose to awaken him, he was able to stand on shaky legs. He continued his way down the mountainside, hardly aware of the terrain.

Vision often blurred or double, Brion Rouwen found himself trying to understand what lay spread in front of him. It was green and lush and he heard soft sounds of wind through grain.

'Paradise?' he wondered aloud. 'Have I died?' He tried to find the tribunal of gods and demons who would barter for his soul, either to enter and live in prosperity or to forever peer in at those blessed and given eternal refuge from hunger and fear.

Rouwen stumbled forward and fell face down into a stream. The sharp knock to the side of his head stunned him more; water rushed into his lungs in a fiery tide. Rouwen struggled to get free, finally rolling over and spitting out the water he had inadvertently sucked into his lungs. He should have died; the curse still held him in its terrible thrall.

'And the other?' Rouwen wondered. Had Sosler lied to her about Kwuway's spell? He had never heard of a spell casket before, yet Kwuway had worked with the spinning silver locket for some time before turning to cast another spell on Diarra. Was there any spell placed on him that would slay those he loved?

'Sorinne,' he muttered. 'I need you so to explain such things to me. You know.'

Rouwen drank slowly from the stream until his thirst was quenched. He found his energy greater than at any time while on the road down from Castle Gan. He stood and called out when he saw two men struggling to pull a cart laden with foodstuffs.

'You there, help me!' Rouwen called. 'I am Captain Rouwen of . . .'

'It's him, him!' shrieked one man. The other cried out in fear, lowered his head and began pulling faster on his pole. The first man added his strength to the cart as they ran off.

'Wait!'

They did not obey him. Rouwen slumped, then smiled when he saw a few parcels had fallen off their cart. He went to the middle of the road and opened the packages, finding dried fruit and bread inside. He ate his fill, then slung the rest in a rude backpack. He looked around the land he had called home all his life. Somehow, the greens were subtly wrong and the azure sky lacked the friendliness he remembered. Rouwen tramped along, not sure where he ought to go.

The Demon's Throat was out of the question. Sosler would have alerted the soldiers guarding the narrow passage to the cursing and banishment. Any of a dozen different ways of death might be his reward, should he try leaving that path.

'Death?' Rouwen laughed harshly. 'If only they could deliver me to Paradise!' But even as the cynical words escaped his lips, he knew they were a lie. His kingdom needed his services more than ever. If Brion Rouwen couldn't die for his kingdom, he would pledge his magically damned life to putting everything right once more.

All day Rouwen hiked and found people shunning him. Word had spread rapidly. Rouwen didn't have to ask to know what had been said about him and Queen Diarra. Anyone speaking or giving aid to the pair would be doomed to suffer the same fate. None of the farmers or merchants he encountered had the slightest idea what that meant, but Kwuway's reputation was such that no one dared risk the wizard's wrath – and if the wizard's actions were ordered by King Priowe, so more potent the shunning.

Rouwen wished he could have spoken to some of the people, to encourage them, to warn them of the dangers they faced. He did not try forcing any of them to listen to his message, fearing that Sosler's revenge might be passed along to innocent people.

At midday, Rouwen stared at the towering spire capped by Castle Gan. He let out a huge sigh. That had been his home for so long; it seemed an eternity. Real eternity loomed in front of him. His gray eyes slid down the steep sides of that rocky column, past the well-kept roads to the Demon's Throat. Commerce would be choked off soon, he thought. This had to be Duke Drioway's plan. Cut off food to the castle, reduce its ability to survive any attack, then bring in the foreign troops. Mion had a smaller, less well-trained army, but if King Priowe's resolve and will to fight had been sapped, victory might be easier.

Rouwen imagined battle pennants fluttering at the head of regiment after regiment marching up the road to Castle Gan, and none of the colors were those of Gannian troopers. That was his kingdom's fate.

The Demon's Throat was only one way out of the valley. He knew two others, both secret ways through limestone caverns under the Shield Mountains. One he hesitated to use since it burrowed directly under Mount Glid. Rouwen was not overly superstitious, but he had no desire to speak with the souls of the dead waiting for transport to Paradise.

The other way might be longer, but it would take him from the Valley of Gan to the outskirts of Mion. What King Nishor attempted in Gan might work against him within his own realm. Rouwen had no firm plan, but the journey would give him time for reflection. Playing the role of assassin had never tempted him. He had spent too much effort preventing killers in the night from reaching any of the royal family to appreciate such a way of shifting power.

What else did he have to offer Gan? If he killed King Nishor of Mion, that would end the immediate threat. Rouwen doubted Duke Drioway could continue his clandestine activity if there was turmoil within the Mionese capital. While this would not put right the injustices already done in Gan, it would give Priowe time to see the error of his actions. He might even come to realize Sosler did not have his or the kingdom's best interests at heart.

If Rouwen's quick blade brought such a change within Castle Gan, becoming a backstabbing executioner might be the only service he could offer. He sank to a shady spot and ate again, ravenous from his hiking. Rouwen touched the scarred spots on his body and remembered the pain of Sosler's dagger driving deep into his guts, the agony of the fall after Diarra had shoved him off the road, the other pain not related to physical injury.

He forced his mind away from the spells. Lingering too long on such matters would turn him bitter. He was a soldier, an officer of the realm, and had a duty to discharge. His monarch might have stripped him of earned rank and denied him the barony he had anticipated, but Priowe could never prevent him from serving his kingdom.

Rouwen heard footsteps along the road. He leaned to one side and looked to the traveller making his way so deliberately. Calling out would do no one any good, but Rouwen found himself starved for conversation. He cleared his throat and this was enough to draw attention to himself. The traveller faced Rouwen and lifted his walking staff.

'Who's there?' the man called. He was dressed simply in brown tunic and sturdy canvas trousers fastened at the waist with an ornate, hand-carved belt. A silver coin had been beaten into a buckle and held the leather ends together. On his feet were boots that Rouwen envied the instant he saw them. Heavy soles, highly polished sides, those boots were more likely to be worn by a noble than a peasant.

'Brion Rouwen, a traveller like yourself.' Rouwen didn't know how much to say, what to admit, what to deny.

'Are you peaceful?'

'As peaceful as yourself,' Rouwen shot back. This was not a standard query in Valley Gan. 'See for yourself. I carry no weapons.'

'I'll believe you, Brion Rouwen,' the traveller said. He walked closer and Rouwen saw that the man was blind, both eyes filmed and sightless. He paused a few paces away, then asked, 'Do I know you? The voice is familiar, as is the name.'

'I must be on my way. This tree gives good shade for a hot spring afternoon.' Rouwen heaved himself to his feet, wincing as various small pains assailed him.

'You are hurting,' the blind man said. 'Don't go. Let me help you with this salve. I find it excellent.' The traveller came over and fumbled in his pack and brought forth a small tin of purplish, waxy paste. 'Put it on your injuries.'

'If I might,' Rouwen said, hesitantly taking the salve. He did not wish to bring trouble down on an innocent man's head, yet the promise of relief from his misery made him take the risk. He applied a small amount of the purplish paste to his belly. He heaved a sigh as a coolness replaced the wickedly hot flame of pain writhing in him. 'This is nothing less than a miracle,' he told the traveller. 'Is it magical?'

The man laughed heartily. 'Nothing so arcane. I am a leather worker and often slip.' He held out his hands, showing numerous scars where sharp-edged tools had slipped and left their mark. 'This healing potion is the best I have found. It comes from Mion.'

Rouwen froze at the mention of Nishor's kingdom.

'You do not like that poor country? Little wonder. They lack capacity to produce food, though many items flow through its ports on their way to more prosperous realms.'

Rouwen shared what food he had left with the blind craftsman, thinking his banishment and shunning might not be as onerous as he had thought. Gan was a large kingdom, and not everyone would know of his disgrace yet. He became so engrossed in conversation with the worker in leather he failed to see the dust cloud in the distance begin to grow, to swirl and come closer. By the time Rouwen heard the pounding of horses' hooves, it was too late to hide.

The blind man turned toward the sounds from the road and said, 'That must be quite a large party. At least ten, I would say. Or a lesser number in quite a hurry to be somewhere else.'

Rouwen counted three uniformed riders, but he wasn't going to quibble over a few soldiers with the blind man. Their leader had sighted Rouwen and pointed, shouting commands that were still indistinct but of obvious intent. Lances levelled, the cavalry troopers rode off the road and attacked.

'Thank you for your kindness,' Rouwen called as he got his meager possessions together. He thought of tossing back the salve, then stuffed it into his own pack and ran.

'Wait, I don't understand. Who are they? Why . . . ?'

That was the last question ever to touch the craftsman's lips. A lance spitted him like a fowl and robbed him of life. Rouwen got only a glimpse of the blind man's death before stumbling and falling to one knee. He swung around, realizing he could never outrun a mounted soldier. Hefting his pack, he gauged distances, speeds and his chance of success. Then he swung, deflecting the lance at the right instant.

Rouwen stepped forward and grappled with the soldier as the man raced past on his courser. The former guard captain's feet were yanked off the ground, but he held on. He kept telling himself he could not die, even if the pain was intense. By hanging on, he unseated the trooper, bringing him crashing to the ground.

The fall knocked the trooper unconscious and gave Rouwen the chance to pull out both his dagger and his sword. He hefted the sword and found it off-balance, but still satisfying in his grip. Letting out a savage war whoop, he rushed forward, swinging fast to weave a curtain of gleaming steel in front of him.

The fiercely swung sword knocked aside the second trooper's lance, and the stolen dagger found a sheath directly under the mounted man's armpit. Rouwen yanked the dead soldier from his seat and tried to mount the now riderless horse. He had scant training as a horseman, but he knew the rudiments of riding. Unfortunately, the horse knew more and resented losing its rider in such an ignominious manner.

Rouwen found himself tossed off the bucking horse, hitting the ground with bone-shaking force and struggling to avoid the kicking hooves, bristling with wickedly sharp battle spurs. He rolled one way, then reversed and avoided the horse, only to find himself facing the third soldier.

'Rouwen,' the mounted soldier said, 'my apologies. You were a good commander, but there is a reward on your head now.'

'Is it worth dying for?' Rouwen asked.

He didn't receive an answer, nor had he expected one. The soldier was too cagy to become embroiled in a verbal battle that might distract him. The trooper charged him, lance readied. Rouwen dodged to the far side and slashed with sword – and missed. He twisted hard, bringing incredible pain to his tortured ribs, and lashed out with the dagger. A long, thin line of red appeared along the horse's flank. He had sought the rider and not his mount, but this worked as well. The horse charged on, then began to stumble. The soldier tried to wheel about for a second attack and found his animal sinking to the ground under him.

Brion Rouwen was the superior swordsman. It sickened him to leave loyal troopers dead on the ground, but he had no choice. He might not be able to die, but the pain within was immense. Rouwen checked himself and was not surprised to find several deep cuts he did not remember receiving in the brief, fierce fray.

Taking what he could from the fallen soldiers, he returned to kneel beside the craftsman. He had been killed with the first lance thrust. Rouwen did not like robbing the dead, but he knew nothing of the man or his family. The boots fitted well, as did the clothing. The belt was tight about his middle, but a few minutes' work with a dagger's point gave enough length to hold a scabbard and dirk.

He wished he could have caught a horse and ridden on his way, but the soldiers' mounts had run off – the ones he hadn't slaughtered by accident. Rouwen began hiking, aware that the entire kingdom was now searching for him. Simple banishment and shunning was not enough for Duke Sosler. He had to order his victims slain when he knew that would only cause pain, not death.

Rouwen's stride lengthened as the day died. The sun dipped behind the circle of high mountains cradling the Valley Gan as Rouwen neared his brother Adan's farm. Adan had always been the grower, the one capable of nurturing and cultivating when others failed. Brion had admired and respected this but had always known his path was different from his brother's.

Now he felt a moment of self-pity that he had not remained with Adan on the farm. Their parents had died years ago and other family was scattered sparsely throughout the valley. Rouwen wished he had maintained closer ties with his older brother.

A fenced area showed where Adan kept his livestock. Neat rows of feeding and watering troughs brought old memories flowing back. It had been too long since he had seen his brother. Rouwen jumped the fence and walked briskly across the field, only to be stopped by a loud cry of welcome.

'Brion! It's you!' Adan Rouwen got to his feet from where he worked on a bent plow, wiped dirt from his hands on an old rag and ran toward his brother. 'It's so good to see you!'

'Adan!' Rouwen threw his arms around his brother and hugged him tight, in spite of the pain lancing into his body. He had come home. He could rest and find some peace and take the time to heal his hideous wounds. He pushed back and said, 'I can't believe . . .'

Brion Rouwen's eyes widened in horror as he looked into his brother's smiling face. Adan's flesh began to flow and melt, bubbling and boiling away from the skull as if a volcano's heat had been turned against it. Adan Rouwen reached to touch white bone, and his hands withered and fell off. His clothing collapsed onto a skeleton, all flesh seared away.

'Adan!'

What remained of Adan Rouwen lay in front of a brother who had dared to love and was cursed by it.

7

A Murder of Crows and Assassins

Brion Rouwen stepped back in horror and tried to call out to his fallen brother. No words came to his shock-numbed lips. He stared in abject horror at the gleaming white skeleton that had been Adan Rouwen a few seconds earlier. The farmer's coarse, plain clothing was unscathed, but the flesh had melted from his brother's bones. And the spell did not stop there. The bones began cracking like thunder, splinters snapping off and sailing into the air like so many missiles.

'Adan, I didn't think, I didn't know. I didn't believe the curse.' Words caught in Rouwen's throat. He dropped to his knees and tried to hide his eyes from the hideous spectacle being enacted in front of him.

The bones stopped breaking and started a slow disintegration. Powdery gray residue remained to stain the inside of Adan's clothing. And nothing more.

Brion Rouwen's eyes lifted to the distant Mount Glid, hoping to catch sight of his brother's soul making its final worldly journey before being summoned to Paradise. There was no hint that Adan's soul had begun the migration that would give it eternal peace and prosperity. All he saw in the sky was the dark wheeling of a flight of crows, harbingers of death. He should have seen the birds and been warned by them – he should have believed Diarra when she told him of Kwuway's real curse. Yet it seemed too incredible.

'No wizard can perform such a spell,' he muttered to himself, still denying the wizard's powerful curse. In spite of his faintly held conviction, he worried that Kwuway had somehow managed to doom Adan to an eternity of peering into Paradise, starving and desolate, never resting, and always longing for what was never to be granted. Kwuway might have cast the spell destroying Adan, but there was no way a mortal, even a mage as powerful as Kwuway, could pass eternal judgment before reaching Paradise.

But the spell did exist to kill any Rouwen loved. He stared at his hands. They were scraped and cut, but otherwise no different from the hands he had known all his life. He had held a sword in those hands, made love using those hands, held newborn animals and embraced his brother and now they killed with a simple touch.

Rouwen's eyes left Mount Glid and turned toward the uppermost regions in Gan. The castle's highest turrets still carried faint highlights of golden sunlight reflected off their pure white. At one time that sight would have brought a thrill of pride to Brion Rouwen. No longer. In that castle resided his worst enemies, and Rouwen was only now beginning to know them.

'Kwuway, you will pay for what you have done in the king's name,' Rouwen promised. 'And Sosler and Drioway. Both of you will find a private pit outside Paradise where you will long for release through all eternity.' Rouwen stopped as he considered his options. They were few. Leaving Gan and killing King Nishor had faded into a vague future. Replacing such a feeble stab with a more forceful thrust entered his mind.

'Priowe is my enemy. He owed me, he owed his wife. He should have listened and investigated the plot.' Rouwen looked back at the empty clothing stretched across the short-cropped grass of Adan Rouwen's pasture. King Priowe had slain an innocent as surely as if he had driven a dagger through Adan's heart.

Rouwen sat and watched the last of the bright sun vanish from Castle Gan's turrets and night descend to a total blackness. Here and there a light blossomed in a castle window, letting Rouwen guess who lurked in those rooms, what they schemed and where they might strike against the kingdom next.

'He must die,' Rouwen said, coming to a conclusion. 'There is no other way. King Priowe must no longer rule Gan, if there is any hope of survival.' Turning the kingdom over to Nishor was disastrous. Only if a stronger hand took control could Gan's prosperity continue, and that meant removing Priowe from power. With this, Rouwen knew he had also to kill Priowe's son, Sped. The drunken lordling would never be able to rule with the strength and determination for the kingdom to survive.

Sorinne must be queen. To achieve this, Rouwen had to kill the woman's father and brother. Rouwen shifted his gaze from the dark bulk of Castle Gan to his brother's powdery remains, now glowing with a faint green radiance. He lifted his hands and looked at them one last time, and determination exploded within him and hardened. He had been trained to kill for King Priowe. Now he had to kill Priowe.

Rouwen settled his weapons and turned to Adan's small farmhouse. He stopped before he got halfway to the house he remembered so well. He and Adan had grown up here, their parents often joyful, sometimes saddened by poor harvests or unexpected twistings of fate, but always loving. Always.

He angled off toward a barn and found the smokehouse behind it. Rouwen filled a rucksack he found with food for his trip. Somewhere within the rocky ring of the Shield Mountains had to be a band of King Nishor's men. Assassins, possibly, but more likely a support team for Duke Drioway. They might pass themselves off as a trade delegation or farmers studying Gannian cultivation methods or even simple pilgrims going to the base of Mount Glid to pray for guidance in their more earthly matters.

Whatever they called themselves, the Mionese would know the secrets of keeping him undetected until Rouwen could use his knowledge of Castle Gan to kill Priowe. He had no sense of how many soldiers sought him, but the small patrol that had slaughtered the innocent blind craftsman and had sought to kill him was only one of many. The Lord Protector of Gan would do nothing by half measures. He had seen Rouwen cursed and knew he could never die. Banishment from Castle Gan and shunning would be little enough torture.

Being hacked and mutilated and unable to die would be the kind of punishment Sosler would delight in – Sosler or Priowe? Rouwen thought he knew his liege, but the events of the past weeks had shaken that belief to the foundations of his being. Priowe had ordered Kwuway's diabolical curses instead of Chertude's physical tortures; Sosler had agreed to the change in punishment.

'Both will die. Both,' Rouwen said, his long legs striding away from his family's farm. He hesitated when he reached the road, wanting to return for one last tormenting look at Adan. Brion Rouwen forced himself to keep walking along the night-cloaked road leading to a small town less than an hour's hike away.

The Lesser Moon shone fitfully on him, clouds scudding above the last nocturnal flights of the crows and their gleaming black wings. An hour later, when the Greater Moon rose, the sky's star-studded dome hid timorously behind thick, forbidding storm clouds. Small bolts of lightning danced from cloud to cloud and even occasionally touched the higher peaks in the Shield Mountains. Rouwen paid no attention to the storm brewing so powerfully above.

Within him raged one even more potent. Before the first heavy drops of chilling rain began to fall, Rouwen reached the outskirts of Wheatown. If Nishor's lackeys were to be found, it would be near the county's largest town. Rouwen knew other possible bases might give better access to Castle Gan, but he had to start somewhere and this was close.

Not wanting to enter the town and force any of the good citizens to recognize him and suffer the consequences, Rouwen scouted the area for any sign of long-distance travellers. He found a half dozen horses, a dray and small crates laden with trade goods in a livery stable behind a wayside inn. Rouwen stared at the stone building with its wooden shutters already pulled shut against the storm. He wished for better eyes to see through the stone and timber to find Nishor's agents. Faint sounds of laughter fought the rising wind and distant thunder to tell of men enjoying their leisure after a day's hard travel, but were these Nishor's pawns?

Rouwen moved closer, peering through a crack in a poorly fastened shutter. He saw two serving girls dancing nimbly between the long tables, avoiding groping hands and mock kisses, as they carried heavy stoneware tumblers of wine to their customers. Identifying the travellers was not possible from outside, but Rouwen had a sense that these were not native Gannians.

A sudden flash of lightning outlined him against the building – and also cast a second shadow beside his. Rouwen pulled his cloak tighter around him as he reached for his dagger. He had to use a weapon quickly.

Rouwen dropped to a crouch, spun and drove his dagger upward, catching the man behind him unawares. The tip of the dagger stopped only when it pinked the man's throat.

'Stay your hand!' the man cried, startled at Rouwen's swiftness of attack.

Rouwen straightened his legs slowly and reached out, catching the man's wrist to pull his hand away from a short sword's sharkskin-wrapped handle. Rouwen encountered no resistance as he opened the man's cloak and studied his clothing. There was nothing to brand him a Mionese spy, but there were subtle clues that alerted Rouwen. Few Gannians used sharkskin on the hilt of their weapons, preferring wound wire to keep the weapons from being wrenched from their hand. Also, the weave of the cloak was coarser than any but the most impoverished wore, yet this man seemed well-fed and far from needing to accept charity.

'Do you serve King Nishor?' asked Rouwen.

'I will say whatever pleases you most,' the man said, lifting his finger to tap gently on the side of Rouwen's dagger.

'I want only the truth.'

'You have the look of a mercenary,' the man countered. 'Do you seek gainful employment with our band?'

'Who leads you?'

'Kennard of Lowpin.'

Rouwen lowered his dagger, still wary. 'Why did you sneak up behind me?'

'Why were you spying on my fellows?'

Rouwen tried to take the man's measure and failed. He was a clumsy stalker, revealing himself through his shadow, but the width of shoulders and thickness of wrist indicated immense strength. The sword showed long use and tolerable care, and the man's clothing was worn but clean for a traveller. In the man's face Rouwen got no hint of intelligence. The eyes were dull and the mouth had a cruel set to it, as if a guard dog had been loosed without proper instruction.

Something warned Rouwen that this appraisal was wrong.

'You are Kennard?' Rouwen asked.

This produced a long laugh that came barking out like a wolf calling a lovelorn song to a distant mate. Rain beat down on the man's square skull and produced small rivers that trickled through matted, dark hair. The occasional lightning flash gave an eerie aspect that caused Rouwen to change his first impression completely. He not only faced Kennard of Lowpin, he faced a dangerous adversary easily his equal mentally – and perhaps even with a sword.

'Yes, yes, I am Kennard. Do you seek employment? We have a position to fill since one of our noble band fell ill with some putrid Gannian influenza and had to be sent home.'

'To Mion?'

'Where else?' Kennard's eyes narrowed as he studied Rouwen with the same intensity that Rouwen had used on him. 'You are more than a simple mercenary, aren't you?'

'I seek those who oppose King Priowe. Are you in that camp?' Rouwen saw the mask of brutish stupidity return to Kennard's face. The man revealed nothing and thought to gull Rouwen into a damning confession.

'We cannot oppose a man who is not our liege. We are a commerce delegation, travelling your fair land to establish trading posts across Gan. We have no stake in your politics, other than the import it lends to our financial agreements.'

'I want to kill King Priowe.' Rouwen's voice came out harsh

68

and packed with more emotion than he intended. He sought to match Kennard in his emotionless aspect. Anything less would brand him as a fanatic looking to engage in a suicide mission. Rouwen intended more, far more.

First Duke Sosler, then Priowe. And Sped. Only then could Princess Sorinne become Queen of Gan and return the land to its usual lofty standards of justice and tranquility.

'We cannot discuss such monstrous schemes,' Kennard said slowly, still evaluating Rouwen. 'We need to speak carefully, as befitting a trade delegation seeking peaceful commerce.'

'Protect me, get me to the gates of the castle, and I will do the rest,' Rouwen said.

This brought another wolfish bark of mirth from Kennard's lips. He shook his head and sent a cascade of rain flying in a thin arc from his long, lank hair. He put a powerful hand on Rouwen's shoulder and pushed him lightly toward the inn's side door.

'I need to find what compels you to make such wild claims to a stranger from a distant – and peaceable – land. Come, enter and have a cup of hot wine with my travelling companions.'

'You will protect me while we speak?'

'I fail to understand this anxiety. You are a native Gannian and yet you fear your own kind. And you want us to dance up the tall spire holding your fine castle, which by all accounts is unassailable? You need us to escort you, but you can enter without our aid?'

'That is correct,' Rouwen said, warily slipping into the inn and looking for a trap to be sprung around him. No one even noticed them as they dripped onto the polished planks. A bawdy song rose from two of the men near the roaring fire, while others swilled the wine from their mugs.

'An enigma,' Kennard said lightly. 'Free passage is the right of all citizens, yet none enters Castle Gan without proper credentials. You seem to have matters turned upside down.'

Rouwen sat at one end of a long bench, wary of the others with Kennard. He jumped when a serving girl came over and stood, waiting for him to give her an order.

'The same as they are having,' Rouwen said, waving vaguely in the direction of Kennard's comrades.

'Mulled wine it is, sir,' she said, smiling a little at him as she left with a rustle of her long skirts. Rouwen wondered if she graced him with the smile because he was Gannian and the others weren't, or if it was simple relief at not being pinched as she took his order. The Mionese were raucous and vulgar, but Rouwen saw that they weren't as drunk as they pretended.

Sizzling wine in a mug appeared in front of Rouwen. He nodded in the girl's direction, but did not look at her. He was aware of Kennard's continued examination. Only when the serving girl left did the Mionese move closer and bend forward, his words barely audible over the loud singing and patter of rain against the inn's shutters.

'What makes you think we seek your noble king's death?' Kennard asked.

'You are no trade delegation,' Rouwen accused. 'You are too well armed and have the look of soldiers, not traders.'

'Matters are not as serene in Mion,' Kennard said in an offhand manner. 'We find ourselves beset by highwaymen at every turn, so we must learn to defend ourselves and our trade goods. Is this so wrong?'

Rouwen hesitated to mention Duke Drioway. If he were King Nishor he would send numerous bands of men into Gan with differing missions, but all aimed at the country's throat. Drioway had succeeded in subverting Sosler, but that did not mean Kennard of Lowpin necessarily knew of this success – or even much cared. If assassination of King Priowe was successful, it would put his drunken son on the throne.

If anything, this would serve Duke Drioway's purposes even better. Sosler would be able to manipulate Sped and have almost absolute power over Castle Gan – and the valley. A treaty, an agreement, a few diplomatic delegations exchanged between Gan and Mion would spell the end of centuries of strength.

Only Rouwen had his own mission. He would not stop at King Priowe, nor would he consider starting there. Sosler and Kwuway must die first, then King Priowe and his son. Princess Sorinne would never submit to foreign powers, especially the King of Mion.

'You want Priowe dead,' Rouwen said flatly. 'I do, also. Protect me, get me up the road to the castle gates, and I shall do the rest.'

'How do you enter Castle Gan? I have never been there, but rumors abound of its impregnability. Steel doors thicker than a man's arm, high walls and boiling oil poured down on unprepared soldiers. Then there are the stories of how hideous magicks protect the castle.'

Rouwen had heard the stories and knew they were partially true. King Priowe used three prongs in his defense. The Lord Protector defended everything within the Demon's Throat. The Captain of the Intrepid Guard guarded both king and castle internally. And Priowe had a third protector: Kwuway.

70

The king could order his wizard to cast spells only they had discussed. What they were or how far-reaching they might be, no one knew. There had never been an invading army penetrate far enough to warrant such magical defense. The Demon's Throat was usually the most effective deterrent, though Rouwen had practiced fending off an army spiralling up the road to the castle's front gates many times, seeking weaknesses and bolstering strengths in his tactics.

'I will get inside the castle in my own way,' Rouwen said, sensing Kennard's interest. 'Get me there and I will do what you seek. What we *both* seek.'

'An interesting proposition,' Kennard said. He drained his mug and banged it on the table to attract the serving girl's attention. 'Damned lazy wench. More wine!' He stood and waved his mug about in his left hand as he passed behind Rouwen.

The soft sound of a blade slipping from a sheath was all the warning Brion Rouwen had before Kennard's razor-edged dagger drove hilt-deep into his unprotected back. He sagged forward on the table, the inn growing dim around him.

8

The Poisoned Dagger

Pain caused his body to shudder uncontrollably. His eyes blinked open, and for a moment all Brion Rouwen saw were beer stains and the rings from the bottoms of dripping mugs set on the table. He gulped, forced himself to sit upright, and reached behind. His groping fingers found the dagger still sunk hilt-deep into his back. He yanked and pulled out the bloodied blade. With all the power he could summon, Rouwen drove the tip into the wooden table in front of him. The blade quivered and hummed for a moment, then simply gleamed in reflected firelight. The inky black blood on the dagger sucked in as much light as the hilt sealed with its sharkskin wrapping reflected.

'It's not that easy to kill me,' he said to Kennard, fighting to keep his voice level. The man's eyes were wide, as much with surprise as with fear at seeing a victim he had thought to slay pull the weapon from his own back.

Rouwen inhaled slowly, letting the eddying current of pain flood through him. He had felt the peculiar liquid discomfort before, and it no longer frightened him as it once did. That did not make it any less excruciating.

Die often enough and the thrill of panic loosened its hold. Rouwen lifted his arm and experienced new agony, but he fought to keep from showing it to the Mionese agent watching him intently. Movement was severely limited in his left arm, and he knew he would never be able to fight Kennard, if it came to that. But one look at the counterfeit trader assured Rouwen that no such fight was necessary.

'You still live. I – I drove the dagger through your heart!' Kennard had turned pale under his deep tan. His square face showed signs of developing nervous tics under both eyes, and his mouth opened and closed for a few seconds until he brought his rampaging emotions under control.

'I can get into the castle,' Rouwen said with pain lacing his words, 'just as I cannot be killed.'

'I have heard of such curses. Have you travelled far?' asked one of the men closer to the fire. 'To see the Lord of Death and Life?'

'I've never heard of him,' Rouwen said. 'The wizard devising this spell is closer to hand. Kwuway is Priowe's pet spellcaster.' Rouwen did not try to keep the bitterness from his voice.

'You would kill the monarch who commands such a powerful wizard?' Kennard's eyes widened even more. He snapped his fingers and got wine poured into his mug. He drained it in one long gulp and demanded more before coming to sit across the table from Rouwen. He stared at Rouwen in disbelief.

'I would, and I know your king also seeks such an end for Priowe.'

'To utter such words inside the Shield Mountains is folly,' Kennard said, choosing his words carefully. 'We are simple traders on our way up the road to Castle Gan.' His dark eyes took in the others in his small band, as if polling them for their opinions. No one spoke. All stared at Rouwen, as if waiting for him finally to die from the brutal backstabbing. Kennard turned back and asked, 'Would you accompany us to the castle on the morrow? We can use a handler for our horses.'

'Your offer is most generous,' Rouwen said. 'I need a place to sleep tonight, also. Undisturbed.' He did not know how long it would take his newly ensorcelled body to repair itself. Before tackling either the Intrepid or King Priowe himself, he had to heal. Already deep inside he felt his heart's liquid sloshing where Kennard's dagger had pierced it, slowly repairing itself – and leaving behind a haunting legacy of pain and weakness.

'That we can offer. None of this group will intrude upon your dreams,' Kennard said with enough vehemence that Rouwen believed him. Too many of them tried vainly to cover the fright they felt at seeing a man who should have died talking so earnestly with their leader.

'You gents want some more wine?' asked the serving girl. She had not seen Kennard drive in the dagger nor Rouwen pluck it out as if nothing had happened. She saw the puddle of blood under Rouwen's seat, wrinkled her nose and went on, not recognizing it and obviously irritated at having to clean up still more untidiness left by drunken customers.

'More wine for all,' Kennard ordered, moving away from Rouwen to confer with his companions. That suited the former guard captain. His hands shook from loss of blood, and he might pass out at any moment from both weakness and pain. He sat and stared into the dancing flames, letting their warmth keep him from chills threatening to possess him totally.

Rouwen jerked around when the inn's door opened letting a blast of cold air and heavy rain pour through. He sucked in his breath and held it when he saw three soldiers. Remembering his encounter with the other patrol, Rouwen knew all Gannian troopers had been put on the watch for him. Sergeant's stars gleamed on one man's tunic. He would pursue his duty most ardently since promotion into the officer ranks might await one clever enough to find Sosler's victim.

Rouwen turned back to the fire and lowered his head, staring at the dagger in front of him. Trying not to move so quickly that he attracted attention, but not so slowly that the soldiers saw the dagger, Rouwen reached out and wiggled it to and fro until the blade snapped free of its berth. Rouwen hid the dagger under his arm and leaned forward even more, a wave of dizziness assailing him.

'Have you seen anything unusual on the road?' the sergeant barked.

'Do you speak to us, Cap'n?' asked Kennard, intentionally promoting the soldier. The attempted compliment did not work. Rouwen heard the contempt for even making the attempt in the trooper's voice.

'You're Mionese, aren't you?' demanded the sergeant. His two men moved to either side, hands on their daggers. Rouwen cursed. They realized the imprudence of drawing a sword in the small inn. If a fight started, they would have the most useful weapons already in hand.

'We are, good sir. We travel to Castle Gan on the morrow. A fine sight it is, too, soaring so tall and white into the sky. Have you been into the castle, Cap'n?'

'We're looking for a traitor,' the sergeant said, refusing to be deterred. 'He's been banished and shunned. No one's to talk to him, and we have orders to kill him on sight.'

'And why is this, after those other punishments?' Kennard framed the question mildly, as if he had no idea what the sergeant meant.

'He has not left Gan. He has been *banished*.'

'And the shunning means none ought talk with him?' Kennard motioned to the serving girl for wine for the soldiers. Rouwen watched from the corner of his eye and saw the sergeant fighting with duty over the need to quench his thirst. The hot wine steamed in its mugs and mouth-watering vapors wafted to the soldiers.

'Any speaking with him risk having the same sentence passed on them,' the sergeant said. He accepted the wine, to the relief of the men with him. They caught up mugs of their own and sipped the mulled wine, nodding thanks in Kennard's direction. The Mionese trader lifted his mug in silent and, Rouwen thought, mocking salute.

'How should we recognize this traitor to the Kingdom of Gan?'

'He stands about my height and wears what is left of a guardsman's uniform. He has dark hair and gray eyes so pale they might be formed of melting ice.'

'I haven't seen anyone of such description,' Kennard said. He turned to his travelling companions and put the question to them. He was greeted with shaking heads. 'So, Cap'n, we have not caught sight of your fleeing felon.'

'Tell me of your travels,' the sergeant said, sitting beside Kennard. 'What is it like in Mion? I have heard tales of a port city where the women . . .' The sergeant's voice dropped so that Rouwen could no longer hear, but Kennard laughed with gusto at whatever bawdy situation the soldier described.

Rouwen stood on shaky legs and wobbled past the two soldiers. One bumped into him and Rouwen mumbled what he hoped sounded like a drunken apology. The soldier did not accept the apology, and Rouwen guessed he wanted to check everyone in the inn without appearing to do so and possibly offend their gracious Mionese host.

'What's with you?' the soldier demanded.

'Too much wine. Good wine. Got to . . . go out back.' Rouwen rubbed his crotch. 'Rain coming down. Too much wine.'

'Get out of here,' the soldier said, shoving him toward the rear door. Rouwen reached for support and dropped the dagger clutched in his right hand. It clattered to the floor where the two soldiers saw it.

'Wait a moment,' the one demanded, starting after Rouwen. 'Why were you carrying a drawn dagger? Did you think to kill us? A backstabber, eh?'

The soldier's challenge brought the sergeant up from his seat beside Kennard.

'What have we here?' His eyes narrowed as he studied Rouwen. The description he must have received was far from Rouwen's appearance now. Blood loss, dirt and the death of his brother had all taken their toll on Brion Rouwen.

'Please, Sergeant,' Rouwen said, his voice quavering. He didn't have to work to put the tremor into his words. He was hardly able to stand and was almost at the point of passing out. 'I didn't mean to do it. I haven't eaten in days. I just thought to exchange it for a meal.' Rouwen lowered his gaze to the dagger on the floor.

'What?' The sergeant picked up the dagger and stared at it.

'Don't arrest me. I'll work for the gentleman to make up for any inconvenience, if he'll have me. I won't try stealing again if he will feed me.' Rouwen glanced in Kennard's direction and saw the Mionese agent smile fleetingly, then put on a dour expression as he came over. He grabbed the dagger and thrust it into the sheath dangling at his belt.

'I never missed it, but it is hardly a valuable weapon. There were no gems on it.'

'You stole his dagger?' The sergeant fought to understand what was going on. His attention was diverted from identifying Rouwen to sorting out the tangled threads of alibi snapping about him.

'I admit it freely. Please accept my promise of work!' Rouwen dropped to his knees in front of Kennard and kept his face averted from the soldiers.

The sergeant kicked Rouwen in the ribs. White pain exploded in Rouwen's side and he gasped, almost doubling over. The ribs had not healed completely. He might not die, but he could suffer – and the non-fatal injuries healed no quicker now than before he received the devilish spell.

'What say you, trader?'

'We can use the help. So much of what we do is menial work. He can load the dray and tend the horses. Maybe then we can see if he deserves a job carrying any pay.'

'You're too generous,' the sergeant said, 'but it is just as well. We have our traitor to find. Dealing with a petty thief would have kept us from our patrol.'

'A big reward has been offered for this traitor, eh?' Kennard asked slyly. 'Would this reward go to anyone, or just you fellows?'

'We seek him for the honor of our company,' the sergeant said primly. 'Unlike Mion, we value honor above coin.' He waved to his two men, who quickly gulped at their wine before leaving the inn. Rain beat through the door and danced in beads across the floor. The serving girl made an obscene comment about the soldiers, then fetched a mop and started cleaning the water from the floor.

'You think fast,' Kennard praised, helping Rouwen to his feet. 'And you have luck riding at your shoulder.'

Rouwen said nothing. He was not lucky. He was the most cursed man in Gan, and possibly in the entire world.

It took Kennard two days to reach the base of the spire holding Castle Gan. The road spiralled around the mountainside, showing white slashes at ever higher levels. Kennard craned his head back and stared at the castle gleaming in the bright morning sunlight.

'No army in this world could ever take that fortress,' he said, admiration in his voice. 'What is it like ruling from the top of the world?'

'There is nothing like it,' Rouwen said with pride. 'Gan is prosperous and the castle assures our freedom.' Rouwen had recovered some strength in the past two days but still rode in the traders' small wagon, glad of the chance to rest. His fight lay ahead, and he needed all his strength for the battle.

'What weapon do you require for your assassination?' Kennard asked unexpectedly.

Rouwen touched the steel dagger at his waist, then fingered the sword. Somehow, he felt less confident now than he had when he vowed that King Priowe must die. Reality intruded, and he realized the king might fall to his blade – but what of Kwuway? The wizard would not allow simple attacks to succeed. He had survived too long to have any vulnerability Rouwen might exploit.

'Inefficient. Here, take this.' Kennard handed him a rag-wrapped bundle. 'You use it as you would a regular blade, but be sure to *twist*.'

Rouwen peeled back the rags to a sudden rainbow gleam of sunlight on glass. Kennard had given him the assassin's weapon, a glass dagger with a poison-filled blade. The pale blue liquid within might be any of a dozen different poisons, but Rouwen knew whatever Kennard had chosen would be virulent.

'You recognize it?' Kennard smiled crookedly. 'But of course you do! You were Captain of the Intrepid Guard and fought against men carrying such weapons.' This seemed to amuse Kennard more than anything else had, and he made no effort to hold back a deep, hearty laugh.

'It will serve me well,' Rouwen said, thinking this might be the weapon to use against a wizard. King Priowe would die of a single thrust of his dagger, but his worries about magical protection Kwuway might have woven around himself faded now. No one, not even a wizard, could counter the lethal effects of an assassin's poisoned blade.

'Let's reach the gates before sundown. The road is steep, and the horses are not as rested as they might be,' Kennard said.

Rouwen rode along in the dray, letting the Mionese trader deal with the knots of soldiers positioned along the road. Once Kennard showed his credentials, no one bothered searching the dray or even giving those with him much notice. Rouwen wasn't sure what Kennard had in the way of permits and visas, but he thought it must be a freedom-of-movement pass from Drioway – and Duke Sosler. Only this would admit the small band so quickly past guardsmen on the lookout for assassins.

Assassins and Brion Rouwen.

The sun dipped low behind the Shield Mountains and occasionally, after taking another steep upward slope, the small party outraced the setting sun for a few more minutes of day. But when the cart creaked to a halt in front of the towering steel doors guarding the entrance to Castle Gan, it was well into twilight.

Rouwen saw no reason to speak to his benefactor. Kennard worked for his own liege, and Rouwen still hated King Nishor almost as much as he had come to loathe Priowe. Rouwen dropped off the cart and fell face down behind a rock. Kennard went through the bureaucratic rigmarole to enter the castle and was told he had to camp until daybreak. The trader might have known this would happen, but Rouwen cared little for Kennard's plans. He waited for the guardsmen to vanish back through their gate before moving away, following the line of the castle wall to a special pattern embedded in the wall.

Twice only had Rouwen used this way, and both times he had left the castle. He ran his fingers over the decorative blocks, finding the right combination. His fingers pushed hard into recesses, but strive as he might, he failed to move them. Rouwen worried that he lacked the strength to open the way into the castle. He stepped back, wiped sweat from his face and tried once more. This time he heard a gentle grating sound and a darkness opened at his feet.

Dropping quickly, Rouwen jumped into the hole. The gateway closed above him with a dull thud. He crouched in the gloom and caught his breath. Even the small exertion of opening the secret door had robbed him of energy. He needed to use stealth rather than power if he was to execute his string of killings.

Duck-walking forward for what seemed hours, Rouwen finally came to a spot where he saw two small points of light above him. He stood slowly, careful not to bump his head in the darkness. Putting his face against the carved stone, his eyes matched the holes and he looked out into the castle's courtyard. By torchlight, troops drilled in formation and at the far side, Rouwen saw one company engaging another in half-speed sword practice. If he had not known better, he would have thought Castle Gan prepared for war.

But he had been gone for too long and knew little of what happened. Perhaps the Intrepid *did* prepare for battle.

Rouwen worried about Sosler being at their head, along with his own troops scattered throughout Gan. The duke might be ruler before the year was finished.

Rotating the slab in front of him, Rouwen opened a door into the courtyard. A squad marched past him but none of the soldiers' eyes shifted in his direction. As far as anyone was concerned, he belonged here. Striving to keep that illusion, Rouwen boldly crossed the courtyard and went to a familiar door in the central keep. He went inside and stopped to catch his breath. Rouwen preferred open, face-to-face combat to such clandestine methods. The strain of what he intended wearied him, no matter how richly Kwuway and Priowe deserved their fate.

He went up the steps and found a smaller branching staircase to one side that led to the royal chambers. Standing guard were two Intrepids, but Rouwen ignored them. He slid behind a tapestry a half dozen paces before reaching their post and sought the small lever mounted high on the wall. He found and pulled it, gaining entry to a narrow staircase running parallel to the one more publicly used.

Rouwen climbed the steep stairs, tiring quickly. He rested to catch his breath too many times. Being this close to King Priowe made Rouwen anxious to finish his task. With luck, he would find Kwuway and Priowe together and finish the distasteful task. Then he could dispatch Duke Sosler and install Princess Sorinne on the throne that rightfully belonged to her.

Rouwen sat on the cold stone step and began to worry about his ability to kill his monarch and the wizard.

'Perhaps it would be best to force Kwuway to lift the spells he has placed on me,' Rouwen said to himself. His hands balled tightly as he remembered the sight of Adan melting before his eyes, horribly dead because of a single touch. He had loved his brother dearly; Adan had been the last of his immediate family. Like so many Gannians, the Rouwen clan was not large due to recurrent starvation and the harshness of life. Valley Gan might fare better than outlying kingdoms, but that did not save it from periodic drought and famine and insect onslaught. Even the best wizards were unable to hold back such privation.

'How to force Kwuway to my will?' Rouwen drew the glass

dagger and looked at the pale blue poison within its gleaming blade. Would the wizard fear death by this poison? Rouwen was not sure what its effect might be. 'Or should I show him that Chertude is not the only master torturer in Gan?'

Indecision began to assail him, sapping his will and promoting doubts of his own ability. Bracing himself, Rouwen shot to his feet, determined to finish the task. He hoped to kill Kwuway first, but if he had to kill Priowe before either wizard or Duke Sosler, so be it.

The staircase narrowed until Rouwen had to turn sideways to proceed. When the width was little more than the thickness of his chest, he came to a wall hanging. Pausing, he strained to hear if anyone moved about in the king's audience chamber. Rouwen's heart almost exploded at the sound of Kwuway's strident tones.

'Majesty, this is absurd. We cannot defend the castle in such a way. I would need hundreds of assistants. Thousands!'

'You claim to be the greatest wizard in the world. Are you saying you cannot perform even simple spells?' King Priowe's chiding was more than a reprimand but less than outright condemnation.

'Simple? These are complicated spells, requiring continuous chanting, magical gestures of incredible difficulty. Your Intrepids can guard Castle Gan better than I with all my spells. You know that – or so I thought.'

'I do not like your tone, Wizard.' Priowe's own voice carried an edge to it, but Rouwen could not decide what bothered his former king the most. Was this irritation over a subordinate's lack of ability or was it closer to fear? What had happened within the castle walls since he had been imprisoned, cursed, and banished?

Rouwen slipped from the secret stairway and positioned himself behind the throne. Decision came upon him in a flash. Torment forever outside Paradise was better than losing his chance to drive the glass dagger laden with poison into Kwuway's foul heart. And with a simple turn he could thrust through King Priowe's bloated belly. Two deaths in the twinkling of an eye!

With luck, he could evade the guards stationed around the audience chamber and reach Duke Sosler before the entire castle was in complete uproar. The audience chamber guards might not spread the word too quickly, fearing for their own necks. Failure was not tolerated by Sosler.

Rouwen pulled out the glass dagger and held it in his right hand. As he reached for his steel dagger with his left, he paused. Soft footsteps approached the throne. He was unable to see into the chamber from behind the throne; he had to whirl around it to kill his enemies, those whom he had once thought his allies.

'Father, I must protest at the way I am being treated,' came angry words from one whom Rouwen loved. He froze. Kwuway's curse slew those Brion Rouwen loved, but did he have to touch Princess Sorinne for the curse to work? Or was merely seeing her enough? He hadn't had time to sort through all that had happened and understand the full evil of Kwuway's demonic spell.

This indecision betrayed Rouwen. A guardsman moving at the periphery of the audience chamber saw him standing behind the throne.

'Assassin! Assassin!' the Intrepid yelled. Then he stopped and his mouth gaped as he recognized Rouwen. 'It's Captain Rouwen!'

Rouwen found himself unable to whirl around the throne and drive his dagger into Priowe's throat.

'Sorinne,' he muttered. Rouwen could never kill her, and he would if he persisted, thanks to Kwuway's curse. Then all thought was past. He had waited too long to make the killing stroke. Rouwen blocked the guardsman's thrust with his dagger and found himself locked in a deadly duel.

9

Escape

Brion Rouwen parried another thrust with his steel dagger and danced away from the Intrepid he had trained so well. Shoving the glass dagger into his broad belt, Rouwen whipped out his sword and turned the tip of the guardsman's sword an instant before being spitted. The thrill of death slashing past him caused the former guard captain to reflect that he could not die now. He could take any cut and not perish.

But he would be injured, debilitated, and would be captured if he didn't fight free. The idea of Baron Chertude torturing him, forever unable to die, sent a shock of fear more potent than that of death through Rouwen. A quick parry *en carte* tied up his opponent's blade long enough to permit him to use the dagger. Rouwen hated to see the life flee from such a loyal defender of his liege, but his own loyalties had changed because of the man on that throne.

Rouwen eased the dying guardsman to the floor and looked up in time to see a half dozen more rounding the throne, all with drawn weapons. He heard frightened bleatings from the audience chamber and Sorinne's high, clear voice ordering calm. From Kwuway or King Priowe there was not a sound, and Rouwen did not dare risk even a quick look. He knew his touch killed; so might his mere glance at one he loved as much as Princess Sorinne.

He spun and ducked back into the secret passage behind the throne, but he did not descend. He found still another hidden niche and pressed into it. The thunder of boots against the hard stone told him the hunt had gone down to lower levels, as he had hoped. But Rouwen had an unpleasant choice ahead of him.

Should he return to the royal audience chamber to seek Priowe or did he flee Castle Gan? If he did, he would lose his best chance to kill the traitors who had cursed him to an eternity of banishment, pain, and death to those he held dearest. He would betray not only his own ideals but the people of Gan as well. Rouwen took his vow seriously to defend the kingdom against all enemies, but what good would that pledge be if he was imprisoned forever?

'Sorinne,' he muttered, coming to a difficult decision. He dared not go into the chamber without risking his beloved Sorinne's life. He must find another way to remove Sosler and the others plotting with him in that vile cabal, even if it meant retreat now to return and fight another day.

Rouwen hurried up a few steps to the seeming dead-end in the hidden staircase, paused and looked for the right stones in the wall to press. In sequence he pushed three off-colored blocks and waited for the deep click that opened a new passage. Rouwen did not tarry. He jumped into the small compartment and found himself in a narrow passage behind the walls on the level above the audience chamber. Now and then Rouwen peered through peepholes and saw augmented patrols marching the corridors. He worried that Sosler or Priowe might order the Intrepids into the secret ways, then chuckled to himself.

Neither would do that, even to catch him. Rouwen realized Priowe wanted these passages kept private if he needed to flee himself. While Rouwen had been Captain of the Intrepid Guard, there had been no such fear stalking the royals in Castle Gan. If the realm could not be toppled by force of arms, it would be gnawed at and rotted from within until it toppled into King Nishor's outstretched arms.

Rouwen made his way to a ladder leading to lower levels. Thick dust made his nose twitch, forcing him to hold back more than one sneeze as he descended. Once he stopped and took a quick peek through a peephole, hoping to catch sight of Duke Drioway. If he had, the duplicitous diplomat would have died then and there. Rouwen touched the poison-laced glass dagger in his belt and wondered if it could find any better use now than being broken off in Drioway's belly.

Weighing the need to keep moving against waiting for Duke Drioway to reveal himself, Rouwen returned to the ladder and finished his descent to a level just above the main courtyard. Entering Castle Gan was difficult, but Rouwen knew more ways. The hardest part was getting up the steep road with its guard points and constant surveillance.

Peering out of his passageway once more, Rouwen saw intense activity. Every trooper in the castle must have been roused to hunt for him. He saw the tight knot of Kennard's phony traders being searched, and wondered if they would find more of the assassin's daggers hidden in the Mionese packs. Escaping with them was out of the question.

A new thought hit Rouwen with the power of a blow to his gut. He sank down to his haunches, sneezed from the ancient dust and tried to keep a clear head. If he left Castle Gan, he might be months returning. Such fervent activity to guard King Priowe would keep anyone from the castle not authorized by Sosler. Those traitors deserved anything he could do to them, and he would be prevented from killing them by the very soldiers he had trained so well. Rouwen's fingers traced the outlines of the dagger thrusts to his stomach and winced as he straightened. The wound in his back still tormented him greatly.

'Goodbye, Sorinne,' he said, coming to a firmer decision. His knowledge of the castle in the plot to overthrow Priowe was invaluable, but he had no idea how best to proceed. Allying with the Mionese killers was no answer. He had to bring the Kingdom of Gan under Sorinne's rule, even if she never saw him again and blamed him for her father's murder.

It was best for Gan, Sorinne – and his own peace of mind.

Rouwen paced the small well at the foot of the ladder, hunting for the lever that would get him out of the castle. It took longer to find than he expected. His memory of the lower reaches of the castle was not as sharp as of the upper chambers where the royal family spent most of its time. The lever moved with ponderous, maddening slowness. The stone grated open just enough for Rouwen to slip through.

Warm, clean air blasted past his face and pulled the dust from the seldom-travelled secret passages out of his nostrils. Pausing for a moment, Rouwen looked down the slope in front of him. The gravelled road was a full twenty feet below without any obvious way to reach it, short of jumping. He couldn't die, but he could be seriously injured, even mutilated.

Ducking back when a patrol searched down the road, Rouwen knew he had to act quickly. Standing exposed as he was invited an arrow through his heart. Weakness still robbed him of full power. Rouwen cautiously peered over the edge and saw the patrol vanish. He had to make his escape now lest Sosler ordered the guards into the secret ways.

He secured his weapons, then dropped to hang by his fingers. Kicking out, Rouwen got far enough from the wall to land heavily on the shoulder of the road. His legs took the force of the impact, but weakness prevented him from controlling his landing. Rouwen went tumbling over the edge and plunged off the far side of the route down the mountain. He scratched wildly and just kept himself from an uncontrolled fall, his feet acting as brakes.

'You, there, come here!' came a loud voice.

Rouwen cast a sidelong glance and saw a corpulent highway guard waving a fist at him. He simply collapsed and lay still, waiting for the guard's predictable reaction. An Intrepid would never do what this one did. Rouwen was grateful the Lord Protector's training wasn't as stringent as his own had been.

The guard grumbled and complained and made his way down the hillside to Rouwen's side.

'What are you now? Drunk, me lad?' He rolled Rouwen over and his eyes widened when he saw the dagger driving upward into his heart. The guard never let out so much as a squeak as he died.

Rouwen fought to keep the man from tumbling on down the hillside. Not bothering to see if anyone saw him, Rouwen stripped off the guard's uniform and shrugged into it. A blood-stain over the heart was hardly noticeable among the wine and food stains already there. Rouwen didn't bother with the trousers belonging to the guard's uniform. There seemed little enough time for him to get down the road to the base of Castle Gan. He skidded another few yards to the road, getting bloodied from sharp, cutting rocks.

'You miserable cur!' bellowed an officer. 'Get to your patrol!'

It took Rouwen a few seconds to realize the officer was addressing him. He tossed off a sloppy salute, not daring to speak. Even if Sosler's troopers were slovenly in their habits and training, that didn't mean they were stupid. Rouwen kept his arm up to hide his face.

'You're on report,' the officer barked, as he spun and started back up the road to the castle. Rouwen watched him go, then relaxed. He started down the road, occasionally stopping to talk with other soldiers to keep from arousing any suspicion. By the time he reached the bottom of the rocky spire, he was exhausted emotionally and physically.

Rouwen looked toward the Demon's Throat and knew he could never escape that way. He had considered it earlier and had discarded the notion of slipping past alert sentries. For all the slovenly appearance of the guards along the road to the castle, he knew many of those on patrol in the Throat had been trained as Intrepids. A wind carrying the last hint of a bright day with it caressed him and gave momentary strength. He needed food and shelter for the night, but he worried that Sosler would turn the hunt for him outward when he wasn't found within the walls of

Castle Gan. His floppy, filthy uniform would never stand strict inspection, either.

Feet moving almost of their own accord, he began walking toward his brother's farm. Even as his feet moved, so did his thoughts. Brion Rouwen found himself remembering better days, days filled with laughter and Adan and their parents. There had been the famines and times when his father had told them bleakly there would be no supper – or breakfast. And yet they had come through those times to prosper in a kingdom increasingly blessed with fertile fields and adequate rainfall.

Rouwen hardly realized he walked along with his hands balled tightly or his jaw grinding so hard that it made the cords on his neck stand in relief. When tiredness assailed him, he slowed his pace but kept walking. As the fatigue passed, he walked faster, varying stride and breathing to match his strength.

Only when he came to his brother's farm did he slow and almost balk at going within the low fence surrounding it. The pile of clothing that had been his brother was obvious, even in the gloom of night. A faint green radiance hovered above the spot where Adan had died so quickly.

'Kwuway, Sosler, Priowe, Drioway – you are all doomed,' Rouwen vowed, growing angrier by the moment when he realized how impotent he was to bring any of them to justice. His excursion back into Castle Gan had been futile and ill-conceived. He realized now he needed a plan of action that would carry him through months or even years to achieve his revenge.

Priowe was unfit to rule, Kwuway was cruel and Sosler was power-hungry. His was the worst crime of all for he betrayed those of his own rank that were honest and loyal in favor of foreign demons like Duke Drioway. Sosler abandoned his own kingdom for what?

Surely, he did not think to rule Gan on his own? Rouwen had never considered what the duke might gain by his faithlessness.

In the distance he heard the thunder of approaching hooves. He skirted the spot where Adan had died and rushed to the barn. He had taken what he wanted from the small house. Food for his trip out of the Valley of Gan was required now. Rouwen packed as much as he could and settling it with double straps in a rude knapsack, slung it on his back. He wrapped the poison dagger in layers of burlap and carefully positioned it to endure all but the most difficult of passages.

When he finished he looked out and saw a dozen riders reining back and jumping from their horses. The moons were down and the night dark, but starlight glinted off drawn blades. Sosler had sent troopers to his brother's house. Rouwen wished that they would stumble over Adan's body and somehow become ensorcelled themselves, but he doubted the spell worked in such a fashion.

A wild idea came to him. Rouwen closed his eyes and considered his love for the men who had served under him in the castle guard and how like those men these troopers were. He opened his eyes to see the soldiers fanning out from the house, their swords poking into the sod as if he might be hiding in a grass-covered shallow pit. None had been affected by his chimerical attempt to associate his love of the Intrepids with these troops.

Love never pranced on such obvious feet. It always came stalking and pounced when least expected, beyond any man's ability to command.

Rouwen headed into the thick woods where he and Adan had played as children, finding the still-remembered old hiding spots, moving easily, keeping ahead of the haphazard search behind him. As he fled, he worried how best to achieve his goals. He needed time to plan, to organize resistance, to regain his strength. The forced march had kept him ahead of Sosler's troops; that he saw clearly now. But it did nothing to help him shuck off the pain from too many homicides forced upon his cursed body.

'A track!' came the cry from behind. 'A new footprint in the mud. See? It only now fills with water from the stream.'

Rouwen bit back a blistering oath on his own head. His fatigue forced him to hurry, and hurrying made him careless. The entire patrol would now descend on him like vultures at a public burial.

Trying not to make any more noise than he had been, Rouwen walked faster and was soon out of the sheltering woodlands. He tried to remember when the moons might rise and couldn't. The royal astronomer had always given the castle watch a detailed schedule including the rising and setting of the two bright moons, but Rouwen had to rely on experience now. He might be off by minutes or hours – and that spelled freedom or capture for him.

A long stretch of barren, wind-eroded fields stretched between him and the foothills of the Shield Mountains. He had once thought to take the hidden route under the mountains to Mion and ally himself there, but that had been before learning of King Nishor's role in destroying Gan.

Or did the Mionese king know of Duke Drioway's mission? And Kennard of Lowpin might be what he appeared, though his intentions in aiding a royal assassin were murky. Rouwen knew so little of politics beyond the ring of mountains.

He barked harshly at the notion that he knew anything about politics *within* the Shield.

'What's that?' came the distant question. 'A wolf?'

Rouwen had drifted into a lassitude from exhaustion and had forgotten why he ran. The soldiers were no closer, but they were far more rested. They rode horses and need only sight him to know their hunt was over. Not knowing the time of moonrise did not slow him as he lengthened stride again and hurried across the empty fields. He remembered the farmer who had worked this land.

Old Kortrim had fought the droughts of ten years back, and it had killed him. Adan had done what he could to help, but the old man had a lifetime invested in this land. Since Kortrim's death, it had lain infertile and unclaimed.

Rouwen cut across the weed-overgrown field and dropped behind a low rise that might shelter him from view. He looked up at the steeply rising mountains and knew he had a long hike ahead, perhaps too long. He tired quickly now and badly needed food and sleep. And from the direction of Adan's farm came the sound of a horse nearing at a gallop. Some sharp-eyed scout had found a careless footprint or a scrap of torn cloth still dangling on a thorny bramble. He had revealed himself twice and did not know how this time.

A quick shrug got the knapsack off his shoulders. He winced in pain and stiffness from the wound Kennard had given him. Dying should end such pain, not augment it, Rouwen thought. He drew sword and dagger and lay in a wind-blown furrow. Thinking to lie in wait, Rouwen almost fell asleep. Only the nearness of the rider and his mount brought him out of his semi-coma.

A dark silhouette loomed unexpectedly, blotting out the stars. Rouwen shifted position, getting his feet under him. He blinked to focus sleep-gummed eyes and judged distances. Long training with sword and dagger came to his aid.

He shot upward like a skyrocket at the Spring Festivals, his sword point driving accurately for the edge of the soldier's armor. Rouwen felt the shockwave course down the steel blade as the point deflected off bone, but he kept driving until he found soft tissue.

The rider gurgled out a warning, turned and fell toward him, further impaling himself on the sword and dropping it from Rouwen's grip. He let the sword remain buried in his victim's side. Rouwen was more concerned with the trooper's horse. He made a grab for the dangling bridle and caught up a leather strap, preventing the courser from bolting.

When the horse had calmed, Rouwen clumsily pulled his sword free from the dead soldier's body and struggled with his knapsack. He worried about taking the time to secure his sparse supplies behind the saddle, then decided he had to. Any misstep or hesitation after he mounted and rode away would be fatal. Even now, he might be seen – or the dead soldier found in the shallow grave that had once been Kortrim's proudly cut furrow.

'This way!' came a distant order. 'We have him on the run! This way. To me, men, to me!'

Rouwen was startled to find another trooper only a few yards away. The soldier wheeled his mount and raced to obey his officer's order. Rouwen held back, then began walking his stolen horse to get a feel of its temper. When he was sure enough of his seat, only then did he turn back toward the base of the sheer Shield Mountains and the secret passage under their bulk.

Sunlight on his back brought Rouwen out of his stupor. He hardly remembered the ride through the night, away from the pursuing troopers. Worse, he ached horribly, every particle of his body screaming in pain. Never one for horses, he knew only the rudiments taught to all Gannian soldiers. But this paltry knowledge had stood him in good stead so far. Two days' ride brought Rouwen within a few miles of the secret tunnel's entrance.

He craned his neck and looked behind him, not so much to see if any tracked him after all this time as to see the majestic spire in the center of the valley and Castle Gan gleaming whitely atop it. Mixed emotions tore at him. Brion Rouwen did not want to abandon the country of his birth, yet he had to. The small skirmish with the soldiers was a taste of what he would endure if he remained.

Banished, shunned, cursed, how could he hope to consummate his plans of revenge? The very people he still considered neighbors would turn him over to Duke Sosler, thinking they did their duty as honorable citizens. And, Rouwen had to admit, in their place he would commit the same mistake.

He was the outlaw in the land of his birth and now he had to kill those who ruled Gan.

All he needed was a plan, a way to achieve such a mad plan.

He rested for a few hours, as much to give his steed a chance to recuperate as to sleep himself. Forage was sparse along the rocky foothills, but the horse found adequate spring grass. Then

Rouwen began his ride in earnest. He didn't know exactly when the idea came to him but Kwuway might be able magically to scry his location. This was not a well-travelled area of Gan, and it would be sheerest chance if any patrol happened upon him.

But magicks. What could Kwuway do? Rouwen had never asked, sharing the superstitious fear of wizards harbored by most of his men. Kwuway had been King Priowe's left hand, the right being Rouwen's Intrepids. As such, left and right never met and knew little about the other's duty.

Rouwen pulled out his dagger and poised it above his chest. A sudden downward stroke would drive it deep into his heart – but he stopped. There was no reason to believe the spell had been weakened by distance from Castle Gan. Some resilience in his body perpetuated the spell. He could not die. He could suffer but never die.

And he could kill. His *love* could kill.

Rouwen swallowed hard as he visualized Adan's sudden death and wished he could join him. The sheer viciousness of the curse on him was that he could not.

Rouwen urged his mount to greater speed. He was still several days' travel from the tunnel leading to the outer world. Brion Rouwen might not greet other kingdoms with open arms, but he would not trade that dubious freedom for an eternity of suffering at Priowe's hand.

10

Wandering Souls

Brion Rouwen paused before urging his stolen horse into the tunnel. Two large rocks hid the entrance from casual observation, and inside a jungle of bushes festooned with wicked thorns made the entrance seem more like a niche in the rock than a natural passage through limestone caverns under the massive Shield Mountains. Rouwen calmed his horse and then went to work pulling back the bushes' limbs. The darkness beyond would frighten off all but the most daring or foolhardy.

Rouwen added another class to that: desperate.

His horse shied at entering the abysmal dark, but Rouwen kept working to quiet the animal. Although not placid, the horse allowed him to lead it blindly until he found a small alcove stuffed with ancient torches. He fumbled around and unearthed a rock, then drew his dagger and began striking the blade along a stony plane until sparks flew. The work was tedious and his horse kept trying to shy, but he finally succeeded in setting afire a small, dry bundle of sticks.

Rouwen snatched up the torch and held it high above his head, not wanting to choke himself on the smoke. The fire mesmerized the horse and it followed without urging now. Rouwen gathered several more of the bundles and put them on the horse. He had never travelled this route before and knew of it only by word of mouth. The Captain of the Intrepid Guard preceding Rouwen had claimed to be the first to explore these caverns, leaving secret marks for those coming after to follow. Lespage had been a notorious braggart and all too often overspoke his accomplishments.

Rouwen didn't care if Lespage had pioneered the route or if it had been done in ancient times before Mount Glid became the pathway for souls migrating to Paradise, or if it was recently charted. He had learned its secrets from his former commander, before he died of infection caused by a brigand's arrow.

He knew the rules of using this secret passage and had already violated the first. He had not replaced the torches he had taken with new ones. Rouwen reflected on this misdemeanor and decided his need was extreme. To take the time to cut enough wood to replace the torches would have jeopardized his freedom.

Rouwen let out a short laugh that echoed in all directions through the immense cavern.

'I carry duty too far,' he said to his horse. He patted the animal's neck to soothe it. 'I still think like a captain in Priowe's guard.'

Bitterness rose to replace any laughter lingering about his lips. He would not be making this journey if it wasn't for Priowe. Rouwen tried to ride his horse, but the animal slipped on the damp rock, and Rouwen feared being thrown. He kept looking up at the vault above him, worrying that low-hanging stalactites might knock him off the horse. Not having travelled this path before turned him cautious. Walking alongside the horse added time to the journey, but it also seemed a compromise between haste and safety.

In silence Rouwen stalked along, seeing huge caverns branching both left and right, but always taking the middle course. Now and again, his horse started and tried to rear because of the strange murmuring noises from deeper within the mountain. Some came as tiny scurrying sounds in keeping with creatures likely to inhabit the caves, but others disquieted Rouwen as much as his horse.

'There, there,' Rouwen tried to soothe, but the third time the horse needed gentling he thought he heard distant voices. Human voices. And they were calling to him by name. Rouwen spun and looked around behind him, torch held high over his head. The bundles of sticks hissed and popped, but the flickering light revealed nothing but damp rock and vast, empty dark chambers. And still he heard the indistinct voices, coming from just beyond the circle of torchlight.

Rouwen tried to deny this was possible. He had avoided the passage under Mount Glid because of the chance that a straying soul might blunder beneath the mountain on its trip to Paradise.

But Brion Rouwen knew it was ridiculous to believe anyone followed him. A soldier would have engaged him in battle by now – or sent for a patrol and overwhelmed him by sheer numbers. He heard nothing more than the creaking of a massif arching over his head, or the slow drip of stalactites forming on the ceiling or even the soft rustle of cave creatures running in fear from his torch.

When he became too tired to walk further, he tethered the horse on a convenient ring of stone cut in the floor by a rapidly flowing stream and slow, primeval water trickling from hidden sources in the shadowy vault above. Rouwen fixed a new torch to last through his sleep, ate a little of his provender, then lay down on the cold stone, wishing he had thought to bring a blanket from Adan's house.

The horse snorted and pawed at the rocky ground, then quieted. As it settled down, so did Rouwen. He tucked his arm under his head for a pillow, twitched as pains assailed him, and finally found a more comfortable position. He slept.

And he dreamed.

Brion Rouwen dreamed of haunted souls coming to him, begging him for release from their endless wandering. They reached spectral fingers for him, touching cheek and forehead before drawing back in a wild cyclone of vapor. And then they returned to plead with him. How he wanted to aid them! But he couldn't. There was no way. He was lost beneath the mountain, unable to find his own way, crushed beneath stone and blind and cut off from anything but a small circle of guttering light. Rouwen came awake, stretched painfully and tried to find a more comfortable position. Sleep took long minutes to return.

And when it did, he tossed and thrashed about but again the specters drew ever nearer. Thin tendrils of fog reached for him, touched his cheek and tried to envelop him.

Help us. Release us to Paradise!

Rouwen moaned when the insubstantial ghosts took on the faces of those he knew and loved and hated. He saw Adan and his parents and Sorinne and Kwuway and Sosler and Priowe. And repeatedly he saw Queen Diarra. The woman's face melted and reformed into increasingly vicious aspects. Fangs slashed at him and thin strands of acid fog reached to sear his face.

Brion Rouwen came awake, mumbling, 'The Lord of Death and Life.' He shook himself and looked around, hand resting on his sword. He heard only the distant creaking of rock settling onto rock and the eternal dripping of water into deep pools. Of the specters he saw nothing.

Shaken, he lay back but sleep would not come. Rouwen silently mouthed the title Lord of Death and Life. He had heard that before and had forgotten it until this moment. But who was the Lord and was he any part of the solution to Rouwen's problems?

In spite of the soft, ghostly importuning returning deep within his mind, Rouwen slept.

Two days' steady travelling beneath the Shield Mountains brought him within view of cherished sunlight. He was grateful for Lespage having told him of the tunnel out of Gan, but he cursed the old commander for not mentioning the ghosts flitting along the way. Not once had Rouwen seen a specter of the dead while awake; they had visited him always in his sleep when his barriers dropped from exhaustion.

He could do nothing to aid them in their search for Paradise. They needed to go to Mount Glid, not prowl under this pile of rock, if they wanted to ascend to their eternal reward. Brion Rouwen tried to shrug off their problem, if there was any. Their appearance might be hallucination or it might be yet another manifestation of the spells Kwuway placed on him. Whatever it was, Rouwen had to find his own path before helping another.

Still, their presence in his dreams worried him. He vowed never again to use this passage in or out of Gan. This time they had spoken to him. The next might find their power over him growing to the point they could do more than haunt him with their pitiful pleas.

'The Lord of Death and Life,' he muttered, turning the title over and over as if he could find truth in repetition. The name obsessed him as surely as the ghostly presences in his dreams. After examining it from all angles, Rouwen deliberately pushed it from his mind. There seemed promise in the name, but he knew nothing of finding him.

Hope had flared for a moment as he considered this aspect of the puzzle he forged for himself. Kwuway had put a spell on him. Could another wizard remove it? He had never heard of such a thing and had always been told spells were so intensely individual that only the caster could remove the curse.

And sometimes, even then it was not possible. Some curses were eternal.

Rouwen mounted when he found drier rock under his horse's hooves, rode forward and peered at last out of the tunnel. The harsh, uncompromising countryside could never be confused with that of Valley Gan. Here and there in the Valley Gan were abandoned farms, their soil so depleted nothing could restore them to fertility. But in this sorry land he saw nothing but wind and water erosion. No oases of green interrupted the endless march of rocky soil and deadness.

The Kingdom of Mion depended more on trade through its three large seaports than it did on farming, but Rouwen knew the dangers inherent in such trade. One bad year of trade and Mion's citizens starved for two. Even in the worst years of drought within Valley Gan, food was available if not plentiful.

'Crops taste better than trade,' Rouwen said to himself, repeating an oft-said phrase he'd heard Priowe and others declare in their lofty speeches.

He turned and looked behind him as he left the caverns under the Shield Mountains. He made note of the tunnel's location, never having seen it on this side before. To Rouwen's surprise, the opening shimmered as if viewed through mist and faded from sight by the time he had ridden to a road less than a mile distant. He turned in the saddle and tried to locate even the foggy edges of the tunnel mouth and failed.

'Magicks,' he said. Hatred grew within him for all wizards. He had not thought the caverns beneath the mountains to be magically carved, but now he was not so sure. The opening inside Valley Gan was properly hidden and not masked by a sight-numbing spell.

Everything was better within the ring of the mountains cradling Gan.

And he had to kill those in power, install his lover and hope he did not kill Sorinne in the process. Rouwen fought down a surge of utter hopelessness and tried to remember his pledge to support Gan against its enemies. All its enemies. He had been successful until he was betrayed by those who ought to have been allies.

'Sosler, Priowe, Kwuway, your lives are forfeit,' he said with great resentment at their treatment of him. Focusing on their eventual fate crowded out some of his despair. While in the tunnel under the mountains, he had considered how best to achieve this end – and their ends.

One man standing against the might of Gan was as a fly buzzing in a giant's ear. He might prove annoying but would never be effective. Without an army at his back, he was not likely to achieve his goals. Diversion could get him back into Castle Gan, and then he would strike as he had tried before. But reaching that point required arriving at the castle gates once more.

He knew Duke Drioway conspired with Sosler, but did the Mionese diplomat have the support of his liege? Rouwen had to find out King Nishor's real involvement in this sorry affair. Nishor might be as responsible for his twin curses as Priowe, or the Mionese king might be innocent. If his envoy acted on his own for his own gain, Nishor might be swayed.

Rouwen knew King Nishor longed for the territory held within the Shield Mountains. What position might he give a former Captain of the Intrepid Guard in return for information about defenses? Rouwen knew he had to test the political waters gingerly. One mistake might cost him his freedom. But was this any worse than letting Baron Chertude torture him for all eternity?

Rouwen laughed harshly. He couldn't die. That single curse might stand him in good stead now as he sought allies against those ruling Gan. But if he was ever to find out King Nishor's true stance, he had to accost him in his capital.

The deeply rutted road showed occasional traffic and the direction most of it flowed. Rouwen rode toward Mion's distant walled capital of Tachre. Not sure how far it was and thinking to take a shortcut across the countryside, Rouwen headed toward the coast and reached the shoreline just as twilight sent shadows dancing across the land.

The ride had been boring. Rocky lands and only occasional sign of habitation had met his eager gaze. Rouwen wanted to find out more of Mion. He had been told all his life that the Mionese were impoverished by high taxes and unable to provide decent food for their families. As with all such tales, there had to be a kernel of truth – but Rouwen had suspected more than a dab of lie had been woven into the propaganda. Even in Gan it was good to feel what you did contributed to a high standard of living and security for your neighbors and loved ones.

Rouwen was astounded at how little distortion there had been in descriptions of Mion. The crash of white-crested waves breaking against the shore brought forth sparkling droplets of salt spray that burned wherever they touched his skin. Rouwen turned back inland and paralleled the beach, seeing occasional evidence of wreckage from ships adrift from their charted routes.

From this grim evidence of lacking a proper course, Rouwen took great meaning. He had to find his star and steer to it. Deposing Priowe was part of his mission. He needed to lift the curses on him, and perhaps King Nishor's court wizard could aid in this. Rouwen knew too little of magicks to be certain what was possible and what wasn't.

The sun dipped farther into the steel gray ocean and finally extinguished itself in a burst of blood red rays. Trying to ride proved increasingly difficult and Rouwen decided to rest. Both he and his horse needed sleep.

A good night's sleep without the tormented ghosts intruding on his dreams, touching him, beguiling him, looking too much like Adan for comfort.

'That looks to be the sort of place we could find a dry bed,' Rouwen told his horse. The animal tossed its head, long chestnut mane flowing in the brisk wind whipping off the ocean. Rouwen inhaled and caught more than a little hint of an approaching storm. He saw distant lightning arching between clouds on the horizon and knew the swells crashing into the beach would soon grow to drenching intensity. A dry bed was more than desirable. It would be a necessity until the storm spent itself.

He turned the horse toward a dark stone hut, slowing as he came closer. Rouwen stood in the stirrups and called, 'I am a traveller seeking shelter.' He waited and got no reply. Dismounting, Rouwen approached the hut.

Even in the darkness he saw that the stone cottage had been long abandoned. Still cautious, he pushed through the rotting wood door, his sword held before him. Only silence punctuated by distant thunder greeted him.

Finding a small lamp, he worked more than ten minutes to light it. Oil sloshed in the glass base, giving him hope of light through the night. He trimmed the wick carefully, letting only the smallest amount of light leak forth to prolong the fuel. Satisfied with his work, he looked around the hut and saw only desolation.

The cottage had not been deserted yesterday or the day before. Years had passed since any had lived within the hut, yet the oil in the lamp hinted at more recent habitation. Poking into debris-filled corners revealed nothing of interest. Checking the roof revealed gaping holes everywhere, but one section seemed more substantial than the rest. Rouwen vowed to make his bed under it.

'Come in and enjoy living like a human,' Rouwen urged the horse. The animal ducked and allowed Rouwen to lead it into the cottage. It stood nervously, startled by sudden creaking and tearing sounds from the roof as the wind increased. Outside, a few heavy drops of cold rain dropped to the stony ground.

Rouwen worked to make a lean-to inside the cottage for himself and did what he could for the horse. Even the patch of roof he had thought intact proved to have holes in it, producing a steady drizzle. The lean-to gave a measure of meager comfort.

Rouwen settled down to eat a scant supper, then lay back and moaned softly as pain assailed him. He had still not grown used to riding the horse, but his real pain came from the deep wounds in back and belly.

Snoring in countertempo to the wind and rain smashing against the stone walls, Brion Rouwen fell into a deep sleep. But his soldier's instincts brought him awake less than an hour later. The storm's intensity had mounted and blotted out casual noises of small animals scurrying, so it took Rouwen several minutes to understand what had awakened him.

A shadow moved across the cottage, coming toward him inexorably. Rouwen snorted and shifted his weight a little, moving his hand to his dagger. The shadow ceased movement for long minutes, then began creeping toward him again. Rouwen wanted to know what he faced before acting.

A scraping noise told him the dimly seen intruder was dragging off his knapsack. In that knapsack lay the glass dagger filled with poison he intended to drive into Priowe's heart. Still unsure how many sought to rob him, Rouwen acted.

He kicked out and produced a loud shriek of surprise. Spinning around, he grabbed a scrawny leg and yanked hard. Rolling, he came to a halt on top of the sneak thief, knees pinning skinny shoulders to the floor. Rouwen stayed his dagger's killing stroke when he got a better look at the man who would have robbed him.

Skeletally thin from starvation, the thief looked up at him with saucer-wide brown eyes brimming with fear.

'Please, master, do not slay me! I meant no harm. I have not eaten in days!'

'And I wouldn't have eaten in still more days if I'd allowed you to steal my knapsack,' Rouwen said. He did not remove the dagger but did slip around to search his captive. Aside from a small knife, more a toy than a weapon, the thief was weaponless.

'I meant no harm,' the thief repeated, but his voice showed less fear. If he hadn't died outright, he might live a while longer. Rouwen understood the logic.

Seeing no threat, he sheathed his dagger and retreated to his dry bed. The thief sat on the floor under a thin drizzle from the roof. He looked more pathetic than menacing.

'I've intruded on your quarters, haven't I?' Rouwen asked, remembering the oil in the lamp's reservoir.

The man's ragged head bobbed and he smiled broadly. Rouwen saw that all the thief's teeth were missing save for the front four. These were bucktoothed and gave him the aspect of a giant gnawing rat. Thin arms and legs showed a lack of muscle and the dark, sunken cheeks hinted at deprivation measured in years rather than days. His clothing hung in tatters. Rouwen tried to guess at the thief's age and failed. He might be sixty or six hundred for all the clues he got from the receding hair and filthy, starved condition.

'In return, let me share some of my poor provisions.' Rouwen carefully apportioned a little of his remaining food. He would have to forage soon or he would be as hungry as the thief.

The old man grabbed the food and gobbled it down, never taking his eyes off Rouwen. After licking the crumbs and grease from his fingers he said unexpectedly, 'Nibbles.'

Rouwen blinked and shook his head. He didn't understand.

'That's what they call me. Nibbles.' The man's mouth worked in mimicry of a chewing rat. In the darkness the image was even more complete. Rouwen had to laugh.

'I'm sorry,' he apologized. 'I didn't mean to make light of your appearance.'

'That's just fine, just fine,' Nibbles said in his squeaking voice. 'I travel far and no one thinks highly of me. And that's to be expected.'

'And desired, unless I miss my guess,' Rouwen said, studying the old man carefully. Behind the emaciation lay an active brain, one that never rested. 'If your victim underestimates you, that makes the pickings all the richer, eh?'

'Something like that,' Nibbles said, curling up into a tight ball. He had found one square yard of space that was relatively dry. He said nothing for several minutes, listening to the rain patter down hard on the roof. Then Nibbles said, 'Why do you carry an assassin's weapon? You don't have the look of a Mionese sneak killer about you.'

'You recognize the glass dagger?'

Nibbles nodded.

'That's a long story,' Rouwen said, not wanting to relate it to someone he had just caught rummaging through his knapsack. 'It has to do with betrayal and magicks and . . .'

'Magicks, you say? I know all about such things, having just come from Nishor's vile court in Tachre.'

The sudden turn dumbfounded Rouwen.

'This interests you, doesn't it?' demanded Nibbles. 'Now why should that be of import to a worldly traveller such as you?'

'I travel to Tachre to petition King Nishor in a personal matter.'

'That's a Mionese dagger, but you're not Mionese. Gannian is my guess. Now why would any loyal Gannian look to Nishor for anything more than to piss in his mouth?'

'I mean him no harm.' Rouwen fought down the anger raging within at the memory of what his own king had done to him. 'I seek King Nishor's wizard to – perform a service.'

'Ah, wizards,' Nibbles said. 'I apprenticed to a wizard once, I did. We spun clouds in the sky like a child's festival candy and pushed the burning sun across the sky and even caused a drop or two of rain to fall.' He jerked his head aside as a drop crashed to the top of his sparsely haired head and ran down his cheek.

'You did all that?' Rouwen said, amused in spite of himself. The tales he had learned as a child told of wizards far underground who kept the universe working properly, but he had never found anyone admitting to serving them.

'More!' claimed Nibbles, getting his feet under him and bouncing up and down in his dry spot. 'I made fortunes and spent them from here to the North Continents and around the Smoking Sea. The water burns there like fire, but there is no heat. I have sailed them.' Nibbles cocked his head to one side, as if waiting to see how gullible Rouwen might prove.

'A world traveller greater than any I have met,' Rouwen said, diverted from his seething anger toward Priowe. 'Tell me of Tachre. What kind of city is it?'

'A filthy place. No one goes there willingly,' Nibbles said. 'Patrols everywhere. The watch will throw you in jail if you are not fleet of foot.'

'I'm sure,' Rouwen said, realizing the same might be said of Gan if you were a thief. 'Have you met King Nishor's wizard?'

'Him? You want nothing to do with him. He doesn't know the words fair play.'

Rouwen wondered if Nibbles knew the meaning of the word truth. He doubted it.

'You doubt me, you do. I see it. But everything I say is genuine, it is. I have wandered the corridors of Nishor's castle and none touched me. I am good at my craft, though you caught me far too easily,' Nibbles admitted ruefully.

'Tell me of Tachre and the castle,' Rouwen said. His interest in the old thief waned and the rain droned on, lulling him back to sleep. Nibbles appeared harmless enough, and Rouwen needed rest before moving on the next morning. He had little idea how far it was to Tachre, or even of the direction, though instinct told him following the coast would bring him to some city. If not Tachre, then another. From wherever he ended up, he could get reliable directions to Tachre, King Nishor and his pet wizard.

'A filthy place, Tachre. Sewage runs in the streets – and in the veins of those who rule there. Avoid it. And it's as if there is a conclave of wizards. You want to avoid them when they travel in pairs, not seek them out. Better to play with *thouse* birds and their poisonous beaks than to confront a pair of wizards.'

'What are you saying?' Rouwen paid only a little more attention to Nibbles's ravings. 'Nishor has more than one wizard at his beck and call?'

'He might not even know of the other one. I think they plot against Nishor, damn his eyes.'

'So the wizards seek to overthrow the king?'

'His very own wizard and that Kwuway, yes, that's what I think they do!'

Rouwen's eyes shot wide open, and he stared at the huddled mass of rags that was Nibbles. Nibbles had guessed he came from Valley Gan. Did the thief toss out Kwuway's name as a bone to be chewed or did he speak the truth?

11

Lord and Specter

Brion Rouwen stared at the glass dagger and the pale blue liquid sloshing within its blade and wondered when he would use it. The sound of rain hammering the stone hut's walls and roof had slackened before dawn, but the weather outside wasn't fit for travel yet and might not be for hours. Would he be able to use that dagger on Kwuway?

Rouwen's gray eyes lifted to study Nibbles. The little rat of a thief sat huddled in on himself, thin arms circling his drawn-up knees. He was a liar and a thief, that much Rouwen knew. But he had known the name of King Priowe's wizard. Had Nibbles mentioned Kwuway only to entice Rouwen and extort more food from him or had it been an honest, unpremeditated comment? Nibbles had accurately guessed the country of his origin. The aged thief might know a considerable amount about the politics of every kingdom. Priowe did not keep Kwuway under an obscuring veil. If anything, the wizard of Gan travelled more widely than most of the king's diplomats.

'On sabbaticals,' Rouwen mused. He wondered now what Kwuway's real missions had been. Were they for King Priowe or himself?

Picking up the glass dagger and balancing it in his hands gave Rouwen no sense of security. It was a coward's weapon. An assassin came in the night and drove such a blade into the back of an unsuspecting victim. Better to face an opponent in open combat.

Rouwen laughed harshly. Such a forthright course was now denied him by Kwuway's spells. Never had he thought it a curse to live forever. Now he considered it worse than a curse. It was abomination.

'Time to go?' Nibbles asked, still groggy from his heavy sleep. Rouwen envied the shabby thief this ability to lose himself completely in pleasant dreams. Although he had not been plagued by the ghosts demanding of him things he could never deliver, Rouwen had not slept well.

'Did you lie?'

'What? Me? Never! All I tell is the truth. What part do you need verification of? After I left the Smoking Sea, I journeyed to a land forever locked in ice and fire. Volcanoes erupting everywhere, lava flowing hot enough to warm even my thin haunches, and all amid glaciers! Talking glaciers. They were alive, I tell you – and they would converse only with me, Nibbles!'

Rouwen let the thief rattle on with his improbable tales of the Northern Continents and beyond. He had no ear for anything not mentioning Tachre and King Nishor. And Kwuway.

'Name Nishor's wizard,' he demanded. Rouwen carefully packed the poison-laden dagger as he listened to Nibbles hem and haw, always avoiding a direct answer. He looked up and asked a final time, 'Name Nishor's wizard or we part company here and now.'

'What? You would travel with the likes of me?' Nibbles seemed genuinely touched that Rouwen had considered him a fit companion. 'Why, that snake Nishor's thrice damned wizard is none other than Anda-Zahn. He is a child strangler and a killer of the helpless. Once I saw him . . .'

'Never mind. What pact might there be between Anda-Zahn and Kwuway?'

Nibbles shook his head. 'I know nothing of alliances between wizards. They tend to distrust one another. Worse than monarchs, they are. Why, some, such as the Lord of Death and Life, go so far as to live far from any other living being.'

'What do you know of this Lord?' Rouwen asked, fascinated in spite of himself. The robber might be spilling out names at random, snippets of intelligent conversation heard over a lifetime of larceny.

'Only that he is the most powerful wizard in the world. No one stands before him without quaking. Even I would do so, had I ever met him.'

'So you admit knowing nothing of him?' Rouwen pushed this aside. Nibbles talked to hear the sound of his own voice. 'Tell me of this Anda-Zahn and Kwuway.'

'Anda-Zahn is Nishor's wizard, but he is not in Tachre now. I know little of wizards' business.'

'Who in Tachre can get me within the castle?' Rouwen asked, slinging the knapsack behind the saddle on his horse. The animal snorted in resignation, seemingly understanding that the rainstorm was ending and they would soon be travelling again.

'One or two might, but why pay for what I can provide for

103

free?' Nibbles bounced around with more energy than he had shown since they had met. 'I can get you into the castle if you want to meet Kwuway. He is Gannian, as you are. Is this why you would meet with him? Why not simply send a message? Surely two countrymen far from their safe little valley would have much to discuss of their journeying.'

'You ask too many questions,' Rouwen said, trying to put irritation into his voice and failing. He found the thief amusing. If even one of Nibbles's tall tales was accurate, the thief would merit the title of world's greatest hero and explorer. And if not, then he was a masterful tale-spinner and worth taking to Tachre for his diverting stories.

A more practical reason for letting Nibbles accompany him came to Brion Rouwen. He knew nothing of the country. Anyone with even a modicum of knowledge could help him avoid obstacles on his way to killing Kwuway.

'You have the look of indecision,' Nibbles said, eyeing him critically. 'To kill or not to kill. Such a decision must be made in the cold light of logic, not when bathed by the white-hot flame of emotion.'

Rouwen shook himself from his mental backwaters. He had vowed to follow a plan, but he found himself filled with indecision at every turn. Too much had happened for him to think clearly. He didn't want Kwuway dead – not until the wizard lifted the curses afflicting him. If anyone could counter the spells, it had to be the wizard casting them.

'Either Kwuway or the Lord of Death and Life,' he said sardonically.

Nibbles bobbed his head as if a spring had been attached at his neck, then scurried out of the stone cottage like a frightened burrow animal. Fitful rain still pelted down, but the worst of the storm had passed. Rouwen led his horse outside and looked across the choppy sea. Better the land than that uncharted expanse.

'Which way to Tachre?' he asked. Nibbles pointed with a gnarled finger and they were off, travelling at a pace slower than Rouwen preferred but one necessary for the decrepit thief to maintain.

'*That* is Tachre?' Brion Rouwen hardly believed this could be the Mionese capital. 'Have they been attacked and overrun by sea pirates?'

'No, not recently. Why do you ask?' Nibbles bounced around then looked up at Rouwen, a slow smile spreading on his face like oil across water. 'Ah, you sense the poverty in the town.

Nishor takes and takes and takes with his heavy taxation. He puts little back.'

'The town reflects that,' Rouwen said. He tried not to doubt Nibbles's sense of direction or probity, but the former guard captain found it hard believing this was the capital of Gan's fiercest enemy.

Holes in the main roads leading into Tachre prevented easy transport of food and matériel from the docks a few miles distant. Lacking pack animals, twice as many workers were occupied lugging their loads along the potholed roads than were necessary. And the walls surrounding Tachre could never hold back a siege of any duration. Huge areas showed lack of repair. A decent siege engine would bring down those already battered sections of wall, allowing any attacking army to rush into the heart of the Mionese citadel.

'Their soldiers aren't too alert,' Rouwen observed. He saw more than one post along the road where the soldiers either slept openly or gambled and drank heavily. Duty was a distant second to more personal pursuits. If he were Captain of the Mionese Guard there would be corporal – and capital – punishments daily until he weeded out those unfit for service.

The failing of a single soldier might cost the kingdom dearly. So Rouwen had been taught and so he believed.

'You wish to find your fellow countryman, although he is a wizard,' said Nibbles. The old thief's eyes gleamed at the prospect of once again entering Tachre. 'We need only go through yon gateway.'

'That's it? We simply ride through?'

'Well, not quite,' Nibbles said. 'There's the matter of a bribe. Without valid travel visas, silver must exchange hands. Is that a problem?'

'How many coins?' Rouwen asked. 'I am new to the country and don't know the going rate for a bribe.'

Nibbles hid a sudden sly expression as he said, 'Five pieces for each guard and ten for the sergeant. Call it twenty pieces to keep peace.'

Rouwen rode along the road, looking into each of the guard stations along the way. When he saw two sleeping Mionese guardsmen, he reined back and slid from his horse. He tossed the reins to Nibbles and said, 'I'll be right back.'

On padded feet he entered the guard station. His dagger slipped the first guard's purse neatly from the belt. The second purse was half open. Rouwen simply reached in and helped himself to what he found. Neither guard awoke during the robbery or after. The bottle of wine tipped over on the table hinted at the reason.

If they had been Intrepids, they would have been executed for dereliction of duty. Then Rouwen checked himself. Such a pair would never have passed the training to become Intrepids.

'You stole their money?' Nibbles's eyes widened at such audacity. 'How much?'

'One gold coin – a lumin, from the worn marking on it. And ten silver cands. That ought to get us into Tachre.'

From Nibbles's reaction, he knew it was far more than would be required. He waited for the thief to insist on doing the bribery himself, but the old reprobate held back. Rouwen smiled slightly. He had been audacious in taking what he needed. There was nothing the Mionese could do to him. He was immortal – until he convinced Kwuway to lift the curses placed on him.

Both curses.

Walking toward the postern gate Nibbles had indicated as their best entry into the walled city of Tachre, Rouwen found himself growing tenser by the minute. When the bribery went as smoothly as Nibbles had said, he relaxed a little. Somehow, he had not believed the guards would be so casually corrupt. Everyone travelling into Tachre had to know of their greed and dishonesty and take advantage of it. Rouwen realized his service to the Kingdom of Gan had left him naive about other countries and their ways.

'You are startled at the ease of entry, eh?' asked Nibbles. 'It is always this way.'

'Have you journeyed to Gan?'

'I could never get through the Demon's Throat,' Nibbles admitted. 'But I have been to even more fabulous places. I have travelled to the once-thought mythical land of Jabbar.' The thief lowered his voice as if not wanting others to overhear. 'It is *true* what they say. There were no men in the entire land, none save I!'

'Oh?' Rouwen listened to the extravagant yarn with half an ear. He was too busy assessing his chances of entering the castle built squarely in the middle of the town. Tachre had been constructed in sporadic fits, probably starting with the castle and its walls, then expanding like some vile fungus to include walls around the entire city. None of the battlements provided significant defense for city or castle. If the exterior walls required serious patching, the castle walls were in even worse repair.

Peasants had stolen large blocks here and there and left gaping holes. He could simply slide through one of those holes and find himself within King Nishor's chambers.

'The only man, I was,' Nibbles said, his tale growing by leaps and bounds. 'They exhausted me. I watched two, three, four of them wrestle together before regaining my manly strength, then I was forced to work my way through an entire harem. Or so it seemed. Truth to tell, they considered *me* their harem. Exhaustion beset me early on, but I rose to the occasion, if you catch my meaning, eh?' Nibbles laughed and did a caper to show how onerous his confinement had been.

'Do we just sneak into the castle?' Rouwen asked.

'What? Oh, no, no! Those are traps built for the unwary.' Nibbles pointed to the holes Rouwen had assumed had been made by stolen blocks. 'Entry is more difficult. Nishor cuts the ears off any guard accepting a bribe to enter his keep. Then he begins the real torture. Tachre is filled with legless one-eared beggars.'

'I suppose everyone is permitted to spit on them,' Rouwen said drily, not believing Nibbles.

The answer chilled him with its ring of sincerity.

'No, everyone is required on pain of death to piss on them.'

'How do we enter?' Rouwen paced slowly, his eyes darting to the guards patrolling high above and the occasional mounted patrol outside the castle walls, making their way through the scatter of customers in an open-air market. Sanitation was not on many Mionese minds, Rouwen decided as he stepped over piles of fresh horse dung already turning odoriferous in the hot springtime sun.

'There, there we enter, if that is your wish.' Nibbles stopped in front of a tumble of stone piled against the wall. Rouwen studied it for a moment, then smiled. He saw a set of footprints leading to a corner of the pile going to the wall but not returning. A secret gate was hidden poorly under the stone.

Rouwen started forward but Nibbles reached out and grabbed his arm. 'What is it you truly desire to find within?' The skeletal thief's concern touched Rouwen.

'Salvation,' he said. He took a deep breath, thought of Kwuway and added, 'That and perhaps death.'

'You are a strange man. Are all Gannians so occupied with losing their heads?'

Rouwen stopped as if someone had pounded him in the gut. He had never considered beheading and its consequences with the curse of immortality on him. Would his head live independently of his body or did they have to be reunited? He touched his throat and then pushed the ugly images from his mind. Only Kwuway could relieve him of his burden.

'Take this, friend,' Rouwen said, handing Nibbles the reins to the horse. He pulled the glass dagger from the knapsack and tucked it into his belt. 'If I do not return, horse and belongings are yours as a reward for getting me this far.'

'It is better if you do not enter on this fool's errand,' Nibbles said uneasily. 'We make a team, we do. The pair of us can go to far-off Jabbar. Or if women do not interest you, the Land of Mentrira is filled with monsters. Two-headed, three-headed ones, all waiting for a noble to slay them. Think of a ten-foot-tall goring bull mounted in your castle's entry! The accolades you would receive whenever a visitor called!'

'You've killed a goring bull?' Rouwen asked, distracted.

'With my bare hands. Well, not exactly with my *bare* hands. I used a stone chipped to a . . .' Nibbles broke off his mendacity to put a bony hand on Rouwen's shoulder.

'Whatever compels you toward this wizard, friend, I trust will not be your death. Walk softly and be not afraid to use that assassin's dagger!'

'Thank you,' Rouwen said, genuinely touched by the thief's solicitude. 'I dare not wait for darkness. Can you create a small diversion so that my entry isn't noticed?'

'Easily done,' Nibbles said. The thief found a box, mounted the horse and rode to the far side of the market. From his perch atop the courser, he began a harangue that was both salacious and funny, berating those in power. A few merchants chuckled and others looked around apprehensively for King Nishor's patrols. But the effect was all Rouwen could have hoped.

He walked to the tumble of stone and found a rude latch on a door barely hidden. Like so much else in Tachre, this was of inferior quality. Ducking inside, he had to bend double to follow a dimly lit route deeper into the castle. At the end of the passage, narrow stairs led upward in a tight spiral. Rouwen's broad shoulders brushed both sides as he began the ascent. Before he had climbed five minutes he heard muffled voices.

The stairway continued upward but on a small landing was a cramped exit covered by a tapestry. Using his dagger to push the concealing tapestry to one side, Rouwen peered out. He had no idea how King Nishor's castle was laid out, but he had the feeling he was in the heart of it.

Angry voices sounded and Rouwen dropped the tapestry back into place. By pressing his face against cold stone, he was able to peer out into the corridor. His heart almost exploded when he saw

Kwuway with a short, heavy-set, bearded man dressed in shabby clothing. The pair walked slowly past Rouwen's vantage and he saw a tarnished golden coronet on the shorter man's head.

His suspicion was realized when Kwuway said, 'But King Nishor, this is foolish. Your ranks are filled with traitors.'

'I will have no more mention of my wizard,' the king said sullenly. 'He thought to depose me.'

'And I have only your best interests at heart,' Kwuway said insincerely. His tone caused Nishor to spin and face him. The shorter man pushed out his ample belly and banged it against the wizard, forcing Kwuway to the corridor wall.

'You are as treacherous as Anda-Zahn, curse his bones.'

'I have done so,' Kwuway said, bowing as much as the king would allow. Nishor backed off and straightened his stained clothing.

'You are all alike, you wizards,' Nishor accused. 'You plot and scheme for your own ends – and those ends are not what the rest of us expect.'

'Duke Sosler and you will both profit, as will I,' Kwuway said smoothly. 'When Priowe is no longer ruining Valley Gan with his insane policies, we will all share equally.'

'Yes, yes, I know. But Anda-Zahn . . .'

'He is dead, Majesty,' Kwuway said more sharply. 'We have other matters to discuss. Urgent matters requiring your immediate attention.'

'Later. I have an audience with some shipping magnate. Somebody from the Northern Continent wanting exclusive trade rights. Or something like that. It is so confusing and difficult to keep straight these days.'

'Majesty,' urged Kwuway. 'We need to plan.'

'Without money from this trade agreement there will be no conquest of Gan,' Nishor snapped. 'Go plan on your own, Wizard. I will summon you when I have finished with this grasping merchant.'

Kwuway bowed slightly, but Rouwen saw the expression on the wizard's pudgy face. Small green sparks marched along Kwuway's fingers as he contemplated a spell on the king, but he held back his curses. Rouwen wondered why Kwuway and Duke Sosler needed Nishor for their overthrow of Gan. They had done well removing King Priowe's most loyal supporters. Both queen and Captain of the Intrepid Guard were banished – and cursed.

Rouwen hoped the wizard would turn back and pass in front of the tapestry. A sudden surge and Rouwen could hold the poisoned dagger to the treacherous wizard's throat. But Kwuway continued along the corridor and turned left. Rouwen had no choice but to follow.

At the junction of corridors Rouwen peered around the wall and saw Kwuway open a door and enter. Rouwen rushed after the wizard. Kwuway half-turned, only to be shoved roughly into the room. Kwuway stumbled and crashed into a chair, grabbing it for support.

'Captain Rouwen, what a surprise,' Kwuway said. He did not seem unduly startled at Rouwen's sudden appearance in Tachre.

'You know why I have chased you across two kingdoms,' Rouwen said, brandishing the glass dagger so that light caught its poison-filled blade. 'Remove the curses you placed on me.'

'Oh? You think magic such a simple task? All I need do is wave a hand and . . .' Kwuway's fingers began to glow with actinic sparks. Rouwen swung hard and hit the wizard in the pit of the stomach. Kwuway folded double and sank into the chair he had been propped against. Gasping for breath, he looked at Rouwen.

Kwuway's eyes held no fear. If anything, he was even more amused at Brion Rouwen's attempts to reverse the spells placed on him.

'You are a fool. Sosler was correct in his appraisal of you. If you had joined us in overthrowing Priowe, you could have been a duke. More!'

'Remove the curses. Both of them or I use this dagger.' He shoved it hard against Kwuway's throat.

'Where did you get a Mionese assassin's dagger? Never mind. Your odyssey to reach this point means little. There is not much you can do to stop us – and there is nothing you can do to threaten me. If I die, the curse will never be lifted!'

'There are others who can remove the spell,' Rouwen said, beginning to panic. His threats didn't carry the weight he had thought they would. Kwuway showed no fear at all of the poison within the dagger's blade, and he was obviously familiar with it.

'No one can remove the spell. I laid it on you. I must remove it, and I will not!'

'The Lord of Death and Life,' Rouwen said, grasping at straws. He was pleased at Kwuway's reaction, though he could read little into it other than annoyance.

'You have to find him before he could reverse the spell,' Kwuway said.

'So there *are* other wizards who can counter your treacherous enchantments!'

'The Lord will never see you. You can never find him. And even if you do, dealing with him is far more difficult than you can ever believe!'

'I know where he is,' Rouwen said, growing more desperate. Time slipped through his fingers like so much water. Kwuway would be summoned sooner or later by King Nishor, and with that command might come a few guards. Kwuway would be forever beyond his reach unless he forced the wizard to reverse his spells now.

'How did you come by this knowledge? He has hidden himself from the world for too many years.'

'I escaped Gan under the Shield Mountains,' Rouwen said, his mind racing. He had no experience of the powers Kwuway played with so casually. Calling on any incident however minor was the only way Rouwen could think of to intimidate him. 'The ghosts talked to me and told me about the Lord.'

'Ghosts? In the tunnels?' Kwuway paled and Rouwen dared to hope.

'Every night they came to me with messages.' Rouwen didn't want to say too much, but he needed to force Kwuway into action.

'The Flame Specter!' Kwuway exclaimed.

'What?' It was Rouwen's turn to be taken aback. He did not understand what Kwuway meant, but the Flame Specter somehow staggered Kwuway more than mention of the Lord of Death and Life. Rouwen covered by asking, 'Where do I find the Lord?'

'The ghosts. What did they say of the Flame Specter?' asked Kwuway. 'I must know. The balance shifts above. There cannot be any interference from . . .'

Rouwen shoved the dagger harder against Kwuway's throat to silence him.

'I ask the questions,' he said fiercely.

'Ask all you like, Captain,' said the wizard. 'It will do you no good.'

Rouwen was unsure what Kwuway did but sparks jumped from the wizard's fingers and touched his torso. Pain exploded and knocked him back into a wall.

'Guards!' Kwuway shouted. Before Rouwen could recover, the door slammed open and four guards rushed in. Kwuway spun from his chair and dashed for the far side of the room, away from any possible danger.

Rouwen was trapped – and unable to use the poisoned dagger on the wizard.

12

Fated to Die Again

Rouwen fought against the guards hanging onto his arms. He kicked and tried to slip free long enough to cross the room and drive his dagger into the folds of Kwuway's dewlaps. He might have escaped two guards but two more crowded into the room and grabbed his kicking legs. The four soldiers heaved, got him into the air, and forced his face down onto the floor until he stopped struggling.

Resignation washed over him like a smothering blanket. He had lost his best chance to avenge himself and possibly save his kingdom from rebellion and civil war.

'You've lost, Captain,' sneered Kwuway, coming over to kick him hard in the ribs. As if the wizard knew of his injuries, Kwuway found the precise spot to cause the most pain. 'I should burn you with a bit of fire, but I won't.' Sparks flew from Kwuway's fingers, causing the guards to recoil. Rouwen tried to use their momentary lapse to his own advantage. He struggled to push the glass dagger forward into Kwuway's leg. The wizard was too quick for that. He danced away and shouted at the guards to be more attentive.

'I'll watch you starve in Paradise,' Rouwen promised. Kwuway only laughed.

'You will never reach Paradise, Captain. You cannot die. Your fate is to roam this world forever, suffering every moment of your miserable trek!'

The guards warily held onto Rouwen, unable to disarm him without letting him unleash his full fury. Kwuway came closer and plucked steel dagger and sword from Rouwen's belt.

'I'm allowing you to keep the assassin's dagger,' the wizard said. 'Perhaps its poison will release you from my carefully concocted spell. As you sit in your cell, ponder that – and eventually you might even come to believe it will give you release from this feeble body.'

Rouwen knew immediately that only terrible suffering would

be his reward if he attempted suicide with the dagger. It was Kwuway's nature to want Rouwen to inflict the wound on himself out of desperation and grief.

'Take him to the dungeons, but do not allow him to use that weapon on you.' Kwuway paused a moment and looked at the guards, then amended, 'I care little if he does. If he kills one of you with the poisoned dagger, give him another once he is in the cell.'

This made the guards even warier of Rouwen. He sagged in their grip as they picked him up bodily and carried him down the corridor, one guard hanging onto each of Rouwen's arms and legs. He watched the flagstones pass under him as he dangled face down and worrying about his fate.

He should never have tried to get Kwuway to remove the curse. Rouwen realized now his first act ought to have been a killing stroke with the poisoned dagger. The plot to depose King Priowe ran deeper than stupidity among officers or even Duke Sosler's perfidy. Kwuway was involved. Who else in Castle Gan sought Priowe's overthrow? Rouwen tried to find it in his heart to forgive his former king, but he could not. Priowe had made a serious mistake in judgment by not trusting his captain of guards and his wife, no matter what appearances had been.

Rouwen sagged even more. He was deceiving himself. He had intended to kill Priowe, and the King of Gan was as much a victim as he had become. Rouwen closed his eyes as the guards took turn after dizzying turn on their way down to the dungeons. Mustering his strength for a forlorn final attempt at escape, Rouwen gauged how hard it would be to reach the dagger still tucked into his belt and use it on one guard. The other three had to be removed quickly and with bare hands.

Just as he made ready for the attempt he heard loud shouts from ahead.

'It's loose, run, run!' came a shrill voice he thought he recognized.

'What's wrong?' demanded the guard hanging onto Rouwen's left leg.

'The king's fire tiger has escaped! It's just down the hall. Run, run, before it breathes. Aieee!' A huge gout of flame blasted past Rouwen, singeing eyebrows and hair. He suddenly found himself face down on the flagstones. Another blast of heat and flame passed above him, causing the guards to scream and rush off in abject terror. Rouwen chanced a quick look up and saw Nibbles in the middle of the corridor. The diminutive thief smiled broadly, then bowed mockingly and motioned Rouwen to follow him.

113

'Fire tiger, fire tiger!' Nibbles kept up the cry.

Rouwen got his legs under him and sprinted forward, vaulting over piles of smelly trash in the corridor. Nibbles had set fire to something volatile and fed the flames with the debris. He threw more liquid from a jug onto the heap to Rouwen's left, then tossed a lantern onto the pile. The resulting flare caused Rouwen's tunic to smolder – and kept the screaming guards at bay.

'Why are you here?' Rouwen asked.

'Excitement, friend, what else might there be to keep me in a town as boring as Tachre?' Nibbles cackled in delight and made sure the other pile of trash caught fire. He scurried on, not waiting to see if Rouwen followed. Rouwen had no desire to stay and see how long it would be until Nishor's guards dared break through the fiery barrier.

'What is a fire tiger?' Rouwen asked as he ran alongside the fleeing thief. 'I've never heard of one.'

'Nor have I, but what matters it now, eh?' Nibbles skidded to a halt and peered around a door opening into a large chamber. Alert guards crowded the room, hands resting on swords and ready for a fight. The escape had already been signalled throughout the castle. For all their slovenly actions, Nishor's soldiers had an efficient communications network in place.

'We can never get past them,' Rouwen said. He touched the dagger at his belt. It was no fit weapon against steel. The poisoned dagger's only use was for assassination.

'Are you so faint of heart? Where is your sense of adventure? Why, I've been in worse predicaments than this. Once, while trekking on foot across the Vahite Desert, I had to strangle a vulture and drink its blood to stay alive to fight . . .'

Rouwen clamped a hand over Nibbles's mouth as two guards hurried toward them. Rouwen spun around, back against the wall and waited. He let one guard pass through, then swung hard. His fist caught the second guard under the nose and snapped his head back so hard it knocked the man out. A quick grab for the fallen sword allowed Rouwen to turn and parry the first guard's thrust at his body.

As Rouwen had suspected, training had lapsed in Nishor's guard. A feint and a quick attack carried him forward, his captured blade slitting his opponent.

'A nice thrust, friend,' Nibbles said admiringly as he went to work stealing what he could from both bodies. 'You display a strong wrist and a quick parry. How did you manage to worm that sword tip under his chain mail so easily?'

'He wore it badly,' Rouwen said, not wanting to debate the

finer points of combat with a man hardly strong enough to lift a sword. Rouwen took both guards' daggers and felt better armed, but where could they run? The fires Nibbles had set were dying and guardsmen crowded close, waiting to rush through.

'The time for fancy swordplay is past,' Nibbles said. 'How are your nerves?'

'What do you have in mind?'

'The king is ready to accept supplicants for his monthly dispensing of alms,' Nibbles said, acid dripping from his words. 'That is, supplicants gather but seldom does Nishor ever attend them. We can be needles hiding among a stack of pins.'

'Hurry, then,' Rouwen urged, pushing Nibbles ahead of him. The guards would see them any instant. The clanking of weapons echoed down the corridor and warned of a fight Rouwen could never win.

Nibbles tugged insistently at Rouwen's sleeve and pulled him into a larger room already filling with guards. As Nibbles passed through, he gathered two long cloaks of a coarse woven burlap from a pile. He tossed one to Rouwen and draped the other over himself. The guards ignored them, thinking they were part of the larger group at the far side of the room.

One guard even aided their cause by cuffing Nibbles and barking, 'Get your worthless ass over with the other beggars.' He sent the thief tumbling with a kick. Rouwen hesitated, considering his chances of running a dagger into this vicious fool's ribcage. Instead he bowed deeply and allowed the guard to punch him. Rouwen did not have to fake the gasp of pain racing through him. The guard had found the spot in the middle of his back where Kennard's dagger had punctured his body.

'Good acting job,' Nibbles said softly when Rouwen dropped beside him, gasping and moaning. 'I'll make a thief of you yet.'

'Out,' moaned Rouwen, faint from the pain. He tried to point toward the distant door leading into the castle courtyard, but his hand shook too much from the pain assailing him. 'We must escape.'

'We stay,' Nibbles said. 'We . . . why, as I live and breathe, my eyes are deceiving me!'

Rouwen turned in time to see King Nishor make a grand entrance into the audience chamber from a small adjoining room, a half dozen retainers sweeping the dirty floor in front of their monarch as he walked. And with him strode Kwuway, gesturing wildly and shouting at the king. Nishor turned and said something that caused the wizard to stop gesturing, but

Kwuway's strident voice carried over the suddenly silent crowd and to Rouwen's ears.

'I want him in the dungeon immediately. He's idealistic and a fool, but he can be dangerous!'

'He can do nothing,' snapped Nishor. 'What will he do? Tell Priowe?'

Rouwen shifted, moving toward the front of the crowd to be closer to Nishor's throne. Nibbles clutched at his robe and tugged.

'Don't be foolish. This is dangerous enough!'

'I must hear what the wizard says.'

'Wizards use ward spells,' grumbled Nibbles. 'They do not take kindly to any eavesdropping on them. Why, once I chanced to overhear two wizards discussing this and that, and they turned me into a newt as punishment for spying.'

Rouwen paid no attention to the thief. He steeled himself against the pain racking him as he moved forward. So much combat had worsened pains he thought well on their way to healing. In spite of his suffering, Rouwen saw that others in the crowd of supplicants were in even worse condition. Some had lost limbs and eyes and all carried the stench of imminent death from disease and starvation.

Dropping to his knees and bending forward so that his forehead touched the cold stone floor, Rouwen found himself less than three paces from Kwuway and Nishor.

'He cannot escape. The castle is bottled up tightly,' Nishor insisted. 'My guards search every room in the castle. It is only a matter of time before they find him.'

'I want him captured *now*,' insisted Kwuway. 'He knows more than I thought. He spoke of the Flame Specter!'

Rouwen almost lifted his head to see Kwuway's expression. The wizard sounded frightened now. What was this Flame Specter? He had never mentioned it, nor did he have any knowledge of such magical things. It had been Kwuway who had put the name to his ghostly visitations while travelling under the Shield Mountains.

'A myth. He rambled on only to confuse and frighten you,' said Nishor as if he hadn't a care in the world. For some reason, the ruler of Mion seemed almost cheerful.

'It is no more a myth than the Lord of Death and Life!' cried Kwuway. 'Powers beyond our control are gathering.'

'Then we must advance our timetable,' Nishor said. 'The sooner we depose Priowe, the quicker we can be in command of both kingdoms. You wizards are too concerned with the magical

116

and find yourself gulled when some commoner drops a name or two.'

'If we are opposed magically, we will never conquer Gan,' warned Kwuway.

Rouwen gripped a steel dagger in one hand and the glass dagger in the other. He was three paces away. A quick leap, a rush up the low steps to Nishor's throne and he would achieve the death of his kingdom's two worst enemies. He tensed for the rush when he felt a hand on his arm holding him back.

'Caution, friend. There are more on the dais,' whispered Nibbles. 'Can you kill them all?'

Rouwen looked up and knew he could fight through any force, even Nibbles's imaginary fire tigers, to reach the trio near the throne. Joining Nishor and Kwuway was Duke Sosler. The three he longed most to kill were within one powerful sword slash.

'I must agree with King Nishor,' Sosler said in his oily tones. 'You are too gullible, dear Kwuway. This peasant soldier has learned how to get under your skin and burrow like some vile cutworm. From all you say, he knew nothing you had not furnished him.'

'He knows nothing, but he reports accurately. There was no reason for him to lie since he thought he could force me to release the spells on his head,' argued Kwuway. 'He described manifestations of the Flame Specter! We must address this if we are to proceed – and succeed!'

'This peasant's prattling matters little now,' Sosler said. 'Rouwen will not escape King Nishor's guard. Even if he does, there is always this.' Sosler reached inside his emerald-embroidered tunic and drew forth a gleaming silver locket suspended on a chain carved from a solid piece of onyx.

'He would spit in a demon's face for that locket,' Kwuway said glumly. 'He might also be tempted to slay the lot of us if he sees you with the spell casket.'

'My life!' Rouwen exclaimed. Rouwen started to rise again, but Nibbles held him back. The three were lost in their own argument and had not heard his outburst.

'The guards, the guards!' hissed the thief. 'They are closing in on us!'

Rouwen saw his opportunity to kill the trio evaporating. The guardsmen were filling the room, circling the crowd with drawn swords and slowly advancing. The supplicants were herded to the middle of the large room.

'It's time for my audience,' Nishor said with relish. He turned and waved to his soldiers. 'Fulfill their hearts' desires, men. Give them the release from their woes they sought from my generosity. Kill the scurvy lot!'

The crowd of supplicants let out a howl of anguish and tried to flee. Several got between Rouwen and the dais, preventing him from reaching Kwuway, Sosler or Nishor before they slipped behind the throne and vanished from sight.

'They're killing everyone,' groaned Nibbles. 'I worried that Nishor was getting the beggars off the streets of Tachre so easily. Now I know how he has accomplished this fantastic feat.'

Swords flashed and hacked as the soldiers worked their way through the crowd, killing indiscriminately. Rouwen considered going after Sosler and the others he longed to kill but found the way blocked by a half dozen guardsmen. One swung his sword and knocked Rouwen back into Nibbles. The pair fell in a heap.

Rouwen struggled to his feet and grappled with the soldier, preventing him from killing another beggar. But Rouwen realized he was trying to hold back an inexorable tide. The men had killed like this often, slaying the defenseless at their liege's command. The guard twisted free and cuffed Rouwen, knocking him back into Nibbles. The decrepit old thief was knocked to his knees by the force of Rouwen's colliding body.

'I was never meant to die like this,' Nibbles bleated like a goat. 'I ought to have died in some seraglio, locked in the embrace of a fine woman. Women! Many women ought to have loved me to death. Or in a counting room surrounded by gold coins. Or – aieee!'

A soldier's sword point was about to rob Nibbles of his life. Rouwen never hesitated. He spun around and interposed his body between sword tip and Nibbles's thin frame.

A shock of pain rocked him as the sword pierced him and the world turned black. Again Brion Rouwen died.

13

Prey of the Sniffer-snake

Rouwen was aware of two things. The first was the strange buzzing that filled his ears. The other was pain so intense it almost drove him out of his mind. No human ought to bear the agony that coursed through his chest, yet he did not die or go crazy from it. Brion Rouwen lived because of Kwuway's curse.

He maintained a stubborn sanity only through force of will.

'Where are we?' he grated out between parched, bleeding lips. He tried to open his eyes, and for a terrifying instant thought he had been blinded as well as skewered. Then he realized from the closeness and stench that he was buried under a pile of dead Mionese citizens. Rouwen forced his way up past inert bodies and finally found hot sunlight beating down mercilessly on him and the mass grave. Rouwen reeled as the odor rose and choked him. He gagged weakly but his stomach refused to yield what wasn't there. Retching so hard it cramped his belly, he bent double and finally controlled himself.

Tears running down his cheeks, Rouwen looked around and thought the world had ended. Never had he seen so many corpses. He remembered one border skirmish used as a training exercise that had been particularly bloody. Twenty of his Intrepids had died and taken with them almost a hundred Mionese soldiers. But that carnage was nothing compared to the charnel pit surrounding him.

Knee-deep in bodies, he struggled to move out of the sea of death. Hundreds, perhaps thousands, had died and were discarded in a deep pit. Rouwen caught at tattered clothing on moldering corpses and pulled himself along until sun and weakness forced him to lie atop the bodies and rest. Vultures circled warily, high in the clear azure sky, unsure now that their repast began moving in a decidedly undead, menacing fashion.

He tried to remember what had happened but so much had fled his memory he couldn't be sure. The jolting pain of the sword piercing his back had jarred him more than any other death. Almost idly, Rouwen wondered if the soldier had twisted as he withdrew his blade.

'Any other death,' he laughed grimly. He had died too many times in the past weeks. Stabbed in back and belly, he had died enough for a squadron of men. The curse had to be lifted, or Rouwen was not sure how he could hope to continue without losing his mind.

Gagging again, he pulled himself a few more yards before his strength gave out. He might have slept. More likely, he passed out from the suffering that refused to die down inside his body. Liquid movement told him of severed arteries and veins deep within. Perhaps even his heart had been pierced one more time.

'No,' he heard someone say in a low voice. 'By the demons along the road to Paradise, no! It cannot be! I have lived too many years not to have seen everything, yet he lives after being impaled by that foul, murderous guardsman!'

'Nibbles,' croaked Rouwen through lips that tried to betray him. 'Help. Help me.' He reached out, not knowing where the small thief might be. Even this feeble gesture was too much for him. Rouwen collapsed once more into the mass grave.

Cheerful whistling awoke him. Rouwen sobbed with pain and clutched at his injured chest, only to find it firmly bound with clean bandages. He tried sitting up, but a firm hand held him down.

'I know nothing of such magicks, but you are truly ensorcelled,' Nibbles said. 'You saved my life, you did, and for that I thank you. How you survived is beyond even magic, if you ask me.'

'I owe you for pulling me out of that . . .' Words escaped Rouwen. He had never seen a mass grave filled with so many corpses. Even after the worst famines in Gan there had never been such incredible numbers of dead. Death had always been private, taken care of by close family and no one else. The magnitude of the slaughter in Mion appalled him as much as it sickened him.

'That's Nishor's Garden, as we call it. It seems he's taken to killing off the supplicants, simply to get rid of them,' Nibbles said. 'Here's where he plants them. Doesn't even bother with lime to keep down the stench and disease from the rot.' Nibbles spat in what Rouwen assumed was King Nishor's direction.

'He's responsible for more than murdering his own citizens,' Rouwen said, trying to take only slow, shallow breaths. This kept his pain to a tolerable level.

'I heard enough to know that he's in league with Sosler and

120

that renegade wizard,' said Nibbles. 'What's this to you? Your aspect is of a military man, but you blunder about so with scant planning that you accomplish nothing. And the way you took that sword in my stead!' Nibbles shook his head in disbelief, although he had witnessed the killing thrust with his own sharp eyes.

Slowly Rouwen related his story, thinking that Nibbles had earned that and more by pulling him from the death pit filling with Nishor's victims. How many could a wizard put into that pit, should Kwuway become interested in mass deaths instead of curses granting eternal life? Rouwen didn't want to know.

'So,' said Nibbles as Rouwen finished, 'you're a knight errant hunting for a way to save your king and queen and kingdom?'

'No, not that,' Rouwen said. 'Diarra would kill me, if she could.'

'You are sure she is cursed in the same manner?' Nibbles picked the gap between his upper front teeth with a sliver of bone chipped off a human thigh. Rouwen shuddered. He didn't want to know what the scrawny thief had been eating that required such attention.

'She cannot die,' Rouwen said, then reconsidered. 'She might carry only the other curse, the one where any whom she loves will perish. That explains why they placed us together in the same cell. Priowe thought we were lovers and would slay each other.' His head began to ache and he stopped trying to sort through all the problems with such a plan.

All that Brion Rouwen knew was that he could not die and that any he loved would die horribly. He had accidentally proven that curse by touching his brother.

'The spell casket dangling around the duke's neck,' mused Nibbles as he continued to pick the only two grooves between his four yellowed, protruding teeth. 'A pretty bauble that would be ever so profitable to steal. It must hold some essence stolen magically.'

'That allows me to die? Or that makes me kill those I love?'

Nibbles shrugged. 'What can a thief such as I say in answer? I have travelled far and seen so many things that it would make you shiver in fear. The sun stopped in the sky for a full day and a new moon joined the other two in the evening sky for a stately pavane, and that caused disease and famine unlike any to touch this fair continent in a century. I have seen all that and more. But this?' Nibbles shook his head in wonder.

Nibbles paused in his catalog of wondrous sights when he heard only loud snores greeting his impossible story. He sniffed in contempt, rose and went to where two horses were tethered. In the days since being tossed by mistake into Nishor's Garden he had been busy. The horses were only part of his treasure trove.

The guards had loaded their human carrion onto carts and brought them to Nishor's Garden, and they had been careless, thinking all their cargo was dead. Nibbles had made off with two horses, equipment and even enough trade goods to allow him back into Tachre to trade for food. He had always returned to the mass grave, knowing this was not a place often frequented by the Mionese. There was nothing to strip from the bodies because the guards did a decent enough job, though they missed occasional gems.

Nibbles touched the poison-filled dagger he had taken from Rouwen. He looked at his fitfully sleeping companion, then carefully wrapped and placed the deadly weapon back in Rouwen's belt. Whistling, Nibbles went about his work of preparing for travel. Leaving Mion seemed more urgent by the moment now that Rouwen was back.

Rouwen awoke with a start. His hands grabbed the poles on either side of his body and clutched hard to keep from being thrown off.

'There's no need to worry, friend,' Nibbles said cheerfully, riding on one of the war stallions he had stolen. He looked back at the travois poles holding Rouwen securely. 'I have you tied down. You thrash about so in your sleep it's a wonder you find any woman to share your bed. Or is that your advantage over others?'

Intercourse was the farthest thing from Rouwen's mind. He rubbed a shaking hand across his face and came away with a thin sheen of fever sweat. He lay back and stared up into the sky. Puffy white clouds billowed on the horizon only to rise in an anvil-head formation, promising a raging thunderstorm soon. Or did it?

He sat up again, this time pulling free of the restraining ties Nibbles had wrapped around him. The jostling motion showed that the horses had not slowed.

'Where are we going?'

'That's a fine way to greet the man who has cared for your every need during the past week. And I emphasize *every* need. You are not a good patient.'

'You're not much of a chirurgeon, either.'

'Nonsense, you're healing nicely,' Nibbles said, grinning broadly. Rouwen closed his eyes and lay back for a moment.

The sight of Nibbles grinning was almost as bad as awakening in a pit filled with ten thousand rotting bodies.

'I do not recognize these lands,' Rouwen said after a few minutes of riding along on the travois, watching unfamiliar trees and terrain pass behind him. He struggled to sit up and almost collapsed from pain. He sat still, silently wishing every horror he could imagine on Kwuway and Priowe for inflicting this curse on him.

'We're on our way to see him,' Nibbles said, twisting around in the saddle, looking like a rat perched on a fighting man's saddle. All around Nibbles clanked swords slung in sheaths, daggers by the dozen and pieces of armor, none of it matched or worth much more than for scaring away excitable birds.

'Who?' Rouwen was too weary to play Nibbles's little word games.

'Why, the Lord of Death and Life, that's who!' Nibbles stood in the saddle and did a precarious caper that threatened to send him crashing to the ground. Somehow, the scrawny thief managed to keep his balance and finally swung around, facing backward to talk with Rouwen.

'You know of him?' Rouwen held his sides and moaned when the travois bounced over a rougher section of the road.

'I know everything,' Nibbles claimed, puffing out his thin chest. Somewhat less enthusiastically he added, 'It took some doing but I found out much after I thought you were dead. A query here, an hour or two spent listening there, and it all came to me.'

'Like a spider in the middle of an information web,' Rouwen said. He opened his gray eyes and stared upside down at Nibbles. 'You said you did this after you thought I had died? Why? Of what import was learning of the Lord to you then?'

Nibbles looked uncomfortable. Rouwen saw the intent to lie flash across Nibbles's face, then change imperceptibly. The old thief cleared his throat for a long story. Rouwen resigned himself to listening to tall tales mingled with truth. He was surprised at Nibbles's seemingly honest narrative.

'The Lord exists, that I have always known. But where, where, I might ask?' Nibbles shook his head. 'The tales were confused and mingled with items that must be impossible. He is a wizard of the first order, but reclusive, always hiding from public acclaim.'

'Or loathing,' Rouwen cut in. 'There are few wizards who openly seek the acclaim of crowds. They do their best work in the darkness, at the behest of more powerful men and women.'

'There's seldom a ruler who hasn't made use of a pet wizard,' agreed Nibbles. 'That is why I was astounded to find that Anda-Zahn was, er, *removed*. He was replaced by this Kwuway, apparently an itinerant wizard, if there is such a rare beast.'

'Kwuway is King Priowe's wizard,' Rouwen said. The wizard played two masters against one another, unless the facts were even more twisted. 'As to his master, I doubt if he has one save himself. He seeks to put Duke Sosler on the Gannian throne.'

Rouwen considered how far Sosler had come to ascending the throne. Queen Diarra was gone, and Priowe was chipping away at those most faithful to him. Rouwen guessed that the Intrepid officer corps had been severely reduced – or the officers replaced with those from Sosler's army. Sped was in line for the throne after his father, but he was nothing more than a joke. True power might be wielded by Princess Sorinne, if she understood the dangers facing her father and the Kingdom of Gan. Rouwen doubted she knew, being more content to look after other matters.

'There is no question that magicks stalk the world,' Nibbles said. 'That meant there is more chittering and chattering about the best of the best.'

'The Lord of Death and Life?'

'Of course, friend, who else but the Lord? He has the power to restore lost life, plucking souls from Paradise to return to this poor world – or he can slay across the world with the wave of his hand. These are his spells, that is his power.'

'He can grant me death?' Rouwen's throat constricted and tears came to his eyes. The pain he felt might come to an end if the Lord performed a simple spell and chased Rouwen's soul to Paradise.

'Pah!' exclaimed Nibbles, becoming agitated again. 'I sought information about him to grant you *life*.' Nibbles stroked his chin and then said, 'If he has such power, he might be able to remove your curse. The Lord is a great wizard, a *great* one, not of paltry powers like Anda-Zahn or Kwuway.'

'Kwuway is mage enough for my taste,' Rouwen said as if the name burned his tongue. Still, for a moment he had dared hope. Nibbles's information was too sparse to aid him, though. Wild tales, hardly more than rumors or tales told to children to frighten them into obedience, mattered little. 'How long have we been on the road?'

'More than a week. We passed the guards at the Mion border five days back and have been making good time for the Isle of Passing.'

'What's that?'

'Why, it is where the Lord makes his home. I paid a young fortune for a map to it! See?' Nibbles held up a yellowed parchment that had been folded and refolded so many times it was falling apart. A slight sea breeze caught the edge and ripped a portion off. Nibbles's quick reflexes saved the fragment from being lost forever to the elements.

'You never paid a young fortune for anything,' Rouwen accused. 'Did the merchant you stole that from know what he had?'

'Perhaps not. Other information relating to the Lord's Isle of Passing came my way before I saw this exquisite map being advertised as an example of fine calligraphy and illumination. It took only a matter of seconds to remove it from a poorly guarded case.' Nibbles rubbed his hand against his tattered tunic. 'Scorpions locked in a case make poor guardians when the thief is as quick as I.'

'How far to this isle of the Lord's?' Rouwen asked, more intrigued than he wanted to let on. Gan was a powerful kingdom, but its favored position in the affairs of nations came from geographic location, good farmland and moderate rains. Wizards had never played a significant role in Gannian politics, although he had heard other countries were rife with magical dealings since they were unable to raise huge armies for invasion and conquest.

'A day's travel, perhaps more. We have been hugging the coastline away from Tachre, a rockier road but one far safer. I sense we are being followed.' Nibbles rubbed the back of his scrawny neck and peered into the misty distance behind them. Rouwen found himself staring in the same direction, aware of an uneasiness he felt also.

'The Lord's island is off the coast? How do we get to it? Surely, a powerful wizard does not maintain a ferry service to reach his domicile.'

'There are ways,' Nibbles said mysteriously. Rouwen interpreted this vagueness to mean that the small thief would find a way once they spotted the island – if they could. The map showed the Isle of Passing less than a hand span from the shore they now travelled. Rouwen had seen ancient maps more intent on artistic delineation and expression than usefulness to wanderers.

'We can swim,' Rouwen said. Kwuway's curse would keep him from drowning, although he was a poor swimmer. No amount of water in his lungs would doom him, however excruciating the experience. What worried him more were the strange denizens of the deep likely to safeguard a wizard's island home. Being devoured by a huge fish and carried in its belly for years and years did not appeal to him.

Not being allowed a human death presented problems he had never considered during simpler, less dire times.

'We can reach the isle with little problem,' Nibbles predicted. 'Once there, we must face an incredible guardian.'

'Giants? Six-headed poison-fanged hydras? Your fire tigers?' Rouwen decided to play Nibbles's game of soaring imagination and ludicrous conclusions.

'Why, no, worse than any such things, even if they existed,' Nibbles said solemnly. Rouwen craned around to look up at the thief. 'The Lord is commander of the Legion of the Air.'

'What's that?' Rouwen settled back down to stare at the ground passing slowly under his travois as Nibbles prattled on and on about invincible warriors of pure air. Nibbles's earlier concern over being followed unsettled him more than it should have, and he could not put into words the reason. Only slowly did the chain of logic work out to tangle around his legs.

'Kwuway has no reason to think I am dead. Nor does King Nishor,' he decided. 'As far as they are concerned, I simply vanished from the castle guards. They didn't know I was hiding among the supplicants. They didn't know I was run through – and that would not put Kwuway's mind at ease, even if he witnessed the killing.'

The wizard had cursed Brion Rouwen and knew the guard captain could not die from mere steel. Only the guards killing Nishor's supplicants thought he had died, and to them he was nothing more than a nameless beggar littering Tachre's streets. Kwuway still wanted Rouwen in a dungeon where he could be watched and tortured.

'What's that, friend?' asked Nibbles. He had been rambling on about the Legion of the Air, and Rouwen wasn't listening. It had taken the small thief some time to realize Rouwen was speaking.

'Nothing. Kwuway would order a hunt for us,' Rouwen said. 'For me,' he amended. 'We need to make all haste. It's been too long and Kwuway will be growing uneasy.'

Rouwen knew little of the wizard's scrying spells, but he had heard Sosler mention more than once how Kwuway used his abilities at far-seeing to scout enemy positions. How this worked or how accurate such a spell was left Rouwen worrying that Nishor's inept soldiers might be dogging his trail. More than a week had passed, and Kwuway had to know Rouwen would take any chance to flee the walls of Tachre – and perhaps even the barren boundaries of Mion.

'When we reach the Isle of Passing, the Lord will protect us,' Nibbles said, assurance in his voice. 'There will be no need to fear Kwuway or Nishor. The Legion of the Air will be our guardian and keep them at bay.'

'Why?' demanded Rouwen. 'Why should the Lord of Death and Life accept our petition if it might mean intrusion on his privacy or worse? The Lord might not appreciate coping with Kwuway and his petty political striving.'

What *would* appeal to a wizard so powerful he could bring back the dead? Rouwen didn't know.

'You lack the ability to sell yourself, friend,' Nibbles said. 'Your plight makes you think ill of all circumstance surrounding yourself. How many immortals not of his own creation does the Lord see in a week's time? Is this not an affront to his self-seized magical power, indeed, to his very name? I say yes!'

'We need to seek shelter,' Rouwen said, eyeing the sky. He cared less about Nibbles's arguments than keeping himself dry. A storm moved quickly in their direction and promised a bone-soaking downpour laced with potent lightning. His joints ached, and he did not want to be exposed to the elements more than necessary. His strength had been returning slowly while they travelled, but he had not become used to deathblows yet. Nor was he ever likely to, he knew.

'From more than the storm, it appears,' Nibbles said, standing precariously on the saddle and shielding his eyes with his right hand. 'A small dust cloud rises in front of the storm, an unusual weather pattern, to say the least.'

Rouwen struggled to sit up. He failed to see what Nibbles did from his higher vantage. Rouwen vaulted off the travois and stood on shaking legs, knowing it was high time that he test his recovery. The dust clouds Nibbles had mentioned were low, close to the ground and moving swiftly.

'Whatever it is dogs our path with uncanny precision,' Nibbles said uneasily. 'Even to the short jog toward the sea we took at noontime. There is not much dust for a full company of soldiers, but this does not bode well.'

'We seek shelter from the storm first,' Rouwen said, estimating that the rain would find them before any tracker. Something gnawed at the edges of his brain about those following his trail, but he was unable to put it into words.

'There is a sharp descent toward the sea,' Nibbles said. 'The map shows a boggy area on the land nearest the Isle of Passing.

We might be able to elude them in the swampy area, though I am loath to slough through the sucking, miserable muck of . . .'

'Snakes,' Rouwen said, turning cold inside. 'Kwuway has released sniffer-snakes on my trail.'

'What are those?' asked Nibbles, abandoning all pretense at knowing everything about all topics.

'They are creatures imbued with magical powers,' Rouwen said grimly. He lengthened his stride to reach the boggy area Nibbles had found on the map as quickly as possible. 'Huge flying snakes that can scent a human and follow him to the ends of the world.'

'And? There is more. I hear it in your words,' Nibbles said. 'Or do I want to know the real danger behind us?'

'They are poisonous and never abandon a scent once they have found it. No one has ever escaped a sniffer-snake. Ever.'

Rouwen worried for Nibbles's safety, but he worried more for his own fate. He might not die of the vicious, implacable magical creatures, but they could rip him apart and inflict such intense suffering that it would debilitate him. As before, death would be preferable to the lingering agony Kwuway had heaped upon him with his curse.

14

To the Isle of Passing

Brion Rouwen pulled his cloak tighter around his body but this didn't do much to keep out the driving rain released by the intense storm. Lightning cracked and danced over his head and once came down to split a tree not fifty feet distant. Hot sap boiled and blasted through the air, scaring the horses and causing them to rear. Loud clanking from the improbable booty they carried echoed through the small stand of dwarfed, wind-tortured trees robbed of all color save that given by the lightning.

Again Rouwen pulled the cloak tighter and put his head down, trying to ignore the aches and pains racing through him. Localizing the worst of his misery proved impossible, though the spot where Kennard had driven his blade seemed worst of all. The fresher wounds had begun healing, promising long pink scars as their legacy. Rouwen shook his head ruefully. There was little doubt he would soon forget the jabs to his belly and chest that had produced those marks.

'What of the sniffer-snakes?' asked Nibbles, huddling beside Rouwen. 'Can they track in such vile weather? I once knew an amphibian creature who was as much at home in a downpour as he was in the sea. A terrible beast, he was, but could he track! Possessed of a huge snuffling snout and a blowhole, he slithered about on the land like a huge slug burdened with flippers. I rode with a band of brave-hearted lads in search of an escaped criminal, a rapist and murderer, he was. This beast performed a true miracle when it . . .'

'They cannot track in rain,' Rouwen said, cutting off another colorful account he neither wanted to hear nor believed. He tried to estimate the storm's strength and decided it might be lessening. As much as he disliked the idea, Rouwen knew it was time for them to move on. The heavy rains would erase their tracks and mask any odor the sniffer-snakes might use to find prey.

The stunted trees afforded some screening from the sniffer-snakes, though Rouwen doubted their vision was good. The best defense against the vicious, magically enhanced reptiles came in the sucking ooze of the swamp they had entered. Travel would be hindered, but any distance put between them and their pursuers would be to the good.

'How far is it to where we might catch a ferry to the Isle of Passing?' asked Rouwen, standing and shaking off water like a duck. Unlike a duck, other droplets quickly soaked whatever portions of his clothing that had remained dry during the storm. He threw down his cloak, giving up any hope of staying comfortable. Looking around, all directions appeared identical to him. He hoped that Nibbles's sense of direction was better than his own. Going the wrong way would only compound their problems.

'A mile or two,' Nibbles said, teeth chattering against the cold rain. 'But why leave now? The storm will clear in another few hours. This is not as comfortable as some inns I have tarried in, but it is better than walking in sticky mud.'

'The sniffer-snakes,' Rouwen reminded his companion. He paused for a moment, considering a different course of action. 'There is no need for you to come with me. There is a good chance the sniffer-snakes have only my scent. You can angle off through the swamp and be free.'

'How will you find your way to the Lord's Isle of Passing?' Nibbles asked, astounded at Rouwen's foolishness. 'You need someone quick of hand and mind to keep you out of trouble. Did I not rescue you from Nishor's Garden and nurse you back to robust health?'

As always, Nibbles exaggerated. Rouwen felt as if he had been walking with the horse on his back, rather than the other way around. Any battle, whether against human or magical beast, would end swiftly – and he would be the loser.

'You have done much for me, and I am appreciative,' Rouwen said, gathering his belongings. 'There isn't any reason for you to share my danger. Remember, Kwuway cannot kill me unless he removes the curse first. I am invincible.'

'You can have your arms and legs chopped off,' snapped Nibbles. 'Unless you are part starfish, what use would you be to anyone then?'

'What use am I to you now?' Rouwen asked honestly. He had no good idea why the thief had accompanied him this far.

'The adventure! What else is there worthwhile in life? I have travelled the . . .' Nibbles cut off his long-winded tale when he saw Rouwen's expression. 'I have only seconds of life on this world,' Nibbles said more somberly. 'Why not live them to the fullest? Seldom have I encountered one such as you.' Nibbles coughed a little and then said, 'Truth to tell, *never* have I had such a quest presented to me. Living by my wits has both rewards and penalties.'

'And what might they be?' Rouwen asked, touched at the small thief's words.

'The rewards are seeing what no one else has, experiencing the thrill of achievement and victory! And the penalties? Being trapped to endure anything less than those few moments of greatness. Glory is over all too soon, and recovering it is a long, hard job.'

'You see in me glory?' Rouwen laughed derisively at that notion. He still didn't understand his own feelings and he doubted if he had fully comprehended the nature of the curses on him. His feeble thrusts to avenge himself had been parried too easily. A new, more potent scheme needed to be forged if he wanted to triumph.

First, he realized, he had to know what triumph meant. Revenge on Kwuway and Sosler and Priowe? Or was Priowe as much a victim as he was? And Sorinne, the lovely, compassionate, effervescent Sorinne! How did he even see her again without killing her instantly? The plot that caused his woe radiated far and wide from Castle Gan, embracing more than a simple captain of the guards. The entire Kingdom of Gan was at risk, and he felt his duty lay as much in protecting the kingdom as in placing on the throne a worthy ruler.

'He failed,' Rouwen muttered to himself, coming to a decision. 'Priowe failed and must be replaced.' He could accept his liege's ordering Chertude or Kwuway to torture him for what appeared to be a gross dereliction of duty, but he could and did fault the king for not uncovering all the facts. Queen Diarra was strangely afflicted mentally, but Priowe should have had more confidence in his Captain of the Intrepid Guard. He should have questioned Sosler and got to the core of the scandal rather than simply bursting in and ordering his most trusted officer to the dungeons.

'We will fail if we blunder about in the swamps,' complained Nibbles. 'Once I was lost for a fortnight in a worse bog than this. Movement was almost impossible. It took all . . .'

'Which direction is the Isle of Passing?' Rouwen considered dumping most of the armament Nibbles had lugged this far, then decided against it. The horse might have a more difficult time sloughing through the swamp, but the armor if left behind would be a beacon pointing the way after them. He should have discarded it much earlier, perhaps throwing it into the choppy sea they had paralleled for a week.

'That way,' Nibbles said without hesitation. One direction was as good as any other to Rouwen, and he had no reason to doubt the old thief's sense of bearings. He grabbed up both horses' reins and started in the direction Nibbles had indicated.

The ground beneath them grew increasingly soft and sticky. When they were struggling to walk through knee-deep ooze, increasingly plagued by the nipping of blood leeches, Rouwen decided they must change direction, even if the coast – and possible discovery – was nearby.

'No, no,' insisted Nibbles. 'We are close. Can you not hear the crash of waves?'

'How can there be any wave action?' Rouwen asked sourly. 'This swamp would be washed clean. The only good point in travelling in the rain is that the insects have sensibly stayed hidden.'

'We are near. I can smell it! I hear it! These old ears might not appear to be sensitive, but they are. I can hear the clink of two coins and know their denominations within a leather pouch. Blindfolded, I can listen to the sound of a coin hitting the bar and tell you which side is up. Many's the bet I have won with this skill. And I tell you, the ocean is close!'

Rouwen plodded along behind Nibbles, cursing himself for a fool. What did the thief know of exploration or scouting? All his tales were lies designed to amuse and entice the gullible. So he was completely astounded when the bottom of the quagmire turned upward, and they soon found themselves not only on dry, rocky ground but looking across a narrow channel to an island that tantalized as rain squalls momentarily revealed and then hid emerald vegetation and a feeling of serenity that had been lacking so long in Rouwen's life.

'That is the Isle of Passing,' Nibbles said with absolute confidence, puffed up by his accomplishment of guiding them to their destination.

'Of course,' Rouwen said, wiping mud and leeches off his legs. He tended the horses next, finding several blood suckers worrying the animals. The rain slackened minute by minute. When Rouwen had finished his crude first aid, the storm between the mainland and the Isle of Passing had vanished.

'It's a pretty one, don't you agree to that, friend?' asked Nibbles. The small thief rubbed his hands together, anticipating overflowing coffers of gold and jewels and how much he might get away with stealing. 'Look at the way the clouds dip low and play across the tallest trees? Not natural, not at all. Some powerful magicks are at work to create such an artistic effect. The Lord must be a true artist, appreciative of all that is beautiful in nature.'

'How do we get to the island?' Rouwen scanned the coastline for any sign of a dock, a ferryboat, a raft that might make the journey to the isle set so intriguingly in what appeared to be a large bay protected by rocky arms reaching out into the ocean. But there were no clues how the Lord of Death and Life came and went from his island retreat – if he did.

'There is a way,' Nibbles assured him. 'There always is, if you are clever enough to see it. Now, let's begin our search . . .'

Rouwen let out a screech of pure fright. He jumped toward the horse laden with their armory of swords and daggers and jerked one of each free. He spun, his sword making a vicious cut at a writhing green-scaled horror that came through the air, supported by gossamer wings that refracted rainbows as it flew.

For all the beauty of the wings, there was none wasted elsewhere on the sniffer-snake. Six-inch-long yellow fangs flashed wickedly, droplets of deadly acid dripping from them as the reptile attacked Rouwen. His sword hit one fang and knocked back the snake's head. He tried to cut the beast's throat with a quick stroke of his dagger but failed. Steel met virtually impervious armor, sending fat blue sparks flying into the air.

'Where are the vital points?' shrieked Nibbles, fumbling to pull a sword from the frightened horse carrying their weapons. He faced a twenty-foot-long sniffer-snake of his own. Rouwen saw that Nibbles had driven a dagger deep into the reptile's back to no avail. A thin greenish ichor dribbled from the wound but did nothing to slow the reptile's slashing attacks.

Rouwen gripped his sword with both hands and let out a prodigious shout to gather all his strength into a single stroke. The sharp blade caught the sniffer-snake just behind the head. A shockwave rippled up the sword and into Rouwen's shoulders causing a jolt of pain in his body that almost made him pass out.

But the sword penetrated and half-severed the sniffer-snake's head. No longer able to stay aloft, the magically enhanced creature flopped to the ground, wings churning the bog. Rouwen dropped to his knees and sawed vigorously until the head was severed from the body.

He scraped the thick, greenish blood off on a rock before turning to aid Nibbles. To his surprise he saw the thief had acquitted himself honorably. A second dagger had penetrated the snake's spiny dorsal ridge. As the reptile had turned to favor the wounded area, Nibbles had used a sword to good purpose to open up a long gash along the creature's belly. That had forced the snake to the ground where a frightened stallion had trampled it savagely to bloody fragments.

'That was a battle well fought,' Nibbles said, panting hard to regain his breath. 'Reminds me of the time when I singlehandedly held off a dozen snapping trifins. I was on the good ship *Encumbrance* out of Lowpin and we'd just spotted a feeding frenzy of . . .'

Rouwen listened with half an ear – and not to Nibbles's narrative. He strapped two daggers around his waist and made sure the glass dagger was securely tucked into his belt. He considered adding a sword to his armament, then decided against it.

'Run, Nibbles, take the horses and flee down the coast as fast as you can.'

'What? Why?'

'Listen!' Rouwen barked at the thief. 'That hissing comes from more sniffer-snakes. There is a swarm of them on our trail. Killing two will seem child's play compared to fighting a dozen!'

'I won't abandon you, friend. You need me. Why, without me you would – no! Nibbles tried to grab Rouwen, but he twisted away and rushed to the rocky shoreline. He never hesitated when he came to the gently rolling surf. He dived cleanly and was swallowed up by the water.

'Brion, no! Come back!' cried Nibbles from the shoreline. 'You can't do this. There is danger!'

Rouwen knew the dangers he faced by his impetuous action. Better to be nibbled by fish than hacked to bloody pieces by the sniffer-snakes. He had been as lucky as he was skillful in avoiding the first two magical reptiles. Strength would fade quickly and his luck would run out. Swimming to the Lord's Isle of Passing was his only chance. The sniffer-snakes might follow, but he had to risk it. Staying on the shore to fight or trying to run along the shore would only result in an eternity of pain for him.

He knew why Kwuway had loosed the beasts. The sniffer-snakes would cripple him. He would suffer intense pain eternally, and Kwuway would be free of him. Acids would course through Rouwen's veins, his arms and legs would be slashed off by the snakes' brutal fangs, they would eat his guts – and he would never die.

It was far better to brave other guardians of magic by getting to the Lord's island and begging for sanctuary.

'Come back, Brion Rouwen. You cannot swim to the island. There are guards, I have heard. Ferocious ones!' Nibbles's cries faltered as he realized he could not continue to harangue his friend without falling victim to Kwuway's sniffer-snakes. The pounding of horses' hooves replaced Nibbles's warnings.

And Brion Rouwen swam. He had never been a good swimmer because of a dearth of places to practice in Gan, but he knew the rudiments. Clothing and weapons weighing him down, he floundered a bit but kept on gamely. Once he rolled onto his back and saw a flash of rainbow colors along the shore and knew the main swarm of sniffer-snakes had found their dead comrades. He didn't know if the water masked his scent sufficiently or if the reptiles' eyesight was keen enough to see him, but he had no choice but to keep swimming while they devoured their fallen in a ghastly banquet.

Rolling onto his belly, Rouwen glided with deliberate strokes through the warm gentle waves breaking around him, preferring a slower pace to expending all his energy in wild thrashing. He quickly changed his tactics when a stab of pain lanced along his leg and exploded in the pit of his belly.

Rouwen shrieked in agony and almost sank as he turned to grab at whatever chewed at his leg. His fingers closed around spines that stung with all the ferocity of a white-hot poker. Rouwen vanished underwater and kicked, struggling to get away from whatever threatened to eat him one limb at a time. Through the murky, blood-filled water he saw a globular fish covered with short, wickedly tipped barbs.

Whipping out a dagger, Rouwen slashed at the fish. His dagger missed and a score of barbs were embedded in his arm, causing him to drop the dagger.

Sputtering for air, he fought to the surface. Rolling and turning, he flailed as hard as he could, hoping to dislodge the spiny monster chewing so hungrily on him. He succeeded only in getting more of the barbs sunk into his flesh. His leg began to numb, and he realized his predicament. He wasn't a strong enough swimmer to make it all the way to the island – and returning to shore was out of the question.

Rouwen could see light flashing off the scales and wings of the sniffer-snakes as they darted about hunting for their prey and he had a moment's triumph when he realized the magical reptiles were not pursuing Nibbles. His small friend had escaped.

Then Rouwen let out a cry of pain and despair when he saw the sniffer-snakes turning toward him. The surface of the ocean had become red from his blood. Whatever scent

135

the snakes homed in on was released and attracting the monsters.

He fumbled out his second dagger and cut and hacked at the globular fish still voraciously eating his leg. His first thrusts missed their target, slithering off the heavy plating covering the fish's body. Then the dagger's tip found a chink in the spiny armor. Rouwen pressed home the blade and twisted savagely. The fish released its hold, leaving behind a few barbed spines in Rouwen's flesh. But he was no longer being devoured from below.

But now the sniffer-snakes were coming at him from above. Rouwen kicked weakly and knew his legs would never respond powerfully enough to matter. He put the dagger back into its sheath and began using his arms like giant windmills to get through the water as fast as possible. He was making progress toward the Isle of Passing, but it was far slower than the flying sniffer-snakes.

One dived on him from above and slashed fiercely at his back. Rouwen dived under the water and instantly regretted the decision. The snakes were reptiles and as at home in the water as they were on land or flying on their diaphanous wings. The sniffer-snake followed him under the surface and came at Rouwen, fangs clacking together in a deadly scissoring action.

Rouwen grabbed the snake just behind its head but knew he could never hold on. His strength slipped away, second by second, and he would soon be left enervated from the struggle. Water would fill his lungs or the acid-dripping fangs would rend the flesh from his bones. Either way he would not die.

He would only suffer excruciating pain.

Something skipped along the surface of the water, pulling Rouwen upward as if by a giant fist. He broke the surface, gasping for breath. The sniffer-snake wriggled free and flopped around on the surface, then took to the air to renew its attack.

Rouwen trod water, wondering what he ought to do. He couldn't die. He could only experience more torture at Kwuway's hand. Or he could abandon himself to the underwater denizens. He knew Nibbles had been right in warning him of the dangerous guardians the Lord of Death and Life stationed around his tranquil-appearing island of verdant growth.

To either side Rouwen saw misty swirls growing on the surface. He wondered if one of them had pulled him up from the depths like a giant suction cup. The twisting pillars of fog were hardly more than five feet tall, small cyclones skipping on the water like flat stones tossed by a child. They danced away from him and gave Rouwen a clear view of the real danger facing him.

The sniffer-snake he had fought had summoned the others in its swarm. Dozens of the deadly reptiles hissed and flapped toward him. There was no way Rouwen could reach the wizard's island and there was no way to fight the reptiles.

All Brion Rouwen could look forward to was intense, outrageous pain engulfing him forever.

15

The Lord's Promise

Rouwen tried to swim, but the intense pain throughout his body
made progress difficult. The swirling mists on either side of him
also impeded his progress, causing a turbulence in the water he
had to fight with every stroke, his numbed leg trailing behind
like an anchor rope in the water.

A new attack of sniffer-snakes caused Rouwen to dive once
more, and again one snake followed him. The magically enhanced
reptile came for him – then suddenly broke off the attack.
Rouwen sputtered, blew bubbles and worked hard to reach the
surface again. His lungs almost exploded as he was lifted out of
the water by one of the misty columns.

The waterspout tossed him aside, and he was again able to
breathe. He thrashed around in the water and watched in
stunned amazement as the columns of mist solidified, whirled
faster, engulfed the sniffer-snakes. A loud, inhuman squealing
filled the air as the reptiles were caught up and whipped around
inside the cyclones.

Rouwen threw up an arm and was momentarily submerged
when a shower of greenish reptilian blood and body parts
came spinning from the vortices not ten yards away. But
the columns of whirling air did not slow. If anything, they
multiplied and increased rotation until the azure sky turned
dark with their ejecta.

Swimming through the floating gore, Rouwen reached the
island and pulled himself forward painfully onto the beach
of brilliantly gleaming white sand. He lay a moment on the
sand, then realized it wasn't hot to the touch as he might have
expected. Its coolness seemed to come from the center of the
world, soothing him, freshening his spirits, bringing healing to
his myriad wounds.

Cautiously standing up, he tried the leg gnawed by the spiny
fish. The discoloration caused by the fish's poison faded as he
watched. He flexed his leg and tried walking a few paces.

The muscle had returned to its normal power and flexibility with no hint of damage remaining. Rouwen stretched and was pleased to note that his other wounds, from the sniffer-snakes and elsewhere, felt better.

Magically better.

He turned and looked at the narrow channel between the Isle of Passing and the mainland. A dozen soaring columns of frantically spinning air darted back and forth, catching the mindlessly attacking sniffer-snakes and whirling them until their bodies came apart. The pieces were casually blown away from the cyclones and caused the blue water to turn green and ugly with death.

'So messy,' came a soft voice. 'But fear naught. The waters will be pure before you know it. The ocean cleanses itself quickly, even after such offal is consigned to its surface.'

Rouwen spun, hand going to the dagger at his belt. He hesitated when he found himself facing a slender young man, hardly twenty years old, fair of face and gentle in manner. The young man smiled almost shyly and bowed deeply.

'Welcome to this humble island,' he said, with a flourish of the hand as he straightened. 'It is so seldom anyone comes to visit.'

'The fish will eat the carcasses,' Rouwen said, indicating the stretch of sea behind him.

'Ah, yes, I am sure they will enjoy the small repast. It has been so long since they got a good meal. But those horrible sniffer-snakes will be more dessert than a true meal. My little pets are *so* voracious.'

'Your pets?' Rouwen was still shaken from the nearness of being devoured by the acid-fanged snakes and the fish. He relaxed and took his hand away from the hilt of his dagger, not wanting to offend this man who seemed so at home on the Isle of Passing.

'Please excuse my incivility. Come this way. I can offer some hospitality, though not as much as in your fine Kingdom of Gan, from which you surely travel.'

'How do you know?' Rouwen was perplexed. Every step he took made him feel stronger, better than he had since Kwuway had put the dual curses on him.

'I have travelled widely myself, before coming to this pleasant island. I recognize your accent, the cut of your hair, the way you carry yourself. A military man?'

'I was,' Rouwen said. His physical woes were receding, and he was better able to concentrate on his host. The young man skipped along like a small child, stopping to pluck particularly

139

pretty or fragrant flowers along the narrow path winding through the stand of low-growing pine trees. In the distance he heard songbirds singing and an occasional *thouse* bird giving voice to a raucous mating call.

'It's always summer on the island,' the young man said. 'It could be any other season, but this pleases me most. I tried autumn but it was so depressing, all the plants dying and no flowers worth mentioning ever in bloom. Spring is so much nicer, but it carries a small chill. That's why I prefer summer, don't you?'

'Doesn't it become boring if there is only one season on this island?' asked Rouwen.

'Ah, a philosopher as well as a soldier. It is so good to have company. So few journey this way. Please join me in a small repast, nothing much, but it represents the viands available here.' The youth bowed Rouwen into a simple one-room cottage.

Rouwen ducked slightly as he went through the low door, then looked around in surprise. He wasn't sure what he had expected, but it was not such simple appointment in furniture and decoration.

'I know what you are thinking. They all do. Why don't I live more lavishly, you are wondering. All I can say is, this suits me.'

'A good answer,' Rouwen said, looking around. He found a chair and sank to it unbidden. His legs were stronger, but he still needed to recover from his trip to Nishor's Garden and the swim to the island and the sniffer-snakes – and so much else.

'Sample a little of each,' the young man urged, holding a platter of small pieces of cut fish, fruit and cheese. 'I've tried to decide which I enjoy most, and I find my opinions changing over time. This is my choice at the moment.' He picked up a small red berry Rouwen didn't recognize and popped it into his mouth. He closed his eyes as he chewed contentedly and let out a small shiver of sheer pleasure.

'Thank you,' Rouwen said, tasting first, then devouring as his hunger mounted. The young man watched in appreciation of his appetite.

'You do me proud. I love seeing someone eat as you are. Thank you for the vote of approval on my selections.'

Rouwen slowed his pace and leaned back. He saw no reason to pass the afternoon with this pleasant young man when he had serious business to attend to. 'I need to find the Lord of Death and Life. I have been told he lives here.'

'Here?' The young man seemed amused as he looked around the simple cabin.

'On the Isle of Passing.'

This produced a laugh of sheer pleasure. The young man laughed until tears came to his eyes. He wiped them away and leaned back in his chair and tried to control his mirth.

'What's so funny?' Rouwen asked, irritated. He sampled some of the wine on a table beside him. The wine was sweeter than he preferred, but it went down smoothly and settled coolly in his belly. A tingling in his stomach caused Rouwen to pull up his tunic and warily examine the flesh there. The bright pink scars from his recent guttings were fading and the skin was healing as he watched. He looked up in surprise.

'You are the Lord,' he accused.

'Of course I am, and you called this the Isle of Passing. How droll! I call it home. Tell me, have you seen death anywhere on this island since you arrived?'

'The winds tore apart the sniffer-snakes,' he said.

'Oh, that was over water. It *is* possible to die here, but only if I assent. Life is so much more interesting. I have seen Paradise and it is boring. Even without the starvation to add some spice or the demons torturing you for petty infractions, Paradise is dull. Whatever do dead people *do?*'

'I never would have thought it,' Rouwen said cautiously. He wasn't sure he believed this young man had seen Paradise and found it wanting.

'I see that this is far from your thoughts.' The young man's eyes turned sharp and bright, and Rouwen caught more than a hint of age-won experience in them. 'You carry two enchantments, each grievous but not impossible to reverse.'

'You can do it? I will be forever in your service if you . . .'

'Get away from me!' The young Lord jumped out of his chair and backed off when Rouwen tried to touch him. 'Don't ever come closer to me than you are now. Do you understand?'

'I'm sorry. I only seek a wizard to remove the curses Kwuway has placed on me.' Rouwen backed away from the Lord and sat down, wondering why such a powerful wizard reacted so strangely. The Lord had banished death from his small island and brought eternal life to it. Such power had nothing to fear from a twice cursed former captain of Gannian guards.

'You do not need me for this,' the young wizard said, settling back into his chair and straightening his simple clothing. 'Kill Kwuway and the curse of eternal life is removed.' He coughed genteelly into a linen handkerchief and then replaced it at his

141

left wrist, hiding it in a linen cuff. 'Why you seek mortality is beyond me, but people's desires are as much a mystery to me as a wizard's spells are to you.'

'And the other spell? Can you remove that curse?'

'Ah, that is a more complex spell, one I would never have expected from such a simpleton as Kwuway.' As the Lord stared at him, Rouwen experienced a moment of vertigo, as if he were falling into a deep well. He jerked erect suddenly, aware that he had somehow been examined more thoroughly than ever before in his life.

'An interesting spell, but one that will not end with Kwuway's death. And, alas, one I have no power to reverse.' The Lord drank deeply from his wine goblet. Rouwen had not seen anyone pour it and wasn't even sure where the goblet had come from.

'What am I to do? Never to love again? How can I stop myself without becoming eaten up with self-hatred?'

'You *are* philosophically inclined,' the Lord said, shaking his head and causing a small lock of sandy hair to fall into his eyes. He pushed it back with a practiced wave of his hand, pursed his lips, then said, 'There is a spell casket holding some vital part of you. Does Kwuway hold it?'

'Duke Sosler has a small silver locket that Kwuway handed him after the spell had been cast,' Rouwen said. 'I have heard it called a spell casket.'

'That is what you must recover, then,' the Lord said. 'See? It is all so simple, as life is on my isle.' He chuckled again and muttered to himself, 'The Isle of Passing. Imagine!'

'I kill Sosler and open the locket – the spell casket? That's all there is to do?' Rouwen hardly believed his ears. He intended to do this anyway. All he needed was a plan and he was on his way to recovering his very soul.

'Ah, no, that's not exactly right. Opening the spell casket without the proper incantations is risky. You might fix the spell forever if you are not careful.'

'Who besides Kwuway knows the proper spells?'

'That is difficult to say. I do not know the intricate patterns of energies used to weave this spell and could not simply wave my hand and remove your curse.'

'Who?' wailed Rouwen, distraught at learning what needed to be and then finding even a potent wizard such as the Lord of Death and Life was helpless to aid him. 'The Flame Specter?'

'What?' The Lord's voice turned to steel. He speared Rouwen with his hard gaze and held him immobile. 'What do you know of the Flame Specter?'

'I . . .' Rouwen hesitated to reveal what little he had heard. 'A name I heard Kwuway mention.'

'Indeed, then it means nothing,' the Lord said.

Rouwen knew the wizard lied. Earlier the young man had appeared carefree. The mention of the Flame Specter caused him to sit with arms and legs tightly wrapped around himself, as if attack was imminent. And more telling, something of his youth vanished. He had aged ten years in the twinkling of an eye, now seeming more middle-aged than youthful.

'I kill Kwuway and win only the right to kill those I love,' Rouwen said bitterly. 'Why bother, except for the right to die?'

'Ah, there is so much more,' said the Lord, relaxing again and sitting forward, hands resting on his knees. He seemed a year or two younger than before, but Rouwen knew the mention of the Flame Specter had turned the wizard apprehensive. 'There is no reason for Sosler, Drioway and Kwuway to further their ambitions by removing Priowe from the Gannian throne.'

Rouwen said nothing. He hadn't mentioned Duke Drioway, but the Lord let the name slide easily from his tongue. The politics of Gan and Mion were better known to the reclusive wizard than Rouwen had thought. Political maneuvering and petty wizards interested the Lord more than he admitted openly.

'Sosler and King Nishor are a force to be reckoned with, though Nishor is an ambitious, overweening fool. I would not have them depose Priowe, though it might not be possible to stop it now that forces are in motion.' The Lord pursed his lips as he thought, then his face brightened.

'There are ways for both of us to profit by this situation. I have no desire to see Priowe deposed, though who sits on the Gannian throne is of little import while Gan retains its present power. Your Princess Sorinne would be a fine choice for queen.'

'What of Sped?'.

'Pah, a fool, a knave unworthy of my attention. Power blocs may shift, but they must remain virtually unchanged.'

'Why?' demanded Rouwen. 'What do you fear out here on your fine island surrounded by your cyclones?'

'The Legion of the Air?' The Lord laughed in delight. 'They are my finest defense. And on this island I am completely impervious to any attack, physical or magical. My interest in Gannian-Mionese politics is only academic.'

Rouwen knew the Lord again lied. No wizard studied the affairs of another without being interested deeply.

'King Nishor has tried repeatedly to storm this island and has

143

always failed. Ask anyone,' the Lord said, seeing Rouwen's incredulity. He let out a deep sigh and leaned forward again, trying to show his sincerity. 'Very well, Captain Rouwen, I will tell you this and nothing more. The balance of power on this continent is of some small import to me. If powers you cannot hope to comprehend are disturbed by Sosler coming to rule both Mion and Gan, it would annoy me.' The Lord straightened, as if he had admitted to great crimes.

Rouwen knew there was more lurking in the wizard's statement. The Lord of Death and Life did not want Gan to fall because of something more than a shift in mortal rule. Some magical power might be released – or constrained – due to the change. Sorinne was acceptable to the Lord, but Sosler was not. Why?

Rouwen decided his interests appeared to coincide with the Lord's – for the time.

And again, as if the wizard read his mind, the Lord said, 'I can help you remove the second curse if . . .'

'If I kill Kwuway? And Sosler and Duke Drioway? What of Priowe and Sped? Are their lives forfeit, too?'

'Kill them or not,' the Lord said testily. 'I promise you this. Kill Kwuway and take his grimoire. Bring that book of spells to me, along with the spell casket, and I will be able to remove the onerous magical burden you now carry. What could be fairer than this?'

'You get Kwuway's spell book, and I will be free of the spells?'

'It sounds so simple, doesn't it?' asked the Lord, leering like an old man spying a lovely young girl. 'It will not be easy, as you have already learned.'

'Not easy,' Rouwen said, wondering what he was not being told. For a recluse, the Lord of Death and Life's concern about mortal politics meant they affected him. He might be impervious on this isle, but the young wizard must travel abroad often to know so much – and was he vulnerable then?

The leer vanished and a harshness entered the Lord's voice. 'I make this promise to you. I also make another. Fail to fetch the grimoire for me, and you will wish Kwuway's spells were all that oppressed you.'

The threat was unmistakable.

'There is no reason to hurry,' said the youthful Lord of Death and Life in his offhand manner. Rouwen saw the expression on the wizard's face and knew that time did matter. How quickly

Nishor and Sosler moved against Priowe mattered, as did their infernal plotting and conniving. It had been far too long since he had seen his lovely Sorinne, yet more time would pass before he was able to hold her in his arms and love her as she deserved.

Time mattered greatly, and it weighed Brion Rouwen down until he almost staggered with the load.

'How do I get back to the mainland?' he asked, not wanting to risk again the spined, gnawing fish. He saw in the distance hazy columns of air whipping up – the Legion of the Air, the Lord had called them. Something warned him that the vicious circular-force winds were the least of the capabilities in those small cyclones. He wasn't inclined to risk finding out what more they might do to intruders to the Isle of Passing.

'Why, it is simple,' The Lord said. 'My island has renewed your vigor, hasn't it?'

'I should swim amid the hungry guardians you've posted? Did you do nothing but fatten me for them?'

'Of course not, my dear Brion Rouwen!' The Lord laughed at what seemed an obtuse jest. 'I would have Kwuway's grimoire in my possession. You require the same since I cannot remove the spell without the book of spells or the spell casket. We *need* one another, you and I!'

'So I swim and you'll hold back the fishes?' Rouwen did not relish the notion of immersing himself in such treacherous waters. For all the Lord's prattling about mutual need, he knew that was not so.

'I cannot hold them back. I am a wizard but my talents lie – elsewhere.' The Lord laughed once more at Rouwen's sour expression. 'All you need do is *walk*. The isle has imbued you with some of its fine powers. For the moment.'

Rouwen started to argue, then decided to show this babbling wizard how absurd such a notion was. He walked across the impossibly white sand and hesitated only a moment before stepping into the gentle waves rolling across the beach. It took Rouwen several steps to realize his feet were not wet.

He walked across the surface of the water.

'The grimoire, dear Brion Rouwen, bring the grimoire and the spell casket!' called the Lord from the shore. The wizard waved and then vanished along the narrow path leading back to his one-room cottage.

Rouwen looked down and saw the vicious fish snapping and lunging at him, only to recoil as if they struck some invisible barrier. He took a deep breath and walked briskly toward the far shore, not certain the Lord's magicks would reach all the

145

way. The schemes racing through the wizard's mind might not be shared, but Rouwen saw a mutual bond between them for the moment.

He had to kill Kwuway, and he had to steal King Priowe's wizard's spell book. That relieved him of immortality. Then all he had to do was kill Sosler and regain the spell casket and its contents, whatever that might be.

'So simple, so simple,' he mumbled as he walked. Rouwen's mind turned over the possibilities and he came to the sorry realization that he had to return to Gan. Kwuway's chambers were laden with the wizard's relics and artifacts. Somewhere in that tangled nest Rouwen would find the grimoire.

He walked even faster when he saw twin columns of swirling air move in his direction. The Lord had made it clear that he was not to tarry. Getting the grimoire was important, but maintaining the balance of power among nations was even more to the Lord's liking.

A few yards from shore Rouwen saw a tiny figure rise up and brandish a sword. He touched the dagger in its sheath, then found the poisoned dagger tucked away safely beneath his tunic. These were pitiful weapons against a sword, but he would fight as hard as he must to win. Rouwen dared not stop or veer away from the half-concealed warrior on the shore without risking either the Lord's Legion of the Air coming ever closer behind or the sudden cessation of the spell holding him above the voracious poisonous fishes.

Rouwen rushed forward, drawing his dagger. His feet crunched against rocky shore and he yelled as he raced to battle. He started to thrust when the figure rose in front of him – and he stayed his stroke.

'Nibbles!'

'Ah, friend, what a tale you must have to relate,' the old thief said, lowering the sword and resting on the pommel after he had placed the point against the ground. 'I've had my share of adventures while you were away, but nothing like you must have experienced, eh?'

'How many adventures could you have had?' scoffed Rouwen, happy to see the lying old thief again.

'How much living can be squeezed into two weeks?'

'What are you saying?' Rouwen dropped to his knees and rummaged through Nibbles's new cache of weaponry. Hidden among a salt cedar's gnarled roots he found a light spiked mace made useless by a cracked handle, a chipped battle-ax, four swords of varying quality and enough daggers for a squadron. He quickly selected weapons for himself and decided the rest ought to rust under the tree rather than being hauled any distance.

'What are *you* telling me?' demanded Nibbles. 'The first day I worried that you might be killed instantly and your body would float high on the tide. The second and third and fifth days passed and no sign. I dared hope. I fought with a detachment of Nishor's bullies and even threw in with a band of brigands for a week's looting of two outposts.' Nibbles pointed at the weapons. 'That was my share.'

'You're lying,' Rouwen said, shocked. 'I was gone only a few hours. The sun has hardly moved in the sky!'

'The sun has come and gone sixteen times,' Nibbles countered. 'After the raids on Nishor's outposts, I went into a small town not ten miles away and listened to the soldiers getting drunk. 'Tis not a pretty sight, that. They are pigs and worse, the entire lot of them. I'm proud to say I fought with the brigands against them and turned them from their strong point.'

Rouwen frowned and tried to make sense of his predicament. Nibbles told wild stories but such an outright lie would not be his style. He might embroider a story and make the truth more exciting, but he would never think so little of Rouwen's opinion to tell such a blatant perversion of truth. To Nibbles more than two weeks had passed.

For Brion Rouwen only hours had gone by.

'The Isle of Passing is oddly named,' Rouwen said, distracted from Nibbles's story of fighting drunken soldiers and stealing their gold. 'It might not refer to life as much as it does to time.' The way he had healed, Rouwen thought was speeded by the Lord's spells, or even something inherent in the isle itself. Now he was not so sure. If time passed slowly for whomever walked the island, a day might equal months on the mainland. Rouwen knew what part of his healing had been truly magical. The scars on his belly and back had faded to thin pink lines; that was the Lord's contribution.

What of the strange passage of time? His rejuvenation was what he would have expected after two weeks' recuperation.

'You look distracted, friend,' said Nibbles, eyeing him closely. 'Are you ensorcelled by the Lord? Are you forced to do his insane bidding?'

'Our needs coincide strangely,' Rouwen said distantly. 'He will aid me if I kill Kwuway and Sosler and work to put Sorinne onto the Gannian throne.'

'How convenient,' Nibbles said sarcastically. 'Why would a

powerful wizard, one controlling life and death, put forth such a plan so congruent with your own?'

'Coincidences happen,' Rouwen said.

His only answer was a disdainful snort from the old thief. Nibbles came around and hunkered down next to him.

'You must tell me every detail of your trip to the Isle of Passing.'

'So you can weave it into your own tales?' Rouwen laughed. He looked toward the peaceful emerald isle and no longer saw the swirling airborne guardians on the water's surface. Without trying it, he knew walking back to the island was no longer possible. Both guardians and escape spell had vanished as completely as the Lord himself.

'Then I shall tell you what I have overheard,' Nibbles said. 'The plan to kill is a good one. He works feverishly to overthrow your King Priowe.'

'Not my king,' Rouwen countered. 'Priowe is no longer my liege.'

'The Gannian king, then,' Nibbles said impatiently. The small thief fingered a dagger he had drawn. He began stabbing it repeatedly into the ground as if he killed giants with every thrust. 'Kwuway has returned with Sosler, and Priowe knows nothing of their treachery. Nishor is preparing to launch a fierce attack against Gan – and it will succeed.'

'Sosler will withdraw the troops from the Demon's Throat and let the invaders flood into Valley Gan,' Rouwen said tiredly. 'This will be the signal to slay Priowe.'

'Are your Intrepids so stupid as not to notice?' asked Nibbles. 'Sosler plays a clever game, and he would not want to be at Nishor's mercy should he let his own army be destroyed.'

'So you believe the real farce will be played out at Castle Gan?'

'Assassination, perhaps, but Sosler has had other chances. I think he plans to discredit Priowe's ability. Driving him insane with rage and grief after losing both wife and Captain of the Intrepid Guard might go far to forcing Priowe into unsound decisions.'

'Sosler and Kwuway gain favor if Priowe becomes too outrageous in his rule,' Rouwen said thoughtfully, resting his chin in a cupped hand. 'That is possible, and it would leave them in charge within the valley.'

'They cannot trust Nishor any more than they trust each other,' Nibbles pointed out. 'This is a game with high stakes. They want not only Gan but Mion as well – and Sosler would not allow a fool like Nishor to be his king. Ever.'

148

'What of Drioway?' Rouwen wondered aloud. He shook off such guesswork. He had to return to Castle Gan because Kwuway, Sosler and the spell casket would be there.

'You mentioned a way under the Shield Mountains,' Nibbles said. 'Can you find it once more?'

Brion Rouwen shivered uncontrollably. The thought of passing under the massive mountain chain and again experiencing the dreams and sobbing importuning of souls lost on their journey to Mount Glid frightened him more than the thought of enduring eternal life.

'I can't go that way again,' Rouwen said. 'But I don't know how else to return.' His tactics were clear – once he got into Castle Gan. Getting there might prove impossible.

16

Stealing the Grimoire

Every minute on the road back to Gan caused Brion Rouwen to fear more that he would never be able to gain entry to the land of his birth. He and Nibbles passed companies of Mionese troopers, marching, drilling, patrolling. They carried rusted swords and feeble crossbows and more than a few sported lances that would have caused any Gannian soldier to break out in loud laughter – but the sheer number of the men worried Rouwen.

King Nishor mustered a large enough army to swarm into a leaderless, disheartened Gan and wrest control from the few soldiers competent enough to take command. And Castle Gan? He worried more of rot from within than any threat the Mionese army posed to the stolid fortress forged of steel and sacred white stone from the base of Mount Glid.

Would Sosler order the gates to be opened to the invading army or would he have a better plan?

Rouwen doubted the treacherous duke wanted Nishor that close to the Gannian throne, with or without a large army at his back. Sosler might offer the castle to the King of Mion as settlement, then betray him. Or Sosler might lure the Mionese army into the Demon's Throat and destroy them totally. Nothing Rouwen had seen promised a legion capable of real conquest of a tenaciously held Gan.

'Dishearten the king, force him into poor choices, decimate the army through careful assassinations and make it look like Priowe's fault,' Rouwen thought aloud. 'Then Nishor's army is destroyed in the Throat, leaving Mion unguarded and at Sosler's mercy.'

'Do not forget Kwuway,' cautioned Nibbles, riding alongside and trying vainly to look in all directions at once. They had encountered four patrols that day, and it was barely noon. If Rouwen wasn't concerned about losing his life, Nibbles was.

'No, I cannot forget the wizard. Or Duke Drioway. They

150

are an unholy triumvirate thinking to seize two kingdoms for themselves, but three is an unlucky number.'

'So right, friend, so right. One will fall prey to the other pair's plots, and then the real battle begins. Who will survive, eh?' Nibbles reined back and pointed. Rouwen nodded absently, having already seen the dust cloud rising in the distance. They had made a zigzagging progress back into Mion and across the barren kingdom to reach the foothills of the Shield Mountains. This close to the Demon's Throat meant dozens of scouting patrols, both from within Gan and by the invading Mionese soldiers. The battle lines were yet to be drawn, but the threat of the forthcoming fight was an electric tension in the air.

'We get closer to the Throat before we camp,' Rouwen decided. He pressed his luck to the limit, but since leaving the Lord of Death and Life's island he had felt time was lamentably short for those he cared about most.

Sorinne! The people of Valley Gan!

'That is not wise, unless you mean to bait them into fighting each other,' Nibbles said. He jerked his thumb behind to indicate a galloping patrol rapidly overtaking them.

'Gannians in front, Mionese behind,' said Rouwen. 'Let them collide while we rest our horses. They are fine coursers and deserve the best before our dash through the Throat.'

Rouwen knew several ways to sneak past the guards along the narrow pass – or thought he did. He had sent his Intrepids against Sosler's troopers many times in practice skirmishes. Always Sosler had demanded a full frontal assault, which was easily won. Twice Rouwen had used stealth and twice had got men through the gorge without detection. Still, escaping Gan might prove easier than attempting to slip into the heavily guarded valley, and Rouwen had never tried that route.

'There's a convenient niche in the rock,' Nibbles said. 'Do we try for it or die out here on the road?'

'I cannot die,' Rouwen grumbled. 'But that doesn't mean I want to be run through again and again. That hurts.'

Nibbles looked at him from the corner of his eye and shivered. The runty thief bent low over the neck of his horse and urged the animal to as much speed as possible. Rouwen followed more slowly, wary of any trap toward which they might ride. He had set up his share of traps. This carried all the earmarks of an ambush worthy of either side in the coming conflict.

Nibbles thundered through and vanished almost instantly, taking a sharp right turn. Rouwen walked his horse between the tall rocks, wary of any lurking men with crossbows on either side.

Seeing nothing suspicious, he turned after Nibbles and found the small thief sawing at his horse's reins, trying to turn the balking animal's face.

'It's a dead end,' cried Nibbles. 'We have to get out or we're trapped! Never, not since my days riding with two headless demons and a brigand out of Squanno have I done anything this stupid.'

'Calm yourself, Nibbles,' urged Rouwen. 'The two groups of riders might see one another and either engage in combat or simply join forces and take a rest. They weren't following us.' Rouwen turned his horse and started back when he heard echoes coming down the narrow gap he had just traversed.

Riders had followed them.

Caught between the high rocks, Rouwen knew he could never fight his way out. He held up his hand to quiet Nibbles. Rouwen's heart raced as he watched two riders pass in front of him, never once looking down the tight channel holding Rouwen and Nibbles. He waited several seconds for more riders. When they did not pass, he rode forward and craned to see the riders. He did not recognize their uniforms and assumed they must be Mionese troopers.

'Specials,' murmured Nibbles. 'I hate them!'

'Where do they hail from? Tachre?'

'What are you saying? They guard the Demon's Throat! Those are soldiers on *your* side of the pass.'

Rouwen frowned. He had never seen those uniforms before, yet Nibbles identified them easily. And what were Specials? He asked the thief.

'They roam the foothills of the Shield Mountains, rounding up peasants and chasing them away – the ones they don't rob and murder. Killers, the whole damned lot!'

Rouwen realized he had centered too much of his attention on the Intrepid Guard and too little beyond the walls of Castle Gan. The plot to overthrow King Priowe must go back months or even years. This speculation did little to cheer Rouwen. He wasn't fighting a plot Sosler and Kwuway had just contrived, but he worried that he should have been more attentive to what went on in the entire kingdom.

Berating himself for doing his duty too well and not overstepping the bounds of his responsibility as Captain of the Intrepid Guard did little to extricate him and Nibbles from their current predicament. He saw nothing of the two Specials and turned to retrace his way out of the tumble of rocks.

'Take care, friend,' Nibbles cautioned. 'We are close to the

Throat. Any combat will bring down the entire roving band of soldiers from the pass.'

Rouwen had no experience with such patrols. He had always thought Gan's sovereignty ended at the outer gates of the Demon's Throat. He rode forward, then reined back. The two groups he had spied earlier were locked in a fight that caused a cloud of dust to rise fifty feet into the air. He heard the loud battle cries and wounded horses shrieking in pain.

'That way,' Nibbles said, pointing toward the Throat. 'If you know a way in, we can slip through while all attention is focused on that skirmish.'

Rouwen nodded briskly and put his heels to his courser's flanks. The horse bolted forward, but Rouwen slowed to a trot and finally a walk as he neared the forts mounted on either side of the heavy gate guarding the narrow passage into the Kingdom of Gan. The weak spots he had hoped to exploit were closed. His Intrepids might have worked their way out of Gan using those routes, but he could never exploit them to enter. Either Sosler was cagier than he thought, or his officers strove to enhance the Throat's defensibility – and had succeeded.

'There's no way I can use the routes I'd considered,' Rouwen said, wheeling his horse around.

'There must be some way in,' Nibbles complained. 'I know how to get into Gan, but not with such security. Look! They search everyone entering.'

Rouwen had seen the heavily armed troops stopping wagons laden with trade goods and searching them thoroughly. An extra needle would never be smuggled into Gan after such scrutiny. It was as if the army had already gone on a war footing.

'I won't use the tunnel under the mountains,' Rouwen said. Somewhere in his recurrent nightmares had come an encounter with his brother's shade – and Adan blamed him for his cursed demise. To face Adan's ghost was more than he could bear.

'What choice do we have? We'll never get inside just by asking.'

'Oh?' A plan came to Rouwen, one he disliked but was far preferable to enduring the wails and whines of lost souls locked in the cavernous passage under the Shield Mountains. 'There might be another path for us, if we show daring.' Rouwen thought for a moment and softly added, 'Or are desperate enough.'

'If we'd used this secret tunnel of yours into Gan, we'd have had to fight our way through, no doubt,' Nibbles rambled on. 'Kwuway must know of it – and surely Duke Sosler does. Why not guard it now that you're free? They might think you would sell them out to, oh, the Magister of Inbion, mayhaps. The Magister has always had designs on Gan, more so than Nishor.'

'We must find those two soldiers – the Specials,' Rouwen said. 'They will be our way into the Demon's Throat.'

'What? We bribe them? We can never be sure they are honest crooks and will stay bought,' protested Nibbles. 'Many's the time I bribed an official only to have him turn on me. Trust me on this, friend, bribery works less often than it seems to those in power. Why, once I convinced this saucy wench to . . .'

Rouwen shut out the ribald tale of bribery and sex to fashion his plan. He touched his belly. It quivered under his fingers, but Rouwen knew there was no other quick way into Gan. Nishor hunted him in Mion, and Kwuway and Sosler would be alert for his presence on either side of the Throat, not sure that the sniffer-snakes had completed their mission. He had to enter Castle Gan before any knew he was nearby, if he wanted to succeed.

In its ironic way, his plan played on the spell he sought to remove.

'There they are,' he warned Nibbles. 'They are coming from the narrow draw. We must hurry if we want to ambush them.'

'Ambush them?' Nibbles called, startled out of his long-winded recitation. 'I thought we were going to bribe them into looking the other way as we sneaked into Gan.'

'Prepare for battle,' Rouwen ordered. He felt a moment's nervousness that vanished as he drew his sword. As always, once his blade met his opponent's he would calmly counter every lunge and riposte. He lowered his blade for combat and put his heels into the courser's flanks, guiding the horse directly at the Special on his left.

The soldier stared dumbly at his attacker, not understanding his danger. Rouwen's sword spitted him like a pig, and the soldier died before he understood what happened. As the dead man twisted, his falling body yanked the sword from Rouwen's grip. Rouwen rushed past, grabbing for his dagger. He pulled his horse to a halt and turned to join battle with the second soldier.

To his surprise, Nibbles had already dispatched the man. Not having the reach to use his sword properly, the small thief had ridden close to his opponent and tossed his dagger with deadly accuracy, the tip burying itself far into the soldier's throat.

'So?' asked Nibbles. 'Now that we have killed these two and can expect to have the entire Gannian army on our necks, what do we do now?'

'Strip off their uniforms.' Rouwen trotted to where the soldier's horse stood, uneasily pawing at the rocky ground. He grabbed the reins and dismounted, gentling his new mount.

'We can't get much for them. The buttons are brass and the material is little more than cheap dyed broadcloth,' complained Nibbles. 'The horses are better traded back in Tachre, but getting there might prove difficult. Perhaps I can use a trick I learned while journeying with a caravan of gypsies to the north and . . .'

'The uniform,' insisted Rouwen, going to the man he had run through. He pulled out his sword and cast it aside. His new weapon was still sheathed at the corpse's belt. Rouwen worked hard to get the uniform off the body, finding it more difficult than he thought. He considered using his dagger to hack off an arm and leg and speed the process, but he decided against it.

He was dressed in the too-small uniform by the time Nibbles had worried off his soldier's trousers. Rouwen cut the sleeves and legs to accommodate his greater height and bulk, then went to help Nibbles put on his too-large uniform.

'Put it on over your clothing,' Rouwen decided. The old thief still looked emaciated and worn, perfect for the role Rouwen intended for him.

'It fills out the cloth somewhat, but I was never destined to be a soldier. I remember once when I enlisted in the Freeman's Army, I . . .'

'Listen closely,' Rouwen said. 'We will ride closer to the Demon's Throat, posing as Specials . . .'

'They'll recognize us. They must know their comrades-in-arms!' protested Nibbles.

'Silence!' barked Rouwen. He settled himself again and continued. 'We will get within a short distance of the main gate. You will begin calling out that your sergeant is mortally wounded and that he must be taken to the castle for immediate attention. Accept nothing less than an escort into Castle Gan.'

'Ah, I see. You will pretend to be injured,' Nibbles said, seeing the sergeant's star insignia. 'Will this work? Are you actor enough to convince them to get castle chirurgeons to look at you?'

'We'll see,' Rouwen said, settling his mind for what had to be done. 'You must not leave my side, but your appearance is enough that they will want you to be tended also. Give them no direct facts concerning our ambush. Be vague.'

'How we, as soldiers, were attacked? Yes, yes, friend, I see the plan. But it is daring – and risky.'

Rouwen listened to Nibbles practice his lies and knew none

155

of the stories would be used. They rode closer to the towering gates and, as they drew near to the patrols, they began to attract attention. Rouwen guessed that Specials did not ride alone as they did and had no reason to enter the Demon's Throat.

He halted and let Nibbles ride a few yards farther, momentarily blocking the gate guards' view of him. Rouwen paused for a moment, then used his dagger on himself. He drove it deep into his guts and pulled laterally a few inches, opening himself up enough to cause a torrent of blood and intestines to spill out. He grunted and doubled over.

'Brion, we – by the demons, no!' Nibbles raced back to his side and put a thin arm around him to keep Rouwen from falling from his saddle. 'You shouldn't have done this. You'll surely bleed to death!'

'Get as much blood on your own uniform as you can,' Rouwen gasped out. 'And do not leave my side. I cannot stay conscious long. Give them the tall tale of your life!'

Rouwen slumped forward and almost passed out. Through gathering darkness and a roar in his ears he saw and heard soldiers rushing to his aid. Nibbles babbled out a story of brigands and Mionese soldiers ambushing them and being gored by rabid duohorns and other improbable tales.

The last thing Rouwen remembered before slipping into warm unconsciousness was being laid flat on a wagon bed and rattling through the heavy gates usually closed across the Demon's Throat.

Soft breeze caressed his face, followed by a teasing touch more ghostly than real. Rouwen stirred, moaned in pain and fought to focus his eyes. He let out a gasp of horror when he saw the wraith hovering whitely above him. He quieted when he realized a thin curtain blew back from an open window and tickled his face.

Turning his head to one side, he saw he was in an infirmary. It took several seconds for him to be sure he had reached Castle Gan. Once he had been sequestered here for injuries during practice and, more often than he could remember, he had visited injured Intrepids given over to chirurgeons' care.

Exulting, he struggled to sit up. Pain lanced into his belly, almost causing him to pass out again. Fighting away the dancing edges of blackness, Rouwen recovered enough to roll to one side. He touched his stomach and found the area covered with clean bandage. He smiled. Gan had always provided the best in medical treatment.

He seemed to be alone in the infirmary, which pleased him. It made his mission easier if he didn't have to sneak past surgeons or attendants. Rouwen rolled to his other side and jumped when he saw someone sitting just inches away.

'So you are recovering, eh?' Nibbles asked. 'It's about time. You frightened me with that dagger trick. How much you bled! And your innards were spilling forth. The guards at the gate paid me no attention, even to ask how you had come to be so severely injured. I was ready to tell them about our dangerous mission against a dozen Mionese brigands who . . .'

'How long?' Rouwen gasped out. His mouth carried a metallic taste, and his tongue had swelled from lack of water. Reaching out, he took a small cup sitting on a low table by the bed. He sipped and almost gagged. Whatever fluid was in the cup, it wasn't water.

'That's medicine your chirurgeon prescribed. I sampled it. Dog piss, that's what it is. I'm amazed he hasn't killed more than he's saved, but then he was reticent about discussing his qualifications and medical expertise. I saw a surgeon once who patched animal parts onto humans, creating . . .'

'How long?'

'Oh, how long have you lain abed while I fought to keep from being sent back to duty as a Special? It has been almost ten days. When the sun sets, that will mark exactly ten days since entering Castle Gan.'

'A day or more to reach the castle and ten days here?' Rouwen fought to drive out the fog from his brain. Dying repeatedly took its toll on him mentally as well as physically. Every time he recovered he seemed a little less than he had been before. He vowed never again to use such drastic methods to achieve his goal.

'That's about it. The food in this so-called hospital is terrible. Eating rats gives a better meal. Why, I once lived off nothing but plankton while adrift on the Smoking Sea, waiting for some passing ship to rescue me.'

'Weapons,' Rouwen said, croaking out his heartfelt desire. 'I need a weapon to kill Kwuway, Sosler and Priowe.'

'You may thank your quick-fingered friend for this.' Nibbles reached under his robes and drew out the poison-filled glass dagger. Turning it hilt first, he passed it to Rouwen. The former captain took it in shaky hands and relished the coolness of its handle before slipping it between his flesh and the bandage holding his guts in.

'Thank you, friend,' Rouwen said. He sat up, dizzy and nauseated. 'What have you learned of Kwuway?'

'He is in Castle Gan. More than this small fact, I have learned nothing. His travels are never mentioned, even in rumor or gossip. It is as if he does not matter.'

'And Duke Sosler?'

'The duke is not within the castle walls now,' Nibbles said, but Rouwen detected some uncertainty about this. 'He spends more time crisscrossing Gan to be sure the army is at its peak of training and readiness. Rumors of war with Mion abound.'

'So Sosler and Kwuway are playing that card – or does this come from Priowe?'

'Who can say where a rumor starts, though it usually ends in my ear. I miss nothing, friend, and I relate it all to you. Spending time in an empty infirmary is boring. With no one to talk to, I have been driven to crazy lengths to amuse myself.'

'Is Kwuway in his quarters now?'

'You think to attack him so soon after regaining your senses?' Nibbles shook his head. 'The food is poor and there is no wine, but it might help you recover your strength. You have lain in a coma for more than a week. Your blood ruined a perfectly good uniform, good except for that unfortunate hole you cut in it when you killed the former occupant, and you need to recuperate more.'

Rouwen saw his friend's point, but time weighed on him. He could not get the Lord's threat from his mind. The Lord of Death and Life had demanded the grimoire and obviously wanted it as soon as possible. In that, Rouwen could agree. The sooner Kwuway died, the sooner one curse would be lifted from his shoulders.

'You're sure Sosler is not in the castle?'

Nibbles shrugged and said, 'I am not privy to all the high command's movements. Priowe is here and rants constantly. I do believe they have driven him to the point of insanity. Should he die, he will never find a decent place in Paradise.'

Rouwen had to admit that his former king's loss of reason presented him with a moral dilemma. The insane were never admitted to Paradise, their souls condemned to wander the periphery of Paradise forever, always trying to enter and always being denied. It was worse being damned, of course, not being permitted to enter and starving constantly just yards away from bountiful meals. The insane at least were fed scraps for all eternity.

'I have to do this now,' Rouwen insisted. He stood on shaky legs. He went to a closet and rummaged through it, hunting for a uniform. The one he had worn was long discarded, but he found a peasant's garb that suited him well. He slipped into the trousers and tunic and found boots that were just a trifle too large.

'You wear clothing from a chirurgeon's failure,' Nibbles pointed out. 'That's unlucky.'

'It's even unluckier being the king's wizard,' Rouwen said. He positioned the poisoned dagger where he could reach it when he found Kwuway. 'Stay here and keep any search from being mounted should they discover me gone.'

'And then what do I do?'

'I'll return for you – or not.'

'Never have I seen a man so intent on finding his own twisted way to death,' Nibbles said, shaking his head. He smiled suddenly and said, 'May luck dog your steps, friend.'

Rouwen left the infirmary, alert for guards or attendants coming to check the progress of their patients. The castle was strangely deserted, even the traditional points where Rouwen always posted guards. Post after post was deserted. He made his way up broad steps to the level where Kwuway had his quarters. Increasingly wary, he stopped and peered out a window.

From this vantage he saw the distant curve of battlements and realized why the corridors were not being actively patrolled. From the flash of light against armor and weapons, every Intrepid in Gan must be on the walls as if awaiting imminent attack. He wondered what had roused them since Nibbles had mentioned nothing of an alert.

Rouwen gave the old thief this much credit. If a rumor roamed the corridors of the castle, it would eventually reach his sharp ears. What he had seen outside the Demon's Throat more than ten days earlier did not indicate any buildup of Mionese troopers capable of threatening Castle Gan.

'Training?' he wondered aloud. He shook his head. He had always kept his guardsmen well honed for any fight. Using them on the walls to defend the castle was a final line of security because they were better used fighting door to door within the castle keep should the need arise.

He guessed that his banishment and shunning had created a power vacuum in the Intrepid, one Sosler exploited now. Even if the Lord Protector of the Realm had not assumed control of the king's finest soldiers, he might be able to divert whomever did command them to his own ends.

Rouwen hurried along the corridor, aware of his own weakness. Stabbing himself in the belly had been necessary to gain entry to the castle, but it debilitated him now. He needed every iota of strength and quickness to kill a wizard as wily as Kwuway.

Rouwen stopped in front of the wizard's quarters, drew the poisoned glass dagger and prepared for the death stroke.

Knocking loudly, he waited for Kwuway to open the door. And Rouwen waited and waited until he realized no one was inside the room.

He tried the latch and cautiously opened the door, peering around the edge into the room.

'Kwuway?' he called. No response greeted him. He slid into the room and closed the door behind him. For a moment Brion Rouwen did not know what to do. He was alone in the wizard's quarters.

The wizard's unguarded quarters. That thought roared DANGER in his mind. Kwuway was suspicious and reclusive. Why would he wander off and not lock his door – or leave some magical guardian?

Rouwen skirted the room, alert for traps. To his uneducated eyes, there were no apparent traps set for an intruder. Bolder, he went to the wizard's shelves and poked through the contents. Dust made him sneeze but nothing else deterred him from touching the rows of magical implements.

A slow smile came to his lips. There might be a penalty paid by Kwuway for laying such potent spells on Rouwen. Other magicks might not work properly, blocked by the pair of spells holding him enslaved to despair. It was a wild hope but one which Rouwen decided to exploit, if true.

'The grimoire!' he cried when he saw the wizard's cluttered worktable. He went to the table and reached for the book of spells.

Rouwen hesitated when a tingling reached up his arm and shocked him lightly throughout his body, but he noticed a particular churning in his belly – the spot last touched by Kwuway's terrible spell of immortality.

Having nothing to lose, Rouwen touched the grimoire, felt the soft vellum of its pages, experienced a curious thrill as he touched the green-glowing letters on the pages of arcane lore and finally let out a cry of delight as he closed the book and tucked it under his arm.

'I have the grimoire the Lord needs to lift my other spell,' Rouwen whispered to himself. Then he thought it might benefit him to study the grimoire. If the youthful-appearing Lord of Death and Life could use the book of spells, so might he. Rouwen started to open the book when he heard loud voices in the corridor outside Kwuway's quarters.

He recognized the wizard's angry tones and looked around for a

160

spot to launch his killing attack. He ducked behind a poorly hung tapestry on the wall nearest the door. Peering out from under the threadbare cloth, Rouwen saw Kwuway enter with an assistant mage. He clutched the poisoned dagger, ready to remove one of Kwuway's curses by slaying the wizard.

17

Love Kills

Kwuway's assistant moved to block any attack Rouwen might make. He shifted, hoping that the two did not see the tapestry stirring. Clutching the poisoned dagger, he waited for his chance.

'Such carelessness ought to be punished,' Kwuway said, 'but these are extraordinary times and I can overlook your malfeasance. Have you prepared the spells for use in the Demon's Throat?'

'They are ready,' the assistant said, grateful to escape his master's wrath this time.

'We will need them to ward off the Flame Specter in the next few months should it escape its bonds,' said Kwuway, more to himself than to his assistant. 'We can escape Gan, should it be destroyed by the Flame Specter, then return after my magicks have contained it again.'

Rouwen hesitated making his attack. Kwuway had mentioned the Flame Specter again, a name that provoked anxiety in both Gan's wizard and in the Lord of Death and Life. The interest they showed made Rouwen wonder how he could turn this Flame Specter to his own benefit. And Kwuway spoke as if all within Valley Gan would die, if the mysterious being won freedom for even a short period.

Freedom from what? Brion Rouwen had never heard of it before Kwuway's mention.

'Are the ward spells powerful enough for that?' asked Kwuway's assistant. 'I have pored over the ancient lore and find no indication that they would hold back an entity as powerful as the Flame Specter.'

'Tending to the Flame Specter is not your primary duty,' Kwuway said sharply.

Each time the name was mentioned, Rouwen felt the grimoire tucked under his arm quiver and begin to warm a little more. The final mention of the Flame Specter produced such heat that his inner arm blistered. With a barely suppressed cry of pain, he dropped the grimoire.

'What's that?' demanded the wizard, swinging around to see what had caused the noise. 'That's my grimoire!'

'Intruder!' cried the assistant, rushing for the door. 'Guards, to Kwuway's quarters! Guards!'

Rouwen wasted no time pushing aside the tapestry and hurling himself at the wizard. Kwuway moved faster than Rouwen would have thought possible – or perhaps his own weakness betrayed him again. He stabbed with the dagger and found only empty air.

Dancing around his worktable, Kwuway stopped and stared at his attacker. 'You!' he exclaimed. 'How did you return to Castle Gan? The entire valley is sealed tighter than a wine jug!'

'I will kill you,' Rouwen promised. The former captain saw that flight wasn't possible for the wizard. That meant Kwuway had to fight or resort to his magicks. Knowing the wizard as he did, Rouwen prepared to endure any onslaught of magic that might be hurled at him. He had already been twice cursed. Anything more would be as a drop of water added to the ocean.

'I misjudged you, Captain Rouwen,' said Kwuway, moving to his right to keep the worktable between him and his adversary. 'We can come to a meeting of the minds. An alliance is to our mutual benefit. It is possible that your position in the new kingdom ought to be higher than it was in the old.'

'You cursed me twice. You must die.'

Kwuway heard the deadly intent in the captain's voice. He shook his shaggy head and said, 'That will not release the spells on you. If anyone told you this, you are sadly mistaken. The spells will remain forever. You will be forever trapped and forced to endure . . .'

'Silence,' hissed Rouwen. 'The Lord of Death and Life told me your death would release me!'

'The Lord! Why, that treacherous . . .'

Rouwen made his attack, grabbing with his left hand to pull Kwuway to him and stabbing out with the glass dagger. The wizard jerked hard and ripped his tunic sleeve to win free. His lips moved but no sounds came out. Rouwen renewed his attack, jumping atop the worktable and kicking hard. His foot smashed into Kwuway's chest and sent the wizard reeling across the room. Kwuway crashed to the littered floor, but his lips kept moving.

And Brion Rouwen began to smolder. His arm had blistered when the grimoire heated. Now his entire body threatened to burst into intense flame. His clothing popped out in tiny sparks, and the skin beneath turned black as Kwuway continued to weave his spell.

'You cannot die, but you can suffer,' Kwuway called triumphantly, getting to his feet when Rouwen stopped to swat at the tiny fires appearing all over his body. 'And suffer you will, for all eternity!'

Rouwen's eyes welled with tears that rolled down his charring cheeks, leaving behind salty trails that stung. Fingers hardly able to close, Rouwen realized he had only one chance.

From atop the table he dived in a flat arc, the poison-filled glass blade held in front of him like a ship's prow. Kwuway screeched when the dagger plunged deep into his chest. He tried to pluck it free, but Rouwen twisted savagely, breaking the glass blade.

'You, no, you don't know what you've done!' Kwuway clawed futilely at his chest, then tried to utter a new spell. Rouwen stopped the chant with a hard fist to the wizard's mouth. He felt teeth crunch into the wizard's face and bones break, but he felt strangely good about the single punch.

His body no longer smoldered and his skin had ceased to blister and burst into flame. But the incredible weakness assailing him caused his knees to buckle.

'You fool, you accursed fool,' Kwuway muttered. Then the wizard died.

Brion Rouwen's entire body shook as if he was caught in the jaws of a giant hunting dog. The tremors increased and razor-edged purple sparks leaped from toes and nose and fingers to arc towards the wizard's grimoire. The actinic charge flowed from Rouwen and entered the book of spells on the floor across the room in a torrent that died as suddenly as it had started.

Sweating profusely, drained of all energy, Rouwen could only lie on his back and stare at the ceiling. Beside him sprawled the dead wizard, and across the room he heard the grimoire crackling and popping with the force that had left him on Kwuway's death.

Unable to move or even turn his head, Rouwen heard the door creaking open. In panic he tried to move and found himself unable to stir even the smallest muscle. The wizard's assistant had returned with the guards!

Rouwen closed his eyes and tried to compose himself. He was vulnerable now to a dagger thrust or a sword's slash. He could die. His only regret was not bringing deadly justice to Duke Sosler, Drioway and King Priowe. Sosler had destroyed him, and Priowe had meekly authorized more than the banishment of a loyal retainer. He was responsible for betraying his entire kingdom.

And perhaps he should have killed King Nishor for his evil ways, too. There were so many and he had done so little. At least, he could die knowing he had not harmed Sorinne.

'Brion?' came a soft voice. 'Are you dead again?' Nibbles shuffled across the floor and stared down at his supine friend. He poked Rouwen in the ribs with the toe of his boot, and Rouwen stirred a little.

'Nibbles, help me,' he shouted. Only faint croaking emerged from his lips, but the old thief saw that his friend lived and helped him to sit with his back against the worktable.

'You killed the old bastard. Death to all wizards,' said Nibbles, spitting on Kwuway's corpse. The spittle sizzled and popped when it struck the wizard's dead flesh. 'There's never any good done by wizards. None.'

'I killed him, and one spell is gone. I felt such a draining when he died.'

'Are you sure?'

'I don't want to test it to find out,' Rouwen said, smiling weakly. 'Help me stand.' Nibbles tried but wasn't strong enough to support Rouwen's weight. Rouwen collapsed to a low stool and tried to catch his breath. He wasn't sure if loss of blood and poor recovery from his self-induced wound was responsible, or if the removal of Kwuway's immortality were on him now. The room spun in crazy circles and he had to hold down his gorge.

But he had killed the wizard! That one thought gave him strength.

'The grimoire! Get it for me, will you?' He pointed to the spell book propped against the far wall under the tapestry. It now looked like any other book. It no longer glowed with its own light, and Rouwen wondered if it ever would again now that its owner had been murdered. Perhaps in the Lord's hand it might regain its power.

Somehow, that thought did not thrill Rouwen as much as it frightened him.

'The least you could do is thank me,' Nibbles said tartly.

'For helping me?'

'For following you! I killed that silly wizardling who came boiling out of here. A quick thrust to the throat, and he was drowning in his own blood. He never got to the guards.'

'Good, good,' Rouwen said, his mind racing. Strength returned to his limbs but slowly, too slowly! 'I learned nothing from Kwuway before he died.'

'So what was there to learn? He would only have lied.'
Nibbles wandered around the small quarters, filching interesting
or valuable items and sticking them into his pockets.

'I need to find Sosler. He has the spell casket. Without it, the
Lord cannot remove the second curse placed on me.'

'Sosler, you say? If your apology had been more heartfelt,
I might have been inclined to discuss this with you, but
. . .' Nibbles gurgled as Rouwen surged from the stool and
throttled him with one hand. Rouwen's fingers almost circled
the scrawny throat.

'What do you know of Sosler?'

'So, your strength returns, eh?' Nibbles pushed away when
Rouwen regained control of his emotions. He had to admit he
was stronger. Still, he would have to use stealth rather than make
a frontal assault when he faced Sosler.

'Tell me!' Rouwen's rage burned away weakness and brought
him to his feet. He worried only that he would not have the might
needed to kill Sosler when the time came.

'I overheard a guard talking,' Nibbles said, stepping back to
survey Rouwen. 'You are a fright. Your clothing is all singed,
and there are unsightly blisters on your arms and face, but then
I have been in lands where such disfigurement was considered a
sexual stimulant. I . . .'

'Sosler!' Rouwen roared. 'Tell me about him or you'll lie beside
Kwuway!'

'Such anger,' Nibbles said, shaking his head. The small thief's
eyes danced, though, as he continued. 'The duke has been
bracing the troops at the kingdom's perimeter and has only just
now announced his return to Castle Gan. Within the hour he
ought to be in the king's audience chamber to report on Nishor's
massing of troops at the mouth of the Demon's Throat.'

'I have him!' Rouwen spun around, hefted the grimoire and
swung it like a bludgeon. 'I'll crush his skull like an eggshell,
then get the Lord to lift the final curse from me.'

'An ambitious course of action for one who can hardly stand,'
observed Nibbles. 'I'd say subterfuge is required more than
brazen assault.'

Rouwen sagged as his energy drained from him. His body
had been buffeted by both physical and magical hurricanes. He
needed another week to recover, and he did not have that luxury.
Propping himself up against a straight-backed chair, Rouwen
looked to his friend for support.

'It's important to you, I know. What do you require of
me?'

166

'Princess Sorinne,' said Rouwen. 'She must be protected until I regain the spell casket and have the curse removed.'

'And Priowe?'

'He can die,' Rouwen said without rancor. His opinion of the king was still too fluid for his own liking. The ruler had made bad decisions and must pay for that. Even worse, he was losing the strongest kingdom on the continent to duplicitous deputies. Rouwen glanced at Kwuway, as if expecting the wizard to rise from the dead.

Kwuway's soul was long bound for Mount Glid and whatever Paradise had to offer. Rouwen hoped the wizard was forever doomed to wander the edges of Paradise, eternally starving and beset by biting insects and petty torments that wore on the spirit. Kwuway deserved nothing less than full damnation.

'A uniform,' said Nibbles. 'You look so dashing in an officer's uniform. Let me fetch one for you.'

'Wait!' called Rouwen, but the thief had slipped from Kwuway's quarters and vanished down the corridor. Rouwen looked up and down the hall, worrying that the Intrepids would leave their drill on the battlements and return to their usual posts at any moment. He did not know how long it had taken to slay Kwuway and gain the grimoire, but the Intrepids' stint on the castle walls had not yet ended.

Rouwen ducked back into the wizard's quarters and closed the door until only a thin sliver of light shone past. He pressed hard against the cold stone wall and, from this vantage, peered along the corridor. He was armed only with his fists. Rouwen lifted his arms and experienced the lethargy that had afflicted him after Kwuway's spell had been sucked from his body and reabsorbed by the spell book.

Opening the grimoire, he began reading the illuminated text. The first few pages were warnings against unauthorized use and unacceptable copying. Following these was a statement of creation, declaring all spells original with Kwuway. Rouwen grew tired of the tedious self-praises and flipped faster. The farther into the book he read, the more the letters began to glow. When he reached the last pages, the letters shone with such an intense green that his eyes began watering.

But Rouwen had convinced himself that he could not use the grimoire to lift the curse. A wizard versed in the arcane phrasings and codes Kwuway had used might work for days to prepare the proper potions and decipher the correct incantations and hand gestures.

Rouwen's attention snapped back to the corridor when he

detected furtive movement in the shadows. He blinked and tried to find the source of movement. Only when Nibbles appeared suddenly in front of the door did he make out the old thief and what he carried. Nibbles beamed and showed his four yellowed teeth.

'A lieutenant of the guard,' the thief said proudly, tossing the uniform to Rouwen. 'A demotion, I realize, but still an improvement on that charred peasant's garb you wear so poorly. Do well,' he went on, 'and perhaps you can gain a new promotion.'

'I was to be elevated to third baron at the Spring Festivals,' Rouwen said. He stopped in the middle of putting on the uniform.

'What's wrong?' asked Nibbles, wandering Kwuway's room again, hunting for more trinkets to steal.

'The Spring Festivals should be in full swing now. I saw no sign of them, or of the festivals having been held.' Rouwen shook his head, trying to remember how much time had passed. His sojourn on the Isle of Passing and long recuperation had robbed him of knowing the time of year. It was late spring; he felt that in the growing warmth and greening of the fields.

'So Priowe has called off the festival. That is nothing more than a missed opportunity to pick a few pockets and tup a wench or two.' Nibbles stuffed one last golden cup into his pockets, twisted from side to side to see if the booty clanked and then smiled in satisfaction.

'No, no, the Spring Festivals are the major Gannian celebration and last for a full month. To call them off would require a major threat to the kingdom.'

'Nishor assembles an army on Gan's doorstep. Would this not be a major threat?' Nibbles jumped onto the worktable and squatted down to watch Rouwen finish dressing in the uniform. He nodded in approval. 'You look so dashing with a chest full of medals and that saber swinging at your side.'

'The armament has changed since I left,' Rouwen observed, drawing the saber and looking at the slightly curved blade. He had armed his men with rapiers, not seeing a need for a horseback weapon within the castle walls. This was yet another indication that Sosler changed the Intrepids to a different mission.

A mission of fighting outside Castle Gan.

'He takes yet another protection away from Priowe,' Rouwen mused. 'The king will be stripped of all friends, trusted advisors and guards if this continues.' He reached down and found large pockets on either side, pockets lined with leather for carrying heavy, bulky loads. This was an improvement over the uniforms when he was Captain of the Guard, though why an Intrepid might need such within Castle Gan was a question Rouwen would never see answered.

'You seek Priowe's death. Does it matter if it comes at your hand or Sosler's?'

'I want the duke and the spell casket around his neck,' Rouwen said. 'Did your excursion give you information about his return?'

Nibbles bounced up and down like a wrinkled, frail monkey, then looked squarely at Rouwen as he said quietly, 'Sosler is returned.'

'Why didn't you tell me straight off?' asked Rouwen. He wondered if the thief had been subverted somehow while he had been off stealing the uniform. Then he saw something more in the thief's mien. 'You want me to leave Gan, don't you? Why?'

'I can steal the spell casket from Sosler,' Nibbles said. 'I am good – better than good! Why risk yourself on such a fool's errand?'

'Sosler must pay for what he has done to me and what he is trying to do to the kingdom.'

'Such loyalty,' Nibbles said sarcastically. 'Or is it stupid revenge you seek and nothing more? Can you continue to be so devoted to a kingdom that has done nothing to come to your aid?' Nibbles jumped to the floor and walked over to stare up into Rouwen's gray eyes. 'I can steal the spell casket from Sosler, and you have the grimoire. Is the feel of blood running over your sword hilt so important? Your life in Gan is past.'

'Sorinne,' Rouwen whispered in a voice so low he knew Nibbles couldn't overhear. Aloud, he said, 'There is more for me to do here.'

'So be it.' Nibbles shrugged his thin shoulders and said, 'The duke is scheduled to begin his audience with King Priowe any time now. Swing your sword and thrust your dagger, if you must, but remember that you are no longer impervious to *his* weapons.'

'Thank you for all you've done,' Rouwen said, his mind turning to the fight ahead. He pictured himself swinging into the audience chamber and seeing Sosler standing on the step below the throne, King Priowe seated and looking regal. A single sword thrust to the back would kill Sosler. A dagger thrust would pin Priowe to his throne, leaving Rouwen precious seconds to prise the spell casket out of Duke Sosler's tunic before the guards reacted.

'Speed,' he said, 'is my ally.'

'You have no ally,' Nibbles grumbled. 'You have a mission that will do nothing but kill you.'

'I'll save the kingdom if I dispatch both of them,' Rouwen said, meaning it. He had been muddled in his thinking. He knew now what had to be done and was able to carry through with it.

'The Intrepids still pace the battlements,' Nibbles said as they hurried along the corridor. 'I know nothing of the alarm Sosler raised that keeps them away from their posts within the castle.'

'Priowe's personal guard will attend him,' Rouwen said, considering which officer might be in charge. If any of rank less than captain served Priowe, he could kill a half dozen people in the audience chamber before triggering a reaction. And only one or two of the lieutenants and the captain would respond quickly enough to stop him from killing Priowe.

Sosler would die, no matter who guarded the chamber.

'There it is,' Nibbles said angrily. 'I trust you have changed your mind.' They had arrived at the king's audience chamber. Rouwen had failed before. He would not do so a second time.

'I must do this alone.' Rouwen began steeling himself for the killing to come. This was combat no different from that he had engaged in dozens of times against Gan's enemies. He drew sword and dagger, getting a firm grip on the wire-wrapped hilts.

'I'll slip behind the throne and distract any guards posted behind the king,' Nibbles said. 'Where shall we meet after you've committed this foul deed?'

Rouwen blinked, his thoughts momentarily confused by the question. He had not considered an escape.

'There is a secret passage behind the throne. Take it up to a landing – it appears to be a dead-end. The sconce in the wall turns and opens a new stairway down to the dungeon levels. We can escape that way.'

'Very well. See you in the passage,' Nibbles said.

Rouwen paused for a moment, watching the old thief scurry off like some rat heading for his burrow. Rouwen smiled at Nibbles's back, knowing how much he owed him. Then he took a deep breath, pushed through the hangings and slid along the wall on the side of the audience chamber.

Sosler's voice echoed hollow and distant, and Priowe muttered replies as the former captain peered past the hanging. Four guards at the corners of the room were too far out of position to stop any real attempt to kill either Sosler or Priowe. No one else petitioned Priowe this day. So much the better for Rouwen.

He moved behind the hangings he had always urged Priowe to remove. Now he was glad that the king had forbidden the removal of the tapestries. Rouwen got within ten yards before hearing a disturbance behind the throne.

Nibbles had engaged a guard there. He had to act now.

Rouwen stepped out and began walking briskly across the chamber, not wanting to draw attention away from Nibbles's attack until it was too late to stay his thrust.

Both Sosler and Priowe turned back. Priowe saw Rouwen first. He started to speak but only choking sounds came out. Sosler glanced over his shoulder, did a double take, then shouted a warning at the guards and grabbed for his sword.

That was the mistake Rouwen had anticipated. Sosler might have lived if he had drawn his dagger. He acted too late to use the slashing sword. Rouwen stepped inside the man's reach and thrust with his dagger. He felt the blade glance off a bone and go skittering along the duke's ribcage.

'I'm killed!' shrieked Sosler, falling away. As Sosler twisted in his fall, Rouwen slashed at the duke. He opened the noble's tunic with his cut and caused another thin line of red to open. Amid the flowing blood shone a silver box.

'The spell casket!' crowed Rouwen. He had intended to kill Priowe next and then retrieve the magical container holding his emotions captive, but the sight of his goal caused him to change tactics.

Rouwen dropped to one knee and used his dagger to pull out the spell casket. He sawed savagely at the onyx chain holding the box while Priowe jumped to his feet and bellowed for his guards to attend him.

'Mine!' Rouwen cried, holding the spell casket in his hands. It felt cool to the touch and seemed to quiver with vibrant energy. He traced over the intricate runes engraved on the exterior and wanted to open it to see what lay within. But he remembered the Lord had cautioned against that. Only proper use of Kwuway's grimoire and the releasing spell could return Rouwen's ability to love without killing.

He tucked the spell casket into his tunic and swung around, sword point aimed at King Priowe. His former liege was fumbling for a jeweled dagger at his side, but the weapon was purely ceremonial and had a dull edge. It might hurt if Priowe stabbed with it, but Rouwen didn't think the dagger could slay.

Not like the saber he held.

'You should have listened to me when I tried to tell you the truth about Diarra and me – and *his* involvement,' Rouwen said, the words burning his tongue. 'You should have been a king and trusted. You should have been a man and loved!'

'Guards!' Priowe's voice firmed as he faced Rouwen squarely.

This made killing him easier, Rouwen thought. To slay a coward was a waste of effort.

Rouwen advanced, only to see a blur out of the corner of his eye. He sensed trouble and did a quickstep forward, thinking to spit Priowe. Rouwen was hit so hard from the side he was knocked off his feet. He went sliding across the floor, spinning toward the main entrance.

He fought to swing his sword at his attacker and failed. He slashed and cut and failed to find any vital point. Only when his opponent released his grip on Rouwen's legs did he wriggle free. He cocked back his dagger for a killing stroke, then stopped.

'Nibbles!' he exclaimed. 'What are you doing? You saved his life!'

Rouwen looked toward the throne and saw Priowe standing in the center of three guards, with more pouring into the chamber from behind the throne. And even worse, Sosler struggled to sit up, clutching at his bloody cuts. From the way the duke bellowed orders, Rouwen knew he had not inflicted any fatal wounds.

'I've failed and you stopped me. I could have killed him!'

'Brion, she is back there. She was waiting to see her father.' The old thief got to his knees.

'What? Sorinne?'

'Yes!'

Rouwen went cold inside. He might have killed Sorinne's father, only to have her come out and see the deed. That wasn't as bad as what the curse might have done to her. He could have killed her as he had killed Adan.

'Thank you, Nibbles, thank you,' he said, helping the old thief to his feet. 'How can I . . .' Rouwen's eyes widened in horror when he saw what was happening. Nibbles's flesh was boiling, just as Adan's had. In the moment of saving Sorinne, Nibbles had caused his own death.

Brion Rouwen had loved too well once again.

He looked up in horror when he heard Sorinne call out, 'Father, what is happening?' The lovely princess moved around the throne to stand at her father's side.

172

18

Death of Hope

Rouwen looked from Sorinne to the sizzling skeleton on the floor in front of him. Nibbles would never again brag about his fantastic exploits. He might have travelled the world over and endured unknown travails and pleasures, but he had met his end at Rouwen's hand – at the hand of Kwuway and Sosler and Priowe.

Rouwen's hand tightened on the sword handle but he knew he would never reach the throne to finish the job he had begun. Too many guards were racing toward him – and Princess Sorinne continued to demand of her father answers to the disturbance. She had not noticed him yet.

Rouwen started to call to her, to tell Sorinne of his love, then averted his eyes, still not knowing if a mere glance might kill or if contact was needed. Both Adan Rouwen and Nibbles had died when he touched them. Rouwen raged as he swung out of the room, sword flashing left and right to clear a path through curious servants coming to investigate the disturbance in the king's chambers. He had developed a fondness for Nibbles, but it had not been until the small, ancient thief had saved him from being near Sorinne that he realized he had come to love him like a brother.

'Like a brother,' Rouwen sobbed out as he ran pell-mell through the castle. Nibbles had become a friend, the only one he had, and it had killed him. Cold rage replaced the fury blazing inside Rouwen. He had slain through no fault of his own.

This was a curse laid by Kwuway at Sosler and Priowe's insistence. The wizard had paid the price for his damnable spells, but Sosler had survived the attack and Priowe was untouched. The king might come to fear that an assassin could enter his chambers so easily, and that meant difficulty in the future reaching him with an unsheathed dagger. But Rouwen had done as much as he could now.

His hand closed over the lump of the spell casket hidden in his uniform tunic. And stuffed into the jacket's voluminous pocket was Kwuway's grimoire. Within his grasp was the lifting of the curses – and with that freedom would come full opposition to Sosler and Priowe. Rouwen could never support King Nishor, and he owed that king's Duke Drioway as much as he did Sosler. But in some way he could remove those who had failed Gan so horribly and threatened to turn a prosperous country into a slave state.

'Lieutenant, wait!' came a shrill call. 'What's wrong?' Rouwen glanced over his shoulder and saw a serving girl coming from her quarters.

'Assassins,' he barked. 'I need to reach the courtyard and bring the guard.'

'I can fetch them for you,' she offered. Rouwen hesitated. He had to find a less exposed passageway if he intended to win free of Castle Gan once more. The girl's quarters might provide such an exit, if he remembered rightly the position and the structure of the walls.

'Do so. I need to patrol this corridor. Tell the captain on duty that Sosler has been castrated.'

'No!' The expression on the girl's face was a curious mixture of surprise and amusement. Rouwen wanted only to cast the duke in as poor a light as possible, but the girl's countenance made him wonder how far-reaching the duke's influence was.

She dashed off, her hand covering her mouth. Again, Rouwen couldn't tell if she tried to keep from crying out or laughing. He waited a moment, then ducked into her quarters, barring the door behind him. In the corridor he heard the heavy thudding of boots as the king's personal guard chased after him.

Rouwen pushed aside the wall hangings and found a narrow window. He had lost much weight during his convalescence, and this allowed him to slip through. He came against a pane of stained glass in the casement and hesitated only a moment before ruining the work of art. Glass crashed down out of the window to splinter in the courtyard three stories below, but Rouwen was pleased to see that he had been right in his estimation. The window opened above a walkway ten feet below.

He knew time was critical. He swung out of the window, hung for a moment and dropped, landing hard on hands and knees. The short fall took his breath. Rouwen realized how weak he was after the repeated deaths he had endured – and meted out.

'Lieutenant!' came the loud cry. 'What is wrong?'

Rouwen looked up and saw four soldiers on the walkway, hands on swords. Two more joined them, crossbows ready.

Fighting his way free wasn't possible, but boldness might win the day.

Rouwen stood and brushed himself off, then said, 'I was after the swine. He came this way, but I fear he escaped. We have to pursue or we will lose him!'

'At once,' the nearest soldier said, saluting.

'Wait!' snapped Rouwen. 'Horses. Get the rest of your patrol and coursers and we will go after him ourselves.' He hoped he had accurately identified the soldiers' insignia as belonging to a patrol unit normally stationed along the road leading to Castle Gan. There had been so many changes, Rouwen was no longer sure which units patrolled where.

'Don't you want your own men riding with you?' asked the soldier.

'You look like doughty fighters. Who could ask for anything more in his command? Do well and I'll have you transferred from your patrol duties to a real fighting unit.'

Rouwen couldn't tell if the soldier was pleased with the promised promotion, but he rushed off to obey an officer's commands. Rouwen wasted no time going after. He let the soldiers get their horses ready before he picked one out for his own use. Mounting, he was glad of the time he had spent riding around Mion as it kept him from appearing a total novice.

'Hurry with that gate!' Rouwen roared in his best command voice. He kept his head down slightly lest anyone recognize him. He need not have worried on this score. The gatekeepers immediately opened one immense gate and his squadron poured forth at a gallop with himself in the lead.

A shudder of relief passed through him as he passed through the gate and again saw the expanse of Valley Gan and the azure dome and the jagged rocky guardians of the Shield Mountains. The castle's defenses had failed, and for that Rouwen was grateful. He had tried to prevent such forays without authorization, but Sosler's command had shaken up the officer corps to the point where only incompetents remained inside Castle Gan.

All the better to expose King Priowe to assassins, Rouwen guessed. If the king was unable to protect himself, he would become more desperate and commit grievous errors of judgment that Sosler and his allies could exploit. A kingdom under Sosler was not progress, as witnessed by the double-dealing the duke had already engaged in to depose Queen Diarra and bring Nishor's armies to the Demon's Throat.

'Lieutenant, dare we gallop much farther?' asked the soldier Rouwen had singled out on the walkway. 'Already they tire.'

'Cut the patrol in half,' Rouwen ordered. 'Halt, and four of you dismount.' He watched as the seven soldiers stopped, tried to decide what was happening, then chose four to become foot soldiers.

'We use their horses as spare mounts?' guessed the soldier.

'We walk a ways, then trot, then gallop and then change to the extra mounts to give our own coursers a rest,' Rouwen said.

'How can the fugitive be so far ahead of us?' asked a soldier from the ground. 'We saw nothing to indicate anyone had come this way recently. And won't the troops stationed along the road capture him?'

'He's a cunning demon,' Rouwen responded. 'We dare not tarry. Are you with me, men, or do you return to the castle like whipped dogs, admitting only defeat?'

'We ride!' shouted a mounted soldier as he rode off. Rouwen followed quickly, not giving the others a chance to think on how strange this mission had become. He had reduced the troopers by half, and he could work on the others as they made their way down the winding road.

He left two soldiers to man a post and stationed another at the base of the road to watch for fugitives who would never arrive. He had three spare horses, and the soldier he had bullied on the castle's walkway would provide a fourth.

'Halt!' Rouwen called. The soldier reined back. As he did so Rouwen kept riding, pulling his saber as he rode. The back portion of the blade struck the soldier on the back of the head and sent him tumbling to the ground. Rouwen had no stomach for killing him, yet leaving him to answer for his dereliction of duty in allowing Sosler's fugitive to escape would see the poor wight in Gan's deepest dungeon.

Rouwen shrugged it off. He had to escape and doing so was going to prove uncomfortable for him. The Demon's Throat would be closed quickly enough, if it wasn't already. Signallers from the castle battlements would have flashed their mirrors or waved their flags to alert the troops in the narrow pass. If he wanted to reach the Lord of Death and Life, there was only one path he could take.

Shuddering, Rouwen scooped up the reins of the felled soldier's horse. He had enough spare mounts to race the wind – and he did. He galloped hard until the horse under him began to falter. He ruthlessly drove it until it stumbled and began to fall. Rouwen lithely jumped off, was momentarily confounded by his own weakness, then pulled himself into the saddle of a second horse. He kept the three others at the same pace, but without riders they did not tire as quickly.

Rouwen ran a second horse into the ground and switched, keeping two in reserve. Only then did he slow his headlong pace and take the time to forage for food for both himself and the coursers.

All day and into the night Rouwen rode until he swayed in the saddle. Another horse failed to maintain the frantic pace he set and he left the winded animal behind to hobble lamely to graze in a lush green pasture. Rouwen envied the horse its future. His own was less secure.

He rode until the Lesser Moon rose half-full in the sky and then used its light to avoid roads that might have patrols hunting for him. By the time the Greater Moon rose, he stood at the hidden mouth of the tunnel leading under the Shield Mountains. Rouwen stared at it and wondered if his quest was worth the pain of going back through this passage.

Turning, he looked back at Castle Gan and past it to Mount Glid. Witch-fires burned on the mountain's sides, souls trying to gain entry into Paradise. Rouwen shivered again and looked into the darkness of the tunnel. The souls unable to reach Mount Glid were trapped within this mountain, and he had to endure their pitiful pleading if he wanted to win through to Mion and from that armed kingdom, to the Isle of Passing.

This time might be different since he knew the passage, but he doubted it. Already he imagined the whines and pleas of the wraiths trapped beneath the massif. Shuddering, he pushed his fears aside. He knew what he had to do.

Rouwen ate some more of the scavenged food he had grabbed on the run to the hidden tunnel, then sat down and found himself unable to stand again. His physical weakness far exceeded any emotional drive he had to leave Valley Gan. Realizing it would do him no good to push on, then collapse, he curled up and was quickly asleep.

Bright sunlight on his face woke him. He stretched and felt better, then remembered what lay ahead. It was a two-day-long journey through the limestone caverns under the Shield Mountains if he travelled at top speed, but this time he would make it without stopping to sleep. The specters flitting through the cavern – and his mind – were more than he could bear.

Seeing either Adan or Nibbles was more than he wanted to bear.

'Come on,' he said, gathering his horses. They had devoured all the grass nearby. Rouwen knew they would need all strength possible for the journey. He led the horses into the cavern, looking back only once at Castle Gan gleaming whitely atop its immense spire. Rouwen didn't know when he would be back, but when he returned he would be free of all curses.

He touched the lump in his tunic to reassure himself the spell casket still rode there, then thrust his hand into the pocket of his uniform coat to touch the grimoire he had taken from Kwuway. All was well. Rouwen swung into the saddle and rode for the tunnel. He ducked down as he went inside, wondering why Sosler had not posted patrols along this stretch of the foothills. The only reason making sense was that the duke didn't know Rouwen used the passageway to leave Gan. Or possibly the duke's control over the army was less than he had guessed. Also he had made good time reaching the tunnel entrance, possibly better than Sosler could match.

Whatever the reason, Rouwen knew he would not be able to use this tunnel again. If Sosler did not close it, King Priowe would. For all his naiveté in the matter of his betrayal, Priowe was no fool. Where Sosler seemed to fail, Priowe would try to succeed.

Rouwen swore that he had not renewed the supply of torches for the trip. He had not thought to be using the tunnel again, much less within a month of his last trip. He took the few bunches of twigs left and lit one, pressing on as fast as he could. The way was safe enough and he now had two horses to maintain his pace.

An hour's ride into the cave, Rouwen switched horses. He tried to estimate the passage of time by how quickly the horses tried, but his own fatigue robbed him of any real sense of time. Swaying in the saddle, he knew he ought to rest. But he couldn't.

Even without drifting into troubled sleep, he saw the filmy white specters moving at the edges of his vision. Every time he snapped around, the wraiths vanished, but he knew they were present. And the soft, distant sounds of dripping water were intermixed with inhuman wailing and whimpering.

'Brion,' he heard after riding seemingly forever in the semi-darkness. His torch failed to hold back the gloom – and the ghosts crowding ever closer. 'Brion, please help meeeee.'

Rouwen swung about, hand on his dagger, though he knew it was impossible to slay the dead. A thick patch of gauzy light flashed and for a split second he thought he saw Adan's face. As fast as this thought formed, it vanished and he screamed.

The almost-human, worried face of his brother changed swiftly to a charred skull, and the entire ghost-being exploded into spinning rings of fire. Rouwen threw up his hand to protect his face, but he felt nothing against his body save dampness from the water dripping from above. Heart beathing, Rouwen relaxed and looked about him. In the darkest crevices of the tunnel danced white flames of insubstantial ghost fire. As he neared each bonfire, it faded and was gone as if it had never existed.

Rouwen rode faster, but the small cries around him continued.

'You run, Brion. You should fight, fight, fight!' mocked another wraith. Rouwen gasped when the ghost took on the form of the old thief he had killed with a single touch. Nibbles floated ahead of him, feet missing the cavern floor by several inches. Tiny whorls of white hid parts of Nibbles's face, but Rouwen recognized him.

'Why do you say that?' Rouwen demanded. 'You always cautioned me against direct attack. And who should I fight now?' Rouwen waved his arm about, sending tiny snatches of ghostly substance fluttering away. Again he felt only wetness as droplets of water splashed on him.

'I know so much more now,' Nibbles said, his voice becoming distant, 'but I cannot tell you. Beware the Flame Specter. It is the cause of our . . . problem.'

'What problem?' shouted Rouwen. 'Tell me, what problem?'

'. . . cannot reach Mount Glid. Too much . . .' The words vanished as Nibbles's ghost seemed to implode, turning into itself and swirling away in tendrils of soft gray fog.

'Nibbles, Adan,' moaned Rouwen. He slumped forward, then firmed with resolve. He didn't know what Nibbles had meant, or if this ghost really was the old thief's shade. Tormenting him with snippets of unexplained warning was as much a torture as anything Kwuway had done. Worst of all, Rouwen had to accept that he had sent both his brother and Nibbles into this frightful limbo.

Or was he going mad? He put his heels into the courser's flanks and trotted on, hooves echoing dully in the cavern. To stay any longer than necessary was to court indecision – and worse.

Almost falling from the saddle, Rouwen emerged at last into Mion a few minutes before sunset. He had no idea how long he had been in the tunnel, having only two exhausted horses to use as a measure. He rode down the slope of the foothills and again looked behind. Finding the entry to the tunnel was almost impossible. Whatever protected entry from this side worked well.

179

He had to sleep. He had before him more than a week's ride to reach the Isle of Passing and freedom from his curse. Rouwen slept.

The way became perilous. Brion Rouwen had to evade constant armed patrols, some setting up posts on the roads and searching everyone and others simply roaming Mion's barren countryside. For a week he dodged and ducked and avoided Nishor's troops, until at last as he was finishing a meal he was spied by three Mionese soldiers.

'You, the one in the torn clothing,' called a sergeant. Rouwen looked up, angry at himself for not finding a better spot to rest and eat. He had ripped and torn the officer's jacket he wore, turning it into an unrecognizable rag. A Gannian lieutenant would not last long in a country set for war.

'Evening,' Rouwen said, respectfully touching his forehead as he had seen other peasants do when confronted by anyone superior in rank. 'What can I do for you?'

'I ask the questions. We got warning of a Gannian spy making his way down the coast. You see anyone like that?'

Rouwen shook his head, not daring to speak. His accent was passable, but the more lies he told to cover any small slip he might make, the more likely he was to have to fight his way to the Isle of Passing. He had only just entered the boggy land leading to the embarkation point for the Lord of Death and Life's island. From where he was camped, the swamp would take the better part of an hour to traverse, and crossing the channel would require another hour, if he had to swim. An hour away from sighting the Isle of Passing and he had to grow careless. Rouwen cursed his bad luck and his own carelessness, then moved a little to better position both dagger and sword for any fight.

'What are you doing in this forsaken land? Only demons and poison reptiles slither here.'

'I noticed,' Rouwen said acidly, staring at the sergeant. The Mionese soldier stiffened, and his hand went to his sword. Then the man's eyes narrowed, for the first time seeing the saber Rouwen wore at his side.

'It's him, men, this is the one Duke Drioway wants!'

Rouwen was mildly interested to know who sought him. Whether the warrant for his arrest carried Drioway's name or Sosler's mattered little. They were allies against their respective rulers, even if it seemed their countries prepared for war. After Rouwen had slain Kwuway and almost cut Sosler in two, a sizable reward must have been offered for his capture or death.

The two soldiers with the sergeant were slower to respond, giving Rouwen the chance to tackle their leader. He dived under the sergeant's wild slash and bore him down to the soggy ground. The sergeant floundered about, stuck in the swampy ooze. Rouwen drew the man's own dagger and used it on him, leaving the hilt sticking straight up from his heaving chest.

'He – he killed Sergeant Cheale!' shrieked one soldier.

Rouwen used their moment of shock to draw his own saber and dagger. Feet spread wide, he waited for the attack. Then a coldness seized him that made him sway and almost faint.

He was no longer immortal. Kwuway's spell had been lifted when the wizard died, rendering him vulnerable to cut and slash once more. Rouwen took a deep breath and calmed himself. He had to avoid being killed now, but this was nothing new for the former guard captain. If anything, it represented a return to normality and he was a better swordsman than either of these green recruits.

'I have no wish to slaughter either of you. He should never have attacked me,' Rouwen said in as even a voice as he could muster. To show any fear now meant a hard battle he might lose. The journey had been tough on him and he had never recuperated fully. 'Take him back to your bivouac and tell your officer he died of some unknown misadventure. He was not a bright man.'

'But you killed him. We can't just go and let you . . .'

The other soldier dug his elbow into his friend's ribs. 'We need to consider,' the more cautious one said. The two soldiers argued briefly. Rouwen watched with growing amusement. He wouldn't have to fight. They sought only to return to their post without being cut to bloody ribbons.

'You must answer our questions,' one said. 'Who are you and what are you doing here?'

'I'm a traveller on my way down the coast,' Rouwen said. 'I was eating when you came upon me.' He had answered, yet told them nothing important.

'That's a good enough answer,' the second soldier said, moving toward his fallen sergeant.

It was then that Rouwen underestimated his foes. His eyes followed the one while the second drew his dagger and attacked. Rouwen barely parried with his own dagger, unable to swing the saber in a short enough arc to do any damage. He drove the hilt into the soldier's ribs as hard as he could and was rewarded with a gusty rush of wind from the man's lungs. But this wasn't enough. The first soldier had launched his own attack.

Rouwen fought with a saber too heavy for fencing and with an unaccustomed curve which threw off his lunges. He launched a quick riposte and found flesh. The soldier yelped in pain and gave Rouwen the chance to turn his attention back to the other soldier, struggling to sit up.

A hard kick to the man's face put him down into the swampy ground. Rouwen stumbled and winced as the other soldier's sword opened a thin gash along his back. The spot where Kennard had driven his dagger to the hilt began to twitch and ache due to the nearness of a new injury, but Rouwen forced this from his mind. He settled down and advanced carefully, measuring every step and using his stronger wrist to intimidate the less experienced soldier.

'Hai!' he shouted at an opportune moment, frightening the soldier. The small jerk of surprise lifted his foe's sword off-line and allowed Rouwen to drive in. The tip of the saber vanished into the soldier's upper arm and caused him to drop his sword. Rouwen followed up quickly with a dagger thrust that killed the man. The soldier slipped to the ground to lie dead beside his comrades.

Rouwen was pleased to find that his strength was returning. He wasn't back to his usual vitality, but the sword fight hadn't drained him as it would have only a week earlier. He quickly searched the three soldiers and took a few coins from each, then added their supplies to his own. Reaching the Isle of Passing would take only a short time, but after he left the island, whole and free of all curses once more, he would need food for his trip back to Gan.

'To Gan and Sorinne,' he said, knowing he would again be able to hold his love in his arms without fear.

Rouwen's head jerked up when he heard the loud noises of a patrol.

'Where in this demon-infested swamp are you, Cheale?' came the choleric demand. 'I'll cut off your ears and feed them to you, if you don't answer me. Men, find that malingering son of a toad.'

Rouwen cursed his bad luck. A much larger patrol had blundered his way. Cheale and the others might have been scouting a path through the swamp for their company. If so, Rouwen could only run and hope to stay ahead of the troopers. Three he could best in combat. Dozens were beyond his skill, especially now that the cut across his back was beginning to pain him greatly. It was a shallow wound, but it bled profusely and hurt like fire ants nipping at his skin.

He tried to make a quiet escape, but his horses' neighing betrayed him.

'There, there he is!' shouted someone behind him. 'And he's murdered Cheale and the other two with him!'

Rouwen put his heels to his courser's flanks, but he made little headway through the heavy mud. He turned toward the coast. The distance to the Isle of Passing was greater this way, but the land was firmer and afforded him a greater chance of outracing his pursuers. The Mionese might become lost or simply give up. Rouwen had nothing but contempt for their low level of training and lack of motivation, from lowest soldier all the way up to their officers.

The Mionese troopers might not have been able to overtake and engage him, but they were more persistent than Rouwen wished for. He reached the coast north of the swampy estuary affording the shortest passage to the Isle of Passing. The Lord's island sat amid the choppy, whitecapped blue waves like a precious emerald.

Rouwen dismounted and judged the distance to the island as being three or four times farther than from the estuary, but he had no choice. He had to reach the Lord with grimoire and spell casket if he wanted to be free of Kwuway's diabolical spell.

He tried to wrap the book of spells in a cloak to keep it from getting wet on his swim when he saw that he need not bother.

The Mionese soldiers had overtaken him. He faced fully a score of them, all furious with him for the chase he'd led them and for the deaths of their comrades.

Rouwen placed the grimoire behind a rock for safety, then drew sword and dagger to face them. He would meet death with saber flashing and dagger ripping the life from their pathetic bodies.

'What are you waiting for?' he called. 'Or are you going to fall on your own swords and save me the trouble of killing you?'

Brion Rouwen began the noblest fight of his life. He only wished that Nibbles could be there to see how a real adventure ended.

19

Hope of Death

Rouwen caught the first soldier's thrust, turned it aside and moved in quickly, his dagger finding a berth in the man's thigh. Yelping in pain, the trooper broke off his attack and stumbled away. Rouwen paid him no attention. He was already engaging a second soldier. He had no chance against them all, but he would acquit himself well and they would grow old telling of his bravery.

'Crossbows!' barked the officer in charge. 'Take him down!'

Rouwen panted harshly as he tried to inflict as much damage as possible before the two soldiers he fought backed off to give the crossbowmen a clear shot. From horseback, four soldiers cranked back the strings on their crossbows and fitted wickedly barbed bolts into the firing grooves. Rouwen edged away, thinking he might be able to swim for the island, but he hesitated. Was it worth saving his life to lose the grimoire and any chance of removing the curse still weighing so heavily?

'No,' Rouwen muttered. Better to use his newly regained freedom to die than to live in fear of loving and slaying.

'You surrender?' called the officer. He held up his hand to stay the bolts from finding targets in Rouwen's body.

'No!' shouted Rouwen. He would not submit to Drioway or Sosler. If he fell into their grasp again, he would rot in the darkest dungeons of Mion or Gan. A clean death under the azure sky and with pure ocean water lapping at his heels was preferable.

'Fire!' ordered the captain.

Rouwen stiffened to attention, waiting for death. He blinked and threw up his hand to protect his eyes when a sudden swirl on the beach kicked up a column of biting sand. Through tears, Rouwen saw four cyclones whirling about between him and the crossbowmen. The soldiers obeyed the order and fired, but the bolts drove through the center of the miniature cyclones and turned to sparkling dust that was caught up in the wind and quickly dispersed.

'Again,' shouted the officer. 'Fire again!'

The four soldiers had no chance to reload and fire. The cyclones danced over to them, bouncing lightly on the beach and then engulfed them. Shrill screams of four men dying inside the Lord's Legion of the Air were drowned out by their horses' frightened neighing. Rouwen watched as the powerful winds whipped the horses around, lifting them off the ground, and, like the crossbow bolts, they also turned to sparkling dust and vanished.

'Stop them! Let them down. No!' yelled the officer. His men suffered a fate different from their mounts. They were spinning wildly inside the cyclones, trapped and unable to escape. Their faces contorted and they obviously howled in fear and anger, but no sound save the soft whirring of the Lord's windy minions escaped to Rouwen's ears.

He changed his tactics of standing and waiting for death to outright attack again. He rushed forward, slashing with both saber and dagger. The soldiers he hacked were taken by surprise. Their attention riveted to their comrades ensnared within the cyclones, they fell easily to his fighting skills.

'Get him, forget the wind!' ordered the officer. He drew his sword and tried to control his horse. The animal had turned skittish because of the wind softly sighing so close – then officer and horse were engulfed by a new cyclone.

This broke the spirit of the remaining troopers. They rode or ran from the beach, shrieking for mercy. Rouwen dropped his guard and fought to catch his breath. The fighting had been short but fierce – and he had been saved by the Lord's wind warriors. Rouwen looked up at the towering pillar of air not ten paces away and saw the officer struggling within. He was being buffeted soundlessly in the prison of spinning air.

As Rouwen watched, the wind's intensity increased and the officer spun faster and faster. Rouwen turned away as the officer exploded into bloody fragments that rained down on the beach. When he dared glance over his shoulder, all five of the cyclones had simply vanished, as if they'd never existed. The only reminder of their presence was the gory pieces of soldiers strewn for a hundred yards along the beach and the gentle mist of blood that still fell.

Rouwen went to the rock where he had hidden the grimoire and grabbed the spell book, relieved that nothing had happened to it during the bloodshed. As he picked it up and held it close to his chest, he felt a familiar warmth growing. He had been blistered by the grimoire when Kwuway had mentioned the Flame Specter.

What caused the warming now? The summoning of the Legion of the Air?

Glancing toward the Isle of Passing, he saw a pair of the Lord's cyclones whipping around on the distant shore. The two columns of air whirled over the water and came toward him. As the cyclones approached, the grimoire grew so warm that Rouwen almost dropped it. Seeing that the heat did not affect cloth as it did his flesh, he slung it in his tunic pocket once more. He opened the pocket a little and saw the grimoire glowing feverishly but felt no heat.

The twin whirlwinds approached the beach. Rouwen nervously touched the spell casket hidden inside his tunic and put his hand over the grimoire, then prepared to do battle with the wind warriors.

The columns of air towered hundreds of feet over him, but they stopped at the water's edge. Rouwen watched as they oscillated slightly, moving toward each other and then parting, as if inviting him to walk between them. He stepped over the body part of one of the slain soldiers and walked slowly to a point between the cyclones.

'Aieee!' Rouwen shrieked as invisible hands lifted him and carried him swiftly toward the distant island. He tried to relax as his feet skimmed the whitecaps breaking under him, but he could not. He stumbled and fell to one knee when the wind warriors deposited him on the crystalline white beach circling the Isle of Passing.

Recovering quickly, Rouwen stood – and faced a giant almost ten feet tall. The huge man was dressed in a shaggy animal skin that hung around his loins. Huge muscles bulged and shone with sweat in the sun. The brutish head had heavy bony ridges over the eyes and tangled, greasy hair hung down over the creature's slightly pointed ears. In one meaty hand the giant held a spear, its shaft thicker than most of the trees on the mainland.

The spear's tip gleamed and shone with finest silver. Rouwen hesitated when he saw that incongruous detail. A creature of such savage demeanor should not be carrying a silver-tipped spear worth a king's ransom.

'The edge is difficult to hone, also,' came the giant's booming voice. Rouwen was taken aback, and this caused the colossus to laugh in delight. 'You are too easily understood, Captain Rouwen.'

Rouwen took his hand away from his saber. The best he could hope to do in any fight with the giant was to slash a tendon behind the ankle or find a small artery in the thigh to sever. A more likely outcome would favor the giant. The length of the spear would keep Rouwen at bay, and the giant need only bat at him to inflict a deadly wound.

'Who are you? Are you the Lord's guardian?'

Again the deep baritone laugh rumbled from the barrel chest and echoed forth to shake the very sky above the Isle of Passing.

'*I* am the Lord of Death and Life!'

'I met the Lord. He is a slight youth, hardly twenty summers old. He . . .' Rouwen bit back any further comment. The giant continued guffawing, and it was honest laughter. Somehow the wizard had altered his appearance. Rouwen remembered how the Lord had seemed to age when the Flame Specter was mentioned.

'You begin to understand what it means to hold the power of life and death in your hand,' the mammoth being said, again correctly guessing what thoughts passed through Rouwen's head. 'Shape means nothing. I can be large. I can be small. But always I control the flow of life and death, granting first one and then the other.'

'Kwuway is dead,' Rouwen said, 'and I have the grimoire.'

'I can feel it. When I sent my Legion of the Air to aid you on the far shore, it began to grow warm with power.'

'It burned me when I took it from Kwuway.'

'Indeed?' the Lord said, uninterested.

He spoke the Flame Specter's name and it burned, Rouwen thought and watched the giant's brutish face for any sign of emotion. The flash of fear convinced him that the Flame Specter was more powerful than even the Lord of Death and Life. Kwuway had feared it – and so did the Lord.

'The grimoire,' ordered the Lord. 'Give it to me!'

'A moment,' Rouwen said, touching the book of spells resting in his pocket. 'The grimoire is yours after you remove the last of Kwuway's curses.'

'Yes, yes, of course,' the Lord said, lumbering forward. A monstrous hand reached out for Rouwen. 'Give me the spell casket.'

Rouwen pulled the silver locket from his tunic and tossed it into the immense outstretched hand. The Lord's fingers closed, and he lifted it high above his head to look closely at it.

The tiny silver spell casket glinted in the sun, just as the Lord's spear tip did. Rouwen wondered if the spear was somehow ensorcelled also, making it even more deadly. Such speculation meant nothing because only the Lord in his present shape and size could hope to wield such a weapon.

'I need the grimoire,' the Lord said. 'Kwuway's spells of binding are hidden in it.' He held out his huge hand but Rouwen backed away, suddenly wary. The Lord was lying.

'You are a powerful wizard capable of changing your shape, of summoning the Legion of the Air, of performing any magicks on this island. Remove the curse now that you have the spell casket, and I give you my solemn promise to hand over the grimoire.'

'I need the book!'

The Lord rushed at him, arms extending on either side to catch Rouwen in a powerful bear hug. Rouwen did not attempt to draw his sword. His dagger slid free, and he stood his ground, waiting for the right instant to attack. Just as the huge arms began closing Rouwen acted instinctively. Ducking quickly and shifting to the right in a feint, he forced the Lord to follow his move – then he drove his body as hard to the left as he could, using his dagger to open a wound along the giant's thickly muscled belly.

Rouwen rolled away and came to his feet, dagger tip dripping blood. The Lord roared in anger and thrashed about clumsily. By opting for size and strength, the wizard had given up swiftness of reflex and agility.

'You need only lift the curse and the grimoire is yours with my good wishes. Why fight me for it?' Rouwen demanded. He darted away from the Lord, using the tip of his dagger again to score a new wound on the giant's forearm. Blood trickled down and spotted the spell casket the Lord clutched in a meaty hand.

'You cannot kill me while I remain on this island,' the Lord said, his face contorted into a mask of rage. 'Do not oppose me. Give me the grimoire!'

Rouwen reflected on the irony of the situation. He had fought so many and lost so much he held dear to lift the curse of immortality, and the Lord stayed on this island because somehow he drew power from it to remain an eternal. But whom did the Lord love? Would he outlive them and mourn?

'Lift the curse,' Rouwen said, mind racing now. He danced back and held out the book of spells. 'Then you can fight the Flame Specter with the hexes Kwuway has collected.' As he mentioned the Flame Specter, the grimoire began turning warm to his touch, but it lacked the fire when Kwuway had spoken the name. Magicks abounded and he knew nothing of them.

'What do you know of such things?' roared the Lord. His brutish face screwed into a look of pure fury an instant before he charged, swinging his spear like a quarterstaff.

Rouwen dropped to the ground and easily evaded the attack. As the giant tried to trample him, Rouwen slashed out and cut the tendon behind the ankle. The Lord shrieked in pain and stumbled off. He might not die, but he lived with the same fate Rouwen had suffered for long weeks. Death was not possible but pain and mutilation were.

'You delve into matters beyond your understanding.' The Lord hobbled around, swinging the spear and trying to jab with it. Rouwen sidestepped and parried the spear thrust with contemptuous ease. The Lord of Death and Life might be a great and immortal wizard on his isle, but he was a poor warrior.

'What are you not telling me?' demanded Rouwen. 'You lack the skill to lift the spell and release my essence from Kwuway's spell casket?'

'You fool!' shrieked the Lord. 'This is the wrong spell casket. It is someone else's! Now give me the grimoire!' Again he lunged at him.

Rouwen almost perished from this attack. He was stunned by the wizard's revelation. It had never occurred to him that Sosler might have more than one spell casket. Queen Diarra had been in the dungeon also when Kwuway performed his grotesque spells.

'Is that Diarra's spell casket?' Rouwen asked taking a small cut in favor of holding his ground. He drove his dagger forward and brought forth a fountain of blood when the tip ripped through an artery under the giant's arm.

'I cannot tell. Give me the grimoire!'

The gigantic wizard made a lumbering, futile attack. Rouwen disarmed him and kicked a foot from under him. The Lord crashed to the ground and found himself pinned with Rouwen's dagger poised over his eye.

'Can you heal yourself if I blind you?' asked Rouwen. From the stiffness in the Lord's body, Rouwen knew he had found another truth transcending magicks.

'I cannot open the spell casket without the person dying. Do you wish that?' The giant's face contorted again in a mask of rage and pain. 'I need the grimoire if I am to do battle with the Flame Specter. Otherwise it will destroy us all!'

'Tell me of it. Perhaps we can strike a bargain. I want my own spell casket and . . .' Rouwen got no farther. The wizard kicked hard and forced Rouwen's blade past his face and into the soft sand next to his head. Rouwen slashed off part of the Lord's ear, but it was a small price to pay for liberty. The giant rolled and came clumsily to his feet. But he did not stand to fight. He hobbled off at a surprisingly fast pace.

'I'll destroy the grimoire,' Rouwen shouted. This caused the wizard to come to a halt and spin about, glaring with stark hatred.

'No, give it to me. I will help you regain your spell casket. I have no love for Sosler or Drioway. They are ambitious fools who know nothing of the powers they arouse.'

'The Flame Specter?'

'Yes! Now give me the book!'

Rouwen started to speak but he saw a golden haze surround the giant. The wizard shimmered slightly, a heat mirage in the middle of a fine summer afternoon. Rouwen blinked and sagged to his knees, suddenly weak and unable to move. The giant came closer, grew taller and more massive – or did he? Through the golden curtain of shimmery fog Rouwen saw an old man hobbling from the severe leg wound he had won in combat.

'Is this the real Lord of Death and Life?' Rouwen asked in amazement. 'An old man with a frightened expression?'

'You see me! How?'

'The grimoire,' Rouwen said, more to himself than to the wizard. The book burned in his pocket now and somehow muted the spell the Lord cast. And through the magicks he saw more clearly, knowing the Lord's true aspect and weakness. An old man wanting to live forever and fearing a change in the politics on the mainland. The Isle of Passing was a refuge, a fortress and nothing more. The balance of powers, both political and magical, was changing in Gan and Mion, and the Lord tried vainly to stem that tide.

The giant vanished entirely and was replaced by a small bird that fluttered away. Rouwen placed his hand on the scorching grimoire and saw clearly again – the old man hobbling along a path that had been magically obscured by a carpet of soft green grass. The Isle of Passing was more barren than it appeared through the Lord's magical powers, but it was still a lovely place. Rouwen concentrated on the fleeing wizard and forced himself to his feet. Whatever spell the Lord had tried to cast left him weak but not debilitated.

Rouwen raced after the mage, closing the distance between them easily. Somehow, the grimoire in his pocket prevented the Lord's spells from working fully, and Rouwen saw with true sight for the first time since setting foot on the island – or perhaps the Lord was so badly injured or frightened that he could not issue the proper spells to veil Rouwen's vision.

'I'll show you! I'll kill you, you, you . . .' The Lord's voice cracked with strain. Rouwen ran faster, seeing that the wizard ran towards a large stone structure very different from the simply decorated cottage he had seen before. He didn't know what the Lord sought in this building but if the wizard could shut him out, if only for a few minutes, it might be enough to conjure a new spell that would overwhelm whatever power lurked in Kwuway's grimoire.

The Lord of Death and Life reached the door and fumbled with the latch long enough to allow Rouwen to catch up with him. Rouwen slammed hard into the wizard, knocking him spinning inside. Losing his balance, Rouwen dropped to one knee. He looked around the interior for any weapon the Lord might turn on him. The rude implements on the table reflected a poor peasant rather than a powerful wizard – or was this merely the Lord's vision-confusing spell?

Rouwen used an underhand toss to fling his dagger at the wizard to keep him away from a golden hunting horn dangling from a leather strap behind the door. What this horn was Rouwen had no idea, but the Lord had fought hard to reach it. That was enough for Rouwen to prevent it.

The mage ducked and slammed hard into the far wall, almost knocking himself to the dirt floor in his frenzied attempt to avoid the thrown dagger. The blade quivered noisily in the timber where the horn dangled. From the expression on the Lord's face, Rouwen doubted that what he saw now was illusion. If anything, he was seeing with clearer perception than ever before. The Lord lived poorly, hardly up to the standards of a Gannian peasant.

'So you traded riches for eternal life,' Rouwen said to the wizard. 'This is a poor place, not the lavish palace you might have enjoyed.' Rouwen realized living well and happily was superior to simply enduring and being eternally fearful of losing life.

'Give me the grimoire,' the Lord said, making a sidelong movement toward the dagger Rouwen had tossed. Did he seek the weapon or the horn? Rouwen thought he knew as he drew his sword and advanced. A single lunge would spit the wizard – and the Lord seemed to recognize that.

'Can you kill me, Captain Rouwen?' came a voice that was only too familiar. Rouwen rubbed his eyes when the injured old man in front of him shifted form and became King Priowe. 'I made mistakes and apologize most abjectly. You wish to be a noble? I grant you your wish. You are now Baron of Gan, my right-hand warrior.' Priowe reached out a hand in Rouwen's direction.

The grimoire in Rouwen's pocket glowed, but he ignored it. He licked his lips, indecisive, and the tip of his sword dipped slightly.

'Priowe?'

'You shame me, my Captain,' King Priowe said, moving closer to the golden horn. 'I listened to Duke Sosler when I should have believed you. How could I have been so led astray? You are my bastion of strength. I doubted you and am now paying the price.'

'Hold,' Rouwen said, lifting his sword. He blinked hard and Priowe's form shimmered slightly. In some inner portion of his brain, he realized he was being ensorcelled, but the spell was good – and powerful.

'You would harm your liege? Not a loyal solider such as you! I grant you your dreams, Captain. You can succeed Sosler as the realm's Lord Protector.' Again Priowe moved toward the golden horn, feet shuffling slightly on the hard-packed dirt floor.

That shuffling caused Rouwen to begin doubting his eyes. Priowe didn't walk with a limp; the Lord of Death and Life did, after Rouwen had cut the tendon in his heel. Rouwen's sword came up to a point where he could lunge and run Priowe through, but he hesitated.

'You aren't Priowe,' he muttered. The grimoire almost burned his flesh from its place in his pocket, but Rouwen ignored it. He concentrated on Priowe and decided what was wrong. Injury, the way Priowe kept moving toward the horn – what was it? Something about King Priowe's apology did not ring true either.

'Priowe would never offer me Lord Protector,' Rouwen said. 'He knows my expertise lies within the walls of Castle Gan!'

Even as he spoke, Priowe shimmered and shifted form again. The spell he wove over Rouwen wavered and then firmed once more. Priowe had gone, and now Princess Sorinne stood in the humble dwelling.

'Sorinne!' Rouwen exclaimed.

'Give me the grimoire, my dearest,' Sorinne said in her soft, sweet voice. 'I can help you if you give me the grimoire.'

'Here it is,' Rouwen said, knowing something was wrong but not able to concentrate on what it might be. He reached into his pocket and pulled out the book of spells and handed it to Sorinne. 'We can be together, my love.' Her long, blonde hair flowed like liquid gold, and eyes a deeper blue than the sky stared at him with such love. The high cheekbones and bow-shaped mouth and the haughty toss of her head all reminded him of his love for her.

Sorinne's hand touched the grimoire, then she – he – shrieked.

Princess Sorinne was instantly replaced by the injured man Rouwen had faced earlier. The Lord looked at his hand where his flesh had brushed Rouwen's. An expression of disbelief crossed his wizened features, then a strange smile crossed his lips.

'I – am – dying. You killed me!' The Lord of Death and Life shivered and stiffened, the flesh beginning to boil from his bones. 'A magic stronger than mine! No, no!'

Those were the wizard's last words. Rouwen stood numbly holding the book of spells in one hand and his sword in the other. The lingering effects of the Lord's spell took several minutes to fade to the point where he could move of his own volition and see without magicks-blinded eyes.

The skeleton on the dirt floor sizzled and crackled, then turned to a glowing dust, just as he had seen happen to Adan and Nibbles.

'You fool, you arrogant fool,' Rouwen said, realizing what the Lord had done. 'Priowe couldn't convince me so the Lord thought Sorinne could, and he was too intent on getting the grimoire to remember *why* I was here.'

In a strange way, Rouwen was relieved. He did love Sorinne, though it would mean her life if he touched her. This encounter with the Lord had been important in spite of still suffering under Kwuway's spell. He had learned that touch was required for the cruel spell to become active. Simply being in the same room or just seeing his love would not affect her.

But what a price he had paid. The one wizard willing to lift the spell, once the right spell casket was found, lay dead at his feet.

Rouwen went to the smoldering bones and plucked the silver spell casket from the ruined body. He tucked it back into his tunic.

The magical ornament had to belong to Diarra, to hold part of her soul. He owed his former queen nothing, but he bore her no malice either. If anything, he might be able to use the spell casket as a trading commodity to obtain his own. Whether Sosler carried it or King Priowe, he didn't know. He would have to find out if he wanted ever to free himself.

Rouwen stepped away from the glowing remains and wandered about the stone dwelling, marvelling at the poverty the Lord endured in return for his immortality. Or did the Lord believe his own illusion? Had the wizard simply imagined magnificent palaces and fine viands, conjuring the vision and enjoying that rather than the reality? Rouwen could never know for certain, but this abode was simple. Too simple. He saw no trace of magical devices or grimoires, such as he had in Kwuway's quarters. The Lord's life was unembellished by such artifice.

Rouwen turned and looked at his dagger sticking in the timber just under the golden horn the Lord had tried to grasp. What magical device was it? Rouwen could not believe the wizard sought the horn for any reason other than to use against him.

'There is nothing else here of value,' Rouwen said softly. He examined the simple pewter plates and drinking goblet, the cup still holding a thin, vinegary wine in it. The few sticks of furniture were uncomfortable, and Rouwen would have chosen a barn over the hard bed pushed into the corner of the room.

'What secrets are locked within the horn?' This seemed the only item out of place in the building.

He lifted it from the peg in the timber and felt a surge of energy pass through him. The grimoire glowed gently in his pocket, assuring him there was nothing dangerous here.

On impulse, Rouwen lifted the golden horn to his lips and blew inexpertly. To his surprise a clear, pure note echoed forth and seemed to blast far beyond the boundaries of the stone walls. Rouwen went outside to blow the horn again and saw twin pillars of wind whirling at the edge of the island. He blew the horn again and the two cyclones became four.

'I can summon the Legion of the Air!' Rouwen stared at the horn and knew the power of the device – and how he would need it if he was ever to lift the treacherous curse on him.

Brion Rouwen slung the horn over his shoulder, felt the grimoire in his pocket, then started walking toward the sandy white beach and the four wind warriors, more confident now that he would succeed than he had been since Sosler and Priowe had ordered him to Gan's dungeons.

Book Two

LEGION OF THE AIR

For the peerless Abner Stein

1

Bloodshed and Death

Rouwen shivered at the notion of having to return to Gan through one of the two tunnels beneath the Shield Mountains. Twice he had left the Kingdom of Gan through a tunnel, and twice the spirits of the dead migrating to Paradise had accosted him. Rouwen closed his eyes and tried to push the memory away. He knew the wraiths trapped there included his brother, Adan, and Nibbles, and they blamed him for their premature deaths. He could never face their spirits again, not until he, too, made his way to Paradise from the upper slopes of Mount Glid. Then and only then could he brave their rightful anger.

'Rise, my warriors, rise and pirouette at my command!' Rouwen laughed in delight and waved his hand at two columns of spinning air. The wind warriors continued their slow circuit of the beach, whirling to the bend of the island and then returning slowly, as if seeking something hidden from them.

'Across the water. Go! Go to the mainland!' Rouwen frowned when the wind warriors resolutely disobeyed. 'What does it take to bend you to my orders?' He stepped away from the beach as one tornado whistled past, oblivious of its new master.

Rouwen crouched down and rested the golden horn on his knee. He felt no great need to form columns with the magical beings and have them march to his command at the moment. Rouwen stood and went back toward the Lord's hut, taking a different path this time. The Isle of Passing was more desolate than he had thought originally, some of its lush vegetation undoubtedly conjured up by the dead wizard, but the island still had much to recommend it to him.

Unusual red-and-blue-striped fruits grew on low bushes, and of these Rouwen ate hungrily. The flavor reminded him of well-hung meat with just a dash of *eng*-spice for peppery contrast. Best of all, a double handful of the berries sated him completely. And along the path he found a small stream bubbling with pure water. Dropping to his belly, he cupped his palm and scooped water to his mouth. At first touch, the water tingled and caused Rouwen to recoil, then he tasted the wine-like flavor and was invigorated by it. As with the berries, a small amount satisfied him.

Rouwen rolled over and sat up, watching white clouds lazily move through the azure sky. The soft breeze blowing off the ocean caressed his face and caused him to drift off to sleep. He had been through so much, had endured so much pain and injury. He deserved the respite.

He came awake suddenly, as the soft whisper of breeze turned into an ear-splitting roar. It took Rouwen several seconds to realize that he heard one of the Lord's – his! – wind warriors whirling into the vegetation along the white strand facing the mainland. He pushed to his feet and settled the golden horn at his side, wondering if he should try blowing it again to gain control over the thick column of rampaging air.

A sudden gust caused him to throw his arms up to protect his face as debris whipped past. Rouwen walked into the teeth of the gale and almost fell face down when the wind stopped suddenly. Curious, he walked back to the beach and hunted for his guardians. The four wind warriors he had summoned were far from the Isle of Passing, pulling skyward thick pillars of frothy sea water.

'Why did they go away from the island?' Rouwen squinted into the hot sun, then turned cold inside when he saw the boats making their way toward him. The dozen or more heavy craft filled with armed men looked like cargo barges Rouwen had seen in Mion's capital city of Tachre, but those had been festooned with gaudy banners proclaiming landings at myriad ports. These vessels had been stripped bare, save for a single colored signalling flag at the prow of each.

'Invaders!' Rouwen turned to shout for the Lord and warn of the attack on his pleasant little isle, then remembered how the wizard had died. Rouwen was alone on the island. If he wanted to hold the invaders at bay, the endeavor was up to him. He forced himself to be calm and make a more complete reconnaissance of the invading forces. He watched the wigwag signals pass from one barge to another and quickly recognized the battle code as belonging to King Nishor of Mion.

Rouwen shook his head as he stared at the twenty barges laden with more than two thousand soldiers. Why would Nishor risk so many men in what might be a suicidal mission against a powerful wizard? There was no way the king could know the Lord was dead.

Then the answer came to him. King Nishor was not the

architect of this assault. Duke Sosler had sent these troops. If the invasion failed, Nishor would be seen as the loser. If the king's hold on his kingdom was weakened as a result, this left Sosler and his Mionese crony, Duke Drioway, in a stronger position to seize both Mion and Gan. And if the soldiers conquered the Lord of Death and Life, that victory would give impetus to the conquest of Valley Gan. No matter the outcome, Sosler triumphed.

Rouwen cringed when one wind warrior dashed across the surface of the water and caught up the leading barge in an airy embrace. For a moment it appeared that the tornado grew arms to hug the barge to its bosom, and a face with a gaping mouth opened. Then the image vanished amid a rain of splinters and sundered bodies.

The faint screams reached Rouwen as he stood on the beach, but a shower of blood told of the deaths meted out by the wind warrior. And the whirling column of air was not content with only one boat. It bobbed and weaved its way toward another boat. Rouwen saw dozens of soldiers abandon the barge, leaping overboard into the seemingly tranquil water. He wanted to call to them, to warn them of the strange and vicious fish protecting the Isle of Passing.

The sea roiled with new blood and froth as the carnivorous fish feasted hungrily. And then new debris became airborne as the Legion of the Air found three new targets and demolished them. Rouwen couldn't see even splinters left behind in the wake of the deadly tornadoes.

In spite of the carnage, the barges pressed on. With only four wind warriors trying to destroy an entire fleet of invaders, one barge had to get through. And it did, not a hundred paces down the beach from where Rouwen watched with a mixture of awe and revulsion.

The soldiers tumbled onto the beach, eager to be off what they now saw was an easy target rather than a means of transport. One officer shielded his eyes and pointed at Rouwen. 'Get him! There's the wizard! Kill him! Double the bounty if we get him!'

Rouwen touched the dagger sheathed at his waist and swung about slightly, feeling the weight of the sword at his left side. The weapons were substantial and bloodied in combat, but Rouwen knew better than to challenge a hundred soldiers. He backed away, cast a quick glance at the battle still being fought between the invading barges and the wind warriors, and knew more of King Nishor's soldiers would beach soon. The tornadoes wrecked one after another of the barges, but there were too many invaders and too few airy minions of death.

Rouwen turned and dashed for the cover of the long-armed willow trees bending low over the beach. He swung around and waited to see how many of the soldiers followed. Too many. Rouwen whipped out his sword and prepared to meet the two troopers who had outdistanced their comrades, eager for combat and honor. With two, he could cope. Possibly their deaths would cause the others to hesitate in their headlong rush to kill him.

He could only try.

The first soldier lumbered past on beer-keg-thick legs, oblivious to his presence. Rouwen swung his sword hard and caught the thickset soldier just above his ornately engraved gorget. Rouwen's blade nicked the heavy metal neckpiece, then glanced upward under the chin strap holding on the man's pockmarked steel battle helm. A clever twist of Rouwen's wrist caused his sword to insinuate itself under helmet and over gorget, slicing the soldier's throat and producing a fountain that gushed forth to stain the Mionese green-and-gray uniform with fresh gore.

Stepping away, Rouwen set his feet to engage the second trooper. This one wouldn't be as easy a target. Rouwen saw officer's insignia gleaming on the man's shoulder and helm and knew an easy kill would be denied him.

'You are the wizard?' the officer called, swinging his long sword with contemptuous ease. Rouwen let the man flaunt his prowess. Such wide slashes with the heavy blade could only tire him. Rouwen's lighter sword might not be a match for the thick blade he faced, but his skill was greater than any Mionese swordsman. Not for nothing had Brion Rouwen been a Captain of the Intrepid Guard and the best swordsman in all Gan.

As the officer whipped the blade around to bring it down in an overhead slash, Rouwen drove forward, getting under the blade and driving the tip of his sword upward. He felt ring mail yield and his sword enter the officer's body.

'What?' The officer's eyes widened in surprise, as if he couldn't believe he had died this easily. He tried to chop at Rouwen and lacked the strength. The Mionese officer stumbled and fell to one knee, then died. His heavy sword dropped to the ground behind him, never again to be hefted in battle.

'Death, that's what,' panted Rouwen, staring at his fallen foe. Shaking himself out of the daze of fatigue descending on him, he looked back down the beach and saw that slower soldiers were almost on top of him. The fight against the first two had been quickly decided, but he had misread the other troopers' determination to take the island – and him.

'They think I'm the Lord,' he said, shaking his head in wonder. How little they knew. Rouwen saw a tall pillar of air whip along the edge of the beach, scattering a few of the obstinate fighters making their way toward him, but not enough to matter.

Rouwen wiped his sword on a tuft of grass and ran for the island's interior. He knew the geography better than those so hot in pursuit, even if he had only seen much of it a single time. They might turn wary of traps and fall even farther behind. Or so he hoped.

Without their officer, the soldiers proved far more reckless than he would have thought possible. Perhaps the sight of the wind warriors frightened them into agitated action, or they had been promised a fine spot in Paradise if they died nobly. Whatever the reason, a full score found the path Rouwen had taken and pounded hard after him, caring nothing if he had set trapfalls.

Sprinting until he was winded, Rouwen found the small spring with the intoxicating water. He dared scoop another palm laden with the precious liquid and again experienced invigoration as it touched his lips. A second drink made him feel as if he could take on all of Nishor's men and best the lot.

'Careful,' he warned himself, knowing he had to guard against the water's magical effect. He had rested, but no one could fight an entire army and hope to win. Rouwen pressed himself against the bole of a large tree a few feet from the spring and heard the angry shouts of his pursuers. In a way, he reveled in this chase. At long last he was able to fight back, even if it was against overwhelming odds. Before, in Gan, with Nibbles, against Sosler and Drioway and Kwuway, he had always played against his enemies' strength. With a sword in hand, he could beat any man – any two.

'A dozen. I can best the lot of them. Bring them on!' he heard himself cry aloud. Rouwen clamped his mouth shut when he realized his excitement had boiled over and made him reveal himself like a tyro going into battle for the first time. It might have been the water or simply his own buoyant spirits after victorious combat. Whichever had caused him to act thus, it betrayed his position.

'There! There he is. Get him,' a Mionese soldier cried hoarsely. But the soldier's voice dropped, he licked his lips in anticipation, and a sly look crossed his leathery, sun-baked face.

'How much are they offering for my head?' asked Rouwen,

astutely understanding the cause of the soldier's sudden silence as he advanced. His opponent was already spending his blood money. 'A few pieces of gold? A dozen? More?'

'A duchy,' the soldier said, moving carefully now to avoid any traps Rouwen might have set. There had not been time for such to be laid, but his slow advance gave Rouwen the opportunity to evaluate his opponent. The first soldier he had slain had been young, brash, thoughtless in his headlong rush to cut his own throat on Rouwen's sword. The officer following him so quickly to Paradise's lush, gentle green fields had been overconfident, thinking a big sword decided any dispute.

Rouwen now was paired off against a battle-hardened veteran who knew the penalty for even the smallest mistake. The sure movement of his feet, the slow flicker of his sword tip as he advanced, the wary expression and the fixed stare all told of many battles fought and won. The promise of becoming ennobled added to the soldier's desire for victory, if the thought of dying did not.

'That's a hefty reward for a lowly soldier such as I.' Rouwen circled, keeping a sharp lookout for other Mionese fighters. 'I am nothing but a cashiered officer, a former captain in the Gannian Guard.'

'You're not a wizard?' Surprise vanished and a broad grin crossed the soldier's face. 'Then you must be Rouwen. You're worth a principality!'

'Sosler values me that highly?' Rouwen didn't know whether to laugh or spit. The Lord of Death and Life merited only a duchy but he, a peasant with aspirations to nobility, would win this soldier a chance at the throne?

'You must die!'

Rouwen parried easily and stepped back, his sword lowered into a comfortable *en garde*.

'What did Sosler really promise you? He thinks to put himself on the throne – the throne of a kingdom combining the lands of Mion and Gan. There is no place for a peasant in his plans, other than himself, that is.' Rouwen riposted and drew a tiny crescent on the soldier's cheek. He had no desire to play with the man; from his deft movement, the soldier was a good fighter.

'Why do you keep naming the Duke of Gan?' The soldier thought to weave words as well as steel to gain his kill. 'Duke Drioway, acting for King Nishor, has pledged his solemn word on . . .'

Rouwen saw the slight hesitation on his opponent's part, the smallest misstep possible, and then the fight ended. He drove his blade inward as hard as he could and tore through the light steel chain mail until he found a vital organ. The soldier gasped, gurgled and died. Pink froth bubbled from his lips for a moment longer, and then there was no remaining sign of life.

'Through the lung,' Rouwen said, pitying the soldier. There were better ways to die. He had seen too many of his own soldiers die from sucking chest wounds.

The rustling of leaves startled Rouwen. The Mionese soldiers had completely ringed him, their swords and lances pointed at him. While he had fought, they had taken their positions.

Now it was his turn to die.

2

Wind and Wave

'What are your orders? Kill me or capture me?' Brion Rouwen asked, hoping to engage the soldiers in dialogue rather than mayhem. He winced as a lance tip nudged his ribs.

'You are the Lord of Death and Life?' The query came more as a statement, though there was an element of uncertainty in the words. The ranking Mionese soldier, a sergeant from the look of his insignia now partially covered with dirt, shifted uneasily. He glanced around at his comrades, as if they might provide him with a glimmering of an answer. He wanted to know if he faced a wizard and was in danger or if Rouwen was merely a peasant doing a wizard's bidding.

'No, I'm not the Lord,' Rouwen said, mind racing to find just the right words to disarm the soldiers. Fighting his way out of the ring of steely points around him wasn't possible. That didn't mean he couldn't get away if he kept his wits about him. 'I can summon him, though, if that is your wish.'

'No!'

The sergeant's sharp command came too late. Rouwen had already placed the golden horn to his lips and let forth a long, low, musical note that rolled across the Isle of Passing and seemed to grow louder as it echoed into the distance. The soldiers tensed but did not spit Rouwen on their swords, uncertain about what he had done with his call. He paused and looked around, worrying that the horn no longer summoned the Legion of the Air.

'Don't try that again,' the sergeant said nervously. 'Men, get him to the barges. I don't think he's the one we're looking for, but . . .'

Immense roaring drowned out the sergeant's orders. Rouwen knew what to expect and dived to the ground, burrowing through fallen leaves and seeking any depression, no matter how slight, in the soft dirt. He found his hiding place barely in time to ride out the blast of wind whipping across the land.

The tornado had formed not a hundred paces away and took a

few seconds to bounce and slide along the fragrant, leaf-strewn forest floor in Rouwen's direction. As if fingers of air ripped at his back, Rouwen felt his tunic being caught up and pulled from his body in tatters that snapped like battle flags. But the carnage being wrought on the Mionese soldiers was far worse than the minor damage Rouwen sustained to his uniform. They had remained on their feet – until the wind warrior struck them.

Screams of agony as the men were lifted off their feet reached Rouwen over the whine of the whirling column of air. Protecting his eyes with his arm, he chanced a look up through the tree limbs to the murky pillar filled with spinning soldiers. As he had seen before, the wind warrior spun faster and faster until the men blasted apart into bloody fragments.

The rain of gore and human parts came down around him, forcing Rouwen to bury his face in the soft dirt. And then a sudden silence descended, making him wonder if he had gone deaf. Wiping off the bloody film from his face, he blinked and tried to see what had gone on around him. Of the soldiers, Rouwen saw no sign. Bodies, weapons, every trace had been removed from his sight.

He snorted and sat up, correcting his first impression. The sheet of blood covering ground and shrub and tree and Rouwen remained as silent testimony to sudden death. But the bodies were gone. Completely.

Rouwen got to his feet and moved back to the path through the forest. Trees had been uprooted by the wind warrior's passage, turning the island to a scene of devastation unmatched in Rouwen's memory. He found his own sword and hefted it. The balance was subtly wrong; he saw a nick taken out of the sword blade, but the weapon would serve him well enough until he could replace it.

He warily went back to the beach and saw more destruction where the new wind warrior had blasted past. Two barges were overturned and their passengers scattered, most dead but a few moaning and trying to put order back into their mission. Rouwen had no trouble picking out an officer badgering his men into ragged ranks. Some order came back to the Mionese invaders as the officer pushed, shoved and shouted. He assembled fewer than twenty men in his re-formed company.

Fingering the horn, Rouwen considered blowing forth a few more wind warriors to take care of the remainder of King Nishor's force. The powerful tornado warriors would make short work of this ragtag band. The officer didn't even recognize the men he now commanded. Rouwen had spent two years as

Captain of Gan's Intrepid Guard and knew the importance of an officer knowing his men, their strengths and weaknesses, and of establishing confidence in that officer's ability to lead. A single challenge would scatter the few paltry soldiers assembling on the beach.

Rouwen looked across the channel toward the mainland and marvelled that the wind warriors he had summoned had so successfully held off a major invasion. Of two thousand attempting to land on the Isle of Passing, only twenty remained. Rouwen held in check his urge to run down to the beach, waving his sword wildly, and rout the disheartened soldiers.

But he did touch the golden horn again, still thinking of summoning yet another wind warrior to finish the task the other five had started. Four had ruined the fleet and the fifth had saved him from capture. What was another tornado whipping around on the beach? Rouwen lifted the horn to his lips but paused as he saw all five of the wind warriors he had summoned swirl into view at the far curve of the island. As if at some master sergeant's bidding, the tornadoes leaped and danced and bobbed in the direction of the soldiers on the beach. Rouwen didn't need to call forth more; the ones already summoned and patrolling the Isle of Passing directed themselves toward the invaders.

Rouwen blinked, for a moment thinking he had seen tiny hands reaching from the core of the whirling vortices. Faces formed and vanished almost as quickly. And then Rouwen's attention turned back to the wind warriors' victims. The soldiers broke rank, in spite of the officer's screamed orders, and ran for the trees lining the snowy white beach.

Their fear saved them. The officer's insistence on keeping order killed him. Rouwen winced as the leading vortex caught up the officer and sent him spinning inside its grip. The officer flew apart, as so many others had done, and ended up an ensanguined coating on the once pure sand. Rouwen put the trumpet to his lips, thinking to make the wind warriors vanish.

The first note sounded remarkably like the others he had blown and a new tornado formed, smaller than its brothers, but still virulently seeking life to snuff out. Rouwen tried again, this time varying the pitch and duration. Two new wind warriors stirred to life and began raging back and forth, joining the other seven in an orgy of destruction.

Uprooted trees flew through the air, to splash down out at sea. Rouwen saw the poisonous fish between the Isle of Passing and the mainland begin snapping at their leafy victims. He wondered if the fish cared what they tore asunder. Remembering his own deadly encounters with the fish in getting to the island, he doubted it.

Another sounding of the horn brought forth still another member of the Legion of the Air. Exasperated, Rouwen stared at the horn, wondering what note it took to make the summoned destroyers vanish.

For the first time, he noticed a warmth in his tattered uniform pocket. Reaching down, Rouwen touched the grimoire stolen from Kwuway that the Lord had wanted so badly. The spell book glowed warm to the touch as he rested his fingers on its cover and then almost burned him as a wind warrior wobbled and spun in his direction. Rouwen retreated toward the center of the island, hoping this would keep the tornado at bay.

It didn't. The wind warrior followed him slowly, ripping apart vegetation and hurling rocks and dirt in all directions. Rouwen ducked as projectiles whistled past his head, forcing him to veer away. As he dodged, Rouwen found himself heading toward the Lord's stone home, almost as if the wind warriors herded him like a stray cow.

Panting, Rouwen ducked inside and leaned against a cold wall. Outside the wind whined as it pelted the hut with more debris ripped from the ground. Rouwen pulled the grimoire from his pocket, hardly able to hold it because of the heat. A greenish glow spread from the spell book and crept along his wrists and arms, but Rouwen did not toss the book aside.

'The counterspell,' Rouwen panted. 'I need a counter to the Legion of the Air.' Somehow, Rouwen had hoped the simple voicing of his request would cause the grimoire to fall open at the proper page. If anything, the book only warmed more and gave him no hint of a way to chase off the wind warriors.

Rouwen opened the heavy cover and flipped through the radiant pages, hoping something might catch his eye. Again he was disappointed. The glyphs so painstakingly written on the pages were of a language Rouwen did not understand. Even if he could have read the incantations and spells entered here, he wasn't certain any would have helped him soon enough. He slammed the grimoire closed and stuffed it back into his pocket, then dared to look out the hut's narrow door.

The Legion of the Air was ravaging the island, tearing trees out by their roots, hurling boulders through the air to crash far out at sea, and otherwise systematically scouring everything above sea level. Rouwen saw that it was only a matter of time before even the Lord's stout home was reduced to rubble and gusted out into the water.

Turning back, Rouwen searched its interior once more for any clue as to how to stop the devastation. As before, nothing came immediately to sight. This time Rouwen began tearing apart the furniture in the hut, poking into crevices, digging into the dirt floor in a vain search for hidden magical implements. He found nothing. Distracted by the increasing destruction being done outside the building, Rouwen felt a flash of fear. He had brought the Legion of the Air to life without knowledge of controlling or banishing them. He closed his eyes and imagined the airy hands reaching for him and mouths filled with dusty teeth opening to swallow him.

'No! There has to be a way of stopping them. The Lord did it. But how?' Rouwen opened his eyes and saw what had eluded him before. The merest scrap of paper lay across the room, fluttering in the brisk wind buffeting everything inside the hut. He scrambled on hands and knees for the paper, praying that this would carry the spell required to silence the winds.

Both fearing and hoping he had discovered the key, Rouwen scanned the scrap of paper. He let out a cry of joy at his discovery.

'This is it. The way to stop them. It . . .' His heart sank when he realized the instructions on the sheet did him no good. His hands shook as he held the thin parchment with the simple words on it. He had to read through twice to be sure he had not missed some nuance of meaning, some small clue that the Lord had hidden in the instructions. 'A golden whistle to stop the wind warriors, and the sequence to use to banish them. But where is the whistle?'

Frantic, Rouwen again searched the building. He threw everything loose into the far corner, then rooted like a hog in the rubble hunting for any hint of gold. As before, he found no magical devices, much less the needed golden whistle. He could rouse but he could not undo the call. Rouwen despaired, but he kept hunting. The Lord must have used such a whistle or there would have been dozens of wind warriors circling the island at all times and they would have turned on him, as the ones Rouwen summoned were now seeking him.

He twisted to avoid a new torrent of wind cutting at him as the roof flew off into the swirling interior of a towering tornado. The ripping wind caught the rubble he had searched and spun it aloft, out of his reach forever. And then Rouwen began worrying that the wind warriors would catch him and blast him apart, as they had already done to the Mionese invaders.

Rouwen fell flat and wriggled toward the door as the far wall crumbled. Rocks sang like catapult-thrown missiles and smashed into the still-standing walls. Fat blue sparks exploded as more debris crashed about his head. He began scrambling for the door, checked for the best way to safety, then took to his heels.

Rouwen weaved between two wind warriors bobbing near the Lord's demolished home and saw three more converging on the clearing. Somehow, his presence drew the tornadoes. It might have been the horn – he could think of no other reason for the wind warriors to dog his path so accurately – but he refused to abandon the hard-won trumpet. He had no intention of summoning more of the deadly whirlwinds, but he didn't know if he might need them later . . .

'After I get to the mainland,' he grated out through grit-caked teeth. Rouwen had no plan for reaching the distant swamp, but even those deadly lands seemed tranquil in comparison with the hurricane-force winds buffeting everything above ground on the Isle of Passing.

Struggling hard, wind causing his eyes to water and face to burn, Rouwen made his way toward the beach where the Mionese soldiers had landed. He remembered one barge still upright. Somehow, he might be able to work the huge vessel back to the mainland, past the wind warriors and poisonous fish and any other magical guardian that might have been placed to guarantee the Lord his privacy.

Rouwen lost track of time in getting to the beach. It was a casual stroll over a short distance before, but now it turned into a deadly battle along every inch. The wind tore at his clothing, but Rouwen stayed low. Once he sighted two wind warriors bouncing in his direction. Rouwen threw his arms around a tree bole and then felt himself being flung high into the air. Startled, the former guard captain let loose of what he had thought a secure anchorage and found himself flying like a seabird.

Flapping his arms against a rising current of air caused him to sail upward as if he had become a bird and had taken wing – for a moment. He shrieked as he fell. The rising current that had supported him moved away suddenly and left him as helpless as a stone thrown at the sky. Rouwen plunged downward and managed to get his feet under him before he hit the sandy beach. He let his knees take some of the shock of the fall, then he doubled over and rolled, ending up half in the soft warm water lapping against the beach.

Rouwen pushed down for support and cut his hand on jagged shards of bone. Parts of an invader's wind-rent corpse had been unceremoniously deposited here. Rouwen recoiled as he found himself sitting in a pool of blood that washed out on the tide as gently as it had washed ashore.

He stumbled back onto drier terrain, only to find himself facing two battered survivors of the invasion force. One held a dagger broken off at the hilt and useless as a weapon. He waved it about weakly, and Rouwen came to the realization that the soldier's eyes were focused on some distant horizon, one no other human might share. The soldier seemed too stunned to notice he threatened no one with his broken weapon and simply stumbled past Rouwen. The other, taller soldier held his right arm tightly to his body. The injury was immediately apparent to Rouwen. A bright white bone from the fighter's forearm had pierced his skin and gleamed in the sunlight.

'Help me?' Rouwen croaked, not sure what else to say. His sword hung sheathed at his side, and the dagger in his belt might not be enough protection against two men, even in their condition, bent on slaying him.

'We must get back,' the dazed soldier said. His eyes never quite focused, but his face turned toward the mainland. In this Rouwen could only agree.

'How? Where's your barge?'

'There,' said the other soldier, trying to point and wincing at the slight movement. 'But how can we hope to make it? We'll be in Paradise long before we traverse *that* channel.'

'I saw what happened as you crossed,' Rouwen said. He bit his lower lip in dread that he had given himself away. Neither soldier noted his verbal slip. He pulled himself farther up on the beach and helped the man with the compound fracture toward the lone barge still upright. Three others were on the beach, all turned upside down and displaying various degrees of damage. Rouwen doubted any would be seaworthy enough to reach the distant shore.

'We might put out to sea and make our way up the coast to Tachre,' suggested the soldier he aided. The other one, still dazed, trailed behind like some dog chasing its master. 'Those damned water spouts don't seem to block that direction.'

Rouwen shook his head. The wind warriors patrolled the entire perimeter of the island. He doubted they had any better chance on the open sea than they would in the channel going for the mainland.

'How do we get it into the water?' Rouwen asked. 'And when we do, we have to keep it moving, no matter what direction we choose.' He had never seen a Mionese assault barge before. He wondered what shores this ancient vessel had attacked, what battles it had seen, and what turn of fate had finally brought it to the end of its usefulness on the Isle of Passing.

A gust of wind pushed the barge into the water and caused Rouwen to fall face down into the surf. He sputtered and tried to stand and found himself unable to. A huge log had been blown across his legs by the wind warrior approaching from inland. To his left he saw two more, and he heard the thunderous noise of others converging on him again. He fought to get free and found an unexpected ally. The dazed soldier worked to lift the heavy log.

'Thanks,' Rouwen said, wriggling from under the pinning weight. His legs were cut and bruised but otherwise undamaged. He got to his feet and grabbed the soldier's hand and pulled him along like a captive child, splashing in the water to reach the barge drifting out to sea. The soldier with the broken arm waved to them from the bow, but his words were drowned out by the tumult caused by the wind warriors.

'Can you swim?' Rouwen asked the silent soldier. The man didn't seem to understand the question. Rouwen kept pulling and finally dived into the waves breaking against the shoreline. If the man who had freed him followed, fine. If not, Rouwen knew there was no hope for either of them if they remained on the island even a minute longer.

'Here, take hold.' A rope splashed down in front of Rouwen's face. He grabbed the knotted end and quickly worked his way up the side of the barge. Glancing back, he saw the mute soldier immediately behind him. Rouwen scrambled into the flat-bottomed boat and lay for a moment, getting his breath back. Then he helped the soldier with the broken arm get his comrade into the boat.

Rouwen paused and stared in astonishment at the Isle of Passing. The Lord of Death and Life's fine little island had been scoured of all vegetation by the seven rampaging wind warriors. Two swirling killers still crisscrossed the denuded land, leveling even the smallest elevation in their way. The pitiful, stripped mound of dirt left behind might never have grown a blade of grass or a spindly bush – or been home to a powerful wizard.

'We need to lower the centerboard,' the soldier told him, nudging him with his good arm. 'That'll keep us from spinning in circles and might keep us on a true course to yon shore.' The soldier lifted his stubbled chin slightly to point toward the odorous, sucking swamps where Rouwen had fought the man's comrades-in-arms twice before.

'How do we give this pile of lumber more speed?' Rouwen saw

a huge rudder at the stern but no other obvious means of propulsion. A dozen men rowing would have hardly propelled the barge with the speed he had witnessed during their initial attack.

'We had a wizard with us. He wasn't much of a mage, but he knew enough magic to spell-move the barges. Said we could go into the teeth of a gale, he did. The fool.' The soldier sank down and clutched his broken arm.

Rouwen wanted to do something to relieve the man's obvious pain. He had set more than a few broken bones in his day, even compound fractures such as this one. But the wind warriors formed into a wall of whirling bluster, as if puzzled by his sudden absence. He didn't know how long it would be until they magically found him again – or was it the golden horn still dangling at his side they followed?

Rouwen lifted the magical instrument, considering the magnitude of his loss if he dropped it into the water. Simply touching the horn caused the wind warriors to wheel about and begin a slow march across the water in his direction. He hastily dropped the horn, but the damage had been done.

'It's as if they can see us without eyes, these miserable mounds of foul breeze,' grumbled the broken-armed soldier. 'Why are they so dogged in their desire to do us in? We wanted only the wizard who lived on the island. You'd think we were a'come to steal away their treasure or something worse.'

'They are the wizard's protectors,' Rouwen said, putting his shoulder to the rudder. He slowly turned the barge so that the bow pointed toward the dubious safety of the distant swampy shore. Never having spent any time in a waterbound vessel, Rouwen's expertise was limited to common sense. Struggling with the sluggish control, he overshot the line of travel he desired on his first try but corrected and got the barge moving slowly toward refuge.

'The demons-damned winds are coming for us!' shouted the soldier. 'How do we fight them? Damn them all!'

The first gusts of wind blasted past Rouwen, causing his eyes to water. He felt his skin burning from the high-speed explosion of air. Then he felt the barge lifting on the crest of a powerful wave and being driven hard for the far shore.

'They're powering us along the way!' Rouwen cried. 'Help me hold the rudder on course. It has a life of its own.' He fought against the bucking handle until the mute soldier joined him. The two of them struggled to keep the barge on a straight path, and Rouwen dared hope they would make a safe landing.

'Tidal wave. A tidal wave's on its way,' called the soldier from the bow where he stood unsteadily looking back.

Rouwen chanced a look over the high stern and saw a wall of water the height of ten tall men curling over and rushing toward them faster than any vessel could sail. The leading wave kept the heavy barge moving, but not as fast as the surging wave.

'No!' Rouwen shrieked as the tongue of water licked over the stern and carried the mute soldier overboard, plucking him up as easily as if he had been a child's doll. Rouwen was buffeted and smashed hard into the stern. He fought to keep a grip on the rudder and failed. The heavy handle snapped about and the barge immediately turned sideways to the wave.

Rouwen called a warning to the other soldier as the barge swung upward, threatening to capsize. But the words were drowned out by the roar of the water – and it mattered little. The soldier had already vanished.

Next moment Brion Rouwen was sucked under, the bottom of the barge between him and the surface.

3

The Wind Warriors Pursue

Rouwen fought hard to get to the surface, but he was trapped under the war barge. He felt strong currents pulling at his legs, trying to force him to the bottom of the channel. Clinging with all his might to a piece of what had been decking, Rouwen resisted the undertow. But his lungs began to burn with the precious air he held inside.

As suddenly as the barge had been turned over by the tidal wave, the barge was lifted high and flung through the air. Rouwen screamed at the unexpected flight and found himself staring down at the water's surface from twenty feet in the air. Then he plunged downward. Still clinging to the broken plank in the barge, Rouwen smashed into the water. The impact drove air from his lungs and made him gasp.

And once more he was forced underwater, this time by a huge mouth fastening around his leg. Sharp teeth pierced his skin, sending tiny spurts of blood into the clear water. Rouwen thrashed but couldn't get free, then calmed enough to realize he would die if he panicked. His dagger slid from its sheath as he dove underwater, not bothering to fill his lungs completely with much needed air.

He never hesitated when he saw the spiny fish worrying at his leg. Rouwen stabbed out, and a new gush of blood spurted into the water. This time it was fish blood, and the voracious beast released its grip long enough for Rouwen to kick free. The blue-green monster swam away just beyond Rouwen's reach and watched, as if waiting for him to make a mistake. Lungs burning again, he had to surface.

From the corner of his eye, he saw the fish begin its attack again. Rolling onto his side, he barely avoided slashing teeth. He raked the fish's side with his dagger and produced new clouds of blood. This was all the punishment the monstrous fish could take. It swiped at Rouwen with a razor-sharp fin and then swam off.

For a long minute, Rouwen was able to float on his back,

gasping for air and recovering his strength. The respite died when he felt the water under him rising again. A new tidal wave picked him up and sent him floundering through a mixture of sky, water, and blood. He didn't know if he was airborne or underwater and trying to breathe froth. Then he slammed down so hard his teeth rattled.

'Another, another's on its way!' came a distant cry. Rouwen trod water and saw the soldier with the broken arm some distance away, clinging with his good arm to a piece from the barge.

Rouwen looked around for the next tidal wave. That wasn't the danger the soldier warned against. Four wind warriors ducked and bobbed across the water, heading directly for Rouwen. Again, he was drawing them to him like a dependable hunting dog sniffing out its master's game.

'Swim for it,' Rouwen called, trying to put as much distance between himself and the Legion of the Air. He saw a muddy outjut of land within his reach. Even as he stroked for it, fish nipped at his legs. One bite was particularly severe, causing his left leg to go numb. The Lord's guardians were nothing if not efficient at their task.

He rolled onto his back and floated for a moment to restore feeling to his paralyzed leg and saw that the Mionese soldier wasn't swimming strongly enough to reach land. Fins cut the water around him, converging on him as if the finest meal possible had been presented for piscine approval. Rouwen rubbed his leg until tingles of sensation returned. He started swimming slowly for the muddy shoal when tortured words caused him to hesitate.

'They're gettin' me. Can't swim, not with a broken arm. Help me!'

Rouwen rolled in the water again and saw the wounded soldier slip beneath the surface, only to fight back a second later. Closer now, four wind warriors whirled across the water, hunting for him. Walls of water surged in all directions as they passed. It would be only a matter of time before a new tidal wave came and inundated him and the faltering soldier.

'Save yourself,' the soldier cried when he saw Rouwen's hesitation. 'I can never make it. Save yourself!'

Again the soldier vanished beneath the waves. This decided Rouwen. He reversed course and ignored the poisonous nipping at his flesh by the schools of fish barely submerged in their haste to feed on human flesh. He cursed himself for a fool as he swam powerfully to the soldier's aid. He should not return. Safety was within his reach and this man had been sent, along

217

with the rest of the invasion force, to take him prisoner or
kill him.

Somehow, this mattered less than the way the soldier had
saved him by casting down the knotted rope from the barge.
The Mionese soldier had not regarded Rouwen as his enemy,
and it had not mattered then.

It didn't matter to Brion Rouwen now.

'Stop, no . . .' The soldier gulped as something powerful
jerked him underwater. Rouwen gulped air and dived, his dagger
flashing. He cut a long gash in a rubbery tentacle. Inky blood
momentarily blinded him, but he felt the soldier's legs weakly
struggling. His arms circled those legs as he drove for the surface.
Rouwen burst forth, gasping, and finally remembered to release
his burden. It wouldn't do to save the soldier from the tentacled
monster and then drown him.

'Don't stay. Got to swim. Hurry, hurry,' the foundering
soldier urged. Rouwen saw that strength seeped from the man
like sap from a cut tree trunk. Tiny droplets, by themselves, were
insignificant but each weakened the whole. Rouwen caught the
soldier as the man sank underneath the water and ran his arm
around his shoulders. Swimming proved difficult and twice he
had to fight off the voracious fish.

Land loomed only a few dozen yards in front of him. Rouwen
swam harder, pulling the soldier along beside him in the water.

'Another one,' the man gasped out. At first Rouwen didn't
understand what he meant. Then he looked behind and saw that
his luck had run out. Three wind warriors had begun their slow
pursuit and were churning up a new monstrous wall of water.
Rouwen felt the beginnings of the swell.

'We can make it,' he said, putting his face down and swimming
as hard as he could. Lances of pain raced up his leg from the fish's
bite. His lungs burned as if liquid fire had been pumped into
them. Worst of all, his arms started cramping from the strain
of holding onto the helpless soldier and stroking through water
that became increasingly viscous. After only a few strokes,
Rouwen thought he swam in molasses.

'Let me go. Save yourself. What do you want, a medal? King
Nishor doesn't give medals to fools.'

Rouwen ignored the soldier and struggled on.

He had lost count of the times he had flown through the air.
This time the massive wave didn't quite lift him because he
was too close to the muddy spit thrusting into the sea. The
wave broke and sent Rouwen sliding across the muddy surface
to slam hard against a half-buried tree trunk. He lay stunned, the

world turned to bright pain around him. The soldier rescued him from the second wave crashing across the muddy finger sticking out from the swampy mainland. As the water receded, Rouwen sputtered and sat up.

More pain dazzled him, but he knew nothing was broken. His arms and legs obeyed, if reluctantly from cramps and bruises, and the few bites he had sustained from the long-fanged fish were minor.

'We cannot stay here,' Rouwen said, seeing the twisting behemoths of air working their way toward him from the water. Huge geysers erupted into the air and spewed out fish, wooden fragments from barges and even human parts. The wind warriors were thorough as they crept away from the Isle of Passing in their pursuit.

Or was it pursuit? Rouwen touched the gold horn still dangling at his side. The strap had remained secure during his travails. He was tempted to try one last blast on the horn to make the wind warriors retreat, but he held back. The message on the scrap of paper had instructed differently.

A golden whistle. Where would he find it? If the Lord had carried it, the magical device was long lost. Rouwen wiped the dirt and salt water from his eyes and tried to imagine the Isle of Passing as it had once been. Seeing the barren knob of dirt rising from the sea required more than memory and imagination. The Legion of the Air had completely ripped away anything thrusting upward more than a few inches. The once idyllic isle had been left a desert.

'Those monsters are a'gaining on us,' the soldier said, struggling to move in the sucking mud. 'We can stay and let them eat us for their supper, or we can rejoin our forces.'

'Where?' Rouwen asked. His uniform was tattered and beaten, but it had once been a Mionese officer's. He had slain the officer before journeying to the Lord's island. If any found out he was not of King Nishor's military, he would be killed out of hand as a spy. But at this thought Rouwen only laughed bitterly.

There were worse punishments. Such as the curse he still carried. His hand crept inside his tunic and touched the silver spell casket.

'Diarra,' he muttered.

'How's that? You calling down the wrath of some demon to stop them?'

'No, not quite that,' Rouwen said, smiling sardonically as he lurched on alongside the soldier. 'I merely remember an old – acquaintance.'

219

The former Queen of Gan's soul lay trapped within the spell casket he carried. This would prove a potent bargaining point. She counted him as an enemy, but they were both victims of Duke Sosler's perfidy. Even if they could never be friends, they might become allies for a common goal. Neither wished to see King Priowe remain on the Gannian throne any longer. And one's affliction might be similar to the other's. If Diarra was freed from the spell placed upon her by Kwuway, then Rouwen could hope that his spell casket could be found and the damnable curse on his head might be lifted.

To kill the one he loved with a single touch!

'We'll have to make better speed than this, friend,' said the soldier. 'Those tornadoes must have sniffed us out. I swear they are coming for us. Seven of them damnable brutes.'

Rouwen saw that the man's eyesight had not been affected. Seven towering wind warriors leapfrogged in unison across the sea toward the land. Their pace was slow, hardly more than a slow walk, but they carried an inexorability that chilled him. They must be drawn to the horn, but he dared not surrender it. He had almost died – he had slain the Lord of Death and Life to gain this horn, though that had not been his intent when he had returned to the Isle of Passing.

Trying to lift a curse, he had killed a powerful wizard and possibly acquired a new scourge. The tornadoes sent forth thin wisps of fog as insects might wave their antennae, sniffing, searching, homing in on him with unerring accuracy. How far would they chase him? To the very gates of Castle Gan?

A crazy scheme was born in Rouwen's brain and died as quickly as it had come. There was no way he could use the wind warriors to regain entry into the valley holding the towering pillar of stone capped by Castle Gan. And certainly he could never direct the tornadoes against the castle itself. It took the better part of a day to ride up the spiral road to the castle's front gate. Although, as Captain of the Intrepid Guard, he knew other entry points, this knowledge gave him little advantage using such magical weapons.

He could not control where and how the wind warriors worked their will. Rouwen wondered if the golden whistle might somehow do more than simply cause the wind warriors to dissipate, if it might also sway them to his fancy.

'I'm Corporal Rol, King's First Reconnaissance Company,' said the soldier.

'May Paradise be yours,' Rouwen said, hardly listening. He had plans to formulate, places to go – and Queen Diarra to find.

She was a noble. She had to know of other wizards who might be amenable to lifting the curses Kwuway had placed on them. With Kwuway dead, though, perhaps Diarra's contacts with the realm of wizards had passed. And treachery was not out of the question. Queen Diarra had never been entirely of rational or whole mind.

Rouwen smiled grimly as he remembered the days and nights Diarra had spend wandering the corridors of Castle Gan dressed only in a thin nightgown, singing to herself and carrying on long, one-sided conversations with portraits of long dead ancestors. None had dared call her crazy, but she was not sound mentally.

That made her all the more dangerous to deal with, Rouwen knew. Also she blamed him for their predicament. King Priowe had conveniently found his naked wife with his Captain of the Intrepid Guard and reached the conclusion Sosler had intended. Two of the king's staunchest allies were removed by a single fiendish plot. Princess Sorinne and her wastrel brother, Sped, would prove no opposition to Sosler when he finally moved to destroy Priowe.

'And Nishor,' Rouwen added, speaking aloud his thoughts.

'What's that?' Rol's steps began to falter but he slogged on gamely through the swamp. 'You think we ought to report straightaway to the king? But he's back in Tachre.'

'The capital's not so far distant,' Rouwen said, covering his lapse.

'Not distant? You must be an officer of the Sprint Troop. Tachre is a fair week's ride. Even the quickest messenger took three days to get new orders to us for the invasion.'

'The Sprint Troop?' Rouwen bit his lip even as he spoke. A proper Mionese officer would know the different units of an attack force. He had heard mention of the Sprint Troop, but had never been exceptionally well-versed in Mion's enemy organization, his duties in Castle Gan being purely defensive, with special attention to internal threat. It had been Duke Sosler's province to protect Valley Gan from external attack.

'Lord Widden's cavalry,' Rol said. The injured soldier turned and stared at Rouwen. 'You aren't jiggled in the head now, are you? We been through much together. Shock and near death turn men's minds to suet. Seen it happen more 'n once, I have.'

'I can't seem to remember – things,' Rouwen said lamely. 'Some things, that is. I try and there's nothing there.' He touched his temple and winced. He had not realized he had

221

sustained a nasty bruise there. Touching it as he had caused it to throb painfully.

'The chirurgeon can get you patched up when we reach bivouac. It's here somewhere, if only I could remember the landmarks.'

'In this swamp?' Rouwen made a rude noise. The low banyans with their prodigious limbs touching down to the ground to form new trees created a green veil beyond which it was difficult to see. On the tree trunks grew lacy mosses, and dangling from the limbs were foul purple parasitic fungi sapping the vitality of the trees. And everywhere on the ground were deep pools of turgid water laden with leeches and fast-swimming reptiles capable of ripping through the toughest boot leather.

'There's one clear landmark, if *they* stay due west of us,' Rol said. He pointed at the seven pillars of the wind warriors working their way toward the mainland. Rouwen could not estimate how long it would be until they reached land, but it would be within the hour. They had not put enough distance between themselves and the magical behemoths.

To be overtaken in this muck spelled certain death. Neither he nor his companion could ever run far enough or fast enough in the swamp, and hiding was an absured idea. The Legion of the Air need not seek. The tornadic winds need only churn up enough swamp to kill.

'I'm sure the chirurgeon can help me,' Rouwen said. 'That invasion was poorly planned,' he added.

'Count Dobesar is not to blame,' snapped Rol. 'He could never have known of *those*.' From the vehemence of his companion's words, Rouwen knew who Rol's commander had been.

'Did he die in the assault?'

'The first barge to be sucked into a vortex,' Rol said solemnly. 'He was a great man. A fine soldier. He was wasted on a mission better suited to a few wizards.'

'How many wizards does King Nishor have in his employ?' Rouwen saw that the question was a mistake from the way Rol swung on him.

'You ask strange questions, even for an officer who has lost his memory. What was your company? Who commanded?'

'There's no time for this,' Rouwen said, trying to divert Rol's attention. 'We must find our bivouac . . .'

'Who are you? Answer now or I'll kill you on the spot!' Rol swung around and lost his balance, falling to a knee. Rouwen tried to keep from laughing, but the charge was serious. He dared not allow the Mionese soldier to question him further.

222

And Rouwen could never rejoin the troops at the base camp. A wounded soldier might be duped by his feeble replies, but he could never answer satisfactorily if serious questioning began.

And, Rouwen had to admit ruefully, he wasn't doing a very good job with Rol. The man's arm was seriously broken and the pain had to be driving Rol crazy. They had been battered, eaten by fish, almost drowned and badgered by the wind warriors and still Rouwen could not mount a tale credible enough to fool the soldier.

'We're both dead if we don't keep moving,' Rouwen said, his hand resting on his dagger. He didn't want to present an overt challenge to Rol, yet he knew he might be forced to kill this man who had saved his life – and whose life he had saved. 'Believe me when I say the Legion of the Air will follow me to the farthest reaches of this continent.' He fingered the horn and knew there would be no convincing Rol without summoning another of the wind warriors.

That Rouwen would not do. He was in enough trouble from his reckless use of the horn on the Isle of Passing. However he worked through his problems, it would be without putting the magical horn to his lips another time.

Rol stared at the whirling giants above the swamp trees and then at Rouwen. 'Who are you? You are no officer of Mion.'

Rouwen spat. 'Nishor tried to kill me, and I killed his wizard – and King Priowe's wizard. Kwuway was playing one monarch off against the other for his own ends.' Rouwen stopped when he considered how much of Sosler's plans for power he ought to reveal. Rol was a common soldier and in no position to help him – or even believe his wild yarn. As a child, Rouwen had listened with Adan to their uncle's graphically told tall tales. He had died a year after Rouwen's fifth Spring Festival, of dysentery. Rouwen wasn't sure he possessed even a fraction of his uncle's skill to convince the skeptical. There hadn't been time.

Rouwen swallowed hard, remembering how many of his family now spent eternity in Paradise.

'You are the one we were sent to capture,' Rol accused. 'You are the wizard . . .'

'No!' Rouwen wiped sticky filth from his arms and knew they had to get free of the swamp soon. Any more time wasted in the muck would give the wind warriors ample time to reach dry land and overtake them. 'I am no wizard. I seek one. I need a spell lifted. Diarra and I . . .'

'Diarra?' Rol frowned, as if struggling with some distant, nagging memory. 'You know her? The Gannian harebrain?'

'What do you know of her?'

Rol winced as he cradled his left arm and moved it to a more comfortable position. Rouwen saw how the soldier had turned white at this simple movement. Rol might not have the strength required for them both to reach dry land, much less the spot where the Mionese had their base camp.

'Tell me,' demanded Rouwen, growing frantic. Time pressed down heavily on him. He had the sensation of being unable to move without knowing Rol's tidbit about Diarra.

'She came to Tachre bragging that she was a queen. No one believed her, though it was rumored King Nishor granted her an audience. The king's whims are notorious.' Rol chuckled, as if Nishor were a comedian bent on entertaining his citizens. Rouwen remembered how the Mionese king had ordered all supplicants to his weekly audience murdered. It removed undesirables in the most cold-blooded way possible. If anything, Nishor deserved whatever fate awaited him at Sosler's and Drioway's hands.

'What became of her? Is she still in your capital?' Rouwen realized as he spoke that he gave proof that he was no Mionese officer. It didn't matter. The wind warriors approached, and he had to locate Diarra if he wanted to enlist her help in finding another wizard.

'I cannot say. She might still be in Tachre. King Nishor is a merciful ruler. He might have kept her on at the court as an amusement. He has a way about him, you know.'

Rol sank to his knees, his strength at an end. Rouwen knew he should abandon the Mionese soldier. If they found the bivouac, any report Rol made would only prove disastrous for him. And yet they had been through so much escaping from the Isle of Passing that Rouwen could not simply walk away. His arm circled Rol's shoulders, and again he supported the man's weight.

The going became harder for Rouwen as his own strength faded. The swamp sucked at his energy as surely as the mud pulled his boots down with every step. The few reptiles mercifully avoided them, as if turning over prime feed to the clouds of buzzing, blood-sucking insects. Rouwen wobbled and staggered, determined never to stop in his flight from the wind warriors. Now and again he glanced over his shoulder to find the towering magical beasts. Sometimes, they seemed to fall behind, but more often they narrowed the distance and came close enough for Rouwen to hear their swirling whine over the buzz of insects feasting on his body.

Just as he thought he could not take another step with the

now semiconscious Rol burdening him, Rouwen stumbled onto a patch of drier land. He dropped to his knees and reveled in the feel of soil between his fingers. And then he heard the neighing of horses. Rouwen jerked to his feet and scanned the terrain for any sign of the sound's source. A low hill blocked direct view of the Mionese bivouac.

Rol stirred and moaned, then called out. Brion Rouwen abandoned his charge then and sought a safer harbor to see what happened if the corporal's moans brought a sentry. A pair of intertwined wind-tumbled trees gave Rouwen his hiding place. Lying behind the fallen trees and peering through their leafy limbs thrusting valiantly skyward gave him a clear view of Rol tossing about on the ground.

'Who's that?' came the challenge. 'Give the password or be damned!'

Rol tried to speak, but his strength failed. He collapsed and lay motionless. Rouwen feared the corporal might have finally succumbed to his wounds, but when two Mionese sentries approached him, Rol lifted his good hand and tried to summon them.

'It's the swine who took all our money in last night's dice game!' one sentry exclaimed. 'Look at him now. He's not so high and mighty.' He knelt and began rummaging through Rol's tattered clothing, looking for the money he had lost in the previous night's game of chance. The guard found nothing. Any money the corporal might have carried on his person was long since lost at the bottom of the channel between the mainland and the Isle of Passing.

'Wasn't he with the invasion force?' asked the other. 'What's he doing back so soon, and in such sorry condition?'

The two guards bent to examine Rol. Rouwen started to circle them and enter their camp before they could return with Rol and report to the officer of the watch. He froze when he heard an all too familiar roaring noise.

The wind warriors had finally overtaken him.

4

Diarra the Discredited

The sky darkened as the two leading wind warriors whirled through the swamp and found dry ground. Rock and dirt joined the muck in the sucking vortex and started a blinding rain. Rouwen buried his head behind one tree trunk and endured the pelting. The soldiers starting Rol's interrogation recoiled when they saw the magical beings dominating the suddenly stormy sky. Both turned and ran for the camp, screaming useless warnings.

Rouwen took a few seconds to gather his thoughts, then left his dubious sanctuary and ran to Rol's side. The corporal moaned and his eyes blinked open.

'So you've not gone yet, eh? Whence do you hail? You are no Mionese loyalist.' Rol coughed and spat as more dirt rained from above. He turned his head and groaned as new pain assailed his tortured body. Rouwen wished he could do something for the man, but such longing was fruitless. Rol required the services of a knowledgeable chirurgeon if he was to survive even another hour.

'I cannot explain. There's no time. Believe this,' Rouwen said sincerely. 'I had no wish to draw *those* to you.'

'They follow you?' Rol's voice was hardly a whisper, almost lost in the thunderous roaring winds brought by the wind warriors.

'Where did you see Diarra last?' Rouwen held Rol's head but the corporal didn't stir. He started to lower him to the ground when Rol responded.

'Diarra? The crack-brained jester Nishor keeps for amusement?'

'The king has her in Tachre?' Rouwen's hope flared. He could hasten there and enlist her aid in dissipating the magical energies binding the Legion of the Air to him. She had been Queen of Gan. She had to know of wizards other than Kwuway, perhaps itinerant wizards pledging fealty to no one and working only as their consciences dictated. Rouwen had never heard of any, other than his almost blind friend Nespizio; wizards were as conniving and greedy as any debater of the law. Yet there had to be one somewhere outside Castle Gan that Nespizio called home willing to help him. If not, Rouwen knew his cause was lost. The wind warriors would trail him forever, until his spirit made the final journey from the peak of Mount Glid into Paradise.

He shivered at the thought that even death might not separate him from the wind warriors. Could they follow him into Paradise?

A sudden whimsy struck him. If only he could come to love the tornadic monsters, all he need do was touch them and they would surely perish.

Rol grunted something in response to his question, but Rouwen couldn't hear. He shook the soldier gently, but there was no response. Rol had died minutes before the wind warriors would whip him aloft along with half the Mionese countryside. Rouwen gently rested Rol's head on the ground and then raced after the two sentries. He quickly found a small clearing in the wooded area where the support base for the Mionese invasion had been established. The normally orderly military encampment was in total confusion, commands being shouted and ignored, officers countermanding earlier orders and still others struggling only to save themselves.

Rouwen gripped the horn at his side, then reached into his jacket pocket and touched the grimoire riding easily there. Somehow the spell book had survived the water and aerial tortures unscathed. Its gentle warmth went far to reassure him that he could get away from the demons pursuing him.

The heavy wagons bringing the supplies for the camp were neatly lined up at the far side of the camp. Rouwen wondered how large an expedition this had been. Surely the barges would have come down the coast from Tachre. These men were only support, though Rol had spent the prior evening in camp playing dice with the guards. Rouwen didn't try to work through the complexities of Mionese strategy. The campaign had been instigated by Sosler, of that he was sure. King Nishor might have authorized it, but the wily Gannian duke had seen the objectives clearly and launched the campaign.

Such tumult in the camp worked to Rouwen's benefit. He skirted the bivouac area and found several frightened horses in a corral. Two were already saddled by soldiers thinking to flee. The others were so frightened that working with them was impossible. White rims showed around brown eyes, and flashing hooves, long since honed and modified for fighting foot soldiers, kicked out at their would-be riders.

The roar of four wind warriors made speaking impossible. The few shouted orders Rouwen heard would do nothing to return tranquility to the camp or ensure an orderly retreat. He used this confusion to push past one soldier and throw open the corral gate. The frightened horses saw their chance for freedom and took it, rushing from the small enclosure. Two soldiers fell to the ground and were trampled by the razor-sharp front hooves. Another barely saved himself by diving over the top rail. And one soldier, who had successfully mounted, was thrown.

Rouwen bided his time and waited for the first saddled horse to race past. He grabbed at dangling reins and was almost pulled off his feet. He had to release his grip or be dragged under the horse in its mindless escape.

'Don't, you'll be trampled,' called the soldier who had dived over the top rail. 'Save a mount for me! I'm the general's aide. Save a mount for me!'

Rouwen ignored the plea. Even if he had been a Mionese soldier, he would not have sacrificed his own life to rescue a general. Rouwen blinked in amazement at the feelings against authority he had developed. Betrayal and treachery and torture did that, he reckoned.

The second saddled horse smashed hard into the corral and knocked rails to the ground, but the small break in the horse's stride permitted Rouwen to grab the bridle and tug hard. Using his own weight to bow the horse's head, he got the huge war beast under control.

The former Gannian captain almost lost his grip when the horse reared, frightened anew at the spirals of air whipping about the camp area. Getting his feet under him, Rouwen kicked hard and clambered into the high-backed saddle. He held the reins tightly with both hands and urged the horse to follow the very route it had intended from the start. Rouwen made no attempt to control the wild gallop from the camp – away from the wind warriors – until the horse began to falter and miss stride some minutes later.

Only then did Rouwen rein back, gentling the horse, trying to calm its fears. If it continued at top speed much longer, its heart would explode and leave him afoot once more. Rouwen doubted he could ever outrace the wind warriors if left on his own feet. They moved slowly but implacably, never stopping and always destroying as they went. He might hope to outride but never outwalk them.

'There, there,' Rouwen soothed his mount. The horse was heavily lathered from its gallop and its flanks heaved, but some of the stark fear had passed. Rouwen got off and walked the horse until its breathing returned to normal. Then he remounted and kept moving at a deliberate pace, not wanting to tire the animal.

Now and again Rouwen saw evidence of the headlong flight from the Mionese encampment. Soldiers here and there trudged along far behind, attempting to put some semblance of military order into their retreat. With the distant columns of tornado-force wind dogging their steps, this proved almost impossible. But Rouwen saw only one other mounted soldier as he sought the road for Tachre.

The man from a hilltop nearby hailed Rouwen. For a moment, Rouwen was unsure what to do, then decided not to create any unwanted suspicion of cowardice or disobedience. Eventually order would return to the Mionese ranks and he did not want to be sought out as an example for a drumhead court martial. The way the sunlight shone off braid and medals, this rider ranked highly in the military command. Rouwen had never seen a Mionese decked out in a bright red uniform before, so did not recognize the man's unit.

'What's gone on back there?' demanded the rider without preamble. This confirmed Rouwen's guess that the man was a high ranking officer. There was no way he could have told Rouwen's rank from the tattered uniform he still wore. It might not even have been Mionese.

'Tornadoes, seven of them. Pillars reaching the sky and killing everything in their path. Nothing can stop them.' Rouwen paused a moment, then added, 'Unless we find a wizard of some power.'

'Wizards,' spat the officer. He looped one long leg across his pommel and leaned forward, as if to get a better look at Rouwen. 'What's happened to you?'

'The whole invasion of the Isle of Passing,' Rouwen gasped out, as if still frightened at the horrific losses. 'Everyone died. No survivors. I was stationed in the swamps as observer.'

'I warned Nishor this might happen,' the officer said. He slid his foot back into its stirrup and straightened his impeccably clean uniform jacket. A quick check assured him that his sword rested easily on his left hip and his medals were properly aligned on his chest. With a dramatic gesture, he unfurled a plum-colored cape and swirled it about his shoulders, hiding some of the gold braid. This seemed to occur to him, because the officer quickly shrugged his broad shoulders and twisted the cape into a small knot behind him. 'Ride with me while I whip these cowardly dogs back into the semblance of an army.'

'I'm carrying a message,' Rouwen improvised. 'To King Nishor. From the commander.'

'From Count Dobesar? He's a fool. He couldn't plan his own breakfast without a staff numbering hundreds. I am the one to be emulated. Do you see my entourage? No! I do my own work, my own planning, and *my* invasions succeed. Strike fast, fade away, fight again another day, that's my motto.'

Rouwen held back the obvious question. Who was the egotistical peacock? He had known a few of the Mionese general staff by name, but mostly he studied their techniques of war, not their faces. King Priowe had wanted it this way, leaving such concerns as opposing personalities to Duke Sosler in his position as Lord Protector of the Realm. Now Rouwen felt the lack.

'But, Lord Widden,' Rouwen said, remembering a name Rol had mentioned in passing, 'this message *must* be delivered immediately. King Nishor will want to hear it.'

'I shall pass judgment on the contents. Tell me your message,' Widden said imperiously. Rouwen had guessed aright. This was the man entrusted with the so-called Sprint Troop, a shock troop able to outflank the enemy within minutes, or to deliver messages quickly or even to project the power of Mion at great distances within a short time. Rouwen knew of the troop through rumor alone and had never been greatly impressed by reports.

'The wind warriors are making their way to Tachre, and the city must be evacuated immediately,' Rouwen said, improvising as he spoke. He wanted nothing more than to be on his way. It appeared that the best course for him was simply to kill Lord Widden. The preening buffoon would never be missed, or if he was, someone might comment as to the reason tactical movements went more smoothly.

'Evacuate the capital because of some local wind condition? I should say not!' exclaimed Lord Widden. 'That is rank nonsense. Take me back to Dobesar, and I shall tell him that to his ugly face.'

'There, there he is now,' Rouwen said, pointing in the direction of the distant wind warriors. As Widden stood in the stirrups for a better view, Rouwen gave the officer's horse a solid whack on the rump. The horse reared and forced Widden to fight to keep his seat. As the horse raced off, Rouwen shook his head. Widden wasn't much of a horseman, for all his prattling about the late Count Dobesar's shortcomings.

Wasting no time, Rouwen turned back north and trotted off.

He had lost valuable time and allowed the Legion of the Air to come closer. He dared not rest until he reached Tachre, and then the only respite would be the time needed to find Diarra.

The journey was long and the horse under him valiant. Brion Rouwen reached Mion's capital city in only five days, weary from the road and hardly able to stay in the saddle. Twice along the way he had badgered food from peasants barely able to spare a mouthful, much less an entire loaf of bread or a large chunk of cheese. He doubted his dire warnings to them of approaching tornado winds sent them scurrying, but he had done what he could to alert them to the tornadic danger now stalking their countryside.

As he rode up to Tachre's gates, he remembered his first visit and how Nibbles had bribed their way past the slovenly guards. That had been before troops were mustered and sent into the field. Nishor had a small army outside the Demon's Throat leading into Valley Gan, and the soldiers remaining in Tachre were more alert to strangers and less likely to accept bribes.

'Hold,' challenged a vigilant guard as Rouwen walked his horse to the main gate. 'What's your business?'

'Can't you tell by my uniform?' Rouwen stepped away from the horse and displayed his rage. Once this had been a Mionese officer's uniform, stolen on his way to the Isle of Passing. Now even the color was unrecognizable. 'I bear a message from Lord Widden for the king.'

'Widden? What's he want of King Nishor?'

'That is for the king's ears, not a peasant turned soldier,' snapped Rouwen, the old edge of command returning easily to his voice. He had put lax guards to death. Overly curious ones were rewarded if they did not meddle in affairs of state. 'Should I speak with your captain about the appropriate punishment for such effrontery?'

'How's that?' The guard scratched himself and leaned heavily against a lance as he studied Rouwen. Whatever thoughts went through the guard's dull mind, he shrugged and motioned Rouwen into the city.

Rouwen stopped in front of the guard and thrust his face forward until their noses almost touched. Rouwen glared, then muttered a curse under his breath and smartly spun and marched away. He had worried about entering the city. He found it almost too easy, simply by relying on his own instincts and training. Never would he have permitted such impudence in one of his Intrepids.

231

As he remembered his lost command, depression assailed him. He had been robbed of so much. Loved ones, his kingdom, all that made life worthwhile. Worst of all, the single person he sought for help not only hated him but blamed him for all her woes. If he did not find Diarra and convince her of their mutual need, Rouwen knew he was doomed to leave Tachre and let the seven wind warriors become a deadly and persistent shadow to his passage.

The stench of the city made Rouwen cough. He had waded through swamps, been surrounded by dead and decaying corpses and still Tachre struck him as loathsome. King Nishor's capital was a disgrace, both to the kingdom of Mion and the king ruling it. Street beggars were more circumspect than before, but they were not badgered as they had been by roving patrols of soldiers. Those minions had been exported to fight battles at the edges of the kingdom.

Rouwen wondered how the forays against Valley Gan went. Unless Duke Sosler allowed the Mionese troops to enter the Demon's Throat, there was no way any army could reach the base of the pillar holding the castle. Treachery, not force of arms, would be Gan's downfall. Rouwen longed to walk the battlements again, the Intrepids at his command.

He laughed without humor when he thought of his new army.

'Windy gasbags, the lot of them,' he said softly. He had ridden fast and hard to reach Tachre long before the wind warriors could traverse the countryside. How long he had before they arrived was open to conjecture, but Rouwen knew better than to rely on luck.

'A golden whistle. All my wealth for a single whistle.'

'What's that, my son? You wish a special instrument to go with your fine horn? Step into my shop and sample my fine wares. The best musical instruments in all Mion are yours for the taking – if enough coin jingles in your purse.' The shopkeeper eyed him warily. Rouwen was not the picture of wealth and prosperity.

'I seek a woman, not a whistle,' he told the shopkeeper.

Rouwen tensed when the man's eyes hardened and a small smile curled the corners of his thin-lipped mouth. The shopkeeper beckoned him closer and whispered, 'For a man of the army, such a request is not out of the question. What type of woman can you afford, in the best sense of that phrase, of course?' The shopkeeper rubbed his hands against the leather apron he wore and looked about, as if this were a trick to trap him into guilty admissions.

'Perhaps you might know her since you are so close to the

palace and it is rumored she is favored by King Nishor,' Rouwen said. 'She goes by the name Diarra. I have a message for her, from the fighting,' he added lamely, trying to give this the best possible light in spite of the shopkeeper's obvious bent toward felony.

'The self-styled queen?' The shopkeeper laughed. The sardonic tone made Rouwen step away a pace and study the shopkeeper more closely. The man's dress was not rich, but there was a hint of better days in the clothing. Bright colors had faded, as was the case with the merchant. Lines cut deep furrows in his forehead and wrinkles around his eyes showed the time spent squinting as he labored at precision work. His hands were strong but gnarled, and Rouwen doubted the man had many days left for crafting the products he so proudly displayed in the doorway to his shop. The sound of joints cracking as the shopkeeper balled his hands into fists made Rouwen wince.

'Diarra. You called her the self-styled queen. What do you mean by that? Watch your tongue,' snapped Rouwen, hand on his dagger.

'I mean nothing by that, my good man. The fingers betray me now and again, but that's the only betrayal you'll find in old Brosy. What do you want with the likes of her? She's skinny. Consider those hips. Too narrow for good childbearing, but who would care on that score? She has the personality of a *thouse* bird. Beware the beak or be poisoned! You want a woman, I can find you one.' Brosy squinted harder, as if wondering how much he could wrest from Rouwen by way of payment for his services.

Rouwen bit back his reply. From Diarra's loins had come the woman he loved. Princess Sorinne was even lovelier than her mother, and she lacked the acid tongue and continual daydreaming that made so many consider her mother peculiar.

'There has been a – death,' Rouwen said slowly. 'I must see Diarra to tell her of a relative's fate.'

'You come from the fighting at the Demon's Throat? How is the campaign there? As good as the news crier's report?'

'I come from the southlands,' Rouwen said, not wanting to get too specific about his claims. He discounted any message given by a news crier. The king's word – or Sosler's! – was more likely to trip lightly from such a tongue than the truth. What monarch would admit to failure in battle, if a simple lie hid his failure?

'You think to find her at the palace?' Brosy shook his head. 'I tell you, she's not your kind. Better allow me to find one who can take any message you might wish to give. I know a saucy little girl, she works for the merchant next door, who is . . .'

'Diarra,' insisted Rouwen. 'Tell me of her.' He stepped closer. He drew his dagger in an easy movement and slid the tip under Brosy's leather apron. The sharp tip punctured skin and made the merchant gasp in surprise.

'Sh-she is no longer in Tachre. She was run out of the city a week back. They stoned her as she left. She is crazy, speaking of being a queen and nonsense like that!'

'Where did she go?' Rouwen lifted slightly and sank the dagger point a little deeper into the merchant's belly. 'Be quick about it, and if you lie, it'll be the last wilful act before entering Paradise.'

'I don't know where she went. I do not!' protested Brosy. The sweat beading his face in spite of the chill breeze blowing down the garbage-strewn street showed the strain Rouwen's blade caused. 'She left by the gate at the foot of Hammerpound Street. It's not much of a gate, but the road from it leads north.' Brosy gasped as Rouwen pushed the tip even deeper into his flesh.

'The truth?' Rouwen asked.

'She might be in the Vahite Desert for all I know! She left with a crowd taunting her. Nishor wanted it that way. Who is this Diarra?'

Rouwen slid the dagger from under the thick apron and tucked it back into his belt sheath. He shook his head and said simply, 'She is Queen of Gan.'

Brosy opened his mouth to protest, then saw the expression on Rouwen's face. The merchant backed into his shop, then slammed and bolted the heavy door. For a moment, Rouwen considered pressing the merchant for more information, then decided there was nothing to be gained. He dared not waste time anywhere, even in Tachre. The wind warriors would arrive and destroy this wretched city, possibly taking King Nishor with it. That would be no loss, but Rouwen could not simply stand by and watch the annihilation.

He turned and mounted his horse. It was the work of an hour before he found Hammerpound Street and the gate leading out of Tachre. The guards on this gate scarcely looked at him as he rode out. Getting into Tachre was now the obstacle. No one cared who left, only who entered.

Rouwen was happy to see the cesspool of a city fall behind, and he wished the populace and its ruler nothing but ill, but he worried about finding Diarra. He didn't think the merchant had lied about Diarra's departure. There had been a ring of callousness in Brosy's words that told Rouwen this was the truth. But where in all of Mion would he find Diarra, if she could wander freely?

He might hold her spell casket, but the former Queen of Gan was not inhibited by seven tornadoes following her every hour of the day. She could linger or speed on her way, wherever fate took her. As Rouwen rode his tired mount, he got the feeling that there were only a few inhabited spots Diarra might have gone. She could ride north and eventually cut toward the Shield Mountains and finally attempt reentry into Valley Gan. That seemed unlikely.

Or she might continue north through the heavily wooded areas to the east of the sea coast. Rouwen knew of a few cities along the coast that might give Diarra safe harbor if she chose not to stay in the Forest of Kelnos. But did she go on foot or had she found a steed to carry her in royal style? From her exist at Tachre, Rouwen guessed she was on foot and not faring well.

There was little call for deposed queens in any kingdom.

By late afternoon, Rouwen and his mount were too tired to continue. The road had turned rocky and narrow, and a storm threatened from off the ocean. Rouwen wondered idly if the power of a full-blown sea storm might stop the Legion of the Air. It would be an interesting spectacle, but one which he had little stomach for witnessing. The farther he rode, the less likely he was ever to see the wind warriors.

Rouwen took a deep breath as he realized he was a man without a country – or worse, he was a man who could destroy any country if he lingered overlong. Never again could he stop for more than the time of travel between him and the tornadic forces at his heels. It was worse than a plague, and yet it seemed fitting. The wind warriors prevented him from finding a distant village and simply quitting on his avowed goal of killing Duke Sosler and deposing King Priowe from the Gannian throne. One curse killed any he loved; another of his own conjuring prevented him from even slowing along the way.

He began looking for shelter against the gathering storm and turned off the pebble-strewn pathway that masqueraded as a road in this part of Mion. Most traffic went along the sea lanes. Very little land transport crossed this windswept, desolate territory. Toward the Shield Mountains were thick forests of linden and pine, but along the coast he saw only places where ships had been wrecked and scavengers like beetles had stripped the fleshy wealth from the carcasses.

Head down to avoid the wind in his eyes, Rouwen continued along the road. At first he thought it only a figment of his imagination. A crowd shouted and cheered, roaring in approval and shouting words too muffled to be understood. Then Rouwen considered it a freak echo of the wind whistling past rocks and the distant surf smashing into weather-worn rocks. But when he topped a rise in the road and saw a small grove of linden trees to the side, he reined back and paid closer attention to what his ears reported.

'Kill her! Kill the whore!' came the cries tossing on the wind, but distinct enough for Rouwen to urge his fatigued horse onward at a quicker clip. The horse sensed something amiss and responded like the good courser that it was. When Rouwen saw the tight knot of men and women gathered around an upright figure, poking and prodding with rakes and scythes, he knew he had arrived barely in time to save Queen Diarra from a fate worse than being stoned and driven from another town.

5

A Wizard Unknown

Brion Rouwen urged his horse to greater speed and reached the group of villagers surrounding Diarra. The peasants held her in the center of a ring of lowered farm implements. An occasional scythe swished through the air barely above her blonde head, but Diarra stood regally, as if she still presided from her throne in Castle Gan. Rouwen had to admire her spirit in the face of such obvious loathing by the peasants.

'I can lead you to heights unknown in your paltry imaginations,' Diarra said, chin held high and her burning, dark eyes focused on some distant point. Rouwen saw that the woman had cast herself free of her senses again and lived in a world of her own making. He had watched her roam the castle corridors, mumbling to herself and offering long harangues on statecraft to pictures of long-dead rulers. That had seemed a harmless pursuit. Now he realized the full depth of her insanity and it was no longer innocent.

Even the threat of death did not sway her from proclaiming dominance over people she had never seen before. Diarra struck a pose and continued her tirade against poor management and the need for her expertise in rule. None of the good people of this village took heed. Several advanced on her, sharp implements ready to separate Diarra from her life.

'Kill her now. I've had enough of her ranting,' cried one woman. 'She tried to steal me child away and suborn him, she did!' She swung at Diarra with a fireplace poker. The former queen endured the blow landing on her arm as if it were nothing more than an annoying insect bite.

'You must fear,' Diarra said in a low, menacing voice. 'There walks in this land demonic powers against which you cannot fight. Not unless you allow me to . . .' A hard blow to her head knocked Diarra to the ground. She stirred, rose to hands and knees and glared at her attacker. The man looked suddenly uneasy at what he had done and backed away. Others in the circle pressed forward for their chance to harry their captive.

Rouwen called out in a clear voice, 'Thank you for your fine work, my brave citizens. This is a dangerous one you have snared for the king. He sends his regards and thanks.'

'What say ye?' The man who had struck Diarra and relented on pressing his advantage turned to face Rouwen. He squinted a little, as if unable to focus at such a distance. Rouwen rode closer.

'King Nishor desires this traitor's presence in Tachre for proper punishment. Turn her over to me.'

'Who might you be? I don't recognize that set of rags you're a'wearing,' the scruffy man said in a belligerent tone. Rouwen surmised this must be the town's headman. Diarra had flown into his town and swept away any semblance of dignity or command he had and he wanted nothing but a return to the old ways, ways with the headman unconditionally in charge of the village.

Rouwen intended to give it to him.

'I am King Nishor's personal lieutenant,' Rouwen lied. 'She is responsible for much the king opposes. Has she tried to usurp your authority, good sir?'

'Why, yes, but she . . .'

'Then that is still another black mark against her. Rise,' Rouwen ordered his former queen. 'Rise and come with me. If you challenge my warrant in this, then you challenge the king's desires!'

For a heartbeat Rouwen worried that Diarra would not accept his way out of sure injury and possible death. He thought he might be able to fight through the peasants, if the need arose, but he had no quarrel with these simple people. They struggled to survive on the barren coastline at the edge of the Kelnos Forest and opposed neither him nor anyone else not bothering their way of life. Simple subsistence took too great a portion of their lives for them to seek out enemies.

'The king?' Diarra asked, rising. She shook her long hair free. The sharp wind off the ocean caught her hair and snapped it in a long, ragged, grimy banner that would have been golden during better times. Straightening her ragged dun-colored robe, she walked with incredible dignity past the headman and stood as docile as a lamb next to Rouwen's horse.

Rouwen saw how appearances often contradicted reality. The fire in Diarra's crazy dark eyes told him of pressure mounting, waiting to explode. He had to get away before she doomed them both with inopportune words or angry invective directed against the headman and his fellow citizens.

'Good day to you. Warm yourselves with the glow of King Nishor's gratitude.'

'Damned little else we're likely to see from him or anyone else in Tachre,' grumbled the headman. Rouwen smiled crookedly and saluted smartly before wheeling his horse and walking it toward the north. To head back south, toward Mion's capital, would be foolish. The seven airy wind warriors still marched after him, he was sure. Distance was his only ally until he could find the golden whistle and banish the Legion of the Air to whatever Paradise belonged to magical beings.

'I will not walk behind a servant,' Diarra said after they had gone a hundred paces. 'I ride. Now!'

Rouwen swung in the high-backed saddle and stared at her. It took him several seconds to formulate a response that wasn't so angry that it would infuriate her.

'I rescued you. We must maintain appearances until their prying eyes are closed to us, my queen,' he said.

'Very well. They were churlish dolts. They refused to listen to reason.' Diarra walked as if she headed the Spring Festival procession, garlands of fragrant, bright red *necoia* flowers on her head and dozens of servants trailing her.

They rode and walked along for another few minutes until Rouwen found a tight knot of linden trees that offered some protection from the increasingly barbed wind ripping at his face and hands. How Diarra walked in such a gale without flinching was a great mystery to him, but then her bouts of insanity took her to realms beyond his ken.

'There,' Rouwen said, turning toward the trees. 'We can find enough shelter to ride out the worst of the storm. I've never seen a land where the weather is always so wretched.' Rouwen almost mentioned the chance of being struck by seven tornadoes, but his sense of irony didn't extend that far. Such humor would be lost on Diarra, and he wasn't inclined to explain more than necessary to gain the former queen's co-operation.

He spat as salt spray wetted his face and lips. With back turned to the ocean, Rouwen heaved a sigh of relief. It was still cold, but the tempest clawed at his spine rather than his unprotected face and hands. The line of trees, bent from constant wind and water, provided more sanctuary than Rouwen would have thought. Dismounting, he led his exhausted courser to the warmest spot in the small grove.

'Why did you save me from those peasants?' Diarra asked,

squatting down in the center of the clearing. The way she spoke, she addressed the trees as her audience rather than Rouwen.

'I feel no loyalty to you, if that thought ever entered your mind,' he said, tending the horse. He wished he had brushes and proper food, but the sparse saltgrass growing in the grove might provide feed enough for it. As he worked, Rouwen found himself craning to listen to the wind, worrying there might be another sound, a roaring brought forth by seven members of the Lord's Legion of the Air.

He wasn't sure the silence on this score quieted his shaky nerves. He knew the wind warriors pursued him in their sluggish, inexorable way. Only constant vigilance would keep him ahead of their whirling destruction. Fingering the horn, he considered tossing it into the sea. But would that accomplish anything? He didn't know. The wind warriors might be after him because he had summoned them. The horn might be irrelevant to the magical beings' quest to catch him.

'It did not. If I had been passing by and the peasants were ready to slay you, I would have kept riding,' Diarra said. She stood and swirled and danced through the grove, touching first this linden tree and then that, as if sampling wooden thoughts or transferring opinions from one to another like some meddling gossipmonger.

'No, I think not,' Rouwen said, taking off the saddle and giving the courser still more relief from its long hard journey. 'You would have stopped to watch them kill me.'

'Perhaps so, now that you have put words to it.' Diarra began crooning to herself and then stopped as suddenly as she had begun. Her eyes fixed on him with maniacal light. 'I will not cooperate with you. My life means nothing. Cast me out, give me back to those swine, it doesn't matter. You caused my banishment from Gan and my darling Priowe's bed.'

'It was Duke Sosler,' Rouwen said tiredly. He did not wish to reiterate the arguments. He and Diarra had been over this ground before, while both were captives in Gan's lowest dungeons. She had not believed him then and nothing had happened since to change her unjust conviction.

'You forced yourself upon me. That was your crime, not mine or Sosler's.' She sank to the ground and lay flat, staring up into the wind-racked branches. Leaves fluttered and flew under the storm's onslaught. Rouwen wondered if she might catch a chill and die from exposure before he had a chance to find what she knew of wizards other than Kwuway. His knowledge of wizardry rested only in talks with Nespizio, a wizard of only small ability and well past his prime.

'Your daughter is my love, not you,' Rouwen said harshly. This brought Diarra to a sitting position, her dark eyes flashing with wildfire. Rouwen ignored her. 'You need not like me, nor I you. But we have a common cause. We both want . . .'

'Priowe dead!'

Diarra's vehemence startled Rouwen. From the way Diarra had spoken just seconds ago, she wanted to return to Gan and her husband.

'Sosler is the architect of our woes,' Rouwen said. He had been loyal to the King of Gan so long he found it hard to imagine himself running a sword through Priowe's belly or driving a dagger into his back. Yet, the king had forfeited the right to any fealty by his actions. He had believed Sosler and Duke Drioway and not the Captain of his Guard or his wife, no matter how crazy Diarra might be.

'You want something from me. That is the price. Priowe's death.' Diarra said it with such finality that Rouwen knew better than to argue. He slowly resolved his own conflict and found himself nodding slowly. 'Good,' Diarra said. 'It is settled. You will kill Priowe and I will do, oh, whatever it is you want.' Diarra lay back on the ground, the wind whipping her tattered robe around her.

Rouwen wondered if the woman thought she was trading sexual favor for her husband's death. He sucked in a deep breath and almost choked. The sharp tang of unaccustomed salt irritated his lungs. He much preferred the more temperate clime within the Shield Mountains, in luxuriant Valley Gan.

'A wizard. I need a wizard to lift the spell on me,' he said. Rouwen fingered the silver spell casket resting coldly inside his tunic. Shrugging his shoulders to cover the action, he settled his shabby jacket the best he could. The lifting of Diarra's spell had to remain the final reward for her cooperation.

First, he had to find the spell casket dooming him to kill those he loved. Rouwen blinked when a particularly loud gust of wind rattled branches all around him.

'First,' he said, verbally correcting his misthought, 'I require a wizard who can counter the Lord of Death and Life's wind warriors. Seven have been summoned and follow me wherever I go. There is a way of controlling them. A . . .'

'A golden whistle,' Diarra said in an offhand tone, as if discussing the latest inconsequential affair among her servants.

'You know of it!' Rouwen swung about and dropped to one

knee, seizing her arm and shaking hard, as if this might loosen her lips. 'Tell me. Where is it? How do I . . .'

'How do you chase off these magical beasts you have summoned?' Diarra's eyes dropped to the golden horn at his side. A crooked smile twisted her thin, cracked lips into a parody of amusement. Rouwen saw how ravaged Diarra had become. Wrinkles laced her face and the once fine skin had turned to leather. Only because he had known her before did he recognize the hidden beauty, so much of which she had given to Sorinne.

'Tell me,' Rouwen said, controlling himself.

'So that will be your payment for killing Priowe. Very well.' Diarra pulled her ragged clothing about her and turned from him, curling up into a tight ball on the cold ground. Rouwen waited for more from her, but over the wind he soon heard her strained breathing. Diarra slept.

Rouwen sat and stared at her, wondering what she really knew. It might be nothing, yet she had told him of the golden whistle before he mentioned it. Diarra possessed the knowledge he required to stop the seven wind warriors stalking him.

She had to!

'You don't know where we're going,' Rouwen accused. 'We've been heading into the mountains for a week and still you haven't told me where we are going or whom we seek.' The pines had become taller, thinner and more shriveled as they reached the foothills of the Shield Mountains. Replacing them were the limberfrost trees of the Kelnos Forest, bushy and low-growing and too hardy to let the fiercest storms and vicious winters intimidate them. The Forest of Kelnos stretched for miles in all directions and only occasionally did Rouwen get the chance to look back along the meandering route they had taken to reach this point.

Once, two days earlier at twilight, he had climbed a small needle of rock and had peered toward the coast. It took several minutes before he made out the seven bobbing, weaving pillars of tornado destroying everything around them. He guessed that a lighthouse was damaged by the wind warriors before they turned slightly inland and worked their way toward the mountains – and him. He had urged Diarra on for another two hours, in spite of the darkness.

'You fear those magical monsters, don't you? Do you fear them more than you do me?' Diarra perched on a rock and basked like a lizard in the warm sun. 'You should not. I am more dangerous by far.' She lay back, her spine arched slightly and her fine, firm breasts pressed hard into the threadbare dress she wore beneath her robe. Rouwen stared at her for a moment, then turned away. At times she looked so like her daughter.

He couldn't keep from thinking of lovely Sorinne. And this only burned like poison in his heart. Torturing himself with thoughts of their love accomplished nothing.

'You will tell me the name of the wizard we seek, or I'll abandon you here and you'll never see Priowe in his grave,' Rouwen said, seeking some small lever to use against Diarra.

'I've been considering this as you forced me along at such a merciless pace,' Diarra said, turning slightly so her face caught the full sun. She smiled, as if she didn't have a care in the world. 'How do I know you will kill him if I introduce you to the wizard?'

'I gave you my promise. My honor is all I have left.'

'A destitute man, indeed,' Diarra taunted. 'We are on the right course. The creatures following us will not overtake us before we find the wizard who can stop them.'

'The golden whistle? He has it?' Rouwen turned from the woman and took a few paces toward the dense stand of limberfrost trees. Their gray-green foliage could hide an entire army. Something stirred nearby and tugged at Rouwen's senses. Stories of the Kelnos Forest abounded in Gan, of trees sucking the spirit from unwary travellers and imprisoning them until the Greater Moon blanked out the Lesser Moon in the second month of harvests.

Rouwen looked around and shivered. The long limbs took on the aspect of groping hands, hands closing as he passed. And the bulbous tops of the trees might be men's heads, with eyes there and mouths screaming beneath and . . .

Rouwen shivered again and forced such wild imaginings away. Concentrating on what his senses told him truly was difficult enough. He was unable to identify the problem, if there was one, and this bothered him all the more. It was more than wind, and less – and then he had it.

A fragrance floated on the soft breeze, totally out of place in the forest. It was a perfume more likely to be found in the royal court than among the silent, haunted limberfrost trees of Kelnos.

'You know that the Lord did not possess a whistle. You told me how you searched his living quarters. Wizards are such packrats. You could not have missed any of his magical toys. He must have controlled the Legion of the Air with simple spells. This wizard will know such a spell to dissipate the tornadoes. He might find the golden whistle, should you want it for some reason.'

Diarra rattled on and Rouwen simply walked away. He drew

243

his dagger and used what forest skills he had to blend into shadows. Rouwen wished he could have performed this stalking feat within the walls of Castle Gan, but he had been banished. He had to adapt to his new life and stay alive long enough to return triumphant to his home in the sky-challenging castle.

Crouching in deep shadow, Rouwen listened hard and heard nothing but the usual forest sounds. The whisper of rising wind through the serrated leaves of the trees caused a curious chattering noise that he had come to loathe, but it was normal for the time and place. His other senses also betrayed him. He sniffed hard to see if he could recapture the scent that had betrayed whoever it was spying on him and Diarra. The fragrant hint had vanished on the wind, making him doubt his own skills.

Rouwen moved deeper into the woods, for the first time considering how few animals he had seen along the trail they followed. Someone used this game trail enough to frighten off the woodland's normal residents. Might it be the wizard Diarra sought? Or were the tall tales correct and the trees themselves sucked in unwary souls?

Another answer came to Rouwen. Diarra might be leading him into a trap. She was capable of any treachery, and time worked against him. How far away were the wind warriors? Any delay would permit their relentless pursuit to narrow the distance and overtake him.

Rouwen pressed into the jagged trunk of a limberfrost tree and peered around it at a small watering hole. In the mud circling the pond he saw a variety of animal tracks, showing recent use. And then he saw human footprints leading away. His hand tightened on his dagger and he moved forward to investigate.

Rouwen froze when a sharp point pressed into his spine.

6

Call the Legion!

Rouwen reacted by diving forward, tucking his head down and rolling, keeping his dagger to one side. He came to his feet and spun around slashing wildly to hold his attacker at bay long enough to measure his opposition. Rouwen found himself waving his dagger at thin air. He took a step back, slipped in the muddy rim at the water hole and fell to one knee.

'I did not mean to startle you,' came a small voice, laden with mirth at his plight. 'Please do not threaten me with your dagger.'

'Where are you? Why do you stick a knife into my back?' Rouwen rose and moved away from the muddy ground, considering the best place to make a fight of it. He had been threatened and now he must make a stand or die.

'I don't have a knife. I left it back at my home. Toit chides me constantly about that.' The small voice floated on the wind, and with it came a hint of the pleasing fragrance Rouwen had scented earlier. Sight availed him little in locating the speaker. He turned and sniffed cautiously, wary of any attempt to choke him with poisonous fumes after luring him with perfume.

'You act as if my perfume is going to suffocate you. Have I used too much again? I really do like it, but a few minutes after I put it on, I no longer smell it. So I add more. Toit tells me I reek, but then he has a very sensitive nose. You must, also. Are you a hunter?'

'Who are you?' Rouwen turned and faced the thick limberfrost tree he had used to shield himself as he spied on the watering hole. Both voice and scent came from there.

'My name is Finola, and I live nearby.'

Rouwen frowned. He hardly faced a phalanx of Mionese warriors, nor did he find himself fighting off a horde of demons bent on sending his spirit to Paradise. Finola sounded like a young girl.

'I'm Brion,' he said, 'but I am no hunter.'

'A soldier,' Finola sighed. 'Toit was right. He almost always is, you know, and it is ever so vexing. He simply refuses to let me forget a single time when he is right and I am wrong. Who are you going to kill?'

'Not you.' Rouwen sheathed his dagger and walked forward, careful to make no sudden moves that might panic Finola. Rounding the tree, he finally saw her. He had been right. Finola was hardly past ten summers and smiled shyly as he peered down at her. The scent from her perfume made his nose wrinkle.

'I don't know your friend, Toit, but he is right. You've used too much perfume. But it is a nice perfume.' Rouwen reached out, palm up for Finola to accept or reject as she saw fit.

She laid her hand across his, just for a moment. She turned her face up slightly and a tiny smile darted across her lips. She had a pug nose and short brown hair raggedly cut just above her eyes and falling like a cap over her ears. Ginger-colored eyes danced with a joke only Finola knew. Her clothing was clean but had a well-worn look to it, as if her life in the Forest of Kelnos was difficult. But this was nothing Rouwen had not already guessed, from other citizens of Mion, from the villagers who had tried to execute Diarra.

'I always tell Toit that I do not hunt, therefore do not need to sneak up on animals. Gathering berries and roots takes only persistence, not stealth.' Finola grinned now. 'They are a long way off.'

'What? Who is? Toit?' The sudden change in the conversation had taken Rouwen by surprise. He had dismissed the girl, save as a way of finding the mysterious wizard Diarra claimed to know in the woods.

'Oh, no, Toit is hunting. He is quite good at it. The seven wind warriors following you are more than two days from reaching Kelnos.'

Rouwen just stared at the little girl. Finola seemed so innocent, and yet she knew more of his dilemma than seemed possible unless she had been spying on him for some time.

'What wizard told you? Toit?'

'Toit? No,' she laughed, 'not Toit. All he ever wants to do is eat mice. But I do know a wizard. Vutorian lives not far from here. You want to speak with him, don't you? I can tell from the expression on your face. You are very handsome, Brion.' This time Finola giggled and looked away. She held a twig and picked off leaves from it, occasionally sneaking a glance at him.

'You poked me in the back with that stick, didn't you?'

'Don't tell Vutorian. Please don't. He is always lecturing me about not being serious enough. He wants me to learn all I can so I can go to Noumet.'

Rouwen's head spun at the sudden changes Finola accepted so easily. She knew of the wind warriors dogging his steps, she apparently was apprenticed to a wizard and yet she believed in children's bedtime stories. Noumet, the City of Mages, was mythical and something used to amuse the youngest and most credulous children before they grew too wise in the ways of the world to believe such tall tales.

'You don't believe in Noumet, do you? I am very good at reading your thoughts, Brion.' Finola reached out and lightly brushed his cheek. Rouwen recoiled when a spark jumped from the girl's fingers to his skin. 'Well, not really reading your *thoughts*. Those are private. But I can tell what you think from the way you stand, your facial twitches, all the tiny little things no one pays much attention to noticing. Vutorian says I am very good and will make a fine addition to the wizards in Noumet.'

'What do your parents say about Noumet?' Rouwen asked gently.

'They're both dead. Perhaps that is why I want to take my place in the City of Mages, so I can help run the world. I really think I would like to specialize in clouds. It would be so nice to move them here and there, shape them into big puffy mounds and finally go whoosh! and chase them from the sky. Of course, this would have to be coordinated with the wizard in charge of the wind. And rain. And the sun. Those would be the very best mages of all, the ones administering to the wind and sun.' Finola looked thoughtful, then added, 'Of course, it could be interesting keeping the Lesser and Greater Moons on their proper courses. Or moving the stars. There are so many to keep track of. Those mages are certainly very good at their job.'

Rouwen shook his head and tried not to rebuke the little girl. There was no Noumet and no City of Mages and no human interference in matters handled by fate. It was nothing more than a pompous claim that the universe had to be tended by wizards. Rouwen firmly believed the cosmos was a huge mechanism set in motion and designed to run forever without interference by human or demon.

'I would meet Vutorian. He might be the wizard I seek who can stop the wind warriors following me.' Rouwen didn't care who had told Finola about the Legion of the Air. What mattered most was finding a wizard able to dissipate the seven tornadoes intent on his trail. And reversing the spell Kwuway had laid upon

247

him. Rouwen caught his breath as he thought of his dead brother – and Sorinne.

'You are sad. Will you tell me what I may do to help?' Again Finola reached out and touched his cheek, and again he was startled by the blue spark leaping from her fingertips. He reached up and held her small, fragile hand gently.

'You are very kind, but there's nothing you can do. Vutorian might prove better at what I need.' Rouwen felt suddenly uncomfortable at the way Finola stared at him. There was age in that gaze, yet it mingled with startling naiveté. He didn't know what to make of the little girl.

'You are troubled by more than the wind warriors. Does it have anything to do with the woman in yonder grove?' Finola gestured vaguely in the direction of the sheltering grove of limberfrost trees where he had left Diarra.

'She is part of my troubles,' Rouwen said, wondering why he bothered talking to this insignificant girl. She was not able to help him, and he had no evidence that she even knew a wizard.

'A small part only,' Finola said firmly. 'I do not think I like her. She does not treat you with the respect you deserve.'

Rouwen laughed again. 'Where is Vutorian? Or Toit? I would like to meet any companion of yours, even one who dines on mice.' The way his belly grumbled from lack of decent food, he might ask to join anyone with as much meat as might be found on a mouse's flanks.

'Toit keeps to himself.' Finola looked embarrassed as she added, 'He is not a very pleasant companion. He is irritable and unsociable. Why he chooses to be with me is anyone's guess. I believe Vutorian has ordered him to watch after me, as if I required it while in Kelnos.'

'You are personable and very pretty,' Rouwen said. He was rewarded with her bright smile again. And deep in her eyes stirred something more than simple wit. Rouwen had the feeling of staring into – infinity. The depths of wholesomeness and intelligence surged up and threatened to consume him. He struggled to get out, even as he wondered why he ought to try.

'You are just saying that to be polite,' Finola said, but the girl's tone told Rouwen she was pleased at the compliment. 'I like you.'

'Then you will take me to Vutorian?'

'Oh, Brion, no, I am so sorry. I cannot! I have just begun a quest and must complete it before I return. Vutorian is very stern.'

'He couldn't object if I explained my need. The Legion of

248

the Air is loosed and must be banished again to wherever it comes from.' Rouwen found it difficult to explain the urgency of stopping the destructive vortices before they overtook him. And then there was the problem of the spell casket. He had to locate this and have a mage remove the spell Kwuway had laid upon him. And Gan. Return to Valley Gan and kill King Priowe, find Princess Sorinne – and make sure Sosler and Drioway received their deserts.

Rouwen's fingers tightened on the hilt of his sword as he thought of the treacherous, power-hungry duke and his Mionese ally.

'Nothing must stop me. That is part of my training. I must learn to overcome any obstacle if I am to be worthy of Noumet.' Finola bit her lower lip and screwed up her face in concentration. 'I see how important it is to you to find the golden whistle. If I give you directions to Vutorian's castle, do you think you can find him? Or should I try to get Toit? He is very good at finding paths through the forest.'

'You can't take me to your master?' Rouwen sucked in his breath and held it. The entire world was filled with swindlers intent on robbing unwise travellers. He wondered how Finola could be a part of any such deceit, but she might be sending him into a trap. A comely little girl soothed any suspicion, then lured the unsuspecting into a trap with scant chance of struggle or escape.

'The quest is too important, Brion. Please believe me, I wish I could.' Her ginger eyes bored into him and she asked, 'Would you ever leave your watch? As captain, would you tolerate a sentry who simply wandered off?'

'Of course not. Duty is . . .' Rouwen bit off further comment. He had not told her he was a soldier, nor had he mentioned that he was Captain of the Guard, yet she knew these details of his past.

'So it is with me. It is doubly important that I learn commitment since I am so young. I must have it ingrained so I will never shirk duties that seem too difficult later. It is a grave responsibility keeping the world working.'

'Yes, yes, it is a complex undertaking,' Rouwen said, venting a huge sigh. Finola had been hoodwinked totally by her mentor. Rouwen could see no other explanation. 'Perhaps I can help you on your quest, then we . . .'

'No! I'm sorry,' she said contritely. 'I did not mean to be so abrupt. This is *my* quest, and I must finish it on my own. That's the only way to learn.'

249

'So Vutorian says?'

'Oh, no, he would never nag like that,' Finola said, smiling again. 'Toit, though, is *always* scolding me. But I have learned where my duty lies. I want to be worthy of acceptance.' Finola stared at him, then used the stick in her hand to draw a map quickly in the soft dirt at her foot. 'This is how to find Vutorian. I am sure he will not mind if you go to him.'

'I'll tell him you said it was all right,' Rouwen said, confused now. This hardly seemed a trap to rob him of his paltry belongings. He wore a stolen uniform that had long since fallen to tatters. Memory of golden coin was all he had in his purse. The horse and saddle might be worth a robbery, but not one this complex unless he was going to be set upon by dozens of children no older than Finola.

The only items he carried worth stealing were the gold horn that summoned the Legion of the Air and the silver spell casket resting within his tunic. Of the pair, the horn might be the most valuable. No one but Diarra would care about the spell casket, and he had kept its possession a secret from her. It would have been too easy for her to demand this as payment for seeking out a wizard to aid him, had she known he had stolen it from Kwuway.

'The grimoire in your pocket will be your guide when you reach this point,' Finola said, again shocking him. He had forgotten the spell book in his jacket. 'This is the base of the mountain. The book of spells will begin to glow, a pale green, I think. Yes, a pale green. It will grow warmer as you near Vutorian's house.'

'How do you know of the grimoire?' he asked. 'And that I was an officer and all the rest?' Rouwen held back a surge of panic. Finola did not lead him into a simple trap to steal. She knew too much and casually revealed her knowledge. But that lack of guile warned him there was more to this young girl than he thought – far more.

She smiled in delight and said, 'Vutorian is a good teacher. So is Toit. When Toit returns from his hunt, I'm sure he will want to meet you.'

'A misanthrope who dines on mice,' grumbled Rouwen. 'My kind of companion.'

'He is far nicer than she is,' Finola said, pointing through the wind-tossed trees toward the spot where Diarra slept. Rouwen instinctively turned to look in that direction. He saw only the darkness and shifting shadows caused by the strong storm winds. When he looked back, Finola had gone as mysteriously as she had appeared. The stick she had used to trace out the map in the dirt remained, its point rammed deep into the spot marking Vutorian's dwelling.

Rouwen removed the grimoire from his pocket and laid his hand flat on its surface. A curious tingling, much like that he experienced when Finola had touched him coursed through his body. There was only a small warmth and no pale green glow to indicate he was on the proper path to Vutorian's. But Rouwen remembered the brown-haired girl had said the book of spells would begin glowing only when he reached the base of the wizard's mountain retreat.

He started back to the camp where Diarra slept, then paused. He was no hunter and his tracking skills were minimal, yet he doubted Finola could have disappeared into the storm without leaving some trace. Returning to where the girl had stood, he found her tiny footprints. He followed the tracks halfway around the limberfrost tree to a spot hidden both from where he had stood and the watering hole – and the footprints vanished.

Looking up into the tree, he thought she might have climbed the trunk to take refuge in the thickly leafed boughs. Rouwen found no trace of the little girl above him. He ranged outward in a semicircle, hunting for any trace of her passage. Finding nothing, Rouwen reluctantly had to admit a ten-year-old girl was a better woodsman than he might ever become.

He shook his head ruefully and started back toward the grove and Diarra. The storm must have hidden the girl's tracks, he decided. She could be the best woodsman in all Mion, but some small spoor would have remained. She did not evaporate like dew in the morning sun.

Rouwen hadn't gone halfway back to the grove when he heard heavy movement around him. Slowing, he bent over and tried to fade into shadow.

'Get movin', you slacker!' came the immediate reproach. 'We got to get into position, or they'll surely get free of us!'

Rouwen drew his dagger and angled toward the hidden man making the demands of him. A burly brute half again Rouwen's size loomed up in the darkness. Rouwen never hesitated. With well-honed skill, he shoved his dagger forward and up, piercing the man's heart before he even knew he had been attacked. The giant stiffened and gurgled, trying to speak. Death had already snipped him free from his spirit. Toppling to the ground, the man lay like a tree trunk waiting to be sawed into firewood.

Dropping beside him, Rouwen struggled to roll the man onto his back and retrieve his dagger. The hilt protruded at a crazy angle from the man's chest. Rouwen slid it free, then wiped it on

251

the lifeless man's tunic. Tugging hard, Rouwen pulled the man's cloak from dead shoulders and swung it about his own. He saw no reason to let a good article of clothing go unclaimed.

'You won't be needing it, even in this foul weather,' Rouwen said softly. He opened the man's purse but found nothing. The only thing Rouwen hated worse than a thief sneaking about in the night was an inept thief.

'Now!' came a cry from ahead. 'Attack now or be forever damned in Paradise!'

War whoops and belligerent shouts drowned out the whining wind for a moment, and then there came an ominous silence from both men and elements. Rouwen shot to his feet and raced through the woods to find Diarra. Six armed men had already seized Diarra by the time he reached the edge of the clearing. One held his horse and another rummaged through the trifling possessions he had stored with the high-backed saddle.

He started to back into the forest and work out a plan of attack. He dared not leave Diarra in the brigands' hands too long. She was so unstable she might believe he had sold her into slavery and would never cooperate with him again. He needed her knowledge if he was ever to be free of the curse weighing so heavily on his soul.

A sword point caused him to yelp in pain.

'Who are ye, eh? You're wearin' Hodie's cloak, but you ain't Hodie.'

Rouwen spun, the cloak flaring in a wide, blinding arc. The cloth tangled the sword and engaged it while Rouwen drew his dagger and stepped forward. He gutted the man, but not before a shriek of pure agony escaped the brigand's lips. The thieves around Diarra – and more from the woods – rushed forward to see the cause of their companion's anguished outcry.

Rouwen faced a full dozen armed and desperate brigands without hope of escape. Swirling his cape again, Rouwen held two at bay while he dragged out his sword. Sword in one hand and dagger in the other, he began the methodical, deadly fighting that had made his reputation among the Intrepids. These ill-trained, poorly disciplined thieves had no chance against an officer of Gan!

Rouwen skewered one with his sword and slashed another's hand with his dagger before they retreated.

'Surrender or we kill you and the bitch,' called the one who must be the band's leader. Rouwen wasn't able to see who spoke in the darkness.

'Let us go and we will forget about the inconvenience you've caused us,' he cried. 'We are simple pilgrims on a retreat and desire only to be left alone.' Rouwen parried and lunged, his blade barely missing its target.

'You're on no religious pilgrimage. You fight like a master,' accused the man Rouwen slowly advanced on. Two of the brigands were already dead by his hand. A few more might convince them to break off their attack and fade into the gloom of the limberfrost trees.

'Come and throw yourself on my blade, as the others have done,' urged Rouwen, blocking a low thrust with his dagger and kicking out. His foot met a face and he felt bones crush under the impact.

For the first time since his escape from Castle Gan, he felt alive, able to ply his trade, to do what he had trained most of his life for. Then Rouwen went cold inside. The thieves had retreated to form a deadly ring about him, three of their number armed with crossbows. They need only stand back and skewer him, and he could never fight his way through the encircling fighters quickly enough to save himself.

'When demons dance, we'll do that thing,' retorted the brigand's leader. He motioned his crossbowmen into position so they wouldn't shoot one another.

'All right,' Rouwen said, realizing he had fallen into a trap of his own making. He had been overconfident and now they had captured him easily. 'I surrender.'

'We don't want you to surrender,' the leader said. 'We want you to die.' He raised his hand to give the order.

Rouwen lowered his sword and touched the gold horn dangling at his side. He couldn't dodge three crossbowmen, and he couldn't fight free of ten other armed thieves. He could summon another wind warrior. But at what cost?

Rouwen lifted the gold horn to his lips.

7

Poison, Wrath, and Wind

'Get him! Don't let him warn anyone else!' The brigand's leader motioned for the crossbowman beside him to fire.

For the briefest of instants, Brion Rouwen stood paralysed by the sight of the triangular-edged broadhead bolt pointed squarely at his head. The thieves thought he wanted to summon aid in the form of humans. Random thoughts flashed through Rouwen's head. They hadn't scouted properly if they believed it possible for him to call down a squad of soldiers lurking in the woods. But this mistake mattered little if the wicked crossbow bolts split his head like a rotted melon.

Rouwen's mouth turned dry from the nearness of death, and his parched lips touched the coldness of the Lord's fabulous horn. He tried to expel enough air to call the Legion of the Air, but no sound issued forth from the trumpet. Sucking in a lungful of air, Rouwen tried again as he saw the crossbowman's finger tightening on the weapon's trigger.

He heard the *twang* and imagined he saw the bolt leap from the crossbow and he blinked twice when he thought he saw a dark mass descend between him and death. A loud squawk sounded throughout the grove, unlike anything Rouwen had ever heard, and then confusion seized the brigands. They shouted and screamed and ran in all directions, arms waving wildly.

Rouwen recovered his wits and whirled around, slashing with sword and dagger. He let the golden horn fall to his side. Why summon a tornado when he had the powers of night defending him? He swatted at feathers falling all around him from the air, then engaged a brigand who was probably a better cutpurse than a swordsman. Rouwen made quick work of him, a parry, another, then a riposte that skewered the thief through the belly.

'Diarra? Are you near? Where are you?' Rouwen called. He touched the spell casket inside his tunic, then went in search of her. The evening and the raging storm masked much in the forest, but he heard the agonized screams of tortured men and the sound of others fleeing pell-mell into the distance. And then came a sound like a war pennant flapping hard in the wind.

A snapping noise followed by a screech of stark fury almost deafened him. A new rain of brown and gold feathers drifted around him – and not a pace away the brigands' leader clawed at a writhing, dark mass obscuring his face. Rouwen had almost been stabbed in the back by this thief, but his strange defender had saved his life. Bloody bits of face and neck flew in all directions, mingled with more feathers and a screeching that chilled the soul. Rouwen circled and watched as the mass on the brigand's face took form in silhouette.

'A *thouse* bird!' he exclaimed. Rouwen had seen only a few of the poisonous birds, and then they had been tiny, hardly more than hatchlings. This creature was twice the size of a man's head, with a wingspread exceeding Rouwen's outstretched arms. The brown and gold feathers continued to fly in all directions, as if the bird molted, but Rouwen knew the involuntary plucking came from the creature's tenacity in battle as it whipped its large white-tufted head back and forth to tear off gobbets of hair and scalp.

Slowly, the thief sank to the ground, no longer feeling pain. Poison from the *thouse* bird's beak had begun its work on his body, first numbing him. As he lay face down on the ground, waves of stark anguish blasted into the dying man's body. Rouwen heard joints popping and bones breaking as the poison worked its deadly magic.

Rouwen had always doubted the travellers' stories that *thouse* poison could down the Lost Cape buffalo, the largest animal on the continent, but now he believed it possible. He had tried to protect King Priowe from a plot to assassinate him with *thouse* poison, and that had been the start of his own personal woe. Now he wished he had ignored the plot and let the treacherous cooks, in collusion with Duke Drioway, have their way with Priowe's food.

Lowering his sword, Rouwen prepared for the bird to attack him. He did not remember hearing anyone say that the *thouse* was a particularly intelligent bird, only vicious. For a single flying creature boldly to attack a dozen armed men and win was ample testimony to its ferocity.

With a single flap of its huge wings, the bird launched itself at him. Rouwen moved with lightning speed – and was too slow by half. The bird's wing knocked aside his dagger, and the serrated beak opened inches in front of his face.

'Fool,' growled the bird. Rouwen staggered as the *thouse*

whipped about and perched on his shoulder, sharp talons cutting deeply into his flesh. 'Take this.'

Rouwen was knocked back as the *thouse* launched itself and became airborne. It flapped into the thick overhang of the trees and vanished within seconds. But at Rouwen's feet lay the prize the *thouse* had clutched in its other claw.

The crossbow bolt that might have ended Rouwen's life had been given to him as a gift.

Rouwen hefted the bolt and marvelled that any beast, magical or flesh, could snatch a fired crossbow bolt in midflight. He ran his finger along its smooth shaft and found the talon marks where the *thouse* had captured it as surely as it might a pigeon or other aerial tidbit for its evening meal.

Then the real import of what had just occurred struck Rouwen. He took a step after the bird and stared into the overhanging branches of the Kelnos Forest. Calling out, he pleaded, 'Wait, come back! You must explain to me what's happening!'

'Isn't it apparent, even to a dolt like you?' Diarra stumbled through the forest to lean against a rough-barked bole. She was covered with blood, though none of it appeared to be her own. Rouwen went to examine her, but she jerked away, turning her face from him.

'I must tend your wounds. If they become infected . . .'

'I am whole. The blood is all theirs.' Diarra made a sweeping motion with her arm that encompassed the whole world. She pulled her arms closer to her body and hugged herself, adding in a bitter voice, 'No thanks to you, I am still intact.'

'My sword and dagger are stained with their blood,' Rouwen said angrily. He cursed himself for walking blindly into a trap as he had done. Even worse, he had been rescued by a *thouse* and had no idea how or why that had happened. The predators were rare, and never had Rouwen heard of a bird aiding a human in this manner. If anything, their only usefulness was in providing the virulent poison so favored by assassins.

'Are you going to let them go free, or will you bring them to justice?' asked Diarra.

'You want me to chase the brigands through the darkness, in their own territory, with the chance of blundering into a trap?' Rouwen snorted. Such foolhardiness was more likely from a raw recruit than a seasoned veteran such as himself, yet there was a dash of curiosity spicing such a venture.

The *thouse* bird intrigued him. Rouwen started to mention his winged rescuer, then clamped his mouth firmly shut. In the heat of the battle and Diarra's subsequent diatribe, Rouwen had overlooked a significant detail: the bird had spoken to him. Never had he heard, even in the wildest of tall tales told at the Spring Festivals, anyone claim that *thouse* spoke as clearly as any human.

'Well? Are you going to stand there, or are you going to bring them back so that I may punish them?' Diarra didn't wait for an answer. She stormed off through the forest, her footsteps quickly covered by the increasingly high wind blowing from the ocean. The storm turned the soft spring into night rivalling midwinter in Castle Gan. Rouwen shivered and pulled his flapping cloak tighter about his lanky frame. He went after Diarra, shaking his head and grumbling as he let her go off in her dangerous pursuit.

So much had happened in the past hour. The fight had been bloody but brief. The conversation with Finola had lasted far longer. As he settled down beside his horse, the saddle acting as a pillow for his head, Rouwen tried to remember all the little girl had said. Though her words burned brightly in his mind they became confused as he tried to make sense of them.

'The map,' he said. 'I remember that. And she knew of the golden whistle and my history. And Vutorian. She knows a mage named Vutorian.' Rouwen closed his eyes and drifted off to sleep, coming awake a few minutes later, his heart threatening to explode in his chest. Sweat covered him, and it took some time to remember the nightmare that had plagued him.

Or was it a nightmare he had endured? Rouwen cocked his head to one side and tried to hear the flapping of huge wings against the gale force winds blowing through the limberfrost trees. His imagination flared and he jumped at moving shadows, thinking each was a poison-beaked fighting demon speaking his name. Rouwen settled back, pulling the cloak closer as his eyes darted about and his heart rate slowed. The flitting masses were nothing more than leaves and tree branches and bits of debris. The trees were not prisons for tormented souls and birds did not speak.

Rouwen snored gently as sleep took him once more. And on the branch above him sat a *thouse* bird, a large yellow eye fixed unblinkingly on the sleeping man.

Rouwen sneezed and rolled over, tangling himself in his newly won cloak so that his arms were pinned tightly as if wound in a shroud. He fought to get free and then stilled when he heard a whispered, 'Quiet, fool. They come!'

Rouwen's head rocked back, and he stared up into the branches above him. He saw only shadows moving within shadows. The dual moons were down, and the storm had brought in heavy rain clouds to suck away any possible hint of light in the dense forest. But the branches moved strangely, as if they were weighted down by something heavy hopping from one to another.

'Who's there?' Rouwen demanded, fumbling to draw his dagger. He cursed himself for not having placed it close to hand before going to sleep. Such oversight might kill him in this forest.

'They come. Three of them slink back. Sleep later, kill now,' came the insistent command.

Rouwen strained to hear other movement in the forest and failed. He kicked free of his cloak and slowly drew his sword, his back to the thick tree trunk. He closed his eyes, then opened them slowly. The dark-adaptation worked. Rouwen saw the brigands returning to finish the robbery they had begun earlier.

Wasting no time, he slipped around the grove and came up behind one man. An accurate thrust with his sword ended one miserable life. Rouwen kicked out and shoved the body off his blade, then rushed forward swinging adroitly. The flat of his blade landed against a second skulker's head, knocking him to the ground. As he passed the fallen man, Rouwen used his dagger to end another life. This left him matched with the remaining robber.

'You!' the man gasped, stumbling back to avoid Rouwen's silent thrust. The brigand hit the ground, rolled and came to his feet, the former guard captain following relentlessly. 'We meant nothing. You killed the others. We meant only to – to thank you! Yes, to thank you. Wolgon was a tyrant. We meant to thank you for releasing us from his servitude!'

Rouwen saw no reason to engage in a battle of words. He wanted only to dispatch the man and get back to sleep, but again it was denied him. The snapping of pinions and the rustle of feathers interrupted the brigand's frightened pleas for mercy. The *thouse* bird savagely ripped once with its talons and left the man bleeding to death from a severed throat.

'Death to liars,' the bird said, landing heavily on the ground and hopping about and pecking at the eyes as if they were a tasty morsel to be savored.

'Are you a carrion eater?' Rouwen asked, marvelling that he spoke with a *thouse* bird. He wanted to explore how far this hallucination of his extended, to see if he could engage the dream bird in dialogue that would finally convince him that, like Diarra, he had gone quite insane.

'One eats what one must,' the bird said testily. Its serrated beak ripped at fleshy cheeks. With a quick toss of its head, the bird swallowed the strip of bloody flesh. 'This is fresh enough for my taste, thought the meat is too stringy.'

'You ought to kill a better class of thief,' Rouwen observed, amusing himself with the idea of such philosophical discussion with a poisonous avian.

'True, quite true,' the *thouse* agreed. It hopped about a few more times, then clawed at the thief's purse and caught up a small coin. Rouwen barely saw it flipping through the air in time to catch it. 'For your trouble,' the bird said. 'You have the down-in-the-mouth look of someone Finola favors. Buy yourself better clothing. Or fencing lessons. You fight like an old lady.'

'Finola?' Rouwen had thought himself past surprise. The *thouse* was only a hallucination, and this sudden unexpected turn ought not to jolt him. But it did. 'You know her?'

'Of course I do. She said you were given my name. Has the poor girl befriended a fool, or are you merely forgetful?'

'Toit? You are the hunter Toit she mentioned? The one who eats mice?' Rouwen laughed at the inventiveness of his own creation. Somehow, he had given birth to both a wraith of a girl in the forest and a talking predatory *thouse* bird.

'I do enjoy an occasional fieldmouse,' the bird admitted, as if confessing a delectable mortal sin. 'Still alive. Kicking and warm and tasty, that's the way I like them.' The *thouse* sounded smug and self-satisfied with its tastes. Rouwen wondered if a blow to his head had brought forth such wild visions. He did not remember being struck, but he had been through so much – or was this another manifestation of the gold trumpet at his side?

Rouwen touched the Lord's horn and worried that it caused its user to go crazy. Yet the feel of his sword penetrating bodies and the sound of the dagger slicing flesh was as he remembered. The feel of battle was unchanged from his days as Captain of the Intrepid Guard, and Diarra reacted not as he wanted but as she chose.

'Couldn't I do better with a dream?' he asked himself.

'I doubt it,' Toit said tartly. 'You are not very smart, no matter how high Finola's opinion of you might soar. She is too impressionable. I tell her not to drag home derelicts such as you, but she will not listen. No, she never does.' The bird clawed at the soft dirt and hopped onto the corpse to drink of the blood clotting at the jagged throat wound.

'I wasn't talking to you,' Rouwen said, trying to sort reality from fancy. He found it difficult because there seemed to be no boundary between the two.

'Then why were your lips flapping? Finola is on her quest, and that bag of bones with whom you travel is just now returning from her futile pursuit through the woods. She is such a hostile person, isn't she?' Toit flapped his wings and stretched, as if preparing to launch into the air.

'Wait,' Rouwen said. 'Finola said you might guide us to Vutorian.'

'Vutorian?' came Diarra's harsh, grating voice. 'What magicks have you used to prise the name loose from my lips? How dare you ensorcel me?' She stormed toward Rouwen, arms waving in mockery of a bird's wings.

'Unpleasant. Ugly, also, though once she might have been passable,' Toit said in a scornful voice.

'What is this? You have a talking bird? But it's a *thouse!* They cannot speak.' Diarra forgot her castigation of Rouwen and knelt to peer at Toit. 'This would be worth a fortune in a travelling circus. A sideshow attraction of . . .'

Diarra yelped and fell back, her finger almost bitten off when she tried to reach out to Toit. The bird hissed and beat its wings to hold her at bay.

'Why must I suffer such indignity?' the bird complained. 'I owe Finola much, but she always commits me to watching after the fools and the preposterous relics from inland kingdoms. No more. I will do her no more favors, even if she becomes the chief mage in Noumet.'

'You believe in the City of Mages?' asked Rouwen, no longer sure he dreamed any of this exchange.

'Who do you think keeps the sun burning and the tides flowing? What of the wind? Why does it blow, if not under a powerful wizard's guidance? Humans,' spat the bird in utter contempt.

'These mages in Noumet,' Rouwen started. He paused and ordered his thoughts. He was past caring if he was imagining Toit and the rest or if the *thouse* was real. 'Can they stop the Legion of the Air?'

'Those seven wind warriors you conjured and can't restrain? Of course they can, any one of them. But Finola is not properly trained.'

'Vutorian is,' Diarra cut in. She had recovered from the wonder of a talking *thouse* bird as if she encountered one every day. 'You will keep your promise, Brion Rouwen. You will slay Priowe for me if I lead you to the wizard.'

'Is this a contest? Must I compete with this hideous crone? I refuse! It is burden enough that I must be a poisonous bird, but now I am forced to prove myself better than a – a –' Toit began sputtering and spitting in outrage at the turn fate had taken.

Rouwen kept his distance, not sure if the bird's spittle was poisonous or if the *thouse* had other ways of injecting its virulent toxin.

'The important thing is to reach the wizard as quickly as possible,' Rouwen said. Before he could continue, Toit cut him off.

'The wind warriors are much closer, and I fear we must go toward them before leaving them behind.' The *thouse* crowed and flapped its wings powerfully. 'Are you going to roost all day or do you wish to take wing and get to Vutorian's nest?' One yellow eye closed, but the other fixed squarely on Rouwen. Toit asked Rouwen this question, not Diarra, whom he seemed intent on ignoring.

'I need to rest more,' Diarra said. 'The uproar of this night has left me drained. More than this exhaustion that reaches to my soul, the woods are dark and we would only get turned around. After sunrise, *then* I shall show you the path to Vutorian's quarters.' Diarra sneered in the bird's direction, as if this would make the *thouse* cower.

Rouwen saw Toit's beak open and close silently. Toit undoubtedly imagined Diarra's throat between those dangerous saw-edged man-killers. To forestall any such fight, Rouwen stepped forward and held out his arm for Toit.

'Come and perch. We need to talk about Vutorian and the Legion of the Air and other matters.'

'You would let me alight on your arm?' The notion struck Toit as funny, and the bird began a raucous cawing that could never be mistaken for a human's laugh. Before Rouwen could respond, Toit hopped into the air and gave two powerful flaps that caused its heavy body to rocket through the air. The impact against Rouwen's shoulder staggered him, and the iron claws crushing his shoulder made him wince with pain. But Rouwen kept a neutral expression.

'You are not strong enough to hold me,' Toit said. 'Thank you for the offer, though. Perhaps Finola saw more in you than I did at first.'

'How far is it to Vutorian?' Rouwen asked. His hand touched the grimoire in his pocket; the book of spells warmed slowly as he spoke the wizard's name. Diarra glared at him, as if he had chosen the wrong source of information. Although Rouwen knew little of Toit's motives – and nothing of Finola's – he trusted the dangerous *thouse* more than he ever could Diarra.

'A day's walk, no more. We can arrive before sunset, if you start now.' Toit watched Diarra for reaction, and Rouwen knew he was caught in a battle of strong wills. He was loath to make the choice between bird or former queen, but he knew the *thouse* had the advantage. Twice the bird had saved him when there was no reason, and somehow Rouwen believed Finola was sincere in her desire to help him. She might be a little girl and one deluded into believing that Noumet, City of Mages, existed but she had been candid. Indeed, her obviously unaffected manner did more to convince him than anything Toit might have said or done.

'We leave right away.' Louder, Rouwen said to Diarra, 'You may accompany us or not, as you see fit.'

'You promised to kill Priowe! You are a liar as well as a traitor to Gan!' She rushed at him, her fingers bent into claws intent on raking him. Rouwen was hampered by the heavy *thouse* perched on his shoulder and could not draw his sword. But he didn't have to. Toit screeched and lifted upright, as if to launch itself into Diarra's face. This stopped the queen's attack.

Seldom had Rouwen seen a look of such stark hatred as that he witnessed on the woman's face. When Toit screeched a hunting cry, the expression changed subtly from hatred to something even more sinister. Diarra pulled back and said in a conversational tone devoid of any fury, 'I can leave right away.' She turned and walked toward Rouwen's horse. The courser stirred uneasily at Diarra's approach, but the woman did not attempt to mount or even touch the horse.

'A dangerous ally,' Toit observed. 'Do you need her?'

'No,' Rouwen said, then reconsidered his answer. 'Yes, I do. We are kindred spirits in our quest.' He touched Diarra's spell casket and knew that he could never be free until she had her curse lifted also.

'Fin said nothing about her. I show you the way to Vutorian's nest because you would never be able to follow the map. The bitch is your concern.'

'Fin? Oh, Finola. How is it you serve her?' Rouwen asked, hefting the saddle and settling it on the reluctant horse's back. He paused when Toit squawked loudly in protest.

'I am not her servant. Fin and I are friends. Equals. Do you understand such an advanced concept?' The latter was more than a rhetorical question. It was a demand from Rouwen that he truly understood the relationship between *thouse* and human girl.

'I apologize for my error,' he said, tipping his head slightly in

Toit's direction. His forehead brushed soft feathers mixed with a sharpness that made him recoil. 'What did I touch?'

'Do you fear the sight of your own blood?' Toit made a disparaging noise and sidestepped along Rouwen's shoulder. 'I do not want your blood on my downy feathers.'

Rouwen probed the small cut on his forehead and stared at his bloody fingers. 'I barely touched you. What caused this?'

'You must have noticed the strikingly lovely golden highlights in my feathers. Those are real gold,' Toit said proudly. 'Some feathers are edged with beaten leaf, quite dangerously so, I might add.' The *thouse* sounded haughty in his vanity.

'Remind me never to embrace you,' Rouwen said dryly.

'There is nothing to fear on that score,' Toit said. 'I would never permit it. Only Finola is allowed to touch me.' The bird lifted its beak, as if disdaining further conversation. Rouwen quickly saddled his horse, kneed it in the belly to be sure the beast wasn't holding its breath against the tightened belly cinches, then mounted.

'Back along the trail already traversed?' Rouwen asked. He shivered involuntarily. He had seen the seven wind warriors as they ravaged the small coastal village and destroyed the lighthouse. To ride back meant daring the Legion of the Air.

'For a while,' Toit said. 'Perhaps until midday. Or later.'

Rouwen knew the *thouse* tried to bait him and did not respond. He rode off, not even bothering to see if Diarra followed. He heard the woman's bitter curses and considered offering her a seat behind him, in spite of the high-backed saddle. Even as the beneficent gesture was born in his brain, so did it die when he heard Diarra's continued denunciation of him as a traitor and fool.

'She repeats herself too quickly,' Toit said, as if this were the ultimate condemnation. Rouwen wondered if the *thouse* engaged in such long-winded cursing, or if the bird made a simple observation on Diarra's vocabulary. His thoughts turned from such petty concerns to more weighty matters. He rode for almost an hour past sunrise before noticing a distant rumbling noise, as if a hundred roebuck ran and battled for supremacy.

'The wind warriors,' Rouwen said, discerning the roaring of tornadic vortices among the other sounds in the Forest of Kelnos. 'They frighten the wildlife and cause it to stampede from the woods.'

'So? They are mindless, even as magical constructs go,' Toit said. 'There is nothing to be gained by emptying the forest of its wildlife, even if you could eat it all.' The bird clacked its beak loudly, as if considering the feast it missed. Rouwen hoped it did not consider his adjacent ear an adequate substitute for the thousands of beasts fleeing before the wind warriors.

'I need to see how close the Legion is,' Rouwen said. He looked for a rise, some elevation to let him spy on the wind warriors. He saw nothing.

'I can scout for you,' offered Toit.

'I'd prefer to see for myself.' Rouwen didn't mistrust Toit, but such information rode better with him if he gathered it himself. 'I can climb that tree and get a good view.' A particularly tall tree, one of the lodgepole pines mixed in with the limberfrost trees, offered an outstanding chance to see the advancing tornadoes. 'Will you watch my horse?'

'I shall watch her, too, if you like,' Toit said, indicating Diarra, who tramped along, puffing and still cursing. Her face had turned into a storm cloud of dark wrath, and rancor etched every line in her once-proud and lovely body.

'Very well,' Rouwen said, his mind already on the task of shinnying up the tree. Pines did not furnish much advantage until far up the trunk. Drawing his dagger, Rouwen drove the point into the tree and tested it for security. It would support his weight when he required it higher up. He began climbing, the sap staining clothing and flesh alike. Sweating, growling at his choice of observation point, Rouwen made his way upward, using the dagger only twice to prevent unwanted backsliding on the rough bark.

At the first strong limb, Rouwen clambered out to rest for a moment. Sudden motion drew his attention. He lifted his eyes and saw Toit perched on the end of the limb.

'You were watching my horse,' Rouwen said, angered that the bird reached this point so easily when his climb had been so difficult. Sticky sap matted his hair and made his hands almost useless, and the pungent odor from crushed needles made his nose run and his eyes water copiously.

'That is more difficult since the wench stole it,' Toit said.

'What?' Rouwen almost fell from the branch as he looked down for the first time. Dizziness assailed him but he saw that Diarra – and the horse – were gone. 'You were going to prevent her from . . .'

The *thouse* bird cut him off. 'Another warning seemed more

important.' Toit turned his head in a half-circle and peered outward, in the direction of the coast.

Rouwen's heart almost exploded when he saw the tall, swirling column of a wind warrior hewing a devastating path through the forest not a quarter mile away.

8

The Wizard's Castle

Rouwen almost fell from the sticky pine tree as he scrambled to get back to the trunk and slide down. Toit simply hopped off the limb, stretched long wings and glided. The *thouse* bird was waiting for Rouwen when he reached the ground.

'You cannot outrun the wind warriors,' the bird observed in an offhand manner. 'Since the wench has stolen your horse, matters are more serious than they might otherwise have been. I would never have trusted her the way you did. Any fool can see how untrustworthy she is.' The bird flapped its wings and lost a few more feathers. Toit preened a moment and added, 'I hate molting season. So many of my best feathers are lost. Perhaps I ought to collect and attempt to reattach them to enhance my beauty.'

'Get caught in the tornado and all your feathers are forfeit,' Rouwen said angrily, starting to run away from the approaching wind warrior. 'Both our lives are forfeit.'

'I need only fly to one side or the other. The tornado does not follow me as it does you,' Toit pointed out. 'However . . .' The bird spoke to thin air. Rouwen had broken into a run to escape.

Toit grumbled and ran a few steps to gather speed, then blasted into the air. The bird almost crashed into a tree as a sudden gust of wind caused by the wind warrior caught him by surprise. Grumbling, the *thouse* beat powerfully and began swooping and soaring through the forest to catch up with Rouwen.

The man had put a considerable distance between him and the Legion of the Air, but it would never be possible to stay ahead for long. The magical monsters moved slowly, but they never stopped. Sooner or later, Rouwen would have to slow or even stop to rest. The distance would then narrow between them until the Legion of the Air caught him and spun him in a wild spin that would burst him apart.

Toit flapped harder and then stretched out his claws. Rouwen looked over his shoulder and tried to ward off the *thouse*, but

Toit kept on his course, smashing hard into Rouwen. The bird's talons caught a shoulder and lifted Rouwen off the ground for a split second. It was long enough to cause Rouwen to stumble and fall.

'What are you doing?' he protested. There was not time to run, much less stand and discuss the grave nature of the threat stalking him. 'You'll kill me. Both of us!'

'You can run but you cannot hide,' Toit said pompously. 'The tornadoes are not human or even a superior avian such as I. They track the one who has called them into existence.'

Rouwen nodded. He had guessed as much. Relieved now that he hadn't thrown the gold horn into the sea, he still did not see a way to banish the wind warriors to their magical netherworld.

'You might consider summoning another one to muddy the path behind,' suggested Toit.

'I'd have eight to dodge. What a birdbrained notion!'

'Your insults flow off my back like a gentle spring rain. I refuse to be ruffled by inferiors.' Toit squawked loudly and tucked his head under one large brown wing, shutting out the world. The gold feathers along the *thouse* bird's back gleamed in the curious light bathing this part of the forest. The very air seemed altered by the nearness of the wind warriors, the sunlight muted and sounds all but vanished as animals fled to avoid the destruction promised by seven tornadoes.

Rouwen tried to dislodge the bird but could not prise loose the strong talons. Toit might have been stuck to Rouwen's shoulder with a powerful glue. The rushing of the whirling tornadoes caused Rouwen to panic. He forced down the rising tide of hysteria that would surely kill him. Various thoughts flashed through his mind.

A dagger thrust might end the poisonous bird's life, but he could not bring himself to that. Somehow, as irritating as Toit was, he was less of a burden than the disloyal Diarra. And Rouwen knew how much Finola thought of the bird.

'I apologize for anything I might have said, anything angering you,' Rouwen said, feeling foolish. He glanced nervously at the way the wind warrior jerked entire trees from the ground and spun them about in its murky column of air. Lateral motion was slow, but the wind speed within the vortex was greater than any storm Rouwen had ever endured, and Castle Gan enjoyed some of the world's worst winds because of the funneling effects of the Demon's Throat and the Shield Mountains.

'When demons dance,' Toit said. 'I have no reason to aid anyone so insulting.'

Rouwen took a deep breath and controlled his urge to run again, bird or no bird on his shoulder. The wind from the tornado whipped his cloak about and told him he had no chance unless Toit aided him.

'I will help gather your feathers and do what I can to help you groom yourself. You're the most beautiful bird I have ever seen.'

'You think so?' Toit looked at him with a huge yellow eye.

'No, damn you, I don't,' raged Rouwen. 'But Finola wanted you to help me.'

'Ah, truth enters your speech. I appreciate such candor. Your apology is accepted. And you are correct. Fin wanted me to look after you, Paradise take you, you silly human.' Toit pulled its head back from under the sheltering wing and looked about, as if noticing the tornado for the first time.

'You ought to avoid that, you know.'

'How? You keep me from running. How can I stop it without the golden whistle?'

'Even then, what could you do?' asked Toit. 'You do not know the commands. It takes a wizard of some ability to learn such magicks, and you are only a – a soldier,' Toit finished, as if this might be the worst insult it could conjure.

'I was that,' Rouwen said, sidling away from the wind warrior, now only a few dozen paces distant. The peripheral winds caught at his cloak and snapped it like a whip. Rouwen fought to keep his balance against the rising barrier of air around him. Throwing up one arm to shield his face, he shouted at the *thouse* over the thunderous roar.

'Can you save us?'

'I can merely fly off at any time,' Toit said in his smug tone. 'You require more potent magicks to save you. Speed alone will never extricate you from this terrible trap into which you have so foolishly fallen.'

A new gust blew Rouwen from his feet. He smashed hard into a pine tree, sliding down its trunk. Clutching it proved no safe anchor. The lashing gale proved stronger than his arms. He was sucked toward the center of the tornado.

'Save yourself then, you foul beast!' shrieked Rouwen as he tumbled into the vortex. 'Save . . .'

As suddenly as the wind warrior had come, this one died. Rouwen fell heavily to the ground, stunned by the fall. He shook his head and looked to the sky, thinking the tornado had skipped over him and intended to wheel around and return. But the azure dome visible through trees still standing was unmarred by the wavering column of dust and debris picked up by the Legion of the Air.

'What happened?' he gasped out. 'Toit, where, what . . .'

'Please control your silly questions,' the *thouse* said, flapping to the ground an arm's length away. 'There are now only six wind warriors following you, and the next closest is an hour's travel away. You have ample time.'

'Time for what?' Rouwen shook his head and immediately regretted it. Blood dribbled from his ears, and the roaring he still heard came from within, not from any of the menacing wind warriors.

'To reach Vutorian's nest, of course. Who do you think stopped that little creation of yours? I?' The *thouse* sniffed in contempt at such an idea. 'There is no reason for me to dabble in such matters. Finola is as near to wizardry as I care to get on a regular basis. She is truly a fine girl, for a human.' Toit cocked his head to one side, as if deep in thought. 'She is a fine person, even for a *thouse* bird.'

'Vutorian stopped the tornado? Where is he?' Rouwen sat up and looked around. Only empty forest met his gaze. Thoughts of fabulous wizardly tricks, of invisibility, of being able to scry and spell at a distance all crossed Rouwen's mind.

'This is the edge of the forest Vutorian calls his,' Toit said with just a hint of bitterness in his tone. 'What a wizard wants, a wizard takes.'

'Can he dissipate the other wind warriors?' Rouwen stood and tried to find the remainder of the Legion of the Air. He fancied he heard the booming sounds of the wind warriors ripping through the forest, but he could not be sure due to the ringing in his ears. He had come close to being sucked into the deadly vortex of one wind warrior; risking another encounter ranked low among the things he needed to do.

'Of course he can, if he stays in the Forest of Kelnos. He's a wizard and his power is great. He's Fin's mentor.' Again the *thouse* spoke with more than a hint of rancor, as if he thought little of Vutorian's skills.

'How long have you worked as his – assistant?' Rouwen asked, trying to phrase the question to prevent another mad sulk. Toit cawed like a crow and took to the air, not deigning to answer. Only when he was aloft and dipping and gliding through the tangled branches above did the *thouse* speak.

'Follow me, if you dare. Vutorian's nest is some distance away.'

'What of Diarra?'

'What of her?' Toit had no time to answer. He flapped powerfully and vanished through the dense forest. Rouwen sucked in a full lung of air, winced at the pain and probed cautiously to be sure he had not broken a rib in his brief encounter with the tornado. Bruised flesh met his fingers and nothing more. He took a hesitant step and another and another until he stretched his muscles enough to begin his long-legged lope after the flying bird. As Rouwen ran, he dared hope the wizard would aid him.

For an hour he ran, barely keeping Toit in sight. The *thouse* tormented him by falling back a few strokes, then putting on a burst of speed to prevent the man from overtaking him. Often Rouwen saw Toit soaring on a rising thermal or banking and spiralling downward to scan the ground for a tasty snack. Rouwen kept on course by remembering Finola's instructions to follow the grimoire in his pocket. Whenever he turned from his course, the book of spells cooled. Only on the right track did it continue to warm and glow a brighter green. This guided him, but did nothing to relieve his exhaustion.

When he was certain he could not take another step, he came upon Toit sitting on a boulder. The *thouse* had caught a fieldmouse and was almost finished devouring it. The bird clacked his beak as a human might smack his lips at a tasty morsel, then turned to face a weary Rouwen.

'So, you have decided to come after all.' The bird preened a moment, then said, 'Do you truly need Vutorian for your silly quest? There must be other wizards able to remove a simple spell.'

'He is the one Diarra sought – and he is Finola's teacher,' Rouwen said, hands on knees and head down as he gasped for breath. He stood and endured a sharp pain in his side that abated as his heartrate slowed. Turning, he saw that he had been running up the side of a mountain for most of the hour. From the tightness in his calves and the pounding within his head, he knew he could not continue much longer.

'There,' Rouwen said, pointing back down the hill. It hardly seemed possible he had exerted so much effort to put so little distance between him and the Legion of the Air. 'There are the six remaining wind warriors.'

'Many hours behind. You have time to reconsider,' insisted Toit. 'Find some other mage to perform your trivial spellings.'

'Trivial?' raged Rouwen. 'They are not trivial. I *will* find Vutorian.' He bit back any more argument as he looked past the rock where Toit sat into the gentle green bowl of a pleasant meadow.

There was a catch in Rouwen's throat, and he had trouble swallowing. How Sorinne would have enjoyed this lovely meadow, with its clear-running stream and tiny groves of shady trees. They might have passed their lives in total contentment in such a valley.

Rouwen stared at his hands and began to shake. 'Damn you, Kwuway, damn you Sosler and Priowe and Nishor and the whole damned lot of you!' A single touch would slay Sorinne, and it was their doing.

'There are the wind warriors, also,' Toit said, eyeing him strangely.

'Do you spy on my thoughts?' demanded Rouwen, furious. He was angry at Sosler, and he was angry at himself and Toit and anyone else who crossed him.

'There is no need. You have so few, none especially original, they become quite tedious and easily discerned.' Toit squawked and waddled about to face the valley.

'Vutorian. Where is he?' Even as the words escaped his lips, Rouwen blinked. He had somehow missed the castle in the middle of the valley, just past one delightful spot where he and Sorinne might have brought a picnic for an afternoon's idyll. 'How did that just appear?' he asked.

'You ask silly questions. Vutorian is a wizard and fond of his petty deceptions. Hiding a castle is the least of his skills, if you care to call them that,' Toit replied. The bird squawked again and took to the air, flapping hard. Rouwen knew he could either follow or leave. But if he left, he lost all chance of speaking with Vutorian. He might never again find this particular meadow or have the castle revealed to him as it was now.

Yet Toit had warned him away from the wizard, going so far as to suggest any mage but Vutorian could aid him. Rouwen shook his head as he entered the peaceful glade. Behind him lay only the six wind warriors and misery. Ahead? He would find out.

The ground had a curious springy quality to it that gave him energy with every step. By the time Rouwen reached the castle, all fatigue from his trip up the hillside had gone. He paused and stared at the open entry, a heavy black iron portcullis drawn up and barely visible under the stone of the gateway arch. Scanning the battlements, Rouwen saw no sign of guardsmen or even the trace of another human. The castle might have been deserted except for Toit swooping down from on high and flying through the gate. The *thouse*

271

landed heavily in the courtyard and beckoned to Rouwen with a golden-feathered wing.

'You may enter only through the gate,' Toit called to him. 'How you leave is another matter.' The bird made a guttural noise deep in its throat and waddled off, without waiting to see if Rouwen came in or left.

With a sure stride, Brion Rouwen entered the castle. As he passed through the gateway, a curious tingling passed through his body, as if thousands of tiny flames danced along his nerves. Within, the sensation vanished. He took a deep breath to calm himself and then studied the castle's interior structure.

Seldom had he seen such opulence. Never! Valley Gan was rich, in minerals, in foodstuffs, in a cheerful, healthy populace. But nothing prepared him for the appearance of the alabaster dwelling Vutorian called his own. Gems of a hundred varieties were inset in the soaring buttresses and the opalescent walls. Doors of teakwood three times Rouwen's height were partly opened and waiting for him to enter. From inside he heard softly soothing music, and the odor of rose and *necoia* flowers made his nose wrinkle with delight.

Truly a powerful mage lived within these walls.

Rouwen paused a moment before entering to meet the wizard, reflecting on the Lord of Death and Life and his simple abode on the Isle of Passing. The Lord had dwelt, a mirage within a hallucination inside a dream. For him illusion had been greater than anything but life eternal. Was all this Vutorian's pipedream?

'It is real, Brion Rouwen,' came a booming voice. 'Enter and be welcome. Finola has communicated to me your difficulties.' A small, dark man with sharp features and the longest, most improbable waxed mustache Rouwen had ever seen stood just inside the teak doors. The man flared a fur-edged cape, bowed deeply, and gestured to urge Rouwen within.

'Vutorian?'

'At your service, dear Captain of the Intrepid Guard. Such a hero is always welcome in my domain.' Fingers moving quicker than Rouwen could follow caused varicolored starbursts in the air. Vutorian laughed and added, 'A bit of magic-derived welcome, nothing more.'

'He thinks to set me on fire,' complained a familiar voice. 'I *hate* fire. My feathers singe and . . .'

'Toit, be off with you. Go roost with the pigeons,' Vutorian said in a stern voice. 'Away!' The wizard shooed the *thouse* off, and Toit obeyed with a surliness reinforcing Rouwen's opinion that the bird did not like the wizard.

'Your hospitality is greatly appreciated. First, I must warn you that I accidentally summoned the Legion of the Air and six wind warriors follow me, even as we speak.'

'An incautious seventh ventured to the boundary of my domain,' Vutorian said. The wizard's nose bristled like a giant sewer rat's, and the long mustaches bristled, reminding Rouwen even more of a rodent's whiskers quivering at the scent of fresh cheese. Hard, dark eyes bored into Rouwen. The only features missing were chisel-pointed front teeth. From this distance, Vutorian appeared to possess only normal teeth, but the rodent image burned in Rouwen's skull as he passed by the wizard.

Rouwen had thought he had gone beyond astonishment at the display of luxury and wealth. He was wrong. Inside, Vutorian's keep proved far more extravagant than its exterior. The sky-light appeared to be crafted from a single crystal of diamond, rays refracting throughout the room in a soft spectrum that soothed and warmed Rouwen. The massive furniture had been constructed by only the most artistic of carpenters, detailed carving at every curve and turn of the finely grained woods. Even the lustrous walls had been decorated; paintings that made Rouwen's heart jump with emotion stretched around the room. He forced himself to stand firm and not reach out to touch them, to experience the thrills promised by both touch and sight. Rouwen turned his attention to the floor, trying not to appear a complete bumpkin. The rug stretched on the floor had been woven with gold and silver threads into a fabric softer than Rouwen would have guessed possible. He bent to touch it, reassuring himself that it truly was of metallic fibers.

'An artisan on the shore of the Smoking Sea weaved it for me in return for a small chore I tended to,' said Vutorian. 'Those chairs, the ones along yon wall, are all carved from living bristlecone pine trees. The roots plunge downward more than a thousand feet.'

'How old are the trees?' asked Rouwen, amazed at such an affectation. Vutorian could never move the chairs, not rooted to the ground as they were.

'Centuries. Who can put an exact date on such ancient trees? Come, let us discuss the matter of the wind warriors. You seem to have an irrational dread of them.' Vutorian's long robes brushed the rug and sent tiny sparks leaping wherever the hem touched. The soft whispering sounds both soothed Rouwen and bothered him, why he could not say.

273

Trailing behind the wizard, Rouwen took an offered chair carved from living wood and tried to find a comfortable position. It proved too difficult, and he resigned himself to sitting awkwardly on the edge of the seat. Vutorian took a chair facing his and appeared quite content with the hardness.

'Finola has told you much, but I am not sure she relayed it properly,' Rouwen began.

'Why not?' interrupted Vutorian. 'She might be only ten years of age, but she is an apt student. Never have I had an apprentice learn so quickly. The young lady has a goal and is steadfast in achieving it.'

'You told her of Noumet?' Rouwen couldn't keep the accusation from his voice.

'Oh, that! Did she rattle on about keeping the sun burning, the winds blowing, or the rain falling? I am sorry for you to have endured her little fantasy. She firmly believes she is in training for the City of Mages. I have never encouraged this mistaken belief – such a place does not exist, of course, but she is young. The skills she learns are quite real.' Vutorian tented his fingers and rested his chin on the steeple. Leaning forward slightly, his long mustache quivered as if a thing alive. For a ghastly moment, Rouwen thought the wizard's hair *was* alive and writhing like a whip-thin snake. He twisted uncomfortably in the hard chair and saw that the movement was only a trick of light within the vast chamber. Light from the diamond dome above reflected off the metallic carpet and gave strange highlights to Vutorian's dark, stylishly well-greased hair.

'Then you did not tell her such a place existed?' Rouwen tried to remember what the girl had said and couldn't – quite. So much of his meeting with her danced just beyond the bounds of easy memory.

'Never! I discourage such talk, but you know how children are. Even talented ones like dear Finola.' Vutorian's eyes bored into Rouwen, who returned the unblinking stare until the wizard smiled slightly.

'The wind warriors,' Vutorian said finally. 'They are easily banished with a spell or two when they intrude onto my domain in Kelnos, but the golden whistle is a more efficient way of doing it, especially if you lack extensive magical acumen.'

'You have the whistle?' Rouwen wondered at the wizard's easy admission to possessing the magical device.

'Would I mention it unless I did?' asked Vutorian. 'Blowing the Lord's gold horn and summoning the Legion of the Air ought to be a joy, not a burden.'

Rouwen started to ask what the mage desired in return. Men of such exalted position as Vutorian were not wont simply to give away the means of their magical power. There had to be price to be paid. A high price, possibly dipped in blood.

'You are skeptical. Ah, then come with me and I shall give you the whistle to prove my integrity. I wish you nothing but the best, my friend. Finola has vouched for you, and you are completely welcome in my home.' The wizard rose. Rouwen quickly stood, also, glad to be off the chair. He towered above Vutorian, but the difference in height seemed unimportant to the mage. The wizard half-turned, then shook his head as if he had seen something in Rouwen for the first time.

'What's wrong?'

'Ah, my little Finola would never approve of my hospitality. She acts as my hostess, the one to whom I turn for entertaining guests. She would never allow me to call myself a host while permitting anyone within these walls to endure such tatters. What was it when new? A Gannian uniform?'

'Mionese,' Rouwen said. 'I took it from a dead officer after I ran him through.' He was not certain why he uttered such harshly threatening words to a man who had been nothing but cordial and courtly toward him, yet it seemed necessary to caution Vutorian about taking him too lightly.

'That explains the traces of blood on the rent,' Vutorian said, his fingers lightly touching the spot where Rouwen's sword had gutted the officer. 'Such rags have long outlived their usefulness, and I'd wager you are hungry and tired. Please accept clothing, a meal, and a bed before continuing our discussion. Rest easily. The wind warriors cannot invade my domain.' Vutorian bowed again, leaving Rouwen at a loss for words. He disliked the man's appearance, but the wizard forced him to amend his impressions with his unfailingly accommodating offers.

'There is only one thing I can say, sir,' replied Rouwen. 'Thank you.'

Vutorian beamed, and the smile seemed genuine. 'Finola would be proud of my remembering. I tend to work overlong and have few visitors. She calls me a harsh taskmaster, and I am. That is the only way to learn the arcane crafts. So many spells, such finesse required in uttering the chants, giving the proper inflections. A mistake, one ignored syllable or wrongly mixed potion and . . .' Vutorian spread his hands as if saying all was lost.

Rouwen stared at the tiny world that spun just above the wizard's palms. It whirled and then exploded, as if the speed of

275

its rotation had proven too great for the material. The incorporeal wisps fluttered like lost spirits on their way to Mount Glid, then vanished.

'An impressive display of your power,' Rouwen said.

'That? An exhibition of petty skills, nothing more. I find it delightful to have an audience worthy of my performance again. But do enjoy my hospitality. I . . .' The wizard stopped in mid-sentence and cocked his head to one side, as if listening to a voice only he could hear. An exasperated expression flashed on his face and Vutorian made an impatient brushing gesture.

'I am sorry. I must tend to matters in my laboratory. My guide will take you to your chambers. You need only ask aloud for whatever you want. Your slightest wish will be obeyed as if it were mine.' Vutorian bowed, then spun, the hem of his robes swinging wide. He did not appear to hurry, but he crossed the vast audience chamber faster than Rouwen could have sprinted across it.

Rouwen wondered what the wizard had meant about guide until he saw a tiny firefly darting about. The glowing insect buzzed loudly and began flashing on and off in an obvious attempt to capture his attention.

'Lead on,' Rouwen said, feeling a little foolish. He relaxed when the firefly buzzed again and shot away in the direction of a set of intricately carved doors at the far side of the audience chamber. Rouwen found that the firefly escort always kept a few paces ahead, no matter how quickly or slowly he walked. Tiring of the game of trying to overtake the magical sprite, Rouwen walked at a steady pace, drinking in the luxury of his surroundings. Paintings of breathtaking skill lined the walls of the corridor down which he was led, and the furnishings were worth more than a king's ransom. Rouwen would have denied such wealth existed in the entire world before seeing it with his own eyes.

The firefly buzzed with a different note as it paused in front of a door covered with soft vermilion-dyed leather held in place by huge brass studs. Rouwen opened the door and peeked inside. Many were the times he had guarded King Priowe in the ruler's personal quarters. The King of Gan did not live as well as Brion Rouwen would that night.

The next item, after drinking in the lavishness arrayed around him, was the closet stuffed with clothing of all descriptions. Rouwen went to it and saw every taste imaginable represented along the heavy iron bar supporting the apparel. He pushed aside the gaudier outfits in favour of one resembling his old captain's

276

uniform. It was functional and felt familiar next to his skin, yet was far and away more ornate than even his full dress uniform.

The firefly's buzzing made Rouwen glance over his shoulder. A sunken tub filled with scented water had been drawn for him. The memory of being scrubbed and clean was so distant, Rouwen never hesitated. He dropped the uniform he had chosen to the floor and stripped his rags off as he walked to the tub. The water closed around him and eased the pains in his body, making even the deepest of cuts feel whole once more.

Rouwen might have drifted to sleep, or he might simply have closed his eyes for a moment, but when he snapped bolt upright in the tub he had the feeling of considerable time passing. He glanced around, but the firefly that had escorted him to these sumptuous quarters had vanished. He slipped from the tub and dried quickly, putting on the uniform he had chosen. He kept his weapons, settling sword and dagger on a finely tooled belt, and he pushed the grimoire he had stolen from Kwuway into his left pocket. Rouwen then added the golden horn to his belt, holding it in place using a double loop of strong silk cord he found. He completed dressing with a pair of boots more supple than the finest leather gloves he had ever worn.

'A man could learn to enjoy a life such as this,' Rouwen muttered as he walked around the room, examining every nook and cranny. He found trays of food waiting for him; he ate vast amounts. Drink from a silver pitcher both intoxicated and left him clearheaded at the same time.

'And the bed!' he exclaimed. Rouwen bounced on it, finding it exactly as firm as he liked. As he lay back, a curious longing developed. He sat up and wondered how he could summon the firefly – or a servant.

Vutorian had sequestered him in extravagant quarters, but Rouwen felt no affinity with the wizard. Their talk had been cordial, unlike the words exchanged with the *thouse* bird, yet Rouwen missed Toit and mistrusted Vutorian. He pushed from the bed and went to the door, expecting it to be locked. He almost fell into the corridor beyond when he put his weight against the door panel. It opened easily.

'Where would I find the pigeons in a castle of such majestic proportions?' he wondered aloud. Rouwen recoiled when the firefly buzzed up and bobbed a few paces away, as if impatient for him to come after it. Rouwen was hesitant at first, then walked with greater confidence when he saw no sentries and encountered no ward spells. It was as if Vutorian had given him free run of the castle, with no reservations.

The firefly guide led Rouwen through twisting corridors and up into a turret he had not seen before from the castle's courtyard. Round and round he turned, taking the steep steps easily now that he had rested and eaten his fill of such fine food. At the top of the turret's stairs, the firefly buzzed once and then winked out of existence. The sudden departure made Rouwen wary. He put his hand on the door's latch and gingerly opened it.

The squawks greeting him and the stench of a pigeon coop told him the firefly had fulfilled its mission.

'Did that eater of bird flesh banish you here?' came the querulous question. Rouwen moved until he had the turret's narrow window at his back and could see the creatures within the circular room. Dozens of pigeon cages lined the walls, and Toit sat atop one cage, looking forlorn.

'I came to find you. I hadn't realized Vutorian meant it literally when he told you to get off to the pigeon roost.' Rouwen looked around for some sign that Toit was more comfortable here than he would have been elsewhere. He found no trace of a nest large enough to hold the immense bird.

'He has no time for me when Finola is gone. She trains constantly, but she always has a kind word for me. Not so Vutorian. Can you imagine it? He *eats* bird flesh. And he enjoys it!'

Rouwen did not comment on this. Roast duck was second only to pheasant to his taste. His culinary preferences would not ease Toit's disgust and might prejudice the *thouse* against him.

'Why do you stay here if you dislike Vutorian so?' he asked.

'For Finola's sake, why else, why else?' Toit squawked loudly and settled his feathers in a fluffy nimbus around himself. 'She raised me from an egg, and I owe her far more than simple life. I will even follow her to Noumet when she begins guiding the sun in its path across the sky, though being trapped underground will be a harsh burden to bear.'

'You believe in Noumet? Vutorian does not seem to.' Rouwen perched on a relatively clean cage and stared through the slit window. He had slept longer than he had thought. The sun was setting, casting long shadows across the castle's courtyard.

'Not really, but Fin believes, and for her sake I will never argue.'

Rouwen snorted and shook his head. Delusion was one thing, self-delusion was another. 'Isn't it Vutorian's duty to steer her in the direction of truth?'

'She is determined to pilot the sun in its daily orbit about the planet,' Toit said, 'in spite of the danger from the Flame Specter.'

'What?' The mention of the Flame Specter brought Rouwen about abruptly. Kwuway had mentioned it, as had the Lord of Death and Life. He reached into the pocket of his tunic and touched the book of spells he had placed there. The grimoire's warmth made him remember how Finola had said the spell book would guide him to this place.

Had its glow increased on his arrival? Or did Toit's mention of the mysterious Flame Specter cause the magical response?

'What do you know of the Flame Specter?' he asked, trying not to sound too anxious. So much intruded on his once serene life, but this unfamiliar name had been spoken by enemy and friend alike.

'Why, it is merely the greatest of all powers in this world. It is an elemental dwelling far beneath the ground.'

Rouwen sagged. More mythology, like Noumet, like so much else told to frighten children. He turned back and watched the setting sun for a few minutes, growing increasingly uneasy. Something in the courtyard below was amiss, and he could not pinpoint what it might be.

Then he saw the reason for his disquietude. A shadow moved, separating from deeper shadow, and dashed toward the teakwood doors of Vutorian's keep. For a moment, the dark figure paused, then vanished within. Whoever – whatever – moved below did so furtively.

9

Dangerous Allies

Toit screeched as he wheeled about in the huge room and came down heavily on Rouwen's shoulder. The man sagged under the weight and then straightened painfully, wondering at the wisdom of his offer to the *thouse* bird to share his quarters. Vutorian might have his own reasons to sequester Toit with the pigeons in the turret.

'The wizard treats his guests well,' the bird said, craning its neck about in almost a full circle to take in every fold of peach-colored, softly scented silk in the draperies and the fine viands spread out on the long ebony table at the far side of the room. 'Better than he treats those with whom he associates daily.'

'You don't like him because he quarters you with pigeons, do you?' asked Rouwen, not wanting to explore this dark side of the wizard – and bird – but not finding other words. His mind kept wandering to the poorly seen figure ducking into the wizard's keep a few hours earlier. He had considered going to the audience chamber and finding out who paid Vutorian the surreptitious visit, but he had refrained. If the intruder was another of Vutorian's guests, it was none of Rouwen's business and might be considered a breach of hospitality. And if the prowler thought to rob the wizard, that was Vutorian's business, also.

Rouwen remembered the curious tingling sensation in his body as he had walked through the castle's gate. It did not seem likely the wizard allowed intruders into his castle. The ward magicks would hold an army at bay, much less a simple night thief.

'Do you mind if I sample the morsels Vutorian has put out for you?' asked Toit. 'I am famished. Pigeons eat nothing but grain and insects, and I refused to dine with them.' The bird spat, showing his contempt for his filthy winged companions.

'Help yourself,' urged Rouwen, glad to have the weighty bird off his shoulder. He wondered if a pad might ease the burden of the sharp talons cutting into his flesh, then shook himself.

He was thinking as if Toit would always use his shoulder as a convenient perch. As soon as Vutorian dissipated the Legion of the Air and lifted the spell Kwuway had placed on him, he would return to Gan.

'Good, very good,' Toit said as he greedily gulped up tidbits of rare meat and sampled strange fruits Rouwen could not identify. 'Far better than the provender given to the wizard's carrier pigeons.'

'Who receives messages from him?' Rouwen asked. 'Pigeons are good only for returning and little else.'

'They don't make a bad snack,' the carnivorous bird said, clacking his beak shut hard, as if in memory of successful hunts and tasty meals. 'But he will not let me eat any of them when I am banished to the turret. I miss Finola. She takes me everywhere with her.'

'How long will her current quest last?' Rouwen lounged on the bed, his head propped up by soft pillows. He found it hard to concentrate as fatigue took its toll on him. The stranger below. The wind warriors. The curse that rested so heavily on him. All were mixed in a strange half-world more dream than reality.

Rouwen imagined Sorinne coming to him, holding out her hand, and he taking it. She screamed with voiceless torment as her flesh began to boil from her bones. In seconds she was reduced to a simmering pile of gray, glowing bones, and all because Rouwen loved her.

'The curse,' he moaned, tossing about on the bed. 'Must stop it. Lift it. The spell casket.'

Rouwen came awake when he felt softness brush his cheek. Less than an inch away he saw Toit's huge yellow eye staring at him. He recoiled and then relaxed. The *thouse* had jumped onto the bed and had waddled close to him as his nightmare took possession of his mind.

'Your dreams are painful,' the bird said softly. 'Was it always so?'

'Kwuway cursed me. King Priowe ordered it, and his pet wizard laid the curse upon my head.' The dream state remained to fog parts of Rouwen's brain. His trip through the tunnel under the Shield Mountains flashed through his nightmare again, his brother and old Nibbles begging for release of their trapped souls to Paradise. Not only did he painfully kill those he loved, he doomed their souls to eternal wandering beneath the massif of the Shield Mountains. Something in the conjuring of the curse had made it impossible for the dead to find their way

281

to Paradise, doubly cursing Rouwen. Without a clear spirit path to Mount Glid, they could never leave their solitary entrapment.

This hideous fate he decreed for them because he was unable to control his love.

'Do not rely on Vutorian to ease your pain,' advised Toit. 'He looks out best for his own interests.'

'Is that why he tutors Finola in magical lore?' Rouwen was coming more awake now, aware that morning light poked through the heavy silk draperies over the windows. He had slept longer than he had thought, but it had availed him little. Fatigue still dragged at his body.

'He sees much in her,' said Toit almost sadly, 'but his motives are other than avuncular. She might be the finest mage who ever lived. Her powers are great, but she is untrained.'

'And she wants to run off to Noumet and keep the sun burning in the sky,' finished Rouwen. He dropped his feet heavily to the warm floor, bothered at the nagging weariness assailing his limbs. The Forest of Kelnos had not provided a good spot for sleeping, and when he found one in Vutorian's castle, the nightmares returned.

'He will want you to dine with him. He considers breakfast the most important meal of the day,' said the *thouse* bird. 'Myself, I prefer to dine in snippets, a bit here, some more there. Nothing is quite as satisfying as snaring a pigeon on the wing. They are mostly feathers – and tough! – but the thrill is as much in the chase as the eating.'

'I'm sure that is so,' said Rouwen, stretching and settling his accoutrements about his waist. He had allowed the *thouse* to stay in his quarters as much out of fear of robbery by the wizard as from any sense of compassion for Toit's plight in the pigeon coop. The poisonous beak would make short shrift of anyone attempting to steal the gold horn.

'Will you join us or are you assigned other duties?'

'Duties!' chortled Toit. 'That's what a meal with Vutorian is, an onerous duty. But I am not welcome at his table. You go. Enjoy the fine foods. He is something of a gourmet, as humans define the term.'

'That's better than the last wizard I met,' Rouwen said, thinking of the Lord of Death and Life. He had subsisted on paltry food turned into decent victuals through magic. Rouwen hesitated at the door to his quarters, looking back over his shoulder and wondering if Vutorian played the same magical tricks. Rouwen shrugged it off. What did it matter if he couldn't tell the difference between gourmet delicacies and magically altered worms?

He strolled the corridors, admiring the wizard's tastes in art and furniture as much as he did the fine views from the occasional windows overlooking waterfalls and secluded groves and sweeping meadows so peaceful they caused an ache in his breast. Without someone to share such vistas of beauty, the landscape meant nothing. If only Sorinne could share it with him. He remembered her touch, the soft breeze of her breath against his shoulder as they slept, the tickling tenderness of long blonde hair brushing his chest.

Rouwen's reverie was disturbed as words echoed down the hallway.

'There you are. I was preparing to send a messenger to fetch you,' said the wizard, coming through a door at the end of the hallway. Vutorian's enormously long mustache quivered like grain in a soft summer wind, forging new images of scurrying rodents in Rouwen's mind.

'Please take no offense. I merely wanted to drink in the beauty of your castle. You have impeccable taste in art.'

'I admire only the best, and collect only the greatest of that small grouping. Come, join us at the table. I have prepared a meal that will be truly memorable.' Vutorian motioned for Rouwen to precede him. The former guard captain stopped and looked down at the shorter wizard for a moment. He wasn't sure if this was the proper time to broach the subject most on his mind, but he did anyway.

'The golden whistle that removes the wind warriors,' Rouwen began, searching for the proper phrasing. 'You promised it to me last night. Perhaps we can . . .' Rouwen bit off further pursuit of the issue when he saw the wizard's expression change subtly. Irritation replaced jovial hospitality. And there was more than irritation at Rouwen's request, but he could not determine its source.

'We shall see about that,' Vutorian said, ice in his voice. 'First, we must dine. Nothing important should be done on an empty belly.'

Rouwen walked briskly to the huge audience chamber. Its colors had changed with morning, now bathing the room in a warm honey-colored light and banishing all shadows. Rouwen held out his hand and marvelled that nowhere did he see shadow. It was as if the wizard had decreed that darkness was not permitted.

'There, please, sit to my right,' Vutorian said, moving to the high-backed chair at the head of the long table. More food than an entire army might consume was arrayed in an artistically pleasing pattern. Anew Rouwen marvelled at the work required to maintain such a castle – or such an illusion.

As he sat down, he froze. Across from him at the table sat Diarra, slumped in a chair. She sneered at him, then greedily stuffed food into her mouth as if she had not eaten in a month. Indeed, she might not have, Rouwen knew.

'It was you I saw sneaking in here,' Rouwen said, settling into his chair. He glanced at Vutorian. The wizard's expression was neutral, but tiny clues gave away his agitation. Vutorian fought to keep his emotions under control, as befitting the lord and master of such a fine mansion.

'Lord Vutorian was kind enough to allow me into his humble abode,' Diarra said, slopping wine down her tattered dress as she sucked at the silver goblet. She dropped it to the table. Vutorian winced as the purple wine stained a fine lace tablecloth. 'He has always been a prince among men,' she said, putting more into the statement than belonged, Rouwen thought.

He locked eyes with her, then saw how the neck of her dress had been torn open. Dangling between her partially exposed breasts hung a golden chain. And on the chain depended a small golden whistle. Rouwen half rose from his chair and started to reach for it when Vutorian grabbed his wrist. The wizard's hand seemed almost fragile around Rouwen's thick wrist, but the power lay hidden. He tried to break free and could not.

'Come, dear Brion, enjoy my feast. It is one of the few luxuries I permit myself.'

'This is certainly a monastic existence,' Diarra said in her nasty, biting tones. 'I can picture you wandering the halls, flagellating yourself, bemoaning your sorry existence. Poor, poor Vutorian.'

'I've worked hard for what I have,' Vutorian snapped, his patience at an end.

'What a pity if it should all come to naught,' Diarra said, leaning back. Rouwen marvelled that he had once sworn to defend this woman's life and honor. He would gladly drive his dagger through her heart, save for the effect it would have on Princess Sorinne. Rouwen could never face the lovely daughter with the news that he had struck down her mother.

'What power does she hold over you?' Rouwen looked at Vutorian, who drummed his fingers on the table. The wizard did not answer, but his long mustaches shook so fast they might have been set to some high resonant frequency.

'Your Legion of the Air, dear Brion, that's what. The six wind warriors have arrived, and poor Vutorian cannot hold them all off, not without this.' Diarra touched the golden whistle. 'I told you I knew how to get it, and I have. Now you must pay for it.' She looked from Vutorian to Rouwen, who saw the madness creeping back into her dark eyes.

'Who? Which of us must pay for it?' asked Rouwen. He reached into his pocket and rested his hand on Kwuway's grimoire. The spell book almost burned his hand. He pulled back, trying not to show his uneasiness at this omen. Powerful magicks were in play, and he feared that the Legion of the Air was closer than Diarra hinted. 'I have promised to kill King Priowe for you. Is Vutorian bidding for that privilege, also?'

'Poor, *poor*, Vutorian,' taunted Diarra. 'He can dissipate one wind warrior or perhaps two, but so many? He is at a loss. His powers are not infinite, even here in the center of his might.'

Rouwen stared at Vutorian and knew the answer was more complex than Diarra allowed. While hardly accidental, the dissipation of the tornado that had menaced him the day before could not be repeated immediately. But why? Something told Rouwen it had to do with Finola and her quest. Or perhaps just the little girl herself. Toit had said she possessed towering ability as a mage. Vutorian might possess the knowledge and Finola the raw power required to challenge the Legion of the Air. With Finola elsewhere, Vutorian might be helpless against six of the magical wind monsters.

Rouwen acted without hesitation. He leaped halfway across the table and snatched at the golden chain around Diarra's neck. She recoiled in surprise, but his fingers had become tangled in the chain. He yanked hard and the golden whistle was his.

'What do I do with it now?' he asked Vutorian.

'Three sharp blast;, dear Brion,' answered Diarra, smirking. Her mind seemed split a half dozen ways, different facets reflecting back twisted light as the world changed about her.

'Three, that's all,' said Vutorian, despondent. He kept his eyes averted.

Rouwen lifted the whistle and blew the required three blasts. He pushed back from the table and went to the huge teak doors and looked outside. The towering columns of swirling windstorms marched back and forth just outside the castle walls. Rouwen repeated the blasts. The tornadoes twitched but did not vanish as their comrade had done in the limberfrost forest.

'There's more,' Rouwen called. 'What else must I do?'

'There's nothing more *you* can do, Brion,' said Diarra grabbing at the whistle. His hand closed over it, the cold metal pressing hard into his palm. He would never return it to her. 'Tell him, Vutorian.'

'She's right. Unless you are of royal blood, you cannot use the whistle.'

'Can *you* use it, Vutorian?' cried Diarra. 'No, of course not. You are not royal, either. All you have are clever little incantations. Real power is denied you, and so it will always be. Aren't those tornadoes getting closer? They might breach the walls at any moment.'

'Can they destroy your castle?' Rouwen stared in wide-eyed amazement at the wizard, who only nodded. His morose expression darkened to a smoldering anger.

'Brion, how can you ask such a question? You know what the wind warriors can do. The Legion of the Air is an invincible army. Only a few have ever been able to neutralize it once summoned. The Lord was one, and that proved his real power, not the prattling about immortality and bringing back souls from Paradise.'

'He could do all that,' Rouwen protested, not knowing if it were true. The Lord had boasted much but had said little. All Rouwen knew of the mage's ability had been guessed – or stolen.

'The whistle, Brion. Give me the whistle.' Diarra held out her hand. Rouwen tossed it to her. She flashed her wicked grin and put the golden whistle to her lips. Three sharp blasts sounded, almost beyond Rouwen's hearing.

And one wind warrior winked from existence, first shaking as if a powerful ague seized it, then falling into itself until only the hint of a dust devil spun. Then even this vanished. The remaining five milled about a common center as if conferring, confused at the loss of another in their ranks, but they soon returned to batter against Vutorian's walls. If anything their power had grown and the debris flying through the castle proved increasingly dangerous.

'That's what it takes to chase them away,' Diarra said with smug satisfaction. 'Being queen of a powerful kingdom such as Gan affords one incredible opportunity to – learn.' Her laugh carried the razor edge of madness in it. She spun around and around as if she were the belle of the cotillion, her small feet performing quick, intricate steps that confused Rouwen's eyes. He pulled away from watching the woman dancing with her fantasy partner and turned to Vutorian.

The wizard shifted his gaze from the spinning wind warriors

to Diarra and back, growing increasingly worried as the queen danced on.

'Use the whistle to get rid of them,' Rouwen said. 'Take it from her. Or use your own magicks to turn them into nothing more than gentle breezes.' The wizard swallowed hard and said nothing, which gave Rouwen all the answer he needed.

Vutorian's power was limited, and he could not drive away the Legion of the Air by himself. Even with the whistle, he was powerless to do any more than Rouwen. Diarra's jibe had struck home about the mage not having royal blood flowing in his veins.

'Coerce her. Use a spell to bend her to your will,' Rouwen went on.

'Be quiet!' snapped Vutorian. 'You do not understand. You toy with powers far beyond your reckoning.'

'Take this. Take it and use the spells written there to get rid of the tornadoes.' Rouwen angrily pulled the book of spells he had stolen from Kwuway and shoved it toward the small wizard. For a moment Vutorian stared at the grimoire. The runic symbols on the cover glowed with a gentle blue that belied the power he had felt earlier when he saw the Legion of the Air battering the castle walls in their attempt to reach him.

'The book!' exclaimed Vutorian. He almost snatched it from Rouwen, but controlled his eagerness at the last possible moment. His hands shook slightly as he took the grimoire from Rouwen. 'I have heard of this grimoire for years but never did I believe it would be mine.' He clutched it tightly to his chest, then glanced sideways at Diarra. The music only she heard must have played itself out because she bowed deeply to her imaginary partner and returned to the doorway. Vutorian hastily hid the book of spells.

'That is payment for two things,' Rouwen said sternly. 'The wind warriors are to be dismissed. The other item is the curse Kwuway placed upon me. Find the spell casket and release my soul.'

'The curse, and the Legion of the Air, yes, yes,' Vutorian said, his hand pressing against the book of spells hidden under his robe. The mage fell silent when Diarra interposed herself between the two men.

'Have they ripped down your walls yet, Vutorian? No? It is only a matter of time. Perhaps not today, but tomorrow or distant tomorrows yet to come. They are persistent.' She turned her wild-eyed stare in Rouwen's direction and mouthed something he could not understand.

Louder, Diarra said, 'You might expel him. The wind warriors follow him.'

'Do that and I shall summon thousands of them!' shot back Rouwen. He touched the gold horn dangling at his side.

'Peace, please. We must work for our mutual gain, not bicker among ourselves,' said Vutorian. He tapped the hidden grimoire significantly, signalling to Rouwen that he would not turn anyone out. Payment had been received and appreciated. But Rouwen wondered what hold Diarra had over the wizard that kept him from banishing her. She could never dissipate the six wind warriors in time if she was driven from the castle's main gate.

'I agree,' Diarra said, startling Rouwen. The madness faded in the woman's eyes, but a steely determination remained. He knew what she was going to say before she uttered the words. 'Priowe must die.'

'I have promised that, but Duke Sosler is mine to slay.' This seemed to appease Diarra, but he could not discern Vutorian's true feelings.

'We all want the wind warriors turned back into noisome little breezes,' said the wizard. 'I agree to see to Priowe and Sosler in return for that.'

'More,' cut in Rouwen. 'Duke Drioway of Mion must die, too.' Rouwen paused and saw that the name registered on the wizard's face. Everyone knew the players in this game of power. 'There is something more. Kwuway cursed me. Find the spell casket and release me from my spell.'

'Dangerous, difficult,' muttered Vutorian, but his fingers outlined the grimoire against his robe. He bobbed his head in sudden agreement. 'We all have stated what we desire most. So be it. The three of us will accomplish much.' The wizard uneasily glanced at the Legion of the Air and then left the audience chamber. Rouwen saw that the soft honeyed light had turned into a more menacing red hue now. How the light filtered through the complex diamond suspended above he did not know. Nor could he know what the coloration implied.

'Do not worry, dear Brion,' Diarra said with mock cordiality. 'I shall sit and blast at those windbags until they are all gone. Just don't go creating any more with your horn. I shall take that as a sign you do not wish to cooperate.' Her teeth ground together as she said, 'Priowe will die. Slowly!'

'The wind warriors,' urged Rouwen. The walls of the castle began to buckle and quake at the repeated attacks by the swirling columns of air. If Diarra did not act quickly, they would destroy Vutorian's stronghold.

Diarra went outside and sat on a step, turning the golden whistle over and over in her hands. Rouwen closed his eyes, fearing the worst, but he heard the sharp notes on the instrument and the eventual sighing of a wind warrior dying. As Vutorian had done, Rouwen quickly left. He had no wish to stay and see Diarra scatter every one of the Legion of the Air he had recklessly conjured on the Isle of Passing.

Rouwen returned to his chambers, worrying as he went. He had forged an alliance with Diarra and Vutorian, but something had been left out. Not being able to pinpoint it, Rouwen feared he had created a dangerous trap for himself that would be sprung when he least expected it.

His hand flashed to his dagger when a brown shape flew at him from across the room. He stayed his hand when he realized Toit was only coming to greet him.

'You respond like a man who has lost a battle,' Toit said, driving his talons deep into Rouwen's shoulder. The man shifted and tried to push the *thouse* into a more comfortable position but could not. He relented and let the bird stay on his fleshy perch.

Rouwen worried that he had done the same thing with Vutorian and Diarra. They had driven their claws into him and he had accommodated them.

'I do not understand Vutorian,' Rouwen said. 'What has he to gain from allying himself with Diarra? I gave him a prize desirable to any wizard.'

'He is not exactly honorable,' Toit warned. 'He will not cheat you or break his word, but you must know what he has agreed to deliver.'

Rouwen shrugged. The contents of the grimoire were closed to him since he could not read the runes comprising the spells. Only the mention of the Flame Specter caused the spell book to burn with a vivid green, intense heat.

'You play another man's game – and you never inquired about the rules.' Toit made a clucking sound that irritated Rouwen more than anything else the bird had said or done. Or was it the truth of the *thouse* bird's statement that bothered him?

Should he have surrendered the grimoire so easily in return for vague promises? What would Vutorian do with the spells written so lovingly on its pages? Brion Rouwen had not found out, and that might be a deadly mistake.

10

Battle into War

'A fine day to die,' commented Toit before making a rude noise deep in his throat. The *thouse* swooped lower and then banked, wings fully extended to make a perfect landing beside Rouwen. 'Three of you pitted against two score of Mionese soldiers. Where should I bury your body, if enough of it survives for proper interment? Or have you got over your squeamishness to allow me to eat your corpse?'

'We'll be fine,' Rouwen said, barely listening to the bird's acid comments. He studied a map of the territory just beyond the Forest of Kelnos at the boundary of Vutorian's castle, trying to decide the strongest points – and the weakest – in King Nishor's defenses. The Mionese capital of Tachre lay beyond their reach for the moment. When he had driven several companies of soldiers from the field, then Rouwen would consider it time to launch an all-out attack on the heart of Nishor's strength.

'Why bother attacking Mion at all?' asked the bird. 'Your enemies lie safe and secure behind the Shield Mountains. You must fly down this Demon's Throat you rattle on and on about before confronting Sosler and Priowe. Go there, not to Mion.'

'Sosler is too wily to be caught in any move we might make, unless we destroy his reinforcements. Who wants a dagger in their back?' Rouwen spoke slowly, his mind still working over details of the coming attack. On the face of it, Toit was right. Three against forty ought to be suicidal, but it wouldn't be only Rouwen, Diarra, and the wizard striking out at the patrolling Mionese troopers.

Rouwen's fingers worked back and forth, smudging the fine gold finish on the horn he had taken from the Lord of Death and Life. That wizard had defended his island for years against all invaders. Even after he had perished, Rouwen was able to fend off a sizable attacking force through sheer luck. With the control of the Legion of the Air promised by both Vutorian and Diarra, Rouwen was sure a few of the deadly tornadoes dropped among

Nishor's troops would kill or scatter them to the most distant points in the world.

'So you destroy Mion, then use this base to make war on Gan?'

'No, not really. There is no way we can assume power in Mion without having to fight half a hundred small insurrections that are sure to spring up around the countryside. Mionese nobles, petty or major, will all decide it is time for *them* to rule, if for no other reason than they claim royal blood. Such discord is the most we expect.'

'You rob Sosler of an ally, then?' Toit preened, taking special care to clean the prized golden feathers. He worked for a moment, then complained, 'I do so hate being a poisonous bird at times. The leakage from the glands cakes my feathers.'

'What?' For the first time Rouwen's attention was pulled away from his maps of the terrain. In the sunlight, tiny dewdrops sparkled on Toit's gold feathers. 'That's poison?' Using the tip of his dagger Rouwen touched a silvery bead left behind as Toit's beak ran along the length of the shining feather.

'What else? I poison myself! In winter it is all the worse. The poison freezes instantly, instead of beading like this. Summer is good to *thouse* birds.' Toit shook himself hard, sending other droplets flying from his back. Rouwen threw up an arm to protect his eyes. The poison from a *thouse* ranked as the most deadly known. The merest hint of a drop in his eyes would mean blindness followed by excruciating death within minutes.

'You are a dangerous fellow, aren't you?' Rouwen carefully wiped the tip of his dagger on a tussock of grass and moved away, to keep from stepping in the envenomed plant during the heat of directing the forthcoming battle. The grass turned black and withered as he watched – the virulent poison worked on any life, plant or animal.

'I am true to my nature,' Toit said. 'Are you?'

'I gave my oath to Diarra that I'd kill Priowe. It is a task which leaves me torn, but one which is better in the doing than in the avoidance.'

'Priowe is the father of your beloved,' Toit pointed out. 'Will Sorinne still think so highly of you when your name is acknowledged as the assassin responsible for murdering her father? Can a woman love the man who killed her father?'

Rouwen didn't answer. That question had plagued him for some time and had made him ambivalent about Priowe's fate. His initial anger at the ruler had been tempered by realization that the overly ambitious Sosler played them all for fools, King

Priowe among them. The duke thought nothing of casting off people no longer of value to his plans, and soon King Priowe would be in that large group.

Losing the Kingdom of Gan might be punishment enough for Priowe, but his former queen wanted more. She wanted him dead, slowly, painfully, tortured or worse. Rouwen did not doubt that Diarra would enjoy tormenting her former husband over decades, stealing his humanity one soulful bit at a time until only a lifeless husk remained. And even then she would not be content. Nothing would be punishment enough to satisfy Diarra's consuming malice.

'I see no way to avoid it,' Rouwen said. 'I need Diarra's cooperation. Only she can control the Legion of the Air once it is summoned. And only she can banish the magical tornadoes back to the place from which they are called.'

'You ally yourself with a madwoman and a wizard, neither partner being what I would call trustworthy.' The large brown bird let out a sudden squawk, shot from his perch and swooped low, scooping up a fleeing fieldmouse in his beak. Rouwen saw the powerful jaw muscles close and break the mouse's back. Toit gulped once, devouring the still-kicking rodent whole and more alive than dead. A quick drag of his talons, a sharp bank to the left and Toit returned to his perch, as if nothing had happened.

Rouwen had to consider not only what the *thouse* said, but other matters also. He had reluctantly aligned himself with a deposed, mad queen. As bad was the wizard whose motives remained as obscure as his true talents. But Toit, for all his warnings, might be as dangerous. Did the *thouse* poison his mind against Diarra and Vutorian for some purpose of his own? Rouwen knew nothing of the creature, other than the introduction given by the little girl, Finola.

Rouwen sighed as he thought of her. She was delicate and pretty yet she had seemed so confident and in command of her world. Rouwen remembered when he had felt that way, although it must have been a thousand lifetimes ago. Something in the way Finola studied him with her wide, direct-gazing ginger-colored eyes made Rouwen both uncomfortable and, paradoxically, trusting of her. After uttering only a few words, she had shown that she read his inner agony, his most secret thoughts – and that she sympathized.

'We will fight the first skirmish in the gully,' Rouwen said to the bird. Toit sidestepped over and craned his head around to look at the map. 'The rising elevation on either side will make escape more difficult in those directions. The soldiers will fight both gravity and a wind warrior.'

'So you puff on your horn and the whirling gas demons appear at either end of the ravine?' Toit made a sound Rouwen interpreted as approval, though its timbre and duration could as easily have indicated contempt for the plan.

'The force will be caught between the tornadoes. After they are defeated, Diarra will blow the whistle and evaporate the wind warriors. Then we move on down the coast until Nishor sees us as a serious threat.'

'Then?' prodded Toit.

'Then we engage King Nishor's main force here.' Rouwen's finger stabbed down at a plain a few miles from the coast. His mind turned over the possibilities of attack on such a battlefield. His wind warriors could sweep in across the sea, from a direction undefended if Nishor expected usual tactics. And forcing the enemy into an increasingly narrow neck would insure Nishor's retreat to Tachre. From his capital the king might retreat across the sea. If so, he abandoned his kingdom and left the Demon's Throat open for Rouwen's major thrust into Gan.

'You want Nishor only to break off attack against Gan so you can attack? A dubious plan,' said Toit. 'Let Nishor and Priowe batter each other, then begin this strange plan of yours.'

Rouwen shook his head. 'The fight between Mion and Gan is engineered by Duke Sosler for his own purposes. I believe he uses the threat Nishor presents to firm up support within Castle Gan. When he gains the allies he needs within Gan, he will lash out and crush Mion. King Sosler, of united Gan-Mion.' Rouwen spat out the words, as if they burned his tongue. This was an ambitious plan, but Rouwen doubted Sosler's zeal stopped there. Kingdoms to the north would fall quickly, if the combined might of Gan and Mion were arrayed against them. And using Gan's highly trained soldiers with Mion's fleet, no country along the coast would be safe from Sosler's aspirations.

'So he lies to Nishor about what is to be achieved? Who can trust a noble? Or a wizard?'

Rouwen looked up and saw Vutorian striding toward him. The wizard had changed from the stately robes he had worn within his castle to jaunty riding gear. He looked more like a young nobleman out for an afternoon's ride than a wizard intent on the opening battle in what might be a bloody war.

'The soldiers enter the gully. Are you ready to summon the Legion of the Air?' Vutorian planted his feet wide apart, as if Rouwen would call forth the wind warriors at this very spot and blow the wizard about. 'Diarra has positioned herself to guide the tornadoes through the Mionese swine.'

Rouwen said nothing. Let Vutorian whip up his courage by thinking the Mionese soldiers were less than human. Rouwen knew they were decent enough fighters, though not of the caliber of Gan's Intrepids. Rouwen bore them no malice, but the road back to Castle Gan had to begin somewhere. These soldiers would be the first to die.

'Very well.' Rouwen lifted the horn to his lips, judged distances and then let out a clear note that echoed through the forest and down the hillside. Rouwen had no idea how to summon the wind warriors at the precise point he desired, but he had not told Vutorian this. Rouwen was pleased to see that the first tornado began its slow swinging at the far end of the gully, blocking retreat.

'Yes, yes, that's it! There!' Vutorian jumped up and down like a small child getting a birthday present. 'They cannot run. Now destroy them. Send another tornado and destroy them!'

'Let them surrender,' suggested Toit. 'Why rip them asunder when they may give up on their own? A battle without bloodshed is the best.'

'They will never surrender. Their officers would never consider it. Another tornado, Brion, another. Now!'

Rouwen held back on this blast of the horn, hoping it would form the tornado much closer. The idea was right but the execution failed. The second wind warrior formed in the middle of the forty troopers. Rouwen winced as their bodies were sucked into the powerfully forming vortex and lifted high. As the tornado gathered force, it spun the soldiers faster and faster, bursting them apart and causing the bloody rain over the countryside that had so sickened Rouwen before.

Battle demanded casualties, but these men had no chance to fight. They were slaughtered magically.

'This is the way you get back into Castle Gan,' applauded Vutorian, still ebullient. 'Kill them all, and you can ascend the throne as conqueror!'

Rouwen started to tell Vutorian his intentions were less lofty. He had no desire to rule Gan, only to marry Princess Sorinne. This thought caused him to pause a moment, wondering if there was any sense in his quest. By honor he was bound to kill Sorinne's father – and do it at her mother's behest. Rouwen knew so little of what happened within the castle walls now. Was Sorinne a victim, as he and Diarra were or was she being sheltered from the truth? It was inconceivable to Rouwen that

Priowe had told his daughter the charges against her mother and her lover. Sorinne would never believe Rouwen had slept with the queen.

Or did Sosler bring in other mages to twist and bend reality, making the princess believe the lies? Had some story been concocted to make her hate him? His foul ally, Duke Drioway, had a way of making the most absurd notion seem plausible.

Rouwen stared at his hands, knowing his lightest caress would doom Sorinne. He clenched his hands into tight fists and watched as the tornadoes began their final pass through the gully. Not a single survivor of Nishor's troops would report on this day's loss.

'We ought to have permitted one to escape,' Rouwen told the wizard. 'The knowledge that we command such vast magicks would have driven a spike of cold fear into the most stalwart commander's heart.'

'Would you have disobeyed an order to attack, should your liege have given it?' asked Toit.

'No, but . . .' Rouwen bit off his reply. The *thouse* was right. A true commander, no matter what the odds, would obey. He would have fought all the harder, even against magical warriors, but he would never have refused an order. Honor would have forbidden it.

'You are a true officer and hero,' Vutorian congratulated him. 'I want you commanding the guard on *my* castle walls.'

'That will be a pleasant change,' Rouwen said bitterly, remembering how Priowe had refused even to listen to his defense. Duke Sosler had poisoned King Priowe's mind. That offense meant death for both men, pretender and king.

The three sharp blasts on Diarra's golden whistle caused the nearest wind warrior to slow its rotation until only tiny pockets of dust were kicked up. The more distant tornado took longer to dispel; she had to use the whistle's commands twice before that whirling column of death blew itself out.

'We are ready to march to Tachre,' cried Vutorian. 'All Mion will be ours before the end of the week. You are a magnificent general, Brion. That Priowe had not promoted you to Lord Protector of the Realm shows his incompetence. Rule should be in the hands of those both clever and able!'

The wizard strutted off, leaving Rouwen and Toit behind. The *thouse* cawed like a crow and settled down into himself, hardly more than a ball of feathers with two eyes peering out.

'What did you say, Toit?' Rouwen gathered his maps and

tucked them away in a watertight cylindrical copper case. The bird kept twittering and cawing to itself.

'He already imagines himself on a throne. Do they have no shame, no sense of proportion? He commands vast magical powers – if he remains in the Forest of Kelnos. But no, Vutorian seeks more. The fool!'

'You mean he loses his magical powers when he abandons his castle?' Rouwen's eyes widened in surprise. He had counted on Vutorian's aid in removing the curse Kwuway had laid upon his head. If the mage was unable to perform the counterspell, Rouwen was being hoodwinked.

'He loses much,' claimed Toit. 'That grimoire you gave him might counter some of the loss. He is a clever scholar, always looking through the old tomes he finds here and there. You should see his library of spell books. Huge. Immense!'

Rouwen considered the situation for a moment and asked, 'Is this Finola's quest? To find Vutorian another book of spells?'

The *thouse* bird lifted his head up and peered hard at him. No answer came, and Rouwen had expected none. The truth was obvious. Vutorian sent Finola out to find books for his library, to enhance his power should he ever venture forth from the castle. With the grimoire Rouwen had given him, some part of the puzzle had been completed, allowing Vutorian freer travel without loss of power.

'So it seems,' Toit said, again appearing to read Rouwen's thoughts. 'The wizard's ambitions are second to none, even to this Duke Sosler you so admire.'

Rouwen heaved a sigh. It might have been a mistake giving Vutorian the stolen grimoire, but it had been necessary. Without it, Vutorian would never have agreed to battle King Nishor's army. If Nishor retained power, Rouwen would feel a sword pointed at his spine.

'We must hurry before Nishor can muster a credible army on the Plains of Tachre,' said Rouwen. 'If we defeat Nishor there, he can never recover.'

'The Plains of Tachre?' came Diarra's mocking voice. 'Why ever would we want to fight there? It is a dreary field, so near the ocean and the unpredictable storms that blow off it.'

'We fight there next to cripple Nishor's army. He will draw back into Tachre to lick his wounds or perhaps even take a ship and flee. Either way, we have a clear field to attack Sosler's forces in the Demon's Throat.'

'No, that's not the way we will do it,' Diarra said, her voice rising shrilly. 'We go directly to Tachre. If we cannot crush

Nishor there, why bother doing it miles and miles outside his capital?'

'He will fight like a trapped rat. His *people* will fight us. We want to destroy the Mionese army, not the citizens of Tachre. If we soundly crush the army on the Plains of Tachre, the populace might rise up to support us.' Rouwen tried to keep the coming battle plan in his head. He needed to summon more than a dozen of the Legion of the Air to assault Nishor's army – if they could be lured onto the plains.

'Vutorian agrees with me. We go directly to Tachre and fight there,' insisted Diarra. 'We will not chase the remains of Nishor's army miles and miles and permit them to hide behind the city's walls.' Her pale face had flushed with anger, and her dark eyes burned with madness again.

'The walls of Tachre are no barrier,' Rouwen assured her. On the two occasions he had entered the city he had marvelled at the poorly patrolled and ill-kept battlements. The soldiers were more intent on extorting bribes from travellers than in defending the city.

'Then you agree. We go directly to Tachre.' Diarra turned and flounced off, her skirts spinning around her like sinister eddy currents in a dusky pond. As she went, she shot him a look of pure hatred. Rouwen wasn't sure if that or the flash of sunlight off the golden whistle around her neck bothered him most. He had learned to tolerate her fiery anger and bouts of insanity, but how could he call forth the Legion of the Air and know only Diarra could stop the wind warriors?

He had no love for Mion or its ruler, yet he had seen the damage done to both guilty and innocent by the rampaging tornadoes. If he brought even one tornado into existence without Diarra's promise to remove it, that whirlwind would begin following him to the ends of the world. Vutorian would not assist him now that he had handed over the grimoire. Rouwen's head spun with the complexity of his plight.

'So I must slaughter thousands of blameless Mionese to depose Nishor?' he asked aloud of no one in particular. Diarra would never answer him, and he knew Vutorian's answer. The mage wanted only Nishor's defeat.

'Why not? War is always thus. The ones who suffer most have no stake in it.' Toit shook himself and sent a cloud of feathers flying in all directions. 'I do so hate molting season. There will be an early winter, mark my words.'

'Why does Vutorian hate King Nishor?'

'Vutorian was once Nishor's court mage. There was a falling-out, possibly a palace coup attempt, and Vutorian chose to seek residence outside Tachre. For years he has hungered for Nishor's head and his own rump on the throne.'

'Let him have it,' Rouwen said, coming to a swift decision. 'We won't tease the generals into engaging us on the plains. We'll fight them within the city.'

'Kill them all, kill them all,' cried Toit, mimicking less intelligent talking birds. Rouwen swung on the *thouse* and tried to grab him by the throat. Toit's reaction speed far outshone Rouwen's. The *thouse* caught the edge of Rouwen's hand in his serrated beak, holding just tight enough to prevent the hand from curling around his neck.

Man and bird stared at one another. As if to emphasize their positions, Toit tensed his powerful beak muscles slightly, pressing down even harder into Rouwen's flesh.

'The poison?' asked Rouwen, almost wishing the bird would slay him.

'No poison.' Toit released Rouwen's hand and made a spitting noise. 'A small additional pressure would have released the poison from gland sacs. Do not trifle with me, silly human.'

Rouwen laughed harshly. He had performed well for the Lord of Death and Life and had been granted mortality once more. He had been cursed to kill those he loved – and to do it for all eternity. Now he only killed.

'You want to live, not die,' Toit chided. 'They make you as crazy as they are.'

'I remember what you told me in the castle. I ought not to play their games, but what choice do I have?' Rouwen's fists clenched again, thinking of the crimes Sosler had committed against him and his kingdom. That could never go unpunished. He had a sworn duty to defend Gan against all enemies. Priowe might have stripped him of rank, but Rouwen still felt the weight of responsibility to honor the oath he had taken. Only now he recognized the kingdom's enemies as both its ruler and his chief advisor.

'Invent new rules,' suggested Toit. The *thouse* squawked and took to the air without saying another word. Rouwen watched the huge brown bird with the golden feathers circle above, then head toward Tachre, toward the next battleground. Slinging his metal map case, Rouwen trudged to the courser Vutorian had given him. It would be a long ride to Tachre, and this battle would be the bloodiest ever seen in Mion.

11

The Destruction of Tachre

'This is wrong,' protested Brion Rouwen. Neither Vutorian nor
Diarra paid him any attention. They rode together a few yards
away, their knees almost touching. Rouwen put his heels into
the horse's flanks and narrowed the distance between him and
his allies. Wizard and queen stopped talking when he rode close
enough to overhear their words.

'We will be at Tachre before sundown,' said Vutorian. 'Are
you prepared to summon the Legion of the Air for this final
battle?'

'We ought to wait,' Rouwen said forcefully. 'Attacking Tachre
is not the way to bring Nishor to his knees. The Plains of Tachre
ten miles beyond the farthest reaches of the city is a better spot.
Nishor might feel he can win there and commit his troops
carelessly.'

'We have the power,' said Diarra, head held high and eyes
closed, as if she sampled the air for the scent of victory. Her
long blonde hair whipped back from her head in a long, silken
banner, and a faint hint of perfume reached Rouwen. There was
no hint of triumph in that fragrance. 'If we do not use it, we shall
certainly perish,' she insisted. 'By now, Nishor knows his patrol
was slaughtered, and if his scouts have done their jobs, they know
the Legion of the Air was responsible – *you* were responsible.'

Rouwen shook his head. He had travelled quickly after the
abortive invasion of the Lord's Isle of Passing. Mionese troopers
had no reason to believe he could now summon the Legion.

'What does it matter if Nishor thinks I am responsible? We
should fight to win, and that means using strategy rather than
raw power. A delicate pinprick is far better than a cudgel.'

'You call yourself a fighting man? You want only to make
excuses for cowardice,' Diarra said sarcastically. 'How did I ever
believe you were the one to bring Priowe to the justice he so richly
deserves? Pah!' She opened her eyes and urged her steed into a
canter, leaving Rouwen and Vutorian behind.

'We must seek victory rather than humiliation or destruction,' Rouwen said, hoping to find more fertile ground in Vutorian's imagination. 'The reason to fight is not to kill but to win.'

'An extension of political force,' Vutorian said in a bored voice. 'We are not yet a political force, but we shall be ere long. When Tachre falls and Nishor is deposed, then they will know a force to be reckoned with!'

'You're as mad as Diarra,' Rouwen said in disgust. 'We will find ourselves fighting peasants armed with gardening trowels if we persist. They have no love for Nishor or his army. Defeat the army away from the city and the peasants will cheer us as conquerors. Destroy their homes and businesses, threaten their lives, and they will flock to Nishor's banner.'

'Do not be ridiculous, Brion,' said Vutorian. 'The peasants have no gardening trowels. They have no gardens!' He laughed uproariously at his own little jest and spurred his horse to overtake the now distant Diarra. Rouwen trailed behind, considering his part in what might be more of a mass murder than a battle. He had no qualms about bringing forth the wind warriors to fight Nishor's soldiers. Using the tornadoes against city dwellers who might become confederates under the proper circumstances rankled. A soldier's duty was to preserve life, not take it.

Rouwen shook his head and put spurs to his courser. There was much to be done, wherever they attacked.

A half hour before sunset they sat astride their horses on the road to Tachre, staring at the gray, walled city. Rouwen knew the battle would never happen if he refused to blow the Lord's horn and whirl up the Legion of the Air. But Vutorian must have powers of his own, either granted through the grimoire he clutched so tightly as he rode or residual from his castle. How far could the former Captain of the Intrepids ride before some magical spell overtook him?

'He's not above turning you into some loathsome reptile,' Toit whispered from his perch on Rouwen's shoulder where he had just landed.

'Are you saying he wants a kindred spirit to appreciate his skill?'

For a moment the *thouse* did not reply, then let out a raucous caw that Rouwen interpreted as laughter. 'That's rich. A kindred spirit! He is a reptile, isn't he?' The bird calmed and asked in a low voice, 'Will you send the wind warriors into Tachre?'

'There is some merit in the plan,' Rouwen said, working the details about in his head to find the small value. The Plains ten miles distant would be a better engagement point, but there was no doubt he had the entire army bottled up within the city walls. A few wind warriors and Tachre would be reduced to rubble. With the capital would go Nishor's power.

'You hate Sosler so badly you would slaughter innocents?' Toit tightened his claws on Rouwen's shoulder to give some hint as to the suffering that might be inflicted.

'I do,' Rouwen answered without hesitation. 'He and Nishor are allied against the people of Gan. That makes me the enemy of anyone in Mion.'

'That is an interesting rationalization that must have kept you awake many nights in the conjuring. I am sure the sleep lost will be nothing compared to the nights to come as you remember the blood raining from the sky. I must query Finola about humans' capacity for lying to themselves.' Toit squawked in surprise when Rouwen reached out and grabbed his legs just above the talons. A deft twist forced the claws to release, and Rouwen held the *thouse* upside down like a chicken waiting to be beheaded and plucked.

'If the sight of battle sickens you, return to the forests. Find Finola and ask all the questions you want.' Rouwen twisted and flung the *thouse* bird away as hard as he could. Toit squawked in protest and struggled to right himself. The big bird extended his wings and caught enough air to swoop, narrowly avoiding a hard landing on the rocky ground.

Rouwen did not watch to see if Toit flew off or lay dead on the ground, as a result of the fall. His eyes fixed on Tachre, and he forced himself to remember the horrors Nishor perpetrated on his own people. Beggars were slaughtered to keep them off the city's streets. King Nishor chose his friends poorly, relying on Drioway and Sosler in a futile attempt to invade Valley Gan. None of them was worthy of continued life or power over others.

Brion Rouwen would reduce them to nothing with a single blast from his horn. He pulled it from his belt and stared at the magical instrument used to call forth the Legion of the Air.

'Do it,' whispered Diarra. 'Summon the wind warriors now. I will send them through the heart of that vile city. Nishor will die!'

'Do it,' Vutorian urged from Rouwen's other flank. 'We should rule, not Nishor, not Sosler!'

The gold horn turned bloody in the rays of the setting sun. Rouwen placed his lips on the mouthpiece and let forth a clear, dulcet note that seemed to vibrate in the air above him. He sucked in a deep breath and loosed another blast. And another and another. Only when he had brought forth eight shimmering columns of moving air did Rouwen hesitate, aghast at what he had created.

'Yes, kill them, yes!' chortled Diarra. She used the whistle to order the wind warriors, to make them twist and turn in lock step directly for the unsuspecting city. No defense could stand against such might. And Tachre did not. Walls blew apart and men were sucked high into the air by the bobbing vortices, their screams drowned out by the harsh roar of the wind.

Brion Rouwen galloped forward, the horn banging at his side. He watched as Diarra sent three wind warriors skirting the outer wall, scooping up peasants and merchants bringing their goods into Tachre for trade. Turning in the saddle, Rouwen shouted to attract Diarra's attention.

For a moment he thought some demon had swooped to earth and replaced the woman. Her eyes blazed with maniacal fury, and the set of her body told him more of her mental state than he wanted to know. She had crossed into the unknown lands of insanity once again, a child given unlimited adult power.

Diarra chased individuals fleeing the city, manipulating the wind warriors to pluck the unfortunates off the ground. She watched as the men and women were spun on high and then blasted apart in the vacuum of the tornado. It mattered naught to her if they wore uniforms or if they were simple citizens. She killed with impunity; she ordered the wind warriors to kill any and all who dared show themselves.

'Diarra, stop the killing! Group the wind warriors at the gates to the city.' Rouwen had seen what the woman had not in her insatiable urge to destroy. Some officer had mustered enough strength to lead a troop against the menace attacking his city.

The companies of soldiers rushed forth, dodging the tornadoes working their way through Tachre. And behind came another company and another. The officers in command had decided it was better to fight to the death than simply wait for the Legion of the Air to destroy them in their barracks.

'Stop them. There. Get them all!' Rouwen could not break the woman's killing frenzy. He searched for Vutorian and saw the wizard a few yards away, holding the grimoire and staring at its cover. Even at this distance, Rouwen saw the bright green glow. Vutorian's fingers danced on the cover, as if burning, but the wizard never moved to cast away the book of spells.

'Vutorian, get her to block the troops leaving Tachre. She is out of control.' Again, Rouwen's words fell on deaf ears. The wizard's eyes had widened, and his long mustache quivered like an insect's antenna as he stared down at the grimoire. His face was bathed in the curious green light, turning him into something demonic.

Rouwen galloped to the mage's side and reached out, grabbing his shoulder. Vutorian showed no sign of noticing. Rouwen shook as hard as he could while astride a nervous courser. The nearness of the tornadoes terrified the horse, and he did not blame the animal. The sight of so many wind warriors working their destructive magic on the city frightened him, also. Rouwen knew Toit had been right in warning him against using the Legion of the Air in this fashion. His own instincts and training should have dictated the course of the battle, but he had allowed Diarra and Vutorian to vent their wrath.

'Vutorian, wrest control from Diarra. She is unable to keep the tornadoes in a battle formation.'

Vutorian looked up, his face drawn. 'The Flame Specter stirs,' he muttered. 'There is so much power to devour. We must work quickly. Quickly.'

'What are you talking about? What Flame Specter? We must force Diarra to control the wind warriors. Nishor's commanders have marshalled their forces and are coming for us.'

'They cannot know three riders cause this massive destruction in their city,' the wizard said, his voice still distant. The glow from the grimoire mounted, as the activity of the wind warriors surged. 'If you need to protect us, Brion, use the horn. Call more wind warriors.'

Rouwen saw hundreds of mounted soldiers bearing down on them. A sentry posted along the city's wall, a traveller along the road, simple military tactics, he didn't know who told the Mionese commander they were responsible. But the commander knew, and soon they would be surrounded by more soldiers than they could fight in a lifetime.

Diarra should have diverted a wind warrior to protect them, but she was too engrossed in the death she wreaked on Nishor and his capital. Rouwen heard her shrill cries over the roar of the tornadoes. Strangely, he looked from her to the sky, hoping to find a brown mass of feathers flying to perch on his shoulder. He missed Toit and his sarcastic advice. The usually bloodthirsty *thouse* had been right about avoiding so much slaughter, and Rouwen had badly misjudged both the strength and determination of Nishor's army.

'A spell,' he said desperately to Vutorian. 'Conjure something to stop them.'

'What? What do you want from me? I cannot summon demons

or make those soldiers disappear,' protested the wizard. 'You are here to kill them. You do it.'

Rouwen hefted the horn again and trumpeted another long, clear note that echoed across the land and bounced off other wind warriors. Not fifty yards away a new whirlwind formed. It spun slowly at first, then gathered strength and speed directly in the path of the approaching army.

'Another, another. Keep blowing until you have woven a wall of defiant air about us,' urged Vutorian. Rouwen glanced at the mage and saw how the grimoire burned brighter now. Every new tornado brought more intensity to the radiant book of spells.

Rouwen knew that they had to retreat in the direction of the coast if they wanted to escape both his wind warriors and Nishor's army units. He reached out and tugged on the wizard's sleeve, pointing toward the rocky shore. Vutorian shook his head, but Rouwen pointed to the towers of air whipping about. The wizard tried to shout his reply, but the wind drowned him out.

Vutorian turned his horse's head and trotted toward the coast, the only possible way to escape death or capture. Rouwen paused, considering what he must do with Diarra. He could not leave her to be captured. The Mionese commander had done well so far. He might understand the situation and coerce Diarra into turning the wind warriors against the man summoning them.

Riding hard, Rouwen came alongside the demented queen. She blew the gold whistle until her cheeks puffed out. He had no idea about the instructions she conveyed, but the tornadoes danced through an intricate pattern that ravaged Tachre but did nothing to protect them. In spite of forming additional tornadoes, the Mionese soldiers were approaching quickly, dodging between the impossibly potent whirlwinds. It had to be more than luck that they so single-mindedly came after Diarra and Rouwen.

'To the coast. We must join Vutorian there,' he shouted in Diarra's ear. The woman paid him no attention. She was too lost in her wanton destruction of a city filled with innocent people.

'I am not finished. I will kill the lot of them. They humiliated me. Nishor used me like a serving wench. He – he tried to use me in other ways.'

Rouwen had seen the reflected glow from the grimoire on Vutorian's face. The incandescence of Diarra's features came from the intense hatred boiling within her. She blew her whistle to continue the cataclysm striking Tachre, not to defend herself. She would perish and never know the reason.

Rouwen reached out and tried to grab her as he had to Vutorian to rouse him from his trance. Diarra recoiled, her face a mask of pure malice unlike anything he had ever encountered. She clawed at him, but this took the whistle from her lips.

Rouwen snatched it and yanked hard, ripping the chain from her hands.

'Give it back! I need that!' She lunged, almost falling from the saddle. 'There is more to do. You cannot let them escape without total punishment. You can't!'

'Come, Diarra, take back the whistle,' Rouwen taunted. He rode a few steps, then swung the golden whistle so that Diarra could see it. He tried to keep the advancing soldiers in sight, but the debris kicked up by the tornadoes prevented it. But they were close, too close for comfort.

A crossbowman fired a bolt at him. Wind caused the projectile to lift and fly off target, but this told Rouwen his time was limited. Foot soldiers approached and tried to circle him.

'The whistle, Diarra. You need it to finish your work.' He saw that she was pursuing him to regain her control over the wind warriors. Diarra cared little for logic now. Hate ruled her completely.

'Give it to me, damn you. May demons take you. I want to kill them all!' Diarra pushed her horse faster until Rouwen thought she would kill it from exhaustion. He maintained a steady course for the coastline where he hoped they might be better able to defend themselves. The Mionese commander would need barges to attack them from seaward, and the slow migration of the Legion toward Rouwen would form an invincible barrier to any counterattack.

Rouwen wished that Toit had not flown off. Aerial eyes would have been useful in finding a spot to make a stand. He needed higher land to look out, but more important than this, he required a place where the Mionese soldiers could not trap him. With his back to the sea, he might have to swim a long way if Diarra did not take immediate control of the wind warriors.

'Vutorian!' he called. 'Here. Come here.' Rouwen waved, tossing the whistle around in his grip so the wizard could see. The small mage's eyes widened slightly, then he put heels to his horse and guided it in Rouwen's direction.

'Give her the whistle, you fool. She is the only one of us who can control the tornadoes.' Vutorian's mustache quivered with rage.

'Make her obey my orders,' Rouwen shot back. 'If she insists on random destruction, Nishor's troops will roast us over a spit before sunrise.' He wished they had attacked at dawn rather than dusk. He saw the tops of the tornadoes whirling about, but he had no idea where or how many soldiers were seeking them. Darkness proved more a burden for the attackers than for the kingdom's defenders.

Again Rouwen wished Toit were aloft to give him constant reports on troop movements against them. It began to look more and more foolhardy for only a trio of adventurers to attack Tachre, in spite of the powerful assistance of the Legion of the Air. Rouwen knew it was his fault if they failed. He was the expert in military strategy and had allowed a madwoman and an unskilled wizard to dictate the tactics of the battle.

'Call more wind warriors,' demanded Vutorian. 'She is beyond our power. Look at her and tell me she is not.'

Diarra had fallen from her horse and huddled on the ground, gibbering incoherently. Rouwen swung the golden whistle on its chain. Air rushing across it caused a shrill keening, but this did nothing to contain the immense power of the wind warriors. Rouwen considered all that he could do, as well as much that he could never accomplish. Four wind warriors marched slowly for the coast, throwing the ranks of the Mionese army into momentary disarray. Rouwen heard the officers' shouts as they re-formed their men for the attack that would stop the offensive against Tachre – or so they thought.

Rouwen shuddered, considering the destruction the wind warriors would cause if they were not sent back into the nothingness from which they had been summoned. King Nishor needed Diarra and the whistle, and he didn't know it.

'Mold them into a wall around us,' Rouwen said, dropping to the ground beside Diarra and shoving the whistle into her hands. She stared at it numbly, as if she had never seen the magical device before this moment. 'Only you can make them fight,' Rouwen said, taking a different course to reach the part of Diarra's brain that functioned rationally.

'Where?' Something inside her rallied, and Rouwen dared hope. 'Where should they kill?'

Rouwen had no good answer for her. He vaulted back into the saddle and settled himself, making sure his sword rested easy on his hip and that his dagger was secure in its sheath. He had to ride into the teeth of the onslaught and return with the information Diarra required.

'Calm yourself and prepare to kill,' he said, hating the way the words sounded. So many had died, so many – and all the wrong people. Nishor's death would have pleased him, but so many loyal, brave soldiers had died needlessly by action of the wind warriors. And the people within Tachre's walls had been slaughtered with no quarter offered. That was unconscionable.

'Keep her here until I return,' Rouwen ordered Vutorian. The wizard tried to protest, but Rouwen had already started galloping hard into the approaching company of soldiers to take their measure.

He rode low, an occasional arrow sailing above his head. The archers fired at random, to keep any defense disorganized. Such a tactic might have worked if they had been arrayed only against humans. The Legion of the Air sucked up such arrows and returned them at speeds a hundred times greater. Cutting to the left, Rouwen rode parallel to the advancing troops. He was startled to see that the field commander had mustered a thousand men or more.

Rouwen doubted his eyes. He rode closer, braving more arrows fired at him and his horse. One bolt from a crossbowman drove into Rouwen's saddle, penetrating leather and tweaking horseflesh beneath. The horse reared and tried to throw him. Rouwen held on grimly to the reins, then managed to worry the bolt free. He tossed it aside and goaded his horse into motion. Standing still gave the Mionese archers and crossbowmen too good a target.

'Men, rally. There are only a few, and they have lost their magical warriors!' The rallying shout carried past the roar of the tornadoes spinning nearby. Rouwen wheeled his horse and trotted closer, trying to see who the commander might be.

'Nishor!' The name escaped Rouwen's lips as a curse. The man he had thought to be a coward led his soldiers into battle.

Rouwen bent low, his head pressed into his horse's neck as he raced back to where Vutorian still tried to soothe Diarra. The former queen spoke calmly enough, but the words were disjointed, wild, totally incomprehensible.

'It's Nishor,' Rouwen panted as he hit the ground running. He pulled to a halt beside Diarra. She held the golden whistle as if she had never seen it before. 'Nishor leads the troops moving to the coast. Channel the power of the wind warriors into a line, march it forward, and you will be the victor. You will defeat Nishor!'

Light burned in Diarra's eyes, as if she understood. The whistle went to her lips and a series of sharp barks boomed forth as explosive as a volcanic eruption. Rouwen turned and saw the wind warriors shiver and shake and begin to move toward Nishor's advancing forces.

Diarra had some control. Would it be enough or would the growing tide of Nishor's soldiers prevail?

12

Nishor's Defeat

'We are doomed,' Rouwen said, seeing how Nishor astutely marshalled his troops at the precise point needed to sweep through the wind warriors and trap the three responsible for this battle. 'There is no way to keep at least a few squads of his soldiers from reaching us. Can you fight off that many?'

'A squad? How many men in a squad?' asked Vutorian, appearing uneasy at the notion of using his magicks to stop an attack. He held the grimoire gained from Rouwen as if this might serve as a shield. The book glowed a hot green. Rouwen wanted to shout out the name 'Flame Specter' and see what happened to the book of spells. But he didn't. He had to deal with the scores of fighters moving into position. He imagined what a sword point driving into his guts would feel like – again. He had accepted the pain of near death from too many strokes. One more would end his life forever.

And would that be so bad? What did he really hope to accomplish? Was hatred alone enough reason to continue his crusade?

'Ten,' Rouwen said, distracted. He considered escape by sea. This might be a temporary haven, though. He saw the distant lighthouse to the south of Tachre winking green and white, signalling to ocean-going marines. Nishor had split his forces, bringing some around in a pincer movement to harry the rear of his attackers. Little did he know when ordering those men to sea that his foes numbered only three.

'We can kill that many,' said Vutorian. 'You can. Summon another tornado. What is one or two more?'

Diarra blew steadily on the golden whistle, but Rouwen saw no evidence of the nearest wind warriors moving to interpose themselves between Diarra and Nishor's troops. Indeed, the first flight of arrows arched into the air and fell short of their target. But the slow march of the soldiers would continue and put the archers within range soon.

'Get her to move the wind warriors into Nishor's forces,' Rouwen demanded. 'She is going to send our souls to Paradise if the tornadoes aren't used properly.'

'I have no power over her. No more than you.' Vutorian winced as the grimoire burned even brighter. Rouwen stared at it, wondering at the change. He hadn't summoned any more of the magical monsters, yet the book of spells reacted. What else caused its incandescence?

Rouwen barely dodged an arrow arching down from above. If Diarra would not protect them, he must. The horn came to his lips. Rouwen paused, looking out of the corner of his eye at the grimoire clutched so tightly in Vutorian's hands. At the first blast on the horn, the spell book shone with a different hue. A second clear note rolling from the horn caused a light more blue than green from the grimoire. And then the brilliant green luminescence returned. Rouwen activated magical energies, but something more than the Lord's trumpet worked through the grimoire's magicks.

'There, you did it. The tornadoes formed directly in front of one company and in the middle of another. They are retreating! We have turned them!' Vutorian danced a complex dance, his feet shuffling and lifting so fast Rouwen could hardly follow the pattern. Somehow, in the middle of the dance, the wizard managed to shove the grimoire into a hidden pocket.

The spell book's radiance was shuttered for the moment, but Rouwen did not doubt that the book continued to glow, powered by magicks other than those taken from the Lord of Death and Life.

'Die,' muttered Diarra, blowing on the whistle but accomplishing nothing. She huffed and puffed, but no sounds issued forth to control the wind warriors. Rouwen peered into the darkness, worrying that there were too many wind warriors ravaging the countryside for the woman to control. A sharp salt-laden wind began blowing off the sea, drawing his attention in that direction.

The lighthouse continued its signals to the ships at sea. Rouwen counted four answering flashes, enough marines on four barges to capture them. He let out a harsh laugh. Any number of soldiers was enough to capture them. He summoned invincible tornadoes but could not control them. Diarra controlled and banished those wind warriors, but she was past sanity. And Rouwen had no idea what Vutorian might be able to do with his grimoire or the residual magical powers he commanded.

'We must move from the coast,' Rouwen said. 'When those barges come ashore, they will easily overwhelm our position.' The slight rise where they stood, letting the chilly sea breeze blow in their faces, was not secure enough to defend, even if he'd had a squad of his Intrepids at his command. This was best suited as an observation post, not a place to fight hundreds of well-trained and armed marines.

'Blow the horn. Send a few more wind warriors into their ships. That's an easy kill.' Vutorian's mood had changed again. He was calm, even serene. He might have been preparing for a late supper rather than being still embroiled in a major battle where a single misstep meant death.

'She must dissipate some of those already summoned,' Rouwen said, pointing at Diarra. 'If she doesn't, the wind warriors will converge on our position. They seek me because I am unable to control them – unless you have a spell or two for that purpose.' He saw Vutorian's reluctance to respond. He wondered if the small mage had thought to sneak away, leaving Diarra and himself alone to endure the meeting with the wind warriors. Such a plan would have left him in sole charge of Mion, if he had the magicks to enforce it.

Rouwen thought the wizard might turn traitor, given such a potential reward. Great power flowed into the book of spells Vutorian had tucked away. How much of that energy the mage might be able to tap was a mystery, but Rouwen didn't doubt that Vutorian's plans did not include a crazy former queen or a cashiered and disgraced Gannian guard captain.

'Perhaps I can convince her to cooperate. We must find Nishor, to be sure he hasn't slipped free of our net.' Vutorian bit his lower lip. Only this small gesture betrayed his nervousness. Even his mustache was free of quiver as he knelt beside Diarra and whispered urgently in her ear.

Diarra tried to push free, but Vutorian held her and continued to speak. Soft, rhythmic chanting reached Rouwen's ears. The wizard sought to beguile the woman with a spell of some kind. Whatever he did, Diarra's madness faded and the blasts on the whistle took on new vitality. She crisscrossed two wind warriors in front of them to protect their front, then sent two more out to sea.

Rouwen took a deep breath and let it out slowly when the distant shrieks of drowning marines reached him. Even if they had been trained in long-distance swimming, few could survive the water spouts being lifted high into the nighttime sky, momentarily blotting out the Lesser Moon's silvered disk.

Hundreds perished before Diarra banished these wind warriors to their airy nonexistence.

'We must find Nishor and be sure he is dead,' Vutorian said, starting toward the front where new cries of pain and suffering rose. 'If he isn't, that condition should not last long.'

'Get rid of more wind warriors,' Rouwen said to Diarra. She obeyed, her eyes glassed over. Whatever spell Vutorian had cast still possessed Diarra, turning her into a compliant slave. Rouwen vowed to keep the wizard from whispering into *his* ear anything close to the chant he had overheard. Vutorian was a dangerous ally.

Rouwen smiled ruefully. Toit had warned him, and he had known full well the treacherous course he pursued.

The whistle's shrilling almost deafened Rouwen but the wind warriors vanished one by one. He had lost count of the number summoned, but Diarra kept blasting long after the Legion of the Air had disappeared. But as she continued to blow the magical whistle, the glassy expression vanished and a dash of her old fire returned.

'Where is Nishor?' she demanded, shooting to her feet. 'Why did I banish the wind warriors? Those tornadoes were my vengeance against Nishor!'

'The battle is over,' Rouwen said, tired to the center of his soul. He walked slowly behind the woman who ran forward to view the destruction wrought on the Mionese army. He arrived some minutes after Diarra, then let out a cry of pure outrage at what the former queen did.

'Stop that. What are you? A butcher, a robber of dead bodies?' He grabbed her slender wrist and forced a dagger out of her grip. She had been going from soldier to soldier cutting their throats. Most were long past caring, but Rouwen saw the gush of blood from one injured man's throat stain Diarra's hands.

'They deserve torture, not sympathy. At least I am giving them a clean death.' The madness did not fire Diarra now, only cold hatred. This was another facet of her that Rouwen recoiled from. How could such vile intent flow from a beautiful woman?

Rouwen pushed her away when he heard the clank of weapons and saw movement from the corner of his eye. A tall soldier, half a head bigger than Rouwen, heaved a long sword up in a two-handed grip and prepared to slice Diarra in half. Rouwen's hand flashed to his dagger and sent it spinning through the air to bury its point deeply into the soldier's exposed throat. The trooper toppled backward, his downward stroke halted. Rouwen quickly retrieved his dagger and looked around for more soldiers.

He saw many stirring as they shook off the effects of the passage of the tornado, and Rouwen knew it would be only a matter of time before an officer rounded them up into a new company.

Even as this thought entered his head, he heard a deep-throated cry for assembly. Many more soldiers he had thought dead began to shake and move, responding to their officer's challenge to fight. Diarra had returned to her throat-slitting task, and Rouwen left her to follow two stunned soldiers moving in the direction of their rallying officer.

As he neared him, Rouwen's hand went to his sword. This was no field officer whipping his men into ragged ranks. None other than Nishor, King of Mion, sat on a nervous white stallion waving his green-and-gold royal standard as a rallying symbol. Rouwen worked his way closer, aware that he might have only this one chance to slay the king.

He paused a dozen paces from the man and saw Nishor had found more survivors than Rouwen would have thought possible. Fully half a hundred men were already moving into ranks and twice that number came from far-flung parts of the killing field.

Rouwen had no chance to kill Nishor and knew it – unless he wanted to surrender his own life.

Suicide was not part of his plan. He could have died a dozen times before, but duty to his kingdom fueled his desire to stay alive – duty and hatred. Only by fighting could he make a difference, slay Sosler, and depose Priowe. He began backing off when he ran into Diarra.

'Him,' she snarled, clutching a dagger in each hand. She was bloody up to her elbows, and the once-elegant gown had gobbets of human flesh stuck to it. Worst of all was the insanity burning inextinguishably in her wild, dark eyes. Whatever beauty had once been there had been deposed, a new ruler in charge.

Rouwen dropped to one knee and thrust out his booted foot, tripping her. She fell face down into the blood and mud of the battlefield. It took only an instant for him to sit across the small of her back and bring the hilt of his dagger down squarely on the side of her head. She stiffened and then went limp, unconscious. Rouwen started dragging her away from the gathering of Nishor's troops when a sergeant saw him.

'You there, stop!' The soldier motioned to others in his squad and they made for Rouwen. 'No raping, now. We've got fightin' to do!'

'Just trying to save her. A peasant who wandered onto the field by accident,' Rouwen said, considering his chances of fighting

312

off the entire squad. He quickly discarded any notion of easy triumph. Even if he outfought all the men in the squad, a company – a regiment! – of men was forming a bowshot away.

'Get away from her now.' The sergeant stopped and stared, his mouth falling open. 'I know you. You're not one of us. You're that Gannian fellow we chased through the castle. You're dead!'

Rouwen's first pilgrimage to Tachre had been less than successful, and everyone had thought he died, or so he had hoped. He had unluckily found a soldier who remembered his abortive attempt to kill Sosler as he conferred with Nishor. He drew his sword as the sergeant bellowed for support.

Rouwen charged, blade flashing in the night. He drove back one soldier and cut another severely enough to prevent him from rejoining the fray. But Rouwen saw that he worked against more than this squad now. Nishor had turned to see what the commotion was, and the king would not permit him to live for more than a brief instant.

'Surrender, Nishor, and I might let you live!' Rouwen shouted at the ruler. 'I control the Legion of the Air. Against those demons you are powerless.'

'Those were no demons,' Nishor said with forced confidence. He didn't sound positive, but he had to communicate assurance if his soldiers were to attack Rouwen. 'Quirks of nature, nothing more. The tornadoes were a message that we ought to fight harder, not that we are defeated.'

This failed to inspire his men. Nishor tried a different tack. 'Kill him and receive your weight in gold. Capture him and receive a duchy!'

This moved the soldiers toward Rouwen. He ducked under a poorly swung blade and stepped forward, his dagger finding a berth in the clumsy soldier's belly. Rouwen grappled with the falling soldier for a moment, using the dead body as a shield against the sergeant and two others who were more adroit with their weapons.

Rouwen's heel caught on Diarra's body, and he almost lost his balance. He stumbled over her and tried to defend both of them. This quickly proved futile. His curiosity had got him into this deadly situation. Only one ally could extricate him.

'Nishor, call off your troopers or I'll summon the Legion of the Air. The wind warriors will destroy you all.'

'Get him. A fleet of merchant ships *and* a duchy to the man who captures him.' Nishor fought to keep his horse under control. The huge stallion bucked and pranced, trying to edge away from the deafening clash of metal on metal. Rouwen fought hard, but realized he had to play his trump.

The gold horn came to his lips and a small note issued forth, creating a moment's hesitation in the onslaught of men. Then the soldiers renewed their attack – for the briefest of instants.

'There, behind us, another one of them air demons!' one soldier shrieked. The frightened man dropped his sword and ran into the night, stumbling over the bodies of his fallen comrades. Another and another took up the cry as the wind warrior grew in size and fury.

Rouwen kept fighting because the sergeant had not relented for an instant. Oblivious to the whirling death behind him, the man fought with ferocious skill. He hammered and slashed, then gently eased his blade around Rouwen's tip in an attempt to spit him. Neither tactic worked, but the sergeant refused to give up.

'Run away, run away,' someone shrieked. Then wordless cries replaced the exhortation to flee. The soldier was hurled aloft by the growing vortex that had formed in the midst of the warriors.

Rouwen struggled to keep Diarra safe from the flying swords and piercing daggers. Only she could turn the tornado or make it vanish, and it was slowly spinning in Rouwen's direction.

'Surrender,' the sergeant urged, using more power in his stroke and beating Rouwen backward. 'I will not let the king have you for torture if you surrender. That is my promise.'

Rouwen didn't bother answering such an absurd offer. If he paused now for even a moment, he would be lost.

Ducking low, Rouwen swung his sword, trying to hamstring the sergeant. The trick almost worked. His sword blade clanged against leg armor and sent the sergeant toppling to the ground, unhurt but shaken. Rouwen turned from the dazed fighter and rushed to Diarra's side. He rolled her over, hoping that she had not suffocated in the muck of the battlefield. Tiny bubbles formed in the mud caking her nose.

Quickly wiping it free, Rouwen shook his former queen to get her awake.

'What happened?' she asked, groggy from the blow he had given her. Rouwen couldn't tell from her befuddled response who she was now. Was she the crazy woman intent on murdering fallen soldiers or had she resorted to the ill-used queen seeking revenge on her husband?

'Blow the whistle. Call off the wind warrior,' Rouwen said, searching through the muck to find the magical whistle. His fingers closed on it as two more soldiers attacked. He parried one and kicked out at the other, driving him back. 'Take the whistle. Use it to stop the tornado. Do it!'

Whether the sharp bark of his command or her own good sense dictated, Diarra obeyed. The huge column of air that had so effectively scattered Nishor's regrouped men whispered softly and began collapsing upon itself until it vanished in a spiral of dust and blood.

Nishor's eyes went wide and his mouth moved. No sound emerged. He let out a wordless cry and put the spurs to his horse. The powerful white stallion with its gaudy trappings had been trying to bolt. Now Nishor gave the horse its head. Like a white jag of lightning in the night, Nishor and his courser took off, scattering the few soldiers still milling about.

Rouwen saw his chance and took it.

In his most commanding voice, he bellowed, 'I have defeated King Nishor of Mion this night. He is no longer your liege. Pledge fealty to me and live! Oppose me and die by the wind!' Rouwen lifted the gold horn to lips, as if to summon a new tornadic champion.

The soldiers did not respond quickly. But they made no move to attack. Even the sergeant struggling to get his bruised leg to support him once more hesitated. The man's eyes fixed on the horn Rouwen clutched in his hand. Seeing his fascination with the magical device, Rouwen lifted it high.

'This is the new symbol of Mion!' He walked forward so all could see the Lord's horn. 'Do not make me call back the wind warriors. None can stand before their whirling might. Tachre is in ruins because of their fierce strength. To me, valiant fighters of Mion, rally to me and be saved!'

Rouwen saw the demoralized soldiers slowly coming to a decision. If he failed to convince them, he would be lost. He pressed the horn to his lips, waiting to sound the single clear note bringing forth a new whirlwind of death. None guessed that Rouwen might die in the center of a vortex produced this close to the horn.

'No, wait, he can only bring forth the wind warriors,' protested Diarra. 'I am the one who . . .'

Rouwen caught the woman's movement from the corner of his eye. He swung the horn about and caught her squarely in the middle of the forehead. Again she tumbled to the ground, stunned by the blow. She still clung to the whistle, his one concern at the moment. Only those of nobility could use the whistle, but nothing was said about the royal blood being

Gannian. A Mionese noble might decide to cooperate and gain a Kingdom in exchange for a few drops of blood.

'What are your orders, my King?'

The question took Rouwen by surprise. He saw that the sergeant he had fought had spoken the words that rippled across the battlefield as if by magic. Soldiers everywhere lowered their weapons and dropped to one knee, pledging their fealty to him. Rouwen smiled crookedly. Soldiers saluting him as was his due as captain did not compare to this.

King Brion. The sound echoed in his skull and sounded better with each reverberation. He could marry Sorinne and not feel the sting of courtly disapproval. He could . . .

He could kill her. Kwuway had cursed him, and his touch would slay any he loved. Fury mounted within Rouwen as the realization of his plight took over from his fantasies.

'Bring me Nishor – alive,' he cautioned. 'I want him to stand trial for the atrocities he has perpetrated on his own citizens.'

Whispered conversations rose and died, as if the surviving soldiers had to come to a decision. Rouwen preempted them once more. He swung his sword around and dropped the flat of the blade onto the sergeant's broad shoulders.

'Rise. You are now Lord Protector of Mion and shall enjoy all rights and responsibilities of that title.'

'L-lord Protector?' The sergeant's eyes widened. 'Thank you, my King.'

'Bring Nishor to me quickly. He must not escape.'

'I hear and obey,' the new Lord Protector cried. He got to his feet and hobbled off, barking orders. What Rouwen had been unable to do, the newly promoted nobleman did. The soldiers picked up their weapons and began forming search parties to find their fleeing King.

Rouwen staggered and sat down heavily as the soldiers rushed off to find comrades and horses and new weapons for the hunt. Nishor had never been a popular leader, and it proved easy for his most loyal troops to turn against him. Almost too easy.

Rouwen sat and put his head in his hands. So much death and destruction. Was it worth the loss?

Was it worth being King Brion?

King Brion!

13

King Brion

Rain drizzled all around. Brion Rouwen looked up and saw the crescent of the Lesser Moon vanish behind a lead-gray storm cloud that had sprung up in the sky after the wind warriors appeared. He stared at the death around him and refused to believe any of it had occurred. The battle had been a strange dream for him, real and yet curiously diffuse, far away even as it touched him greatly. Rouwen shook like a dog and brushed rain from his face.

'King Brion,' he muttered, wondering if it had been a dream. Then he saw Diarra and knew it had not been an illusion. She glared at him as if he had been the one to banish her from her home, to abuse her, to drive her beyond the bounds of sanity.

'You took all the credit for the victory,' she said, snarling. Her lips pulled back like some feral animal, and for a moment Rouwen thought she might try ripping out his throat. Diarra advanced and reached for him, then let her arms fall limp to her sides. The expression that had doomed him seconds before now changed mercurially into one of utter befuddlement.

'We must find Vutorian. He is on the field somewhere,' Rouwen said, taking his former queen by the arm. She allowed him to lead her like a lost soul hunting for Paradise. The drizzle became a downpour, and they were drenched before they reached their horses.

'Bodies,' Diarra said dully. 'So many bodies. They are all around me. How did I get so bloody?' She held out her hands and let the rainwater lave away some of the gore.

'We won,' he said simply, thinking this would quiet her. Instead Diarra flew into another of her wild rages. She yanked free and dashed into the night, screaming incoherently. Rouwen climbed into the saddle of his shaking, exhausted horse and started after Diarra but quickly lost sight of her in the driving rain.

'Diarra!' he called. 'Come back. We need to talk. Vutorian

needs us!' No matter how he cajoled or threatened, Diarra would not return. For all Rouwen knew, she had thrown herself off a cliff into the raging sea. The storm had mounted to the point where no one would be safe along the shore.

Turning his horse's head from the teeth of the storm, he walked slowly through the battlefield again, past the rotting bodies and toward Tachre. The Legion of the Air had devastated an army. Granted, Nishor's attack had been hasty, but Rouwen knew the result would have been the same in any event. The wind warriors were too powerful for any mortal army to conquer, no matter their training or armament. Even with a powerful wizard, the Legion might be invincible. Only the Lord of Death and Life had been able to control the tornadoes completely.

Rouwen wondered if he would use the Legion in the Demon's Throat to gain entry to his homeland. With Diarra gone, perhaps temporarily or perhaps forever, would he allow those whirling demons to destroy Gan just to gain revenge on Duke Sosler and King Priowe? Rouwen's head throbbed with pain from the battle, from the use of magic, from his worry over his future.

'King Brion,' he muttered. Mion was not the greatest of all kingdoms – he considered Gan far better. It might become a rival for the verdant valley kingdom, should he rule wisely and long. Ascending a throne to become sovereign had never occurred to Rouwen since his duty had always been serving others. 'King Brion.'

He liked the sound, but was such a position too much for him to handle? The Legion of the Air gave him momentary power. Without a way to dissipate the wind warriors after using them in battle, he was helpless. The threat of such magicks would endure only until someone else rose to challenge him for the throne. Since he lacked even a drop of royal blood in his veins, that might not be long.

He dared not make the mistake of believing the nobles of Mion were any less proud of their kingdom than he was of Gan. They would fight to keep rule in the hands of a native-born Mionese.

'Why would I want to be king?' he said to himself. The more he turned the notion over in his mind, the more ludicrous it became. What he knew of ruling an entire country could be etched on the point of a pin.

'Majesty!' someone called through the downpour. Rouwen rode on. 'Majesty, wait. We have found him. Nishor!'

Rouwen reined back and looked down at the sergeant he had elevated to Lord Protector of Mion. The man had slogged through the mud and might have been freshly washed ashore from his bedraggled appearance, but his face shone with pride. His new liege had given him an order, and he had obeyed.

'You have done well, Lord Protector,' Rouwen said, trying to sound pleased. He could play the role of king for a few more minutes. He needed Nishor's surrender to free Tachre, then he would worry about the assault on Valley Gan.

'The sentence is being carried out,' the sergeant said, wiping rain from his face. Rouwen wondered whether the man might drown if he kept looking up into the deluge.

'I don't understand. What sentence?'

'Your viceroy ordered Nishor executed. So many men volunteered that your viceroy had to . . .'

'Describe this man, the one who claims to be my viceroy. Does he have a long, thin mustache? Short, dark, carrying a book that glows from within?' Rouwen went cold inside as he spoke. Rouwen didn't need the sergeant's brisk nod to know his description had been accurate. He could not even be king for a few minutes without Vutorian usurping his authority.

'Lead the way. Now, my good man, now!' Rouwen's horse broke into a trot as the sergeant took off running through the sucking mud of the battleground. The horse had difficulty keeping its footing, but the soldier ran easily and well, no doubt worrying that he might be stripped of his title if he did not set a brisk enough pace.

'There, Majesty, there's your viceroy.' The sergeant pointed. Vutorian sat on his horse, staring down at a tight knot of men gathered nearby.

Rouwen rode ahead, no longer needing the sergeant's assistance. This was a fight between him and the wizard. Nishor had to pay for his crimes against the citizens of Tachre and Mion, but he had to do it after a public trial.

He started to call out, to order Vutorian to stop, but the blade already flashed through the air. Two men held Nishor's arms stretched straight from his shoulders, forcing his head down slightly. The sharp sword flickered in the strange light cast by the grimoire, alien light reflecting off water droplets on its length.

The sound of a razored edge slicing into bone made Rouwen cringe. The first stroke had not been powerful enough to sever Nishor's head completely. The dying king thrashed about, stronger than the two men holding him. He slipped free and tried futilely to stanch the flow of blood from his neck. The second stroke completed the task. Nishor's head lay face down while his body twisted about and thrashed for several seconds until finally realizing it had died. The force of the storm seemed to lessen with Nishor's death, the drizzle replacing the hard-driving downpour.

'He should have been made to pay publicly,' Rouwen said angrily. He dismounted and stormed over to the wizard, who stood with the book of spells clutched tightly to his chest. From his expression, Rouwen couldn't tell what thoughts ran through Vutorian's head. 'He had to be humiliated, brought to trial, and the people of Mion ought to have executed him.'

'He is dead. That is good enough,' said Vutorian.

'No, it isn't,' Rouwen said, trying to keep his ire in check. 'You might have made him a martyr. If his crimes had been paraded before the people of Mion, they would have lined up for a chance to execute him. Now, some clever noble will turn his death into a laudable defense of his country against foreign invaders. We – never mind.' Rouwen saw that Vutorian cared little for the niceties of politics. He had different goals, and Rouwen had yet to figure out what they might be.

Rouwen mounted and rode through the rain, finding consolation only in the fact that Diarra had banished the wind warriors. He could ride wherever he wanted without being dogged by their tenacious stalking. But what did he do now?

The question burned brightly as Rouwen rode without direction through the lightless drizzle. He had seen how unreliable Vutorian and Diarra were in battle. He had called forth too many of the Legion of the Air to control and had begged the woman to remove them. He dared not fall prey to blackmail if she threatened not to remove them. After all, he would be the one followed to the ends of the world, not Diarra or Vutorian.

His mood turned even darker as he saw the evidence of the overwhelming destruction his wind warriors had brought to Mion. But this hadn't been enough. Vutorian had to add Nishor's miserable life to the death roll to be admitted to Paradise. Rouwen took scant satisfaction in knowing Nishor would wander outside the boundaries of Paradise for all eternity, starving and cold and begging to get into the gentle fields where there was never any want. The king's crimes transcended mere human law. The demons would exact even more punishment, but this was impersonal. Rouwen would have taken pride in seeing Nishor brought to justice by his own citizens.

The clatter of stones passing beneath his horse's hooves took more than ten minutes to penetrate Rouwen's somber reflections. Although he could not see in the drizzle, he knew he had found the poorly repaired road to Tachre. Or did it lead from Mion's capital? He could not tell in the cold rain. And it didn't matter to him which way he rode.

Somehow, though, he wasn't surprised to see that he was riding into the walled city. Always in disrepair, Tachre now seemed a more open city because of the tornadic destruction wrought on the city's battlements. Rouwen's lips thinned to a line as he saw how the citizens of Tachre had suffered. The slaughter on the battlefield had been unfortunate, but those men knew the penalties of failure. They went into action with the full realization they might never see another dawn. The people of Tachre had been killed in their homes and businesses, not knowing the reason they died.

The streets were choked with debris turning soggy from the incessant rain produced by the action of Rouwen's wind warriors along the coast. Such suction lifting air normally layered along the ground to the upper atmosphere created currents from the ocean. As the cooler air reached warm land, rain began falling. Rouwen had not only killed thousands with the Legion of the Air, he doomed the city's survivors to a miserable, wet night.

'Please, Lord, anything,' begged a woman on her knees in the street. 'I am left homeless.'

'So are others,' Rouwen said. 'I will see what can be done for all of you.' He snorted and caused twin plumes of condensed breath to jet forth like quicksilver. 'After all,' he said with more than a touch of irony, 'I am King Brion.'

He rode slowly through Tachre, winding along back alleys and riding up the middle of the main thoroughfare. Everywhere he saw the same suffering and devastation. Looters had little to steal, and those with food greedily ate it rather than have it taken from them.

The most significant change Rouwen noticed, though, lay in the lack of soldiers patrolling the city. Before, squads and even companies of Nishor's troopers had kept the peace and imposed their huge bribes on travellers and merchants. Commerce, both legal and illegal, had come to a halt as the city slowly died.

Rouwen walked his horse in the direction of Nishor's palace. The sprawling structure had occupied much of Tachre's center, the jewel in Mion's tarnished crown. Now the jewel was shattered and the crown twisted beyond recognition. Walls had fallen under the onslaught of impossible winds; the once carefully tended gardens were turned into fields of chopped salad; the stained glass dome that had once soared over Nishor's audience chamber lay in a million multicolored shards. Anyone standing in that chamber when the wind brought the dome crashing down would have died

321

a death of a thousand cuts. Vitreous missiles would have sliced and slashed more thoroughly than Mion's entire army wielding knives.

Rouwen didn't dismount. He rode directly through the audience chamber and stopped at the foot of the dais where Nishor had once held court. Rouwen dismounted and climbed those five steps, glass grinding noisily under his boot soles. He paused for a moment, staring at the throne. It had been knocked askew. Rouwen grabbed the arms and heaved, dragging the heavy throne back to its usual place.

Turning, Rouwen stared across the deserted audience chamber. He thought he might have seen a few corpses in the corners, but he couldn't be sure without checking. He had seen too much death this night. With the rain pouring through the shattered dome, Rouwen sat carefully to savor fully the sensation.

'The court of King Brion the First will now assemble!' he called with great bitterness. Hands on the arms of the throne, he tasted power and found it unpalatable. What decree might he sign to bring back those who had died needlessly in the assault by his wind warriors? Did he have the proper law to impose that would make everything right?

He had no quarrel with the people of Mion. King Nishor was no more, but another would rise to take his place on this throne. Perhaps the new king would be more caring – or less. It wouldn't be Brion Rouwen.

The drip of water running down the walls and the thunder and lightning in the sky drowned out any reply Rouwen might have received to his summons of petitioners. He leaned back on the throne and experienced an overwhelming weariness. He considered his future and knew it was as bleak as life in Mion would be for years to come.

But that was his destiny, not guiding Mion into prosperity. Heaving himself to his feet, Rouwen walked to his horse and mounted. He patted the horse on the neck and said, 'Perhaps I should have elevated you to a noble's position. You deserve a title. Or perhaps you'd simply prefer a bag of grain.'

The horse nickered in agreement, and Rouwen smiled for the first time.

Another bolt of lightning lit the interior of Nishor's ruined audience chamber. Rouwen jerked about, hand going to his dagger. Darkness moving across darkness alerted him to something unusual in the sky. Squinting against the rain, he failed to make out the signal. He relaxed, deciding he was overtired but ready for the next move toward Valley Gan.

'Down the Demon's Throat, more wind warriors, more death, then –' Rouwen left the rest of his pledge hanging. No conquering army in history had ever vanquished the Kingdom of Gan, and he intended to invade with only a sword and dagger, a wizard of dubious power, and a former queen more demented and vengeful than reliable.

Riding back into the street running alongside the palace, Rouwen started to return to the battlefield in the hope of finding Diarra and Vutorian. But the clank of chains and the rattle of heavy wheels caused him to urge his horse into the wind-ruined shell of a nearby building.

Shouts and the clatter of riders alerted him to something important happening. Rouwen peered out and saw a fine carriage, unscathed by wind or war, coming to a halt a dozen yards away. Surrounding the carriage were ten guardsmen, their dark cloaks pulled tightly around their bodies. Rouwen tried to get a better look at their insignia and couldn't. They revealed nothing of their unit emblems or medals. Something in the way they set guards at precisely the positions Rouwen would have ordered put the spying man on alert.

'See how they cover all possible entry and exit points?' he asked his horse, patting the strong neck to keep it quiet. 'They might have been my soldiers.'

Rouwen sucked in a deep breath and held it when he saw the carriage door open. Stepping out, resplendent in the full dress uniform of Lord Protector of the Realm was Duke Sosler. The dark purple tunic was only partly hidden by a swirling cape, and the Gannian medals marching in precise rows across his chest betrayed him, if the intricately wrought insignia on his hat and the gold and silver buttons did not.

Standing in the rain for a moment, Sosler tapped his highly polished foot as if impatiently waiting for a visitor. Rouwen dismounted and tethered his horse, needing to get a better look at this strange assignation. Working his way through the tumbledown building, Rouwen struggled to get to the second floor to peer down on the carriage and its occupant. The flooring gave under him several times, but he made his way to a window and saw Sosler take off his cap and wipe rain from his face.

He had not expected Sosler to be in Mion, but the treacherous nobleman travelled freely between Gan and Mion, even as the two armies skirmished at the Demon's Throat. Now that the backbone of the Mionese army had been broken and the country's king executed, Sosler might find himself in a precarious position. Why had he not fled when it became apparent Nishor would lose?

Or had that information reached Sosler? Rouwen doubted much got past the cunning duke. As Lord Protector of Gan he knew as much, and perhaps more, of Mion's war-waging capabilities as had Nishor. The sight of the Legion of the Air towering above a battlefield should have warned Sosler to leave the country immediately. Any wind warrior appearing in Mion would soon be threatening Gan.

'Where is he?' the duke asked his aide-de-camp in irritation. 'I will have his tongue and eyes for ornaments if he doesn't get here soon.'

Two guardsmen, one Rouwen recognized as having been an Intrepid and now wearing the uniform of the Lord Protector's Regiment, marched forward smartly, stopped and reported. Rouwen could not hear their low voices over the patter of the gradually diminishing rain.

A new lightning bolt tore the night sky and forced him back into the building. If any of those alert guardsmen spotted him, he would never be able to fight his way out.

'I can end Sosler's life now,' Rouwen said softly, touching the gold horn dangling at his side. One small blast from the Lord of Death and Life's horn would generate a vortex directly over Sosler's heavy carriage. The swirling wind demon would surely suck up the duke and his men – and possibly himself, as well. But did that matter? Rouwen felt rancor against King Priowe, and had promised Diarra he would kill him, but Sosler was his true enemy. Sosler had engineered the plot to take over Gan. The Captain of the King's Intrepid Guard had been an obstacle to overcome, nothing more.

Sosler had persuaded Priowe with his clever machinations. Sosler was the source of Rouwen's woe, having ordered Kwuway to cast the spell on him. Kill him now, screamed the thought in Rouwen's brain.

Even as it crossed his mind, Rouwen saw the silver flash of a spell casket dangling from a chain around Sosler's neck. His heart almost exploded. With it, he could be free of the curse and find Sorinne and . . .

Or he could kill the duke with the Legion of the Air. Rouwen lifted the horn to his lips, only to stagger away when a heavy weight crashed down on him from above. The roof had collapsed and left holes in a score of places. He didn't even know which of the openings provided the entrance for the *thouse* bird.

'Don't be more of a fool than you must,' Toit cautioned. The *thouse* twisted sideways and almost ripped the horn from Rouwen's tensed fingers. Sitting on the trumpet's bell as he did, the bird forced the horn away from Rouwen's lips by sheer weight.

'That's Duke Sosler,' Rouwen said, furious at the interruption. 'Let me kill him.'

'Where is your curiosity? Do you not wonder why a man of his power stands in the rain?' Toit refused to make the killing any easier for Rouwen. The bird twisted left and right until Rouwen stopped trying to blow the horn.

'You just don't want me to die along with him,' accused Rouwen. 'Why not?'

'Finola, the demons only know why, has taken a fancy to you. She ordered me back to watch over you, to keep you from doing anything monumentally stupid.'

'He stole my life,' Rouwen said hotly. 'I can avenge myself.'

'Some revenge, not knowing if Sosler really dies in your tornado. What if the wind warrior kills you, but he somehow escapes? Where is the satisfaction? Would you not prefer to drive your sword through his putrid guts and *feel* him die? And this curse. What if the wind warrior kills Sosler but leaves you alive? The spell casket, should Sosler have it on him, will be gone forever. Sosler will have triumphed, and your continued wretched life will be proof of it.'

'Damn you,' Rouwen said, lowering the horn and finally strapping it back to his waist when Toit jumped onto a broken roofing timber. Everything the *thouse* said was true. Rouwen had to deliver Sosler's soul to Mount Glid personally, both for the satisfaction of revenge and to retrieve his spell casket.

'And there's simple, unpretentious nosiness. Don't tell me you aren't just a little curious about the person he meets. I have your interest piqued. I can tell.' Toit laughed, a raucous sound that echoed through the night. The soft fall of rain had almost stopped and no longer deadened sound.

'Quiet,' Rouwen urged, moving back to his post at the window. No one below had been alerted by the bird's shrill call, and Rouwen hadn't missed anything. The guards still alertly patrolled, and Sosler still impatiently paced.

'There. There he comes,' said Toit, the wide yellow eyes sharper at night than Rouwen's.

A small figure walked briskly down the center of the street and came directly to Sosler's side. The guards moved farther away when their lord's visitor arrived, to be out of earshot.

Rouwen might not have heard what they discussed, but he recognized Duke Sosler's confederate.

'So Vutorian plays both sides,' Rouwen mused. He had passed

beyond being shocked at the double-dealing he discovered among wizards or nobles.

'Of course he does, my boy,' said Toit. 'Who doesn't?'

Brion Rouwen had no answer to that.

14

The Duke's Bride

'You show potential, my boy,' said the *thouse*, stretching its wings and flapping a few times to undo the kinks in the strong pinions. 'Finola sees much in you, for whatever reason. Perhaps she is right.' Toit cawed and added, 'She usually is. In spite of the trouble I give her, she is usually correct in her judgments of people. And magic. She is going to be one of the great mages of all time.'

'Not if she insists on wasting her life searching for Noumet,' Rouwen said, still peering at the carriage around the corner of the destroyed building. Sosler had finished with the wizard and dismissed him – or perhaps it was the other way. Vutorian clung to the grimoire as if his life depended on it, and well it might. The spell book's green glow was dazzling, so brilliant now that Rouwen could not stare directly at it.

More telling, Sosler continually shielded his eyes from the glare, as if being threatened by the book of spells. Who was in command? For the first time, Rouwen wasn't sure of Sosler's power. With the grimoire in Vutorian's possession, the wizard might have turned the superior card in this game of deception and domination. Rouwen lifted the magical horn, wondering if even a small noise might cause the grimoire to glow more than it did.

'Have you decided to die?' Toit asked softly.

'Other thoughts intruded,' Rouwen said. He lowered the horn and imagined the spell casket dangling around Duke Sosler's neck. With that in his possession, he could freely summon the Legion of the Air and eliminate his enemies.

Vutorian now belonged in that camp.

'How do you intend to deal with the wizard?' asked Toit. 'I am bound to him through Fin. She is naive, but she is no fool. Alas, being honor bound is as bad as being a blockhead. I can do nothing against Vutorian while he is her mentor.'

'What quest did he impose on her?' Rouwen watched as Sosler climbed into his fine carriage and the driver whipped the team

327

into motion. The guards quickly found their mounts and trotted behind. Within seconds only Vutorian remained. He held up the spell book, as if offering it to the bolts of lightning still lashing the sky. The rain had stopped and the gleam from the book of spells allowed Rouwen to see the mage's face. Not even at King Nishor's execution had the wizard looked this alive, this much in control of his world.

The shifting sands of power had somehow brought Vutorian to the fore.

'I cannot say. She is close-mouthed about her training, as if it matters to me.' The *thouse* hopped to the edge of the window and peered down. Vutorian tucked the grimoire back under his tunic and hurried off, oblivious to those spying on him. 'Such talent wasted in that one.'

'Vutorian?'

'Who else, who else? He could have been one of the greats, but no, he frittered away his talents in Nishor's court. The king caught him doing some horrible thing, probably plotting to overthrow the government, and banished him.'

'Vutorian got his revenge.' Rouwen picked his way through the fallen timbers and jumped to the floor below. His horse pawed nervously, not sure where his rider had gone. Rouwen mounted and hardly minded when Toit fixed himself to Rouwen's right shoulder. He was getting used to the bird's weight.

'Do you seek out Vutorian or go after Sosler?' asked Toit.

'Neither,' Rouwen said, his mind working out the intricacies of the plots boiling around him. 'I would like to know why you returned. Was it only because Finola sent you?'

'Of course it was,' the *thouse* said, almost angrily. 'Do you think I enjoy flying through such foul weather, getting my feathers wet and then having to hunt through this miserable pigeon coop of a town to find you in a burned-out hovel?'

'I saw you earlier. I thought it was only a shadow in the sky, but it had to be you.'

Toit said nothing for a moment, then, 'Your eyes are not as good as mine. Why were you hiding from me?'

Rouwen did not bother answering. He rode slowly through the empty streets of Tachre, appalled anew at the destruction surrounding him. He should never have agreed to do battle so close to the city. The Plains outside town would have given latitude for movement, or even retreat, and the huge numbers of people would not have perished. Already the stench rising was enough to make him gag.

Nishor had sent many of his own people to the lime pit outside town. Even more would now decay in that huge mass grave, and this time the murderer was not Nishor.

'We had planned to use the Legion of the Air to enter Gan. The Demon's Throat is the only way open . . .'

'That's not what Finola told me. There are two tunnels under the Shield Mountains. Why not take one of them?' Toit twisted his neck and turned an eye up to stare at Rouwen. The former captain said nothing to this. He had been through one tunnel twice and had met too many spirits, souls he could not again face.

'How does she know of such secret ways?' Rouwen asked, trying to divert the bird's attention from the real question. 'Only a handful of people in Gan have ever known of those tunnels, and as far as I've ever heard, no one outside the kingdom has discovered them.'

'She is a mage,' Toit said as if this explained everything. Seeing how skeptical Rouwen remained, the bird added, 'She wants to use the tunnels as a passageway to Noumet. The City of Mages is below Castle Gan, you know.'

Rouwen laughed heartily at this. A city beneath the massive spire holding Castle Gan was outrageous. As Captain of the Intrepid Guard, he would have known of any inhabitants sneaking about under his feet. Never had Rouwen even heard a whisper of such a place.

'She wastes her time seeking the City of Mages,' Rouwen said, but the merriment such a notion provided him lightened his mood. As he rode, Rouwen noted the storm clouds had vanished and the stars shone brightly. The Lesser Moon was setting and the Greater Moon was mid-sky and crescent. Nights such as this invigorated him and made him feel as if he could go on forever.

He stared into the northeast and knew the Shield Mountains lay in the darkness, far beyond his vision. Still, Rouwen imagined he could see them – and the Demon's Throat leading into the kingdom he had once thought of as his own. For seven generations his family had lived in Valley Gan. Perhaps, if all went well, he and seven more generations would be there in honor.

'If you are not looking for Vutorian, that can only mean you want to talk with Diarra,' Toit said, dejected. 'She is quite mad. She will never be a reliable ally.'

'No, but she might become a useful weapon.' Already, plans formed in Rouwen's brain. Vutorian and Sosler were allied for some purpose that could only mean woe. A more cordial arrangement with Diarra might assure Priowe and Sosler's deaths – and liberation for the Kingdom of Gan.

Queen Diarra was an instrument best played gently, carefully, with great skill.

'They will follow us into the deepest grave,' chortled Vutorian. The small wizard rubbed his hands together, twirled the tips of his long, heavily waxed mustache and then thrust his hand beneath his tunic. Rouwen knew the mage made sure the grimoire rested safely within, as if he could not tell otherwise.

The spell book's glow was so intense now that it shone through even two layers of cloth. That it was a cold light saved Vutorian from serious burns. Rouwen considered what he had surrendered for the wizard's help. The grimoire might be more important than the gold horn dangling at his side. But both magical devices carried penalties. Rouwen could not read the runes in the grimoire and, once called, he could not shoo away the Legion of the Air. He needed Vutorian to read the spells in the grimoire to protect them magically, as they both needed Diarra to use the whistle to control and finally dissipate the wind demons.

'Leading such an army against Priowe makes me burn inside,' Diarra said. Rouwen had been unable to talk with her over the last three days. She had alternated between catatonic and completely mad, dancing with imaginary partners and singing to herself tunes unshared by any other mortal. Vutorian had used those days to whip together the Mionese army and assemble it for the attack through the Demon's Throat. The small wizard had proven more adroit in military discipline and morale than Rouwen would have thought possible.

Perhaps the long nights spent poring over the radiant grimoire had something to do with Vutorian's new-found expertise.

'The army is ready, Majesty.' For a moment Rouwen did not respond. He had not become accustomed to thinking of himself as King Brion, in spite of the short stay on the throne of Mion where Nishor had ruled so terribly.

He looked at the sergeant he had made Lord Protector of the Realm. The man's ability had likewise astonished him. It was unusual for a sergeant to take so quickly to supreme command.

'You are a man of vast talent, Laslo,' he said to the new Lord Protector. 'You have found more deserters than I would have thought existed, and you have turned them back into soldiers.'

'My liege is too kind,' Laslo said, obviously pleased with the

330

praise. 'Your viceroy has done much to retrieve the men from their hiding places.'

'Magicks?' Rouwen asked, knowing the answer. He spoke only to appear occupied while he considered the assault on Gan. Even with the Legion of the Air destroying fortifications along the narrow walled canyon, entry into Valley Gan would be difficult. Not many of the soldiers entering would ever see their homes again. For Diarra and Vutorian, this was not a concern. The soldiers, whether Mionese or Gannian, were expendable. Rouwen surprised himself worrying about casualties on both sides.

'They returned as if drugged with *necoia* flower tea. Their eyes were open, but they did not see. And few could speak. Your viceroy sat in his tent and muttered long chants, and they continued to flock back.' Laslo seemed uneasy with the notion of a spell controlling a soldier's mind. Rouwen did not bother agreeing with him that this was a dangerous precedent.

The battle would be met soon. That mattered most.

'Get the army moving, Lord Protector,' Rouwen ordered. 'And send out scouts to find other units patrolling along the way. All are to join the attack on Gan.'

'At once, Majesty.' Laslo raced off to obey. Toit pulled his head from under his wing, stretched mightily and looked about, as if assuring himself any conversation would not be overheard.

'He calls Vutorian 'your viceroy'. Your new Lord Protector does not consider Vutorian his leader,' the *thouse* bird observed.

'With good reason. Vutorian coerces the wayward soldiers with his spells.'

'The grimoire must contain potent enchantments. Was it wise to give him the book of spells? Vutorian had done little besides betray you.' Toit stretched again and settled his wings. Rouwen had taken the precaution of putting heavy padding into his shoulders for the *thouse* to grip as it perched. He had only the bird's weight to contend with as he rode.

'Why should he be any different from anyone else?' Rouwen asked. 'We go into battle side-by-side, but once Priowe is dead, I have no doubt Vutorian will try to cheat Duke Sosler of the Gannian throne. Let them fight it out.'

'Then you will slay the victor of that contest.' Toit squawked and shook all over, sending a cascade of brown feathers into the air. 'Not a bad notion, letting them weaken one another before you swoop down and devour them. What of Diarra?'

'I need to speak with her,' Rouwen said, seeing his former queen riding a course parallel to that taken by the main body of soldiers. He tugged on the reins and got his huge horse moving

331

in Diarra's direction. She paid Rouwen no attention as he pulled up beside her.

'Good day, Diarra,' he called to her. Her head remained frozen, eyes fixed on the terrain ahead as if by force of will she could see past the Shield Mountains and into Valley Gan.

'Vutorian is dealing with Duke Sosler,' he said, wanting to see if this had any effect on her. Rouwen thought a muscle twitched in her cheek, but he wasn't certain. He rode closer. 'I saw them together in Tachre three nights ago. They have allied and plan to see us . . .'

'Lies!' Diarra raged with the suddenness of a summer storm. 'You think to split up our alliance before the battle. You want Priowe to wriggle free. You have no honor, Brion Rouwen. You think to break your promise to kill him. Well, you won't. I hold you to your promise! Kill Priowe or be forever damned!' With that, Diarra dug her heels cruelly into her horse's flanks. The animal tried to rear at such treatment. She savagely sawed at the reins and got the horse galloping toward the Shield Mountains.

'She is so understanding, so compassionate, so thoughtful,' Toit said. 'You find only the best in compatriots.'

'You're here, aren't you?' Rouwen snapped, angry at Diarra and Vutorian and himself. 'How do you plan to betray me?'

Toit was taken aback. The *thouse* sidestepped to the far end of the pad on Rouwen's right shoulder and peered at the man. 'I am here because Finola asked me to look after you.'

'Go to her, then. You have no reason to stay. There will only be more death. Unless you want to peck out dead men's eyes, go, go!' Shrugging his shoulder and shaking hard, Rouwen loosed Toit's grip. The brown bird flapped wildly, then caught enough air under his pinions to swoop and fly off. Rouwen thought Toit might have circled twice and then arrowed off in the direction of the Forest of Kelnos where Finola was still engaged in her meaningless quest. He wasn't able to tell where Toit flew, and that bothered him almost as much as the bird's departure. If he could have called the *thouse* back, he would have.

Somehow, he felt as if he had lost his only friend.

'I found him, Majesty,' Laslo reported. 'Your viceroy has pitched his camp not a half-hour's ride down the road. Do you wish a squad to fetch him?' Laslo's eyes gleamed at the idea of soldiers dragging the wizard into the presence of their king, but Rouwen was not going to allow any rift to show. When they marched into battle the following morning, all the soldiers had to believe their leaders were in complete agreement. Anything less and

332

they would be unsure. In battle against the fortifications along the Demon's Throat any hesitation meant unnecessary death.

'I'll ride to his camp and confer. Has he had any other visitors?'

'No one, not even Diarra.' Laslo shifted slightly to see if the demented woman was near. 'She has not been in any condition to speak, even if they had met. Is she dangerous, Majesty?'

Rouwen understood Laslo's worry but chose to misinterpret the Lord Protector's concern. 'She will not harm herself. She is too focused on the battle and victory. See to the troops. I'll return before dawn to instruct the officers in our battle plan. It will be simple, yet will require the utmost bravery on their part.'

'We await your orders, Majesty.' Laslo saluted. Rouwen returned it, his mind already drifting to Vutorian and his grimoire. The book of spells must not be turned against the Mionese troops once the battle began – but would Vutorian use it to hinder the Gannian soldiers along the Demon's Throat? Rouwen had to find out where Vutorian's loyalties lay for the coming battle.

Overall, Vutorian was loyal only to his own interests, but tomorrow? Rouwen shook his head. He had to be sure no more died than necessary as they invaded the invincible Valley Gan. For a man out for revenge against Sosler and to lift a curse on his own head, Rouwen found himself worrying too much over what became of soldiers he had once denigrated as poorly trained and even cowardly.

The Mionese army required hard training to equal that of the Gannian, but the finest army in the world would never stand for more than an instant against the Legion of the Air. But what spells did Vutorian conjure for Sosler? Was a spell contained in the grimoire capable of rendering the wind warriors' attack futile?

Rouwen shook off the feeling of impending dread. The only way he would enter Gan was down the Demon's Throat. To get there he had to fight. Reduced to those elements, the battle sounded simple.

Rouwen dismounted when he reached Vutorian's tent. From within came the bright green glow he now associated with the grimoire. Whatever magicks activated it, they now were more potent than at any time Rouwen had held it.

'Vutorian!' he called, not wanting to startle the mage. Wizards had a way of laying protective spells about them. 'A word with you.'

'Enter, dear Brion, come in and rest. We have a busy day ahead of us. All should be over by this time tomorrow.' The small wizard motioned for Rouwen to take a stool next to a folding table. Where Vutorian had got so much furniture was anyone's guess. But the king's viceroy might command more than the king himself – or at least Vutorian might ask for more.

'A busy day, yes, but I need to know which side you favor. I will not ride into the Demon's Throat against men I still consider countrymen if you seek to destroy me.'

'Why, Brion, whatever gave you such an absurd idea? You have purchased my cooperation with this marvelous spell book.' Vutorian rested his hand on the radiant volume.

'I saw you speaking with Sosler in Tachre, just after I destroyed the city.'

Vutorian's mustache twitched slightly but other than this he maintained a neutral expression. Rouwen wondered if he had practiced for this moment or if his self-control mounted as he read from the grimoire. The wizard cleared his throat and spoke slowly.

'I saw Duke Sosler in the Mionese capital, but it was not to betray you. We are allies, friends. I hope our friendship can grow and deepen after this unpleasant matter is behind us.'

'Why?' Rouwen refused to accept platitudes. Let Vutorian make his pretty speeches to the peasants. If they believed – or allowed themselves to be led astray – that was their concern.

'So blunt. You will never rule wisely or long in Mion if you reduce everything to such simplistic terms.' Vutorian placed his other hand over the grimoire, as if drawing strength from it. His eyes took on an inner glow matching that of the book of spells. The magicks were being filtered through him now, but was Vutorian a vessel or a pawn of the book of spells?

Rouwen tried not to address that matter directly. He knew little enough of wizardly doings. But he did know of loyalty.

'So you say. What proof do I have that, when we enter the Demon's Throat, you and Sosler will not work together to defeat us?'

'Us? You place yourself in the Mionese camp now. Interesting.' Vutorian closed his eyes and held up one hand that appeared to have been dipped in flowing green dye. 'Peace. I have made no deal with Sosler. I sought only to gain information that might aid our mission against King Priowe.'

'Sosler carries part of my soul in the spell casket around his neck. That spell casket – and Sosler's life – are the reasons I gave you the grimoire. It is Diarra who desires Priowe's death the most.'

'You do, also. I see it in your face. He betrayed you. He

tortured you and cast you out. Priowe disgraced you before your men, and revenge burns within you. Information only of King Priowe is the reason I spoke with Sosler.'

Rouwen knew the wizard lied.

'What did you find of importance?' Rouwen doubted any honest answer would be forthcoming.

'Maps. I have maps of the fortifications along the canyon leading into Valley Gan. And once there, I have other maps showing the traps set on the road spiralling to Castle Gan. Sosler has no love for your monarch, either.'

'When were you going to share these with me? Before the attack?' Rouwen knew everything Vutorian claimed to have received from Sosler and already had warned his officers of the defensive capabilities.

'Of course, Brion, before the attack.'

'Why did Sosler give you the information, and what did you pay him for it?'

Vutorian laughed. 'He gave it willingly. There is much dissent within Castle Gan now. His wife insisted that he pass along any facts that might aid us. She is eager to see a new regime within her kingdom.'

'His wife?' Rouwen asked, coldness growing in his belly. 'The duke isn't married.'

'But of course he has a wife, Brion. Did you not know? Only recently he has married Priowe's daughter, the Princess Sorinne.' Vutorian laughed at Rouwen's expression and kept laughing as Rouwen left without uttering another word.

15

Down the Throat

'This is your finest hour. Why are you so glum, other than it appears to be your true nature?' Toit walked from one shoulder to another across Rouwen's neck. The man tried to brush the *thouse* bird off, but Toit was too quick for him. Since he had grabbed the bird and heaved him away, Toit had been more cautious. Rouwen wished he could have apologized for that rash act, but the weight of the invasion rested more and more on him. He couldn't waste time on soothing the bird's hurt feelings.

The Demon's Throat loomed ahead. Sheer walls of red rock rose vertically on either side of the mouth, a heavily fortified pass with more than a regiment of men stationed to defend Valley Gan. Even if the twin fortresses on either side of the road leading into the valley were taken and the massive gate swung wide, the advance down the aptly named corridor would prove deadly.

Rouwen knew a retreat, should the fortresses begin to fall, would provide adequate personnel for harrying any invading army. Men on the steep cliffs and along the rim could push down boulders and let those massive missiles do their work. And should an army penetrate the fortresses and rush into the rich farmlands of Valley Gan, there remained the soaring pinnacle with Castle Gan atop it. Fighting up the spiralling road would sap the strength of more than a kingdom.

To the best of Rouwen's knowledge, only once had an army penetrated the Demon's Throat and made it to the base of the rocky spire holding the castle. The army had fought every step of the way to reach the massive steel gates of Castle Gan and been crushed by a rested, well-fed and armed legion from within the castle.

The task was daunting, but Rouwen led not a simple army, though most of the Mionese soldiers were hardly more than illiterate peasants. He touched the horn dangling at his side and wondered if he could trust Diarra to recall the Legion of the Air when he loosed them against his own kingdom.

'It will not be easy taking Gan,' Rouwen said. 'I have no wish to make my people suffer for the acts of Sosler and Priowe. If I could find a way to kill only those two, I'd take it in a flash.' He turned and peered squarely into Toit's yellow eyes. 'Why not fly into the castle and bite them both? Your poisonous beak will slay instantly, and if that doesn't work, you can always talk them to death.'

'Poison beak, poison tongue,' Toit said equably enough. The bird seemed to have forgotten his last ignominious launching and wasn't holding it against Rouwen. That didn't make the man feel any better.

'Will you stay at my side or do you wish to fly above and bring back information on their troop deployment?' Rouwen sought a way to keep Toit from harm. If he stayed on his shoulder, Toit would find danger everywhere. On the wing, up above the fighting, Toit would be safe.

'You can use a defender at your side,' Toit said reasonably. 'Finola has entrusted me with seeing that you do not get too many scratches. Why she cares about your hide is beyond all reason, but she knows more of the world and its ways than either of us ever will. That is required of a master mage in Noumet, you know.'

'I could use her to move the sun to my back so the enemy troops squint into the light,' Rouwen said, pointing to Gan's defenders. He attacked northward, into the Throat. The Gannian forces knew he massed an army, but he hoped they were not prepared for the onslaught of the wind warriors. If only he knew the nature of the pact between Vutorian and Sosler, it might tell him the risk he now faced. Was Vutorian playing Sosler and Rouwen against each other, or was the wizard's game something else?

None of it made sense. Duke Sosler was no fool. He had seen the destruction in Tachre and knew he faced forces more potent than any human army. Rouwen thought hard and came to an uneasy idea.

'Toit, is it possible Sosler wants us to devastate Gan's army? How can he gain power if I destroy most of the frighting men?'

Toit chuckled and then squawked loudly, as if clearing his throat before replying. Rouwen waited and finally the *thouse* spoke.

'You are correct in this, I fear. If Sosler needs any proof that King Priowe is unable to rule well, letting an invading army into Valley Gan will suffice. The other nobles might support him if he can offer a way of defeating the trespassing masses from Mion.'

Rouwen nodded slowly. He was being forced to kill men he

might have served with, fought with side-by-side, to aid Sosler in deposing Priowe. Yet he had little choice but to play the wily duke's game to its conclusion. He needed the spell casket dangling about Sosler's neck if he ever wanted the curse on him lifted.

Rouwen's thoughts turned briefly to his brother and the thief, Nibbles, who had died because he loved them. And he had slain the Lord of Death and Life because the Lord magically assumed the shape of Sorinne. Rouwen had only brushed his fingers across the Lord's face and the mighty wizard was dead in seconds. Rouwen held out his hands and knew Princess Sorinne would die if he touched her now.

Duke Sosler deserved death for his role in this curse. And Priowe would die with him because he had been so easily duped.

'You fail to ask the proper question,' Toit said as Rouwen started to give the signal for Mion's army to advance.

'What's that?'

'How does Sosler think to stop you once you reach the base of Castle Gan? Your wind warriors are invincible. No human force can stand against them, yet he has no fear of letting you roar down the Demon's Throat and reach the base of the castle.'

'What does he have waiting for me when I reach the castle?' Rouwen knew Toit's valuable insight had saved him from a fall later. The best answer would be alliance with either Diarra or Vutorian.

Rouwen knew the duke and wizard had met and parted on amiable enough terms. Neither had tried to kill the other during their brief meeting in Tachre.

'Vutorian will betray me,' Rouwen said, nodding his head.

'Kill him now and save yourself grief later,' Toit urged. 'The wizard is no good. He has not taught Fin all she needs. He withholds tiny snippets, important details in his lessons so she will not grow too strong magically and leave him. He uses her mercilessly, and she never complains.' Toit's claws gripped harder on Rouwen's shoulder, indicating the depth of the *thouse* bird's feelings for Finola and against Vutorian.

'Why have you chosen this moment to tell me of your dislike for Vutorian? Before, you always skirted the issue.' Rouwen found himself eye to eye with Toit again. The bird let out a raucous squall and shook his head vigorously.

'I am bound to him through Finola. She makes me obey him, because she believes he can teach her lore needed to enter Nourment. I told her Vutorian does not even believe in the

City of Mages. I now fear Vutorian works against Fin because he has scented more fragrant game. He has tasted power.'

Toit panted harshly, and Rouwen saw tiny droplets of poison forming on the bird's serrated beak. This, as much as the words, confirmed Rouwen's belief that Toit was not a willing pawn in any game played by Vutorian. But unwilling? He could not say, and he doubted if the *thouse* could, either.

'We must watch Vutorian closely, but not let Diarra run too far afield, either,' Rouwen said. He knew Vutorian was untrustworthy and feared Diarra might become so if madness seized her too firmly.

'Majesty, are we ready?' asked Laslo, riding up. The former sergeant looked apprehensive. This would be the grandest battle of his life. 'The men are nervous.' The Lord Protector of Mion swallowed hard, and tried to force saliva into his mouth.

'Where is Diarra?' Rouwen asked, directing the question more at Toit than Laslo. But it was the Lord Protector who spoke.

'There, Majesty. She is guarded by ten of my best men. Your best men.'

'Ours, Laslo, ten of *our* best,' Rouwen said, putting the man at ease. 'Let the attack begin.'

He lifted the horn to his lips and sounded a long, clear note that reverberated off the steep cliffs and echoed down the length of the Demon's Throat. A returning blast came, followed by a gust of wind that almost took Rouwen from the saddle. He fought to maintain his seat in the powerful gusts of winds returning from the Throat.

'What magicks await us inside?' worried Laslo.

'I cannot say, but I think the wind might have been caused by my own hand.' Rouwen stared at the trumpet, then cocked his head to one side and listened hard. He heard the roaring of the wind warriors, many of them. Perhaps dozens.

'The echo,' Toit said apprehensively, 'created more than you intended. Is Diarra able to handle so many?'

'We will find out.' Rouwen raised his arm, signalled the guidon bearer to lower the flag and charge. For a moment after the flag lowered in the direction of the twin fortresses on either side of the huge gate closing off the Demon's Throat, nothing happened. Then the Mionese army began to move, to flow like some aquatic beast slithering out of the ocean and onto the beach.

Rouwen raced along, Laslo at his side. He watched Diarra, who worked diligently on her whistle. He knew many of the whistled commands the wind warriors obeyed, but the thundering hooves, the war cries and the general cacophony of attack drowned out most of Diarra's work. Looking above the huge gates, though, convinced Rouwen his former queen signalled properly. Two towering vortices whirled and crashed, killing anyone foolish enough to be exposed behind the gates.

From the fortresses came flight after flight of arrows. Now and then a heavy rock arched upward from a trebuchet on either side of the gate. After the initial rush had burned out most of the nervous energy, Rouwen kept his army moving steadily, avoiding the missiles and hoping the dense cloud of arrows did not inflict too many casualties.

'Majesty, the men are faltering. The arrows are taking too many lives for them to advance.'

Laslo's caution matched Rouwen's assessment of the problem. The first ranks of his army had slowed and were beginning to spread along the line of battlements facing the defenders. In this way they would be slaughtered quickly. Rouwen lifted the horn to his lips and sounded a new blast, this one less intense. Wind warriors appeared on either side of the gate, sucking up the arrows and even swallowing whole the huge rocks tossed by the trebuchet. The sight of the wind-driven allies rallied his troops.

'To the gates. Destroy the gates!' shouted Laslo, as he rode off to enforce the order.

Rouwen gave a short blast on the Lord's horn and created still another wind warrior, this one against the massive gates that had protected Gan for so long. The slow spin of air strengthened and more debris was kicked up in the tall column forming so powerfully. By the time Laslo and the first elements of the Mionese army reached the gates, they were ripped from their hinges and cast aside, as if by a bored giant child.

'Through! We are through!'

Rouwen saw the army he commanded surge past the gates and into the Demon's Throat. For only the second time to his knowledge, an army had penetrated the exterior fortifications.

'Those fortresses will makes fine roosting areas,' Toit said. 'So many windows, so many drafty places for nests. Fine, fine.'

'Are you planning on staying behind?' Rouwen asked. 'Or are you suggesting we go no farther?'

'You will do whatever you want,' Toit said testily. 'I merely comment on what I find.' The *thouse* edged over and used the end of a wing to lift the chain around Rouwen's neck. The silver spell casket tumbled out.

'Don't.' Rouwen's hand clamped firmly over the magical container. He glanced about to see if Diarra had noticed. The woman and her tight knot of protectors rode through the gates, paying heed to nothing but the wind warriors. She blew the golden whistle continually, giving orders the Lord's magical monsters obeyed reluctantly.

'That is what you seek, save that it dangles from Sosler's neck?' The bird blinked at him, as if questioning his sanity.

'I need the spell casket Sosler has, and a mage capable of using it. An improperly cast releasing spell will doom me for all eternity.'

'Ah, I see. This is how Vutorian came by the grimoire you carried. You think to pay him in advance for his services.' Toit clucked like a hen. 'Look at him and tell me if you believe a word he says. Look and see if he appears the least bit human!'

Rouwen knew a moment of the fear that had beset Laslo before the attack. Vutorian rode alone – but surrounded by a green nimbus. The grimoire in his hands radiated so much light Rouwen had to squint. Somehow, the use of magicks near the book of spells caused it to burn ever brighter.

'Summon a new wind warrior,' urged Toit, 'and then call on the Flame Specter.'

'Why should I do that?' But the horn was already on its way to Rouwen's lips. The Flame Specter was a mystery to him, yet it was tangled up with the grimoire he had so freely given Vutorian. Vutorian claimed it was a myth, but neither Kwuway nor the Lord of Death and Life had shared that belief. Rouwen thought that Vutorian lied.

A new trumpet blast brought forth a single tornado spinning along the vertical wall of the Demon's Throat. As it began spinning itself to magical life, Rouwen whispered, 'The Flame Specter.'

The unexpected brilliance blasting forth from the grimoire temporarily blinded him. He felt the flesh on his face crinkling, as if he had been too long in the summer sun, and his clothing hissed and popped.

'Damn him!' protested Toit. 'My feathers, my precious feathers. Scorched, and all because of Vutorian.'

'What is the Flame Specter?' asked Rouwen, wincing as Vutorian's grimoire sent out new waves of intense light. 'The mere mention of the name gives more power to the wizard.'

'Does it give or does it take?' countered Toit, moving to Rouwen's left shoulder to put the man's head between him and the wizard. 'You know something now of the magicks with which you play. Use them wisely.'

'I know nothing!' Rouwen's eyesight returned, yellow and blue dots dancing in his vision. 'Tell me more.'

'I have told you all I know,' the *thouse* protested. 'Finola knows more. Ask her. She would be inordinately excited if you did. She becomes an imbecile whenever someone thinks enough to ask her opinion. That comes from Vutorian and his haughty ways.'

'Rouwen, we must hurry. The Demon's Throat is a hard day's journey and we do not want to be caught between the walls at sunset.' Diarra and her soldiers had come close enough to hail Rouwen.

'You're right, Diarra,' Rouwen answered. 'The defenders in the fortresses have retreated. We ought to keep them running all the way to the castle.'

'Retreated?' she scoffed. 'They were abandoned. We fought only a skeleton force. Sosler knew we would easily breach his walls. We fight shadows.'

'Shadows are killing the men at the head of the column,' Laslo reported, looking as if he had been in the fight of his life. Rouwen knew the man might well have been, since the Mionese army had never seriously engaged in battle before this hour. 'We struggle to gain even a foot. They have dug into the walls and roll rocks onto our heads, then fill us with arrows if we try attacking.'

'The wind warriors will do us little good against them,' Rouwen said. 'The tornadoes are difficult to control and directing one against a handful of men is not using their power to its best.' Rouwen didn't want to exhaust Diarra before they reached Castle Gan. But the woman had blood in her eye and would not rest until they stood over Priowe's mutilated corpse.

'I can destroy them. Show me the pockets of resistance.' As if to illustrate her resolve, Diarra lifted the whistle and blew a complicated set of long and short blasts. Three wind warriors returned from their ravaging along the canyon floor and whirled in a complicated threesome toward a fortified area halfway up the side of the cliffs.

Rouwen had watched as some of these positions were built. Some were reachable only from the canyon rim. Soldiers would be lowered on lines to take their posts until relieved. Other pockets in the soft red rock of the walls were staffed by men coming through tunnels painstakingly cut through the rock.

The wind warriors would kill everyone in the fortified position if the men there had been lowered. In a way, he hoped they would find retreat through tunnels and reach Castle Gan safely. He had no desire to fight them again in even more treacherous battle, for Rouwen had led these men. They were his countrymen, no matter what Laslo and the others called him.

He wasn't King Brion. He would prefer being Brion Rouwen, Captain of the Intrepid Guard.

'There, they've died. Each and every one. I *can* fight this battle now that you have given me the weapons.' Diarra rode off whistling until she must have panted with exertion. Rouwen followed, worrying that the real bloodshed lay ahead.

16

Up the Spiral Road

'They cannot stand against us,' Diarra claimed with manic fury. She danced about in such tight circles that Rouwen worried that the madness descended on her once more. 'We will beat them, we will have Priowe's ugly head on a pike!'

'Their army flees,' gloated Vutorian. He stood to one side, pressing the glowing grimoire to his chest. It was no longer possible to separate the green radiance of grimoire from wizard. The small wizard's mustache twitched like a mouse's whiskers as he moved restlessly, never doing more than pausing for an instant before pacing, rocking, bobbing. 'The Legion of the Air is invincible.'

'We will be turned into bloody rags if Diarra fails to control them,' complained Rouwen. He had watched as Diarra lost domination of first one and then another of the mighty tornadoes. Columns of whirling air had piled up against the far canyon wall and vied for supremacy, raining down rock and debris until Rouwen had pleaded with her to dissipate both wind warriors.

She had done so, but Rouwen worried that the others his echoing first trump had created might prove even more tenacious now that Diarra was tiring. He lacked good numbers from Laslo but doubted the Mionese soldiers had taken more than one in ten casualties, mostly from their own ineptitude. For an army entering the Demon's Throat, this was nothing less than miraculous.

'We press on,' Diarra cawed, sounding more like a bird than Toit. This drew even Vutorian's attention. The green-glowing wizard moved away, as if distancing himself from such madness.

'Remove two more wind warriors,' ordered Rouwen. 'We need only a few to flush out the resistance remaining.' He saw the woman wasn't responding. The distance in her eyes bespoke of madness coming with victory. 'Speed,' Rouwen urged her. 'Let's not be encumbered by too many tornadoes. The only ones we need are those driving the Gannian army toward the castle.'

344

'We must make haste,' Diarra said, a semblance of sanity returning. She blew on the whistle, giving commands Rouwen found strange. He saw no immediate change but heard the echoes down the canyon. Straining, he thought there might be less roaring, as if wind warriors had been sent back into the magical realm of their birth.

'Toit,' Rouwen said softly. 'Can you reconnoiter for me?'

The bird gave Rouwen a nasty look, stretched its long wings, preened a moment, then launched so hard that he almost staggered. Rouwen nearly fell against Vutorian, but when he came within a few feet, warmth mounted until he wanted to shriek. He caught himself and pulled back from the wizard.

'What is it about the grimoire that makes you glow so brilliantly?' Rouwen asked.

'Power,' whispered Vutorian. 'The power mounts, and one day I shall tap it! I have translated more than half the book of spells. When it is all done . . .' Vutorian cut off his boasting. A horrified expression crossed his face, as if he had admitted to a guilty secret.

'You do not forget why I gave you the grimoire?' Rouwen squared off against the wizard and watched the transformation on Vutorian's face. Shock at what he had said turned into a neutral expression that Rouwen interpreted as being guileful. Whatever the wizard answered would be a lie wrapped in just enough truth to make it palatable.

'I will not fail you, King Brion,' said Vutorian. 'Count on my talents when you need them most.'

'We ride hard now to get out of this canyon.' Rouwen grew increasingly edgy because of their trapped position within the Demon's Throat. He feared Sosler might send a few companies around behind somehow and try to bottle up the Mionese, a fighting force at the gates to prevent retreat and all of Gan and its might ahead. To thwart any such plan, Rouwen had left a considerable number of his soldiers guarding the entry into Valley Gan. They could live the easy life while in the twin fortresses, and he had set them to repairing the destruction caused by the Legion of the Air so that the gates could be locked once more.

Whether they required safety during the attack or after Gan had fallen did not matter. The gates must be rehinged and put into place.

A loud squawk from high above alerted Rouwen to Toit's return. He braced himself and was still almost bowled over when the heavy *thouse* hit his shoulder.

'Consider a softer landing,' complained Rouwen.

345

'Consider a softer landing place,' snapped Toit. 'Three wind warriors remain, and they scour this miserable canyon clean of all life. The few troops I saw make no effort to fight. They run directly for the castle sitting atop its pile of rock.'

'Thank you,' Rouwen said, walking to his horse. He cast a quick glance over his left shoulder at Vutorian. Of Diarra he saw no trace. The demented woman might have ridden ahead to watch the destruction caused by the twisting air columns. Struggling under Toit's considerable weight, Rouwen climbed into the saddle and urged his courser to a quick trot. Rouwen's keen eyes picked out the fortifications along the walls, all abandoned.

'Sosler pulled the soldiers back to Castle Gan,' Rouwen said to Toit, using the *thouse* as a sounding board for his thoughts. 'That means resistance will be even stiffer at the base of the road.'

'Your Legion of the Air will make quick work of any defense,' said Toit.

'It should,' Rouwen agreed reluctantly. Vutorian rode some distance away, entirely within the pulsating green nimbus caused by the spell book. Rouwen thought of a dozen reasons his wind warriors would never penetrate Castle Gan, and most of those reasons rode along with the wizard. Magicks of prodigious power grew, and Rouwen did not quite believe Vutorian when he said he had yet to master them.

'Majesty, King Brion, they make a stand!' Laslo galloped back, waving his sword wildly in the air. 'At the mouth of the pass leading into the valley, there're ten thousand soldiers waiting for us! A trap, a huge ambush!'

'Calm yourself and give a decent report,' Rouwen snapped. He considered lofting Toit again, but the bird might refuse. Beyond this, Rouwen felt disinclined to risk Toit's life. Among the Gannian soldiers were counted some of the best archers anywhere. A single arrow might rob Rouwen of his finest and most trustworthy ally in this preposterous invasion of an invincible kingdom.

'Sorry, Majesty,' Laslo panted. His eyes were wide with fear and sweat poured from him like an artesian spring. 'The leading squad marched into the valley and was immediately set upon. I ordered the cavalry to engage and defend the foot soldiers and found that this wasn't enough. I got a report back from the sole survivor of the first squad that ten thousand men had attacked and worked to hold us in the Demon's Throat.' Laslo looked upward with some concern, as if the skies might open and spill acid on his head.

'This is strange. Why would Sosler abandon the chance to

fight along the canyon floor when . . .' Rouwen's eyes narrowed. 'Laslo, the soldiers your men face. What of their armament?'

'Arms, Majesty? Why, they come at our soldiers with rocks and scythes and . . .'

'Enough,' Rouwen said. 'We do not face an army. These are the citizens of Gan fighting to repel the invaders. They saw how Sosler pulled the defense, so they formed into a ragtag army of their own.'

'But they fight like soldiers!'

'They fight like free men who have been betrayed by their leaders,' Rouwen said grimly. 'Sosler considers them expendable.'

'He thinks to further discredit Priowe,' cawed Toit. 'Those still alive will demand their king's execution.'

Rouwen fell silent, thinking hard. He had sworn to defend the people of Gan, not just the lords of the kingdom. He certainly did not want Sosler to gain by anything he did, but how did the duke plan to stop the wind warriors? Rouwen looked at the green-glowing Vutorian and shook his head. The key to that question lay with the wizard, not Diarra.

'I'll lead the troops,' Rouwen told Laslo. 'Take me to the fiercest fighting.'

'But, Majesty, you can't do that!' Laslo seemed genuinely shocked at the idea of Rouwen seeking the keystone to Castle Gan. 'No king rides with his men into battle. You must stay back where it is safe and lead us!'

Rouwen laughed harshly. His notions of leadership differed greatly from King Nishor's. He ignored his Lord Protector's advice and rode forward, winding through the final turns of the Demon's Throat and into Valley Gan. Rouwen's heart jumped to his throat as he saw the verdant green of the fertile, well-irrigated fields. Odors of growing crops made his nose flare and his eyes water slightly. And the sight of the mighty pillar supporting Castle Gan shone brightly in the sunlight, Mount Glid appearing off to one side. It might have turned twilight in the Demon's Throat because of high vertical red stone walls, but the sun graced the white castle with its full rays.

This was home.

'There are men and women being slaughtered,' Toit said, pointing by lifting its beak to indicate a particularly bloody skirmish. The Mionese troops seemed to have command of the field, but Rouwen saw the battlefield differently. The soldiers' officers had led them into a trap. The citizens of Gan might be taking casualties now but they would soon cut off the tiny pocket of troops and massacre them, giving two or three to one for the injury received.

'We will stop it soon enough,' Rouwen said, sounding more confident than he felt. He galloped forward, trailing Laslo and a dozen other soldiers acting as his personal guard. The lot of them did not equal a single Intrepid, but Rouwen knew such training took years. Attitude as well as skill went into being the finest.

As he rode forward, the fortunes of battle changed subtly. The Mionese soldiers began falling back from the ambush they fought into, and the Gannians slowed their attack as if to renew their energies.

'Parlay,' Rouwen called. 'Call for a truce!' His shouts were met with obvious relief by the Mionese officers. The four still commanding the field lifted their swords and daggers above their heads in a steel X to show their intent to parlay. The Gannians halted their fight, fell back and debated this sudden turn in their fortune. Somewhat reluctantly, they acknowledged the parlay, reinforcing Rouwen's contention that the Gannians ruled the field.

Rouwen motioned for Laslo alone to accompany him. But he was curiously happy that Toit decided to remain on his shoulder. Rouwen had come to rely on the *thouse* bird's steady view of the world and suspicions of others' intent.

'This is dangerous, Majesty,' Laslo said uneasily. 'They are not soldiers. What if they violate the truce? They kill our king with nothing risked on their part.'

'We will talk,' Rouwen insisted. 'Remain quiet, unless there is direct danger.'

'As you will, Majesty,' Laslo said with poorly concealed anxiety.

'Of course he will,' Toit said, revelling in the position of authority on Rouwen's shoulder. 'He is king, isn't he?'

Rouwen waited in a meadow for a half dozen Gannians to advance, as if they expected to be struck down by lightning. The grizzled man leading them squinted at Rouwen, then tensed when he recognized him.

'You,' the farmer spat. 'Traitor!'

'Rest easy, Danen,' Rouwen said softly. 'You were my brother's neighbor for many years. You watched over Adan and me as we grew up.'

'You betrayed King Priowe, and you now lead these . . . these . . .' Words failed the old farmer.

'I will not fight my neighbors, but I will not allow you to follow a false leader. Priowe has betrayed you,' Rouwen said firmly. 'The real fault lies not with Priowe but with the Lord Protector. Duke Sosler wants this army to slay many of you so he can depose

Priowe. Sosler has designs on the thrones of Gan *and* Mion. If your anger is to be directed against a traitor, seek out Duke Sosler!'

'You and Queen Diarra were driven from the kingdom in disgrace,' Danen said, still not convinced.

'We were – by Sosler. He lied to Priowe, and the king believed him. Know this, Danen, friend and neighbor for most of my life. I seek only to place a true ruler on the throne of Gan.'

'Who? Prince Sped?'

Rouwen had to laugh. Priowe's wastrel son was less fit to rule than Danen. 'I serve the Kingdom of Gan, and it is my belief that the fittest to rule is Princess Sorinne.'

'The Duke's wife?' Danen sucked in a breath and let it out slowly. 'That places Sosler next to the throne.'

'If he sits on the throne, it will be with a sword through his vile heart!' Rouwen calmed himself.

'What are you suggesting? I cannot control these poor people,' Danen said, indicating the fringes of the meadow. Here and there Rouwen saw the glint of sunlight off metal farm tools. A surge of pride raced through him. The people of Gan fought for their homes; he had seen little evidence that any in Mion would do likewise for their kingdom.

A solid core of honor remained in these people, in *his* people.

'I do not want the Mionese army gutted by your fighting. It is hard to ask you to trust my intentions. I seek only to remove Sosler.' Rouwen's hand went to the spell casket around his neck. He needed the one Duke Sosler still carried if he was ever to be free of the curse placed on him.

'You command those tornadoes?' Danen made a vague gesture toward Castle Gan. Rouwen saw that three wind warriors had begun the long march toward the base of the castle, sweeping troops ahead of their fierce winds.

'I do,' Rouwen said, 'but they will not be used against any citizen of Gan.'

'You would retreat if we decide that is in our best interest?' Danen made an outrageous demand and knew it. He pressed to see Rouwen's true intent.

'There will be no Mionese soldier left in Gan after Sosler is dead. What happens to Priowe will be up to the people of the kingdom.' Rouwen heard Toit muttering in his ear, telling him he lied. The price Diarra demanded for her control of the wind warriors lay in King Priowe's death.

'What if you cannot take the castle, even with your tornadoes?' Danen looked more inquiring than skeptical now. Rouwen knew he was winning over the farmer.

'Then there will be no Mionese soldier left because all will be dead. I promise you this. Give us unobstructed passage to the spiral road and not a single Gannian citizen will be harmed. We will not pillage, and any soldier caught doing so will be turned over to you immediately for any punishment you deem fair after trial. That is my promise.'

'You can never fight a war without causing suffering in the kingdom,' countered Danen.

'Sosler's death will aid Gan more than anything else.'

Danen conferred with several others, then stepped back. 'I knew your family, I knew you as you grew up. Our neighbors' farms failed in bad years, but the Rouwens worked hard to help however possible. I cannot believe the charges brought against you, Brion Rouwen.'

'Thank you for your confidence,' Rouwen said, knowing he had won free passage to the road leading upward to Castle Gan.

'We have seen Sosler's actions,' Danen said, turning angry with the Lord Protector of Gan, 'and how he withdrew troops intended to protect us. Go, Rouwen, but know this. We will watch carefully.'

'I know the power of Gan,' Rouwen said soberly. 'And know this. I will never be anything else but a citizen of Gan.'

Danen nodded briskly and herded the farmers away, busily discussing what had occurred. Rouwen waited until they had vanished into the distant groves of trees circling the meadow.

'Get the troops moving toward Castle Gan,' Rouwen ordered Laslo. 'No man steps off the road, no man harms a single Gannian citizen, regardless of the provocation. I will see half our soldiers dead before striking a blow at these people.'

'But, Majesty!' protested Laslo, seeing where his new king's real loyalty lay.

'And when we reach the base of the spire, we will begin our real fight,' Rouwen finished. 'Give the orders while I talk with Vutorian and Diarra.'

'As you will, Majesty,' Laslo said, opposed to the orders he received but determined to carry them out. He rode away, muttering to himself.

'He is a loyal follower, but is he a leader?' asked Toit.

'It won't matter,' said Rouwen. His eyes turned to the gleaming Castle Gan sitting high atop the rocky spire. Soon it would be different within the walls of that impregnable castle. The Legion of the Air would see to that.

Then real destruction would begin.

17

To the King's Chamber

'No guards,' mused Rouwen, staring at the empty broad road hewn in solid rock spiralling upward to Castle Gan. Such dereliction and abandonment would never have occurred had he still been Captain of the Intrepid Guard. Not even the Lord Protector should have given an enemy free passage up the side of the rocky spire. An army fighting every step of the way would reach the summit tired, dejected, and decimated.

Removing any threat in front of the gates of the castle would be a simple matter after such attrition, not one that would bring death and destruction to those within. But Sosler had chosen not to post a single sentry along the road to the castle. That worried Rouwen as he led the Mionese army upward.

'It's a trap,' complained Toit. 'Sosler is no fool. He knows the power of the wind demons. Why should he permit you to arrive with your army intact?'

'He must know that he has lost support among Gan's people, also. He should never have thought to use them as a buffer between us.' Rouwen rode slowly, eyeing the fortifications and traps set for the unwary. He pointed out a few of the more intricate devices to Laslo, who sent ahead a team of sappers to dismantle or destroy any snares.

'Perhaps Sosler is dead and Priowe has followed his wife into insanity,' suggested the *thouse* bird. Toit squawked loudly and flapped once, then settled down. The soldiers marching closely behind their king fell back, uneasily discussing their liege's new bodyguard. 'That would explain the lack of defense.'

'Not at all. Sosler is holding the troops in reserve. He must feel he cannot fight the wind warriors, so there is another battle to be fought – and it involves only me. When I am dead he has control of Gan's entire, rested army.'

'He might think to take control of this army, also, though why he would want it is a mystery known only to those on the other side of Paradise,' said Toit. He cast a hard look at soldiers sidling closer to overhear their king's conversation. The men fell back fearfully when he motioned them back.

'If I still controlled the Legion of the Air, it would be suicidal. I would have both armies trapped at the top of a summit. One or two tornadoes would resolve any conflict.' Rouwen knew this meant Sosler was confident of his ability to gain the horn and kill any opposition to his power. Or did the duke have a way of neutralizing the wind warriors?

Feeling the threads of power about him hum and sing, Rouwen touched the horn and considered summoning the Legion – and killing Diarra for the whistle. He couldn't use it, but there would be no need to. The wind warriors would destroy Castle Gan and all within it, including Sosler and King Priowe.

And Princess Sorinne.

He sighed. He could never doom her, nor would he wantonly slaughter so many soldiers with whom he had served. They were as much due his respect and concern as any of the farmers below him on the floor of Valley Gan. Rouwen did not lie to himself about the potential for death. Many would die who were undeserving of their trip to Paradise, but it was the only way to rid the kingdom of Duke Sosler.

Those needless deaths would be on Sosler's head, not Rouwen's when it came to judgment at the gates of Paradise.

His eyes lifted from the steep road to the crest of Mount Glid. All souls slipping from their bodies migrated to its precipitous slopes and from there to Paradise. At night, especially when both the Lesser Moon and the Greater Moon were visible, witchfires of dead souls danced along the slope before arrowing into the sky. Sosler's soul would join many others before Rouwen finished.

The road carried him around its spiral and Mount Glid vanished from sight, hidden by the bulk of the mountain supporting Castle Gan. Rouwen considered all the ways he might be betrayed by Vutorian and found none that didn't require Diarra's cooperation. The wizard might have gained power through the mere possession of the grimoire, but he was far from the spell-caster that the Lord of Death and Life had been.

'I must talk with Diarra. How far ahead is she?' he asked Toit.

The *thouse* made a rumbling sound deep in his throat. 'Half a turn, no more. The sappers hold her back as they work. She is furious with them. Can you not hear her protests?' Toit turned his head to one side, as if listening.

'Perhaps your ears and eyes are sharper than mine,' Rouwen said. He knew the *thouse* wanted to get into an argument, as much to break the boredom of the ride as for any other reason. Rouwen had too much to consider before standing before the gigantic steel gates of the castle and demanding that Sosler come forth.

'Of course they are. All your senses are dull because *you* are dull.'

If Toit expected argument, he was disappointed. Rouwen rode to the verge and peered far below. The army he led spiralled around the thick base at least twice. He was king to more than two thousand soldiers, but their skills were insignificant compared to the power he carried in the gold horn. He touched the cold metal and considered calling forth a few tornadoes to protect both the rear of the column and the head. Diarra would have to work double duty to manage them, but he cared less for her complaints than he did her obedience.

Vutorian must not control her until the castle gates were flung open. Rouwen had no illusions about his troops fighting the Intrepids and winning. If Sosler had pulled back Gan's entire army, the battle was even more one-sided, but stealth rather than brute force would win the day. Rouwen had learned subterfuge and, as much as he hated the notion, a dagger slipped into the back proved more effective than massive movements of unwilling, untrained armies.

'Diarra!' he called, seeing her astride her prancing chestnut mare. He trotted ahead and stopped abreast the former queen. Diarra's eyes burned with an intensity that warned Rouwen that she was on the edge of insanity once more. She had come too close to achieving her goal to lose, no matter the adversity.

'Why do we waste time like this?' Diarra pointed at the sappers working to remove a deadfall. 'We send ahead expendable forces. Let them trigger the traps. The remainder of the army can march on, on the backs of the valiant dead. They should be willing to die so that I may kill Priowe!'

The shrillness of her voice carried and caused more than one combat engineer to look up uneasily. If their king commanded they should be feed for the hungry traps they found, they would simply stop working.

'There is no need for such haste,' Rouwen told her, more to reassure the men than to quiet Diarra. 'We need to agree on how we enter the castle and what we do afterward.'

'We kill Priowe. You promised me the king's death.'

'Yes, of course, of course,' soothed Rouwen. 'But we should remain together. Only you can guide the wind warriors to the proper points, and only I can summon them.'

'A tornado forming around Priowe,' she said, rubbing her

hands together in anticipation of such a violent end. 'Yes, that amuses me. I want to watch him spun apart, turned into bloody stew and then spat out across his filthy kingdom.' Diarra's passion for this torture caused her to drool slightly.

'We need to stay together,' Rouwen said again, peering over the shoulder of the road and trying to find the green haze that betrayed Vutorian. One entire circuit down the side of the spire he saw the wizard, hunched over his book of spells and muttering constantly. At this distance Rouwen was unable to make out the wizard's words, but nothing was to be gained by eavesdropping. Vutorian might be practicing the spells contained in the grimoire or he might simply be looking forward to his victory.

Rouwen considered eliminating the wizard and taking back the grimoire. If he did this he would have to find another mage capable of reversing the curse placed on him – and that would be after he took the spell casket from Sosler. Rouwen tried to evaluate Vutorian's worth to him, knowing the wizard was in league with Sosler.

'He is dangerous, but useful,' he decided aloud.

'Kill him. Let me peck him. My poison will do him in before he can utter a single spell,' Toit claimed. 'Fin would be outraged at losing her mentor, but I can always tell her Vutorian died nobly. She wouldn't believe it, but she might not be too angry with me.'

'He is still more useful alive than dead,' Rouwen said. 'We need to make haste, though. Vutorian is only twenty minutes behind us, since we are so close to the summit.'

Castle Gan towered above, only two more twists in the road away. The sappers had done their finest work, and Rouwen knew they would be supremely challenged before they cleared the last of the traps from the roadway. Before they completed their work and the main body of the Mionese army moved into position in front of Castle Gan, Rouwen intended to be inside the walls actively hunting for Sosler.

'Diarra, we go now. You have convinced me that we ought to range ahead.'

'You know secret ways into the castle, don't you? Priowe never told me of those hidden gates, the tunnels, the ways of escaping. That proves he never trusted me. I'll cut his ears off first, then . . .' Diarra's voice faded as she worked out the various torments she would inflict on her husband.

'Into the castle? Just the three of us?' asked Toit. For the first time since Rouwen had known the *thouse*, there was a suggestion of apprehension in his voice.

354

'You can remain aloft, watching and reporting to Laslo,' offered Rouwen. In a way, he hoped Toit would accept such a post above the castle. The troops needed a steady source of reliable information. This might prevent many from dying under the rain of arrows shot from the battlements.

'Fin would pluck me like a chicken if I deserted you in your hour of need, though it might be better to be alive so she could pluck me,' the *thouse* argued. 'But she is a clever wizard and might find a way to make me suffer for eons.'

'When you finish debating with yourself, let me know. We are not far from where Diarra and I must advance on foot.' Rouwen saw that the sun was drifting behind the distant Shield Mountains circling Valley Gan. The gathering shadows provided the only cover he was likely to get as he advanced on the castle's foundations in search of hidden doorways. Rouwen hoped that Sosler had not turned these secret ways into deadly traps. He had escaped Castle Gan twice using his intimate knowledge of the architecture.

Rouwen dropped to the ground and handed the reins of his horse to a sapper, saying to him, 'Tell Lord Laslo that he is to bring the entire army in front of the gates, then demand immediate surrender.'

'But they will never do that!'

'Have Laslo give them one hour before the attack begins,' Rouwen said, knowing he would have succeeded or died by then. If dead, what Laslo did was of no concern to him. If he succeeded, there would not be a battle. He would control Castle Gan and sit on two thrones, Sosler's dream.

And his?

'Sorinne, you will be queen,' he said softly. 'Perhaps it will please you to marry King Brion!'

Rouwen motioned Diarra ahead and ignored Toit's snide remarks. He vowed to remain silent and not let his innermost thoughts slip from his lips again. The *thouse* managed to ridicule everything he said, with only an occasional constructive comment.

For twenty minutes, Rouwen and Diarra slipped from shadow to shadow, hunting for the spot on the mountainside that would give them entry to Castle Gan.

'Are we going to risk our lives falling off this accursed rock while you search in vain for a door Priowe must have closed?' Diarra sat heavily, dangling the golden whistle in her hand. Rouwen wished there was time to find out where she had got that whistle and what he could do to get it from her. After Sosler and Priowe were dead, Rouwen toyed with the notion of giving Sorinne the whistle. He could summon the Legion of the Air, if needed, and she could steer it against their enemies. Gan-Mion would become the most powerful kingdom on the continent, in the world!

Rouwen pushed that from his mind as his fingers pressed into hidden crevices seeking the small lever he remembered from his study of the castle's defenses. Just when he was about to admit defeat, he touched the cold metal bar.

'Here, here it is. Stand away. Sosler might be waiting for us.' Rouwen gripped the rod and pulled hard. On silent hinges, a section of the rock peeled back to expose a dark cavity. This tunnel led directly under the dungeons. Following hidden stairways he knew within the castle, Rouwen had complete confidence in finding Sosler and killing him. The duke would never even know his enemies were behind him!

'I see nothing within,' Toit said, nervous at the tightness of the tunnel. The *thouse* would be unable to fly until they reached the dungeons, and even then his ability to take wing would be limited by stone walls.

'This is your last chance. Come with me, or stay free and report troop movements on the castle walls to Laslo.'

'He makes my feathers molt. I could die of suffocation as they fall from my body! Why you promoted a sergeant to Lord Protector is one of the many things I have yet to understand about you, Brion. You have a compassionate streak in you. If you don't control it, it will be the death of you.'

'There, ahead,' Rouwen said, spotting two tiny pinpricks of light. He hurried forward to shove his eyes against one, aware of Diarra close behind, muttering to herself. Catching only an obscene word here and there, he knew the nearer she got to Priowe's death, the crazier she became. Rouwen worried that Duke Sosler might have cast some additional spell on the woman. He touched the spell casket dangling around his neck and realized the power he might have had, if Diarra had been sane. The promise of return to a normal life would have bent her will to his in all matters.

As it was, she felt little burden from the curse laid upon her. Diarra did not love – perhaps it was impossible for her now – and dwelt only in lands of hatred and despair.

'Hurry, we must not hesitate. He knows we come for him. I feel it in my bones.' Diarra tried to push past but Rouwen held her back.

'Take a look through the spy hole before rushing into the

dungeon. It should come as no surprise that Sosler keeps the dungeons filled these days.' He pulled back and rubbed his eyebrow, freeing it of the accumulated dust from the spy hole. The dungeon was crowded with prisoners, most hanging from chains as they awaited execution. Only a few guards patrolled the area, but they were more numerous than Rouwen cared to deal with at the moment. Any alarm and his plan to sneak up on Sosler would be forfeit.

'We can kill them all before they know it. You are good with that sword. I've seen you.' Spittle formed on Diarra's lips. She didn't wipe it away as she continued to peer into the lowest level of dungeon in Castle Gan.

'Take the ladder upward to the next level. Our chances for entering undetected might be better there.' Rouwen staggered as Toit flapped once and managed to shoot up the narrow shaft leading higher into the castle. As he climbed Rouwen studied the dust on the iron rungs driven into the hard stone. No one had been this way in long years. He took heart in this and counted on the secret passages being unguarded and free of traps.

'No one here,' Toit told him, gripping the edge of a loose stone to stare through another spy hole. 'Do we enter here? My feathers are getting dirty. It will take months of preening to restore their luster.'

'Wait,' cautioned Rouwen. He heard Diarra struggling up the ladder behind. He did not want to risk everything on a quick excursion into this part of the castle, yet he needed to leave this series of passages if he wanted to enter those leading to the upper levels – and the king's audience chamber and quarters.

'Why do we halt there?' Diarra pushed past him and thrust her eye against the peephole. 'No one. We go!'

Before Rouwen could stop her, Diarra pushed against the stone slab. It grated loudly as it swung out into the dungeon. Cursing, he followed her, hand resting on his sword. He heard Toit's protests but paid them no heed. It was as he had feared. The narrow field of vision through the peephole and Diarra's rush to enter had betrayed them. Three guards lounged on straw pallets on the far side of the chamber.

'Who's there?' called one guard, half-drunk. He lifted a jug, as if to offer some refreshment to his unknown guest.

'Is that some of the cook's finest brew?' asked Rouwen, walking quickly toward the three. 'I haven't tasted a drop of that potent liquor for . . .' His sword slid from its sheath and ended the life of the generous guardsman. Rouwen whipped around and tried to steal the second man's life but found himself tangled in dangling chains long enough to allow the guardsman to roll free.

This man wasn't drunk. His sword came from his sheath easily, and he fell into the stance Rouwen had drilled into his Intrepids. The man might not wear the uniform of the elite guard but he fought like an Intrepid. Rouwen wasted no time pressing an attack. The longer he lingered, the harder it would be to kill Sosler.

'No, not so easy,' the guard he fought chided, easily deflecting Rouwen's blade. 'You fight like a Mionese whore. Ah, I see you are wearing their uniform. How did you find your way into the castle?' The guardsman fought with economical thrusts and parries, talking only to keep Rouwen's mind occupied. There seemed no real curiosity as to how the foreign invaders had penetrated this far into Castle Gan.

'You fight well. It will be a shame to kill you.' Rouwen had not fought a decent swordsman in months. It took him a few parries to settle into his usual skillful style. As he began the sharp riposte and the quick-stepping toward a kill, the guardsman realized he fought no common foe.

'You are good, but can you give me a poem as you duel? No? Well, allow me. "I once saw, I do declare, a . . ."' The guardsman screamed and clutched his throat, then sank to the stone floor, dead. Toit had watched for a few seconds until the proper moment, then swooped down and ripped out the soldier's throat. Whether the rending of the flesh or the *thouse* poison stripped the Gannian of his soul, Rouwen could not say. In a way he felt cheated.

'I could have taken him,' he complained to the bird.

'You can fight the entire castle, for all I care,' Toit said, 'but you are neglecting another in our party.'

'Diarra!' Rouwen spun and looked around the silent dungeon. The third man lay on the straw pallets with his throat slit from ear to ear, Diarra's handiwork. But of the former queen there was no sign. 'Where did she go?'

'Up yon stairs, though where it leads is a mystery. I have never explored this miserable pile of cold stone. What you see in such a place is beyond me. I vastly prefer a nice nest tucked into the branches of a limberfrost tree and – Brion! Wait for me. Don't leave me!'

Rouwen hurried up the broad stone steps, hoping to overtake Diarra. He almost crashed into two guardsmen making their way down into the dungeons. He pushed one into the other, twisted around so they didn't have a good view of him or his uniform, and barked, 'Watch where you're going, Corporal.'

'Sir, sorry, I meant no . . .'

'Carry on with your duties, unless you care to walk off the battlements onto the Fingers of Providence. I have sent better men than you to their fate!'

'Sir, yes, sir!' The two men fell over themselves to continue down the stairs. They vanished around a curve in the stairs. Toit cawed and hopped along before launching himself to land heavily on Rouwen's shoulder.

'What are these Fingers of Providence?' Toit asked.

'They are spires of rock at the base of the castle. It takes twenty seconds for a man thrown from the battlements to impale himself on those knife-edged pillars.' Rouwen had passed the guardsmen, but they would return quickly when they found their companions dead below. He hurried up the stairs and stopped when he came to a dirty section of wall.

'More passageways?' inquired Toit. 'I fail to see why you simply don't grow wings and fly. I enjoy the sensation, and it keeps me out of such drafty cellars as this. And these staircases of yours! Tiny, so confining.' Toit gasped as the wall sank inward and Rouwen whirled about, crushing himself and the *thouse* into a tight cylinder.

'No talking,' Rouwen whispered. 'Anything you say will echo upward as if you are trapped in a chimney.'

Rouwen began climbing, using protruding stones as a crude ladder. He tried to remember where this upward shaft led but couldn't. He had studied the secret passages of Castle Gan but had never traversed all of them, seeing little need. Now he wished he had been more diligent, if only to better guard the king.

'Be careful,' squawked Toit. 'You are crushing me against the wall. The space isn't *that* narrow.'

'Quiet. I warned you that we might be overheard,' whispered Rouwen, his self-recriminations fading. He had done his job as Captain of the Intrepid Guard the best he could and had kept King Priowe from danger. If Priowe fell now it was because he had foolishly listened to Duke Sosler's beguiling advice.

Rouwen banged his head unexpectedly and almost fell back down the confining shaft. He gingerly reached up into darkness and touched a solid block of stone.

'What have you got us into, friend Brion?' The *thouse* bird's tone was thick with sarcasm. 'Perhaps we should wait for someone to light a fire at the bottom of this miserable chimney.'

'Quiet,' repeated Rouwen. 'This blockage isn't supposed to be here.' Feeling around in the dark, he found the edges of the stone barricade and knew that he would have to find some other way. He started back down, wondering what had happened. The secret passages were not supposed to have obstructions in them.

'Where are you going?' asked Toit. 'There is a small ledge to your right. And unless my eyes are mistaken, tiny peepholes.'

'What? No, that can't be. This is supposed to go directly into Priowe's chambers.' Rouwen stopped his descent and reached out carefully, finding the narrow ledge Toit's sharper eyes had found in the unlit shaft. Swinging over to the ledge, he twisted around and saw slivers of light shining from under two metal disks camouflaging the spy holes. He slid one back and peeked into the corridor.

'Oh,' Rouwen said softly. He gazed into Sorinne's bedchamber, the room where he and the princess had spent so many enjoyable nights. The hangings were gone and the furniture looked tawdry now that all decoration had been removed. He remembered how he had last come to this room to seek Sorinne's aid, only to find Sosler and his guards waiting to capture their escaped prisoner. Sorinne had been removed to unknown quarters and had never returned.

'She is married to Sosler, but it cannot be of her own volition. He forced her,' Rouwen said.

'I am going to bite your ears off if we do not get out of this hole,' Toit complained. 'I am going crazy. I need to be free, to fly, to soar! Imprison me one more second and I will not be responsible for my actions, pledge to Finola or not.'

'We can reach Priowe's quarters from here, unless the patrols are heavy or the king has taken new rooms.' Rouwen found the catch and pushed open the secret panel, worrying that he had never know of this way into the princess's suite. Anyone aware of this shaft might have watched as he and the lovely Sorinne were in bed together.

'Sosler,' Rouwen said, more to himself than Toit. The duke had known of Rouwen's dalliance with the princess. This might explain why. The duke had kept the woman under scrutiny, spying on her, indulging his voyeuristic tendencies. And he had learned more than the Captain of the Guard would have ever wanted revealed.

Rouwen quickly crossed the deserted room and opened the door to look into the sitting room. It was bare, also. Rouwen went to the outer door and chanced a look into the hallway. The corridor, always guarded when he had been in charge of castle security, was bare. Dust formed a thin film on the corridor floor, showing no one came this way any more.

'I hear chanting from the battlements,' Toit said. 'Laslo must have arrived, and the Gannians are taunting him.'

Rouwen touched the gold horn at his side. If Diarra hadn't vanished, he would have blown the horn to summon a wind warrior. That would keep the castle's defenders occupied and might even break the massive gates protecting those within. But Rouwen did not want to call forth the Legion of the Air. The battle between Mionese and Gannian forces was not to his liking, and without Diarra and the golden whistle, the wind warriors would be uncontrollable.

And the Legion would slowly seek him out with their magical homing sense. He had to work unencumbered, at least until Sosler had paid for his foul crimes.

'If Priowe is to be found anywhere, it is in the audience chamber,' Rouwen said. 'With the army battering away at the castle gates, he will have his Lord Protector at his side.'

His hand closed around the hilt of his sword. Blood pounded hard in his temples as he imagined the satisfaction to be gained by running his blade entirely through Sosler's body.

'Do you stand or do you lead the way to this mythical chamber? I grow weary of the wait,' said Toit.

'This way. Be wary of leaving footprints. Some sharp-eyed sentry might see our steps.' Rouwen pressed his back against the stone wall and edged along, disturbing only a bit of the dust in the corridor. He smiled ruefully when he heard Toit's scornful answer. He had started thinking of the bird as a human. The *thouse* flapped off and landed at the end of the corridor perched on a chair, waiting for him.

Rouwen hurried and silently pointed to stairs leading up. He and Toit worked their way through the castle until he came to a flight of stairs that would come out behind tapestries to the left of King Priowe's throne in the audience chamber. Even to Rouwen's less sensitive ears came the sounds of angry argument. He recognized Priowe's voice.

'Sosler *is* with him,' Rouwen said grimly. He drew his sword and took the steps two at a time. He slowed as he came to the head of the stairs, ready to kill the guards posted to protect the king.

Rouwen was too slow. Toit swooped and silenced one guard before the man knew there was any danger. With a dexterous twist, the *thouse* rolled over and clawed at a second guard, forcing him to drop to one knee. Rouwen lunged and spitted the guard through the throat.

'You took your time deciding what to do,' grumbled Toit, but the bird had already hopped back onto Rouwen's shoulder, content to follow the man's lead.

'How is this possible?' came Priowe's voice. 'You were never to return to Gan.'

'You scorned me, you turned me out, you banished me, but I have returned, dear husband. I have returned with an army to kill you!'

Rouwen recognized Diarra's mad voice. She had somehow reached Priowe before him.

He pushed aside the tapestries to join the former queen before she alerted Sosler and sent him running. Rouwen needed the spell casket from around the duke's neck. Without it, he could never be free of the curse that burdened him.

18

Victory – and Defeat

'Diarra, stop!' Rouwen called frantically. He quickly scanned the audience chamber for other guards, but the ones he and Toit had killed were inexplicably the only ones to be seen. Rouwen guessed that Diarra had left several dead along the way, exposing King Priowe to her insane wrath.

Spread before the throne were dozens of maps, some with small colored markers showing the placement of the Mionese army and others indicating strengths Rouwen knew nothing about. All this he took in at a single glance before he centered on Diarra. She advanced on Priowe with a dagger in her hand. The king sat on his throne, leaning forward looking slightly apprehensive but not frightened at the sudden appearance of the wife he must have thought long dead.

'Diarra,' Rouwen said rushing forward. 'He is not our enemy. It is Duke Sosler. He is the one we must kill.'

'You!' raged Diarra, spinning on him. Rouwen staggered as Toit took flight in the huge room and began circling high above, wings beating slowly. 'You promised to kill him. You failed. You coward!'

'I will kill him after we find Sosler. The duke is the only one who can release the spells binding us. Here,' Rouwen said, reaching into his tunic and pulling out the silver spell casket. 'It is *your* soul trapped within this magical device. I need the one Sosler carries – mine! Then we can deal with an unfaithful monarch.'

'Unfaithful?' asked Priowe, as if he spoke at an elegant state dinner. 'You and this cuckolding swine are the unfaithful ones.' For the first time real passion flowed through Priowe's veins. He rose but did not move from his throne. As he stood, Rouwen had the momentary impression of Priowe being yet another marker on his maps, as large as life but no more powerful than any of the tiny figures representing armies.

'Sosler is the source of our problems,' Rouwen said, moving quickly. He worried that the huge audience chamber might flood with soldiers at any instant. Why Priowe was virtually unguarded was a mystery unless all troops had been stationed along the battlements waiting for Laslo to attack. That hardly seemed likely when a dozen Intrepids could protect Priowe easily.

The only explanation for the lack of protection had to mean Sosler intended Priowe to die.

Rouwen studied the balcony running along the sides of the gallery, fearing crossbowmen might appear with their deadly weapons. All he heard were the echoes of words. For the first time, Rouwen heard how hollow those phrases were.

'We are all Sosler's pawns, King Priowe,' Rouwen insisted. 'He lied to you. There was never any tryst between your wife and me.' Rouwen swallowed hard. 'It is your daughter I love. For Sorinne alone I will die!'

'You are lying, and why not? You have nothing to lose,' Priowe said, returning to his neutral, spiritless tone. He sank back into his throne, as if held there by invisible chains. The king of the most powerful kingdom on the continent slumped like an old man.

'I have nothing to gain.' Rouwen leapt forward and grabbed Diarra's raised arm. She had reached the foot of the dais and was preparing to advance on Priowe and drive her weapon deep into his body. Diarra struggled, squealing incoherently. Rouwen fought to hold her prisoner while avoiding the sharp tip of her dagger.

Rouwen heaved and threw Diarra to the floor, then knelt on her. She kicked and tried to bite, but he had control of her arms and pinned her down. He looked up at Priowe as he had done so many times from this spot and saw only an empty man. Whatever will had been in the monarch was now drained.

'I have everything to lose,' Rouwen insisted. 'I have spent long weeks hating you, then making excuses for your treacherous decisions. Finally, I have come to pity you. What man is so easily manipulated who sits on the throne? You have lost the valor and determination that brought you the Kingdom of Gan. It is time for another to replace you. But first, I want Sosler's death for all he has done!'

'The duke is defending Castle Gan against your filthy Mionese allies,' Priowe said, again without fire in his words. 'Without him, the kingdom would have fallen.'

Rouwen shook his head sadly. He had no time to convince a man determined to ignore the facts. As shocking as Priowe's attitude was his own former admiration for the king. Weakness flowed from the throne now, a palpable river of coldness.

'Sosler,' Rouwen said, the bite of command in his voice. 'Where is he? I want the spell casket around his neck, then I want his life.'

'The duke is . . .' King Priowe stiffened and his face turned into a contorted mask of pain. He slipped sideways on the throne, then twisted and fell across his maps. A huge bloody spot spread rapidly on his back.

Rouwen pulled away from Diarra, letting the woman twist lithely, the dagger still in her hand. He stared at the dying king, wondering what had happened.

'Access behind the king's throne is a privilege you never knew, Captain Rouwen,' Sosler said, stepping out from behind the hangings at the side of the throne. The tall, hatchet-thin, sandy-haired duke held a bloody sword in his hand. 'I took the liberty of reworking Priowe's throne. A small slit, true, but one large enough for a sword to thrust through, when the proper moment arrived.' Sosler held the sword above his head and laughed.

'It's your turn to die, Sosler,' Rouwen said, advancing.

'No, it is *your* turn, Rouwen. After all, to all appearences, haven't you just killed King Priowe?' Sosler laughed again.

Rouwen stumbled when Diarra shoved him aside to get to Sosler. Screaming, she raced up the steps toward him, brandishing the knife and shouting, 'You robbed me of his life. Die for robbing me. Die!'

Diarra gasped and sagged to the floor when Sosler slashed downward with his sword, the tip cutting Diarra open from shoulder to belly. On her knees before the duke, she still tried to stumble forward to stab him. Sosler stepped back, gauged the distance with deadly intent, then lunged, his blade impaling her body.

Rouwen tried to sever Sosler's hand while the duke tried to pull his blade free of Diarra's body. His sword sang through the air but he was slightly out of position. Rouwen's blade glanced off Diarra's falling body and saved Sosler any injury. The duke danced away, sword ready to do battle.

'You are more resilient than I thought,' Sosler said, his icy blue eyes on Rouwen. 'It is incredible how you found your way into the castle and stabbed King Priowe in the back. How vile!' Sosler laughed harshly but parried easily when Rouwen launched a long, slow thrust in his direction. Sosler whirled his heavy fur-rimmed cape around and momentarily tangled Rouwen's sword.

'The spell casket,' Rouwen grated out between clenched teeth. He fought harder and harder against Sosler, wondering how the duke had improved his fencing skill. Or was he himself slowing? He had not practiced since leaving Castle Gan. 'I want it.'

'And who will remove the curse I ordered Kwuway to place upon your head?' Sosler began to enjoy the fight, seeing that his skill and reactions outdid Rouwen's. 'Surely not Vutorian. He is in my employ. Since Kwuway was murdered, and I know you had a hand in that death, I have required a wizard of consummate skill.' Sosler beat against Rouwen's blade, then lunged. The point slid down Rouwen's arm, opening a bloody gash.

Rouwen recoiled and almost had his leg cut from under him as Sosler whirled his sword about in a slashing attack. Stumbling, trying to fight defensively until he could recover his composure, Rouwen retreated to the center of the audience chamber. From this vantage he saw Priowe's body slumped over one arm of the throne and Diarra's body face down on the dais beside it. He didn't remember how it happened but the markers on Priowe's maps had been scattered, better representing the true defense of Castle Gan than anything the king had symbolized on the diagrams.

'An easy fight. I hadn't realized how poorly prepared you were to meet me in combat, Captain,' said Sosler, swinging into the attack again. He beat Rouwen back. Rouwen felt his muscles weakening and he considered using the horn dangling at his waist to summon the Legion of the Air. This would be suicidal, but it would take Sosler and his foul plans of conquest with them.

Sosler gave Rouwen no respite. The duke's wrist was strong and he kept him on the defensive, weakening him, driving him back. Rouwen tried to circle and slipped in a patch of his own blood. He fell heavily and saw death shine on the blade.

Sosler laughed in delight and put the power of his shoulders behind the downward strike. But the laugh turned to a howl of outrage when the blade deflected off a hurtling brown body.

'Toit!' cried Rouwen, seeing Sosler's sword glance away from the *thouse* bird's body. The bird flopped to the floor, struggling to get upright and launch again. One wing had been broken, but Toit's vile curses distracted Sosler for an instant.

The duke turned to finish off the *thouse* and gave Rouwen the chance to kick out, his legs tangling in the duke's. Sosler grunted and toppled backward, crashing hard onto the polished floor. His sword flew from his grip, spinning across the floor. Sosler wrenched about and scrambled to retrieve his weapon, giving Rouwen a few seconds to gather his wits.

'Toit,' he said, his heart going out to the bird. 'Are you all right?'

366

'My wing is broken,' squawked Toit. 'Help me.'

'Here,' Rouwen said, holding out his arm for Toit to walk up. But Rouwen jerked away as Toit, at his touch, tensed and fell back, his feathers smoldering. Toit tried to speak, but the curse laid by Kwuway had taken another life. Rouwen had inadvertently loved the bird, and his touch had killed the *thouse* as surely as it had his brother and the old thief, Nibbles. Toit's body shivered and began to boil away, until only a slight avian skeleton remained. And then the glow from the curse set in, reducing the gray bones to a molten pool.

Rouwen whirled around, wild-eyed. He screamed and launched himself clumsily at Sosler, who had retrieved his sword and was returning to finish the fight.

Sosler easily parried Rouwen's reckless attack but could not follow through with a killing stroke. Rouwen turned and started back for Sosler.

'The curse,' Rouwen panted. 'Toit died because of the curse. And my brother and my friend.'

'The curse?' taunted Sosler. 'You mentioned it earlier. Can this be what you seek, you poor fool?' Sosler pulled the spell casket from his thick doublet, dangling it on a silver chain so that it caught the light and mocked Rouwen all the more.

'I'll kill you. I don't care about the curse. I'll kill you!' Rouwen fought with crazed fury, his skill replaced by brute strength and utter hatred. Sosler fell back, hardly able to keep Rouwen at bay.

'Is my death all you really care about, Captain? I think not. There is more to you than mere revenge.' Sosler parried and kicked Rouwen's foot from under him. He tried to spit Rouwen but missed by a fraction, only opening a thin scratch on Rouwen's belly.

Sosler stepped away and waited for the next out-of-control attack. But it didn't come. The thrill of pain from the light scratch brought Rouwen back to his senses. If he wanted to kill Sosler, it had to be through skill. He began duelling, his every stroke economical and deadly. Sosler immediately saw that any advantage he might have had was evaporating as Rouwen fell into the deadly style that he had learned so well as Captain of the Intrepid Guard.

'A trade, Captain,' Sosler panted out, tiring. 'The spell casket for that horn. I will let you leave Castle Gan under a truce, and you can remove the curse.'

'I'll never let you have the horn,' Rouwen said, knowing that such power in Sosler's hand would turn him into a worldwide conqueror. Mion and Gan would be stepping stones to every other kingdom on the continent – in the world!

'Can we not trade? Your life, your love' – Sosler shook the spell casket to capture Rouwen's attention – 'for the Legion of the Air?'

Rouwen tried a low-line attack and opened a cut on Sosler's calf, severing both heavy boot and flesh beneath it. When the duke's boot filled with blood, he would find fencing more difficult. Rouwen would kill him the instant his foe began to weaken.

Sosler realized his dilemma even as Rouwen renewed his attack. Sosler yelled, 'Vutorian, to me!'

Rouwen glanced over his shoulder and saw the wizard, cloaked in his magical green nimbus, step out from behind Priowe's throne. The wizard's hand rested on Sorinne's shoulder. She appeared drugged or under Vutorian's spell.

'Sorinne!' Rouwen found himself torn between killing Sosler and risking his love's life. He had already inadvertently killed Toit.

'Bring her closer, let her touch him,' urged Sosler.

'Brion, is that you?' Sorinne walked as if in a daze. Her slender hand reached out in his direction as she started for him.

'Stay back, Sorinne. Don't get too close.'

'You will kill her, Rouwen, unless you give me the horn. The spell casket for the horn. What will it be?' Sosler again tormented him with the choice, this time with Sorinne's life added to the deadly mixture. To keep the pressure on Rouwen, Sosler attacked, slashing and hacking.

'Sorinne, stay back, don't come any closer.' Rouwen circled to put Sosler between him and the woman he loved.

'What's wrong, Rouwen? Don't you want to feel her touch again? She might be my wife but she still talks of you and your *love*.' Sosler laughed and Rouwen knew he was destined to failure, to bring death to those he loved most, unless he did something quickly.

Rouwen dived past Sosler, cutting at the man's legs again. He opened a new cut on the duke's thigh, but it was hardly noticeable. The real tactic lay in coming up beside Diarra's body. Rouwen rolled the woman over and frantically sought out the golden whistle she used to control the Legion of the Air.

'Do you seek this, dear Brion?' asked Vutorian. The wizard held the whistle. He had already stolen it.

Rouwen grunted as he lashed out hard to divert Sosler's sword from a killing stroke. Rather than relying on his fencing skills, he charged, his arms circling Sosler's body in a bear hug. The men struggled and went down in a heap.

Rouwen tried to wrestle with Duke Sosler and at the same time keep the ensorcelled Sorinne at a distance. Those he had loved and killed had all been by contact, but Rouwen worried that his love for Sorinne was so great mere proximity might slay her. And she kept walking toward him, as if she stumbled through a dream.

Rouwen's fingers closed on the slender silver chain wrapped round Sosler's hand. Yanking hard, the chain separated and he clutched the spell casket.

'Mine!' Rouwen cried, rolling away and coming to his feet. But his hand shot to his left hip. As he had struggled to prise the spell casket free of Sosler's grip, the duke had cut the silk cord holding the gold horn to his belt.

Brion Rouwen had his soul back and the chance to remove the curse on him, but Duke Sosler controlled the horn summoning the Legion of the Air. And Vutorian held the whistle in one hand and the radiant grimoire in the other.

For a moment, Rouwen stood still. Then Sosler and Vutorian laughed in triumph. They had won.

'Go to him, dear Sorinne. Go to your lover and embrace him!' Sosler pushed Sorinne in his direction. Rouwen saw no recourse open to him but to turn and flee.

'Sorinne, know this. I love you dearly. I do!' Then he bolted from the room and into the arms of a curious sentry coming to discover the cause of the uproar in the king's audience chamber. Rouwen kicked out and caught the guard's heel, taking his leg from under him. The guard hit his head on the floor and lay stunned. But down the corridor came a half dozen more soldiers.

Rouwen ran in the opposite direction, determined to find a secret passage. Only in that way could he escape. He turned down a branching hall and then another and another. From behind came the shouts of guardsmen hunting for him.

'There, *there*,' gasped Rouwen aloud, finding a sconce and twisting it to the left. Stone grated and a secret panel slid open just enough for Rouwen to squeeze through. He immediately pushed the panel shut and pressed his ear against it. Feet pounded in the corridor, and men cursed at having lost him.

Rouwen leaned forward, his sweaty forehead cool against the stone. He had the spell casket, but at what price? Rouwen had to find a wizard to remove the curse, and he wasn't likely to find one within Castle Gan. Vutorian had the grimoire, the whistle and power rivalling Sosler's.

'Sorinne, dear Sorinne,' he muttered, then turned to find a way from Castle Gan before Sosler mounted a systematic search for him. Brion Rouwen had a gigantic task ahead of him, and he had to start immediately.

Book Three

THE FLAME SPECTER

For Howard Morhaim.
#85 and still going. Thanks!

1

Death, More Death – and Defeat

Rouwen found a dusty ladder leading to a lower level and pressed his eye to a small peephole. He chewed his lower lip at the sight of dozens of soldiers patrolling the hall. When an officer approached the wall and began fumbling at the secret catch, Rouwen knew his hiding place was in jeopardy. He darted back to the ladder and considered escaping to lower levels. From the dull thudding of boot soles along the heavy stone corridors of Castle Gan he heard echoing from below, and knew the entire guard had been alerted and were searching for him. Escape was becoming more of a phantom.

Rouwen climbed back to the level of the king's chamber, mind racing. A small wedge of light shone past a secret panel; soldiers were entering the passages. From his tracks in the dust, Rouwen knew they would have little trouble following him.

'Attack, don't retreat,' he muttered. The need for Sosler's death burned brighter than ever. He swung around on the rusty rungs of the ladder embedded in the castle's stone and climbed to a higher level as soldiers burst into the passage. Rouwen, fortified with new resolve, squeezed through the ever-narrowing chimney and finally found a small stone ledge. He swung about and sat on it. Through a peephole he saw a tapestry-hung corridor.

Empty.

He tried to remember the exact layout and believed this passageway led to the mezzanine above the king's audience chamber. From that vantage Rouwen knew he could drop near the throne and finish his deadly mission by slaying Sosler. The mezzanine was seldom used by any but guards of the Intrepid company trusted with protecting their monarch.

King Priowe was dead. But Sosler had yet to install himself on the throne, even if he had married Sorinne. There would be no reason for guards to patrol these ways now. Or so Rouwen hoped. He squeezed through a small opening and dropped onto the walkway. Crouching for a moment, he prepared for what must be done. He drew the dagger at his belt and tucked the spell casket inside his tunic where it would be safe.

Rouwen moved quickly along the narrow walkway and pushed past a tapestry, gaining a good view of the audience chamber. His heart sank when he saw the room was empty save for the bodies of Priowe, Diarra and poor Toit. Where would Sosler have gone? The perfidious duke and his wizard might be gloating. The duke's chambers? Rouwen wasn't sure where Sosler thought it safe enough to sleep.

He started to retrace his steps when Sorinne's voice echoed in the chamber. Rouwen sank down, peering over the low wood railing. His heart skipped a beat when he saw her blonde beauty enter the room below him.

'I don't remember anything. What has happened?' she demanded of Sosler. The duke walked at her elbow, gently guiding her away from the bodies of her mother and father.

'The grippe, my dear,' Sosler said in an unctuous voice. 'You were taken ill. Luckily, Vutorian countered the sickness with a few magical waves of his hand.'

'Why does he glow green?' Sorinne asked, a touch of irritability entering her voice. 'There is something happening and you are not telling me everything.'

'My dearest wife, you know all you need. Now run along,' Sosler said, pushing her toward a side door. She had not seen her parents' corpses. Rouwen almost yelled to draw her attention but held back. He would only put her life in jeopardy, much as he wanted to reveal to her Sosler's true character. The duke must have used powerful magicks to so befuddle the woman's usually clear mind.

'Has she gone?' came Vutorian's querulous tones. Rouwen straightened and peered directly below to see the wizard striding into the audience chamber from a side door. From the set of his body, Rouwen knew things were not proceeding well for Vutorian – and that pleased him greatly. Confusion and death to his enemies!

'She is so troublesome,' Vutorian went on. 'Why you insist on keeping her alive is beyond me.'

Sosler sneered as he replied. 'She gives me much pleasure in bed, something about which you know nothing.'

Rouwen seethed. His hand tightened on the dagger's hilt. He longed to drive the weapon deep into Sosler's putrid flesh – and the chance presented itself.

Vutorian turned and walked off, drawing Sosler to a spot in the middle of the audience chamber. Rouwen never hesitated. He got his feet under him, gauged distances and launched into the air. His dagger point cutting through the air ahead of his body, he drove directly for the duke's body.

Rouwen cried out in joy when he felt the dagger sink deeply into Sosler's torso. And then he flashed past to land hard on the marble floor. The impact dazed him for a moment. He shook off the shock and whirled around to finish the killing.

Sosler stood before him, hand on the dagger's hilt. A pained expression crossed Sosler's hatchet-thin, pale face, but the cold blue eyes bored hard into Rouwen's. The duke pulled the razor-sharp blade from his side and cast it away, as if it meant nothing. It clanked on the stone floor with an ominous sound, the peal of death and failure.

'That was your last chance at murdering me, Rouwen,' the duke said in a firm voice.

Brion Rouwen looked past Sosler and saw a dozen guardsmen crowding into the chamber. And from behind he heard Vutorian ordering more troopers to the duke's aid. He was surrounded. And defeated.

2

Strange Fire

Brion Rouwen knew he had only a heartbeat moment to strangle Duke Sosler. He launched himself, trying to find the man's throat. He slipped on the slick floor then felt swords pricking at his body. Flat on his belly, he looked up at his nemesis.

'You are persistent, if not too bright,' Sosler said, stepping toward Rouwen now that the guards had him pinned to the floor. He clutched the spot where Rouwen had stabbed him, a small red splotch expanding, but Rouwen saw that his blade had been robbed of death by hidden chain mail. 'I do admit, though, that I misjudged you. Your persistence far outstripped my expectations.'

'Is that all I was? A diversion?'

'Oh, yes. I needed to manipulate Priowe until I gained support within the castle, in the courts of Mion and . . .' Sosler bit off his explanation. Rouwen's eyes widened. Sosler's ambitions reached farther than he had thought. King Nishor of Mion was a pawn; he had known that. But what other realms turned to Sosler's will?

'You could have just ordered my execution,' Rouwen said, more to himself than to Sosler.

'I could, but Priowe needed a visible enemy. You and his unlamented queen provided a grand opportunity. She was quite crazy, you realize. She might have had the vision, as many claimed, but her nude wanderings of the castle made even a loving husband believe the worst.' Sosler laughed harshly and circled Rouwen. He took a sword from a guardsman and used it to prod his captive.

'You ought to have died. I needed my wizards to practice their crafts, hone their skills and find just the right incantations for my military conquests. Who would have thought you could have reached the Isle of Passing and retrieved this marvelous horn from a wizard as powerful as the Lord of Death and Life?'

'He had his weakness. He was afraid to die,' Rouwen said. 'That kept him on the isle – and cowering.'

'Ah, yes, immortality. You tasted it. Perhaps I should have Vutorian practice on you and grant you immortality once more?'

'No!' The word ripped from Rouwen's throat. Along with the curse of death to his most beloved, Sosler's wizard had prevented him from dying. Rouwen had suffered maiming cuts that would have killed him half a dozen times over. He touched the long scars on his belly where swords had run him through. Almost as if magically activated, the spot in the center of his back where a dagger had lodged began to itch unbearably. Never dying, killing those he loved, shunned in his kingdom, Brion Rouwen had become a pathetic figure.

But the spark of hope had never died. Whether it was need for revenge or the insane belief that he might triumph, Rouwen didn't know. But faith burned like a banked fire in his breast.

'So there is life yet within you,' Sosler said, pleased. 'I enjoy thinking up novel tortures. The combination of seemingly propitious spells to give utter pain amuses me. Eternal life and the inability ever to love – that was a master stroke, if I do say so. What other curses might be placed on your head? What would vex you most of all? Something concerning Sorinne, of course, but my use of her is not at an end until I am secure on Gan's throne.'

Rouwen had slain Sosler's wizard, Kwuway, and been released from the scourge of eternal life – what the Lord had sought and lost. And the spell casket gave him hope that the second curse might be lifted, too. That dream had died when he failed to kill Sosler and again fell prisoner. Rouwen began to believe he might be better off dead, freeing Sorinne of death at his hand.

Sosler's words about sitting on the throne brought him back to his senses. Sorinne would never be safe until the duke was worm food.

'She is nothing to you? You married her only to secure the throne?' Rouwen spoke now to keep Sosler from killing him outright. The longer he lived, the better the chance for escape. A sword cut sharply into his side, forcing him flat to the floor. Rouwen raged at his impotence. He had been so close. To have failed at the last instant . . . There seemed no chance for escape from the guards he had trained himself.

'Nothing at all,' Sosler said in an affected, offhand manner, as if other matters were vastly more important. The duke waited for a moment to be sure Rouwen seethed at his words, then added, 'Oh, that's not quite true, my dear, amorous Captain. What I said to Vutorian earlier is true. She is quite good in bed. Did you teach her those things, or did she practice with

379

others? I suspect she had much practice before you arrived at her bed.'

Rouwen refused to be goaded to anger. Sosler sought only to annoy him. That the slender noble did only made Rouwen mad at himself. He remembered the tortures he had endured in the dungeon after he had been arrested for consorting with the queen. Sosler had arranged a fake escape simply to give him hope and then dash it. There had been faint whispers Rouwen had thought came from Sorinne, urging him to be strong. Those came from the throat of some unknown minion of Sosler's.

Or perhaps the long-nosed Mionese Duke Drioway had been responsible for that particular torment. Under the guise of an informant, he had betrayed Rouwen more than once, the last time luring him into Sosler's well-baited trap. There were so many whose lives were forfeit, if Brion Rouwen only had the chance.

His hands clenched and unclenched in futile rage. Rouwen looked up and saw the ring of soldiers step back a half-pace, waiting for his attack. He read nothing but determination and death in their expressions. With them he had no quarrel. They obeyed orders, even if they followed the wrong lord.

'Where the lovely Sorinne learned her tricks matters little, my dear Captain. I am in control of Gan now that Priowe and Diarra are dead, thanks to you. And King Nishor is now no barrier to ruling Mion, also thanks to you. The use of the Legion of the Air was a tactical masterpiece.'

'We destroyed Mion. What is left will be of little use to you,' Rouwen said, taking some small satisfaction in that. He, Diarra and Vutorian had loosed the wind warriors on Nishor's walled city. Tachre had been left in ruins.

'What are the lives of a few peasants to me?' asked Sosler. 'And Tachre? Mion's capital would have been plowed under to rid it of disease and infestation. I intend establishing a capital farther along the coast, one of enduring grandeur with a deep-water harbor. Lopin, perhaps. Do you not agree, Vutorian? After all, that is near your precious Forest of Kelnos.' Sosler's gaze turned to Vutorian's green-glowing figure.

'When I left the forest to join forces with you, King Sosler, I abandoned all interest in that petty kingdom.' Vutorian spun about, sending a new robe whirling away from his frame, preening like a peacock in summer feathers. He seemed to revel in the new-found treasure, though Rouwen had seen riches aplenty in the wizard's castle. Like Sosler, the wizard played his own game. The grimoire that produced the green glow surrounding Vutorian like a nimbus figured prominently in that plan, though what it might be, Rouwen could not say.

'I now have the most powerful wizard in the world as my dearest friend and ally.' Sosler went to the wizard and slapped him on the back in a gesture of camaraderie. Sosler's pale eyes widened slightly as his hand brushed the fringes of the shimmering curtain of magic. Recoiling, he pressed his stung hand against his tunic. He covered his momentary lapse with an insincere smile.

Vutorian laughed, and Rouwen wondered if the wizard was foolish enough to believe such a blatant lie. Vutorian had the Lord of Death and Life's grimoire and the whistle needed to control the Legion of the Air. Only for those reasons did Sosler court his friendship. Rouwen wished he knew what spells were contained in that grimoire. He had carried it and felt its magical response many times, but he had used the spell book in trade to Vutorian for what he now knew was even more treachery. Vutorian had always been in league with Sosler, from the first moment Rouwen had stumbled across Vutorian's pupil in the forest.

Rouwen's cynicism rose in a tide of choking bile. Was the young girl, Finola, also Sosler's pawn? He had liked her when they had first met. She was earnest and sincere for one so young – and she had sent Toit to him as a guide and guardian. Rouwen's eyes slid along the floor to the pile of burned feathers that had been the *thouse* bird. His love had killed a valued comrade, even if Toit had not been human.

'How do you intend to dispose of him?' Vutorian pointed at Rouwen, as if he were nothing more than a horse's droppings.

'His death serves no purpose, even if a public execution of a traitor to the kingdom would be an object lesson for the grumblers. He has been my experimental animal before. Why should dear Captain Rouwen cease to give me great pleasure?' Sosler motioned to the guards, who moved quickly to bind Rouwen's hands behind his back.

Rouwen winced as the thin leather strips cut into his wrists and caused tiny trickles of blood to flow. If the leather bands stayed on too long, the blood would begin to dry, making them shrink. The agony would be intensified tenfold. But Rouwen doubted he would live long enough to enjoy such a commonplace torture.

'There, in the center of the room.' Sosler walked briskly to the throne and mounted, seating himself heavily. A moment's pain crossed his face, the only sign that Rouwen's dagger thrust had almost taken the duke's foul life. 'Now get away from him.'

Sosler drew forth the gold trumpet and put it to his lips. He paused long enough to savour Rouwen's expression of horror and distaste. The duke laughed gleefully.

'This is the sort of life I intend living. Never again under the thumb of a petty, stupid tyrant like Priowe!'

Sosler pushed the horn to his lips and let forth a single long, clear note that would summon an air elemental.

Rouwen struggled to get his feet under him. Sosler summoned the tornado to where he crouched. He might escape if the wind demon whirled off-center enough to force back the soldiers. He blinked when he saw the misty whirlwind beginning to form, but something appeared different – wrong.

Rouwen had summoned too many of the twisting minions of death not to recognize their usual patterns of birthing. Deep within the core of this misty whirlwind he saw sparks. The flecks of curious dark flame danced and grew brighter. Worrying that Sosler's royal blood had allowed him to summon a vortex of wind and flame, Rouwen fought to slide away from the newborn tornado.

'Keep him in the center. Feed him to that monster,' ordered Sosler, relishing the fear on Rouwen's face. 'And Vutorian, bring over the whistle. I need to control the wind warrior. There's no reason to let it rage aimlessly when I can direct it wherever I desire.'

Rouwen saw Vutorian's hesitation. The wizard had stolen the gold whistle from Diarra. The queen had been able to shepherd the wind warriors because of her royal blood. Vutorian lacked even a drop, if Rouwen was any judge. That meant the whistle was worthless to him, save as a bargaining tool. Sosler sought to prise this loose while surrounded by soldiers loyal to him. What possible reason could Vutorian have to deny the duke the means of controlling and banishing the Legion of the Air?

The wizard reluctantly handed over the whistle, even as he clutched the grimoire tighter to his body with his left hand. The hue of green around the wizard deepened and took on alien shapes, hands reaching forth and mouths gaping and eyes burning with manic intensity. Rouwen found it impossible to look away from Vutorian and the green, dancing cloud surrounding him, in spite of the wind warrior bobbing and ducking a few paces away.

'Good, very good,' crowed Sosler. He put the whistle to his lips and blew a few tentative notes. The tornado kept growing and did not obey his commands. Sosler frowned and blew harder, intent on sounding the right number of notes.

The wind warrior grew stronger and paid the duke no heed.

382

Rouwen looked from the green-shrouded mage to the tornado and felt suddenly weak. This was no powerful windstorm billowing up inside Castle Gan. It was something more, something more horrible than mere air.

Fire lapped and licked at the marble, turning the hard stone liquid. Molten trails sluggishly flowed downward into a pit being dug in the audience chamber and churned and bubbled like a caldron. As Rouwen watched, the rotary motion strengthened and the tornado's core turned into eye-searing fire.

'See!' cried Sosler, standing in front of the throne. 'See the power at my command. None will dare oppose me now.' He put the whistle to his lips and sent forth shrill notes ordering the wind warrior toward Rouwen. But the column of fire and air did not budge. It weaved and circled in place, intent on consuming the marble floor – and growing in size.

'Sosler, something's wrong!' shouted Vutorian, backing from the tornado. 'This isn't the kind of wind warrior Rouwen summoned. It's different. There are black flames within, as well as bright ones. Send it back to oblivion!'

Rouwen kicked and struggled to get away from the tornadic force building up between him and Sosler. Vutorian was correct in saying that this wasn't the magical guardian he had brought forth. The lightning searing from side to side within the column of misty air was quickly hidden by fire so intense the heat caused Rouwen's face to blister. He turned away from it but could not escape the mounting inferno.

'How do you get rid of it?' Sosler asked, still not frightened by his creation. The duke seemed more curious than anything else as the tornado whipped about in rising frenzy. He blew on the whistle and nothing happened.

Vutorian screamed in pain, dropping to his knees and clutching his chest. The grimoire burned with a dazzling green light equalling the fire within the wind warrior. It consumed Vutorian, ate at his flesh, turned him into a skeleton by melting away his body. The wizard's shrieks of agony were quickly drowned out by the thunderous roar of the demonic *thing* Sosler had summoned.

The duke appeared not to realize the full horror of what he had brought into the world. He had not seen tornadoes mild in comparison that Rouwen had sent against Tachre to destroy the Mionese capital. Sosler might have believed this wind warrior was a magical norm. Rouwen shied back even more, his flesh blistering more severely.

In spite of himself, Brion Rouwen could not look away from the core of the whirling column. The flecks of fire had become a raging inferno – and within that white-hot blaze he saw – eyes.

You are the one.

Rouwen had no idea where the voice came from. It welled from deep within his brain and soul. But those eyes! They were merciless and glared at him with a hunger that frightened a man who had fought wizards and courageously faced magical beasts of inhuman ability. For the first time in his life, Rouwen knew true fear.

'Tell me what to do, Vutorian. Get rid of it.' Sosler's voice carried the sharp edge of command, but the wizard wasn't listening. A huddle of glowing bones beside the throne was all that remained of the mage. Or so Rouwen thought until the skeleton stirred and rose.

Vutorian's eyes had become those of the fire fiend. Although no flesh clung to the wizard's bones, the hand rising to point a bony finger in the direction of the tornadic column had a solidity to it far exceeding anything made of bone. Tongues of fire jumped from the column and blasted into Vutorian's outstretched finger, causing the wizard to shine brighter than the sun itself.

Sosler's mouth worked but no words came forth. He backed from his ally, realizing the wizard had become something more than a dupe. The duke held out the pitiful whistle, as if this might appease Vutorian. The wizard turned slowly, sending pinwheels of fire about the huge audience chamber. Everything touched by the fire melted or simply burst into a million pieces. Rouwen thought he might escape in the confusion, but he found himself the focus of Vutorian's unwanted attention.

'Stop,' the wizard said. The command boomed in Rouwen's ears, deafening him for a moment. He fell to one side, his bound hands throbbing painfully. Thinking to blot out the world by squeezing his eyelids tightly closed, Rouwen found this tactic did not work. He still saw Vutorian perfectly so brightly did the man burn.

The pillar of wind and fire rose higher until it burned through the stained glass dome of the audience chamber. Rouwen wondered if it might reach all the way to the Lesser Moon. From the way the base thickened and energy poured into the surging pillar, it might reach the Greater Moon and never slow. Rouwen imagined the fire devouring the sun and stars, the entire universe and still remain hideously, inhumanly hungry.

'Vutorian, banish it,' Sosler said, his voice quavering as he began to fear that the man who had once been his ally might now be his master. 'Use the whistle. This thing is destroying the castle.'

Rouwen shielded his eyes as he watched Vutorian take the whistle, but the wizard did not put it to his mouth. He opened his arms and held the whistle out, as if offering it to the wind warrior. A tiny golden mist formed around the whistle, and then it vanished utterly.

'You fool!' shouted Sosler. 'You lost the only way we have of controlling this monster.' He stepped away as if to run and stumbled against the throne he had plotted to ascend. Sosler reached around and lifted the magical trumpet. The instant he touched it, a change occurred within the column of fiercely burning flame. It shifted slightly and moved toward him.

'What's happening, Vutorian? Tell me. If this is a joke, I am not amused.' Sosler's voice was shrill with fear. He tried to lift the trumpet, perhaps thinking to summon a second wind warrior to do battle with this wayward one.

Rouwen was blown across the room when a tongue of fire blasted from the column and engulfed Sosler's hand. The trumpet for summoning the Legion of the Air puffed out of existence in a golden mist. The duke was wrenched off the throne and tossed aside. He landed hard on the floor and skidded, scrambling to regain his balance. As if ricocheting, the lightning bolt of pure energy shot toward the green-glowing Vutorian.

The wizard staggered as the fiery bolt reflected from the grimoire he held in his hand. Rouwen shrieked as the rebound of energy smashed into his chest. The brilliance dazzled him, even as the pain in his torso exploded with the force of a thousand battering rams. By the time Rouwen's eyesight returned and the duke found his balance, the spinning pillar of flame had disappeared. A few vagrant breezes blew through the audience chamber, but the only evidence of the fire demon's presence lay in the melted flooring, small black flames still licking at the edges of the pit. After a few seconds, even the curious black fire vanished.

Rouwen blinked and tried awkwardly to wipe his eyes against his shoulder. Sosler seemed stunned – but it was Vutorian who startled Rouwen most. The wizard stood stock-still and completely whole. There was no sign that the flesh had burned from his frame. And the green haze had dissipated until only tiny clouds hung about his knees and feet.

When Sosler saw that Vutorian was not going to respond to his question, he spun and angrily shouted for his guards. 'Take that one to the dungeons. Execute him!'

All hope fled Rouwen when the guards seized him and dragged him from the room. He did not understand what had happened, nor did it matter now. He would be worm food before the sun rose again.

3

Soft Voices

'Get that traitor out of here. Call Baron Chertude and have him perform the execution,' Sosler said, his voice quaking with emotion. He glanced from Rouwen to the molten, smoking crater in the middle of what had been the king's audience chamber. The duke turned to his wizard. Vutorian stood quietly, looking more composed than Rouwen had ever seen him.

All hint of the flesh-devouring magicks that had held Vutorian in their fingers was gone. He might have just returned from a leisurely walk in the castle gardens for all the distress he showed. The wizard held the grimoire in his hand, and it had ceased glowing.

'What of it, Vutorian?' demanded Sosler. 'Did you banish it?'

Vutorian turned to his lord and smiled beatifically. He heard but his attention was focused elsewhere. Before the wizard could respond, Sosler turned and angrily gestured to the guards surrounding Rouwen.

'I told you to take him to the dungeons. Do it now or you shall join him. Chertude will use your worthless bodies for his experiments!' Small red spots appeared high on Sosler's cheeks. Other than this, he remained pale and trembling. Any vestige of courage shown by the guards vanished before his wrath.

They dragged their former captain from the audience chamber, and Rouwen was glad to be away from that magic-racked room. Sosler had thought to summon a wind warrior and had brought into being something far worse than the seemingly invincible tornado used by the Lord of Death and Life to protect himself and his island hideaway. The stench of dissolution hung heavily in that room, Toit having perished, but Rouwen found himself more relieved by the separation from Vutorian. The wizard had changed drastically in the few minutes between Sosler's summoning of the Legion of the Air and the strange banishment of the column of flame. Something within that turbulent shaft

387

of flame had sucked the energy from Vutorian's grimoire – and been satisfied.

Rouwen worried that the magical hunger might not remain sated long.

'You might be the lucky one,' a guard said as he dragged Rouwen along the corridor outside the audience chamber. 'Even if Baron Chertude takes his time and lets you die slowly, you might be better off than the rest of us.'

'Hush, Bullo,' the second guard cautioned. 'The duke hears everything we say.' The smaller guardsman looked about, as if Sosler would storm up and order him beheaded for his opinions. Rouwen wondered if the strength of Sosler's grip on Castle Gan had turned a fearless fighting force into a gaggle of cowards. It seemed that way, and it was a pity. The valley had been the finest place in the world to live, and Castle Gan provided the strong core for the kingdom.

'I can walk, if you let me stand.' Rouwen's bound wrists had gone from painful throbbing to numbness. Circulation had failed totally, turning his fingers into swollen bulbs incapable of gripping a sword or even wrapping around Sosler's throat to squeeze out the tyrant's life, should he be given the chance. Almost as bad as this pain was the burning in the center of his chest where the reflected energy bolt had rebounded from Vutorian's grimoire to strike him. He tried to rub the spot, but his bound hands prevented even touching his chest.

'Let him,' said Bullo. 'It's in the way of a last request, don't you know?' His comrade grumbled about the duke's spies being everywhere, and he refused to relent when he saw a diminutive officer striding toward him.

'You've come a long way in a short time, Smel,' Rouwen greeted, still on his knees. The small man looked Rouwen squarely in the eyes. Then Smel turned angrily and shoved his face into Bullo's.

'Get Captain Rouwen to his feet,' Smel ordered sharply. 'He is to be honored, not . . .'

'Sosler ordered his execution, Captain Smel,' cut in the more frightened of the guards. He looked behind him, again as if he expected the duke suddenly to appear in full wrath to order more deaths – *his* death.

'So, that's hardly unexpected, is it, Rouwen?' Smel looked up at his former commander with a hint of sympathy.

'No, it's not, Captain,' Rouwen said, doubting he would get the one-time corporal of the guard to aid him. Smel had never been an outstanding soldier, but he had always executed his duty faithfully. There was no reason for him to oppose his sworn liege lord to help a former, disgraced officer. Especially one who had led an invading army to the castle gates.

'I've been lucky, and more than a few ahead of me in the chain of command have come to untimely ends.' Smel smiled crookedly, as if remembering how some of the others had died. The leap from corporal to captain was extreme, and Smel knew such a leap might happen again under Sosler's rule for someone else.

'He is to be given over to Baron Chertude,' the nervous guard announced, too loud and too shrill not to be noticed.

'The kingdom's premier torturer will enjoy this task, I am sure,' Smel said drily. Of Bullo, he asked, 'Is Sosler in his audience chamber? There has been a disturbance deep within the castle.' Smel frowned and shook his head, speaking more to himself now. 'It's as if the castle's foundations burned. Stone cannot burn, but it did with a strange black fire. This might be some evil weapon turned on us by the Mionese.'

'It's my doing,' Rouwen spoke up. 'But you should ask Sosler. Or Vutorian.'

'You have your orders. Take him to the dungeons,' Smel muttered to the guards, worried that Rouwen was giving him more information than he needed or wanted.

Smel, Captain of the Intrepid Guard, marched off without looking back. That suited Rouwen. If the chance arose, Rouwen needed to be able to kill the short captain without remorse. Any slight hesitation might doom both Rouwen and the kingdom he sought to save from Sosler's ambitions.

The journey down into the bowels of the castle failed to provide Rouwen with any chance for escape. When he reached the lowest dungeons, his moment of hope had faded and despair replaced it. Bullo and the apprehensive guard shoved him toward a cell with its door standing open. Rouwen had been imprisoned here before, and his escape had been tainted by the curses put on him by Sosler's wizard. The only way Rouwen had of getting free of these heavily guarded cells was through death. Even then, they might let him rot in the cell rather than give him a decent burial or throw him from the castle's battlements onto the Fingers of Providence, those needle-sharp spikes of rock almost a mile below Castle Gan's uppermost turret.

'May your shade find its way to Mount Glid,' Bullo offered as he shoved Rouwen into the prison cell. This was all the help Rouwen was likely to get. He stumbled and dropped to one knee to keep from smashing into the far wall of the stone dungeon.

The door crashed shut behind him, plunging him into heartless darkness. But the true sense of futility came when the locking bar dropped into place, forever barring him into the tight confines of his prison.

Rouwen dropped to the floor and sat with his back to cold stone – or so he would have thought. He let out a yelp and moved away when the rock proved almost too hot to touch. Whatever demon Sosler had summoned chewed its way up through the castle's center and left behind a fiery trail. Rouwen remembered Smel's mission to find Sosler to tell of burning stone throughout the lower reaches of Castle Gan. It was a shame he wouldn't live long enough to see how Sosler coped with this unleashed menace.

Rubbing against the wall to cut through the leather straps binding his wrists proved more difficult because of the heat and the strain it placed on his burned chest, but he persisted until the leather gave way. He gasped in relief when the band parted. Then he moaned in pain as blood flowed once more into the cold, lifeless fingers. It seemed that years passed before Rouwen could bear the misery of returning circulation. Once it did, he became active, seeking any weakness in the cell to exploit for his escape.

He swallowed hard when he peered through a large crack in the door. All he could see in the dungeon was a strangling post. Dangling from it were three cords with bloodstained knots showing where the executioner had been too eager and had drawn blood from his victims. Baron Chertude was infamous for his ability as a torturer, and Rouwen doubted those cords belonged to him.

That didn't remove the threat of immediate torture and death. Did Sosler want him to suffer more? Would Chertude be allowed to prolong his death through endless hours of agony, or would the baron simply snuff out his life and move on? Castle Gan faced dangers unknown in its history and required every sword in its defense – if a sword was the necessary weapon for defense. Rouwen shivered as he remembered the fiery monster Sosler had summoned unwittingly.

He heaved a deep sigh, then attacked the wooden door as hard as he could, putting his shoulder to it. He smashed repeatedly into the thick planks, once getting a small creaking sound from them. But his shoulder yielded before the door gave way. Rouwen shifted his tactics to more subtle attempts to make the door yield. Prising loose a long splinter, he tried to move the heavy outer locking bar through a small crack in the wood. After this attempt failed repeatedly, Rouwen turned to the hinges, hoping to find a weakness in either rock where the door was mounted or in the metal itself.

Exhausted after hours of effort, Rouwen sank down. How long would it be until Chertude strode arrogantly into the dungeons to carry out Sosler's execution order? Rouwen felt the hand of time squeezing him tighter and tighter, limiting his options and making escape look hopeless.

Rouwen wiped sweat from his face and realized he was drenched from his efforts. Usually, dungeon cells were cold and damp. The heat radiating from the cell walls turned the cramped space into a sultry steam bath that wore him down second by second. Rouwen tried to press his hand against the wall but pulled it away, his flesh blistering even from the lightest touch.

'What *has* Sosler done to Gan?' he wondered aloud. Vutorian and the grimoire might have banished the fiery demon this time, but its memory lingered. If the demon returned, what would Vutorian – or Sosler – do then?

Rouwen sat in the center of the tiny cell, arms around his drawn-up knees, head down. The throbbing of his chest wound slowly died and permitted him to consider sleep. He tried to take a nap, but the mounting heat bothered him and a faint vibration beneath him grew in intensity minute by minute. Rouwen shook himself out of his stupor when the entire room trembled so hard he thought an earthquake had struck. Never in the history of Castle Gan had such a disaster threatened. The wizards had always assured Gan's rulers that nothing could harm the lofty fortress, but then, never had such magicks prowled.

Reaching to support himself, he was still tossed against the burning hot wall. He kicked out and forced himself away from the dangerous stone, but the quake continued to intensify until Rouwen's teeth were rattling in his head. By the time the vibrations died, he found himself wishing that Chertude would come to end it all for him.

'No,' Rouwen said to himself, summoning his courage and anger at Sosler, Nishor, Vutorian and all the rest. Revenge would be his. How and when, he couldn't say, but he would never surrender easily. If Chertude came at this moment, he would have the fight of his life before snuffing out the spark of Rouwen's soul.

Rouwen shot to his feet and pressed hard against the cell door, hoping the earthquake had weakened the planks or hinges. He sagged when he discovered the portal remained secure. Pounding his fists weakly, Rouwen fought against defeat. He swung about and paced the narrow confines of his cell, feeling the vibration

391

under his boot soles and avoiding the burning heat from the wall nearest the castle's center.

'Brion,' came a voice so low he almost didn't hear it. He turned, trying to find its source. 'Do not lose hope. Try the door.'

'Who's there?' he cried. No answer came. Rouwen paced the cell again, hoping to find a crack in the stone or some way out he had missed in a dozen earlier examinations.

'The door. Use the door and flee. There is little time left before they come for you.'

'The door?' Rouwen laughed harshly. The hallucinations had begun. He had smashed into the door, tried to lift the bar, used his wiles and strength and never had it budged. 'Who are you? Are you the phantom of some poor, lost soul on its way to Mount Glid?'

'The door,' insisted the soft voice.

'See?' Rouwen took two steps and kicked hard to show his unseen visitor the futility of that approach. Rouwen tumbled forward, his leg skittering from under him when the door crashed open. He pushed up from the cold stone floor outside the cell and stared. The locking bar had been removed, but his benefactor was nowhere to be seen.

'Who are you?' Why help me?'

'There is no time. Please, Brion, do not argue. Do as I say and escape.'

Rouwen had been duped before by Sosler. He thought he had escaped the dungeon on his own, only to find that Sosler had enjoyed giving hope and then dashing it. But would the duke repeat this sick ploy now that the entire castle burned from within?

'Guards approach, Brion. Use the exit at the far end of the dungeon, the one leading downward into the subcellars.'

'Who *are* you?' He swung about suspiciously, trying to find the source of the muted voice. He couldn't even identify the speaker's sex, though he felt it was a woman. 'Why should I believe you?'

'You are free, aren't you?' A titter came that was childlike rather than evil. Though he had been deceived too many times to remember, Rouwen decided he had nothing to lose by following his rescuer's advice. He knew the little-used passage, but going below the castle's foundations availed him naught. There were no exits from Castle Gan in the storage cellars.

Rouwen smiled grimly. His belly growled from lack of food, and his mouth felt like dusty summer in the Vahite Desert. If nothing else, he could get food and water from storage tuns.

He might be trapped, but it wouldn't be in a hot cell with a shaking floor.

He ducked under the low stone arch and brushed aside sticky cobwebs. The passage was darker than the intestines of a ten-foot-tall goring bull, but Rouwen plowed on hoping to find his mysterious benefactor before falling down an unexpected flight of stairs or breaking his ankle in a shadowy pothole.

'Stop! Don't move another step,' came the urgent whisper, almost in his ear. Rouwen reached back to find the speaker but encountered only more filmy spider webs. 'Above you is a narrow chimney fitted with iron rungs. Take it up to the next level. If you continue here, you will be trapped. Guards have discovered your escape and follow.'

Rouwen was tempted to press on, to enter the storage cellars he knew. Never in his lengthy explorations of Castle Gan had he found such a chimney as described, leading upward from the dungeon levels. Reaching above and expecting to find only solid roof, Rouwen was startled when he flailed about in empty space.

'To your right is the first rung. Hurry. They are in the passage behind you. Eight guards, all with orders to kill. Baron Chertude is most aggrieved at losing a prisoner.' The whisper died and Rouwen heard the pounding of heavy feet behind. The inky darkness turned into his ally. Even if the soldiers brought torches with them, they wouldn't be paying much attention to the arched roof. Rouwen's fingers closed on a rusty bar.

A quick jerk upward won him a second rung. Then a third and a fourth so he could get his toes over the lowest portion of the ladder. He had barely pulled himself up from the tunnel when rising smoke made him sneeze. The billowing torches carried by the soldiers caused both smoke and flame to lick at his boot soles. This gave Rouwen the impetus needed to begin the climb.

But as he did, his feet scraped on ancient metal and sent flecks of brown rust cascading downward. He had attracted the attention of the squad.

'There, above us. He's found a chute leading to the upper dungeons.'

A sword clanged just under his left foot. Rouwen wished he had a sword of his own, or a dagger, or even a pocketful of rocks. All that remained of his armaments and belongings was the spell casket hard-won from Sosler. Climbing for his life, Rouwen tumbled into another tunnel, this one faintly lit from either end by torches. He hesitated, wondering if he should turn back toward the dungeons or go in the unknown direction.

How he wished he had explored the lower levels of Castle Gan as thoroughly as he had the upper!

'Left,' came the ever-present voice. 'From there you may escape, if you are fleet enough of foot. Be brave, Brion, and we will be together soon.'

'Where does the passage end?' he asked, but he found himself talking to air. The clamoring below warned him that he had only a few minutes before the soldiers reached him. Rouwen dashed for the faint light at the end away from the dungeons. He couldn't force himself to return to those death pits, even if it meant possible escape.

Before he reached the end of the corridor, Rouwen noticed the quaking had died down. Castle Gan no longer shook on its foundations. Rouwen had no way of knowing if the intense heat threatening to melt the rock under the castle had abated, but the cessation of the shuddering boded well.

Reaching the T-junction, Rouwen looked both left and right. He sighed in relief because he knew where he was again. To the right lay a small postern gate cut through the castle wall. Once to it, he could reach the road spiralling around the stone pinnacle holding the castle. Sosler would have the road heavily patrolled, but Rouwen knew a few tricks to get past them.

As he turned right, the voice spoke more urgently than ever. 'No, Brion, the other direction. Left! Go to your left. This way leads only to capture.'

'It leads out of the castle,' he snapped. Rouwen had tired of the unseen guide's advice, though it had served him well to this point. He had the feeling of being toyed with. At some point he would find the true motives of his guide, and he doubted if he would like the answers. Too much time had been spent in Gan's dungeons awaiting execution for him to trust easily anyone again.

'Left,' urged the soft voice. 'You must go that way! You must!' The voice turned frantic, and this firmed Rouwen's resolve. He had got into his worst trouble when listening to the advice of others. Go to the Isle of Passing, he had been told. He had faced the Lord of Death and Life and almost perished from attacking monsters, both magical and natural.

'That way leads back down,' Rouwen said, straining to remember this section of the castle's passageways. 'I have no desire to be trapped in a storeroom.'

'You must do down. That is the only safe route!'

Rouwen ignored the now almost hysterical pleading and raced for the postern gate. He put his hand on the locking bar and hesitated. The voice sobbed pitifully and choked words urged him to reconsider. Rouwen touched the spell casket dangling around his neck. Without a wizard capable of lifting the curse, life held little for him. Revenge against Sosler and Vutorian might sustain him until they lay in their graves, but what after that?

To love and kill because of it was worse than achieving all his dreams. While the curse remained, a void filled his heart and robbed him of true life.

'Thank you for getting me this far,' he told his unseen ally. Rouwen tugged at the bar and pulled it free. 'If we ever meet face to face, I'll stand you a tankard of ale!'

He swung open the door and froze. Four soldiers stood guard there. His noisy unlocking had alerted them, and they had their swords drawn. Rouwen slammed the door shut as hard as he could, but one sword blade got caught between door and frame; he couldn't shut the portal without first snapping off the blade.

Then his luck vanished entirely. The guards following him from the lower dungeons swung around, blocking retreat. He was caught between the four outside the castle and three within.

'Kill him,' ordered the leading soldier, already advancing to follow his own command.

4

Mark of the Specter

Brion Rouwen widened his stance and judged distances carefully. Unarmed, he stood no real chance against the soldiers, but he could die trying to escape. Being sent back to the dungeons and Baron Chertude's merciless knotted strangling cords proved less enticing than a foot of cold steel rammed through his guts. He preferred to die fighting for his freedom.

Rouwen sidestepped the soldier's lunge and released the postern gate at the same time. He got an unexpected advantage when the guards outside the castle burst in, tumbling to the corridor floor. This pile of flailing humanity and wildly swinging steel robbed the attacking soldier's thrust of accuracy. Rouwen stepped up, grabbed a thick wrist, and wrenched the sword free, using his elbow to knock the soldier to the stone floor.

Dancing lithely around the tangle of guards, Rouwen faced three more coming up from behind. He lunged and used a strong wrist turn to disarm his opponent. Rouwen would have thrust home for the kill except for distance. He was too close to get the point into the man's body. Instead, he smashed his forehead into the soldier's face, causing a bloody ruin of the man's nose.

'Stop him, you fools,' cried the soldier who had lost his sword to Rouwen. 'We're all *thouse* food if he gets away.'

The guard struggled to his feet amid the pile of others from outside. Rouwen tried to get past by shoving the soldier back to the floor and then trampling the others into the ground to win free. His tactic worked in part. He got to the open postern gate and found his way blocked by a pair of soldiers armed with battle-axes.

One was too startled by Rouwen's sudden appearance to respond. The other's heavy ax was already swinging. Rouwen tried to avoid it, but the guard's aim was too good, too accurate, too deadly.

To Rouwen's surprise – and the guard's – the ax blade drove squarely into his chest but did not penetrate. Rouwen yelped in pain as the shock from the impact went through him. But no blood flowed. He hadn't been cut in two pieces. And he had a chance to slip past the guard and reach the distant road spiralling down around the rocky pinnacle holding Castle Gan. He had led the Mionese army to Gan's massive gates, leaving Lord Protector Laslo in charge. If he struggled a turn or two up the road, he might be able to rejoin those foreign forces and save himself.

If the army hadn't been destroyed by now.

Gan's military might had been arrayed against the weaker Mionese army, lured through the Demon's Throat and then all the way up the spiralling road to the gates. From the pockets of guards Rouwen suspected had slipped out of hidden gates, fighting back down the road would prove far more difficult than anything the Mionese veterans had faced thus far.

Bringing up his sword hilt, Rouwen knocked away the smooth wooden handle of the war-ax and pushed hard using his fists into the stunned guardsman's shoulders. The soldier stumbled back, more in fear at seeing a man who ought to be dead continue to fight than from any fighting prowess on Rouwen's part.

'He took my ax cut, and he still lives! He's a demon!' The guard turned pale and fled. Rouwen blinked in surprise, thinking that the soldier would never have qualified for the Intrepid Guard while he was captain.

'I'll stop him,' cried the second guard, finally bringing his ax around for a feeble swing. Rouwen ducked under the clumsy attack and drove his shoulder into the man's soft, exposed gut, knocking the air from his assailant's lungs. Rouwen went down on top of his foe, fighting to get back to his feet.

His chest burned like liquid fire where the first guard's ax had touched it, and his vision blurred from sweat running down his face. Rouwen realized how out of condition for real fighting he was. Too much deprivation and too little training now took its toll on him. He half-stood and drove his knee into the fallen guard's gut again, making sure he wouldn't renew the attack.

He had vanquished two ax-wielding men, but the others still inside the castle recovered and poured from the gate, swords levelled. Three of them had yet to engage him and were fresh to the fray. They laid into him with a fervor fed by fear of what Sosler might do if they allowed a prisoner of Rouwen's importance to escape.

It took only a few minutes of fierce fighting before Rouwen's shoulder ached from swinging the sword. Seeing this weakening in their opponent, the guardsmen turned cautious and circled him, keeping him from running and cutting off any escape save back into the postern gate – and the dungeons.

'Surrender,' urged the guard in command. He had picked up a fallen ax and swung it uncertainly, obviously more accustomed to using the sword now in Rouwen's hand. 'Chertude won't torture you. He'll give you a quick death. That's a promise.'

'No way of making you pay if the promise is broken,' gasped out Rouwen, fighting harder than ever. He would die in the bright light of day with a sword in his hand rather than return meekly to the slaughter awaiting him in Gan's dungeons.

'How'd you get free?' The guard pressed him to answer, to take away concentration from his defense. The ploy didn't work. Rouwen was an old hand at fighting tricks. He kept the guards at bay with wide, slashing moves and put full pressure on a single soldier. If that guardsman weakened for even an instant, Rouwen thought he might be able to dash past him, enter the gate and bar it from inside. It was a faint chance but all he had.

Using a strong disengage, Rouwen forced the soldier's blade off-line, then rushed forward. He elbowed the guardsman out of the way and almost reached the door. Almost. He fell face forward when the guard's commander tossed his ax between Rouwen's legs, causing him to stagger. The guards piled on top of him and quickly disarmed him.

The commander seized his own sword and started to swing it at Rouwen's exposed neck for a death blow, only to have his attack stopped by a heavy hand.

'Don't make things worse for us,' came the advice. 'Let the baron have him and report back *his* success to Sosler.'

'He stole my sword!' protested the guard.

'Explain that to Sosler. Explain to the duke how your prisoner got away. A fine day for an execution. Sunny and bright. But whose execution will it be? His or ours?'

The guards argued among themselves for a few more seconds, but Rouwen had no chance to stand. The sword points kept him pinned, giving him time to seethe at the nearness of freedom. If he had got through the gate, he might have gained long minutes of freedom to make good his escape.

'Get him back to the dungeons. Chertude will be there any time now,' the guard whose sword Rouwen had taken gave in. The soldier's tone said much more, though. He hoped Rouwen tried to escape so he would have the chance to snuff out the life of a man who had humiliated him. With any luck, Rouwen would give him the chance. He did not want to die in a windowless dungeon.

They shoved him along the corridor, to the fork in the passageway. Rouwen let out a tiny sigh and wondered if escape truly lay in the other direction, as his mysterious guide had urged. He had doubted and now would pay with his life. He ought to have gone in that direction. His fate could not have been much different.

'You are stubborn, Brion, and it vexes me to do this,' came the soft voice. He looked around for the speaker but saw no one. The guards ahead and behind showed no sign of having heard the words. Rouwen kept walking, tensed and waiting for something more to happen.

They turned in the direction of the dungeons, but Rouwen ran into the guardsman preceding him.

'Who are you?' the guard demanded of some unseen person in the passage. 'Make way. We're returning a dangerous prisoner to the dungeons.'

'Please let him go,' came a voice hauntingly familiar. It carried a different timbre than when speaking only in his ear, and now it reminded him of someone he knew. Rouwen tried to place it and couldn't. He was shoved back by the leading soldier, who drew his sword.

'You find only death unless you move, little girl. We are under the personal orders of Duke Sosler.'

'Duke Sosler,' came a titter. 'He is Vutorian's pawn now. Or so Vutorian thinks. The truth is that neither enjoys free will in their lives.'

'Away!' The guard drew back for a thrust. Rouwen reached out and gripped the soldier's elbow long enough to cause the attack to miss his target. The guardsman roared with anger and tried to spin around to strike at Rouwen.

'Don't fight,' came the voice again. Rouwen tried to peer past the guard to see who spoke but found himself stepping back to avoid being struck.

The guard whirled back and roared a new command, then froze. He dropped his sword and ran, blundering into Rouwen and bouncing off to collide with the other soldiers in the patrol. For the first time Rouwen saw his benefactor.

'Finola!' he cried, pleased at seeing the young girl again but fearing for her life.

'Come with me, Brion. You disregarded my advice before. Do not argue now.' She held out a tiny hand for him to take. He did so and felt a curious tingle pass through his arm.

'Stop, stop or we'll have to make you,' piped up another guard, braver than the first.

'No, leave us alone,' Finola said in her tiny, girlishly pitched voice. She began glowing a faint pink that turned into a rainbow of blues and greens and reds until Rouwen had to shield his eyes from the brilliance. 'Go away.'

Choked cries of pain from the soldiers filled the confined passage. They danced back, swatting at their clothing as if they had been set on fire. The rainbow flares died around Finola and she turned to Brion with a curious expression.

'Something mutes my power. They should not have endured the spell I cast for more than a few seconds.' She frowned and shook her head, her brown hair swinging slightly. 'I really must find Vutorian and ask what I did wrong.'

'Not Vutorian,' Rouwen said, unwilling to face the wizard again. His chest began to burn anew, as if the wizard was present and holding his grimoire.

'It is good seeing you again. I knew you needed help, so I came.' Finola smiled almost shyly as she looked at him.

'I cannot thank you enough for saving me. Whatever spell you cast was good enough.' The soldiers had fled and there was no sign they would return. Still, Rouwen was uneasy. Sosler still ruled Castle Gan and at his side was Vutorian, Finola's mentor. He hesitated to ask but had to. 'Does Vutorian know you rescued me?'

'I haven't seen him in weeks. He sent me on a mission to fetch some roots for a potion. I returned to his castle, only to find him gone. I had other tasks to complete, so I did them – then a curious feeling came over me. I thought on it and your likeness kept appearing in my meditations.' The young girl smiled more confidently now. 'I knew you needed me and so I came.'

'From Vutorian's castle?' Rouwen frowned. 'That's quite a distance for you to get here so fast.' He couldn't fathom how she had traversed the Shield Mountains, even by taking the hidden tunnel under the massif, and got into Castle Gan so quickly. The Mionese army still stood at the gates and would not let anyone past, much less a young girl who so proudly claimed to be Vutorian's protégée.

'It didn't take long. I *saw* you in the prison cell and came right away. Well, not really then. There was an unsettling feeling, *then* I knew you were in prison. Why do your own people imprison you?'

'We can discuss it later,' Rouwen said, growing nervous at the idea of the guards mustering their courage and returning for him. He didn't know what form Finola's spell had taken, but fear of

Sosler and Vutorian would soon override anything Finola might conjure.

'Vutorian is in the castle, isn't he? I tried to contact him, but he didn't answer. It was as if a curtain had been pulled around him, insulating him from my requests for aid.' Finola chewed on her lip as if this had never happened. 'He is normally responsive.'

Rouwen remembered what Toit had said about the wizard using Finola's vast talents for his own ends. Memory of the *thouse* bird brought a sudden wave of anguish. He put his hand on Finola's shoulder, knowing he had to tell her of the bird's fate.

'He's dead,' Rouwen said, not marshalling his chaotic thoughts too well. 'Toit. I killed him.' Rouwen snatched his hand back, as if he might bring similar death to the young girl. 'He saved me from Sosler's blade, and I touched him, and I killed him.' It sounded lame to him, but his misery knew no bounds and Finola recognized this.

'Your curse, the one Sosler ordered to be placed on you,' she said simply. 'There is a darkness to your soul, and this is such a burden for you to bear. I am sorry, Brion. I wish my skills were greater.'

'We need to get to safety,' Rouwen said, knowing nowhere within the castle walls where he could rest for even a moment. Sosler sent guardsmen into the secret passages to hunt for intruders. The duke might not know the full extent of the hidden ways, but enough of the Intrepid Guard searching the narrow corridors would flush out anyone trying to hide there.

'We can always return by my path,' Finola said. 'It is virtually unused.'

Rouwen almost laughed. He didn't know how she had entered Castle Gan, but it would not be unused. Rouwen knew every gate and every other means of entry – and so did Sosler. Finola's chance of having found an unknown way in or out of the castle was unlikely.

'Perhaps I ought to speak with Vutorian first. There is too much within these walls that troubles me. A power stirs most distressingly.'

'Vutorian and Sosler are now allies,' Rouwen said bluntly. 'Let's find a hiding place, for the moment, and I will tell you what has happened.'

'If Vutorian is near, I can convince him that the duke does not have his best interests at heart.'

Rouwen did laugh this time. Finola saw everything in such starkly contrasting ways. Good and evil. Friend or foe. She didn't understand the complex game Vutorian played, hoping to win not only a kingdom but the entire world. Sosler lacked the magical powers, even if he did have the political sense. Together Sosler and Vutorian had triumphed, but it was an uneasy alliance doomed to failure. The men's unbridled ambitions would see to that.

'He is beyond that. The grimoire I gave him as payment for helping Diarra and me has taken complete control, though its effect diminished when Sosler tried to call the Legion of the Air.' Rouwen rubbed the burning wound on his chest again. The mere memory of the fight in the king's audience chamber made it ache.

'Is something wrong, Brion? You touch your chest as if you've been hurt.'

'Sosler tried to call the wind warriors and got a column of fire instead,' Rouwen said. 'A bolt of lightning from it ricocheted off Sosler and struck Vutorian – struck the grimoire. It bounced around and hit me.' Rouwen almost groaned as the pain drove him to his knees. Finola hurried to him and ripped open his tunic. Her brown eyes widened in disbelief and she stepped back.

'No, Brion, no! This is terrible!'

'It hurts, but I'll heal,' he told her. But Finola's face told him there was more.

'This is like no wound dealt by mortal hand. It is far more – and far worse. You have been marked by the Flame Specter!'

5

Grimoire

Finola's diminutive fingers tentatively touched the spot charred on Rouwen's chest. He winced as new waves of agony rushed through him, even at this soft a touch. Finola drew back, her expression of concern growing.

'This is serious,' she said in her solemn voice. 'The mark of the Flame Specter is dangerous.'

'What is this Flame Specter everyone prattles on about?' Rouwen had heard the name mentioned repeatedly, by Kwuway who had owned the grimoire, by the Lord of Death and Life who had wanted the spell book, even by Vutorian who now possessed it, but he had never received an explanation worthy of the name. Like so much else dealing with magicks, Rouwen thought of the Flame Specter as a tale told in the dark of night to frighten children. He didn't know what Sosler had summoned by using the gold trumpet, but it had not been any Flame Specter. That was only a tall tale, even if Finola was convinced of it.

In spite of his skepticism, Rouwen worried that it was working into his thoughts as a distinct possibility.

'Is it fatal?' His fingers traced the unburned edges of the rectangular wound. He could imagine an imprint of the grimoire being drawn on his flesh using a finger of fire. 'I've had injuries that hurt worse.' Rouwen smiled without humor as he remembered the killing wounds he had sustained while cursed to live forever. The pain had been far greater then, but he had the uneasy feeling that this wound burned more than his skin.

'The Specter's mark is not lightly placed. You have been chosen.'

'For what?' Rouwen saw that Finola either didn't know or couldn't say. She worried at her lower lip and shook her head slightly. He turned back to the T-junction in the corridor and remembered how the mysterious voice had urged him to take the other branch. He started down it, going a few paces and then turning to wait for the girl.

'It was you who freed me from the cell and guided me this far, wasn't it?' Rouwen saw the pleased expression on her face and knew it had been Finola's doing. 'Why didn't you show yourself instead of whispering from shadows?'

Rouwen had tried to locate the source of the quiet voice urging him to escape earlier and had been unable to do so. Leaving the dungeons seemed more important then. Now his curiosity about the young girl's motives burned brighter.

'I wasn't here yet. It took me some time to get into the castle,' she answered, leaving Rouwen with more questions than answers. The pressure of time weighed down on him again.

He looked around and asked, 'Where does this lead, other than to subcellars used for storage?'

'Why, it's the way I entered Castle Gan. The entire core of the pinnacle holding the castle is hollow. I simply followed the path from below.'

'There is no path,' Rouwen said bluntly. He had been Captain of the Intrepid Guard and would have known of any such pathway. King Priowe had been many things but tight-lipped about such a way into his castle was not one of them. Rouwen found it impossible to believe the king of Gan would not have known and revealed such a way. The defense of the entire kingdom depended on such knowledge.

'I've known about it for, well, for all my life,' Finola said. She struggled to tell him, as if explaining a complex notion to a small child. 'Since I am in training to enter the City of Mages, all that is beneath the surface is my province.'

'Show me this way,' Rouwen said. He took a few steps and grew dizzy, having to thrust out his hand to support himself against the rough, dripping stone wall.

'The grimoire,' Finola said anxiously. 'It is the key to your mark. I did not realize it might be the summoning tool for the Flame Specter. Vutorian never told me he wanted to bring forth such elemental power. He is a good wizard but not of *that* caliber.' For the first time, Rouwen heard something of scorn in the girl's voice, a sentiment about Vutorian reflecting Toit's cynicism.

'Sosler will have everyone watching for me. Perhaps you can . . .' Rouwen bit off the uncharacteristic thought. He had almost suggested that Finola retrieve the grimoire while he hid in the subcellar. To have her engage in such a pursuit without him also risking his life was unthinkable. She ought to stay out of sight while he tried to find Vutorian and steal back the grimoire. He was the one carrying the curse.

Dizziness passing, Rouwen reached for the thin chain dangling around his neck, pulled out the silver-chased casket, and stared at it. The answer to his problem was at hand. He held the spell casket out for Finola to see.

'Can you lift the curse on me?' he asked anxiously. 'I stole this from Sosler.' The spell casket dangled on the chain, catching faint rays of torchlight and turning them into rainbows. In spite of himself, he found his eyes captured by their light.

'Brion, I'm sorry,' Finola said, breaking the visual hold it had on him. 'If I tried to lift the curse, even with the spell casket, I might do more harm than good. If I had been the one who laid the curse, it would be different, but styles vary and the slightest misstep on my part could make the spell permanent and then not even the wizard who put it on you could remove it. A wizard of surpassing expertise needs to perform the removal. Or the one who laid the curse.'

Rouwen snorted in disgust. Sosler's pet wizard, Kwuway, had cast the spell, and Kwuway was dead by Rouwen's hand. That death had lifted one spell, but not this one. The magical result had been locked within the spell casket. Rouwen suppressed a surge of despair. Then another idea occurred to him.

'Could you do it if you held Vutorian's grimoire?' For a brief instant, hope rose. Then Rouwen saw Finola's deepening frown and knew the answer before she spoke.

'No, I don't believe so,' she said after a moment's consideration. 'From what you say, the grimoire contains important information about the Flame Specter, not lifting soul-binding spells. With the grimoire, I might not be able to do much, but all the knowledge I can gain is helpful in avoiding future encounters with the fire elemental. We *don't* want to do anything to antagonize it.'

Rouwen felt the need to retrieve the grimoire, simply because Vutorian had taken it under false pretenses. Rouwen had stolen it from Kwuway and had used it as a means of bargaining ever since. It was time to stop dangling it before others' noses and use it himself. If only he could decipher the runic inscriptions. Perhaps with Finola's help he might succeed.

'I'll get the spell book back somehow,' Rouwen said, coming to a decision. Would Sosler's troopers still be hunting him? What fool would remain inside the castle after escaping from a detail taking him to the dungeons for execution? If Sosler turned his attention outward, into the mass of Mionese troops at his gate, such a fight might occupy him for days. All Rouwen needed was a few hours – or even minutes.

405

Find Vutorian, steal the grimoire, escape. It sounded so simple when he thought of it that way.

'Brion, do you hear voices deep inside your head?' The little girl stared up at him with her solemn eyes. Rouwen thought he saw a hint of fear lurking there, too.

'I have heard only your whisper when I was in the cell,' he said, wondering why he hesitated before speaking. He tried to put his finger on his unvoiced concern but couldn't. There was something just beyond words he could not touch.

'I want to come with you,' Finola said. 'This is the first time I've been inside Castle Gan. All my life I've heard how grand it is, so I want to see for myself.'

'Vutorian's castle was better appointed,' Rouwen said truthfully. The wizard had lived well in the Kelnos Forest. Why ambition had flared so brightly that Vutorian wanted to leave his keep was a mystery to Rouwen, but greed for power was a fickle mistress.

'That might be,' Finola said, 'but I spent scant time there. He was always sending me on quests to improve my skills.'

Again Rouwen remembered Toit's words. He thought Vutorian exploited Finola's superior talents for his own ends. The thought of the *thouse* tore at him. How could he have been so foolish as to care for the sardonic, acid-tongued, acid-beaked bird? It had killed poor Toit.

'It isn't the royal corridor but we can take a back stairway to the upper levels,' Rouwen said, turning from the subcellar entrance and heading back toward the dungeons. He knew several ways to reach the upper levels, but most depended on the guards' careless patrolling. If they had been under his training, he knew that was a bad assumption. They would be alert and ready to carry out the execution order handed down by their new liege.

He kept a careful watch for guards but saw none. He finally commented on this to Finola, who had been craning her neck to look up at the elegant wall hangings and the various pieces of statuary decorating the halls.

'Did you kill the guards who had captured me?' He halted and waited to be sure no one patrolled a crossing corridor before proceeding. 'That would explain why they haven't raised a hue and cry over my escape.' He knew that fear of the duke would carry them only so long. Word would spread among the soldiers that a prisoner had escaped – it was a worse crime to let Brion Rouwen slip free than to admit he had momentarily eluded a patrol, only to be recaptured.

'The spells I used were somewhat different. I don't enjoy

killing.' She brushed a tear away from the corner of her eye, and Rouwen knew she thought of Toit. 'The guards saw – things.' Finola shuddered delicately, as if sharing some of the horrors she had visited upon the soldiers. Rouwen didn't ask what they might have been. He had seen demons of his own too often.

'There's so much I need to ask of you,' Rouwen said, hesitating. He brushed away another bout of dizziness, wondering what caused it. He couldn't remember the last meal he had eaten, but he was trained to endure long periods without eating. This weakness stemmed from something more than bodily frailty, coming from outside rather than from within.

Rouwen pressed his hand against the burn on his chest and knew he had located the source of his debility.

'I know, Brion, I know,' Finola said almost sadly. 'You have been through so much, and I have seen so much. Together, we must forge a . . .' Finola cut off her sentence and cocked her head to one side, as if listening. All Rouwen heard were the usual sounds from deep within the castle.

Faint creaking told of the ponderous mass of Castle Gan settling slightly. Uneven heating by the sun and cooling due to shadow on the exterior walls caused more sounds, and the weight of heavy boots marching along the battlements accounted for more noise than he cared to think about at the moment. Or was the sound caused by Lord Protector Laslo beginning his siege with battering rams against the massive gates? Rouwen doubted Sosler would permit an attack of any power being launched, unless he had other motives in permitting the Mionese army to camp on his doorstep.

'He has used the trumpet,' said Finola. 'Sosler summoned the Legion of the Air and the Flame Specter answered the call.'

'It wasn't what I've come to expect from a wind warrior,' Rouwen admitted. As frightening as the tornado of fire and wind had been, Rouwen found it hard to believe this was the Flame Specter so talked about, and so feared, by wizards from here to the Isle of Passing and back.

'Everything is in flux,' Finola said, her features hardening as she decided on a course of action. For a moment, she looked years older than ten summers. 'I sense magical rumblings within the castle that make me believe Duke Sosler will try summoning the Legion of the Air again, no matter that his castle burns around him. Unless we find the grimoire and insulate ourselves from the Flame Specter, we might be killed.' Her hand stretched out, then stopped just above Rouwen's chest. She had started to touch his brand but hesitated at the last moment, as if the evil might rub off.

'How does Sosler change anything?' Rouwen was confused and staggered slightly, catching himself at the last moment. He sank down to sit with his back to the wall. Weakness came and went in giddy tides that sapped his resolve to do more than simply sit.

'In Noumet the wizards keep all the elementals in their proper place,' Finola said, looking increasingly worried at Rouwen's condition. 'The City of Mages is the most important place in the whole world. The wizards keep the sun shining and moving through the daytime sky, just as others move the stars in their course at night and control the destinies of both the Lesser Moon and the Greater. Tides, winds, the movement of the earth and ice, all are within the realm of those residing in Noumet. It is a heady task, keeping the different parts of the universe working together.'

'Noumet,' muttered Rouwen, breaking into a sweat. If a single soldier appeared now, he could never hope to defeat him in combat.

'The balance is shifting, thanks to the summoning of the Flame Specter,' Finola went on. 'There cannot be one elemental supreme over the others. The tension within the castle makes returning the elementals to their true position more important than ever.' She chewed at her knuckle, then hastily stopped, as if she had been warned about such childish gestures. Finola's brown eyes bored into Rouwen. 'Your inept summoning and control of the wind warriors helped create the imbalance, making it possible for the Flame Specter to break free.'

'It's broken loose from some magical bonds?' Rouwen had his breath back now and the flash of fever passed. Strength returned to his limbs and he dared stand. To his surprise, his legs didn't buckle.

'Not yet, but it is trying. It would burn up the whole world, just as the sun is aflame. That's why the mages of Noumet work so diligently to keep order. The Flame Specter is *powerful*. I fret over that mark on your chest. It sees in you something more than another human.'

Her sincerity convinced Rouwen that some power beyond his reckoning threatened Castle Gan, but he had never set any faith in Noumet or the notion that legions of wizards kept the world functioning. That magicks entered the world was no surprise, but Rouwen doubted any power greater than the Legion of the Air. Perhaps the trumpet did summon an air elemental, but that did not mean other elementals were likewise amenable to their summons.

'I don't think Sosler will be able to call the Legion of the Air again,' Rouwen said, his mind clearer now. Strength flooded through him like a refreshing stream washing through the last vestiges of a frozen winter. 'At the same time as the brand was placed on my chest, the trumpet melted.' Rouwen tried to remember the exact sequence and couldn't. The shock of being struck by the magical bolt had addled his wits.

'The trumpet melted?' Finola sounded incredulous.

'Evaporated is closer to what happened. It turned into a golden mist and simply blew away when the wind warrior – the fiery tornado – exploded.'

'The Flame Specter seeks dominion over the atmosphere by destroying the magicks able to summon the Legion of the Air. Finding the grimoire is more important than ever, if my fears are right.' Finola took his hand but Rouwen pulled away. He lived with the constant threat of killing those around him. He hadn't meant to feel any emotion for Toit, yet he had killed the *thouse* with a single touch. The curse lay too heavily on him to forget his vigilance for even a moment.

Finola seemed to understand. She stepped away and closed her eyes. Lips moving in a silent spell, she finished and looked at him as if he might turn into some disgusting animal.

'What was it you did?' he asked. 'I was recovering my strength. Now I feel entirely whole!' Rouwen touched the spot where the demon had burned him and found no trace of hurt remaining.

'A simple enough spell to blot out the pain,' Finola said. 'It won't last long. Where should we look for the grimoire?'

'Vutorian had it before the magical bolt drained him of his energy.'

'What?' The sharpness of Finola's question stopped Rouwen. He turned to look at her.

'Contact with the spell book caused a green cloud to form around him. The bolt of energy turned him back to normal.'

'The Flame Specter tried to destroy the spell book but failed. The grimoire's energies might be drained, but so was the Flame Specter. The grimoire *is* our key to controlling the fire elemental! I must find it!'

'What will you do with it then? I don't want to insult you but you aren't a fully trained wizard yet.'

'The mages in Noumet will know what to do with it if I take the grimoire to them for study. They know everything.' Finola sped along in front of Rouwen, searching for the flight of steps leading upward to the highest reaches of Castle Gan. Rouwen followed, not wanting to point out a logical inconsistency to her mission. If the wizards running the universe knew everything, they also knew the grimoire's contents and didn't need the spell book.

'You are wrong, Brion,' Finola said, reading his thoughts as they climbed up flight after flight of stone steps, winding first to the right and then, from a landing halfway to the royal levels, spiralling up stairs to the left. 'Kwuway must have compiled the spells in the grimoire for his own evil use. An elemental is a potent ally, but it is also dangerous. Only the best can hope to control it for even a few seconds.'

'Kwuway wasn't that good a wizard,' Rouwen said, 'but the Lord of Death and Life was – and he wanted the spell book.'

'The City of Mages is always so engrossed in the minutiae of running the world it sometimes forgets others of surpassing power and knowledge roam the surface.' Finola sighed and shook her head sadly. 'Experts ignore lesser talent at their own risk.'

'A lesson you have learned?' Rouwen asked, amused at hearing such an aphorism.

'Vutorian, for all his faults, *is* a good teacher,' she said. 'I fear ambition has overtaken his abilities – and good sense.'

'Wait,' Rouwen cautioned, holding her back. The girl pressed flat against the wall as Rouwen pushed ahead. Three guards marched in step down the corridor. He allowed them to go past the mouth of the stairway before slipping out. Rouwen feared they might turn and attack, though he felt strong and quick enough to best the trio.

'It's Finola's spell,' he muttered to himself, suspicious of even spells intended to aid him. He could not tell when the magicks might evaporate and leave him weak and wretched as he had been only a short time before.

'I feel a disturbance, a slight one to be sure, but a use of magic alien to me,' Finola said. Almost as if she walked in her sleep, she wandered down the corridor, going in the direction opposite to the guards' round.

'Might the grimoire have been destroyed along with the gold trumpet?' Rouwen followed her, asking the question to cover his growing nervousness at this frontal assault on Sosler's power. The duke was nobody's fool and would have surrounded himself with the finest of the Intrepid Guard, if for no reason other than the presence of the pitiful Mionese army scratching like a sick kitten at his gates.

'It is a magical tool, as the trumpet was,' Finola said in a monotone devoid of any life. 'Its energies might have been drained by the Flame Specter, but the grimoire wasn't destroyed. As the trumpet summoned the air elemental, so might the grimoire bring forth fire. I sense the spell book nearby. Somewhere. Somewhere . . .' She went into a suite of rooms belonging to a minor noble. King Priowe had reassigned many of the sleeping quarters after Rouwen had been imprisoned and the curses laid on him, but these rooms were too cramped for most nobles. This one was empty, stripped of its once fine furnishings and left to gather dust.

Rouwen was quick to see why Finola had been drawn to this room. He walked to a section of bare stone wall and placed his hands against the panel, pressing firmly on a section just above eye level.

'Brion, how did you find the secret passage so quickly?' asked Finola. She came out of her trance long enough to marvel at a non-wizard locating a magical trail so easily.

'The dusty floor betrayed Vutorian, or whoever has come this way.' Rouwen pointed to the footprints scuffed in the thick dust. The wall swung inward; the secret catch lay under a dirty hand print. Whoever had preceded them had not been careful or worried about pursuit.

'The stirring is greater within the wall,' Finola said, her voice falling back into the level tones of intense concentration. She walked forward and slipped through the panel. Rouwen quickly followed, closing the panel behind him. Any guards might see what he had in the dust and on the panel, but they had no reason to come after them without provocation. Royalty often engaged in assignations not meant to be witnessed by lesser ranks.

'Can you hear the grimoire? Or is it more like a magical sense of feel?' Rouwen asked. The cramped, dark secret passage wore on his nerves as Finola made her way along faster and faster. 'Are we getting closer?'

'Closer? No, no, no!' Finola started to cry. 'It seemed so close, then it just faded away like an echo. I don't know what happened to it.'

Rouwen took her in his arms and let her bury her face against his chest. Her hot tears of frustration burned anew on his wound, and he pushed her away.

'Try to find it. We both want to recover it,' he said. Their reasons might differ but the grimoire was important. Even if the reason for stealing it away from Vutorian was little more than preventing its use, that was a worthy motive. 'Confusion to our enemies,' Rouwen said softly.

'But it is I who grow more confused by the moment.' Finola

411

spun around and around in the tight passageway before she stopped. 'I hear voices, but the grimoire is gone! I can't detect any magical stirring from it at all!'

Rouwen was almost blinded by the sudden flare of light pouring through a door that opened in front of him. A half-dozen guards stood there, swords drawn.

6

Haunted Visions

Rouwen reacted rather than thought. He rushed forward, sword swinging about as a club. Catching the leading soldier across the knees produced a yelp of surprise that turned into pain as Rouwen kept running. He bowled the man over and sent him reeling into his comrades. The sword whipped around, still not a cutting or stabbing weapon. Rouwen clubbed the second man and kept him down. The others blundered into each other, yelling curses.

'What are you doing, you fool?' shouted a guard from the bottom of the writhing pile. 'You're clumsier than . . .'

Rouwen didn't let him continue his diatribe. He swung hard and caught the man on the side of the head with the flat of the blade. The *whack!* stopped his complaints and sent the others scrambling to regain their feet.

Rouwen felt a hand pulling him upright. He kicked out and knocked a foot from under a struggling guardsman, sending the off-balance soldier back to the floor. Finola kept tugging at him, saying something he couldn't quite understand. Then her voice cut through the rising din of obscenities and clanking of weapons.

'I can't put a spell on them. There are too many and it takes too long. Get back!' Finola heaved and sent Rouwen sliding back into the secret passage.

'I can fight them,' Rouwen said, confused by his own surge of irrational courage. He tried to fight free of Finola but found himself unable to stand again. The dizziness made him sick to his stomach now.

Mine!

'Let us in. What do you mean by attacking us?' The shouts from the corridor echoed down the narrow passageway where Finola and Rouwen crouched. The guardsmen began angrily pounding on the secret panel. It wouldn't take more than a few seconds for the men to break down the thin door.

'We must run, not fight,' Finola said firmly. Rouwen blinked

413

at her and started to speak, but she held up a small hand and signalled him to silence. 'The guardsmen will fight among themselves, if you can keep the panel closed for a minute longer.'

Rouwen nodded and moved to jam the spring catch while Finola started her low chanting. He tried to focus on her words, but she muffled the words with her hand. From out in the corridor came sounds of fists striking flesh and increasingly angry shouts.

'That will do for the moment. It will take a while for them to calm and remember they were entering this secret passage,' Finola said. She shrugged and added, 'Almost secret passage. It seems everyone knows of these ways now.'

'Sosler has judged it better to let his soldiers know of the passages than to have me sneak up on him.' Rouwen hesitated when they came to the narrow staircase winding back down into the depths of the castle. He wanted the grimoire for reasons transcending mere protection from the Flame Specter. Rouwen wasn't sure he believed much of what Finola had told him of the fire elemental, but he had seen enough to know Sosler played with forces beyond his control. Vutorian might contain the power released by the gold trumpet, but he didn't think this would last long. The green glow had been drained from the wizard, leaving Vutorian strangely peaceful.

'Subverted,' he said suddenly. 'Vutorian has been recruited by this Flame Specter of yours,' he said to Finola. 'We *have* to get the spell book back or . . .'

'Or nothing, Brion,' she said calmly. 'The grimoire would be useful, but what is gained if we die? Come, we can reach Noumet before another day passes, if we hurry.'

'You're just not taking me out of Gan but to the City of Mages?' Rouwen found this funny, but he held down his amusement to a small smile. 'What of the Mionese army knocking on the castle's gates? Is there anything you can do to defeat Duke Sosler?' She looked at him with eyes that glowed with a fierce inner light he had not seen before. For a ten-year-old, Finola possessed an unconquerable will.

'Listen well, Brion. I can do nothing more. The grimoire is either beyond my reach or – hidden.' She shook her head and small strands of unruly brown hair poked forth. With a womanly gesture, Finola smoothed them back into place, tossing her head haughtily.

'When we reach Noumet, we will tell the wizards of the danger. They might already know, but I think the Flame Specter is

414

growing strong enough to slip free of its bonds. If so, and it is crafty, the wizards might not realize the full extent of the problem. That is more important than the grimoire.'

From behind, Rouwen heard the guards hammering once again on the sliding panel. A few well-placed blows would break the flimsy wooden panel and open the path directly to the fugitives. Rouwen swung down the staircase, taking the narrow steps two at a time. Finola followed in a more leisurely manner but managed to keep up.

'I want to see your route into the castle,' Rouwen told her. Two levels lower, he paused and considered a foray of his own to find Vutorian and the grimoire – or Duke Sosler. He had a good sword and the will to use it. If he killed Sosler now, their troubles would be at an end. The internal fighting for power would rip apart the kingdom, but factions would eventually unite under some more beneficent ruler.

Or would they? Rouwen frowned as he considered Vutorian's power. He knew so little of how the wizard had been touched by the magicks released in the audience chamber. His burn began to throb again, distracting him.

Soon.

'The Flame Specter!' Finola spun about in a tight circle, her hands reaching out. The girl's fingers worked in curious patterns weaving magical spells to ward off the powerful elemental. 'It is hunting for you. The mark is a gateway. It seeks to explode into the world, Brion, and it will come through you!'

Rouwen doubled over, clutching his belly as he tried to retch. Deep within his head he heard echoes, echoes of pain and death. A part of him was beguiled and wanted to explore more fully. Another part recoiled from the stark, raw, hungry power drawing him ever inward. Rebellion and iron will won out. Rouwen forced his way back from the brink of being sucked into a blackness relieved only by a single glowing spot.

'I fought it off,' he said in a weak voice.

'We did, Brion,' came Finola's soft voice. The girl looked at him with concern in her ginger-colored eyes and put her hand against his chest. He shrieked in agony at the light touch. 'The Flame Specter tried to break through. *Here.*' Her fingers pressed more insistently, and curiously the pain began to recede. 'You are its way into the world to regain its power.'

'Regain?' Rouwen was too shaken to think straight. He had won a battle he had hardly known he was fighting. 'What do you mean?'

'The Flame Specter once ruled supreme. Slowly, over millennia, the earth and wind and sea quelled it and developed an equilibrium.' Finola let out a little sigh. 'It is very complicated how this balance came about. Someone in Noumet might explain better. I just know it happened. And now the Flame Specter is trying to rule once more.'

'Did I cause the imbalance?'

'No, not you, Brion.' Finola laughed a little at the notion. 'Kwuway might have been responsible, or the Lord, or even Duke Sosler and Vutorian. Every use of power causes a countering weakness somewhere. The Legion of the Air might have sapped important restraining energies from the sea and land, probably the land since the Flame Specter has tried to appear in your king's throne room.' She bit her knuckle, pulled it away and chewed a few seconds on her lower lip, lost in thought, before continuing.

'We must not waste any more time. The sooner we reach Noumet the better off we will be.' She helped him stand straight. For the moment all pain had passed and Rouwen again felt a crazy, irrational sensation of invulnerability.

He could see Sorinne, touch her, make things right with her the way it used to be. And Sosler? He was nothing! A fool whose ambition outstripped his ability. Choosing allies such as Vutorian and King Nishor showed how puny an opponent he was. Rouwen sucked in a deep breath and choked on heavy dust. This forced him back to reality.

'I'm not well,' he said, hating to lean so heavily on a little girl but seeing no way around it. 'The thoughts that run through my head. They're crazy – they are making me crazy.'

'You might be experiencing desires of the Flame Specter. If you feel, nothing can harm you, this is a sure sign. You are a more cautious man, Brion. Bold when needed, but never foolishly reckless.' Something akin to adoration shone in Finola's eyes. He smiled and started to speak when shouts from behind cut off any discussion.

'This way,' Finola said, taking his tattered sleeve and pulling him along like a toy on a string. She expertly traversed the tight, winding passages, working lower until they came out in a main corridor filled with soldiers milling about. For the first time since Finola had pulled him along the hidden ways, Rouwen came to his senses. He was sweating hard, and his hands shook so badly he could barely hold his sword.

'How do we get past them?' asked Finola. She cowered

416

back against him, apparently not expecting to see a company of guardsmen hurrying about their duties at this level of the castle.

Cocking his head to one side, Rouwen heard distant alarm bells. He wondered if the Mionese army attacked, or if Sosler had tired of having so many armed men, even if most were little more than poorly trained peasants, camping at his gates. The appearance of the Flame Specter might have caused him to change his plans.

'He lost the trumpet,' Rouwen said. 'That has changed his schemes. He must rely on more conventional armies now.' The trumpet had dissolved in a single blast of golden mist thanks to the demon Sosler had inadvertently summoned. The loss of the trumpet meant increasing imbalance between the elementals, giving more power to fire and less to air.

A pair of soldiers stared curiously at Rouwen and Finola but kept walking, obviously in a hurry to reach a post elsewhere. Rouwen took this as a sign that daring would be rewarded. He grabbed Finola's hand and started walking briskly, looking neither to left or right as he strode along. Twice he brushed men out of his way. They grumbled but didn't stop to question his curious uniform – Rouwen took it as great luck that no one identified the Mionese commander's uniform he had stripped of all insignia – or recognized him as the escaped prisoner. Whatever mission spurred them to such activity occupied their attention fully.

'There, down there,' Finola said, gasping for breath. She darted down a short flight of stairs, bringing them out just before the door leading into the subcellar she had guided him toward earlier. 'I didn't think we would make it. You were so sure of yourself.' Again she looked at him with more than a hint of hero worship.

'Necessity forces us to do what we must,' Rouwen said. He sagged against the door, regaining his strength. He felt as if he had embarked on a strange journey, riding high for a few minutes, then falling to the blackest depths afterward. Finola might be right that the fire elemental sought to use him as gateway into the world and that he sampled the Flame Specter's thoughts and desires.

'We will be out of Castle Gan before you know it,' Finola assured him, once more her cheerful self now that they had got past the flurry of activity. 'I care little for most people. I have lived alone much of my life, save for the lessons given me by Vutorian.'

'And Toit,' Rouwen added sadly. 'He was your friend. He would never quite admit it, but I knew how much he cared for you.'

'And I for him. He was a noble bird. I shall miss him terribly. He was the only true friend I've ever had. Becoming a wizard is such a lonely job.' Finola looked somber for a moment, then hurried on, forcing Rouwen to run to keep up with her. They passed through the lowest storage levels, down into the hard rock of the mountain spire holding the castle's foundations. Rouwen stopped for a few minutes, letting Finola forge ahead, while he stuffed food into a burlap bag and found an old wineskin that would hold enough water for a few days' journey.

If Sosler brought the full force of the Gannian army against Laslo and his ragtag army all these supplies might be exhausted soon. Rouwen shook his head, thinking how quickly Laslo had risen through the ranks.

Before King Nishor had died in his capital city, Laslo had been only a sergeant of the guard. Loyalty to Rouwen had caused a rapid promotion to commander of the Mionese army, a post for which the man was poorly suited. Rouwen had not cared about capable officers as much as he had in getting his revenge on Sosler and lifting the damnable curse on his head. Now he wished he had a more seasoned field chief battering at Gan's gates. If Sosler took such an assault seriously, it would give him and Finola a much better chance of escape.

He looked around the poorly lit subcellar. Someone had left a smoldering torch in a sconce. It gave off a small amount of light and even more smoke, choking Rouwen and making him wish for the windswept battlements high above Castle Gan. A pang of regret came now as he realized he would never again be Captain of the Intrepid Guard or inside these walls he had called home for so long.

'Are you ready, Brion?' Finola's soft voice carried a curious thrill to it, as if she anticipated the journey with relish.

'Have you found a rat hole to squeeze through?' he asked. The only way out of Castle Gan at this level had to be through a small hole burrowed long since by some tunneling animal. As Captain of the Guard, he had never inspected these rooms, but his junior officers had. The penalty for sloth while on duty was death. He trusted them to find any breach in the wall or hidden way into or out of the castle.

They hadn't reported any such path to him, therefore it didn't exist.

Rouwen blinked and started to speak but no words came when

he saw the door Finola held open. Stairs led downward to an even lower level that couldn't possibly exist. He slung the food-laden burlap bag over his shoulder and settled the wineskin at his hip where the magical trumpet had hung and cautiously approached the door. Fetid air blew against his face. From the look of both door and rock behind it, this portal had been in place for decades.

'My intelligence reports about the castle weren't as good as I thought,' Rouwen muttered. 'Does this come out farther down the road?'

'No, not at all. The spire under the castle is hollow. This leads all the way down into the planet, to the City of Mages.' Finola bounced from foot to foot in her eagerness to reach Noumet and the wizards who supposedly kept the world functioning.

Rouwen looked back over his shoulder, thinking of Laslo and the fight that must be ready to explode. He might keep the fight from being a slaughter, but the Mionese would never occupy Castle Gan. Rouwen's best chance with Laslo and the army would be to form a decent retreat down the mountain and from there into Valley Gan. The citizens of the kingdom had let the Mionese soldiers through because Sosler hadn't properly defended them. No army should have been allowed through the Demon's Throat unopposed, yet Sosler had withdrawn quickly and left the fertile valley open to any invader.

Duty tore at him, as much to save Laslo who had befriended him and, for a Mionese who had shown great loyalty, as to keep Sosler from destroying the Kingdom of Gan.

'Let's go,' Rouwen said, coming to a decision. He had escaped recapture only through the judicious use of Finola's spells and a huge serving of luck. From now on, he would have to find his own course and be less a pawn of fate.

That thought caused the burn on his chest to pulse and throb as if it had a life of its own.

Rouwen stepped through the door and entered another world, one he had never suspected to exist beneath his feet. The air tickled his nose with a staleness bespeaking hundreds of years of imprisonment, but more than this it carried a curious scent. It was elusive and as if something burned – but not quite. The walls glowed a dim green and illuminated the path winding down into the distance. Rouwen expected to find a central shaft from what Finola had said, but this was more a tunnel cut through stone than a shaft. He breathed a sigh of relief on this point. Clinging to a rocky wall as he edged his way along the lip of a thousand-foot fall had

419

not appealed to him, even if it meant getting away to fight Sosler again.

'We can make good time, though I am glad to see you brought food. I overlook so many things,' Finola said, chastising herself. 'Vutorian says the details will come around and bite me when I least expect it.'

'How far to Noumet?' Rouwen need not believe in such a place but he had not expected to find such a fine pathway, either. 'A day's travel? Longer?'

'Less, if we hurry,' Finola said. 'I do not want to spend more time here than I have to. There are too many . . . memories.' Rouwen couldn't see her face to garner more information from her about this. She stepped along the path, setting a pace Rouwen was hard pressed to equal. Finola didn't want to speak; she picked up the pace every time Rouwen sought to question her about his surroundings.

Settling into a long-legged stride, Rouwen followed the girl and tried to figure out how this path came to be hewn through what he had believed to be solid rock under Castle Gan. The walls were rough and the phosphorescent moss clung with frantic tenacity. Each time Rouwen tried to scrape some off as he went by a patch, he came away with only a few strands for his effort. Reaching out, he pressed his hand against the rock, thinking it would be cool. Again surprised, Rouwen drew away with burned fingers.

'The entire shaft is warmed by the planet's inner fires,' Finola said. Rouwen hadn't thought she had been paying any attention to his minor experiments. 'The moss grows and glows because of the heat generated below. More than this, I cannot tell you.'

'An army could have driven squarely up through the core of the castle, had anyone known of this route,' Rouwen marvelled. 'How did you learn of it? And does Vutorian know?'

'Everyone in Noumet knows this course, but then they know so many things,' Finola said. 'Come along, Brion. We dare not tarry.'

'Why not? From the air, nothing has been in here for long years.'

The girl didn't answer, making Rouwen mad. She had adopted the wizard's manner of answering only those questions suiting her. He calmed when he remembered she was only ten years old and had many years left to learn better behavior. After all, wasn't he King of Mion? He had defeated Nishor and led his army to the gates of the most invincible fortress in the world! He was more powerful than Sosler and . . .

'Finola,' he called in a weak voice. 'I think the Flame Specter is trying to take over my thoughts. It's as before. Invincible. Powerful. Everyone else is a fool.' Rouwen sank down to a rock and put his head in his hands, shaking uncontrollably. His chest ached and breathing became harder.

Submit. You weaken.

'Brion, it's all right,' came a voice he remembered all too well. He looked up and saw his brother, Adan. Rouwen tried not to recoil. His brother had been the first to die because of his curse. Rouwen had watched the flesh boil off Adan's bones, leaving him a pile of gray ash. 'But you owe me. Listen to your inner voice and obey. You can become supreme!'

Rouwen turned away and tried to rise, only to collide with a wall. He bounced back and landed hard on his rump, staring up at the Lord of Death and Life. The slight man laughed in glee, mocking as he always had.

'A fine sight you are. A world conqueror? *I* should have been the one. The spell book was my ticket off the Isle of Passing.'

'You were immortal. The island was a paradise. You chose to live otherwise.' Rouwen licked dried lips and scuttled like a crab to avoid the Lord. The wizard had been far more powerful – and more vulnerable – than Rouwen had realized. Even as this thought crossed his mind, Rouwen saw the Lord's visage fade and become that of Princess Sorinne.

He closed his eyes and tried not to move. If he touched her, Sorinne would die. He loved her and she would die from his curse. But the voice crashing into his ears wasn't that of his lover. At first grating, it became musical. Rouwen finally realized two voices spoke, vying for supremacy.

'He loved me more,' came one grating voice.

'No, me,' came a second, shriller one. 'You look like a rat. I am a proper creature, beautiful by any standards. See my feathers?'

Rouwen chanced a look and saw both Nibbles and Toit arguing over which he had loved more – and which he had slain the faster for that love. Toit spread a tail fan of brown feathers edged with gilt. Nibbles worked his teeth like a rat chewing through a grain sack, and Rouwen put his arms over his head to keep them all away.

Their voices rose in his head and flutterings brushed his face and hands and neck until he screamed to be left alone.

'Away! Go away! I killed you all. I admit it, and I'm sorry. Go to Mount Glid and leave me be!'

'Brion, what's wrong?'

He didn't recognize the voice. Had he slain someone else because he dared to love them?

'Are you suffering from exhaustion?' A small hand tugged at his arm. 'Please, Brion, this is serious. Are you possessed?'

'Haunted,' he grated out. He opened his eyes and saw Finola – and behind her the legion of those he had killed, either with his unbridled emotion of love or a sword. He had killed hundreds in Mion using the Legion of the Air. As Captain of the Intrepid Guard he had killed hundreds more. He was a bloody-handed butcher slaying with both love and steel.

Rouwen ran, stumbling as he went, trying in vain to escape the cacophony of jeers rising behind him. He slammed into a rock and spun about, falling to his knees. Reaching out to support himself, he almost fell. Somehow, he had come to a ledge and looked out over a huge cavern. Filling the cavern was the most resplendent city he had ever seen.

'It's Noumet,' came Finola's soft voice. 'We've reached it!'

The City of Mages.

7

City of Mages

'It exists,' Brion Rouwen muttered, staring at the high, soaring towers of clear, pure crystal and the incredible streets that glowed as if they were rivers of molten gold. The vista was more than he could take in with a single glance. He sank to the rocky edge and dangled his feet over the precipice, kicking slowly and banging his heels against stone. The solidity forced him away from the voices calling after him, the voices of those he had killed.

'Yes, it exists,' Finola said behind him. She came and stood behind him, oblivious of the hundred-foot drop into the city itself. 'Are you all right, Brion? You are so pale and drawn. The past day's travel has been hard, but . . .'

'The last *day?*' Rouwen whirled about so fast he almost slid off the ledge. Finola grabbed his shoulder and steadied him. He pushed her hand away when he regained his equilibrium. Somehow, the rock seemed less solid under him when he heard her offhand comment. 'What do you mean? We've only been walking a few minutes. We left the castle and took a single bend and then they came and . . .'

Sweat popped out on his forehead again, though the wind whipping up from Noumet was cool and should have evaporated it quickly. The last, long hours were filled with tormenting voices of the dead, shades of those he had killed during his life. The army of ghosts had tried to touch him and . . . what? He didn't know what they wanted from him. Sympathy? Apology? How could he ever apologize to Adan, Nibbles, and Toit when he had loved them and caused their deaths? Many he had fought in battle and killed fairly, but his brother and the others weighed on him most. He had loved and killed, and what did their phantoms want from him? Could he somehow give them release? How? How?

'They haven't been able to reach Mount Glid and go into Paradise,' he said, pain etching every word. 'I should help them reach Paradise where they belong. They deserve better than endless wandering, trapped in some middle land between life and death.'

'Brion, you worry me so,' said Finola. The girl sat cross-legged beside him and stared intently at him. 'What are you talking about?'

'You didn't hear them? What sort of wizard are you?' He laughed at himself. Finola was no true wizard. She was a little girl, but even she ought to have heard the loud cries from the spirits trailing after him. The more he had run, the louder they had chanted his name, imploring him to – do what?

He didn't know. He just didn't know.

'The Flame Specter tries to emerge,' Finola said. 'I sense some disturbance, but not as powerful a one as before. Perhaps it has shifted tactics from brute force to something more subtle. You must fight it, Brion. Only by being vigilant can you prevent the balance from shifting. The entire world will be bathed in flame.'

He tried to make a joke when he said, 'Do you mean those in Paradise will see a new sun if I let this elemental use me?'

'Yes.'

The simple reply made him shiver. As a child, he had suffered bouts of the ague that caused symptoms similar to the ones he experienced now. Rouwen tried to believe he had caught some foul disease in Castle Gan and nothing more than minor illness troubled him. But the voices still echoed deep within his mind, and he knew he only lied to himself. His body was whole. It was his soul that carried the seeds of true sickness.

'Can the Flame Specter enter Noumet?' He blinked away sweat and tried to focus on the vast city. Never in his life had he thought the tales of the City of Mages might be true. Even as a child he had scoffed at the stories of the wizards hidden away beneath the surface, working their magicks to keep the world whole. His system of beliefs changed in fundamental ways.

'An elemental can go anywhere, if the balance shifts drastically,' Finola said, again sounding dozens of years older than her years. 'We will find someone to help you.' She reached out and put her hand under his elbow, lifting it slightly.

To Rouwen's surprise, she picked him up off the rocky ledge. He shouted in fright when they drifted slowly off the ledge and began descending toward the city with nothing but thin air below their feet. Rouwen calmed himself and tried to enjoy the short descent to the edge of the city.

The crystalline towers and the golden, glowing streets vanished behind a wall of granite as they settled on the floor of the cavern. Rouwen's strength surged once more, as if some enervating blanket had been pulled from his shoulders.

He shot to his feet and wondered if he could vault over the wall.

'Why not use your magicks to put us down on the far side of this barrier?' Rouwen asked. He touched the stone and recoiled when a shock raced up his arm and exploded in his shoulder. Staggering, he stared at his hand as if it had turned traitor.

'We must wait for a few minutes,' Finola said, laughing at his plight. 'No one enters Noumet without approval. The feeling isn't permanent. It is a warning to keep at bay those who have come this far.'

'Who has ever reached Noumet?' Rouwen walked along the wall, suspiciously studying it for more traps. The granite appeared normal, yet he knew it held magicks enough to stop him from trying to scale it. 'Other than wizards wanting to work there?'

'Why, many explorers have sought and found it. The way isn't easy for people unversed in spell casting, but it can be done.' Finola closed her eyes and her lips moved in a silent chant. Then she opened her ginger eyes and smiled. 'We have been approved for entry.'

'After your quest for Vutorian, did you come here?' Rouwen asked. 'This world holds few surprises for you.'

'I was here,' she admitted. 'I returned to Kelnos Forest and found Vutorian gone. The magical hints of what he attempted were everywhere. Use of the trumpet and the Legion of the Air left a charged agitation that was quite unmistakable. I decided then to come directly to Noumet, in spite of Vutorian's warnings.' Finola smiled almost shyly and looked at the ground. 'A wizard has to know when she is ready to move on.'

'Outgrowing Vutorian is the best thing that's ever happened to you,' Rouwen said.

'Oh, no, there're other things.' Finola stared at him intently, took a deep breath and said, 'Let's go into the city. I'm dying for you to meet some of the wizards who keep the universe in proper order.' She took his hand. He tried to pull away, fearing contact with anyone he didn't intend to kill, but Finola was firm. She tugged gently and turned toward the solid wall. Confidently, she walked forward – and through – the wall.

Rouwen trailed her by a half step, wincing as millions of needles pricked at his skin. Then he was through the wall and at the end of a golden street. The beauty of the City of Mages assaulted his senses anew. Not only was the architecture unusual and stunning, there came a dozen other perceptions telling him about the city. A soft hum filled the air; he heard the susurration of wind through the treetops and across the surface of the ocean and movement of feet on soft dirt.

Turning slightly in the direction of the hum changed his perception to one of liquid, of spray against his face, a softly warming spring rain mixed with biting cold blizzard.

'What is happening?' he asked, hand reaching for his sword. Scents of salty ocean spray and cooking bread and burning leaves made his nose wrinkle. And then came the tastes struggling for supremacy within his mouth. Every meal he had enjoyed and loathed mingled and taunted him. Rouwen spat, trying to clear the taste, but too much remained.

'Stop it,' he ordered Finola. 'I am going to choke if you don't keep the tastes away.'

'Some do find the cavalcade of sensations overpowering,' Finola said. She began a silent chant and the taste left Rouwen's mouth. A slightly metallic suggestion remained, but he could live with this. 'No one is trying to enforce any of the stimulations on you. They are excess, you might say.'

'I don't understand,' Rouwen said, hand still on his sword. The streets were singularly deserted for a city this size. He had the uneasy feeling of being watched – and led into a trap.

'Consider a boiling pot,' Finola said, reveling in the chance to explain to Rouwen. 'What remains in the pot is tasty, but so much escapes. Scent and froth and even some of the meat, perhaps, from a thick stew. Noumet is like that. The wizards work their spells and some small magicks overflow. The surplus is harmless, even invigorating.' She took a deep sniff and then skipped off happily. Rouwen followed, less enthusiastic about the continual onslaught on his senses.

As he walked, he peered into the buildings. Many were finely appointed but many had the look of destitution, filled with threadbare furniture and wall decorations laden with dust and neglect. He looked at his feet and saw how he sank slightly into the golden paved street and how the road lent vigor to his stride. Then Rouwen saw two people, a man and a woman, leaving a house a few paces along the street. They might have been peasants starving during a long drought. They were shabbily dressed, shuffled tiredly and had the look of malnutrition about them.

'Who are they?' Rouwen thought he knew the answer. In any city of such splendor, there had to be an underclass responsible for the menial labor. Such peasants might live in fine buildings but their lot would be poor compared to their wizardly masters.

Finola's answer stopped him in his tracks.

'Why, those are wizards on their way to work. A shift change in the water section is due. A wizard works for twelve hours and rests for twelve.'

'They are starving!' protested Rouwen. He hastened along the street until he came level with the pair. Their eyes were glazed and their pasty faces were haggard. He had seen survivors of the Great Plague who seemed more lively. If he had thought Finola was right about this being the mythic City of Mages, he now doubted everything she said. How could these be the most powerful mages in the world?

'Please, Brion, don't trouble them. They think constantly of their duties. Many work two and three shifts without rest. Their work is as important as that, and it is so difficult to find apprentices willing to assume the duties of running the world.'

Rouwen fell back and let the two alleged wizards shuffle on. They turned at the next corner and vanished from sight. He could not doubt Noumet existed – or could he?

'Is this some magicks-spawned illusion you've wrapped about me?' he asked. 'Are you trying to gull me into believing we have walked for a full day down the inner spire and found this?'

'I am not fooling you, Brion!' The outrage in Finola's voice convinced him she was not responsible for the fantasy world surrounding them, but that did not mean the source of the illusion did not also enfold her. 'Noumet is filled with great wizards!'

'Are you suggesting that the most powerful in the world, the wizards entrusted with moving the sun and stars and tides, are famished?' He pointed after the pair who were long out of sight. No others had emerged from the buildings. The sense of being in a deserted city began to gnaw at Rouwen and make him increasingly edgy. He almost longed for the company of the spirits of those he had slain who had pursued him to this place – almost.

'They sometimes forget to eat, so great is their attention to duty. And you are wrong. The greatest wizards in Noumet do not guide the stars. That job is left to apprentices. After all, who would notice if a star or two in the nighttime sky moved out of place?'

'The royal astronomers might,' Rouwen said, yielding the point to her. Unless a major star pattern shifted, the Chariot becoming the Crippled Bear or Lost Hero, who *would* notice? 'If the work is so onerous, why does anyone persist? Why do you want to assume it?'

'It's the highest responsibility anyone can have,' Finola said haughtily. 'Few are capable enough to reach Noumet. Even fewer can learn the spells required to labor here. I have worked hard. Vutorian might be an avaricious dunderhead, but he taught me well. A student who wants to learn can surpass the master.'

'You want to move stars about?' Rouwen's head swiveled from side to side as he took in the sights and sounds and smells in the City of Mages. He wished he had found such golden pavement earlier. It not only cushioned his tread, it also imparted energy he had lacked for too long. And the constant hum proved intriguing, also. He caught the hint of voices and sounds he had known all his life – and many he had never heard before.

'To start. Eventually, I want to control the sun,' Finola answered. 'What can be more important to the world than that? Only the best are permitted to apprentice there. They must deal with all the elementals, including the Flame Specter.'

Rouwen winced at the mention of the elemental. A nerve spasmed in his chest, causing the burn to throb with new life. He pressed his hand against the brand, but it did not cease its insistent pulsation. Opening his uniform tunic and exposing the wound, he saw that the edges smoldered, causing small columns of smoke to rise as if he had been set afire.

'Brion, no,' Finola said, putting her hand over her mouth. 'This is terrible. The Flame Specter is trying to burst forth again, and I don't know the spells to hold it back. We must find a wizard who can do something.'

'The one controlling the sun?' he suggested. The pain turned him giddy. Although he hardly believed Finola's claims for Noumet, he had half-hoped entry into the city would hold to a minimum such suffering as he now endured. Since the pain mounted with inexorable power, he again doubted his senses and thought the whole City of Mages to be an illusion spun to fool him. But who had such magical power? The Lord of Death and Life might have, but he was dead. Vutorian lacked the imagination for such a deception, even goaded on by Duke Sosler.

He sank to one knee and took power from the golden street. Under his hand it felt softer than velvet, yet his feet told him that, though cushioned, it was harder than rock. Rouwen didn't care what it was because it drove away the pain when he lay down and rolled over, pressing his chest into the golden paving.

'Good, good,' Finola said. 'I had not thought to do that. Come along, Brion. We must reach Gerberria and find what can be done for you.' She lifted him to his feet. Rouwen experienced a moment's disorientation, then went along willingly enough because movement kept the pain from returning. The idle thought of walking constantly to hold away the torment passed through his mind, discarded almost as quickly as it had come to him.

'Is Gerberria in charge of Noumet?' he asked. The girl turned down a broad boulevard lined with ruby-and-sapphire-fronted buildings, searching for a particular edifice. She broke into a run when she saw the two-story building capped with a shining globe representing the sun. Rouwen followed her but proceeded more cautiously as he entered and glanced around the large room.

As with many of the other buildings, the interior was dilapidated and adorned with inferior works of art. It was as if the decorator had been ten years old like Finola and had thought this constituted sophisticated tastes.

'Here, Brion, this is Gerberria. She is one of only three powerful enough to control the sun. She has been struggling to hold back the Flame Specter – and she has succeeded.' Finola turned to the bent-double old woman with tangled gray hair and a hooked nose as if introducing the greatest person in the world.

'You have the mark. You are the one we must watch,' the old crone rasped. Gerberria's finger curled as she pointed in his direction. Rouwen found it impossible to believe she was a wizard, much less one keeping the heavens in their proper order.

He had seen people delude themselves before. Some thought they were royalty, others proclaimed themselves deities or more. And all he had met making such claims were crazy.

'What should he do, Gerberria?' Finola moved closer to the old woman to hear the reply. The croaking whisper faded from Rouwen's ears. All he heard was nonsense that had nothing to do with him or his plight. He turned away from Gerberria and walked around the room. Filthy, the room showed even less care and attention than he had thought at first glance. For a supposedly puissant wizard in a city of stunning beauty and grace, Gerberria lived like a rustic.

'Take him and let me get about my duties,' Gerberria said in a hoarse voice.

'Have you eaten today?' asked Finola. The girl tried to hand a plate of spoiled food to the old woman. Gerberria ignored it and shuffled away toward a door leading into a dimly lit room beyond. Rouwen went to the portal and looked inside the next room.

The darkness was so intense he thought he had gone blind for a moment. Then he saw a tiny speck of light moving across the ceiling. It took him several seconds to recognize the pattern on the face of the speck as being the Greater Moon. A few seconds later, another pinpoint of light, the Lesser Moon, chased after it.

'Does Gerberria control the moons, too?' Rouwen threw up his arm to protect his eyes when the room exploded in a blaze of light.

'Brion, leave her to her job. It is so demanding. Gerberria must keep track of the moons to guide the sun along its proper course. She works long hours at her task since there are only two others capable of the intricate spells.'

Rouwen let himself be led from the door and back into the squalor of Gerberria's quarters. He felt dirty simply standing amid the tasteless paraphernalia. It seemed to him that the inhabitants of Noumet were so self-engrossed that nothing mattered but their own delusion. Believing Gerberria really controlled the sun was far beyond Rouwen's imagination. The Lord of Death and Life had lived in virtual poverty but had used his spells to make it appear that his quarters and viands were of the finest quality. Vutorian lived better than most nobles of Gan, and Gan was the richest kingdom on the continent.

With magical ability, it was easy to summon up the illusion of something finer than this.

'Let's go outside and let Gerberria work in her laboratory,' Finola suggested. Nothing pleased Rouwen more than being outside. Here he was surrounded by elegant buildings and the hint of so much activity he could never identify it all. Inside Gerberria's quarters, he had to fight off his feeling of contempt. She was old, ugly, starved and not likely to want to change her squalid lifestyle.

More than this, Rouwen doubted she was a wizard of any talent, much less one as exalted as Finola thought. If Gerberria had been a mage of any power, she would have mentioned the curse still resting on Rouwen's head. He had not broached the matter to her because he knew only the finest of wizards could remove the diabolical spell. Rouwen touched the spell casket dangling around his neck and felt a new surge of anger at Sosler for all he had done.

'Gerberria suggested I petition other wizards working with air, water, and earth elementals. When I get them together with Gerberria, they can decide how best to aid you.' Finola looked worried, her forehead furrowed.

'What's troubling you?' Rouwen feared that the old crone had filled Finola's head with groundless concerns. They had more than enough to do opposing Duke Sosler. By now, assuming Finola's estimate of time spent reaching Noumet was correct,

Sosler could have vanquished Laslo and the entire Mionese army. At the first sign of real battle, those peasant soldiers would have broken rank and run all the way down the spiralling road leading to Valley Gan.

Sosler would have killed them at his leisure.

'Your mind wanders off on strange paths, Brion,' answered Finola. 'I want only to help you. Why don't you enjoy the entertainment area at the end of the street while I seek the others? The quicker they meet with Gerberria, the quicker you will be free of the Flame Specter's mark.' She started to reach out to touch his chest, then pulled away as if nearing a blazing fire. Rouwen experienced no discomfort now.

They are weak, you are strong.

'Very well,' he said. 'I wouldn't mind relaxing a little after all I've been through. A few minutes can't harm.' Rouwen decided this might be a chance to explore the city streets and decide once and for all if Noumet was only illusion or if Finola's claims were accurate. He could roam about more freely without the young girl at his side.

'The park is special,' she said, skipping along beside him. He found it easy to forget she was only a child until moments like this when her innocent enthusiasm bubbled out. 'You can do anything you can imagine. It takes no special skills.' They reached the edge of a grassy area dotted with benches and individual chairs. Rouwen sat in the first one and found it surprisingly comfortable as he sank into its padded depths.

'Start with something simple,' urged Finola, still eager to show him an example of the city's attractions. 'Picture something to eat.'

Rouwen smiled and shook his head, then to please the girl he tried. He closed his eyes and experienced a lethargy settling over him that threatened him with sleep. But he fought to form a picture of a full banquet meal. In his mind he saw it – and when he opened his eyes the same meal was laid out on a long table before him.

'You can eat it,' Finola said, grinning from ear to ear. Tiny freckles twitched on her cheeks and dimples came forth. 'You can create anything within the boundaries of the park. It's all harmless, all amusement.'

Rouwen sampled the bread nearest at hand. He felt it and smelled it and the soft pressure against his tongue faded into a delectable taste.

'Can I really eat it?'

'Well, no, not really. It is an illusion, but you must admit that

431

it is a fine one. You did quite well for a first try. I must go, but I won't be long. I promise.' Finola hesitated, then bent and gave Rouwen a quick kiss on the cheek. Then she rushed off, humming to herself.

Rouwen watched the girl leave, then settled down in the chair, marvelling at the meal he had conjured. He had no spell-casting ability, yet he had summoned forth a meal rivalling anything he had seen served in Castle Gan. To be sure he hadn't relied on Finola's abilities in some unknown way, Rouwen brought forth images of riders engaging in combat and strange beasts he had heard of and ones that were physically impossible. He marched them about as if they were ranks of soldiers, then made them vanish.

As if he were ten years old himself, he laughed at his creations and for a while forgot his woes. But eventually his thoughts strayed as he tired of playing with imaginary beasts and fighters and food.

'Sorinne,' he said softly. 'Why shouldn't I enjoy your company for a brief moment?' He closed his eyes and pictured the princess exactly, savoring the smallest detail of her. The curve of her neck and the flare of her hips, the firmness of breast and the lyrical quality of her voice. All this and more Rouwen remembered. And conjured.

Opening his eyes, he saw the lovely blonde woman standing a few paces from him. He rose and took a tentative step toward her.

'Sorinne, is it you?' he asked, his voice quavering with emotion.

'I have missed you so much, Brion,' came his answer. Sorinne's arms opened to greet him as he deserved. He rushed forth and threw his arms around her, his lips pressing into hers. The instant he touched Sorinne, the world exploded into a multicolored spray of sharp-edged jags that ripped and tore at his body and brain.

Rouwen screamed and screamed and screamed as he fell endlessly through infinite space.

8

Untimely Demise

Rouwen's chest felt as if it would explode. He rolled on the ground, clutching himself tightly, hoping to hold inside all that threatened to erupt. The swirling lights around him faded, and the sensation of falling endlessly decreased until he could sit upright and not fall over. Looking down at his torso, Rouwen saw new spots of charring where flame had lapped at him. Other than this, he was unharmed from the tumultuous spasm occurring when he had invoked Sorinne's image.

'Sorinne,' he muttered. It took him several seconds to remember all that had happened. When he did, Rouwen got to his feet and looked around, almost expecting the princess still to be on the grass. 'All a trick, a filthy magical trick,' Rouwen grumbled.

Although he didn't see the princess, he did see a poorly dressed man lying face down a few yards away. Rouwen looked about, wondering if his wrenching experience had affected another in the park. He hurried to the man's side and knelt, rolling him over.

Eyes already misting over in death stared sightlessly at Rouwen. He carefully closed the eyelids, not wanting to look into those death-dimmed orbs. He stood and wondered what was wrong within Noumet. In the distance he heard shouts of anger or terror. Unable to tell which and not much caring at the moment, he turned his attention back to the man on the ground. The expression frozen on the corpse's face held out no assurance of a peaceful death. He had died in utter agony, perhaps caught in the same vortex that had whirled Rouwen about and thrown him aside.

'He must have been a wizard,' Rouwen decided, since Finola had hinted that no one, save mages, lived within the granite walls surrounding Noumet. Like the others Rouwen had seen, this wizard was shabbily clothed. No self-respecting Gannian peasant would be seen publicly in such filthy rags, nor would any but the most impoverished have the desolate look of malnutrition about him.

'This is indeed some place you've chosen to spend all your life in, Finola,' he said in disgust.

The clamor rose and forced Rouwen to heed it. Dozens of men and women ran down the broad boulevard leading to the park, all shouting incoherently. Behind them Rouwen saw a sheet of fire dancing along the street, melting everything it touched. Buildings sagged, the street buckled, and waves of blistering heat forced Rouwen to turn his face away. He bent over and let the hot wind blow past before turning to see what had happened.

'Some wizards,' he muttered, seeing the destruction wrought along the wide street. Then a chill settled over Rouwen as he remembered the devastation caused by the Legion of the Air when he had loosed the wind warriors on Tachre. No amount of spell casting would have thwarted those magically powered tornadoes. And no amount of spell casting could have prevented the scorching swell from liquefying both buildings and golden pavement. It had come too fast, and it had come too unexpectedly.

Rouwen noticed that the coolness within the city was changing to a sultry temperature that threatened to rise past the bounds of tolerance. He wiped sweat from his face. This time he came by it honestly. Even the ground was becoming so hot that he danced about, shifting weight from one foot to the other to avoid the intensifying heat.

Rumbling noises alerted Rouwen that more was to come. A small volcano erupted on the other side of the dead man, forcing itself upward in a liquid bubble and then spewing forth molten rock. Rouwen had a few seconds to run for cover, dodging people in the street. If the City of Mages was going to be destroyed, Rouwen wanted to find a quick way out.

'Finola!' he yelled, hunting for the young girl. She knew the city better than he, and she must know a path to safety. If Finola didn't, she might use her levitation spell to lift them above the confusion seizing Noumet.

Rouwen staggered along as the ground began shaking. He had ridden out an earthquake before, in the dungeon of Castle Gan and he had not yet forgotten it. Rouwen was thrown to his knees and skidded along the golden-paved street. It hardly surprised him that the energy he had once derived from contact with the pavement no longer flowed. Whatever magicks vivified the street had vanished with the rising temperature.

'Finola, where are you?' He found his way past small fumaroles gushing forth noxious fumes to the two-story building where Gerberria had her laboratory. Rouwen forced his way into the structure, wary of two fallen support beams. 'Finola? Gerberria?'

No answer. He searched the outer room quickly, then stopped in the doorway leading to Gerberria's laboratory. Darkness still reigned within the laboratory, the two moons having moved to spots almost directly overhead. Of the blazing sun Rouwen saw no trace.

'What have you done?' came the old woman's trembling voice from beneath a pile of rubble Rouwen had only dimly seen. He began throwing the debris aside, hunting for Gerberria. A thin arm showed him he wasn't wasting his time. When the hand began twitching and then helping to remove the fragments of ceiling that had fallen, he knew the wizard still lived. Only when he threw off the last large piece of wreckage did he see the woman's mouth working in silent chant.

Gerberria turned rheumy eyes on him and repeated, 'What have you done?'

'I've done nothing,' protested Rouwen. 'Where's Finola? I can't let her roam the city with it coming down around her ears.'

'The wizard on the green. He is dead, isn't he?' Gerberria's hand clutched at Rouwen's sleeve with surprising strength. 'Tell me. Torgon is dead, isn't he?'

Rouwen shrugged. He had no way of knowing the dead man's name. 'Many have died in Noumet. A wave of heat rolled through the city, melting buildings and destroying pavements. Was it spawned by the Flame Specter?'

'You killed Torgon. You and your damnable curse!' Gerberria shrieked now. Rouwen tried to pull free, but the old woman's hand held him firmly.

'What do you know of it?' Rouwen's free hand touched the spell casket dangling around his neck. He recoiled. The spell casket had turned so frigid his fingers stuck to it. If it had been left outside in the polar regions it could not have been colder.

'You summoned an image of someone you love, and then you killed Torgon. You unutterable fool! Look at the disorder you have caused. The sun has stopped in its circuit of the planet! The flow of night to day is interrupted. However shall I correct it? What are the right spells?' Gerberria released Rouwen and hobbled to the center of the room. Her arms rose and sparks flew from her fingertips, arcing upward to strike the tiny dots representing the Lesser and the Greater Moons.

Rouwen didn't know what to believe other than that the City of Mages was falling apart around him. He backed off, intending

435

to leave. An unexpected paralysis held him captive just inside the door to Gerberria's laboratory.

'Find the girl. Find Finola,' ordered Gerberria. 'She must replace Torgon. That is what I, as Sunkeeper, decree. Do it, outsider, get her and bring her to me!'

Rouwen grunted as a powerful force lifted him and threw him into the outer room. He crashed to the floor, smashing into one of the fallen beams. Moaning, Rouwen rubbed sore ribs where he had collided. Dark bruises already rose to challenge the burned spot on his chest for title of most painful wound.

He left the building and stood in the street outside, not knowing where to look for Finola. Noumet had turned from a deserted city into one filled with shouting, cursing men and women. Rouwen hoped that none of the obscenities carried the weight of a full spell behind it. If any of the improbabilities he heard came to pass, the world would be a vastly different place peopled by half-human, half-animal brutes.

Amid the confusion, he tried to remember Finola's exact words. She had gone to find others working with elementals, but where in the city would they be? At compass directions? Rouwen didn't know but thought he might find out more directly than guessing. As a small, mouselike man rushed past, Rouwen thrust out his powerful arm and caught the man around his thin neck.

Swinging hard, Rouwen slammed the man against the wall and shoved his face into one resembling a weasel with skin eruptions. If the citizens of Noumet were all wizards, they did little magically to help their own appearances.

'The young girl, Finola, where can I find her?' demanded Rouwen. If the man he had caught knew Finola's whereabouts, he could be scared into telling. If he didn't, Rouwen thought he was a good enough judge of human nature to see. He would just release the man and find someone else to interrogate.

To his surprise, Rouwen felt the small man slowly break the iron grip he had around his throat. The man shoved him back with contemptuous ease, and then Rouwen realized magicks were a'play. He tried to lift his arms and felt heavy weight increasing with his effort. As he relaxed, the weight vanished.

'Can you tell me where Finola is?' Rouwen asked again, this time with more deference in his tone. The man looked at him as if he were a forest slug leaving trails of slime wherever he crawled. Without a word, the man walked off, leaving Rouwen furious and still unable to find Finola.

Rouwen looked about frantically. The heat rose to such a level in Noumet that he worried the granite walls around the city might melt. Twice he had travelled in the Vahite Desert and seen the infamous mirages dancing with great and deadly enticement. The curtains of heat shimmer over Noumet rivalled any he had seen in the desert. Silver flecks formed and vanished as he watched, and then indistinct images came into sharp focus.

The writhing beasts he saw shifted into flame and back into more substantial creatures, but different and all deadly. Rouwen had the feeling of being trapped within a cage and unable to escape because of the evil beyond.

He sucked in a deep breath to calm himself and choked on the fetid odor. He had been intrigued upon entering the City of Mages with the strange aromas carried on the air. The exotic mixture of scents were now transformed into a cloying stench that gagged him. His eyes watered and deep in his skull he heard a distant thrumming as if vast legions had begun a long march.

'Finola!' he cried. 'Where are you?' Rouwen was less interested in obeying Gerberria's command to bring the girl to her than he was in fleeing Noumet. The magicks assaulting the underground city were of prodigious power; a single glance at the visions of horror smashing against the walls around the city reflected that. He could never escape if he had to levitate back to the ledge before finding the path up the spire and into Castle Gan. He might never break free, even if he managed to climb the granite wall surrounding the city. The Flame Specter – or whatever beast slavered without – would make short work of any mortal trying to elude it.

He got no answer to his shouts. Rouwen stumbled along the heaving streets, wondering if the entire planet might break apart beneath his feet. Finola had claimed the Flame Specter was one quarter of all power in the universe, that it was held in check by air, water, and earth. With Sosler's destruction of the wind warriors' summoning trumpet, this might have crippled the air elemental enough for fire to rush in.

Was the fire elemental now half of all power? With the destruction of Noumet, would it be more and set the world afire like the noonday sun?

Rouwen shoved such questions from his mind. He was no wizard. He was a soldier and a good one, trying only to survive. With Finola his chances were better – and he had to admit he had done poorly by a child who thought highly of him. He had slain her only friend and showed up her mentor to be a betrayer of her trust.

'Brion, here,' came the girl's voice. He swung about and saw her seated at a table just inside the door of a simple building.

The single-story structure had suffered greatly from heat and earthquake, but it still stood.

'We have to get out of here,' Rouwen called, going to her. He started through the open doorway but was flung back by an invisible hand. Shaking himself to clear his head he tried to thrust through again. Once more the magical barrier held firm and repelled him.

'Don't try to get inside, Brion. They've cast a ward spell to keep me safe while I work.' She hunched over a table, two spell books open before her. One glowed the strange green he remembered engulfing Vutorian before the Flame Specter drained its energy. The other grimoire pulsed with every color of the rainbow, from deep, angry red to eye-searing violet.

'If I can't get inside, can you leave? It must be the Flame Specter trying to destroy the city.' He stepped back and looked down the street. He no longer saw vicious beasts flinging themselves against the magical bubble encapsulating Noumet, but he had the feeling the magical attack was only in a lull and would continue soon.

'I have been impressed into working for the wizard you killed,' Finola called. 'I am sorry. I never thought to warn you of the dangers.' She wiped away a tear. 'I never thought there would *be* any problem. You do love her, don't you?'

'Torgon was the wizard's name. Gerberria wants you to see her immediately,' Rouwen said earnestly, hoping to lure Finola away from her work table. Once free of the magical barrier, they could attempt to flee to safety. If anywhere in the world was safe with volcanoes erupting and the temperature rising catastrophically. He wiped sweat from his forehead, then tied a headband into place to soak up any excess.

'Torgon was a capable wizard,' Finola said, her voice distant now as she thought of things other than escape. 'I studied some of his spells. When he wasn't working in the illusions park, he helped contain the Flame Specter. Now I must do that.'

Another quake shook the ground so hard Rouwen was knocked from his feet. He crashed into the wall, then recoiled as the magical spell cast him out.

'Finola, please, we have to go. Noumet is being destroyed.'

'I cannot leave now, Brion. By killing Torgon, you doomed me. I am the only wizard able to assume his role, and there is so much to learn, so much to do. It is very complicated. A single mistake and I will die. If only I knew more.' She began sobbing, her thin shoulders trembling with the force of her emotion.

Rouwen experienced a moment's giddiness. As the fit passed

438

he knew he could never entice Finola into leaving her post. She must be held by powerful magicks or simple duty might keep her at work.

Then Rouwen realized there could be more to the girl's decision to assume Torgon's duties. Without any check on the Flame Specter, it might rampage freely. Finola would earn her right to be counted among the wizards of Noumet long before her apprenticeship ended.

'Brion,' came her faint words, as if she spoke from a thousand miles away. 'The grimoire. Vutorian's grimoire. Get it. I need it to . . .'

A new earthquake knocked Rouwen from his feet and sent him tumbling down the street. When he recovered he saw that he was cut off from Finola by a river of flowing lava. Heat and fumes drove him back, away from the only one in the City of Mages who could help him.

9

Twisted Time and Space

Traversing the molten rivers flowing through the streets of Noumet proved difficult, but Rouwen returned to the now tumbledown building that had once held the replica of the sun atop it. He forced his way into the room where he had spoken with Gerberria, hoping to find the woman there. Not seeing her, he went to the door leading into her laboratory. Sunlight blinded him, and he averted his face.

'Gerberria!' he called. 'I can't bring Finola here. She is trapped in a building not far from here. I need your help.'

'Go away, you worthless maggot,' came the hoarse reply. 'Can't you see the cosmos is a jumble?'

Rouwen used his arms to shield his face as he looked toward the wizard's ceiling. Both moons and the sun were clustered near the zenith in an unusual configuration. He didn't know what to make of it – he wasn't even sure he believed that Gerberria or any other wizard in the city commanded the world as they claimed.

'The sun halted in its course. I need to concentrate to bring about a regular cycle of day and night. The world will fry on one side and freeze on the other if I am not successful. Go. Go away and leave me alone.' The force of the words sent Rouwen reeling backward, but he refused to be deterred.

'Finola needs the grimoire in Vutorian's possession. Can you help me retrieve it? Can you lift the spell on me and . . .'

'No!'

The answer to his plea drove him back into the street where red molten rock flowed sluggishly in his direction. Excruciating heat and a heavy sulfur odor gagged him. Eyes running from the fumes, he sought a way back into Gerberria's laboratory. He knew no one else in Noumet who might free Finola and aid him. The spell casket around his neck weighed him down more heavily than ever. Killing brother and friend because of the curse was one thing. He had slain a powerful wizard and had hardly known what happened.

'I've disturbed the balance of the elements even more,' he muttered as he tried in vain to find another entryway into Gerberria's building. Failing, Rouwen jumped a narrow streamlet of lava and made his way back to where Finola was trapped. He caught sight of the girl hunched over her grimoires, chanting her spells and never once looking up. She seemed years older with the burden of the magicks placed on her young shoulders. Shouting, jumping about, waving his arms to draw her attention, every ploy failed.

Rouwen didn't want to leave her, but he saw that he would never have a chance of escape himself unless he left Noumet quickly. Fumaroles appeared everywhere, and the way the rock flowed threatened the very structure of the cavern holding the City of Mages. He had no idea if the wizards sought to counter the Flame Specter's presence or if they simply attended to individual problems, letting Gerberria – or Finola – worry about the greater dangers facing both their city and the entire world.

Rouwen stopped to think what he was doing if he fled now. He had not done his duty for the Kingdom of Gan. Sosler still sat on the throne enforcing their marriage on Sorinne, sanctifying his position with magical compulsion. Rouwen didn't delude himself into thinking Laslo could defeat the armed might of Castle Gan. That left the kingdom entirely under Sosler's thumb. Worse, the scheming tyrant could expand his dominion to other countries, with Gan and Mion as a base.

'Duty,' Rouwen sobbed out. He had failed his kingdom. He had killed his brother and friends. Abandoning Finola, hoping that he could somehow retrieve the grimoire and bring it back to her, was as much a dream as anything around him.

'None of this is real!' Rouwen spun about shouting and stamping his feet in an attempt to dispel the illusions enshrouding him. When his boot touched the edge of a stream of lava, leather hissed and burned away. The sharp pain in his foot caused Rouwen to rock back and stare. If he lived in an illusion, it transcended any route of escape he commanded.

More careful now, Rouwen jumped the lava flow and made his way through the once beautiful city to the granite wall at its perimeter. He stared at the high wall and knew he could never scale it. Simply standing near it almost fried him. The rock itself was too hot to touch. The Flame Specter worried at the magical barrier in its attempt to destroy Noumet and the only control remaining on it.

Rouwen touched his sword and knew his usual weapons were powerless against the elemental. The spell casket bobbed at his chest, brushing over the wound on his chest. Rouwen pressed the cool chased-silver into his flesh and winced, but he couldn't tell if the pain was magical in origin or simply the result of a sharp edge cutting him. He had been branded by the Flame Specter as its own, but did this give him any cachet? Rouwen hesitated to use its possible power fearing he might fail. And if he failed, Finola was doomed.

A quick look over his shoulder at Noumet told Rouwen the city could not long survive. Even if he stole the grimoire back from Vutorian, returning with it to this underground world might take too long. He began walking along the base of the high wall, seeking some answer to his dilemma. A gust of cold wind from the city supplied it to him.

On the heels of the rush of cold wind came a rush of water more powerful than any tidal wave Rouwen had ever seen. The water blasted him against the granite wall and drove him to his knees. As he tried to stand up to the torrents soaking him, the packed dirt beneath his feet began to erode – or simply part. He couldn't tell. Rouwen plunged into a steep-walled sinkhole and was washed along, his startled cries drowned out by the rush of wind past him.

Crashing hard into a stalagmite, Rouwen lay stunned for a few seconds. Like a dog shaking water from its coat, he got to hands and knees and shook all over. By the time he could see clearly and understand what he saw, the sheets of flame licking at Noumet had shrunk under the onslaught of air, water, and earth.

'They fight back,' he decided. Whether the counterstroke came because of Finola's efforts or those of the other wizards, Rouwen didn't care. His chances for reaching Gan and securing the grimoire had just improved greatly. With the Flame Specter driven off, the path back into the castle lay open to him. Rouwen found the ledge where he had dangled his feet and first looked across Noumet, then began scaling the rugged face. It took the better part of an hour to return the few hundred feet Finola had crossed with a simple spell, but Rouwen felt a sense of accomplishment as he heaved himself over the rim and lay flat for a moment, panting to catch his breath.

Rolling over, he sat up and stared at the City of Mages. It had changed drastically since he had first seen it. The vaulting towers and lovely sapphire and ruby arches had melted away, leaving behind molten ruin. Here and there he saw unscathed stretches of the golden roadway, but most were buckled or completely missing. A scent of brimstone rose and caused his nose to wrinkle, but most perturbing of all was the *feel* – or lack of it.

Before, there had been a deeply felt hum that both soothed and stimulated. Now the only sensation he got from the city was one of utter doom.

Rouwen wasted no time in picking up the wineskin and the burlap bag with rations he had packed before leaving Castle Gan. He was happy he had discarded them before Finola had levitated them to the cavern floor below. They would serve him well on the way back. Rouwen started hiking along the narrow rock pathway he did not even remember traversing before. Worrying that the spirits of the dead would return to haunt him, Rouwen kept looking over his shoulder and straining for the smallest hint of ghostly discontent.

All he heard was a silence so profound it weighed on him like a pile of rock. Walking faster, he started to worry that he wouldn't again hear the spirits. Contact with them was unsettling for him, but it was the only chance he might ever have of speaking once more to his brother, Nibbles or Toit. But he remembered what had precipitated the crisis in Noumet.

'I dare to love and ruin a world,' he moaned. He stopped walking, his legs tired from the climb. Looking back along the path, he was startled to see he had come only a few paces. From his level of exhaustion Rouwen would have guessed he had tramped along for the better part of an hour.

Belly complaining, he ate a large meal from his provender and drank deeply of the tepid water in the wineskin. Rested and sated, he began walking again.

For hours he walked, refusing to rest. He had to reach Castle Gan and find the grimoire for Finola's sake. Only with the spell book could she escape the servitude forced on her by the wizards of Noumet – and only using it could she imprison the Flame Specter again. It struck Rouwen as unfair that such a burden was placed on a girl so young. He had seen no mage in Noumet less than ancient. Even the few who had been apprentices were many summers older than the oldest in Gan.

Back aching and legs turned to lead from the exertion, Rouwen stopped and looked about for a comfortable place to sit. To his surprise, he saw the spot he had eaten his meal not ten feet away.

'How could I walk in circles?' he protested aloud. 'That's not possible. There are no side tunnels, and I came down the path straightaway before.' Rouwen turned and started walking toward the debris left from his meal, only to find that he made no progress. Walking faster had no effect on the distance, nor did breaking into a run. He slowed and came to a halt, hands on knees and out of breath.

'Perhaps this is why Finola thought it took a day's travel from the castle. I might be less than a few hundred yards away.' Even as he voiced this, Rouwen knew he had to be wrong. The spire capped by Castle Gan was immense. Even with a good road it took a day or more hard travel from base to castle gate. There was no reason to believe Noumet was positioned anywhere else than far below the base of the hollow spire.

'I don't know what peculiar twist of time causes this, but I reached Noumet on this path. I can get back to Castle Gan the same way.' Rouwen hefted his burlap bag and started hiking in earnest, putting any tiredness behind him. For long hours he walked and gained only a few feet along the trail.

Exhausted, Rouwen slept for what seemed hours. He feared his dreams might be visited by those spirits denied entry to Paradise, but his sleep was sound and devoid of nightmares. He rose, ate, and began walking again. By midday he wished again Adan and the other spirits would come to him and relieve the boredom of the walk. For every hour he hiked, he saw less than a half-dozen paces of progress.

'Adan, Toit, Nibbles, are you there?' he called. He licked his lips and then added, 'Torgon? Is your spirit also denied flight from Mount Glid? I meant none of you harm. Quite the reverse. Is there anything I might do to ease your burden?' The more he talked, the less he came to fear the spirits of the dead. But they did not respond.

Past midday, Rouwen stumbled and fell to one knee, a surge of dizziness robbing him of balance. He fought to get to his feet and found he could not. Most disturbing of all, he scented the brimstone more strongly than ever.

There is no escape.

And then the ground began to quake alarmingly. Rouwen clutched at seemingly solid rock for support, only to find himself tossed through the air, still clinging to the rock. He crashed hard to the ground – and fell.

Rouwen had experienced the sensation before, when he had touched Sorinne's mirage in the illusion park. This time he held his panic in check and tried to analyze the fall, the wild shards of parti-colored reality slashing at him, the cause behind the commotion.

The first thing he noticed was the throbbing in his chest where he had been branded by the Flame Specter. The skin turned translucent and shone with a vivid red light that tried to force its way outward. Rouwen closed his eyes and concentrated on

444

remaining whole. His arms crossed over his chest and held back the onslaught from within.

To his surprise this helped, though it did nothing to stop the tumbling sensation or the vicious incisions made by the many hued fragments whirling about him. Rouwen gathered his feet under him and spun like a ball. At the moment he deemed best, he extended arms and legs in an attempt to slow the rotation.

The spinning did not stop but he was granted a quick look at a world that terrified him. Molten streamers of raw rock rose and fell violently into lava pits. Nothing but heat and light existed in most of this world; the solid matter passed from that state directly to heat, to fire and poisonous smoke that would gather around any human daring to enter the world.

Brion Rouwen saw the Flame Specter's sphere of influence and understood its hunger and hatred for . . . the cold ones.

Know my power. Fear it!

Hitting the ground hard, Rouwen smashed against solid rock again. His eyes flashed open wide and he stared around in panic, sure that the elemental came for him. To his surprise he was again on the path leading upward to Castle Gan, but he held small bits of the Flame Specter within him. Worse than heartburn, the tiny fire inside gnawed at his heart and soul. He had visited the elemental in its lair and taken on more of its essence.

'No, I deny you, I don't want this!' moaned Rouwen. In his thrashing about, he found the spell casket still around his neck. Parts of its case had turned liquid, flowed and coalesced into a new shape. Rouwen clutched it frantically, examining the magical device holding captive part of his soul and worried that the Flame Specter had managed to steal from the tiny casket.

Rouwen rocked back and pressed hard into cool stone until his pounding pulse slowed and he recaptured some semblance of sanity.

'I'm whole. All I need is a wizard powerful enough to counter the curse. When I get the grimoire back to Finola, Gerberria and the others in Noumet will be in my debt. One of them will remove the curse.' Rouwen calmed further when he realized that Gerberria had known of the curse on his head without being told. For all her apparent physical weakness and age, she possessed the ability of a true master mage. Rouwen wasn't sure he believed that those in Noumet truly controlled all that happened in the world above ground, but Gerberria had certainly considerable magical skill.

'Let them delude themselves, wizards or not,' he said, calming further. 'I'll fetch the spell book, let Finola restrain the Flame Specter once more and then I can be free of my curse.'

He looked around for the first time since being thrown about and forced back new fear. The pathway had changed completely. Six different crevices radiated from the spot where he sat. Only one – the path to the castle – had stretched before him minutes earlier.

Rouwen stepped into one crevice and listened for sounds. He heard distant wind. The second crevice brought forth a blast of heat that singed his eyebrows and drove him back. The third also carried hints of the Flame Specter's presence. The fourth and fifth cracks that had opened in the solid rock made Rouwen suspect that oceans lay ahead. Salt spray and cool mist blew into his face in one. The other carried the roar of flowing water back to him. The final crevice might spiral upward to the castle, but Rouwen doubted it. The odors of the dead came to him. Cemetery scent was particularly strong when he took a few tentative steps forward.

And then the crevice tried to close on him. Rouwen twisted and dived back into the safety of the center of the radiating pathways. Looking back where he had been, he saw only the huge crack in the rock again.

He might have imagined the walls collapsing around him, but he doubted it. Of the paths open now, none matched his memory of the one taken from Castle Gan. And all seemed to hold new dangers.

Sitting down to review his chances of making any progress toward the castle now that he was confronted with so many choices, Rouwen noticed how famished he had become. His belly grumbled and his hands shook from lack of food. He began eating from his larder until it was almost gone.

'I didn't feel this hungry after going a week without food during training,' he muttered to himself. He drank deeply, reducing his water still further. Only then did he turn his attention back to the new tunnels broken through solid rock. None necessarily led to safety, but he reasoned several were more deadly than others.

Rouwen dismissed exploring the two carrying the taint of the Flame Specter. Those with watery rumblings did not appeal to him either, and the rocky crevice where he had almost been crushed ranked last on his list to try. The one with fresh air blowing in his face drew him. Some sense told him the air elemental crippled by the loss of the gold trumpet and the Flame Specter's hunger for supremacy resided within this crevice. He had somehow become the focus of a new fight between the elementals, and the Flame Specter had receded into its own lair.

For a while.

Rouwen slung his diminished larder over his shoulder and walked courageously into the wind. He experienced a moment of rejuvenation and then picked up the pace. If he walked into death, he would do so at a brisk march and with a sword in his hand.

Rouwen took three more steps and then stumbled, falling down a long shale slope. He came to a graceless stop halfway down, the bright sun in his eyes. He blinked and looked around, trying to get his bearings. Behind him rose mountains with a familiar cast to them, and ahead lay the Rocky Coast.

In a mere four paces, Rouwen had left the hollow spire beneath Castle Gan and ended up on the far slopes of the Shield Mountains, facing the Smoking Sea. He was farther than ever from his goal!

10

Wizard and Pretender

Rouwen had trouble keeping his sword belt cinched tightly enough. He had lost considerable weight during his ordeal underground. Even after eating every last morsel in his burlap sack, he felt hunger pangs that refused to go away. In the bright light of noontime, he had little chance of finding anything worth hunting. He would have to wait until twilight when the smaller animals came out to feed before catching himself an easy supper.

But what seemed a simple wait stretched into endless hours. Rouwen lay back under a limberfrost tree and stared through the narrow green and silver leaves at the sun. It hung stationary above him, not moving so much as a twig's width the entire time that he lay. Rouwen drifted off to sleep and awoke refreshed and having the feeling that a considerable time had passed.

The sun remained in its position directly overhead. For the first time, Rouwen began to worry that the wizards of Noumet truly controlled wave and wind, sun and stars. Gerberria had been shaken by her encounter with the Flame Specter. Rouwen remembered how the sun and the two moons had swung back and forth in a position directly overhead. Squinting, he blocked out enough of the sun's brilliance to see the Greater Moon to the right of the sun and the Lesser Moon just below.

Day might never end unless Gerberria regained control of the sun's path around the planet. Worse than eternal day was the prospect of the Flame Specter rising to supremacy.

Belly still complaining from lack of food, Rouwen foraged for nuts and berries and then found a slowly flowing brook that replenished his empty water bag. The sun still had not moved in the sky. Rouwen rolled up his sleeves and set off for the coast, thinking to find a small village there and some decent food before trying to re-enter Valley Gan through the Demon's Throat.

Although he knew the tunnel beneath the Shield Mountains would be quicker, he had come to fear meeting the spirits of

448

those he had slain again. While under the castle and walking up the path inside the spire, he had convinced himself there was nothing to fear from the ghosts of those still seeking Paradise. A chance to reflect on it – and the Flame Specter's influence – had brought back his old trepidation.

By Rouwen's reckoning, he had walked for a half day when he sighted the column of soldiers riding along a little-used road. Ducking behind a tree, he peered around the trunk in an effort to get a look at the soldiers' banner or gear. The Mionese army had been slaughtered by now, or so Rouwen figured. Laslo might have been a brave soldier and true to his beliefs, but he was no general. His sudden promotion to lord and commander of the army had been bolstered by Rouwen's tactical expertise, Vutorian's magical ability, and Diarra's ability to control the Legion of the Air once Rouwen summoned it.

He could never withstand even a simple foray against his ranks. And for this Rouwen mourned. Laslo was a good soldier.

Rouwen frowned as he studied the soldiers riding down the lane. They sported no pennant or battalion banner, and all insignia had been stripped from their uniforms. But the wine-red and silver chasing was that of the Gannian King's Guard. These men had been Priowe's, and now they rode along a road in the back country of Mion.

More curious than anything else, Rouwen found a path through the forest paralleling the travelling soldiers. Brigands abounded in this part of Mion. Rouwen had run foul of them before. The back-stabbing thieves would waylay any traveller, young or old, male or female, and massacre them without warning. While he entertained the notion that a Gannian patrol had been ambushed, killed, and their uniforms stolen, Rouwen kept noting details that made this unlikely.

For all the attempt to hide insignia and unit, the uniforms were not ripped or torn and appeared to be reasonably clean. Any fight to the death would have left blood and dirt smeared on the uniforms. From all Rouwen had seen of the brigands, they were not inclined to spruce themselves after a fight.

'Halt!' came the command from the head of the soldiers' rank. Rouwen moved to get closer to the officer in charge. He didn't recognize the voice, but there were many officers in the King's Guard he did not know. The Intrepid had been a separate unit, charged with maintaining castle security. The King's Guard had acted as Priowe's personal bodyguards, more nursemaids than fighters to Rouwen's way of thinking.

He threw himself face down into a tangle of shrubbery when

an officer rode closer. Rouwen worried he might have given away his position, but the rider only trotted to the rear of the column to have a few words with his sergeant. Rouwen had seldom been on a horse before being cursed and leaving the Castle Gan; these men were accustomed to riding. This reinforced his belief that they were truly soldiers of the King's Guard. King Priowe had enjoyed his parades and often rode throughout Valley Gan to visit the citizens and put on shows of pomp and ceremony.

'Will that cursed wizard allow us any closer wit'out abasing ourselves?' grumbled the sergeant. The grizzled old man's voice cut like a knife through the silence of the forest. Rouwen couldn't hear the officer's reply, but the sergeant retorted, 'May the demons take 'im and 'is own! We're soldiers of the kingdom, not 'is personal servants.'

Rouwen did hear the officer's reply and it startled him.

'We serve King Sped, not the wizard. Keep that in mind. If it pleases our liege to heed the wizard's counsel, that's his business and not mine – or yours, Sergeant Yint.'

'As you prefer, Captain,' the sergeant said in a disgusted tone. 'I know my place.'

The captain said something more that Rouwen missed and then trotted to the head of the column and dismounted. Watching carefully, Rouwen saw the officer walk slowly toward an empty glade. As he approached two limberfrost trees, he began to shimmer as if seen through a heat haze. Remembering the onslaught of the Flame Specter, Rouwen called out involuntarily. No one noticed because of the loud crackling sound that echoed back from the twin trees.

What had been an empty glade seconds earlier now held several voluminous tents constructed of brilliantly colored silks. Tent flaps blew in the gentle breeze caressing the glade, waving invitingly. But Rouwen did not move from concealment.

Striding from the first tent came Vutorian. And close behind followed King Priowe's indolent son, Sped. The youth sauntered out, threw back his head and sucked in a deep breath, then spat a berry seed high into the air. He laughed as it turned about and landed a few paces distant. Vutorian watched with ill-concealed disfavor such inappropriate behavior from a prince.

Rouwen worked his way forward on his belly, getting closer to the edge of the glade. Sped and Vutorian waited for the guard captain to salute before motioning him into their tent. Any hope of his overhearing the conversation died. Rouwen knew the tent would be magically screened against prying ears.

He wondered if Vutorian maintained his magical wards around

the entire glade now that the patrol had returned. Sped would never think of such things, but Vutorian was wily – and cautious.

Rouwen wondered why Sosler's pet wizard returned to his own territory. The Kelnos Forest lay only a few days' travel to the north, where stood the most fabulous palace Rouwen had ever seen. Vutorian had lived better than the King of Gan, and yet he had given up that life when Rouwen offered the grimoire as payment.

'The grimoire,' Rouwen said under his breath. If Vutorian was here, so was the spell book. So the fight between the Flame Specter and the other elementals had benefitted him when he had thought it would only slow his quest. Emerging from the underground world on the far side of the sky-touching mountains enclosing Valley Gan had seemed a setback, but he had emerged almost on top of Vutorian.

The only question puzzling Rouwen was the speed with which Vutorian had left Castle Gan, ridden with the soldiers down the spiral road to the valley floor, out the Demon's Throat and a dozen days' travel to this point. If he had travelled hard for three weeks he might only just have arrived.

He watched a squire struggling with a half-dozen of the soldiers' horses. The men had walked away to an encampment of their own, leaving the young boy to tend their mounts. Rouwen saw his chance. He pushed clear of the shrubs and boldly walked forward.

'Is that the captain's charger?' he said in his most commanding voice. 'He wants it posted just outside the tent.'

'What?' The boy blinked in surprise. He hadn't seen Rouwen come up, and he had no instructions concerning the captain's mount. 'No one's to go near His Majesty's tent.'

'If you won't do it, I will. I'm no fool. Disobeying the captain's direct order is folly.' Rouwen grabbed the reins from the youth's hands, keeping the bulk of the charger between him and the frightened boy. He strode off, tugging on the horse's bridle to keep it moving. For a moment, he worried that Vutorian's ward spell still protected those within the glade.

The horse reared and had to be gentled before entering the grassy area surrounded by the thick forest. Rouwen passed the twin trees marking the entrance without incident and decided the horse had been frightened by nothing more than its own shadow moving quickly along the ground in front of it.

Rouwen looked to the sky and saw the sun sinking quickly into the west, as it should. The preternaturally long day was ending –

and it was ending with an abruptness he had never experienced before. Rouwen stopped a few paces away from the tent where Sped, Vutorian, and the captain conferred. Trying to eavesdrop would gain him little.

He wanted the grimoire. If Vutorian carried it on his person, as he had for so long, he had to attack the wizard when he was alone and unsuspecting. His best chance of that was in the wizard's own tent. From the layout of the camp, Rouwen guessed the next gaudily colored tent housed the wizard. Looping the horse's reins to a tent stake, Rouwen looked around to see if anyone noticed him, then ducked into the purple-and-gold silk tent.

The tent's cool interior reminded him of how fiery the day had been outside, with the sun never moving. Rouwen moved about slowly, letting his eyes adjust to the dimness. As he worked his way around the outer tent wall, he searched for any possible hiding place where Vutorian might have placed the grimoire. If the spell book still glowed with its vivid green, he would have found it quickly.

Rouwen remembered how the Flame Specter had drained the grimoire of its power, leaving behind a book similar in appearance to dozens of others he had seen. The exceptional qualities lay within the grimoire now, in its information Kwuway had garnered and carefully recorded about the fire elemental.

'You search in all the wrong places, Captain Rouwen,' came a cold voice from behind. Rouwen spun, his hand flying to his sword hilt. He half drew, then paused. Fighting a wizard with steel availed him little. A simple pass of Vutorian's hand might cast a spell that would freeze him solid or turn him into a boneless maggot.

Vutorian closed the tent flap behind him and secured the strings for the sake of privacy. 'I assume you hunt for this.' Vutorian reached into his robes and drew forth the grimoire. It carried a small greenish tint, but it had not returned to its former brilliance.

Rouwen laughed easily and sat on the edge of Vutorian's cot. 'You know my plight. I seek you out to lift *this* curse on my head.' Rouwen drew forth the spell casket.

He had not anticipated Vutorian's reaction on seeing the altered magical device. Vutorian muttered a ward spell and held out the grimoire, as if it might protect him from some savage magical assault.

'You have come through much, Rouwen,' the wizard said, his eyes fixed on the spell casket. 'The power required to alter a spell casket holding its magical secret is extreme.'

452

'Explain to me what happened in the audience chamber.' Rouwen assessed his chances of stealing the grimoire Vutorian held so lightly now. He decided he would not be able to take it without a hue and cry being raised. Vutorian's ward spell would protect him for long enough to bring down the entire company of King's Guard.

'What? Oh, that!' said Vutorian, as if struggling to remember. 'Sosler summoned the Legion of the Air and somehow got the summoning wrong. Nothing more.'

Rouwen knew Vutorian lied, but he expected nothing less from the wizard.

'You should lift the curse on me,' Rouwen said, dangling the misshapen spell casket in front of Vutorian. 'You promised.'

'I did,' Vutorian said, 'but our situation has changed, hasn't it? How did you disappear so completely from the castle? Sosler thought to have you executed, but patrols simply vanished and others could not seem to remember their orders or duties. I suspect a touch of magic.'

'No magic. Just knowledge of the castle and its secret passages,' lied Rouwen.

'A pity. Sosler had Nespizio tortured to death, thinking he had aided you. I tried to intervene, you realize, simply to save a fellow practitioner of the arcane arts from such misery, but the duke would have none of it.' Vutorian smiled, and Rouwen had seen friendlier expressions on the faces of hungry wolves.

'Nespizio had no hand in my escape,' Rouwen said. He was sorry to hear that the aged wizard had died in such a manner. Another he had called friend had perished because of him. Rouwen hoped Nespizio's spirit easily climbed Mount Glid and made its way into Paradise, as it so richly deserved. He had been a good man, even if his wizardly powers were diminished with age.

'How did you evade Sosler's search? He opened every secret way in the castle, against my advice, of course. Now he must continually fear assassination through those exposed routes.'

'Sosler will never find out, and neither will you,' Rouwen said sharply. He considered for a moment how Vutorian spoke. A flash of insight came to Rouwen and he asked, 'How did you escape Castle Gan? Surely Sosler's men would not have permitted you easy flight.'

Vutorian's eyebrows rose and the mage began pacing. As he walked, he tucked away the grimoire in the folds of his voluminous cape. Rouwen kept estimating distances and striking range, thinking he might gut the wizard before a hand could be

453

lifted in a spell. For the nonce, though, he preferred to hear the tale of Vutorian's exit.

'He is a faithless fool,' Vutorian said with poorly concealed malice toward his former liege. 'He tried to double-cross me. Me!' Vutorian forced himself to be calm. His lip curled into a sneer. 'He will not profit by betraying my confidence, not after all I have done for him.'

'Remove the curse on me, and we will both see his head on a pike,' offered Rouwen. Again he held out the spell casket and let it swing slowly. Vutorian's expression changed subtly and the sneer became a broad grin.

'Your proposition interests me, but I have a new liege. Nothing can be done without his approval.'

'Do you mean Sped?' Rouwen couldn't keep the contempt from his voice. Sorinne's brother had been a wastrel all his life and never fit to ascend the throne to rule. Rouwen had found him to be slow-witted, extraordinarily arrogant, and unworthy of any position more demanding than that of assistant hostler.

'You haven't just come into our camp. You know he is forming a government in exile. These past months have been tedious since we fled the castle but . . .'

'What?' Rouwen's sharp inquiry stopped Vutorian. 'How long has it been since you escaped Castle Gan?'

'Why, more than two months. We roamed aimlessly for half that time. Sped thought he could find refuge in the Dorman Highlands, but all we found were Sosler's spies and toadies. They harassed us at every turn until we struck out for the Rocky Coast. I know the region well and believe we can prosper here.'

Rouwen tried to keep his face impassive as he considered Vutorian's astounding claim. Rouwen had lost track of time, but he had not been underground, in Noumet and after, for more than a week. Perhaps less because his food would have given out before that. To claim two full months of wandering pushed his gullibility to the limit, yet why would Vutorian lie about such an innocuous matter?

'You thought he could obtain an alliance with others more quickly? So did he,' Vutorian said in disgust. 'But we shall prevail. He is of the royal line, and the peasants will rally to him once we raise a sizable army.'

'What of Sorinne?' Rouwen heard himself asking. He didn't want her used as a lever against his resolve, yet he had to know her fate.

'You worry that the spells used on her will turn her completely against you? Sosler has her under his control and isn't likely to relinquish it,' Vutorian said. 'She is the symbol of the old, even as Sosler promises more to the citizens of Gan. Sorinne was always a charitable and kind princess, from all tales.' Vutorian studied Rouwen for any reaction. Rouwen did not give the wizard the satisfaction of asking further after Sorinne's condition.

'I worry about the length of the day,' Rouwen said in an attempt to turn the conversation to less personal matters.

'The curious movement of the sun and stars is a matter of concern,' Vutorian said. 'Days that last minutes or a week become trying. It is the uncertain tide that proves the most inconvenient, though. How can we launch a ship if the tide might not come in for days? Or goes out unexpectedly. All nature is in an uproar.'

'Because of Sosler,' Rouwen said flatly.

'Who knows the reason? Don't flatter him with more power than he has, Rouwen. Remember how he lost the gold trumpet. Sosler cannot again summon the Legion of the Air, nor could he control it even if he had sounded the proper peal.'

Rouwen swung around when he heard unexpected noise at the flap of the wizard's tent.

'What goes on in there?' came Sped's petulant question. 'Open immediately or I shall order the guard to burn down your tent.'

'My liege,' Vutorian said in exasperation. He unfastened the cords holding the tent flap and let Sped and a cold night wind into the tent. Somehow, Rouwen wasn't too astonished at the rapid dying of the light outside. If what Vutorian said was true, the length of the day and night had been uncertain for most of the time since their departure from Castle Gan – which corresponded with Rouwen's entry into Noumet and his unfortunate encounter in the illusion park.

But months passing since Torgon's death? Rouwen found that doubtful. Too much occurred without explanation.

'It's you. I ought to have guessed. There was some confusion in the squire. You know the one I mean. The youngling who tends the horses; the one I do so adore. He told me that a man answering your description had duped him.' Sped popped a berry into his mouth, chewed for a moment, then spat the seed against the tent wall. Vutorian steadfastly ignored the young prince's behavior and stared straight at Rouwen to gauge his reaction.

'We have something in common now, my lord,' said Rouwen. 'You have been driven from Castle Gan, as have I. We should join forces to depose Sosler before his grip becomes too secure on the reins of power.'

'My idea exactly,' Sped said, showing how easily led the young man was, given the proper argument. Rouwen didn't doubt that Vutorian took full advantage of Sped's self-centered nature.

'Rouwen has graciously consented to lead your army. You need a field general of unsurpassed ability. Lord Brion is the one you need, King Sped.' Vutorian grimaced as he forced out the title. The former Captain of the Intrepid Guard couldn't tell if the distaste came in naming Sped king or Rouwen lord.

'General?' Sped swung about on the wizard. 'This man is a traitor. He and my mother . . .' Sped's face contorted into a mask of unadulterated hatred.

'What Queen Diarra did is of no consequence now, Majesty,' Vutorian said smoothly. 'There is strong evidence Sosler lied to you about the entire matter. We shall discuss this at length later. Consider this: Lord Brion swears fealty only to you.'

'I do,' Rouwen said, willing to say anything if Vutorian removed the curse laid on his head. Sped could never be a menace to Sosler. The duke's death would come at the tip of Rouwen's sword, as it should.

'I'm not sure,' Sped said, vacillating. 'Oh, very well, Vutorian. If you say so. Come here, Rouwen.'

Rouwen went to the youth and knelt when he saw Sped's intent. The youth drew his sword and held it above his head with both hands, point downward.

'In the name of Gan, forthwith shall I recognize you as General Rouwen, Lord Brion!' Sped's grip on the sword weakened and the sword plunged into the ground. It struck a rock and skittered to one side, leaving behind a trail of bright sparks.

Rouwen shook his head. This wasn't an auspicious start for a general, especially since he detested his new king as much as he had Sped's father.

11

Battle and Grimoire

'This is it?' Brion Rouwen stared at the double rank of mounted soldiers in disbelief. 'You mean this is your personal guard? The remainder of your force is elsewhere?'

'Why ever do you say that, my good General Rouwen?' asked Sped. The effete young man sniffed delicately at a yellow and orange flower he had picked. The pollen caused him to sneeze violently, sending petals flying into the air. 'These are stout fellows, each and every one worth a dozen of those fools Sosler has in his army.'

'What size is the army of Gan?' asked Rouwen. 'A hundred times this number guard the castle. And a hundred times that rode under Sosler's personal command while he was Lord Protector of the Realm. We cannot go into battle with so few fighters.' Rouwen saw that his argument fell on deaf ears, at least as far as Sped was concerned. Vutorian smiled slightly, and Rouwen didn't know if it was in response to Sped's ignorance or for some other reason. Vutorian played his own game – always.

'Sosler's army is somewhat diminished,' Vutorian ventured. 'The fight with the Mionese army that you led to the castle gates caused a few casualties.'

'How did the battle fare?' Rouwen wanted to know how well Laslo had fought before dying.

'It took more than a week of fighting before the Mionese were forced back down the road to the valley,' Vutorian said, startling Rouwen. 'They fought like cornered rats, never giving a pace without demanding payment in blood. It was rumored that more than half of the Mionese are still hiding in Valley Gan.'

'Times have changed, and not for the better,' Rouwen lamented. An invading army should never have entered the Demon's Throat without considerable losses. He had led the Mionese without casualty all the way to the gates of the castle, with the blessing of Gan's citizenry. Now Vutorian hinted that those same citizens, once the kingdom's greatest asset, now hid foreign soldiers from their own troops.

'Sosler need not fear a ragtag band hiding in holes and running from their own shadows.' Vutorian squinted as he peered into the sky at the sun directly overhead where it had been for more than six hours. 'Even casting a shadow these days is difficult.'

'Do you have any explanation for the unusual track taken by the sun?' asked Rouwen, fishing for information. He wondered if Vutorian considered the strange happenings the result of trouble in the City of Mages or connected it with the appearance of the Flame Specter when Sosler had tried summoning the Legion of the Air.

'These things happen,' Vutorian said in an offhand manner, dismissing any more questions on the subject. He pointed at the double rank of cavalry and asked, 'What can you do with them, General Rouwen? Sped desires a quick return to the throne so he can get on with his reign.'

Rouwen tried not to laugh. Sped wandered about picking flowers and blowing their fluttering white seeds into the air. A small child might do this, though Rouwen couldn't imagine Finola ever doing it. Rouwen's amusement died. She had been robbed of a childhood because of Vutorian and his desire to use her magical talents.

'So few soldiers cannot launch any real attack against Sosler's guard,' Rouwen said. 'We can begin a nibbling attack, chewing at an exposed post or ambushing a lone patrol. More than by chivvying Sosler, we can't hope to succeed.'

'But you are a brilliant general, Lord Brion. Vutorian says so,' spoke up Sped. Rouwen hadn't realized the young pretender was listening to their conversation. He damned himself for a fool. Sped seemed ill-equipped mentally but this might be a façade to lull others into misjudging him. Sped hadn't survived in Priowe's castle through intervention by the king alone.

Rouwen tried to remember the times Sorinne had spoken of her brother. She had seldom mentioned Sped, and when she did it was always in a diffident manner. Rouwen didn't like admitting it, especially now that he was so dangerous to her, but they had spoken little of their own thoughts and ambitions while together. Mutual passion had ruled them completely.

'The most illustrious tactician can do nothing if the soldiers are not up to the task,' Rouwen said. 'I do not say these men are lacking in training or bravery. Rather, they are lacking in comrades to ride at their shoulder.'

'So? Find more. This entire country seems undeveloped. Go

into the countryside and find others willing to ride under my banner, wherever it is.' Sped looked around, as if confused at the lack of pennants flying over his tent or at the head of the column.

'Majesty, we have removed your banner, fearing spies will report to Sosler,' Vutorian said.

'Put the banners back on their staffs,' Rouwen ordered. 'It won't hurt advertising our presence. Mion is a ruined country. It was never strong under King Nishor. After we devastated Tachre, there wasn't more than a handful of soldiers left.'

'And those you led against Sosler,' Vutorian finished. 'You claim there are no men left in the country willing to flock to our banner?'

'We'll do better getting into Valley Gan and reassembling those men who rode to the castle under Lord Laslo's command,' Rouwen said. He hesitated to name himself commander of that expedition, though the army had followed him. He had not been Mionese. Only Vutorian's magicks and Diarra's control of the Legion of the Air had kept him in such an exalted position.

Rouwen heard the pounding of horse's hooves and saw the grizzled old sergeant who had braved his captain come riding up. Sergeant Yint ignored his officers entirely and dropped to the ground in front of Vutorian. He shot a sour glance in Rouwen's direction, taking in the tattered Mionese uniform shorn of its ornamentation, then reported briskly to the wizard.

'There's a company of troops not an hour's ride away. We can ambush 'em if we 'ave the will.'

'Report this to your general, not to me,' ordered Vutorian. 'I am only King Sped's advisor, not his military commander.'

'This one's a general?' Yint snorted, wiped his nose, then spat on the ground not an inch from the toe of Rouwen's boots. 'Next you'll be telling me it's 'im doing the sun up that way.' Yint pointed at the sun, now beginning its slow sink, this time into the east where it had risen almost eight hours earlier.

'Been Sergeant of Cavalry long?' Rouwen asked, walking around Yint. The sergeant tried to follow Rouwen but a sharp command brought him to stiff attention. 'I doubt you have ever learned how to deliver a proper report. I served as Captain of the Intrepid Guard, an elite unit. I never inspected the lesser units.'

'Lesser!' raged Yint. 'We're the best there is! Give us the chance to prove it!'

'Indeed,' Rouwen said, content at having roused the sergeant's ire enough to put some military flash back into him. 'Bring your captain, give a decent report, then we shall discuss what can and cannot be done with your unit. Dismissed!'

Sergeant Yint saluted and did a sharp about-face, marching off to fetch his company commander.

'Well done, General,' complimented Vutorian. 'We might have a chance against Sosler after all. I applauded your skill before, when you rode at the head of the Mionese scum. With true soldiers, there can be hope.' Vutorian wandered off, muttering to himself. Rouwen wanted to stop the wizard and get him to lift the curse then and there, but he knew that would never happen.

Even if they rode triumphant into Castle Gan, Vutorian might never lift the curse. That promise was his hold over Rouwen, and Rouwen knew it. A better course of action would be stealing the grimoire and getting it back to Noumet for Finola's use. Rouwen examined the sun and its erratic path through the sky, seeing there would be more hours of daylight than he estimated just a few minutes earlier. As if realizing its mistake, the sun stopped its easterly setting and worked back up to zenith to slide down toward a western sunset.

'Gerberria, you have lost control,' Rouwen said, finally believing those in the City of Mages controlled the universe as Finola had claimed. He paused to wonder how the young girl fared. So much responsibility had been placed on her. Whether the other wizards in Noumet were aged or simply ancient beyond their years due to the rigor of their magical work, Finola had to perform far beyond her training.

Again Rouwen considered asking Vutorian his opinion of the City of Mages. Vutorian had once decried Finola's insistence that she was bound for the ranks of wizards controlling the world's conduct.

'General?' The cavalry captain strode up, Sergeant Yint following closely. 'Who are you to take command of *my* troops?'

'I'm King Sped's military commander,' Rouwen said tiredly. 'If you have a problem with this, take it up with him.'

Yint laughed derisively. All three of them knew what would happen if any sensible question was put to the king.

'Report, Sergeant. Tell me how we can ambush Sosler's patrol and turn it to our advantage.' Rouwen sat on his heels as the sergeant began his rambling report. He watched the captain, evaluating his usefulness. The man seethed at being relieved of his command. Practically, a general would command the cavalry directly, there being little chain of command when only fifty soldiers were involved. Rouwen considered ways of involving the captain and defusing his anger at being demoted to a position little higher than his crusty sergeant.

'So you believe we can get them to surrender and join us?' Rouwen's eyebrows arched in surprise at this notion.

'There's dissent in their ranks, General,' Yint assured him.

'So? Captain, is this likely?'

'Why are you asking me?'

'You will lead the troops. Your opinion is important. Do we stand the chance of, say, doubling our force if enough of this ranging company surrenders?'

Rouwen listened with half an ear to the captain's conviction that Yint was right. When the captain paused for breath, Rouwen shot to his feet. 'Enough talk. We act. I will assume you and your sergeant have done good scouting work and that the ravine is a good ambush point. Be ready to offer generous surrender terms. Any officers surrendering will retain their rank, unless it exceeds yours.' Rouwen got a blink of surprise and a slow smile of approval.

'As you will, General.' The captain saluted and rushed off to prepare for battle. Yint gave Rouwen a knowing look, chuckled, and went after his officer.

Rouwen almost called Yint back to ask him what the captain's name was. He had neglected to find out. He sighed. It hardly mattered. If all went well he would promote the captain to a higher rank. If the attack failed, none would be alive for recrimination.

'Fight gallantly, General Rouwen,' Vutorian said in his mocking voice. Rouwen turned and faced the wizard.

'You are coming with us,' Rouwen said. 'We will need the powers you control. A spell here and there will turn the tide for us. You might be our only advantage.'

'I must protect our liege,' Vutorian said easily. 'My magicks are all that stand between him and . . . disquiet.' Vutorian made a vague gesture encompassing the entire world.

Rouwen said nothing, his mind working over details of sneaking away from the battle to return and find the grimoire. He had no reason to remain with Sped. He loathed the man, and he did not trust Vutorian to lift the curse on his head.

'My mount!' Rouwen bellowed. The squire Sped fancied came rushing up, leading a sway-backed mare that had seen too many fights and too few days of rest. Rouwen pulled himself into the hard saddle and adjusted his sword so it would draw more easily. He surveyed the troops he led and thought he ought to have insisted on a new uniform. The old Mionese uniform he wore might confuse the soldiers in the heat of battle. Then he shook off such a notion. These men fought their former comrades-in-arms. Rouwen's different uniform would not confuse the fighters as much as having to attack those bearing Gannian insignia.

Such was the rationale of a pretender fighting a tyrant for the throne.

Rouwen rode alongside the captain and talked of older, better times in Castle Gan. He learned the captain's unit, its strengths, and how the officer had risen through the ranks after being a farmer not twenty miles from Rouwen's family farm. But Rouwen never learned the officer's name, which bothered him greatly.

The captain was the first to die in the ambush.

Whether Yint had not properly scouted or the old sergeant had been duped and lured into the ambush by Sosler's troops, Rouwen found hard to say. An hour's ride remained before reaching the ravine Rouwen had chosen for the ambuscade.

He found his guardsmen caught in the jaws of a trap, attacks coming from front and rear quarters. Rouwen saw immediately that the opposing commander sought to force Rouwen's men to flee either left or right, splitting the force.

'Rally the men. Straight forward. Attack!' Rouwen bellowed. The confusion rippling through the ranks of his men settled when they saw someone in charge. The captain slumped to the side, unable to sit upright in the saddle. Yint rode to the officer's side and pushed. The captain fell from his shying horse, a crossbow bolt buried to the fletching in the man's chest.

'Attack, Sergeant Yint, attack!' repeated Rouwen. He whipped out his sword and led the charge, crossbow bolts singing around his ears. One bolt buried itself in his saddle and caused his horse to falter. Rouwen kept pressing the attack, much to the shock of the soldiers blocking the road ahead.

'Our rear, General, our rear. They are stronger there,' reported Yint. It was as Rouwen had suspected. Sosler's commander had assumed the attack would either split the enemy ranks into two easily conquered sections or precipitate a retreat. If Rouwen had tried retreating, he would have met the strongest portion of Sosler's troops. By launching his attack ahead, he unerringly found the weakest portion of the enemy position.

'We're through, General. What now?' demanded Yint.

Those surviving the frontal assault reformed their ranks, but Rouwen knew he could never take the initiative. He lacked numbers for an effective assault, even if he had surprise on his side. The unscathed and unbloodied bulk of the attacking troops lay behind.

'A geyser!' someone shouted as the earth opened and a ten-foot column of water blasted skyward. Mud began falling over his troops. Rouwen ordered them to hold back for a moment to assess their position. He was glad caution had dictated his next movement.

The heavy quake shaking the ground drove many of the cavalrymen from their horses, leaving them on foot. If he had committed his troops and the earthquake had hit, he would have been cut to bloody ribbons by Sosler's crossbowmen.

The rain of mud and the shivering ground subsided. Rouwen ordered the attack.

A deep crevice opened along the road, keeping some of the enemy from attacking directly. Those troopers on the same side as Rouwen's soldiers found themselves quickly vanquished due to lack of command from their officers.

'Surrender and none shall be put to the sword,' Rouwen called. 'You will be permitted either to join King Sped's troops at your present rank or simply be stripped of weapons and sent on your way.'

The message was slow to flow through the opposing guardsmen but finally the battle wound down and Rouwen found himself in command of almost twice as many soldiers as before the attack. Many of the company's officers had either died when the earthquake struck, when the huge chasm yawned, or had been caught on the far side and unable to command their men.

Those troops had retreated to fight another day, but the remainder had surrendered to Yint, only a few choosing to be stripped of their weapons and sent on their way back to Valley Gan.

'A victory, General,' Yint chortled. 'Who'd of thought it, eh?'

'Yes, a victory,' Rouwen said tiredly. So many had died, and they had all been loyal Gannian citizens. Civil wars were the worst, each death being a neighbor's or friend's. 'Prepare a roll of honor. Put the captain in for a medal.'

'What rank, General?'

'Your decision, Captain Yint.' The old sergeant's eyes narrowed a little and a smile began to change the contours of his leathery face.

'Thank ye grandly, General. I'll see to it. What are ye doing now?'

'Returning to camp with news. See the men – all the men – back to camp, Captain. And watch for their former comrades to ambush you, if the opportunity comes their way.'

'As you will, General.' Yint saluted smartly and set off to assemble his new company.

Caked with mud and wary of more earthquakes and geysers, Rouwen rode at a brisk trot back to the camp, slowing only when he neared the glade and heard the flapping of Sped's tent in the rising wind. The sun had finally set for the day, finding its proper resting place in the west. Dismounting, Rouwen tethered the horse and circled the camp.

Knowing nothing of Vutorian's ward spells, Rouwen approached the rear of the wizard's tent cautiously. He expected lightning to fall from the sky or the wild shrieking of ward demons to alert the wizard to unauthorized intrusion. Nothing happened when Rouwen lifted the back flap and slipped once more into the tent.

This time Rouwen could hardly believe his good fortune. The cape Vutorian had worn earlier lay spread over the cot, as if the wizard had used it as a blanket for a nap and then left it behind in the heat of the day. Rouwen picked up the cape and fumbled in the silk lining. His hand brushed over a hard, rectangular shape.

Rouwen's heart stopped beating for a second when his fingers closed around the spell book. He drew out the grimoire and stared at its leather-bound cover.

Rouwen flipped the book open and let out a breath he hadn't known he was holding. This was a grimoire, but not the one he had given Vutorian. He had to keep searching for the spell book that would relieve Finola of her burden and imprison the Flame Specter again.

12

Down the Throat

'Stay under cover,' Rouwen urged his captain. The coal-black sky opened with huge bolts of vivid lightning, and a torrential downpour drenched his ragtag band of soldiers making their way across Mion toward the Demon's Throat.

'Where?' came Yint's quarrelsome reply. 'This 'ere's a damn, empty desert after so many 'quakes. There's no place to take cover. No place what's dry.'

'Find it,' Rouwen said, irked at Yint's attitude. He tried to see through the sheets of water pouring down. He couldn't. Even the orange and yellow bolts of lightning no longer showed the way in the intense dark. He tried to remember when the sun had last shone and given some thin hope of warmth and dry clothing. Without the daily transit of the sun, he was lost in estimating time.

It might have been as long as three days since the sun had risen to warm the land. He shivered and pulled his red-and-silver cloak around his shoulders. His Mionese uniform had rotted off him as he made his way through fields filled with fumaroles, all spewing sulfur fumes. Rouwen had lost a horse in a sinkhole in a trip from one side of a field to the other, and had thought he would never get his troops across because of constantly spewing miniature volcanoes.

He had won across this field, after a series of earthquakes rearranged the terrain, lifting a small mountain range and levelling rolling hills in other places. And the wind! Never had he endured such gale force wind. The only bright spot in the journey to the Demon's Throat, if Rouwen dared call it lucky, lay in the absence of the Flame Specter's fiery touch.

'We can get through the Throat if we push on,' declared Captain Yint. 'We're no untried soldiers. We 'ave the will.'

'There's no rush,' Rouwen insisted. Somewhere ahead of the soldiers travelled Vutorian and Sped. The wizard supposedly eased the way for them with spells that guided enemy patrols from their course. The two brief skirmishes Rouwen had engaged in showed no sign of any ward spells working against Sosler's troops.

Rouwen rode through the storm, deciding he could not get any wetter. He watched carefully for any sign that the lightning above him would turn into a gout of fire from the Flame Specter, but all he saw was ordinary, though unrelenting, lightning. As he rode, he considered his decision to attack Valley Gan through the Demon's Throat again. He had successfully led the far larger Mionese army into Gan between the twin fortresses protecting the canyon mouth, but he had summoned the Legion of the Air to weaken resistance.

Depending on Vutorian gave him no sense of comfort. The wizard played his own game, and Rouwen couldn't decide what it might be. After finding the spell book in the wizard's cape, he had replaced it. Had Vutorian left the false grimoire as bait for a trap, or did he have more than one spell book, the grimoire Rouwen sought so desperately being still on his person? More than once in the past week Rouwen had considered asking Vutorian about the spell book and had always hesitated. To show any interest in it might anger Vutorian, and as much as retrieving the grimoire, he wanted the curse on his head lifted.

'He's using me,' Rouwen grumbled as he rode through even heavier rainfall. 'He wants Sosler deposed so he can install Sped and be the power behind the throne.' The citizens of Gan would never permit a wizard to sit on their throne. This prejudice ran deep and with good reason. More than one mage had ruled, using magicks as well as force of arms to maintain order.

They had always been assassinated because of distrust. Mention of demonic dealings always grew into something more. The last of the wizard-kings had been Ulonto, a hundred years earlier. From accounts, Ulonto was beneficent, as rulers went, but his use of arcane powers convinced his people that he was in league with demons. When confronted, he grew more aloof and haughty. The castle guard had murdered him in his sleep, and no one in Valley Gan cared.

'He'll keep Sped on the throne,' Rouwen decided. He sat straighter in the saddle when dim shapes appeared ahead on the muddy road. Reining back, Rouwen tried to make out the dim forms.

Two men on foot talked earnestly. One waved his arms about, giving him a strange birdlike aspect when repeated lightning flashes illuminated him. Rouwen couldn't identify him, but the calmer speaker was Vutorian. The wizard tried to quiet the agitated man but failed.

The lightning died for a few seconds, and when a new jagged flash lit the sky, Vutorian stood alone in the road. The wizard turned and walked slowly away. Rouwen considered finding out whom the wizard had consulted but knew the futility of tracking in this downpour. He rode on, overtaking Vutorian as the wizard mounted his steed.

'How far to the Demon's Throat?' called Rouwen, words muffled by the heavy rainfall. 'The men aren't going to be in any condition to fight if this rain keeps on much longer.'

'I have no power to control the weather,' Vutorian said testily. His argument with the unknown man on the road had left him irritated and he had no desire to speak with Rouwen. He whirled his cape around him to keep out the worst of the rain and rode ahead. Rouwen followed, refusing to be put off.

'The storm can be a blind for our attack if you guarantee the guards will sleep.' Rouwen pressed the wizard to gain any advantage, no matter how small. If Vutorian grew angry enough, he might reveal one or two of his secret plans for this invasion. Rouwen wasn't gullible enough to believe that Vutorian's motives stopped at putting Sped on the throne and pulling the marionette-king's strings.

'When do you begin to cast the spells and how do you keep Sosler's wizard from discovering them?'

'What wizard? Sosler trusts no one with arcane power after I . . .' Vutorian bit off his reply.

Rouwen smiled slightly, his face hidden under the drooping hood of his cape. It was as he had guessed. Vutorian had tried to depose Sosler and had lost the struggle. Rather than return to his mansion in Kelnos Forest, Vutorian had taken up with Sped in an attempt to regain some of the power he had let slip through his fingers. A second attempt on Sosler's power might not be any better executed, but Rouwen knew that Vutorian would try.

'My troops will be ready for an attack within the hour, after you give the signal,' Rouwen said. He had been denied seeing familiar landmarks because of the continual storm, and the time of travel was a mystery with the sun hidden for so long. Both factors might work to his advantage if they reached the Demon's Throat. Constant night and the cloak of rain might get them closer than any other attacking force. Without the power of the wind warriors at his beck and call, only stealth would win them entry.

'Yes, yes, soon, Rouwen.' Vutorian put his heels into his

horse's flanks and galloped off, vanishing quickly in the rain. Rouwen turned his charger's head and walked slowly back to where Yint had bivouacked the meager hundred men in the invading force.

'Well?' the captain demanded. 'What of it? Do we go into battle soon?'

'Tell the men to sleep while they can,' Rouwen said. 'The attack won't occur for a few hours yet.'

'You've sighted the Throat?' An edge came to Yint's voice. They were returning home as an invading army. Rouwen experienced many of the same emotions, though he had lived them before and they were no longer unique for him.

'Soon,' Rouwen assured his captain. He had no idea how far away the Demon's Throat lay, but they must be close. Finding shelter proved impossible so he rode constantly, heading back to the spot in the road where he had seen the unknown man arguing with Vutorian. Rouwen tried to trail Vutorian's mysterious visitor but failed. He eventually took refuge on the lee side of a hill and settled down to consider who might be meeting Vutorian.

Unless the plots were layered more thickly than he could fathom, Vutorian had not met with Sosler or anyone representing him. Perhaps Vutorian thought to buy influence with someone on Sosler's staff. That idea appealed to Rouwen since it matched his conception of the wizard. If so, it might be an alliance going back to when Vutorian was in the duke's good graces.

He settled down, head resting on drawn-up knees, letting the rain pelt him mercilessly. He missed Finola and hoped she fared well as she struggled to contain the elementals running wild in the world. The lack of sun told of trouble in Noumet, but the Flame Specter had been absent since the single eruption on his way back to the surface. Rouwen's hands rubbed the burned area on his chest and winced. It was a wound past healing, beyond mere physical existence. Somehow, this was the Flame Specter's gate into the world, and similarly, it gave Rouwen a window on what the fire elemental thought and did.

Rouwen might have dozed in spite of the wet discomfort of his position, but he became immediately alert when he heard the sucking noise of horses approaching through mud. He found his mount and climbed into the saddle, settling down for what might be a fight. Before he could loosen his sword in its scabbard a flash of lighting showed him Yint waving.

'General, the word's out. We go now. The damn wizard's said so.'

'Forward,' Rouwen ordered, seeing that Yint had formed the

468

small company into four columns. Two would approach one fortress and the remainder of the force would assault the second. If luck held, and Rouwen did not count on it, Sosler would not yet have repaired the fortresses after the attack made on them by the wind warriors.

And Vutorian would have lulled the guards to sleep with soporific spells.

''e sent word, he did,' grumbled Yint, 'telling us to get our arses moving. It's a good thing I saw you by the road. What were you doing over there, all curled up like that?'

'Thinking, Captain, just thinking.' Rouwen cut off further conversation by cantering along the muddy track, still unable to see more than a few paces ahead. When his horse's hooves clacked on paving stones, Rouwen reined back and called his troops to a halt. They had reached the base of the twin fortresses guarding the Demon's Throat. Night still clung tenaciously to the world and the rain refused to let up for even a heartbeat. If Vutorian had carried out his part of the assault, they might win entry to Valley Gan and not suffer any casualties.

'The deed is done, General,' came Vutorian's somber voice. The wizard rode through the rain, a tiny bubble of dryness in the storm. He maintained a spell warding off the rain, though Rouwen saw that some leaked through in annoying drips. It was a measure of Vutorian's lack of skill as a wizard that he couldn't hold a perfect spell.

'Shall we take the fortresses or proceed through?' Rouwen didn't want to linger longer than necessary. The posts along the canyon walls in the Demon's Throat might be manned. Under the cover of night and storm they could escape detection. The time needed to kill, imprison, or recruit the guards in the fortresses might stretch into long hours better used reaching the base of the spire holding Castle Gan.

'Go through. There are few guards. Sosler's forces range far afield to conquer territory for him.' The bitterness in Vutorian's tone told Rouwen that the wizard and the duke were not in league. The hidden figure Vutorian had conferred with hours earlier did not represent Sosler in some twisted turnabout of loyalties.

'Yint, you've heard. Get the men moving as quickly as possible. We are on our own territory now. Make all possible speed down the Throat and into the valley.'

'Consider it done, General.' Yint flashed hand signals to the men and got the four columns moving directly to the massive gates that had been twisted from their hinges by the Legion of the Air. Scant attempt at repair had been made – and why

469

should it? Gan was pre-eminent among kingdoms and no external threat existed. After the fall of King Nishor in Tachre and the destruction of the Mionese army, the only enemies Sosler need fear came from his own ranks.

'Is Sosler in Gan?' The notion that he rode into the enemy's stronghold, only to find its leader absent, had not occurred to Rouwen. He wanted the grimoire. He also wanted Sosler dead.

'Ah, yes, he is not one to leave the security of his castle.'

'How difficult is your sleep spell to cast? Can you use it on dozens more, if we reach the castle gates?'

'Castle Gan is too large. If one guard did not notice, another out of range of the spell would and raise the alarm. You must find another way to enter, but you are so clever at finding secret passages that will be no trouble, will it, Brion?'

The sardonic way Vutorian spoke put Rouwen on edge. He waved to Yint and then joined the soldiers as they wended their way through the gates and into the narrow canyon leading to Valley Gan. Twice he had done the impossible, breaching the once impregnable defenses of a powerful kingdom. Rouwen felt no triumph.

Gan was *his* country. He was returning home, not invading. Before he had led Mionese soldiers. This time he rode with others from the Gannian army. Somehow, that didn't make the ride down the center of the Demon's Throat any easier.

'To the castle!' came the loud cry from behind him. 'To Castle Gan for your king!'

Sped raced by at a full gallop, oblivious of the deep holes hidden by water and the need for quiet until they reached the wide, fertile valley. Rouwen heaved a sigh and went after his liege, worrying even more that his choice of allies was deadly.

13

Elementals Gone Wild

Brion Rouwen stood in creaking, wet stirrups and stared across storm-racked Valley Gan. He tried to remember when he had thought of this lush farmland as his home. It might have only been months ago – or was it longer? He had trouble analyzing the strange time-stretching sensations while underground in Noumet and later. Eons now separated him from his neighbors.

'The storm's breaking up,' commented Yint. 'We can almost see the castle.' The grizzled captain's voice carried great emotion. He, too, was coming home with mixed feelings.

Rouwen couldn't see Castle Gan but knew just where it would eventually appear through the storm clouds. And hidden behind both cloud and castle would be Mount Glid, the pathway to Paradise for those spirits able to make the journey. Rouwen swallowed hard, thinking of Adan and the others still wandering aimlessly, chained between this world and Paradise by the action of his curse. He had slain and trapped them in a nonexistence, a double curse.

'We ride hard for the castle,' Rouwen decided. 'Sosler must have patrols out to keep order. We dare not engage them or the attack will be delayed by interminable skirmishes.' He remembered how agitated the citizens had been when Sosler pulled back his forces to Castle Gan and let the Mionese army enter the valley unopposed. That might have been a good defensive tactic since Rouwen commanded the Legion of the Air then, but it had alienated his own subjects. Rouwen doubted Sosler would ever win back the goodwill of the citizenry.

'Road's out,' observed Yint. He squinted and wiped rain from his eyebrows to see better. 'Looks to be 'ard going for the lot of us. Might be better to take off 'cross country.'

The well-maintained highway leading to the castle had been cut by more than one fast-running stream driven down from higher in the mountains. Rouwen knew the number of times the road soared in bridgework across streams and rivers. If the road was

471

poor here, so close to the high country of the Demon's Throat, it had to be in grave disrepair farther on.

'Do it,' Rouwen decided. He walked his horse away from the road, letting the animal choose its path carefully over the slippery, treacherous terrain. Behind him, Captain Yint ordered the hundred soldiers to find their own way through the fields. The broken country approach would serve them well, Rouwen thought, but an uneasy feeling began gnawing at him.

He heard Sped yelling and cursing, threatening Sosler with a variety of improbable tortures for exiling the true heir to the throne. Rouwen pushed the young man's vociferous calls for a war from his mind. The storm was dying, but the distant crash of thunder along the Shield Mountains drowned out all but the loudest of Sped's cries. Rouwen doubted any scout sent out by Sosler would hear enough to become suspicious. He worried more about being sighted now that the impenetrable sheets of rain were thinning.

His horse slogged through the mud, then reared suddenly. Rouwen thrust out his hand to signal Yint. When the captain did not obey, Rouwen bellowed, 'Halt!'

Two men walked from the edge of a lightly forested area, farm tools clutched in their hands. Rouwen recognized one man as Danen, a farmer who had agreed to passage of the Mionese army earlier.

'You're back,' Danen accused, when he recognized Rouwen. 'You going to do any better getting rid of that bastard this time?' Danen cocked his head to one side and studied the men arrayed behind Rouwen. A crooked smile came to the farmer's face.

'As you see, I lead King Sped's troops now.' Rouwen was greeted with harsh laughter. He looked around nervously to see if either Vutorian or Sped noticed the contempt in this citizen's attitude. Where those two were, Rouwen couldn't say. He no longer heard Sped's shouts, and for that he heaved a sigh of relief.

'This isn't much of an army, if you intend to take Sosler down. You did better with that pack of Mionese peasants,' Danen said. 'I suppose you want to cut up our fields on your way to the castle?'

'Your fields are destroyed by the torrential rain,' Rouwen pointed out. The uneasy feeling grew. He wondered if Sosler had recruited Danen and his friends and this was a trap. Nowhere along the edge of the field did he see massing troops, but the feeling of a trap closing could not be denied.

'What are your plans this time? Our patience has grown

472

thin, Rouwen.' Danen gripped his scythe even tighter until his knuckles turned white. 'We're tired of armies moving back and forth, killing our crops and livestock – and worse.'

'The men riding with me are members of the King's Guard,' Rouwen said carefully. 'They are not brigands living off the land – or their neighbors.'

The man with Danen spoke for the first time. 'The Mionese aren't such a bad lot. They don't try nothin' but what's right and they're hard workers. Better'n some of the scum from the castle, I say.'

Rouwen digested this information. Vutorian had said Laslo was defeated and the Mionese soldiers sent running, but he had also hinted that as many as half of the invading army had eluded Sosler.

'Do you give the Mionese shelter from Sosler and his troopers?' asked Rouwen. Danen's angry response was clear as he turned to his friend and whispered something harshly, the scythe swinging back and forth dangerously close to the man's legs.

'We want nothing but to return to our crops,' Danen said fiercely. 'Take your wars and be damned. Don't trouble us.'

'Tell us what you can about conditions within Castle Gan, and we will move on as quickly as possible.'

Danen looked at him suspiciously. 'What do you want to know?'

'Does Sosler move his army into the valley or is it still stationed along the road up the spire and within the castle?'

'We don't count them as they go by, but many soldiers have ventured out of Gan,' the farmer said, carefully choosing his words. 'What else?'

'Sorinne,' Rouwen said, choking out the name. 'What of Princess Sorinne?'

Danen snorted and swung the scythe around and laid it over his shoulder. 'The princess is in the dungeons, or so it's rumored. She found what Sosler has been up to. Seems the poxy wizard the duke used to befuddle her senses lifted the spell before getting exiled himself.'

Rouwen didn't venture the information that Vutorian rode with him as Sped's advisor. Like most farmers, Danen had no love for the wizard or any dealer in the arcane arts. Too often in the past, wizards had claimed the ability to grow crops magically, only to ruin entire fields for a generation.

'Is she well?'

'Who can say, except the others in the dungeons. Sosler has been putting more and more of us in his cells for treasonous deed and thought.' Danen moved back a pace and turned to go. Over his shoulder, he called to Rouwen, 'Remember, no destroying our fields as you go or you're no better than the duke.'

'We will float through the countryside like a gentle breeze,' Rouwen promised. Danen and his comrade vanished into the woods, but Rouwen's sense of impending danger grew. He sat for a minute, eyes seeking any clue within the woods. He saw nothing.

Power can be yours. Obey me.

'Yint!' Rouwen called, wondering where the voice came from. 'Did you speak?'

'Not a word, General.'

Rouwen shrugged it off. He was edgy being so close to Castle Gan – and Sosler – again. 'Send out scouts. No action against our citizens. No interrogation, no prisoners, no fighting.'

'Understood, General,' Yint said. 'I grew up not far from 'ere. Danen is an old curmudgeon, but then who isn't, eh? An 'onest man, 'e is, and to be trusted with your life.'

Rouwen saw a half dozen scouts fan out to find a course through the fields – and to discover what caused his uneasiness. As he turned in the saddle, his chest began to twitch and burn. Opening his uniform tunic, Rouwen stared at the Flame Specter's brand on his chest.

He shrieked in pain when the skin began to scorch from the spread of tiny flames around the edges of the mark. The charred flesh glowed with inner light and a curious translucence spread until his chest might have been mistaken for a stained glass window.

Mine!

'Recall the scouts,' Rouwen moaned. 'There is – danger.'

He heard Yint bawling out the order, and then the world swung in wild, crazy circles around Rouwen's head. He swayed in the saddle and almost fell. His hands clutched fiercely at his pommel as fire rose in a semicircle before him.

'Demons!' cried a soldier. 'There's demons being sent to take us to Paradise!'

Being damned was worse than a demon leading a spirit to Paradise, but Rouwen couldn't tell his troops this was no demon. The Flame Specter was one of the four elementals vying for supremacy and had chosen this moment to make a new bid for freedom from Noumet's imprisoning spells. Rouwen's horse bucked and tried to run through the flames. It couldn't break through.

The fire licked at Rouwen's legs and body, but the real pain came from his chest. The brand blazed brighter than the sun and burned his clothing.

Yield, let me through!

'We can't reach you, General. Turn back. Get back!' Yint's voice carried well but the Flame Specter's roar drowned out most of the captain's instructions and invective.

Rouwen tried to turn his horse's head, only to find the semicircle of fire spreading rapidly. He was walled in by twenty-foot-tall flames, crackling loudly and blistering his flesh. The circle began to tighten about him, and he was sure that Finola had finally failed. The Flame Specter had escaped the tenuous bonds the young girl had placed on it and now roared free into the world. Its first victim – sacrifice – would be Brion Rouwen.

Rouwen screamed as he tried to break through the ring of fire. Then he shrieked in fear as the ground below his horse rose, carrying charger and rider ever higher into the air. The plug of dirt erupted above the top of the licking circle of flame and threw him over. Rouwen separated from his horse, flailing as he fell through the air. He landed hard, spattering mud in all directions. For several seconds he lay in the mud, stunned and unable to move. Then he forced himself to his elbows and saw the column of fire contracting still further, solidifying into a core of sun-hot flame that scorched the ground for yards and boiled off pools of water too near the edge.

Rouwen fell onto his back, gasping as the pressure within his chest mounted. He felt as if a thousand horses pounded hard against his chest, trying to burst outward. Gasping, he pulled back his burned tunic and exposed his chest to the sky.

New torrents of rain fell, drenching only him. And the earth began heaving under him, throwing him about like a small child tossed high on a tautly stretched blanket. His ears rang from constant thunder and when he tried to stand, a hurricane force gust of wind blew him back to the ground.

'General, we can't get to ye!' came Yint's distant words. 'The ground's opening up something fierce under us. Crevices a mile deep all around!'

'Get away from me. Go!' Rouwen shouted. He rolled onto hands and knees, arching his back to escape the pain in his chest. Every breath became a nightmare of agony, and through it all he *heard* and *saw* and *felt* the Flame Specter's presence.

Triumph surged within him as the elemental sought escape. But through it all, Rouwen thought he heard a faint chant in a voice he knew well. Finola's words caused the Flame Specter to writhe in anger, and Rouwen tried to feed whatever energy

475

Finola might use in her binding spell. He knew nothing of magic. He might have aided her, or he might have hindered by giving the Flame Specter new territory to exploit. Rouwen knew only that he endured for an eternity before the suffering suddenly ceased.

He fell face down into the mud, the soothing, cool mud, and lay there until his lungs threatened to burst. Pulling himself up enough only to breathe, Rouwen tried to look around. The pillar of fire must have burned half of Gan. Nothing so intense could have done less damage. But he saw nothing unusual in the middle of the field save his horse lying on its side and kicking feebly.

'Yint,' he mumbled around a mouthful of mud. 'Where are you? Save the troops. Retreat.'

'Right 'ere, General,' came the gruff captain's words. Hands clutched Rouwen's shoulders and rolled him over. 'By all the demons, what's 'appened to ye?'

Rouwen's eyes fluttered open and he saw Yint standing over him. Beyond, in the sky, Rouwen saw puffy white clouds and a sun blazing down on a perfect summer's day. The storm had passed, as had the firestorm caused by the fire elemental.

'That's none of your concern,' Rouwen said, pulling his burned tunic closed the best he could to hide the brand on his chest. Although the wound felt warm to the touch, the intense inner pressure had abated. For the time being. 'The soldiers. What of them?'

'A few got caught when the ground opened.' Yint pulled Rouwen to his feet. Rouwen staggered slightly, then regained both strength and balance. 'More than a few,' Yint admitted reluctantly. He made sure Rouwen could stand under his own power, then moved to the brink of a crevasse more than ten feet wide.

Rouwen joined his captain and stared into the abyss. The evidence of such power being unleashed so close frightened him. The Flame Specter had tried to take him for its own, possibly drawn by the curse he sought to have removed, possibly for reasons he could never guess. And as the fire elemental surged upward, earth, wind, and water had retaliated to drive it back underground.

'Never saw anything like it. There was some 'uge worm coming up through the ground making this cut. And above, I swear I saw a wet, slimy beast with eyes glowing yellow, flashing like lightning.' Yint shuddered. 'There's more in Gan than there used to be.'

Rouwen tried to pull his eyes away from the deep fissure but couldn't. Was that a hissing he heard from far below at the bottom? And eyes of unblinking red? Even as he began putting details to the monster he saw, it vanished.

'My horse is injured,' Rouwen said. 'It must be put out of its misery.'

'What 'appened?' Yint stepped back from the crevasse and settled his uniform in a nervous gesture.

'The horse and I went flying,' Rouwen said. 'I had my fall cushioned by the mud. It was too heavy for the distance it fell.' He knew Yint's question had been broader but Rouwen didn't feel like telling his captain more than he needed to know. Yint and the others would surely abandon the attack if they thought he was a lodestone for a war being fought between elementals.

After putting the horse out of its misery, Rouwen walked around the field until he found a span that could be jumped. Yint followed and they rejoined the soldiers, all nervous and frightened. Rouwen looked round for Vutorian and Sped but didn't find them.

'Where's the king?' he asked of Sped's squire. The youth pointed in the direction of Castle Gan. 'He's gone ahead by himself?'

'He h-has. He w-wanted to be the first to the gates to call out the d-duke for mortal combat.' The squire stuttered so badly Rouwen almost misunderstood him.

'We ride. Now!' Rouwen called, accepting a new mount from the squire's trembling hand. This might be one of Sped's personal horses, but Rouwen didn't care. The young kingling would find death if he presented himself at Castle Gan's gates, and only Rouwen was likely to risk his life rescuing him.

14

The Grimoire of the Flame Specter – Again

'Why bother with 'im, General?' Yint asked the question that burned inside Rouwen's brain as fiercely as the Flame Specter's brand had burned in his chest. He wasn't sure he had a good answer, but it had to do with Vutorian.

Rouwen touched the spell casket dangling about his neck. Vutorian would never release him, and Rouwen wasn't sure he trusted the wizard even to try but, more than freedom from the spell that had plagued him for so long, Rouwen had to retrieve the grimoire for Finola. The catastrophic upheaval in the field proved that.

'I need him for my own ends,' Rouwen said simply. He had chased after Sped for the better part of a day, or so the sun told him as it burned down with its unwinking, manic fury. It normally took far longer to reach the base of the castle from the Demon's Throat, but a day's ride had taken on new meaning since the sun began its chaotic travels in the sky.

Yint nodded, as if understanding the deeper meaning behind Rouwen's words. Rouwen guessed that the captain's mind had raced ahead, past the immediate wars being fought, to the time when Sosler was no longer on the throne – and neither was Sped.

King Brion. Again. He had crowned himself king of Mion and had led an army to destruction. This time wasn't proving very different. He counted his guard as they rode by. More than a dozen had been lost to the yawning chasm opening under his feet as elemental fought elemental, with him as the prize.

As that thought came to him, he was shocked. The very forces of nature fought for a prize: Brion Rouwen. The brand on his chest meant more than simple possession. The Flame Specter needed a conduit into the world, and if it ever succeeded in opening it, Rouwen knew he would be snuffed out like a puny candle flame in a hurricane.

'Disperse the men along the road leading to the castle,' Rouwen

478

ordered his captain. 'We cannot make any frontal assault without being slaughtered.'

'What do ye plan, then?' Yint cocked his head to one side and peered at him with a squint that reminded Rouwen of a one-eyed man. He wondered if Yint was going blind in his right eye.

'You'll be in charge of the troops until I return. If Sped is so eager for a full attack on the castle, we'll let him make it.'

'With his wizard and his general?'

'Something like that,' Rouwen admitted.

'Suicide, it is. Purely a way of getting yourself killed, General. Don't go dying for 'is like.' Yint gestured vaguely, possibly meaning Sped but more likely wanting to include Vutorian in the advice.

'If I had a solid gold Mionese lumen for every time I've died, I'd be rich by now,' Rouwen said. Yint snorted in disgust and shook his head, wondering at his leader's strange choice of words. Rouwen didn't enlighten him on the number of times he had died. That curse of immortality had died with the death of the wizard who had laid it on him. If only Kwuway's death had also removed the curse still haunting his every waking second as well as his dreams.

'Ye want us to melt into the countryside if ye don't return soon? The lads would appreciate seeing their families again. Rumors 'ave it that those Mionese bastards are taking to settling down while we're out 'ere dying.'

'Muster out the lot of them for service to Gan,' Rouwen said, watching as Sped and Vutorian foolishly rode directly to the first gate along the road spiralling upward to the castle. They stopped as a guardsman emerged from the stone tower. Vutorian spoke for a few minutes and the guard returned to his post.

Rouwen saw Sped and the wizard ride through, vanishing within a few minutes along the winding road. Vutorian had used a mind-numbing spell to gain entry. Rouwen's path wouldn't be as easy. He had only his sword to rely on as he followed them to the castle. For Vutorian to allow Sped this foolish offensive meant the wizard had plans other than those including Sped.

'Before I go, bring the wizard's belongings to me.' Rouwen met Yint's square gaze without blinking. The captain shrugged and rode off to obey. Meddling with a wizard's possessions merited a horrible death, if the thievery was discovered.

Rouwen dismounted and began going through every bag, every box, every fold of Vutorian's clothing. When he finished he hadn't found the grimoire he sought.

'What do ye look for, General?' asked Yint. 'Might be I can 'elp ye out with the 'unting.'

'A spell book,' Rouwen said in disgust. His eyes raked the thick shaft of the rocky needle holding the castle and came to rest on the gleaming white castle atop the spire. Rouwen's mind raced as he turned over the myriad possibilities and finally one seemed to be more logical than the others.

'Up there. Vutorian abandoned the grimoire in Castle Gan. Perhaps Sosler has it or knows where it is. That's why he wants Sped to enter and kill the duke.'

'Sped 'as problems killing a fly. No fighting skill in the boy. A layabout and nothing more, I say,' commented Yint. The captain spat and added, 'Seems to me ye might need a knowing 'and getting into the castle. Never know I was riding at your elbow, if ye let me come with ye.'

'The men need a reliable commander. You are that and more, Yint.' Rouwen had already considered ways up the road without causing any alarm among the guards. There hardly seemed a way, unless he posed as a messenger bound for Sosler himself.

'Dismiss them, then let's go,' Yint insisted.

'Thanks,' Rouwen said, 'but this is my fight. You'll never know the woe Sosler has given me nor the pleasure I will take in slitting his throat.' Rouwen's hand clasped the hilt of his sword. He squeezed so hard the muscles in his forearm knotted painfully. Trying to relax availed him little. He wanted Sosler's death almost as much as he wanted his curse lifted.

'You're a good leader, General. Don't think it would pain me over much to call ye my liege.' Yint saluted and wheeled his horse around, trotting off without a backward glance. Rouwen hesitated and considered how different his attack on the castle might be with a stalwart comrade at his side. He quickly pushed the notion from his mind. This was his fight, not Yint's.

And it was a fight for more than killing Sosler or lifting the curse. He had to recover the grimoire if Finola was to contain the growing dominion of the Flame Specter.

Rouwen pulled insignia from his uniform, leaving only a basic red-and-silver denoting the King's Guard. Swirling his cape around his shoulders, he put his heels into his horse's flanks and was rewarded with a leap that carried him almost to the road. The horse had been bred for parade ground appearance as well as speed, and this helped Rouwen convince the guard he bore a message for Sosler.

And so he worked his way up the side of the spire, always behind Sped and Vutorian with his magical spells, but making good time nevertheless. Whether the guards posted along the road were still groggy from Vutorian's spells or they truly believed Rouwen to be a courier bound for Duke Sosler mattered little. He reached the broad expanse in front of the massive gates of Castle Gan just before the sun traced out a lazy figure-eight pattern in the sky and sank in the west.

Dozens of merchants milled about, peddling their goods to one another and occasionally calling to guards posted in front of the open castle gate. Rouwen moved closer to the portal, cape pulled tightly around his frame to keep from showing himself as a soldier until he had a plan to enter.

'A ripe fruit from the valley harvest, good sir?' asked a short, stocky vendor. The man shoved a rotted fruit in Rouwen's face. As four guardsmen came through the gate, Rouwen turned and pretended to be interested in the garbage being offered.

'I've seen better,' he argued, to give some life to the merchant's argument. 'This isn't good enough to fling at Duke Sosler.'

'What? You have no love for our dear sovereign! Treason!' the merchant called out, but a small smile wrinkled the corners of his lips. 'A man of your breeding can see how fine this fruit is.' Again he thrust it at Rouwen.

From the corner of his eye Rouwen watched the guardsmen march past. The gates stood invitingly open, but the few soldiers outside were only a hint at the number inside. It took more than fifty men to close the gates, and they were always on duty. Rouwen had no chance of sneaking inside. And where had Vutorian and Sped gone? It wasn't possible for the wizard to cast his somnolence spell on this many soldiers. Rouwen had noted gathering exhaustion in the wizard after he had cast even a simple spell more than three times. To reach the gates without raising an alarm would force Vutorian to cast a dozen spells.

'Where's the courier?' bellowed a sergeant from behind Rouwen. 'We've had word of a courier making his way to see the king. Show yourself!'

Rouwen tossed the fruit back to the merchant and said, 'Can't afford it. No coin.' Rouwen edged closer to the stocky merchant when the soldiers pressed behind him. He was aware that his cape betrayed him as a soldier of the King's Guard, but Rouwen didn't turn as the others pushed past him.

'You have connections inside the castle, good sir?' asked the merchant, a sly expression on his round face. 'A helping of my excellent wares for your assistance in reaching those who buy for the castle's kitchen.'

'Very well,' Rouwen said. 'But I need a favor more than a

sample of your goods.' He poked the fruit in the merchant's hand. A tiny river of putrescence oozed out. 'Fling this fruit at yon officer.' Rouwen indicated the guardsman at the gate. 'Don't be obvious about it. He has been my bane for weeks. If I stand one more extra watch because of him, my arches will fall flat.'

'In a few minutes. You'll be here to watch?' The merchant sounded skeptical, but Rouwen knew he would do it – or have it done by any of the dozens of urchins ducking in and out of the crowd.

'Do it and I'll introduce you to the assistant cook,' lied Rouwen. He poked the fruit again and wiped the juice off on his muddy tunic.

'Where's the courier?' came the shout from deeper in the crowd of merchants. The soldiers began fanning out to find the courier who was to report to Sosler even as Rouwen walked closer to the gate.

Less than five minutes later a rotted fruit arched up and landed at the guardsman's feet. The soldier looked up, angry. A second fruit struck him on the shoulder and a third came apart in midair and pelted him with a dozen fragments. The officer yelled and summoned a squad from inside the gates to stop the attack.

As the soldiers rushed out, more fruit rained down. The urchins throwing the fruit started laughing, and the merriment was communicated to others. Rouwen sensed that Sosler's rule was not greatly popular, and the soldiers now bore the brunt of that dislike.

Rouwen joined part of the squad rushing out, yelling and waving his arms. Within a few seconds he had been hit by a fruit, too, and this suited his purposes well. It took more than five minutes to disperse the crowd and the officer to order, 'Get back into the castle. And clean yourselves. You are a disgrace, the lot of you!'

With head bowed, Rouwen joined the others returning to the castle. No one noticed one more returned than had sallied forth to quell the disturbance. Once inside, Rouwen veered away from the soldiers' barracks and found his way to the kitchens.

He stole a few crumbs from a preparation table, enjoying the taste of real food again. Then he started up the broad stairway used by the kitchen staff when they served the king in the main dining room. Rouwen paused for a moment and saw that no affairs of state were likely to be held in the huge dining room. Chairs had been overturned and left on the floor and the table had been hacked apart. Whatever had happened in the room hinted at greater disturbance in Castle Gan.

Finding a minor stairway to the upper levels brought Rouwen out on the corridor leading to the king's audience chamber. He wondered where Sosler might be. The duke wouldn't sit on the throne all day, and Rouwen doubted he held audience. The fruit-throwing was only a hint of what might happen if Sosler allowed in any number of Gannians.

'You won't find him there,' came a cold voice. Rouwen spun, hand flying to the hilt of his sword. Behind him stood Vutorian, looking glum.

'Where is he?'

'Sosler or Sped?' Vutorian waved his hand. Rouwen tensed, thinking the wizard might be casting a spell. From the haggard look, Vutorian was at the end of his strength and unable to summon the energy for any arcane dabbling.

'Either, both,' snapped Rouwen. 'Sped will get himself killed if he thinks he can meet Sosler in combat and beat him. The duke is a soldier and a fine swordsman.' Rouwen spoke with some bitterness. He had duelled with the duke and had lost. The dissolute Sped would have no chance at all.

'We both seek the same thing, Rouwen,' said Vutorian. 'Let Sped do what he will. He is beyond my control now.'

'You only used him as a cat's-paw to get into the castle. For the grimoire?' Rouwen realized then that his suspicion had been correct. Sosler had somehow wrested the grimoire from the wizard and now Vutorian wanted it back.

Just as Rouwen wanted it back, though for different reasons.

'Sped has his uses,' Vutorian said. 'And in return for the grimoire, I will lift the curse on you.' He reached out and tapped the spell casket under Rouwen's tunic. Rouwen drew back, the Flame Specter's brand on his chest beginning to burn again. He didn't know if the nearness of a wizard caused the reaction or if the elemental threatened a new thrust into the world.

'Noumet exists,' Rouwen said, to see Vutorian's response. The wizard's eyebrow rose slightly. He didn't seem unduly surprised or interested. 'And Finola is there trying to contain the Flame Specter.'

'What?' Mention of his former student finally caused reaction in the wizard. 'She never returned from the training assignment. I thought she had given up on becoming a mage.'

'Hardly. She ranks with the most powerful in Noumet.'

Vutorian laughed contemptuously. 'Why do you make up such lies? I have already promised to remove the curse from you – after we recover the grimoire. You need not lie to convince me to do more.'

'The Flame Specter is partly the reason for the disarray in the weather. It strives for complete dominance of the world.' Rouwen saw he had sparked Vutorian's interest, but the wizard did not believe in the danger. This only convinced Rouwen that the grimoire belonged in Finola's hands, not Vutorian's. Still, he asked, 'What use do you have for the spell book?'

'The Flame Specter can be used to achieve great power. The Lord of Death and Life knew this. So did Kwuway. That is why he compiled the spells in the grimoire. He sought to chain the elemental to his will!'

'Guards!' warned Rouwen. He grabbed Vutorian's arm and pulled him into an alcove until the soldiers ran past, their weapons drawn for immediate use. 'Something's alerted them. Do you think it is Sped?'

'Probably. He had no idea how he was going to kill Sosler. Stab him in the back, I urged. Sped wanted to face him in a noble contest of skills.' Vutorian spat angrily. 'We have little time. Where would Sosler keep the grimoire?'

Rouwen's mouth opened and closed. He had thought Vutorian was in contact with the spell book's power. Wizard and book had been joined magically, both glowing with intense green light. Whatever bond had been forged must now be severed.

'The king's vault is the most secure spot in the castle. We . . .'

'I have looked there. The counting room is filled with gold and other plunder Sosler has extorted, but the grimoire wasn't there.'

'That's the counting room, not the king's vault. Priowe had a special room built off his sleeping quarters, a safe room if any internal trouble developed.' Rouwen looked around to get his bearings and found stairs leading upward to the royal levels of the castle. He took the steps two at a time and collided with a guard at the top as the soldier started down.

Rouwen never hesitated. He drew his sword and smashed the hilt into the soldier's face. The guard yelped in pain and reached for his damaged nose, spurting blood. Rouwen's second blow on the side of the man's head dropped him to the floor, dazed and moaning in pain.

He stepped over the fallen soldier, then spun when he heard a death rattle. Vutorian had plunged a dagger into the stunned soldier's throat. The wizard glared and said, 'You are soft, Rouwen. He would have trapped us by raising an alarm.'

'A dead body won't?' Speed, not blood, was their only ally. Rouwen struggled to pull the corpse from the hall, leaving behind a trail of blood. Vutorian uttered obscenities as Rouwen dropped the body into a servant's empty sleeping room.

'We waste too much time. Sped will have found Sosler by now. When that young fool . . .' Vutorian trailed off, grumbling to himself.

Rouwen ran down the hallway and skidded to a halt in front of the door leading to Priowe's sleeping chambers. If he understood Sosler's way of thinking, he would have moved into these chambers. His ego would accept no less than the same King Priowe had enjoyed.

Pushing the door open with the tip of his sword, Rouwen peered inside. He expected to find Sosler here. The room was deserted, and a curious hollow feelling settled on him. He tried to keep his priorities straight. He wanted the curse lifted, but he needed to retrieve the grimoire more. Sosler's death finished a poor third on Rouwen's mental list.

'Behind those hangings,' Rouwen said, pointing with his sword blade. He let Vutorian make a quick sweep of the room to determine that they were alone. Rouwen shoved aside the tapestry and studied the blank block wall behind. By accident he had watched Priowe open the door once. His fingers searched out the depressions in the wall and found three. He pressed his fingers hard into the dents and waited for the locking mechanism to open.

'Let me,' insisted Vutorian, pushing Rouwen aside. Rouwen yielded and watched as Vutorian exerted his own powers against the wall. Vutorian's eyes closed and his lips moved in silent spell. The wall began to glow a dim blue, but the indentations Rouwen had sought and only partly found shone with a pure azure light.

'There are five spots on the wall,' Rouwen said. He reached past Vutorian and found the two indentations he had missed before. A solid click sounded and a section of wall swung inward. Rouwen wasted no time seeing if the king's vault was occupied. Lowering his sword to impale anyone in front of him, he rushed in.

The room was poorly lit by a thin slit window high on the opposite wall letting in the last dregs of daylight. In the center of the room stood a large carved wooden table, two chairs pulled up to it.

'There. There it is!' crowed Vutorian.

Both he and Rouwen reached for the grimoire at the same instant. Hands resting on the spell book, both men stared challengingly at the other.

15

Death, Dungeon and Door

'I can slay with a single spell,' Vutorian said through clenched teeth. He pressed his hand down even harder on the leatherbound grimoire as he glared menacingly at Rouwen. The spell book vibrated as if it were developing a life of its own. Rouwen refused to yield now that the fate of the world lay under his hand.

'Try and you'll be speaking through a second mouth.' Rouwen leaned forward slightly, the tip of his sword gouging Vutorian's throat and drawing a drop of blood. The stalemate could not last. He vowed to end the wizard's life before any more magic could be conjured when he heard the clatter of armed men in the king's chamber.

'We'll both forfeit our lives if you kill me,' Vutorian said.

'The grimoire is mine.' Rouwen refused to give up.

'Keep it, then, for the moment. We can settle the matter when we get out of this accursed castle.'

Rouwen held his tongue. It wasn't Castle Gan that carried the curse. It was even more than Brion Rouwen being accursed. The entire world would fall prey to the Flame Specter's burning lust for supremacy if Finola didn't get the grimoire. He slid his hand under the spell book and noted how warm it felt to the touch.

Victory!

Rouwen staggered slightly as the thought came to him. A greenish glow pulsated around the book, as it had before. But this time the green wasn't the lovely emerald green reminding him of growing things and gentle spring days. Now the green was that of pus, a sickness growing worse. Rouwen hastily dropped the spell book down the front of his tunic, wincing as the magical tome touched the Flame Specter's brand on his chest. As he had thought, the Flame Specter somehow activated the glow in the book.

'Four guards,' Vutorian said softly, peering around the corner of the tapestry hiding the king's vault. 'They don't seem inclined to budge from their easy post sprawled on the bed.'

Rouwen put his finger to his lips to silence the wizard. He moved forward and strained to hear what the soldiers said among themselves.

'The young fool's got to be around somewhere,' said one soldier. 'He might know the castle but he can't hide forever the way we're searching.'

'Why bother stopping him? Is he any worse than what we've got on the throne?'

'Silence!' snapped a third. 'That's treason. No matter that Sped is of the royal blood, Sosler is our liege now.'

'Some liege. Half the officer corps has been tortured to death. Who's to say we won't follow? He uses a man and tosses him aside the instant it suits him. Why show loyalty to anyone like that?'

'Smel was a traitor. He was in league with the wizard,' claimed the first soldier.

Rouwen caught Vutorian's expression out of the corner of his eye. He now knew who had met Vutorian on the road to the Demon's Throat. Smel had formed an alliance with the mage after seeing how Sosler's rule would ruin the kingdom. The diminutive Captain of the Intrepid Guard had chosen the wrong side in the battle for ascendancy within Castle Gan.

Vutorian looked at Rouwen, and shrugged slightly, whispering, 'He would have killed Sosler at the proper time. Sped ruined everything we had planned.'

'Smel was a good enough soldier. I'm sorry he died like that.' Rouwen gripped his sword more tightly, then relaxed and took a breath before flinging aside the tapestry. The move into the king's quarters took Vutorian by surprise. It also dumbfounded the four soldiers waiting in the room.

A quick, powerful overhead slash removed one soldier's hand. Yelping in pain he twisted away, clutching it to his belly. Rouwen recovered and thrust, the point entering the second guardsman's chest. The point turned off a rib and then plunged through his heart. A step brought Rouwen back into fighting position again. He made a long thrust that snaked around the third guard's sword point. The blade ended abruptly in the man's throat, coming up under a gorget.

Rouwen pulled back, whipped about and swung the blade in an arc that ended in the fourth soldier's belly. He doubled over and fell to his knees, suddenly white from shock and blood loss.

'Come along,' Rouwen called to Vutorian. The stunned wizard obeyed without comment. Rouwen had no time to lose. If these four had been positioned in Sosler's quarters it meant the entire castle swarmed with guardsmen, thanks to Sped's ill-timed assassination attempt on Sosler.

Rouwen engaged two more guardsmen, both Intrepids, and mourned their deaths as he flew down the stairs to the lower level where the audience chamber was filled with more guardsmen than he could count. He backed off, motioning Vutorian to a small ladder in an alcove. They scrambled up to the mezzanine overlooking the floor of the audience chamber. Crouching behind the low wood railing, Rouwen took in the scene with a single glance.

It was as bad as he had thought it might be. Fifty or more soldiers circled a single figure, swords and pikes lowered and ready to spit him. For his part, Sped did not cower or whine. Rouwen counted that as a step toward Sped's attaining a semblance of adulthood though that maturity would be short-lived.

'You have been in the court all your life,' Sosler said angrily. 'Surely, a boy of your background would have tried something more effective than throwing a dagger at me.' Sosler cast aside a dagger balanced for thrusting, not throwing. Rouwen tried to keep from groaning. Sped had been ill-prepared for the attack. He had even used the wrong weapon for the assassination attempt.

'Release my sister immediately,' Sped said in a voice carrying only a hint of fear. 'Take my life, but free her.'

'Why should I bother doing that? You are my prisoner, if you hadn't noticed.' Sosler signalled and six pikemen moved forward, the tips of their weapons gouging into Sped's body.

'You loved Sorinne. You married her. Let her go.'

'I never loved her. I married her for . . .' Sosler caught himself, realizing he spoke in front of a chamber filled with soldiers. Even if he ordered them all killed, word would flash through the castle as to everything that had been said before such a slaughter. 'She turned traitor. How can I love a woman who betrayed me?'

'I'm sorry I failed when I threw the knife,' Sped said, most of the bravado burned out of him.

'There might be a way of redeeming yourself,' Sosler said as he sat in the throne. 'There is no reason you should not regain a notable position in my court. I have no love of traitors, but I cherish those who are loyal and truthful.'

'No, no, you fool,' moaned Vutorian. 'Do not listen to him.'

Rouwen saw the trap Sosler laid for the youth, too, but he huddled over, pressing into the rail and trying to keep from crying out. The grimoire burned his flesh with new fury and the brand on his chest began throbbing as if every muscle in his body turned spasmodic and knotted,

The grimoire. Use the grimoire!

'You and Vutorian left the castle. Did he come with you?' Sosler's words were honeyed. To Sped they were a way out of a predicament he had never envisioned.

'We both returned. The wizard used sleep spells to get by your guards. And . . .' Sped stopped, as if catching himself admitting too much.

'Yes,' Sosler urged softly. 'What else is there?'

'Brion Rouwen, my general. He has a troop of men waiting below in the valley to attack the castle.'

'What!' Sosler shot to his feet, his face livid. 'You lie! Rouwen is dead! He died months ago.'

'He is my general. Vutorian suggested that appointment, and it has worked well. We recruited almost twice the number of soldiers in this room, just from those we defeated in combat.' Sped spoke nervously now, chattering on without knowing what he said.

'Is Rouwen in the castle? With Vutorian?'

'I don't know. Only the wizard and I came, but Rouwen voiced his intention of joining us.'

'Kill him,' Sosler snapped. His pale blue eyes shone with icy intensity as he watched Sped sink to the floor, dead from a dozen wounds. 'Get a squad to my sleeping quarters. A company! And search the castle. Find the wizard, and if that traitor Rouwen is with him, bring him, too! Ten thousand pieces of gold to the men who capture them. A duchy, more! And death to those who let them escape again!'

'We've got to leave,' Vutorian said, shaking Rouwen's shoulder. Rouwen groaned as he tried to stand. The pulsation in his chest grew worse, and the hideous burning sensation grew by the minute. He feared that the Flame Specter was trying to reassert itself here and now. It had appeared once in this chamber in an attempt to burst free of Noumet's wizards. Rouwen worried that it felt a weakness again and tried to use him as its way to freedom.

'You're sweating,' Vutorian accused. 'Are you so afraid of him? Give me the grimoire and . . .'

'No!' Rouwen clutched the spell book to his flesh, though it burned as if he had dipped himself in acid. 'We can get away. I . . . I know a route. It leads to Noumet.'

'Noumet,' scoffed Vutorian. 'Go on. Show me the way.'

Rouwen walked on rubbery legs to the tiny stairway leading

to lower levels. He feared that the alarm would spread so quickly that even these minor staircases would be blocked off, but he dared not use the secret ways, either. If the guards knew of them, those would be the first places they would search, as Rouwen had used them so successfully before.

'Where is Sorinne imprisoned?' asked Rouwen as he made his way down the stairs. As he walked, his strength returned and the horrible burning in his chest faded. But with the returning vigor came a new terror to torment him.

The castle's walls began shimmering, turning misty and indistinct. He stepped forward and found himself walking on air, the nearest substantial support for him hundreds of feet below. But the floating carried him away on an airy tide so fast that he had no time to fear. Half-seen, misty flashes of a scene, a half-destroyed city, perhaps Noumet, lay beneath him. And tiny, distant voices rose in a singsong chant.

As unexpectedly as the scene had intruded, so did it fade to leave him shaken and pale, still in Castle Gan. He didn't understand the significance of the waking dream, but he took heart from it.

'You can't see her,' said Vutorian, not aware of the slide through time and space Rouwen had just taken. 'Better let her stay where she is. Sosler won't harm her as long as he has a use for her.'

'I know the use he has for her,' snapped Rouwen.

'If you touch her, she dies,' Vutorian reminded him, the wizard taking demonic glee in his pronouncement. 'There isn't time for me to remove the curse either.'

'We'll free her. She need not know who is responsible. If she can escape the castle, more power to her. It is all the legacy I can give,' Rouwen said, realizing his destiny lay underground in Noumet. He had to get the grimoire to Finola and let her use the knowledge contained within to stop the Flame Specter.

'By the demons, no!' gasped Vutorian, colliding with Rouwen. Rouwen peered past the wizard and saw the source of his fright. The castle walls were turning liquid and flowing. Tiny spots sizzled and burst like grease in a hot skillet, and in others small flames of black and orange danced. Stone didn't burn.

Unless the Flame Specter touched it.

'The entire castle might be devoured,' Rouwen said. 'We've got to get away *now*.'

Vutorian ran after him. The few soldiers they encountered were running in stark fear of what they had seen. Everywhere streamers of flame turned the corridors into infernos no human could bear. Vutorian uttered spells constantly in an attempt to ward off the might of the elemental. Rouwen knew he had no such power, yet a bubble formed around him more effective than the wizard's ward spells.

'The grimoire,' he guessed. He pushed on, not sure how long the spell book would protect him. How he wished he could read the runic writing within and use it!

'There, there's the way into the dungeons,' he said to Vutorian. 'Either you go and free Sorinne, or I'll find some way to do it myself. But if she dies, there is no reason for me to continue.'

Rouwen lied; the glowing grimoire had to reach the City of Mages, but Vutorian heard only truth because of his own soaring panic. The wizard was weakening from magical exhaustion, his ward spells protecting him less and less. Without the bubble of safety surrounding Rouwen, Vutorian would never survive.

'I'll do it,' the wizard said. 'But I won't let her know who is responsible. She would think it a trap.'

'Do it however you like,' Rouwen said, 'but just do it!' He used his sword on a dungeon guard blundering up from the lower level to see what the commotion was about. The fire elemental had yet to touch this level with its fiery tongue of strangely colored flame, but the smell of brimstone and the slow drip of molten stone down the staircases warned of its spreading.

Rouwen followed Vutorian halfway down the stairs to the lowest level, then let the wizard continue by himself. He heard the whispered instructions to Sorinne and the snap of a locking bar being pulled free. And he heard Sorinne's voice.

'Let me thank you, whoever you are. Please!'

'No, stay in your cell until I've gone. You cannot look on me. It means both our deaths if you do.'

Vutorian crashed into Rouwen on the steps as he hurried up. Rouwen heard the princess running through the dungeon, trying to catch a glimpse of her benefactor. He turned and fled, not daring even to gaze at her. His body was a playground for magicks. The curse alone might kill her, but the energies flowing through him created by the Flame Specter might give additional pain before she died. Rouwen refused to take the chance of killing the woman he loved as he had done to his brother and his friends.

'There,' Rouwen gasped out, pointing down the corridor Finola had used when she had rescued him from the dungeons months earlier. Or was it years? Hours? Time meant so little to him.

'I can hardly move,' panted Vutorian. 'The heat is stifling. It sears my lungs as I breathe. How do I know this isn't some trick of yours, that you don't intend killing me?'

Rouwen whipped around, sword pressed into the wizard's midriff. 'All I need do is shove,' he said, twisting the blade slightly, 'if I intended you any harm.' Rouwen tried to understand why he bothered with the wizard. The grimoire rode uneasily inside his tunic; why not leave Vutorian behind? The wizard was a double-dealing, overly ambitious, conniving despot.

The answer was simple: He didn't know why he spared Vutorian's life.

'Down into the subcellar. There is a door leading lower. Much lower.'

'To Noumet?' the wizard asked. 'I hardly dare believe you when you say my pupil was there. Noumet is – was – a myth. I truly desire to see young Finola again.'

Rouwen pushed Vutorian down the steps and through the dimly lit storage cellar. Again he stopped to pack food and take water from a big, open cask, but Rouwen noted the diminishing reserves. Sosler did not take seriously the threat of a siege outside his castle. With the Mionese army defeated, who could mount any significant attack? But Priowe had always maintained the storage cellars against drought or famine. Sosler was not as far-looking or prudent.

'There, there it is,' said Rouwen. He heaved open the wooden door revealing the rocky path through the center of the rocky spire cradling Castle Gan. Vutorian entered but Rouwen hesitated when he heard the pounding of feet behind. He turned, ready to fight.

'Where do you go? There is no way out down here,' Sorinne called. Rouwen caught sight of the lovely woman, a dim, almost ghostlike figure fluttering through the cellar hunting for her benefactor. A lump formed in Rouwen's throat. How he wanted to invite her along, but to do so meant her death. Why save her from the ravages of Sosler's cell only to kill her in the most hideous manner possible?

Rouwen could not bear the knowledge of having committed such a heinous crime.

He spun through the wood portal and pulled it shut behind him. He heard Sorinne rush to the other side and begin pounding, begging to be let through. Quaking with emotion, he held the door securely until she stopped. Only when he was sure she had left to seek other escape from the fire-devoured castle did he turn, tears in his eyes, and race after Vutorian on the path to Noumet.

16

Worlds in Chaos

Rouwen tried not to think of Sorinne and her anguish on the other side of the door and how the Flame Specter was devouring Castle Gan. He hoped she could win free if she stayed on the lower levels. For whatever reason, the fire elemental worked on the upper levels, possibly drawn by the royal suites. Or Sosler. The duke had been the one summoning the Legion of the Air when the Flame Specter broke free and destroyed the trumpet.

Rouwen hoped the duke and the fire elemental merged. He had seen what the Flame Specter could do and wished only the worst onto Sosler.

Not paying attention to where he ran, Rouwen smashed into the tunnel wall and rebounded. Rubbing his arm, he tried to find Vutorian. The wizard had outraced him easily, having enough of a head start to put a considerable distance between them. But Rouwen remembered the curious troubles he had encountered returning from Noumet. He had walked for what seemed days, only to traverse a short section of the path. And when he had thought he would spend the rest of his life trudging uphill slopes, the crevices had starred the rock around him, giving him six options for escape.

Rouwen wondered if he would encounter that junction soon. If so, it posed problems he needed Vutorian to solve. After the six cracks had broken through the rock, the path behind him to Noumet had vanished. Rouwen knew no way to find the true course, unless the grimoire he carried somehow provided a clue.

He kept up a brisk pace but failed to overtake Vutorian. Rouwen slowed and finally stopped, out of breath. He tried to estimate how long he had run. Even with the sun sailing through crazy gyrations, he had some idea as to the passage of time. With only the gentle phosphorescence of the moss to guide him, he only had his inner time sense.

'Vutorian!' he shouted. His call echoed along the passage and disappeared without being answered. Rouwen sat on a large rock and fumbled inside his tunic to pull out the spell book. He didn't know what he had expected, but a quiescent tome was not it.

Surrounded by magicks, the grimoire ought to have been glowing or pulsating or responding in some other way. It weighed down his hand without giving any clue to its importance in rechaining the Flame Specter. Idly leafing through the pages, Rouwen saw runes he recognized as having pored over before. This *was* the grimoire he had stolen from Kwuway. It just didn't respond to magicks as it had before the Flame Specter touched it.

'Drained,' he decided. 'The usefulness of the grimoire might be past.' He tucked the spell book back into his tunic, wincing at the tenderness of his chest wound. Ichor began dripping from the edges of the brand, forcing Rouwen to remove the grimoire. With the spell book settled in the burlap bag containing his larder, the chest wound stopped oozing. Rouwen took a deep breath and knew he had a long journey ahead.

As he stood, vertigo struck him. Rouwen reeled and tried to stand. He fell heavily to his knees. Blinking hard, he tried to make sense of what he saw, but his senses refused to help him sort out the enigma. He had been in a stony tunnel when he stood. Now a long, green meadow stretched to the horizon. Rouwen jerked around, hunting for the Shield Mountains guarding Valley Gan.

No mountains.

The deep scent of grass mingled with salt. Rouwen looked over his shoulder and saw the sandy expanse of beach. Again the flatness of the world stretched to the haze-shrouded horizon, no mountain or island breaking the monotony. Rouwen spun, trying to find his way back into the tunnel. Only within the rocky spire could he find the City of Mages.

'Vutorian!' he shouted. 'Where are you?' If he had blundered into this 'other place', the wizard must had preceded him. That explained why Vutorian hadn't responded when he shouted after him in the tunnel. 'We cannot stay here.'

But he didn't know where 'here' was. This was a land unlike any he had seen. The Vahite Desert was barren, but the sand dunes broke the long line of horizon and lent some character to otherwise unremarkable terrain. And the Smoking Sea changed constantly, unlike the ocean stretching behind him. He took a few paces, hunting for signs of life other than the lush grass crushing so noisily under his boots.

If life existed, other than his own, he saw no hint of it. Burrows for small animals usually dotted the land. He found none. Fish washed ashore and reeked as they decayed. The beige sand was unblemished by shells, seaweed or any fish struggling out of its watery home. A quick survey of the sky likewise did not give any hint of birds or other flying beasts.

'The sun is back in its orbit,' he said to himself. Rouwen held out his arm and waited a few minutes, watching the shadow move slowly. He had a general idea where east and west lay, but this told him nothing useful. If he headed north or south, what was he likely to find? Rouwen doubted he would see evidence of life there any more than he did in this spot.

'Vutorian, did the demons steal you away?' Rouwen took a step forward and fell. And fell and fell and fell. He smashed hard into a rocky wall, rebounded and collapsed to the path. Whipping about, Rouwen saw he had returned to the tunnel leading to Noumet. Or a tunnel enough like it to fool him.

'Vutorian! Where are you?'

'Here,' came a weak answer. 'I have blundered into another – world. Help get me out of here before . . .' The wizard didn't finish his plea. A throaty roar loud enough to cause Rouwen to clap his hands over his ears blasted through the tunnel. For a moment he thought the Flame Specter had erupted ahead of him, but the grimoire remained cool in his burlap bag and no pain etched his chest wound.

Rouwen got to his feet and started along the tunnel, only to tumble over Vutorian's prone body. The wizard cowered on the ground – and what ground it was! Rouwen had abandoned the empty world only to find himself in a dense jungle. Not ten feet away, a jaguar crouched, fangs bared and ready to jump. He dropped his bag and put his hand on the hilt of his sword.

'Kill it. I tried a spell on it, but nothing happened. My magicks failed!' whimpered Vutorian. He curled into a ball on the ground, no use to Rouwen in fighting the giant cat.

Rouwen stepped to the side to lure the jet black jaguar away from Vutorian, but as he moved, the cat's outline began to dim and blur and flow into a rainbow of colors. By the time Rouwen had taken three steps, he faced a hulking, shaggy-haired creature. The beast lifted impossibly long arms in his direction, but what captured Rouwen's attention weren't the filthy talons or the yellowed teeth. The beast's eyes shone with intelligence.

'We mean no harm. We want to leave,' Rouwen said in a soothing voice. He sidestepped back to Vutorian and knelt, keeping his eyes on the shaggy monster. Shaking the wizard to get him out of his panic did little good.

'Vutorian, what spell did you use? Did you try to change its shape?'

'That's not possible. I don't know those spells. I don't know!' Vutorian's teeth rattled as Rouwen shook him harder. This settled him for a moment. 'I tried to put him to sleep. It's the only spell I truly know.'

This startled Rouwen, but this was no somnolent creature. Rouwen stood and put his hand back on his sword as the beast lumbered forward – and changed again. The hairy arms shriveled and flowed back into the main body. As the animal moved, it sank to the ground and became more snakelike, wriggling toward Rouwen.

'Stop,' warned Rouwen. He drew his sword, knowing he could never hack away fast enough at a serpent so large and kill it before it killed him. He aimed the tip of his sword between the snake's eyes, intending to make one lunge that could penetrate the thick skull and enter the brain.

The reptile hissed, a forked tongue snapping out like a whip's lash to curl around his sword. Rouwen jerked back and sliced off part of the tongue. The snake went berserk, thrashing about.

And as it thrashed, again it changed. This time it became a hybrid monster Rouwen couldn't name. Part cat, part horse, part winged monster, it stamped and snarled and flapped razor-edged wings at Rouwen. He retreated and fell over Vutorian, landing hard.

The odor emitted by the monster made him gag. To his credit, Vutorian fought back his fright and began a low chant Rouwen recognized as the sleep spell. But Rouwen found himself affected more than the monster. His eyelids drooped and lifting his sword proved almost impossible.

'The spell. I'm going to sleep. Don't,' warned Rouwen. He sank to his knees, trying to keep the monster in view. The last thing he saw was the beast rising up, using its wings to become airborne. It crashed through heavy jungle vines and sent bright green leaves flying. Rouwen passed out.

He came awake with a start to see the wizard bending over him. Rouwen forced himself upright and saw only the rocky tunnel.

'What's going on?' he demanded. 'That monster was real. I smelled it, I heard it, I *saw* it.' Rouwen reached out and pulled his sword to him from where it had fallen. After the encounter with the shape-changing brute, he no longer felt as confident of his ability to fight and win against any living creature.

'I took a turn in the tunnel, and I was suddenly there,' Vutorian said, shock still in his voice. 'What is this place you've brought us to?'

'It's changed from the last time I went down it,' Rouwen

496

said. 'Nothing like this happened, but maybe that was because of Finola.'

'Finola?'

'She might have held the beastly manifestations at bay with her own spells.' Rouwen didn't remember the girl performing any complicated spell casting. She had seemed eager and alert rather than reflective like a mage intent on a spell. 'Can you cast a ward spell to keep us on course?'

'No,' Vutorian said in a low voice. 'And I taught Finola nothing she could have used to prevent what we've just endured.' The wizard shivered and hugged himself tightly. 'She studied constantly, but I watched her studies. She thought only of Noumet, which I doubted even existed.'

'You believe now?'

'I . . .' Vutorian crouched down and shook. When he got control again, he said, 'I cannot doubt what I have experienced, but there is no evidence of Noumet's existence. Unless you claim all this is the City of Mages.' Vutorian tried to indicate the strange worlds they had slipped in and out of, but his hand shook.

'It took a few minutes – a day,' Rouwen corrected, 'to reach Noumet.' He swallowed hard, remembering how he had been beset by the spirits of all those he had killed, both through the terrible curse on his head and by the strength of his swordsmanship. His conversations with the spirits lost on their way to Paradise had shrouded the real time in getting to Noumet. But now?

'We can't go back,' Vutorian said, more to himself than to Rouwen. 'The Flame Specter is devouring the castle. Its walls melt and flow like honey. No one can possibly survive that. But here? What are we doing to ourselves?'

'We're going to Noumet,' Rouwen said, putting his hands under Vutorian's arms and heaving the wizard to his feet. Vutorian shied away, as if Rouwen's touch might kill. Rouwen laughed harshly at that notion. The curse destroyed those he loved, not those he hated. 'The sooner we get on the way, the sooner we'll arrive.'

'There is no Noumet,' insisted Vutorian, but he took a hesitant step behind Rouwen. When nothing happened, Vutorian took another and then began walking slowly. The wizard began walking faster, muttering to himself. Rouwen trailed along, trying to fit his sword back into its sheath. His attention strayed and he collided with Vutorian – in yet another world.

'No, no! I tried to prevent this. My ward spells should have worked,' wailed Vutorian. The wizard ripped at his hair and spun in a tight circle, shrieking in anguish.

Rouwen went pale when he saw the sky darken and felt the ground begin to shake. He grabbed Vutorian's shoulder and jerked him to face the danger. The ground rumbled and began splitting into a vast chasm. And from the chasm rose a sheet of steam that would have boiled the flesh from any living being unlucky enough to be nearby.

'We've got to run,' Rouwen said. 'The elementals are battling. Look! The sky! See the storms?' The blue dome above darkened as clouds formed with startling speed, then lit the world with prodigious bolts of lightning. Water poured down on them, but Rouwen saw something even more ominous than the storms threatening them. In the clouds were yellow eyes peering down.

And from the crevice shone green eyes. And then Rouwen went blind as a thick column of fire blasted upward from the ground and pierced the cloud. Wind howled and the rain hissed and turned to steam as it beat against the column of flame.

'We can't survive this,' Rouwen shouted in Vutorian's ear. The wizard nodded, unable to speak. His face was gaunt but a greater sign of his fear was his hair. It had turned pure white from fright. 'A spell. Cast a ward spell.'

'I tried in the tunnel. We were still drawn here.' Vutorian screamed as they were cast aloft by a strong gust of wind, only to be dropped as the flames spread under them. They tumbled downward into the fire but did not burn. They were tossed from side to side, as if in a boat, but only inferno surrounded them.

Rouwen's eyes watered from the brilliance and his chest began to bulge. The Flame Specter spoke to him, laughing, teasing, cajoling him to merge and join and become one. To surrender.

Surrender to me and become powerful!

Rouwen bellowed in rage and clutched the burlap bag holding the grimoire close to him. His flesh charred from the spell book's touch but he refused to release it. Fire within and outside gnawed at soul and body, but Rouwen endured and rode out the flow.

The water elemental tried to drown him to prevent him from joining the Flame Specter's cause, and the earth elemental poured tons of dirt atop him. Even the weaker air elemental blew past, sucking breath from his lungs, but the Flame Specter was worst of all.

'I deny you all. Leave me alone. Go away, go away,' moaned Rouwen. As suddenly as the storms had come, they vanished. Firestorm vanished, and the rainstorm died to a whimper, and the earth receded, and the air returned to normal.

Dirty, caked in mud, cut and burned, Rouwen swung about and put his back to a rocky wall. Again he had come back to the tunnel leading downward to the City of Mages. Beside him lay Vutorian, gasping to keep his lungs from collapsing.

'We're back,' Rouwen said.

'For how long? I cannot bear any more. Those monsters did things to me. Inside, they tried to tear me apart, my soul, oh, the demons, the demons!' Vutorian skirted the bounds of insanity, and Rouwen did nothing to pull him back. He fought too hard to keep a grip on his own rampaging emotions.

He got to his feet and took a few tentative steps. Fearing what might lie head, Rouwen hardly believed his eyes.

'Vutorian, Vutorian! We're here. We've found Noumet!'

The wizard crawled up next to him and peered straight ahead. Somehow, they had survived the treacherous trail from Castle Gan to arrive at Noumet. Rouwen recognized the city immediately, in spite of the extensive damage done to its soaring towers and golden streets. It might have been through a long war, but Noumet had survived. It had kept the Flame Specter at bay and survived.

Rouwen went to the arch of rock and peered down at the cavern floor. Finola had levitated them down before. Now he had to climb down, weak and distraught as he was. Rouwen didn't know if Vutorian could follow, considering his condition.

'Who's that?' asked Vutorian. 'There. Coming after us on the path?'

Rouwen drew his sword and faced the solitary figure running after them. He hadn't heard anyone in the tunnel, but with the strange shiftings he had endured, an army might have followed. Rouwen swallowed hard when he saw a woman's silhouette.

'No, Sorinne, you shouldn't have followed. No!'

Then Rouwen saw a slender, athletic woman with brown hair, not Sorinne's gorgeous blonde, come bounding up. Perhaps twenty-five years old and almost matching his height, she gazed at him with animation in her lovely features. She stared at him for a moment, grinned broadly, then threw her arms around his neck and hugged him, crying, 'Brion, you came back!'

Rouwen pushed her away gently and shook his head. Too much had happened. He didn't know who the young woman was.

'Who are you?' he asked. 'Do I know you? You look so familiar, but I . . .'

'Oh, Brion, what's happened to you? You know me. I'm Finola.'

The world spun about Rouwen again, and he slumped into the woman's outstretched arms.

17

A City Crumbles

Rouwen struggled to regain consciousness. His chest burned and deep inside his head he heard an insidious whisper.

You are mine. The curse makes you mine. Do my bidding and we shall rule forever! Together, forever!

Rouwen tried to cry out but only choked. He turned his head to one side, trying to figure out where he was. His head lay on softness and cloth brushed his cheek. Then came a soft hand touching him. He jerked upright, head spinning.

He swung about and stared at the woman who had been cradling his head in her lap. She smiled almost shyly, and Rouwen recognized her.

'You are Finola,' he said in a shocked voice. 'But you're old! Older,' he corrected. She was beautiful and no longer the young girl he remembered. In that ten-year-old he had seen the seeds of such beauty, but never had he thought he would see her blossom so. And not when he was hardly older than when he had left Noumet. 'What happened to you?'

'A better question is what happened to you, Brion,' she countered. 'You ought to have recognized the way time was twisted out of shape when you reached the surface.'

'The cracks radiating from that chamber,' Rouwen remembered. 'When I reached the slopes of the Shield Mountains it seemed as if only days had passed. Months had,' he said. 'Vutorian and Sped had been exiled for months, and Sosler had consolidated his power by destroying Laslo and the Mionese army.'

'Time has been flowing strangely since the Flame Specter almost destroyed Noumet,' Finola told him. 'The wizards responsible for keeping time intact and linear were killed. Those taking over were apprentices. They have learned so much since.'

'But the real time shift had to have occurred after Vutorian and I left Castle Gan,' Rouwen said, trying to piece everything together. He touched his chest, worrying that the Flame Specter had touched him in ways other than the obvious. Was he insane?

'The Flame Specter tried once more for total conquest. I cannot say what happened on your trip back, but a month must have passed for every hour spent on the trail.'

'Vutorian and I slipped in and out of worlds so different from this one,' Rouwen said, shivering at the recollection. 'Creatures I'd never seen before abounded – or there were none, leaving only an empty plain to walk across. And one world existed where the elementals battled for supremacy. The Flame Specter was driven underground by the air, earth, and water elementals. I – I don't know if that was some other world or this one.'

'Both; neither,' said Finola. She shook her head and looked worried. 'Noumet has been in such an uproar since you left – fifteen years you have been gone.'

'Fifteen?' Rouwen's head threatened to split apart and he clutched his chest again. 'It can't be. It's impossible. The magicks. The spells. But how?'

Finola smiled and patted him on the shoulder as if assuring him all would be well. 'I have learned much and worked hard, and still we have difficulty maintaining the proper order of the world. Too many of our number were killed during the attack you experienced and in subsequent ones. The Flame Specter is immortal and never sleeps. We must be eternally vigilant, something not easy for mortals.'

'If it breaks free, everyone will die?'

Finola nodded again. 'There will be nothing but an incandescent ball of gas remaining where there is now the world, with its humans and sea and air.' She took a deep breath and said, 'I'm so glad to see you again, Brion.'

'Is it truly you, Finola?' came Vutorian's stunned words. He had stood nearby, staring open-mouthed at both city and woman. 'Is this truly Noumet? It's real!' The wizard stared out across the city, a look of complete astonishment on his face. 'I always doubted its existence. I thought you were a silly girl for believing. But this is the proof.'

'The best wizards in the world are here, Vutorian,' said Finola. 'But there are so few of us left. The Flame Specter has killed many, and the duties of those left behind are onerous. We work long hours, with so little reward.'

'The sun never quite followed its ordinary path in the sky,' Rouwen said, remembering the most obvious manifestation of discord. 'I never realized how accustomed I was to a daily regime until the day lasted for weeks – or minutes.'

'We must get back into Noumet before the Flame Specter tries to stop us. Any magic used outside the ward spell surrounding the city is instantly detected.' Finola reached out and took both Vutorian and Rouwen's hands. She stepped into the air and gently glided down to the cavern floor as she had before. Rouwen found it impossible to think that it had been fifteen years earlier, though for Finola it had been.

'This is a dangerous path I follow, though this is a simple spell, and we need to hurry.' She tugged at both men's hands, pulling them along the granite wall. Rouwen saw that the barrier between Noumet and the rest of the world had changed. Huge cracks had been driven through the solid stone, in places large enough for him to slip through. Finola led them to a small gate that he had not seen before.

'Is this new?'

'The magicks holding back the Flame Specter's onslaughts stop at this point and have for a dozen years. It is the only break in the bubble around us.'

'Won't the elemental slip through when you least expect it?' asked Vutorian, hesitating at the shoulder-wide opening.

'We watch this point carefully.' Finola shot Rouwen a smile that was laden with as much sorrow as it was happiness. 'Once inside we might never leave. The situation is as uncertain as that.'

'Perhaps I ought not to enter,' Rouwen said, hanging back. But he wanted to be with Finola, to find out who this girl grown into a woman was. She seemed capable as she had before, but the added experience gained over the years he had been absent had made her more confident.

'Don't be silly. We have come so far. I risked the use of a minor spell levitating us down to the floor. If we stay outside the city's protection too long, it will surely find us.'

'It can find me whenever it wants, wherever I am.' Rouwen pulled open his tunic to reveal the bright pink area on his chest. The skin throbbed and pulsated as the forces within tried to burst out. He experienced some small discomfort from this perpetual struggle going on inside, but most of all he feared his entry to Noumet would tilt the balance in favour of the Flame Specter.

'You were in the city before. We can work on this.' Finola sounded confident but Rouwen saw the lie etched in her face.

'Is Gerberria able to work the spell to remove the conduit the Flame Specter has forged within me?' he asked. 'Or some other mage?'

Finola sighed. 'Gerberria is dead, some ten years ago. The

elementals battled and caught her in the middle of their fight. She tried to control the Flame Specter as she did the sun and found herself too weak. The fire elemental destroyed her.'

'I'm sorry,' Rouwen said. He looked past the young woman to where Vutorian still hesitated at the gate. The wizard moved slightly, as if bracing himself to enter, then backed off a pace and stared. Rouwen wished he could see Vutorian's face to judge what the real dilemma was that was holding him back.

'Go on,' Rouwen called to Vutorian. 'You never believed in Noumet. Now you can see it firsthand.'

'We can never leave if we enter?'

'Perhaps not,' said Finola. 'Everything depends on subduing the Flame Specter.' Even as she spoke, the stone floor beneath their feet began cracking. Rouwen staggered and fell to one knee. Finola supported him and kept him from tumbling into a crevice the width of his body that started at the far side of the cavern and raced along the granite barrier, sucking in debris as it went.

'The earth elemental is hardly more a friend or ally to us than is the Flame Specter,' she said. 'The fight for balance seldom takes humans into account.' Finola lithely jumped the crack in the cavern floor and turned sideways, slipping past Vutorian and entering the gate. Pale pink sparks jumped from an invisible sheet and danced along the woman's contours.

'There is no danger to the city and the wizards in it by my entering?' asked Rouwen. He hesitated.

Finola laughed without humor and said, 'There is no safety left in the world. The Flame Specter has come to think of itself as a god worthy of worship. But hurry. We can talk inside the protective barrier.' Finola gestured for Rouwen and Vutorian to hurry.

'There is something amiss,' Vutorian said. 'I want to study this more carefully.' He made a gesture in the air, leaving behind trailing purple sparks. Though he was no wizard, Rouwen knew Vutorian had made a serious mistake.

Whether it was the surge of power he felt within his body or the change in the air outside, Rouwen couldn't say. The small magical spell drew the Flame Specter's attention and sent Rouwen staggering.

'Can't move,' Rouwen gasped. 'It is trying to use me to reach you.' Rouwen clutched his chest, as if this would hold back the might of a fire elemental.

The ground shattered into a thousand small cracks, and the single large crevice began widening, threatening to swallow both Rouwen and Vutorian. The wizard tried another spell; this made Rouwen wince in pain.

503

Surrender. Do not fight me. We are the same, you and I. We will be supreme rulers!

Rouwen understood the message echoing in his head, though it did not come in words or images he could understand. The elemental worked through him, for its own purposes and would destroy him in an instant if he relented. What inner strength did he call on to hold back such a monster? Rouwen didn't know.

'Vutorian, stop casting your spell,' cried Finola from inside the barrier. 'The few of us left cannot hold the ward spell against the Flame Specter when you weave magicks so close.'

'Very well,' the wizard said uneasily. He saw Rouwen writhing on the ground and moved away from him. He stepped through the gate. Rouwen sensed a pressure lift on him, but he still could not move. On the ground, eyes screwed shut tightly, Rouwen *saw* worlds that were not his. Flames danced everywhere, and heat! More heat than he imagined, and even this was not enough for the Flame Specter. It wanted to evolve into a star, a sun blazing hotter than solid matter could contain. It wanted to explode across the cosmos, leaving a trail of incandescent fury behind.

And it wanted Rouwen to be a part of this great journey.

'No!' he denied, finding the strength to roll. He focused all his anger, his hatred at Sosler and Kwuway and the Lord of Death and Life and the Flame Specter itself, and drew power from it. He remembered his brother and Nibbles and Toit and his love for them.

He remembered Sorinne.

Brion Rouwen rolled and got his feet through the gate. He felt Finola grab his ankles and begin pulling. For an eternity she pulled, and Rouwen thought he would be stretched a mile long, ten thousand miles long. The pull of the Flame Specter on his chest held him back, even as Finola tugged him into Noumet's sphere of influence.

He denied the Flame Specter its strength using hate and love and passion and courage. He burst through the gate and lay staring upward at a silvery dome above him. For long seconds, Rouwen wasn't sure what had happened. Then he heard Finola.

'You made it!' she cried. The woman knelt and cried hot tears as she pressed her face into his shoulder. 'We're all inside, safe, protected.'

'That's the shell?' He pointed upward at the mirrored ceiling arching above.

'We cannot see out any longer. We radiate back every bit of magical power we can to keep the city safe.'

504

'It's not safe,' Vutorian said, wandering toward an intact golden roadway. 'I sense the weakness all around. Noumet is doomed.'

'Not if we all work to keep it intact,' Finola shouted at him. 'Now that you are here, you must help by doing whatever you can. I know you lack any real magical ability now, but . . .'

'What are you saying, girl? I am Vutorian, Wizard of the Kelnos Forest! I am more than a match for you or any of these so-called wizards in this tumbledown town!'

'Prove it,' challenged Finola. 'Come, join the web of wizards. Fight to return balance to the world.' She and Vutorian strode off, leaving Rouwen behind. He stared at the silvered dome and then rolled to one side and watched the pair heading for a nearby building, more destroyed than whole. He tried to call to them but his voice clogged in his throat. Standing was out of the question, so Rouwen rolled to his belly and began crawling.

He had so much he wanted to tell Finola. She had never asked about the grimoire. He could give it to her and she would destroy the Flame Specter, making the world complete again. But Rouwen realized he was moving too slowly. Time flowed in curious eddies around him – and the force of the fire elemental seeking exit through him became almost unbearable.

But Rouwen would not surrender. He crawled, dragging the burlap bag holding the grimoire. He crawled and he succeeded in reaching the door to the building where Vutorian and Finola had entered. As he did, the silvery sheen of the dome over Noumet began to change. He saw patches appear, transparent sections that opened onto other worlds, worlds far stranger than the ones he had visited on his trip from Castle Gan back to Noumet.

As quickly as those windows opened, they closed, but from within the building he heard the groans and sobs of men and women pushed to the limits of their endurance. The Flame Specter mounted another attack, and even with Vutorian's assistance, the wizards of Noumet were flagging.

Mine! came the ominous ringing in Rouwen's head. *The time is right for me to claim the world as mine!*

18

The Grimoire Revitalized

'Finola, I have it. Please, come take the grimoire,' Rouwen called hoarsely. His frantic words were hidden under a continual roll of resonant thunder throughout Noumet. The city shook with earthquake and lightning, thunder and the ominous hissing of fire burning unchecked in the buildings. Rouwen struggled to pull himself to a sitting position. His legs twitched and shook, as if he had been pinned under a tree log, but only magicks held him in place.

Surrender. Know my power!

Rouwen closed his bleary eyes and fought even harder against the prodigious influence exerted by the Flame Specter. As he battled, the elemental's power weakened. Rouwen's elation at this minor victory grew, but he saw why the Flame Specter chose to divert attention elsewhere. Above the City of Mages writhed the liquid-bodied, green-eyed water elemental, intent on driving the Flame Specter back into its niche deep within the bowels of the planet. The wizards added their magical power to the fight, and for this reason alone the fire elemental turned from its human conduit into the world. The brand on Rouwen's chest still throbbed hideously, but the fire deep inside began to cool.

I will not be denied.

He took this chance to pull himself to his feet and stagger forward in search of Finola and Vutorian. To Rouwen's surprise, the building was empty. Just inside the door he spun about in a complete circle, staring in disbelief at the cobwebs and thick dust clinging to the old dilapidated furniture within. It took several seconds for him to understand what had happened. The city endured the same time-warping he had experienced on his way from Castle Gan.

'Finola, can you hear me? Where did you go?'

No answer came. To escape the mocking echo of his own voice, Rouwen stumbled outside into the street and took note of how badly the city fared in the conflict. He endured the

506

sudden shifts in the ground, the occasional falling piece of tall building, and the stomach-wrenching surges of unseen tides of potent magicks being unleashed as he stumbled along what had once been the main thoroughfare in Noumet. The silvery dome developed sickly splotches, showing how the conflict went.

The battling elementals suddenly vanished, leaving a preternatural calm over the city. Rouwen spun about, trying to figure out what to do. Nothing moved as far as he could see. He tried calling for Finola again but didn't expect an answer – and he got none.

Rouwen sat on a crumpled section of the golden paving and rummaged in the burlap bag for the grimoire. It had once burned with intense green light. After the trumpet summoning the wind warriors had been destroyed by the fire elemental, the spell book had returned to a more normal color and feel. All that had passed.

The grimoire blazed with an actinic light that forced Rouwen to squint as he stared at it. Before being drained magically by the Flame Specter, the book had been infused with greenish light, almost pleasing in hue. Now the purple illumination cut through his eyes and bored directly into his brain to explode in painful fireworks. He dropped the spell book to the golden paving and pushed open the cover. A new flash of light, more intense than ever, slashed at his face like a knife, burning his cheeks and forehead.

Rouwen shielded his face with his hands and peered at the first page of the grimoire. The runic writing dazzled him, but he tried to decipher it and recite the words in the distant hope of aiding those defending Noumet – and the entire world.

Try as he might, he couldn't make any sense of the lettering. Before, when the intensity had been far less, he had puzzled over the words. Rouwen doubted those slithering, snakelike letters would change but he had to make the effort.

Although unable to read the book, Rouwen knew it contained the solution to harnessing the Flame Specter. There was no other reason for the book of spells to become so energetic. The fire elemental had drained it once, robbing the magicks contained within of any true power – or had the spell book kept the Flame Specter chained a little longer?

Vutorian had been left docile and had fallen prey to Sosler's ambitions in a completely uncharacteristic way, but the book had again become saturated with magical energy from some source, perhaps the same fountainhead giving Noumet its special place in the world. Rouwen was in no position to judge, wishing this battle could be ended with a quick thrust of a sword or a simple push off Castle Gan's battlements. He had to get the book to Finola if there was to be any hope of beating back the Flame Specter's onslaughts.

New sizzling and cracking sounds over his head alerted him to the failure of the ward spell over the City of Mages. The silver dome faded and finally vanished. At the spell's failure came another pause, the moment before a storm when the true destruction begins. Rouwen kicked the grimoire into the burlap bag with his toe, not daring to touch the spell book. Even so, his boot began smoldering from the incredible power locked inside those pages.

Scooping up the bag, he slung it over his shoulder and looked for high ground. If Finola was to be found, he would have to do it quickly. A slow smile came to his lips when he saw a distant globe shimmering a dull silver. He guessed the mages had retreated to that far spot and now held their ward spell over only a small section of Noumet. In the eerie silence of the city, Rouwen began running for that stronghold standing unfailingly firm against the Flame Specter's might.

He ran and ran and the distance seemed never to diminish. Panting harshly, he began to worry that he had again encountered a patch of terrain like that in the tunnel leading back to Castle Gan. He might walk for days and traverse only a few feet. Worst of all, the hair on the back of his neck began to tingle as it rose with the growing presence of the Flame Specter.

Do not fight. Open yourself to me. Give me what I want. Power! Destroy the spell book. Let me through!

Rouwen staggered but kept moving as the words formed in his head. He caught sight of vistas not meant for any man, molten pits of lava, glowing gases so hot they turned metal into mist. At the same time, there were flames of pure ebony, cold and even deadlier than their fiery brothers. Worst of all was the inhuman exultation of being free to destroy anything in his – its – path. The Flame Specter needed to expand, to incinerate, to destroy all material things.

Anathema to fire lay water and air and earth. The Flame Specter sought destruction and expansion across the entire universe. Not for it were boundaries and balance.

'Why don't you just take me?' gasped out Rouwen as he ran. 'You're powerful. How can I hold you back if you want to burst forth?'

Release them. Let them go and you will be totally mine!

Rouwen didn't understand, and then he did. Hints came

from the Flame Specter itself but Rouwen put more together himself, finally finding answers to why he had been condemned to wear the fire elemental's brand. Just as the curse drew the fire elemental to him, so the curse kept the elemental at bay. The spirits of those he had slain because of the curse were bound to him. His brother, Nibbles, Toit, even the Lord of Death and Life, all hovered near since they were denied entry to Paradise. Their spirits acted as a shield between him and the Flame Specter.

If they reached eternal rest in Paradise, the Flame Specter would surge through him and the world would end. And if Rouwen kept the fire elemental from destroying the world, he condemned his brother and the others he loved to aimless, eternal wandering, to miserable nonexistence between life and the delectations of Paradise, a fate worse than any torture found in the dungeons of Castle Gan.

The world lived, and those he loved suffered for all eternity.

You cannot evade me. I will burst forth through you.

Rouwen didn't doubt the Flame Specter's promise, but he knew it would be better to doom those he cared for most in the world than to condemn the world for all time. Untold unborn generations would prosper if the fire elemental was forced back into its uneasy alliance with the other elementals.

'My duty is to the world,' he panted. 'The world, not those I love. To love me, to have me love them, is to suffer.' Rouwen dropped to his knees in front of an intact building near the middle of Noumet. Through the shimmery silver of the ward spell he saw an old man, bent double with the weight of his years, painfully walking.

'Vutorian?' Rouwen forced himself closer. His hands smarted as he touched the outer envelope of the ward spell. 'Is that you, Vutorian?' Shout as he might, he couldn't draw the wizard's attention.

'So old. Has the fight aged you – or has time shifted like sand under me once more?' A coldness grew that threatened to make Rouwen give up all hope. If Vutorian had aged so many years in what seemed to be only a few minutes, what of Finola? Had she become an old woman because of the magicks playing back and forth in Noumet?

He shoved harder against the unyielding magical barrier. The harder he pressed, the more forcefully he was pushed away. Rouwen stood with his face almost touching the magical screen and shouted at the top of his lungs, trying to draw someone's attention. He saw several wizards shuffling about within the spherical magic bulwark, but they ignored him, as had Vutorian. Knowing he could never gain entry with physical force, Rouwen stepped back to consider what he might accomplish with a different tactic. A slow smile crossed his lips. If brute force wasn't the answer, and subtlety failed him, that left pure magic. Rouwen flung the burlap bag holding the grimoire against the shield.

The explosion knocked him back. He fell heavily and lay stunned for several seconds. The bag sizzled and smoked but did not burst into flame. Rouwen crawled to it, intent on throwing it against the barrier again to draw attention. Such force had to send shockwaves throughout the structure and bring some response from the wizards maintaining the spell. He stopped when he saw Finola's worn, pale and utterly lovely face staring out at him.

Her lips moved but no sound came to him. He knew she called his name from her expression and the way she reached out for him. Relieved that she had not aged any more than when she had greeted his return to Noumet, Rouwen held up the bag and pointed at it, mounting the word 'grimoire'.

Finola's eyes widened. He wished he had not been so stunned at the sight of her being fifteen years older when she had come to him. Rouwen knew she could have used the grimoire immediately to stifle the Flame Specter and regain a semblance of natural order in the world. But all would be put right now. She turned and gestured to other wizards. He saw them move slowly, painfully, as if any activity strained their bodies to the limit.

Finola turned back and pointed to a spot at her feet. Rouwen saw the silvery dome begin to fade slowly to a dark spot that spread, as if a hidden door was prised open. He moved forward quickly to enter, to give the spell book to the wizards and complete his mission.

A shudder passed through the cavern floor and sheets of fire leaped in front of him, cutting off any possible entry into the center of Finola's ward spell. Heat drove him back. He tried to dodge around but found the sheet of fire bending, curling and enclosing him.

Destroy the spell book and you will become powerful.

'No, no, I won't.' Rouwen clapped his hands over his ears when he heard not only the Flame Specter's silent voice deep inside his skull but the painful mourning of his brother. And Toit squawked, chiding him for being so human. And Nibbles. The old thief begged him for mercy, for justice, for release.

They will go to Paradise if you destroy the grimoire.

'You'll destroy the world if I do,' sobbed Rouwen. He flailed about with his fist, striking at the fiery barrier around him. His flesh was seared and he recoiled as stark pain battered its way into his body. Turning in a tight circle, he tried to run, to escape the deadly prison around him, but there was no release. The fire elemental had him boxed in and threatened to extinguish him as the walls danced and bobbed ever closer.

Rouwen held up the coarse fabric bag containing the grimoire. The entire sack now shone with a purple light so bright even closing his eyes didn't keep out the light. The actinic glare burned through eyelid and brain, boring directly to the center of his soul. What had Kwuway compiled in that accursed book? And could any be more accursed than Brion Rouwen?

He swung the bag with the book around in a circle and the flames arched away, as if touch might harm them.

You are mine. You are my channel to ascendancy.

Rouwen kept the bag whipping about until the ground shivered so hard it drove him to his knees. He dared open his eyes to stare at the cylinder of flame working its deadly way toward him. A shout of pure terror died on his lips as he was driven flat on the ground. He rolled onto his back and stared up in time to see a wall of water descending. Like a tidal wave the water struck him, even as he was accelerating upward into it. Wind buffeted him, but the trembling of the earth beneath his body shook him far worse.

'Finola!' he cried, hoping she could hear. The blood hammered in his ears and he knew he was going to die. 'Adan,' he groaned. 'I'll be with you soon.'

'No,' came a soft sigh. 'No, dear brother, no, you won't.'

And then Rouwen screamed as he was hurtled high into space, tumbling wildly, the ground far below him. In midair he pitched over and saw the planet far below him. A fall from this height would leave him indistinguishable from a squashed insect when he hit the ground. But as he fell a new torrent of water crashed into him, spinning him around and forcing air from his lungs.

Instead of falling, he was drowning. And then wind slashed past his face, pulling water from his lungs and leaving only hot, dry air that seared with every breath.

No, you are mine. I need your body. I need your soul!

The Flame Specter's words were submerged in the rush and roar of being pitched around in the atmosphere. Rouwen had no idea how long he was buffeted by wind and water before he landed so hard on the ground that his lungs refused to take in new breath.

'Finola, I've failed you,' he gasped, curling into a tight ball to keep from being injured more. Somewhere in the back of

Rouwen's mind a tiny pinpoint of question formed. He hadn't died. Had he failed Finola? He still had the grimoire and his life. The Flame Specter had failed. The fire elemental had not gained entry into the world yet.

Rouwen pulled the burlap bag closer and huddled by a rock until his senses returned. He tried to figure out where he was. He remembered incredible speed pushing him down hard. He had been underground in Noumet and then the earth had erupted and thrown him far into the sky. Water, wind, the elementals had each tried to take him in their turn. And he had not succumbed.

'The grimoire. It has to be the grimoire.' He stared at the burlap bag and winced as daggers of light drove into his eyes, burning them, tearing at them. Rouwen turned his face away and still the cold light worked its magic on him. The grimoire had saved him as it had doomed him.

Rouwen wiped tears from his eyes and tried to focus on the dark shape in the distance. At first he couldn't make out what it might be, then realized he stared directly at Mount Glid. The Lesser Moon shone down on its jagged slopes, but something was amiss. It took him several seconds to comprehend the vast change that had occurred.

Mount Glid stood alone.

The Shield Mountains that had formed an impenetrable barrier around Valley Gan for so long were missing, stolen away as if by a giant's thieving hand. Rouwen shot to his feet and staggered, then steadied as he turned in a full circle to get a clearer look at the land of his birth. Only the part of the mountain range closest to Mount Glid had vanished. The rest remained, though not as tall or jagged as he remembered.

'The castle,' he sighed, seeing that Castle Gan remained atop its soaring spire. In the light of the Lesser Moon he saw the snowy white radiance of the castle walls. His world had changed but not enough for the center to have evaporated like dew in the morning sun. The castle remained pre-eminent atop its rocky spire, even if he could not see any details in the valley itself.

Rouwen started walking toward the castle long before a plan formed in his muddled head. As he walked the Greater Moon rose and sent its bright silvery light on the countryside, reminding him of the magical shell over Noumet. And with the memory of the City of Mages came a rush of emotion.

'Finola,' he said softly. 'I wish you were here with me. There has been too much misery.'

But there was nothing to be done except get the spell book

into the hands of someone able to use it. As he walked, the spell casket around his neck banged against his chest, reminding him of both his curse and his blessing. He both attracted the Flame Specter and held the fire elemental at a distance because of it.

Rouwen cocked his head to one side when he heard distant sounds. At first he thought Adan's blighted spirit might be returning to haunt him, but the sound was only a dog howling at the moons working their way higher in the sky.

Rouwen concentrated more on the land around him, taking care not to step in a hole and break his leg. Everywhere the depressions stretched like some vile pox on the land. At a large hole, he knelt and peered down. The sides of the hole were glassy, as if intense heat had turned the ground to brittle obsidian. He realized this was only one indication of the battle between elementals. Somehow, the earth elemental had been vanquished by the Flame Specter. He stood and kept walking until long after the twin moons had sunk behind the diminished Shield Mountains in the west.

To his surprise, the sun rose and moved across the sky in an orderly fashion, but Rouwen wished that it had remained dark. This was Valley Gan, but not as he remembered it. Once lush and fruitful, Gan had been the most prosperous kingdom on the continent. The valley looked as if a firestorm had ravaged everything above ground – and it might have. Rouwen tried to remember all that had happened to him after being blasted upward from the underground, out of Noumet. Memories were vague and confused, but walls of fire marching toward him played a large part in what he did recollect.

'All gone,' he sighed, seeing the devastation. The ground was poor and the streams were thin and polluted or even dried-up beds. Valley Gan had been turned into a rocky desert. And along with the crops, the people seemed to have vanished. Until past midday he walked and never saw another soul. Only the howling dog in the distance convinced him the kingdom wasn't entirely devoid of life.

'The castle survived,' he told himself. 'There will be people there.' At last he reached the road leading to Castle Gan. Along with the easier walking along the road came a nebulous plan that solidified the closer he came to the first guard post on the spiral road leading upward.

His kingdom had been vanquished and destroyed past redemption. His brother and others he loved were prisoners of the curse on his head, as surely as he was doomed. Returning to Noumet might be possible but Rouwen had to be honest and admit he might never be able to reach it again. The last time had added fifteen years to Finola's age. Could the wizards in Noumet hold out against the Flame Specter if he took another fifteen to return?

Rouwen didn't think so. The grimoire had to be given to someone who would use it against the Flame Specter, someone who would imprison the fire elemental and give the other elementals a chance to regain something of their former power. Only in this way could he see balance returning to the world.

He walked, he slept, he cried openly for the destruction he saw throughout the countryside, and eventually he came to the road leading upward. The guard post had been abandoned long ago. Simple repair might have saved the post from collapse years earlier. The road itself remained in decent repair, but it had been hewn from solid rock. Only in places had earthquake or flood washed away parts.

Even here, Rouwen felt heartsick at what it meant. No heavy wagons made their way to the castle to supply those within. The deep ravines cut across the road would prevent all but the most nimble from travelling upward.

'My world is gone,' he said sadly, gazing across the valley. Thick patches of forest grew where tilled fields had once stretched verdant green and alive with the odor of growing oats, barley, and hybrids. From the size of those trees, Rouwen guessed more than fifteen years had passed in Valley Gan. Perhaps far more.

He was no longer contemporary in this world or any other. Truly was he accursed.

Foot-weary and tired to the soul, Rouwen finally turned the last bend in the road and stared at the impregnable Castle Gan. The huge steel gates had been ripped from their hinges years ago. Gaps in the thick stone wall large enough for an army to rush through had never been repaired. And the signs of neglect he saw past these sundered walls told that the castle itself was in no better shape.

Castle Gan wasn't dead, but it was dying a death of indifference and slow decay.

Clutching the burlap bag with the grimoire, Brion Rouwen entered Castle Gan with no hope of finding anyone able to read the runes so painstakingly entered and so brightly burning on every page.

19

The Castle Dies

Rats.

Rouwen heard rats running through the rocky debris of Castle Gan's walls. He stumbled over a large block, then worked his way past into the once great courtyard. Deathly silence met him, interrupted only by squeaking, chittering, red-eyed, black rats and their quick scurry-scurry to investigate him. Rouwen drew his sword and banged the flat of the blade on a stone block. The ringing of steel, an unaccustomed sound in the castle, frightened the rats away and let Rouwen pretend, if only for a moment, that he had just stepped out of the officers' barracks to inspect the Intrepid Guard.

His eyes rose to the once proud battlements. Here and there large blocks had fallen from the walls. Rouwen tried to guess how long the castle had been abandoned and couldn't. For him very few weeks had passed since leaving Gan. For Finola at least fifteen years had passed. And for the kingdom? He shook his head.

Walking slowly toward the great hall, he paused when he heard something more than the sounds of rats. It might have been a foot stepping across gravel. Or it might have been nothing more than the settling of a decaying fortress. Rouwen listened intently, still hoping to find someone who might decipher the runes in the grimoire. Nespizio was long dead, and for that Rouwen grieved. The old wizard hadn't been skilled, but he had known everything that happened within these walls. He could have started him on the path to finding a wizard of surpassing skill able to remove his curse.

'Old friend, how I wish you had survived Sosler.' But Nespizio had not, any more than dozens of others he had known. Rouwen touched the spell casket dangling around his neck. It had become an anvil, a weight far exceeding its size, yet it was partially responsible for holding back the Flame Specter.

Rouwen killed and those spirits roaming between worlds acted as a buffer against the Flame Specter. How long that would last when the other elementals weakened, Rouwen couldn't say. He sheathed his sword and tossed the burlap bag over his shoulder, marching through the deserted hall and into the offices where the affairs of a kingdom had been conducted. Dust had accumulated in thick layers, all records were long turned to brittle yellow flakes in forgotten books. Rouwen slammed open a door and sent echoes down long corridors.

Empty. It was all as empty as Rouwen's heart.

He left to work his way higher in the castle. The magnificence of Castle Gan had turned into decline. A part of him wanted to cry with joy. Sosler had failed. He would never have left this center of power. The barrenness also meant Rouwen had failed in his duty to the kingdom. He had loved Gan and it had died, too.

He froze when he heard the distant shuffling of feet across stone. He moved quickly to the inner wall and pressed his back into it. The sounds of movement came from above. He worked upward slowly, careful not to expose himself to needless attack. He tried to decide if time again flowed in weird surges or if what he experienced now was only natural anxiety.

He heard someone moving within Castle Gan. Friend? Foe? Princess Sorinne?

The thought that his love might still be here turned his stomach into a knotted rope that pulled back and forth in his abdomen. He played a desperate hand and might fail, but if he succeeded in imprisoning the Flame Specter once again, Rouwen did not want to endanger the princess. To win the battle against the fire elemental and forever lose the woman he loved would be no victory at all.

Rouwen came to the head of the spiral staircase and looked up and down the hall. He saw only scuff marks in the thick dust on the floor but was unable to tell where the sounds had come from or gone. This level held dozens of smaller rooms for conducting affairs of state. Rouwen turned toward one and heard new scratching noises, accompanied by a deep-chested sneeze.

Going to the door of the audience chamber, Rouwen peered in. Sitting on the throne that had once rested on a dais in the king's audience chamber four levels higher in the castle, sat a timeworn Duke Sosler. The Lord Protector of the Realm had always been razor thin. Now he was emaciated. And old. He was older than anyone Rouwen had ever seen.

Sosler's nose hooked over until it almost touched his upper lip, and he had lost all but a fuzzy white corona of fine hair. The pale blue eyes that had frozen with a single glance now appeared murky. A hand with parchment skin stretched tautly lifted as

516

Sosler made a sweeping gesture, as if addressing a gathered multitude.

'I grant you all pardons, if you will turn over the traitors to me,' he said in a weak, gravelly voice. 'I am king and you will obey!' The duke shot to his feet with startling speed.

For a moment, Rouwen thought Sosler had seen him, then realized the old man acted out his own fantasies. He started to slip from the room and continue his search of the castle for someone who might help when Sosler spied him.

'Rouwen! You have come back!'

'I have returned,' Rouwen said, walking slowly toward the old man. He felt no sense of victory. Time had beaten Sosler, not Brion Rouwen. 'I need information.'

'The traitors are all over the kingdom. They sneak up when you least expect them. And she is the worst. She hunts me like an animal!' Sosler quieted and a sharpness returned to his dim eyes that had not been present earlier. 'Are you still cursed?'

'I am,' Rouwen said, seeing no reason to deny it. If Sosler tried any attack, he could kill him with a single blow. There would be no need even to bloody his sword in a fight. How different from the last time they had fought. Sosler's skill with a sword had been the stuff of legends. Rouwen had once fallen under his clever, strong parries and thrusts.

'Where is Princess Sorinne? Is she the one of whom you speak?'

'She is, the bitch. She escaped years ago. How, I do not know. There was destruction in Castle Gan, and she somehow escaped the dungeons. How I rue that day!'

'This destruction was caused by the Flame Specter?' Rouwen smiled slightly, knowing he and Vutorian had been successful in freeing the princess. For years, Sorinne must have dogged every move Sosler made. Rouwen had never underestimated Sorinne's beauty or her determination.

'Yes, yes, it ruined the castle. Nothing was the same after that. The other forces came rushing in to do battle with the fire elemental. Water and earth and even wind – I didn't completely lose control of the Legion of the Air – all fought over Gan. The kingdom died, but I lived.' Sosler coughed and a firmer note came to his voice. 'So did Sorinne and her band of traitors!'

'She leads others against you?' Rouwen wondered why they hadn't been more successful. A simple shove would break bones in Sosler's chest. A punch would end his life. Deposing this frail skeleton would not be a hard task.

'Sorinne tries, but I keep her out.' Sosler cocked his head to one side and fixed an uncomfortably intense eye on Rouwen. 'How did you enter? There were no vibrations in my ward spell.'

'Your spell?' asked Rouwen. 'You have a wizard in the castle?'

'You think to remove the curse, don't you?' Sosler cackled, but Rouwen saw the cunning returning to the man instant by instant. 'I can remove it, but I won't! I want you to suffer for all the woe you have brought me.' Sosler sank into his throne and hoisted one thin leg over an arm. His eyes no longer appeared murky. They hardened into the icy pits Rouwen remembered.

'I dragged the throne down from above years ago, when the roof collapsed,' Sosler went on, answering Rouwen's unspoken question. 'After the fire elemental ravaged the castle, nothing was the same.'

'Your wizard. Where is he? I need help with a more pressing matter than the spell casket.' Rouwen flipped the silver-chased box out of his tunic and let the magical device dangle in plain sight. If this fueled Sosler's contempt for him, so be it. Rouwen needed a wizard of some power to use the grimoire.

'I have no wizard assisting me now,' scoffed Sosler. 'Why encourage anyone to usurp my power? After the elemental devoured half my castle and everyone fled into the valley, I found Kwuway's old books in his workshop and learned to read them. They were not difficult. Anyone can become a master wizard, given the time and effort. It requires no talent or great intelligence.'

'So you studied and became a wizard on your own?' Rouwen remembered how hard Finola had studied to master the arcane arts, just to be worthy of a post in Noumet. Toit claimed she had a great magical talent, and still the young girl had worked long hours to hone her skills and learn what spells Vutorian could teach. 'Just like that?' Rouwen snapped his fingers.

'Yes, just like that,' retorted Sosler, 'more than thirty years! I have placed ward spells around the castle to keep Sorinne and her terrible cutthroats out. And the Flame Specter. It does not trouble me any more because I am such a powerful wizard.'

At this Rouwen laughed. The Flame Specter fought opponents infinitely stronger than this old man and won. Still, he knew he had to find a mage capable of deciphering the runes in the spell book soon. The battle might be lost in Noumet, or it might still rage. That the sun shone and days were of the right length boded well for the continued existence of the City of Mages – and Finola.

'So how else do you pass your time in Castle Gan, other than studying ancient tomes of magical lore?' Rouwen walked closer, aware that Sosler's breath quickened. The duke dropped his leg off the throne's arm and leaned forward.

'You have the grimoire. I can feel it. Bring it to me. I can defeat the fire elemental with it. Bring me the grimoire. It supplied power to the Flame Specter once to destroy my ability to summon the Legion of the Air. Now I can retaliate. After all these years, Kwuway's grimoire! I can control the Flame Specter!' Sosler rocked forward and moved on arthritic legs toward Rouwen.

The former Captain of the Intrepid Guard had time to consider his course of action. He had come so far. What was there to lose letting Sosler look at the spell book?

'Here,' he said, dropping the burlap bag on the floor in front of him. 'Examine the grimoire, if you dare. It has become re-energized.' Rouwen did not go into the details of the fight for Noumet. Instead he asked, 'How long has the sun been keeping its normal orbit?'

'Eh? What? That? The seasons returned some years ago. Can't remember when. When the fire elemental attacked the castle and did so much damage, the world turned crazy, unpredictable. But some time after, everything returned to normal.' Sosler hobbled forward and dropped to his knees in front of the bag.

'I can feel its power. It *is* the grimoire.'

Sosler reached for the bag. Rouwen hoped he was doing the right thing even showing the spell book to the old duke. Somehow, his hatred of the man had abated. Pity replaced much of his anger. He shoved the bag forward, aware of the intense energies boiling forth from the grimoire.

'Why is it so important?' Rouwen asked. 'Kwuway spent his life compiling – what?'

Sosler cackled as if quite mad, and Rouwen wondered if the old duke might not be. He scrabbled at the burlap, ripping it with long, cracked nails. Dropping the contents to the stone floor, Sosler sat cross-legged and put his hands on either side of the brilliantly radiating spell book.

'It contains the binding spell for the Flame Specter,' Sosler said. 'Whoever uses it, forces the fire elemental to his will. I'm not sure from where the power for the spell derives, but it must tap into the most basic forces in the universe. What else could be potent enough to hold an elemental in check?' Sosler reached for the spell book and Rouwen recoiled, his chest feeling as if it might explode.

Reeling, he staggered away from Sosler and the grimoire. The duke gripped the book in his hands, oblivious to what must be searing pain. Rouwen's eyes clouded over with tears and he clutched at his chest.

Near. Soon. Release me, release me!

Rouwen heard the Flame Specter's words but could not warn Sosler. Something in the grimoire would allow the fire elemental to blaze free of all constraint, and Rouwen could not speak. He tried to force more than a gasp from his lips, but the might of the Flame Specter kept him silent.

Rouwen raged but could not shake free. He felt humiliated at being duped like this. He had delivered the spell book to one who would release the bonds in mistaken belief he was controlling the fire elemental. He, Brion Rouwen, would be the agent of destruction for the world, not its salvation.

His dirty, torn tunic sprang into a lively blaze, but it was a cold fire now, not the blistering heat he had experienced before. The skin on his chest bulged outward like the sides of a teapot but throbbing with energy, pulsating and threatening to blow apart his body at any instant. Rouwen didn't know what would happen when his skin yielded. He feared he would quickly learn.

'Adan,' he muttered, trying to summon the spirit of his brother. The spirits had held back the Flame Specter's full power before. Now they must prevent the fire elemental's eruption into the world. 'Toit, Nibbles, if the world dies you will be lost forever. Don't let it happen. Don't.' He grated out the words but Sosler didn't listen – and the spirits of his lost loved ones did not respond.

The power of the Flame Specter was too great.

'The words, the chant, are important. The cadence of the words. To have such a being at my command. I have longed for this power all my life!' Sosler flipped open the grimoire and letters blazed so brightly Rouwen could not focus on them. Sosler had no such trouble. A shaky hand began tracing out the letters. Everywhere his finger touched and he recited the word, it changed from blazing purple to a more subdued magenta.

'Yes, yes, I have it. I learned Kwuway's secret codes. I know what he meant by these words.'

Sosler began chanting words that made no sense to Rouwen, but he experienced new agony as the Flame Specter struggled within him, ready to burst forth. A part of Rouwen worried that he would die when the fire elemental blasted forth – and another part worried that he would not.

'ANENABITE, LUSHATINE, SOWEABLITE. And what's the next word? What can it be? IMLORITE, yes, that is it,' Sosler said, his confidence growing. 'Yes, yes, these are the words of power, the ones binding the fire elemental. How brilliant Kwuway was. Why did I not see his usefulness while he lived?'

Sosler carefully repeated the words of power and added new ones to every recitation. Rouwen listened, in spite of himself, in spite of the fire blazing in his chest. He was frozen to the spot, tormented by the knowledge that he had done the wrong thing in giving the spell book to Sosler. The old duke was freeing the elemental, not binding it. The Flame Specter surged in Rouwen's body, exulting in its imminent release from all bonds.

'UNNAWATE, INCHLIONORY, RANATION CHLIPHI-BLATE DRIOCAY,' Sosler raced on, repeating the magic words of binding over and over, as if savoring a fine new wine or a succulent morsel prepared by a master chef. 'I feel the power. I feel it, yes!'

Hurry, hurry.

The Flame Specter's unspoken words rang like a bell in Rouwen's ears. He was past being able to do more than utter small trapped animal noises. The conduit he supplied because of the curse on him took form. He sensed the speed within, the heated rush, the ultimate triumph of the fire elemental.

'There!' cried Sosler. 'That is the spell needed to bind the Flame Specter.'

Brion Rouwen's chest erupted as the fire elemental burst free, spinning, turning, burning. Where it had once used incandescence, now its fire was cold. But still it melted. The walls in the room winked out of existence as if nothing more than a snowflake in a farrier's kiln. With them went the ceiling and floor.

And Sosler. With wide, frightened eyes the old man stared at the thick shaft of effulgence streaming out of a quivering Rouwen's body. The duke tried to scream in fear but had no chance. The lance of light speared him, and he winked out of existence, superheated to bloody mist in a split second.

Rouwen recoiled when the Flame Specter blasted high into the air, cutting a tunnel for itself through solid stone. It had been unleashed before – temporarily. Now he knew its ecstasy.

Free. Free!

The Flame Specter began its destruction of Castle Gan in celebration of newfound emancipation.

20

Sorinne

Rouwen shook all over, trying to crawl toward the molten pit that had been Sosler and the stone floor under him. His strength flagged and he fell to the floor until the pain forced him to roll on his side. His hands tried to pull free the clothing on his chest and found his tunic seared to his flesh. Closing his eyes, he tried to keep from passing out as wave after wave of pain rushed through him.

Free!

The taunting cry of the Flame Specter was worse than any pain Rouwen felt. The balance of nature had changed, and now the fire elemental would devour the world, turning it into a fiery ball rivalling the sun. Proportion between the elementals would fade, giving dominance to fire at the expense of earth, water, and air.

As if this symmetry already shifted, Rouwen found it harder to breathe. Forcing his eyes open, Rouwen stared at his chest. He cringed at the depth of the wound. Huge hunks of flesh had been burned away mercilessly when the Flame Specter erupted. How the fire elemental could have used him as a road into the world and not killed him was a puzzle to be pondered another time.

His attention turned from the deep charred pit in his chest to the vast cavity in the castle's ceiling. Far up in the sky, Rouwen saw a blazing dot spin and twist and knew it was the Flame Specter enjoying its liberation.

He craned his head back and crawled toward the pit melted in the stone floor, hunting for the grimoire. If the spell book had permitted the Flame Specter to escape, then the runes scratched on its pages must give hope of recapturing it. Rouwen wasn't sure how Sosler's mumbling of the odd words had freed the elemental when the duke had thought he was chaining the Flame Specter to his will. Magicks and their consequences were imponderable, and all Rouwen knew for certain was that Sosler had been no wizard.

'Get it back for Finola, get it back,' he grated out between clenched teeth. The absolute agony raging in his ravaged chest died down a little, permitting more movement. What had he ever done to deserve such misery? He killed those he loved and now he had presided at the death of the world. Not only his kingdom but his world lay forfeit by his hand.

Rouwen pulled himself to the edge of the crater in the floor and saw that the Flame Specter's entry to the world had also destroyed the grimoire. Like Sosler, the spell book had been reduced to a black, sooty smear that hinted at the elemental's real victory.

Drops of molten stone began falling around him, though he felt no heat. Rouwen pushed himself up to a sitting position, barely able to move. Half his chest had been blasted away but the rest of him would be liquefied if he stayed in Castle Gan much longer. The Flame Specter saw the castle as a symbol to be destroyed.

Struggling to pull himself along the floor, Rouwen got to the door before the ceiling in the room behind him crashed down in a soggy lump. The curious lack of heat as the stone melted spoke of the Flame Specter's immense power now. Before, fire had been its weapon. Now it controlled both white fire and cold, black flame.

The ebony flames danced along fallen timbers, causing them to vanish slowly. And wherever those strange sparks touched, stone flowed into pools. Rouwen didn't have to remain to know the hungry remnants of the Flame Specter would continue dining until nothing remained. The entire spire on which Castle Gan sat might be devoured before the flames were sated – or maybe not even then.

Rouwen shivered as he considered that the Flame Specter might have begun its destruction of the world starting with the highest point: Castle Gan. The black fire might never cease until the entire world swung beneath its two shining moons as a cinder. Rouwen didn't know what future the fire elemental intended for the world, but it did not include human life.

Long hours passed before Rouwen got out of the castle and started for the winding road down the side of the rocky spire. Now and then he chanced a look up at the castle. The soaring battlements sagged and fell in on themselves, feeding pits filled with towering black flares that sucked in both stone and sky. Destruction of the symbol of human triumph was almost complete.

Rouwen half-walked and half-fell down the road, forcing

himself to keep moving. His strength refused to return no matter how far he got from the top of the spire, making him think that he might be forever robbed of strength by his experience.

'Why couldn't I have died in Priowe's dungeons?' he moaned as he stumbled along. He had killed and he had witnessed the death of both kingdom and world. Where were the spirits who had badgered him before? He longed to see his brother again, even as a spirit, to beg him for his calm, wise opinion. Or Nibbles. The old thief saw everything in terms of food and gain. Where was the gain in anything that had happened to Rouwen? Even enduring Toit's scolding would be a relief for him. But the spirits were not at hand.

A sudden eruption at the top of the spire blasted forth a molten cloud of tiny, sizzling pebbles and knocked him from the road. He rolled down the side of the mountain, tumbling out of control until he fetched up hard against a large boulder. And then he shrieked as droplets of molten rain cascaded on top of him. He began burrowing under the rock and found some protection from the hot rain. Like a small frightened animal hunted by a carnivorous predator, Rouwen curled up in a tight ball and tried to sleep.

Rouwen came awake with a start, kicking out, reaching for his sword and not finding it.

'There, there, calm yourself,' came a voice trying to be soothing. It was too gruff to succeed. 'Come on out of that hidey-hole and let us get you away from here.'

Several pairs of hands fought to reach him. Rouwen was too weak to resist for more than a few seconds. Or was it a year? Time flowed in curious spurts now, the pain stretching to eternity and any contentment fading to a flicker.

'We cannot stay here any longer. We saw you take the tumble down the hill. Come along now. Come along.' More hands pulled him from under the rock and passed him along like a bag of grain. Rouwen fought but only succeeded in helping them move him to the back of a wagon. He fell heavily into the bed and quickly passed out again when the rattling, bumping ride began.

The next Rouwen knew, he stared at a sky turned unnaturally dark. Soot filled the air and choked him when he tried to breathe. He sat up and looked around the small camp. Lightning-struck trees showed where a forest had once stretched over lush, fertile soil. Sky, trees, land, all were uniformly black now.

'You've come back to us. A good sign, though there's precious little gained by living these days.' A burly man some twenty years

Rouwen's elder squatted by a small fire fitfully burning. 'Don't seem right, does it?'

'What's that?' Rouwen shook his head and instantly regretted it. Huge hunks of his brain bounced about inside, giving him more pain. He cautiously explored the burn on his chest. Whoever had dressed it had left off bandages so the pain would be more bearable. Some sticky paste had been smeared on the wound, but Rouwen found little to show healing had begun. The deepness of the burn worried him. He had seen men with lesser wounds who had perished.

'Can't keep a proper fire burning and up there,' the man pointed vaguely in the direction of Castle Gan, 'the fires don't ever go out. But then, they're black and here we deal only with real fires.' He poked the twigs in the fire pit again and got a more cheerful blaze to burn. But it quickly died, as if intimidated by the knowledge that a fire elemental now ruled the world.

'How long have I been unconscious? You rescued me from the castle road. I remember that much, but nothing after.' Rouwen slid down from the wagon bed and took a tentative step. His legs didn't buckle. That was all he could lay claim to that was good. Nausea rose and his belly growled, whether from lack of food or some other damage from the Flame Specter's touch. And his chest. He pressed his fingers into the scorched flesh on the sides of what had been little more than a brand.

He tried to remember how he had felt when the Flame Specter had blasted forth into the world. Rouwen wasn't too surprised to find that blocks of memory were closed to him. He sank down beside the man at the fire and stared into the dark distance, swallowing hard when he saw only a jagged peak remaining where once Castle Gan had stood so proudly.

A part of Rouwen died when he saw how complete the destruction was. He forced himself to look away, and this was no better. He remained in Valley Gan, but the fertile valley had changed as drastically as the more obvious symbol of its prosperity. No one could farm this land of black soot and sluggish creeks filled with poison.

'We been thinking on leaving the valley. There's not much to keep anyone here now that he's dead. Sosler is gone, isn't he?' The man lifted a stick and stabbed in the direction of the castle.

'He is. I was there when he died.' Rouwen bit his tongue. He knew nothing of this man or the others who must be with him. To admit too much jeopardized his life.

Rouwen settled down a bit more and stared into the erratic

525

fire. What difference did it make? He had done all the damage possible. The only way he knew of helping had been destroyed with Sosler and the grimoire. Noumet must have been reduced to black ash by now, and with it Finola, Vutorian, and all the others. He had failed. There was nothing that could be done to him now.

'You saw the old vulture? We been after him for years, but he was always too quick for us. He knew every inch of that bedamned castle. Even my wife couldn't ferret him out. When he got hold of them magic books of his, there was no way we could corner him.'

'Your wife?' Rouwen was mildly interested. 'Did she once work in the castle?'

The man laughed heartily, the only truly cheerful sound Rouwen had heard in more weeks than he cared to think about.

'She was a princess, she was. Heir to the throne. Why, she . . .'

'Arno, don't be such a braggart,' came a voice that caused Rouwen to whirl about. He almost fell face down in the dirt when he saw Sorinne walking up, lugging buckets of water like a scullery maid.

He tried to speak but no words came to his lips. She was older, far older than he expected. Finola had aged fifteen years and had become a lovely young woman. Sorinne was still pretty, but more than thirty new years bowed her shoulders and added more furrows to her face than the best tended field at planting. Her once fair complexion had hardened into brown leather, the result of exposure to unfavourable conditions. She dropped the buckets of water and came to Rouwen.

He tried to speak but weakness assailed him at seeing her once more. He pushed her away but she was too determined.

'Arno should never have let you up and about,' Sorinne said firmly. She pressed her fingers into the wound on Rouwen's chest, causing him to blanch with the pain – or was it stark fear that she would die?

She did not turn into a pile of magically smoldering bones that burned to gray ash. Sorinne frowned and said, 'Your wound is unlike any I have seen.' Her blue eyes with the memorable gold flakes floating within bored into his brown ones. She frowned and the furrows on her forehead deepened even more. 'I know you. Where have we met?'

'We met at a Spring Festival,' Rouwen said, finally getting back the power of speech. He moved away from her, still fearing she would perish from the curse placed on his head. How long had he labored under that vicious spell? In his mind it was a span of months. For Sorinne, it would be more than thirty years, a full lifetime of heartbreak and misfortune.

'You joke. There hasn't been a Spring Festival since I was a young girl.' A far-off look of remembrance came to her and a small smile curled the corners of her lips. How Rouwen remembered that smile! He backed off even more, not wanting to get too close. A touch would kill, as it had before.

But why hadn't Sorinne died when she examined his wound?

'A jest, nothing more,' Rouwen said, staring at her and not knowing what to say. 'How long have you and – Arno been married?'

Sorinne smiled again, remembering even more pleasurable events. 'We married soon after we met. When was that, my love?'

Rouwen started to say he had no idea, then realized Sorinne spoke to the hulking man still poking at the reluctant fire.

'You escaped the castle and came down into the valley. That was when I first set eyes on you. What a beauty, what a beauty,' Arno said, as if confiding a deep secret. 'Couldn't believe she was a princess, not at first. More than a month passed before I got up the nerve even to speak to her.'

'Then he wouldn't be quiet,' Sorinne said, laughing with true enjoyment now. Rouwen held his breath as Sorinne went about her chores, pouring water into a cook pot to boil the pitiful roots someone had collected and piled nearby. It would make a poor stew, yet it looked as if it was all there would be for this meal, or any future one.

'We worked together with a band of Mionese who had tried to depose Sosler. It . . .'

Rouwen cut into her reminiscence. 'Do you remember the Mionese commander? A man named Laslo?'

Sorinne's eyes widened in surprise. 'Why, yes, of course. But how do you know him? You are hardly old enough to remember the Isolation, much less Laslo.'

'Isolation?' Rouwen's head spun. He pulled up his knees and tried to close in on himself. The emptiness in his chest prevented it. Rather than look at Sorinne as she spoke, he directed his attention to the dark sky. Jagged lines of blue fire cut through the firmament as the Flame Specter consolidated its claim on the entire world. The air was vanishing and would eventually be totally burned away. How much longer for the oceans and planet itself? Or did it matter, if there was no air to breathe?

'You speak strangely, in the old manner. The Isolation.

Everyone knows of it. The Demon's Throat closed and the mountains on either side of Mount Glid began to dissolve. The elemental ate down the stone but could never quite finish its meal. We were cut off from the rest of the world, from Mion and . . .' Sorinne stopped and stared at Rouwen, as if remembering who he was.

Rouwen waited for his princess to speak his name. She didn't.

'So Valley Gan was cut off? What of the tunnel under the Shield Mountains leading to Mion? Was that closed also?'

'I knew of such a way out, but no one else did. How do you speak of it?'

Rouwen started to identify himself. It cut to his very heart that Sorinne hadn't known him immediately, no matter that three decades or more had passed. But because he thought so of her did not mean she should remember him.

A hollow feeling entered him, one more chilling than ever. Did he truly love her? Love wasn't likely to die because Sorinne failed to recognize him. Love was not that fragile, but had he changed? Rouwen held back tears, thinking that he might be incapable of love again. This triggered still other wild thoughts. If he didn't love, he couldn't kill, but was life worth living then?

The confusion covering him so completely made Sorinne edge closer and put her hand on his shoulder. She squeezed, as if to reassure a small child.

'The world has changed since the old days, and not for the better. We can leave the valley when the Flame Specter eats through the rest of the mountain range.'

'Leave, yes,' Rouwen said. 'I've lived here all my life, but we should leave. There is nothing left for us.'

'Arno, can't you make the fire any hotter?' Sorinne went to scrape the roots before dropping them into the pot. She worked like a cook as she prepared their meal. Rouwen huddled even tighter, pulling his knees up to his chest. A princess of the realm working as a scullery maid, and this after she had fought Sosler for so long.

'You really must tell me how you know of Laslo,' Sorinne said, not looking up from her work. 'He was a dear man. And the tunnel. I have never told anyone of it.'

'You told me,' said Arno, finally finding the right combination to make the fire flare brightly. 'Or was that the way under Mount Glid? I can't recollect.'

'I can't either,' Sorinne admitted.

'Why bother?' Rouwen asked unexpectedly. 'Why bother continuing existence?'

'It's better than the alternative,' Sorinne said easily. 'The valley is haunted with the spirits of those denied entry into Paradise. I can't remember when it occurred to me that the Flame Specter barred entry with its assault on Mount Glid. The holy mountain has remained inviolate since the Isolation, but it cannot endure much longer.'

'Those who haven't reached Paradise will be caught forever?' Rouwen pitied Adan and the others, but he would soon join them. Would his curse carry into the grave and beyond? For all that he had done to destroy the world, he knew that it would. He would remain an outcast, even trapped between life and reward.

'We can only guess,' Sorinne said. 'Oh, there they are. The others are late. Go greet them, Arno.'

The hulk of a man rose and lumbered off to speak with a half-dozen others rolling up in a larger wagon. Rouwen saw that they lacked a draft animal and that four of the six worked to pull the flatbed wagon with their own muscle power.

Rouwen only poked at the thin stew Sorinne gave him and did not enter into conversation with the others. His future was as bleak as that of Valley Gan – and the world. But he did not dwell on lack of a tomorrow as much as he did on the knowledge that she had forgotten him. She remembered Laslo and other events that, to Rouwen, had happened only weeks earlier, but she had not endured over the years.

And Rouwen no longer loved her. He came to accept that as the evening wore on. What shocked him most of all, he might never have loved, not the way he should have.

He rested his head on his knees and fell asleep, sobbing quietly for the horror that was his life.

Rouwen spun about, hand flashing toward his sword when he was shaken awake. Arno towered above him.

'Time to move on. You're welcome to come with us, if you have a mind to,' Arno told him. 'Sorinne's taken quite a fancy to you for some reason.'

'She was always looking after stray animals,' Rouwen said with more than a hint of bitterness. 'I doubt she has changed.'

'You knew her? Ah, you are making a guess at her nature. Well, good sir, it is a good guess. She's got a kind heart, but don't let that gull you. There's steel within her, there is.'

'The war against Sosler?'

'That and more. She never quits.' This Arno said with a slightly different note in his voice. Rouwen realized the man was giving him as much advice as he was likely to get. Don't give up.

'Where do we go?' Rouwen asked, getting painfully to his feet. 'I don't think I can pull my weight with your wagon, not like the others did last night, but I can scavenge with the best.'

Arno laughed and slapped him on the back, almost knocking Rouwen over. 'That's the way to talk. We're heading to the south and east of the old Demon's Throat. Sorinne heard that a new canyon has been eaten by those infernal black fires. We can skirt those, she thinks, and get on out to the sea.'

'To the sea,' Rouwen said, 'to the Isle of Passing and beyond to other lands.'

'Where's that? Never heard of any place called the Isle of Passing.'

'The Lord of Death and Life lived there once, a long time back,' Rouwen said. He was speaking to a man who might not have been born when the Lord died – when Rouwen's curse killed that master wizard when he assumed the face and figure of Sorinne.

This memory from distant times kept Rouwen walking most of the day. He had loved Sorinne. That proved it, even if the proof lay so far in the past. The Lord had thought to trick him and had taken Sorinne's image as his own. A brief touch and Rouwen had killed the world's pre-eminent wizard.

'I did love you, Sorinne,' he said softly, staring at the woman working a few paces away. Her once lustrous blonde hair now hung in thick, dirty strings, but there remained a nobility to her. 'And that's enough, for now.' This knowledge warmed Rouwen enough to keep pace with the others, though the way was hard and getting worse.

After midday, their progress suddenly halted. The sky had been crackling with violent fire most of the morning, or what Rouwen had come to think of as morning, and then the ground started to respond to the thunderous explosions aloft. He was tossed about as if he were nothing more than a pebble on a broad blanket being snapped by a dozen strong men. He fell to his knees, then grabbed out to steady himself against Arno's wagon.

'Away, get away from the wagon,' shouted Arno. 'There's no way to save it!'

Rouwen heard but he couldn't obey. A noise louder than any thunder sounded and a huge chasm raced along the roadway, separating him from the others. They had taken dubious cover in a shallow ditch beside the road. He saw the pit widening and knew he could never jump across it. Peering down into the pit, Rouwen saw unblinking green eyes peering up. The earth elemental was trying to fight back, and Rouwen saw that the creature was losing.

Rain began pelting down from above, burning like acid with every drop. And the wind began to blow in fitful gusts, too weak to blow a true storm into what had been Valley Gan.

Rouwen crouched down, using the wagon bed as shelter from the erratic storm. The skies burned with new fire, and it wasn't from a thunderstorm, the melding of air and water. It was pure flame, cold and sharp and belonging to the Flame Specter.

Rouwen clung to the wagon as it rattled and shook under the onslaught of earthquake and biting rain, then was lifted and thrown into the mud when a column of fire blasted the wagon apart. Rouwen looked past where the wagon burned with a cold black flame to where Sorinne and her husband peered over the verge of the road.

Rouwen's vision blurred and he knew his life slipped away, along with Sorinne, Arno and all the others.

The fire elemental was slowly wresting the world away, destroying all balance.

21

Finola

'Sorinne!' he called. Rouwen forced himself to his knees, only to be knocked back down by a new buffeting caused by the ground shivering under him. The chasm opened and the woman drifted away, farther with every passing second, as if she stood in a boat drifting from the docks on a hidden tide.

Mud splashed in his face, but Rouwen cleared it when he heard a tortured creaking. The wagon slowly slid down an incline and tumbled into the crevice. It vanished into the depths, and Rouwen made no effort to see what had happened. He tried to squirm away from the abyss, but the crack widened faster than Rouwen could move.

He clung to a half-buried root as his feet slipped into the chasm. Rouwen thought he heard Sorinne call his name, but it might only have been the crack of energy spraying in vivid fans across the black sky. Rouwen clenched his teeth and tried to get a footing to pull himself away from the mouth gaping to swallow him.

As his hands began weakening, the earthquake stopped and the crevice ceased its quick advance. Rouwen hung with his feet dangling in air for a second, then fought to pull himself upward. Every muscle in his body – those he still had left – screamed in protest, but Rouwen managed to roll over onto his back, safe from the death awaiting him in the depths of the pit.

He stood and tried to find Sorinne, Arno and the others. His eyes widened in surprise when he discovered they had gone. Whether a quirk of time had removed them or the island of land to which he clung had floated far away, he couldn't tell. Nowhere in the soot-filled distance did he see any trace of another soul, lost or living.

He walked around the tiny island that had broken off and been isolated when the chasm had opened. It would require a considerable jump to reach solid ground on the far side, but Rouwen saw nothing to lose by trying. He could not remain on this patch of soil long without food or water. Being pelted by the sporadic acid rain only wore at his patience. He gauged the distance, then put all his power into a single jump. He sailed and landed heavily. But now he was even farther from Sorinne's party, more cut off by the wide crack in the ground that stretched as far as he could see in either direction.

Settling his sword at his side, Rouwen began walking along the newly gouged canyon, aware that he might spend the rest of his life looking for a lost love. Or should he call Sorinne a love lost?

He walked on gamely until he became too tired to continue. The distance was shrouded from view by the heavy layer of black ash that continued to fall in a relentless curtain. Here and there the ground burst into tiny flames, some a cheery orange and giving heat and others the cold black soul-devouring fire of the freed Flame Specter.

To keep himself amused, he tried to recall the words Sosler had uttered to harness the Flame Specter. They jumbled in his mind, and this made the game all the more interesting. Rouwen realized this might be the last enjoyable thing he experienced before the fire elemental claimed the entire world.

Rouwen thought he heard distant laughter but wasn't surprised to discover it was only a trick of the ground creaking and shifting. The Flame Specter no longer used him as its highway into the world. He had served its purpose and counted for no more than any other insect crawling on an unwanted body of dark matter.

'ANENABITE, LUSHATINE,' he intoned. The words rolled off his tongue like honey, but Rouwen hadn't expected the bolt of black fire from above that seared his path. It was as if the Flame Specter warned him not to utter the words. He had no reason to fear the Flame Specter now. The elemental could do nothing to him that hadn't already been done.

Again he tried the words and again he was almost devoured by a pillar of cold fire.

Laughing, Rouwen danced about, taunting the fire elemental. It was childish but gave him a feeling of power again.

Then came a distant voice, 'No, Brion, do not do that. It draws the Flame Specter to you.'

Rouwen hesitated, thinking he had started hallucinating. He had gone without solid food for so long, this was possible. Staring at the sky, he waved his clenched fist at the lines of fire slowly marching to and fro.

'It is occupied with larger battles, but it senses your power,' a voice told him. Rouwen frowned, swung about, trying to find who spoke. In the distance, a white spot emerging from the curtains of soot, came a woman. Rouwen blinked and wiped at the cinders in his eyes, wanting to believe but not daring to.

'Finola?'

'Stay there, Brion. It will take me a few minutes to reach you. The distance is far greater than it appears to you.' The ghostlike figure shimmered and then became a focused pinpoint of the purest white. Against the gray-black backdrop, Rouwen counted it as the most beautiful sight he had ever seen. He hopped from foot to foot in anxious need to see her again.

'Finola!' he cried when she surged forward. The light appeared to explode and there stood the woman, looking no different from the last time he had seen her in Noumet.

He reached out to take her in his arms, then checked himself. He backed off, trying to keep her at a distance. What he felt now for her far surpassed any feelings he had ever experienced while with Sorinne. Rouwen didn't want to slay Finola as he had the others he had loved.

'The words, Brion. I need the words now.'

'What happened to Noumet?' His question brought tears to the woman's eyes. The tracks left down her cheeks shone and refracted rainbows of color in the iron-blackness of the new world.

'It is – different,' she said in a small voice that reminded him of her much younger self. 'A few wizards survive and continue their work. Although you cannot see it, the sun follows its usual course and other vital parts of the world function properly.'

'At what cost?' He wanted to hug her, kiss her. It was as trying a torture to him not to be able to do so as anything else he had endured recently.

'Fully half the wizards are dead. They were unable to cope with the Flame Specter when it blazed through the city. Those of us remaining gathered in a tiny building where we could maintain our ward spell. From within we did what we could. I guided the sun for some time, but my talents were needed elsewhere.'

'You came for me,' he said.

'I would have come before the Flame Specter destroyed the world,' she said, smiling shyly. She reached out but he recoiled. She hesitated, then nodded in understanding. 'There was another reason to quit my post and come for you, though. How did you read the grimoire?'

Rouwen explained how Sosler had recited the words and the result. He opened his cloak to show the devastation in his chest. 'How I survived the Flame Specter using me as a pathway into the world, I cannot say.'

'The spirits of those you killed,' Finola said. 'They were released from their nothingness when the Flame Specter shot forth.'

'Adan is gone? To Paradise? And Nibbles and Toit?' He dared hope they had found their eternal reward after all he had inflicted on them.

'I – I don't know, Brion. I am sorry. Their spirits might have simply vanished into another nothingness, one at which we can only guess. Whatever happened to them, they are gone for all time.'

'I choose to believe they found their way to Mount Glid and into Paradise.' Rouwen swallowed hard. So much sacrifice and all for him. A pleasurable eternity might be denied his brother and the others simply because they had insulated him from being destroyed as the fire elemental escaped unchecked into the world.

'I hope so,' she said. Finola's face was pale but colored spots came to her cheeks. 'The words, Brion. The ones Sosler uttered. Do you remember them?'

'They did him no good. I think the spell he used released the Flame Specter.'

'Yes, and it can also chain it again!' Finola stepped forward and reached for him again. He resisted the urge to let her touch him.

'Finola, please, don't. I – my feelings for you have changed. You were an appealing child and nothing more. But now.' Rouwen swallowed.

'Brion, from the first time I saw you I have loved you. But we need to bind the Flame Specter again immediately. What were the words Sosler used?'

'I was trying to remember them, as a game to keep me occupied,' he said, straining to retrieve those curious sounds from his mind. 'Then came black fire, as if the elemental wanted me to stop.'

'It feared those words. You can put it in chains once more, Brion.'

'I'm no wizard. How can I do that?'

'You are no wizard, but I am. Say the words aloud and I shall repeat them. All the power remaining in Noumet will feed through me. Now, please, Brion, do it. Hurry. We have no time left.' Finola stared up at the sky. The darkness seemed more complete until Rouwen saw the faint glow of white-hot incandescence at the periphery. The Flame Specter had destroyed with cold fire and now ignited the ball of ash remaining to rival the sun in brilliance.

535

'ANENABITE, LUSHATINE . . . SOWEABLITE,' he said. 'Yes, those were the words. Then Sosler had trouble with IMLORITE.' Even as he spoke the words, the world trembled under his feet. The very planet was breaking apart.

'More, Brion, the rest. What are the rest of the words Sosler read from the grimoire?' Finola's distress caused Rouwen to lose his concentration for a moment. He reflected on all the chances he had missed before to stop the Flame Specter. The grimoire had been the key to the spells, but Sosler had unleashed the elemental.

Rouwen shook his head ruefully. It made no matter if Finola's use of the spell did anything worse. There wasn't anything worse than the dissolution of the entire planet with all its life.

'UNNAWATE, INCHLIONORY,' Rouwen said, straining to remember. He had thought he would never forget. The pain in his chest had immobilized him as Sosler read from the spell book.

'The final words, Brion. I need the rest. How many are there?'

'RANATION CHLIPHIBLATE DRIOCAY,' he finished in a rush. 'That's all.'

And Rouwen was almost destroyed by anvil-heavy hunks of black fire descending on him. He bent double and threw up his arms to protect his head, but it was his chest paining him most. New stars blossomed within his flesh and expanded, exploded, tore at him.

'ANENABITE, LUSHATINE, SOWEABLITE, IM-LORITE, UNNAWATE, INCHLIONORY, RANATION CHLIPHIBLATE DRIOCAY,' came words louder than any thunder.

Rouwen forced his head up and saw Finola standing a few feet away, arms crossed over her breasts. She shone with an uncorrupted white light that pushed back the darkness all around – and where that whiteness touched the incandescence billowing at the edges of vision, it charred and turned the brilliance to night. No matter how the Flame Specter changed or fought, the binding spell contained it.

'Is it over?' he asked, dazed. Rain still fell, burning his back and arms, and the ground quivered with new quakes threatening to swallow him.

'Hardly. The other elementals now find their power equal to that of the Flame Specter's. It will take years – more – for true balance to return. But the fire elemental is no longer reigning supreme.' Finola reached for him, but he flinched back.

'You forget the curse,' he said. 'I don't dare let you stay within sight. I might kill you as I did Toit.'

'No, you won't do that, Brion.' With a motion faster than he could follow, Finola grabbed for the silver chain around his neck. She jerked free the spell casket and held it aloft. Drops of rain glistened on it, but the rain did not burn or pit the surface. The precipitation now falling lacked the acidic bite it once had.

'It is a complex spell, one only Kwuway could have performed,' Finola said, her eyes glowing. She stared at the magical device and started it spinning slowly, as if hypnotized by its movement. 'He was a far more accomplished wizard than any knew, even Sosler and Priowe.'

'You can't undo it without harming yourself,' Rouwen said, pleading with her to stop before she doomed herself. 'The Lord of Death and Life said that . . .'

'Don't believe anything *he* said. The man was a notorious liar. Besides that, his powers were limited. I know. I have learned, oh, how I have learned.' Finola spun the spell casket faster and faster. Her eyes widened into soft brown pools that expanded to infinity.

Rouwen watched, not understanding what she did. Then he felt a pinprick deep within his body. Trying to touch it, he found his hand resting on his gouged-out chest. The spot grew and grew, and Rouwen gasped when it engulfed him totally. He flopped on the ground, trying to escape. There was no escape. He finally ran out of strength and simply endured.

'Payment for all the horror I've caused,' he moaned out.

'No, Brion, it's payment for all the good you have done. The curse wasn't your doing. And you gave me the spell needed to bind the Flame Specter. You are a hero, not a villain.'

'I don't feel too heroic. Mostly I feel empty.' He looked at his chest cavity, then sucked in his breath. A new feeling permeated him, one that he remembered – almost. He looked up at Finola.

She smiled, then dropped to her knees and kissed him soundly. He tried to get away but the woman was too determined. And nothing happened to her.

He finally broke off the kiss and stared. 'I thought I loved you. It feels as if I do, but . . .'

'You do, you do,' she said, flushed and breathless. 'And I love you, Brion. Remember, I am a wizard who has guided the sun and stars and kept the Flame Specter at bay for years. Your spell wasn't too complex for me to unlock. I've lifted the curse.'

He kissed her again, enjoying the feel of his arms around her, and hers around him.

They sat in the mud and soft, warm rain for some time before Rouwen asked, 'Are you going back to Noumet? With so few wizards left, they'll need you.'

'There's no place for you in the City of Mages,' she said.

He tensed and tried to move away. She prevented him. 'Silly man. I'm not going back because there's nothing for you there. They don't need me. Let the elementals find a new balance. That's beyond the power of any wizard to control.'

'We can find new land,' he said, thinking aloud. 'Valley Gan is a wasteland, but the Northern Continents might be in better shape. Or Mentrira.'

'Or Jabbar,' teased Finola. 'The women there keep men as love slaves.'

'Hmm, that's not too bad,' Rouwen joked.

Finola clutched hard at him and said, 'I'm not sharing you with anyone. Not now, never!'

Rouwen thought for a moment and asked, 'What of guiding the sun and the stars?'

'They have enough for those chores. The world might not function as we remember, but does it matter? The most important things will work.'

'I've always been skeptical about that, anyway,' Rouwen said. Finola's head rested on his shoulder. 'Maybe they deluded themselves into thinking they controlled the world. I'm not denying their power when it came to harnessing the Flame Specter, but the other things. I don't know.'

'Hush,' she said kissing him again. As Rouwen began kissing her lips and cheek and throat, Finola lifted her hand and made a small gesture.

Together with the Greater Moon and the Lesser rose a third moon, a new moon, to shine down on their love.